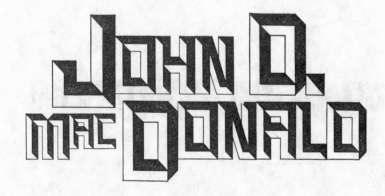

JOHN D. MAC DONALD

TIME AND

Nelson Doubleday, Inc.   Garden City, New York

TIME AND TOMORROW

TOMORROW

Wine of the Dreamers

the Girl, the Gold Watch, & Everything

Ballroom of the Skies

CONTENTS

Wine of the Dreamers

I

THE SOFT PURR OF THE TURBINE WAS ALMOST LOST IN THE ROAR of wind as the gray sedan traveled south through the New Mexico night. The night air, as always, was cool. Night in this land, he thought, is different. The land seems to rest from the heavy fist of the sun.

Step out of the cool shadows of early morning and the sun is a vast white blow between the eyes. The sun sucks greedily at all liquids. A man lost for a full day in the wastes of rock and sand will be found in the blue dusk, curled in fetal position, lips black, body withered and mummified like the long-dead.

Parched, wind-driven air dries the membranes of mouth and nose. The sun gaunts the men, pinches wrinkles into the flesh around the eyes. It fades colors and drabs the women.

At night, in the blue desert dusk the jukes sing out the plaintive old ballads, and the young girls dance with a determined abandon. For the young girls know that the sun makes short work of youth, and juices are soon gone. Flat bronzed Indian faces look in at the dancers, and their eyes are polished obsidian. They know that they alone are bred for this land, and when the pallid laughing ones are gone, they will remain.

There are racial memories, more of a faint pulse of blood and ache of bone than a true memory. The sun is a god. The god is angered because the tall pyramids are no longer used. The sun has long since baked away the faint stains on the pyramid crests, on the stone bowls, the time-worn channels. At dawn the sun hears no chant, sees no black upraised glint of stone knife, sees no blinded virgin awaiting the clever twisting thrust that rips the pulsing heart from its hot membranous nest.

Maybe, he thought, big hands resting easily on the wheel as he drove, they are closer to truth than we are. We and our learned talk of hydrogen-helium reaction.

Speed at night was a hypnotic. The speedometer needle held steady at ninety-five. Faint vibration from the road surface. White onrushing flick of an insect caught in the hard bright headlight beams. And weariness. Bard Lane knew that his weariness was of a very special type. An all-inclusive type, compounded of physical, intellectual and emotional strain, each carried to the threshold of tolerance. For a moment the car seemed to be standing still while the road ahead leaped toward him and was snatched under the wheels. He bunched his shoulders, shook his head violently to thrust back the impulse toward sleep that for a moment had brushed his eyelids. He adjusted the side vent a bit to throw a stronger current of the cool air against his face.

Far ahead the Christmas tree of a truck appeared, heading in the same direction. He came up on it slowly, made a pass signal with his lights and swept by, noting that it was a truck train, with heavy quad trailers. Once by the truck he sat a bit higher in the seat so that he could use the rearview mirror and the diminishing glow of the truck lights to check on the prisoner who slept curled on the back seat.

Far ahead he saw the lights of a lonesome town. He diminished speed gradually, saw the single traffic light ahead turn from green to red. In the glow of the lights along the deserted sidewalks, he glanced at the girl who slept beside him. She had slumped over toward the door so that her head appeared to be uncomfortably braced in the angle between door and seat back. Long legs were stretched out under the dash, and both hands, palms up, fingers curled, rested in her lap. She looked remarkably young and quite helpless. Bard Lane knew that there was nothing at all helpless about Sharan Inly. At the southern outskirts of the town he picked up speed again, and felt the heaviness of eyelids begin anew.

He shook his head again, reached out and punched one of the radio buttons, turning the volume down so as not to disturb the girl.

". . . and remember, when you're bored, drink Wilkins' Mead, spelled em ee aye dee. Wilkins' Mead is non-alcoholic, non-habit-forming. Four out of five doctors know that Wilkins' Mead cures boredom through a simple process of intensifying your reception to all stimuli. Three years ago, in May of 1972, Wilkins' Mead was placed on the market. Since that time, one hundred and sixty million Americans have learned that you have never really seen a sunset, enjoyed a kiss, tasted a steak until you have first had your handy lip-sized bottle of Wilkins' Mead. And now for your Wilkins' Mead reporter, the man the Senate couldn't silence, Melvin C. Lynn, with his nightly Wilkins' Mead summary of news of the world. . . ."

"This is Melvin C. Lynn, reporting the news for Wilkins' Mead and the Wilkins Laboratories, where the secret of your happiness was developed.

"This has been a quiet day on the international front. The Paris Conference continues and an informed source stated late this afternoon that the delegates have not yet lost hope of reaching an agreement on the basic problems confronting them. The Pan-Asia delegate has flown back to Moscow for further instructions on the Siberian agreement not to launch snooper satellites until new orbits have been assigned to each major power. The South American Coalition has refused to back down on their claim to five thousand miles of their moon base, even though they admit that it is almost a month since the last weak signals were received, and all expedition personnel must be assumed dead. Tomorrow, and throughout the world, as well as at the conference, there will be the customary sixty seconds of silence to commemorate the anniversary of the loss of the first manned rocket to Mars . . .

"And now for the national news front. Bliss Bailey, the Staten Island ferry boat captain who barricaded the ferry-boat bridge and chugged off toward Bermuda, was brought back under guard today. The commuters who took the inadvertent cruise with Captain Bailey have reported that once it was discovered that the ferryboat was heading east across a calm sea and nothing could be done, most of them turned it into a holiday. The identity of the nude blonde who jumped overboard the first night out has not yet been discovered. Bailey is quoted as saying, 'It just seemed like a good idea at the time.' Witnesses say Bailey appeared slightly dazed. His employers have not yet made public their decision regarding Captain Bailey. His cruise passengers are circulating a petition for his reemployment.

"Well, tomorrow morning the new slot-machine divorce law goes into effect in Nevada. Thirty machines have been installed to handle the expected rush of business. Applicants will slide a fifty-dollar bill into the waiting slot, then give their name, address and reason for requesting a divorce in a clear, low voice into the mike, then press their right thumb firmly against the exposed sensitive plate. Six weeks later they will return to the same machine and duplicate the procedure and the decree will fall into the hopper.

"Speaker of the House, Wally Blime, was severely reprimanded today in the public press and over the airwaves. This reporter feels, as others do after yesterday's childish display, that bubble gum and a pea shooter are rather poor substitutes for the dignity expected of a public figure in high office. Blime's only defense is that 'Something told me to do it.' And this, my friends, is from the same man who, two years ago, broke fourteen windows on New York's Madison Avenue before he was restrained by the police. His defense, at that time, was the same. Wally, this is a word from a friend. This reporter feels that it is high time you returned to private life.

"Larry Roy, national TV favorite, today jumped or fell from the forty-first story of a New York City hotel. Melly Muro, Larry Roy's seventh wife, told police that she could think of no reason for suicide, unless it could be a breakdown due to overwork. Melly, you will remember, is the redheaded woman who figured so largely in the divorce of Franz Steeval, composer and conductor, three months ago. Larry Roy was her sixth husband.

"Martha Needis, the Jersey City landlady who, last Tuesday, murdered her six roomers in their beds with a steak tenderizer, is still at large.

"In Memphis, debutante Gayla Dennison was today acquitted of murdering her guardian. She wept tears of joy.

"At Aberdeen Proving Ground in Maryland, government psychiatrists today disagreed on their diagnoses in the case of Corporal Brandt Reilly, the enlisted man who, ten days ago, turned an aircraft cannon on a company formation, killing sixteen and wounding twenty-one.

"And here is a light note in the news. Today, Pierre Brevet, French artist, is in serious danger of being lynched by irate American womanhood. He has been in this country for three days. He told reporters that he heartily approves, for French women, the new beachwear consisting of halters only, but after a visit to Jones Beach yesterday, he feels that this is one daring style this country could do without. He stated that his objections are deep-seated. Could that be a pun, Pierre?"

"You have just heard Melvin C. Lynn with the Wilkins' Mead news. And now do you hear that? Know what it is? You—pouring your first full golden glass of Wilkins' Mead from its handy lip-sized bottle. And tonight you have that date you've been waiting for. The big important date with the 'one and only.' Take her a bottle of Wilkins' Mead too. And then you can be sure that the two of you will enjoy one of the most——"

Bard Lane grunted and punched at the radio button. The airdale voice was mercifully silenced.

Sharan Inly said wryly, "No mead for me. But a beer would go good, if the man can arrange it."

"Did I wake you up with that racket? Sorry."

"You didn't wake me up. That creamy little voice of Melvin C.'s is insidious. It crept into my dreams, licking its chops at sudden death, Bard. I listen to him and feel that we're in an age of decay, and he is its prophet. Wonder what compulsion makes him go all oily over a nice juicy hammer murder?"

"You work all the time, don't you, Sharan? Always the psychiatrist."

He could feel her eyes on him. "You always shy away from psychiatry. There's always a little bitterness in your voice when you bring it up. Why?"

"If I start telling you my attitude, it will turn into an argument. Looks like a beer spot ahead. How's our boy?"

She knelt on the front seat and reached into the back as he began to slow for the neon flicker far ahead. She turned and plumped down into the seat with a sigh. "He'll keep for another three hours without a booster shot. Better park where it isn't too light, so nobody will get nosey."

There were a few shining new cars in the large parking lot, a larger number of dusty heaps, some pickup trucks and a few huge trans-state trucks. Bard parked near a weary-looking clump of live oaks, and carefully locked the car. He straightened up and stretched stiffness out of his joints. Sharan, standing nearby, made the time-honored and infinitely feminine gesture of looking back down over each shoulder to see how badly her skirt was wrinkled. The night breeze molded the thin skirt against the long clean thigh-lines, the trim hips. He felt the stir of pleasure in looking at her, along with the knowledge of the trap. Biological trap. Nature takes clear fresh skin, and youth and a slim body, and the child-bearing ability, holds it up and says, "This is what you want." And the pulse responds.

The acid twang of a jukebox cowhand quavered on the night air. ". . . *She never reely tole me that she loved meeeee . . .*"

There were metal tables on the patio, on the stones that were still warm underfoot from the sun-heat of the long day. He held a chair for Sharan, then went inside, walking the cramped tiredness out of his legs, muffling a yawn with the back of his hand.

Inside there were booths and dancers and girl-laughter and soft drinks held under the table edge for the quick jolt from the package store bottle. He stood at the beer bar and waited patiently, a tall tanned man with blunt bones in his face, with widow's peak slanting sharply back into the crisp brown hair, gray-touched, with an odd look that combined both mildness and authority. He wore a rumpled khaki hunting jacket over a faded blue work shirt, open at the throat.

He carried the two frosted bottles and one glass out to the table. Sharan was making up her lips, turned in the chair so the light from the doorway struck her mirror at the right angle. She smiled up at him, capped the lipstick and dropped it back into her white purse.

"How are we running on time, Bard?"

"We can kill a half hour and still get there a good hour before the conference."

"Want me to drive for a while?"

"No thanks. It's better to be doing something."

His big brown fist rested on the table top. She patted it with a quick, affectionate gesture. "Don't let it get you down. Screening wasn't your responsibility.'

"My responsibility is to get the job done. I couldn't pass the buck if I wanted to."

The light behind her haloed her cropped curls. She was indeed pleasant to look at. A face that was almost, but not quite, thin— with eagerness, mobility, sensitivity. She held her glass in both hands, like a child. Thrown together on the job, they had kept their relationship on the plane of friendship, mutual respect. There had been isolated moments—bending together over a desk, a quick glance across a crowded office, an inadvertent touch— when he had become conscious of his own awareness, and hers. But by unspoken agreement between them they always forced a return to an unemotional status. Maybe one day there would be time. Maybe one day the pressure of responsibility would be taken away, and there would be time for play.

He had wondered about her in the beginning. This new crop of young professional women no longer had any consciousness of fighting for equality. It existed. In the beginning he had accepted the idea that her amorality would be no less casual than that of the other women her age on the project. For a time he had skirted the idea of asking her to add the self-evident closer aspect to their association. But, at the time, he had decided that his duty was to maintain all his energies at the highest possible peak.

Now he was glad he had made that decision, for as he had come to know her better he realized that a casual amorality would not integrate with the rest of her character. In fact, she would probably be decidedly old-fashioned in that regard. And, had he asked her bluntly, he suspected that something in their relationship would have ceased to exist in the moment she denied him.

Women who played for keeps were becoming so rare as to be refreshing.

Until the all-pervading, all-important, capital J Job was done, Sharan Inly would remain Dr. Inly, Project Assistant in Charge of Psycho-Adjustment.

"The General," she said dolefully, "is going to be *muy irritado*."

"That is an understatement. Fat blue sparks are going to crackle off his fingertips."

She finished her glass, refilled it from the bottle. "How about that argument we're going to have? Want to start now?"

"You want to hear someone attack your profession, Dr. Inly?"

"Sure. I'm a missionary. I'll bring enlightenment to your poor layman mind."

"Here goes. Ever since Freud and Jung, you people have been honing certain basic weapons. I am a layman in psychiatry. However, I am a scientist. As a scientist, I am disturbed by your acceptance of the truth of your basic assumptions. Take the case of the critter we've got out in the car. I'll use a little of your gobbledegook language. He's been screened two ways. Loyalty and, in your province, stability. You hunted for all the garden-variety neuroses and couldn't find any of any importance. Ergo, we've got a stable guy. No delusions of persecution, no manic-depressive tendencies, no control so excessive it smells of dementia praecox. Doesn't miss his mother, save lady's shoes or draw pornographic pictures. Your ink-blot tests, properly fitted into statistical distribution charts, show that Mr. X is a nice clean-living ambiverent, ideal technician material."

She frowned. "You quarrel with that?"

"Not at all. But the neat little tests assume that this stability is a permanent state."

"They do not! The tests and the whole theory admit that in the face of unexpected strain, even the most stable, the most adjusted, can become psychoneurotic in one way or another. My goodness, that's why I'm employed out there. It's my job to detect the presence of any change in the face of strain and . . ."

"Now you're stating my point. I say that one of your basic assumptions is that there has to be an environmental change to create the strain which results in an alteration of this basic quotient of stability. I say that the assumption is too hasty. I say that there is something further to study. I think the shift from stability to instability can come in the twinkling of an eye and come without reference to any outside stimuli. Forget hereditary weaknesses. Forget the old business about escaping from a life that is unbearable. I say that you can take a perfectly adjusted guy, put him in a situation where his life is satisfying—and boom, he can go off like that. You've seen it. I've seen it. Why? Why does it happen? It happened to Bill Kornal. One minute he was okay. The next minute it was as though something . . . quite *alien* took over his mind. So now we've got him out in the car and there's four months' work lost."

"Are we going to go back, Bard, to the old idea of being possessed by devils?"

"Maybe we should. How about the news we listened to? What keeps perpetually messing up mankind? Jokers who go off their rocker when they've got every reason not to. No, you people are doing a good, but a limited job. Floating around somewhere is an X factor that you haven't found yet. Until you do I'm looking at psychology and psychiatry with a limited and dubious acceptance, Sharan."

There was a whisper of sound. He searched the night sky until he saw, against the stars, the running lights of a jet transport, losing altitude for the Albuquerque landing, the six flame-tongues merged, by the altitude, into a thin orange line.

The breeze stirred her hair. She said slowly, "I should rise up in mighty wrath and smite you hip and thigh, boss. But a still small voice within me says there might be something in what you say. However, if I admit you might be right, I'm also admitting the impossibility of ever isolating this X factor. How can you find something that hits without warning and disappears the same way?"

"Possession by devils," he said, grinning.

She stood up, slim against the light, more provocative to him in her complete, thoughtful, forgetfulness of self than if she had posed carefully.

"Then," she said, "the devils are more active lately. Oh, I know that every generation that reaches middle age believes firmly that the world is going to hell. But this time, Bard, even at my tender years, I think they may have something. Our culture seems like a big machine that's vibrating itself to bits. Parts keep flying off. Parts that are important. Decency, dignity, morality. We've all gone impulsive. Anything you want to do is all right, provided your urge is strong enough. It's a . . . a . . . ."

"Sociological anarchy?"

"Yes. And there, Mr. Lane, you have my motivation. Now you

know why I'm so desperately anxious for you to succeed. I keep feeling that if mankind can find some new horizons, there'll be a return to a decent world. Quaint, aren't I?"

They walked across the lot toward the car. He looked at the night sky, at the stars which seemed closer, more attainable here.

"Elusive devils, aren't they?"

She caught his wrist as they walked, her nails biting into the flesh with quick strength. "They won't stay elusive, Bard. They *won't.*"

"Four years now, that I've had my little obsession, Sharan, and they seem as far away as ever."

"You'll never give up, Bard."

"I wonder."

They had reached the car. Through the rear window, open an inch, came the soft sound of Bill Kornal's snores.

"It makes me feel ill to have you talk of giving up," she said in a half-whisper.

He leaned over to put the key in the lock. His shoulder brushed hers.

Without quite knowing how it had happened, he found her in his arms. She stood tightly against him with upturned lips, and with a small, plaintive sound in her throat. He knew that he was bruising her mouth, and could not stop. He knew it was a forgetfulness, a little time stolen from the project, from the endless drain of effort and responsibility. He had expected to find in her all the warmth and passion of any healthy young adult. He was pleased that her intensity matched his own.

"This is no good," she said.

She stood a little aside, her head bent. He knelt and swept his hand back and forth across the gravel until he found the keys. He straightened up.

"Sorry," he said.

"We're both tired, Bard. We're both scared to death of what General Sachson might do. We were clinging to each other for . . . comfort. Let's forget it."

"Let's not exactly forget it, Sharan. Let's shelve it for future action."

"Please," she said sharply.

"All right, so I shouldn't have said that." He knew that his tone was a shade indignant.

He unlocked the door. She slid under the wheel and across to her side. He chunked the door shut and drove out in a long curve onto the highway, accelerated viciously up to cruising speed. He gave her a quick glance. She was staring straight ahead, her face expressionless in the reflected dash lights. A big jack bounded from the shoulder into the road, startling him. He felt the tiny thud in his wrists as the wheel hit it, heard her sharp intake of breath.

"Just say I was possessed by one of those devils," he said.

"Probably we both were," she said. He glanced again and saw her smile. She moved a bit closer to him. "Besides, Bard, I'm a prim kid, I guess."

"Didn't taste very prim."

"That's what I mean," she said, enigmatically. "Now be good."

The gray sedan droned through the night.

2

AS THE GRAYNESS IN THE EAST BEGAN TO PALE THE CONFERENCE room lighting, Bard and Sharan sat with the other three persons awaiting General Sachson.

Gray, shaggy Colonel Powys, Projects Coordinator, rolled a yellow octagonal pencil against the polished top of the conference table, pressing so hard with his palm that the pencil made an irritating clacking sound as it rolled. Major Leeber, Sachson's aide, sleek and demurely pompous, nibbled at one edge of his moustache. The lean enlisted stenotype clerk turned a glass ashtray around and around and around.

Bard glanced over at Sharan. She gave him a wan smile. There were bluish shadows around her eyes.

"The general's very upset about this," Powys rumbled. His words dropped, like stones, into the pool of silence. There was an accusation behind his tone. The inference was that no one else was upset. Bard Lane restrained the impulse toward sarcasm.

The wall clock had a sweep second hand. Each time the hand made one full revolution, the minute hand jumped one notch with a tiny grating clack. Leeber yawned like a sated cat. He said, in a soft voice, "You're quite young for all that responsibility, Dr. Inly."

"Too young, Major?" Sharan asked politely.

"You're putting words in my mouth, Doctor."

"Major, I use that prefix for state occasions. I am Miss Inly."

He smiled at her, sleepy-lidded.

As the sweep second hand touched the hour and the minute hand clacked, the door swung open and General Sachson came in, small blue eyes full of electric crackle, neat heels striking at the rug. He was of minimum stature for Army requirements, with a face like a dried butternut, a man of snap and spit and polish and a score of uniforms tailored by experts.

"Hen *shut!*" Powys brayed. Only Sharan remained seated.

Sachson rounded the corner of the table, flicked his eyes across them in the moment of silence and then sat down, indicating with a chopping gesture of a child's thin brown hand that they should do the same.

"Meeting to order!" he snapped. "For God's sake, Sergeant, get the names right this time."

"Yes sir," the sergeant said in an utterly uninflected voice.

"Report damage, Dr. Lane. And keep to the point."

"Kornal broke down the door of the lab where the control panels were being assembled. He was alone in there for an estimated ten minutes. Adamson estimates that Kornal set us back four full months."

"I assume," Sachson said in a deceptively mild tone, "that the door was not considered sufficiently important to be guarded."

"There were two guards. Kornal knocked them down with a piece of pipe. One is all right. The other is in danger. A depressed skull fracture."

"The military, Dr. Lane, has discovered that the use of a password is not exactly a childish device."

"Kornal was privileged to secure a pass at any time to enter that lab. He was working long hours."

Sachson let the silence grow. The sergeant sat with his waiting fingers poised on the stenotype keys. The blue eyes swung slowly around to Sharan Inly.

"As I understand the theory of your work, Dr. Inly, it is your responsibility to anticipate any mental or emotional breakdown, is it not?" Sachson asked. His tone was replete with the mock gallantry which showed his distaste for the involvement of women in such projects as the one at hand.

Bard Lane saw Sharan's pallor increase a bit. "As William Kornal had access to all portions of the project area, General, it is self-evident that he was a double A risk on a psychological basis."

Sachson's smile was thin-lipped. "Possibly I am stupid, Dr. Inly. I don't find things to be as 'self-evident' as you seem to think they are."

"He was given a routine check three days ago, General."

"Possibly the error, Dr. Inly, is in applying so-called routine methods to special cases. Just what *is* a routine check?"

"A hypnotic is administered and the employee is asked a series of questions about his work. His answers are compared with the answers he gave on all previous checks. If there is any deviation —any deviation whatsoever—then the more exhaustive special investigation is instigated."

"You can prove, of course, that Kornal was actually given this routine check?"

Sharan blushed. "Am I to consider that a question, General?"

"Forgive me, Dr. Inly. I am a very blunt man. I have seen post-dated reports before. It merely occurred to me that——"

"I can back up Dr. Inly on that, if you feel she needs proof," Bard said in a harsh voice.

The blue eyes flicked over toward Bard. "I prefer, Dr. Lane, to have my questions answered by the person to whom they are directed. It saves confusion in the records of the meeting." He turned back to Sharan. "Why are not all the tests special rather than routine?"

"They could be, General, if my staff were tripled and if the persons to be tested were relieved of all project duty for a three-day period."

"That would build up quite an empire for you, Dr. Inly."

Sharan's eyes narrowed. "General, I am perfectly willing to answer your questions. I realize that somehow I should have anticipated Kornal's violent aberration. I do not know how I could have, but I know I should have. I accept that blame. But I do not have to accept innuendos regarding any possible dishonesty on my part, or any desire on my part to make myself more important."

"Strike that out of the record, Sergeant," Sachson snapped.

"I would prefer to have it remain in the record," she said quietly.

Sachson looked down at his small brown hands. He sighed. "If you feel that the record of this meeting is inadequate, you are privileged to write a letter to be attached to all copies that go forward from this headquarters. So long as I conduct these meetings, I shall direct the preparation of the minutes. Is that quite clear?"

"Yes sir," Powys said quickly, sitting at attention in his chair.

"Sergeant," Sachson said. "Kindly stop tapping on that thing. This will be off the record. I wish to say that I have had a reasonably successful military career. It has been successful because I have consistently avoided all those situations where I could have been given responsibility without authority. Now I am faced with just such a situation. For any ranking officer, it is a death trap. I do not like it. I cannot give you orders, Dr. Lane. I can only make suggestions. Each time you fall further behind schedule, it affects my record, my two-oh-one file, my military reputation. You civilians have no way of knowing what that means. You can switch bosses. Things are forgotten, or overlooked. I always answer to the same boss. There are always Siberias to which an officer can be sent."

"Isn't this project considerably more important than any one man's reputation?" Bard asked, hearing Powys' shocked in-suck of breath.

"That, Dr. Lane," Sachson said, "is a pretty ethereal point of view. Let me tell you exactly what I think of Project Tempo. On all previous extraterrestrial projects, the armed forces have been in complete control. Civilian specialists have been employed on a civil service basis in a technical and advisory capacity. Our appropriations have been part of general military appropriations.

And, I might add, those projects which I was privileged to command were all completed on or ahead of schedule.

"Now, Dr. Lane, you are in command, if I may use that word. You have the authority. I have the responsibility. It is a damnable situation. I know far too little of what is going on up in your hidden valley in the Sangre de Cristo Mountains. I know that a properly run guard detail, along military lines, would have prevented this . . . this accident. Now I am making this request of you. As soon as we start talking for the minutes again, you will ask me to detail Major Leeber to the project area in an advisory capacity. Major Leeber will report directly to me on all matters which, in his good judgment, may tend to endanger the promptness of completion of the contract."

Bard Lane tensed at the threat hidden behind the words. "And if I object?"

"I have given this considerable thought, Dr. Lane. If you object, I shall ask to be relieved of all future responsibility in connection with Project Tempo. That will, of course, make a stink. It will be wafted to the nostrils of our lawmakers. Already there is some discernible pressure for a senate committee to investigate this project and the apparently endless number of dollars required. My resignation will crystallize that move. You and your project will be investigated."

"And?" Bard Lane said softly.

"And you will find that many people in Washington, many important people, will have the same idea that I have: the only way to deep space, my scientific friend, is through further perfections in physical propulsion units, such as the current A-six tubes. All this Einsteinian space fold, time field stuff is so much dreaming."

"If you're so certain of that, General, why don't you recommend that the project be discontinued?"

"That is no part of my responsibility. My responsibility is to get your ship, the Beatty One, off the ground. If it fails in flight, it is no reflection on me. If you can't get it off the ground, we can use the hull for a military project now under consideration. You have your choice, Dr. Lane. Cooperate in the matter of my assigning Leeber, or reconcile yourself to giving up the project."

Bard Lane took long seconds to organize his thinking. He said,

"General, let me be presumptuous enough to summarize recent history of interplanetary travel. Ever since initial work on the old chemical propulsion V-two at White Sands over twenty-five years ago, it has been a history of failure. Those failures can be divided into three categories. One—technical deficiencies in staff and the ships. Two—espionage and sabotage. Three—weaknesses in the human factor.

"Project Tempo, General, has its own answer to each category of failure. Placing full authority in the civilian technical staff is the answer to category one. Secret location and careful loyalty screening is the answer to two. Dr. Inly and her staff are the answer to three. I am still in command, as you say. I will take Major Leeber under three conditions. One—he will not discuss technical problems or theory with any member of the staff. Two —he will wear civilian clothes and conform to all rules. Three— he will submit to class A security clearance, and to an extended stability test given all new employees."

Leeber flushed and stared at the ceiling.

Sachson said, "Dr. Lane, do you feel you are in any position to set up those restrictions?"

Bard knew that this was the focal point of the entire meeting. If he backed down Leeber would soon acquire his own staff, a nucleus of a military headquarters, and inch by inch General Sachson would take over control. If he did not back down, Sachson might do as he threatened. Yet such a resignation would not look well on the General's record.

"I will not accept Major Leeber on any other basis," Dr. Lane said.

Sachson stared at him for a full ten seconds. He sighed. "I see no reason not to meet you halfway, Doctor. I do resent the implication that any member of my personal staff might be a poor security risk."

"General, I can remember the case of Captain Sangerson," Bard reminded him gently.

Sachson appeared not to have heard. He looked at Leeber. "Get the prisoner, Major," he said.

Leeber opened the conference room door and spoke softly to the guard. Bill Kornal was brought in immediately.

Sharan Inly gasped and hurried to his side, examined the purple swelling under Kornal's left eye. She turned toward the General, her brown eyes suddenly brittle. "This man is a patient, not a prisoner, General. Why has he been struck?"

Kornal grinned miserably. "Don't make an issue of it, Dr. Inly. I don't blame the guy who clobbered me."

"Strike that off the record, Sergeant," Sachson said. "Take that chair, Kornal. You are—or were—a technician."

"More than a technician," Bard Lane said quickly. "Kornal is a competent physicist with over five years at Brookhaven."

"I'll accept that," Sachson said. His eyes were cool. "But it shouldn't be necessary to keep reminding you, Dr. Lane, that I wish answers from the person addressed." He turned his attention back to Kornal. "You smashed delicate equipment. Do you know the penalties for willful destruction of government property?"

"That isn't important," Kornal said bleakly.

General Sachson smiled. "I consider that to be a very peculiar statement. Possibly you can explain it to me."

"General," Kornal said, "the Beatty One means more to me than I could explain to you. I've never worked harder for anything in my life. And I was never happier. I don't care if the punishment is boiling in oil."

"You have a strange way of expressing your great regard for Project Tempo. Maybe you can tell us why you destroyed government property."

"I don't know."

"Possibly you don't want to tell us who employed you to smash the panels?" Sachson said in a silky voice.

"All I can do is tell you the way I told Bar——Dr. Lane, General. I woke up and couldn't get back to sleep. I put my clothes on and went out for some air and a smoke. I was standing outside when all of a sudden the cigarette fell out of my hand. Like somebody took over my hand and opened the fingers. Like I was being pushed back into a little corner of my mind, where I could look out, but I couldn't do anything."

"Hypnotized, I suppose," Sachson said acidly.

"I don't know. It wasn't like when they give you that hypnotic drug. My own mind wasn't fogged up. Just shoved back into a corner. That's the only way I can describe it."

"So there you were with your mind in a corner. Continue, please."

"I went over to where the carpenters had been putting up a new bunkhouse. The plumbers had left some lengths of pipe around. I picked up a short length and shoved it inside my belt. Then I went over to the lab and walked up to the two guards. They knew me. All this time you've got to understand, my body was doing things without my mind telling it to. And I had the funny feeling, sort of on the *edge* of my mind, that it wasn't right to be building the Beatty One. It was nasty, somehow. Dirty. And all my friends, all the people sleeping in the area, they were enemies and not . . . very bright. You know what I mean?"

Sachson stared at him. "I think that needs a little more explanation."

Kornal scratched his head. "Look. Suppose you went into an African village at night, General. They were all asleep. You would feel a lot smarter and superior to those savages, General, and yet you might be a little afraid of them waking up and ganging up on you. It was like that. I pulled out the pipe and hit the two guards, backhand and forehand. They dropped and I broke the door down. I went in, and it was like I'd never been there before. The equipment, the panels and all, they weren't familiar to me. They were dirty, like the Beatty One, and I had to smash them. I had ten minutes in there before they got me. As soon as they grabbed me, I was myself again. I did a good job in there. Adamson cried when he saw it. Cried like a baby. The thing that took over my mind and body . . . it was a kind of devil, I guess."

Bard intercepted Sharan's quick, startled look.

"The devils had you, eh?" Sachson said, his eyebrows arching up toward his hairline in mock astonishment.

"Something had me. Something walked in and took over. There wasn't a single damn thing I could do about it, either. After I was myself again, I tried to kill myself. But I couldn't do it."

Sachson turned to Colonel Powys. "What's S.O.P., on such cases, Roger?"

Powys had a rusty, rumbling voice. "We can't bring it to trial, General, if the suspect knows too much about any top secret project still under process of completion. When that man tried to blow up the Gettysburg Three he had almost the same story this man has. The head doctors thought up a name for it, and we stowed him away in the nut house until the Gettysburg Three took off. Of course she turned unstable at five hundred miles up and crashed off Hawaii——"

"I didn't ask for a history of the Mars flights, Colonel. What happened to McBride?"

"Well, sir, when Gettysburg Three was done for, the head doctors said McBride had recovered and so we brought him to trial. Because he was an enlisted man, we were able to give him five years at hard labor, but as I see it, this Kornal doesn't come under us."

Sachson gave Powys a frigid glare. "Thank you, Colonel. Brief and to the point, as usual."

Bard spoke to Kornal. "Bill, I think you'd better come back on the project. Want to try it?"

"Want to?" He held out his clever hands. "God, how I'd work! Adamson says four months lost. I could cut that down to less than three."

Sachson said harshly, "Are you completely mad, Lane?"

Bard ignored him. "What do you think, Sharan?"

"If he can pass the original psycho-screening tests, I don't see why not. We are using the best tests known. If he can pass them, he should be as acceptable as anyone who can pass them. Major Leeber can take them at the same time."

"I go on record as objecting to this," Sachson said.

"Me too," Powys rumbled.

"Sorry, General," Bard said. "Kornal is a highly trained man. We need him. If this was a temporary aberration, and not part of a repetitive pattern, he can help us undo the harm he did. I haven't time for thinking about fitting punishment to crime. Bill will punish himself more than anyone else ever could."

Sachson stood up. "It seems to be your baby. But it's all in the minutes. When he loses another four months for you, Project Tempo will either be disbanded, or have a new director. Sergeant, Dr. Lane will give you the exact wording on his request for Major Leeber. Meeting adjourned. Take Leeber with you when you drive back."

They stood in silence as the little general strode out of the room, favoring them all with a final bleak nod.

As soon as the door closed behind the general, Major Leeber said unctuously, "I know that you folks are thinking of me as a thorn in your side. It wasn't my fault the Old Man pushed me down your throat. But, believe me, I'll stay out of your way. Tommy Leeber can be a real happy guy. All the boy needs is that five o'clock jolt of firewater and a few shell-pink ears to whisper into. Couple of times a week I'll mail the old man a double-talk report and we can all live happily together in the mountains."

Leeber had a lazy grin on overly-full lips under the dark military moustache, but under sleepy lids his eyes were steady, cold, unwinking black.

"Happy to have you with us," Bard said without warmth.

Sharan stood up. Leeber moved closer to her. "And how about you, Miss Inly? Are you glad to have me aboard?"

"Of course," she said absently. "Bard, how soon are we starting back?"

"Better make it noon. That will give some time for a little sleep."

The others left. The sergeant looked expectantly at Bard. Bard smiled at him. "You know your boss. Write it up in any way that will make him happy, just so long as the conditions I imposed are included. Do you have them down?"

"Yes sir. Want me to read them back?"

"No need of that." He walked toward the door.

The sergeant said, "Uh . . . Doctor Lane."

He turned. "Yes?"

"About Major Leeber. He's very smart, Doctor. And he gets along fine in the Army. I think maybe someday he'll be a general."

"A worthy ambition, I suppose."

"He likes to make a . . . good impression, where it counts most."

"Thanks, Sergeant. Thanks very much."

The sergeant grinned. "Mention it not, Doctor."

Back in the room assigned him in the B.O.Q., Bard Lane lay awaiting the steep drop into exhausted sleep. He thought of what Kornal had said. Possession by devils. A devil that could invade the unwilling mind, use the reluctant body as a tool. Were the ancients closer to the truth than we, with our measurements and dials and ink blot tests? A man could not face the theory that there is a measure of built-in instability in the mind, that insanity can come with the next breath. Even a theory of devils is more comforting than that. Maybe, he thought, we share this planet, have always shared it. We are . . . things that the Others can use to amuse themselves. Maybe they can slip gently into the human mind and exercise their evil humor. Maybe they visit us from some far planet, a gaudy picnic for them, a stained excursion. And perhaps they laugh. . . .

3

RAUL KINSON'S WORLD HAD WALLS. IT WAS A WORLD OF ROOMS, of ramps, of corridors.

There was nothing else. Thought could not reach *beyond* the walls, beyond the furthest rooms. He had tried to thrust his thoughts *through* the walls, but thoughts cannot encompass the idea of nothingness, and so his thoughts curled back, repelled by a concept beyond the authority of the mind.

When he was ten years old he had found the opening in the wall. It was an opening you could not crawl through, because it was covered with something you could look through as you look through water. Yet the substance was hard to the touch.

He was not yet old enough then to be permitted to dream.

Dreaming was for the older ones, the ones who had grown big enough to join the mating games.

In the ancient micro-books he had found the word for that hole in the wall. Window. He said it over and over. No one else read the micro-books. No one else knew the word. It was a secret that was precious, because it was not a made-up secret. It existed. Later, of course, he found that in the dreams there are many windows. They could be touched, opened, looked through. But not with one's *own* hands. That was the difference. In the dreams you had to use other hands, other bodies.

He would not forget the day he had found the window. The other children angered him. He had never liked the games they played. They laughed at him because he was not frail, as they were. His games, the muscle-stretching games, hurt them and made them cry out. On this day they had permitted him to play one of their games. The old game of statue dance, in one of the biggest rooms on the lowest level. One spindly girl held the two white blocks and as they danced the girl would unexpectedly clap the blocks together. At that signal everyone stopped as though turned to stone. But Raul had been off balance and when he tried to stop he crashed awkwardly into two of the frail boys, knocking them to the floor with shrill yelps of pain and pettish anger. They were angered but his anger surpassed theirs. The translucent floor glowed softly amber.

"You cannot play, Raul Kinson. You are rough. Go away, Raul. We won't let you play."

"I didn't want to play anyway. This game is silly."

He had left them and gone down the long hall that led through the maze of the power rooms where the air itself seemed to vibrate. He liked walking there as it gave him a strange but agreeable sensation in the pit of his stomach. Now, of course, he knew what the power rooms contained, and knew the name of the soft gray metal of the corridor walls in the power area. "Lead" it was called. Yet knowing what was in the power rooms had never decreased the pleasure he felt walking through the humming air, through a vibration below the range of audibility.

The day he walked away from their games he had wandered aimlessly. Memory was clear, though it had been fourteen years ago. He had been bored. The rooms where music played endlessly, had been playing since the beginning of time, and would play on forever, no longer pleased him. The grownups he saw ignored him, as was the custom.

Seeking some kind of excitement, he had stepped onto the moving track which carried him up through twenty levels to the place of the dreamers, where all children were forbidden to go. He had tiptoed down an empty silent corridor until he came to where the dreamers were, each in a thick glass case set into the wall.

He looked in at a woman. She lay on softness, curled, cat-slack, one hand under her cheek, the other touching her breast.

Her mouth was distorted by the fitted metal plate between her teeth. Shining cables coiled up from the exposed edge of the plate and disappeared into the wall behind her shoulder. Standing close, he could feel a tiny throbbing, very much like that near the power rooms, but weaker.

As he watched her she suddenly stirred, and his sudden fright held him transfixed there as she took the plate from between her teeth, laid it aside, and reached down for her loose-woven robe of soft dull metal wadded near her feet, her movements slow and fumbling. As she began to yawn and to reach to push open the door of the glass case, she saw him and her slack sleepy face tightened at once in anger. He fled, knowing what the punishment would be, hoping that in the dimness she had not recognized him. He heard her call, sharp-voiced, "Boy! Stop!"

He ran as fast as he could, aware that if he took the track that moved slowly downward, her shouts might alarm someone on a lower level who could intercept him.

And so he dodged and ran up the stationary track that led to the twenty-first level. Once before he had explored up there. The silence of the rooms had awed him, had frightened him so that he had hurried back down, but on this day the silent rooms were refuge.

Higher and higher. The twenty-first level did not seem safe enough. He continued on up to the next level above that and collapsed, his mouth dry, a great pain in his side, his heart thudding. He listened above the sound of his heart and the stillness settled around him.

It was then he had noticed, close to his left hand, the edge of the great wheel that moved the track. It was like the wheels at the lower levels, with the one astounding difference—it was stilled.

Raul touched it gently. An odd new thought began to form itself in his mind. This might be a thing that was . . . broken. That had ceased to run. The thought dizzied him because it was outside his experience. All things ran—that is, all things designed to run did so, quietly, perfectly and forever. He had known of the tracks that were still above the twentieth level, and had thought that it was meant that they should be that way. And now he was confounded by this new concept of "brokenness." One of the women had broken an arm. She was shunned because it was now a crooked misshapen thing. He knew that he dared not talk of this new concept as it applied to the tracks above the twentieth level. Such a thought if expressed would be heresy, pure and simple.

It was hard to think in such a fashion. It made an ache deep in his head. If this track had ceased, for some reason, to run—then it followed that these upper levels were to be used by all the Watchers—and were shunned now merely because of the physical difficulty of walking up the steep slopes. He knew of no one, adult or child, who had gone higher than the twentieth level. There was no need for it. On the lower levels were the warm perfumed baths, the places of wine and of sleep and of the taste of honey. On the lower levels were the food rooms and the rooms that healed pain.

He suddenly wondered how high the levels stretched above him. Would it be possible to go to the top? But was there a top? Was there an end to it? Or did the levels go on and on, higher and higher, without ever an end to them. The strength of his desire for an answer to this question shocked him. He could taste the shrillness of fear in his throat, but at the same time excitement fluttered inside him with soft frantic wings.

He was dressed, as were all the children, in the single long strip of soft metal fabric. It was wound around the waist, with the trailing end brought up between the legs and tucked firmly inside the waistband. When one was old enough to be permitted to dream, one was given either the toga and thongs of a man, or the robe of a woman. When death came, when the dead one was slipped, naked, into the mouth of the oval tube to speed down into unknown blackness, the clothing was saved. He had seen the room where it was stored in shining piles that reached to the highest point a man could touch.

He stood up, took a deep breath, tightened the band at his waist and walked solemnly up the next motionless track. And the next, and the next. He tired of the steep climb and rested, realizing that he had lost count. The corridors down which he glanced had a sameness about them, and a silence.

At last he came to a track which moved upward, its neighboring track moving downward, silently and perfectly. He stepped onto the track which carried him up, wondering how long it had been since other bare feet had stopped there.

Up and up and up. The familiar things were a frightening distance below him. But fears were lulled by the familiar silent motion of the track, which created a wind to touch his face.

With the sudden shock of a blow, he saw that at last there was no track to carry him higher, and thus no level above the one he had reached. The corridor was smaller than the others. He fought against a fear that commanded him to turn quickly and descend. The silence was the worst. No pad of feet against the body-warm floors. No distant voices. No sound of children. Just silence and the glow of the walls.

This, then, was the top of the world, the top of eternity, the summit of all. Fear faded into exaltation and he felt larger than life itself. He, Raul Kinson, had gone, alone, to the top of the world. The sneer at the others formed in his mind. He stuck his chest out and carried his chin high. The old ones said there was no limit to the world—that the silent levels went upward into infinity, that those who slid down the tube of death fell forever, turning slowly through the blackness, until the end of time.

He walked down the corridor. It curved slightly. He stopped. There was a picture, a large picture, at the end of the corridor. He knew of pictures. There were thousands of them on the eighteenth level and no one really understood them.

He walked to the picture with the contempt of familiarity. He walked close to its oddly shining surface. A low sound bubbled in his throat, the darkness rushed over him and he had no feeling of impact as he fell.

He struggled back to consciousness and knelt and looked at the picture again. He knew that it was no picture. It was a revelation. It was a truth so fantastic that he heard, on his lips, the meaningless sounds that infants make. He knew that from this day forward, he would be apart from all the others who had not seen this, who did not share his concept.

Outside of the levels, beyond the walls that glowed, everyone was taught that there was nothingness. Often he had gone to sleep trying to visualize "nothingness." It was all a lie.

All of the levels were located in an enormous, frightening

room. The ceiling, impossibly high, was a deep purple color, with hard shining dots of light in it, and one enormous round deep-red light that hurt his eyes when he looked directly at it. The floor of the room was tan and brown and gray. The most horrible aspect of the enormous room was his inability to see the walls. They were beyond vision, in itself a new concept. It dizzied him to stare down at the remote floor. Far off, to the right, the floor was humped up into a jagged series of mounds much higher than the level of his eye. And, in the foreground, six objects towered, standing neatly in a row. The glow of the round red light made them look silvery. The longer he stared, the more accustomed he became to perspective and the more accurately he could assess the height of those six cylindrical featureless objects with the blunt snouts and the flared portion that rested against the tan of the floor. As he watched he saw movement. A bit of the floor came alive, lifted up into a tall whirling column. He could not understand why it did this thing. He watched it move, still whirling, toward the high rough mounds. Soon he could see it no more. He touched his mouth to the hard surface of the transparent substance and drew back with startled speed. In a world where everything was warmed, the surface had a strange chill.

The gnawing of hunger at last took him away from the picture which he later found was called a "window." He went all the way back down to the deep familiar levels. He spoke to no one of what he had seen. He walked in a daze, feeling shrunken and small against the enormities of what lay outside the known world. He ate and slept and bathed and walked alone, seeking always the chance to slip away, to return to his window that looked out on another world which dwarfed his own.

Once, full of the importance of new knowledge, he had tried to tell one of the old ones about what he had seen. Wrath exploded and Raul Kinson picked himself up off the floor, with bleeding mouth, determined to speak no more.

With Leesa, of course, it was a different thing. As his sister, she shared, to some extent, that wry biological joke which had given him a deep chest, broad shoulders, strong column of neck, muscle-bulge of thigh and calf in a world where physical strength was useless.

He remembered that he had been twelve and she was ten when he took her up to the window. At ten she was taller and stronger than the other girl children of the same age. Like Raul, her hair was blue-black and abundant. It set them apart in a world where hair was thin, dry and brown, lasting usually until the age of twenty, seldom beyond.

They had talked, and he knew that Leesa shared his vague feeling of disquiet, his aimless discontent—but her releases took a different form. Whereas he strove constantly to learn more, to understand more, she made a fetish of wildness and childish abandon.

He was proud of the way she refused to show her fear. They stood at the window. He said, proud of his new words, "That is 'outside.' All of our world and all the levels are inside of what is called a 'building.' It is cold out there. That red round light is a sun. It moves across the ceiling, but never goes completely out of sight. I have watched it. It travels in a circle."

Leesa looked at it calmly enough. "It is better inside."

"Of course. But it is a good thing to know—that there is an outside."

"Is it? Why is it good just to know things? I would say it is good to dance and sing and be warm—to take the long baths and find the foods that taste best."

"You won't tell anyone about this?"

"And be punished? I am not that stupid, Raul."

"Come, then. And I will show you other things."

He took her down several levels to a series of small rooms. He took her to one room where ten chairs faced the end of the room. He made her sit in one while he went to the machine which had taken him so many months to understand. He had broken four of them before he at last found the purpose.

Leesa gasped as the light dimmed and the pictures appeared, by magic, on the wall at the end of the room, the end that they faced.

Raul said quietly, "I believe it was intended that all children should be brought to these rooms to watch the images. But somehow, a long time ago, it was given up. Those marks under each picture mean nothing to you, Leesa. But I have learned that they are writing. Each thing has a word, as you know. But those marks can mean the word. With those marks, if you could read, I could tell you something without talking."

"Why would you want to do that?" Her tone was full of wonder.

"I could leave a message for you. I can read the writing under the pictures. There is an uncountable number of these spools to put in the machines. Each room holds ones more complicated than in the previous room. I think that this room was for the very small children, because the words are simple."

"You are clever, Raul, to understand those marks. But it seems like a hard thing to do. And I don't know why you do it."

Her wonder had changed to boredom. He frowned. He wanted someone to share this new world with him.

He remembered a place that would interest her. He took her down several levels to a much larger room. This time the pictures moved and they seemed to have real dimensions and the persons, oddly dressed, talked, using strange words scattered among those more familiar.

Raul said, "That is a story. I can understand it because I have learned the strange words—at least some of them." In the dim light he saw her leaning forward, lips parted. The people in peculiar dress moved in strange rooms.

He turned it off. "Raul! It's . . . beautiful. Make it appear again."

"No. You don't understand it."

"It is like what I imagine the dreams must be, like they will be when we're old enough to be allowed to dream. And I thought I could never wait. Please, Raul. Show me how to make it happen again."

"No. You have no interest in these things. In women that wear strange colors and men that fight. Go on back down to your games, Leesa."

She tried to strike him and then she wept. Finally he pretended to relent. "All right, Leesa. But you must start like I did. With the simple pictures. With the simple writing. And when you learn, then you can see all this again and you'll understand it."

"I'll learn today!"

"In a hundred days. If you are quick and if you spend many hours here."

He took her back to the first room and tried to help her. She wept again with frustration. At last the corridors dimmed and they knew that the time of sleep had come. Time had gone too quickly. They hurried back down to the others, hiding until the way was clear, then strolling in with exaggerated calm.

At sixteen Raul Kinson towered above every man in the world. He knew that it was time, and that the day was coming. He knew it from the way the women looked at him, from a new light in their eyes, a light that troubled him. They could not speak to him because until he was empowered to dream, he was still a child.

There were those who had certain duties. And, in each case, they instructed a young one of their choice in these duties in preparation for the time of death. There was a woman in charge of the rooms of childbirth, and another who cared for the young children. A man, fatter than others, organized the games of the adults. But of all those with special duties, Jord Orlan was the most powerful. He was aloof and quiet. He was in charge of dreams and the dreamers. He had wise, kind eyes and a face with a sadness of power in it.

Jord Orlan touched Raul Kinson lightly on the shoulder and led him to the far end of the tenth level, to the chambers where Jord Orlan lived alone, apart from the community life.

Raul felt a trembling excitement within him. He sat where Jord Orlan directed him to sit. He waited.

"After today, my son, you cease to be a child. All who are no longer children must dream. It is the privilege of being an adult. Those of you who come to me come with many wrong ideas of the dreams. That is because it is forbidden to discuss the dreams with children. Many of our people take the dreams too lightly. That is regrettable. They feel that the dreams are pure and undiluted pleasure, and they forget the primary responsiblity of all those who dream. I do not wish you, my son, to ever forget that primary responsibility. In good time I shall explain it to you. In our dreams we are all-powerful. I shall take you to the glass case of dreams which shall be yours until the time of death. And

I will show you how to operate the mechanism which controls the dreams. But first we shall talk of other matters. You have remained apart from the other children. Why?"

"I am different."

"In body, yes."

"And in mind. Their pleasures have never interested me."

Orlan looked beyond him. "When I was small, I was the same."

"May I ask questions? This is the first time I have been permitted to talk to an adult in this way."

"Of course, my son."

"Why are we called the Watchers?"

"I have been puzzled about that. I believe that it is because of the dreams. The source of the word is lost in antiquity. Possibly it is because of the fantastic creatures that we watch in our dreams."

"You say that those creatures are fantastic. They are men?"

"Of course."

"Which, then, is the reality? This constricted place or the open worlds of the dreams?" In his intense interest Raul had forgotten to use only the familiar words.

Jord Orlan looked at him sharply. "You have strange language, my son. Where did you obtain it? And who told you of the 'open worlds'?"

Raul stammered, "I . . . I made up the words. I guessed about open worlds."

"You must understand it is heresy to ever consider the creatures of the dreams as reality. The machines for dreaming have a simple principle, I believe. You are familiar with the vague, cluttered dreams of childhood. The machines merely clarify and make logical these dreams through some application of power. They are limited in that there are only three areas, or worlds, in which we can dream. In time you will become familiar with each world. But never, never delude yourself by believing that these worlds exist. The only possible world is here, on these levels. It is the only conceivable sort of surroundings which will permit life to exist. We become wiser men through dreaming."

Raul hesitated. "How long has this world of ours existed?"

"Since the beginning of time."

"Who . . . who made it? Who built these walls and the dream machines?"

"Again, my son, you come close to heresy in your questions. All this has always existed. And man has always existed here. There is no beginning and no end."

"Has anyone ever thought that a larger world might exist outside the levels?"

"I must ask you to stop this questioning. This life is good and it is right for all of the nine hundreds of mankind. Nothing exists beyond the walls."

"May I ask you just one more question?"

"Of course. Provided it has more sense than your previous questions."

"I have seen that this world is large, as though many more men once lived in it than do now. Are our numbers smaller than in times past?"

Orlan abruptly turned his back. His voice came softly to Raul's ears. "That question has bothered me. I have not thought of it for a long time. When I was very small there were over a thousand of us. I have wondered about this thing. Each year there are one or two togas or robes for which no children are born." His voice strengthened. "But it will be of no importance in our lifetime. And I cannot believe that man will dwindle and die out of the world. I cannot believe that this world will one day be empty when the last person lies dead with no one to assist him into the tube."

Orlan took Raul's hand. "Come and I will take you to the case assigned to you for all of your life."

Orlan did not speak until they stood, on the twentieth level, before the empty case. Orlan said, "At your head, as you lie therein, you will touch that small knurled knob. It has three stations for the three dream worlds. The first station is marked by a line which is straight. That is the most beautiful world of all. The second station is marked by a curved line which stands on a base. You will find that world frightening at first. It is noisy. The third station, marked with a line with a double curve, is to direct the machine to create the third world, the one we find of least interest. You will be free to dream at any time you desire. You will shut yourself inside, set the knob for whichever world you desire, then disrobe and take the metal plate between your teeth and bite down on it firmly. The dream will come quickly. In your dream you will have a new body and new, odd, pointless skills. I cannot instruct you how to acquire change and mobility in the worlds of dreams. That is something you must learn by doing. Everyone learns quickly, but the actual procedure does not lend itself to words. You will dream for ten hours at a time and at the end of that time the machine will awaken you. Then it is best to wait for a new day before dreaming again."

Raul could not resist the chance to say, "When the lights are bright in the walls and floors, we call it day, and when they are dim, we call it night. Is there any particular reason for that?"

Jord Orlan's hand slid quickly down from Raul's naked shoulder. "You talk insanely. Why do we have heads? Why are we called men? Day is day and night is night."

"I had a childhood dream where we lived on the outside of a great globe and there was nothing over us but space. The other globe, which we called the sun, circled us, giving light and heat. Day was when it was overhead. Night was when it was on the opposite side of the globe."

Orlan gave him a queer look. "Indeed?" he said politely. "And men lived on all sides of this globe?" Raul nodded. Orlan said triumphantly, "The absurdity is apparent! Those on the underside would fall off!" His voice became husky. "I wish to warn you, my son. If you persist in absurdities and in heresies, you will be taken to a secret place that only I know of. It has been used in times past. There is a door and beyond it is an empty coldness. You will be thrust out of the world. Is that quite clear?"

Sobered, Raul nodded.

"And now you must dream of each world in turn. And at the end of three dreams you will return to me and you will be told the Law."

Jord Orlan walked away. Raul stood by the case, trembling. He lifted the glass door, slid quickly in and lay on his back on the softness.

He unwound the band of fabric and thrust it from him. The soft throb of power surrounded him, tingling against his naked limbs. He set the knob at figure 1, which Orlan had not known as a figure, as a mathematical symbol.

The metal plate was cool to his touch. He stretched his lips and put it between his teeth. Putting his head back he shut his teeth firmly against the metal . . . and fell down into the dream as though he fell from the great red sun to the brown dusty plains near the ragged mountains.

He fell remote and detached in the blackness, limbless, faceless. . . .

All motion stopped. This then, was the precious dream? Absolute nothingness, absolute blackness, with only the sense of existence. He waited and slowly there came to him an awareness of dimension and direction. He hung motionless, and then detected, at what felt like a great distance, another entity. He felt it with a sense that was not sight or touch or hearing. He could only think of it as an awareness. And with the power of his mind he thrust out toward it. The awareness heightened. He thrust again and again and it was a sudden merging. The thing he merged with fought him. He could feel it twist and try to turn away. He held it without hands, pulled it toward him without arms. He pulled it in and merged it with himself and pushed it back and down and away from him so that it was shrunken into a far small corner.

And Raul Kinson found himself walking on a dusty road. His arm hurt. He looked down at it and he was shocked to see the stringy leanness of the arm, the harsh metal enclosing the withered wrist, the dried blood where the metal had cut him. He was dressed in soft rags and he smelled the stink of his body. He limped on a bruised foot. The metal band on his wrist was in turn connected to a chain affixed to a long heavy pole. He was one of many men fastened to one side of the pole, with an equal number attached to the other side. Ahead of him, bare strong shoulders, oddly dark, were crisscrossed with wounds, some fresh, some very old.

The thing he held pressed down, writhed, and he released the pressure, a pure mental pressure he could not understand. It seemed to flow up into his mind, bringing with it strong fear and hate and the strange words of a strange tongue which, oddly, had meaning to him. These others were his comrades. Yes, they had fought together against the soldiers of Arrud the Elder, seven days' march away. Death was better than captivity. Now there was nothing to look forward to but an empty belly, a life of slav-

ery and savage punishment, a ceaseless, hopeless desire to escape
and return to the far green fields of Raeme, to the cottage where
the woman would wait for a time, where the children played by
the mud sill of the door.

Vision and other senses began to fade. Raul found that he had
released the mind of this man too far, that he had given the man
the power to thrust him back into the nothingness. So once again
he exerted control. In a short time he found the necessary delicate
balance—with the captured mind thrust down, but not so far that
language and circumstances became meaningless, yet with a
sufficient control so that his own will would not be thrust out.
With the maintenance of a proper balance, it was as though he
existed on two levels. Through the mind of this man, this person
who called himself Laron, he felt the hate and the hopeless anger,
and also, through the alien invasion of his mind, a secondary fear
of madness.

He trudged along in the dust. The soldiers guarding them
carried long pikes with metal tips and walked lightly, joking
among themselves, calling the prisoners foul names.

Raul gasped with pain as the pike point stabbed his upper arm.
"Scrawny old one," the soldier said. "You'll be lion meat tomorrow, if you live that long."

Ahead the dusty road wound back and forth up the flank of a
hill. Beyond the hill he could see the white towers of the city
where Arrud the Elder ruled his kingdom with traditional ferocity. It appeared to be a march of many hours. What had Jord
Orlan said about change and mobility? A knack to be acquired.
This helplessness and the pain of walking did not seem to promise much.

He let the captive mind flow back up through secret channels,
once again taking over will and volition. Senses faded, and as the
nothingness once again enfolded him, he tried to thrust out toward the side, toward the soldiers. Again the feeling of grappling
with a strange thing that resisted. The moment of control, of
pushing the other entity down into a corner of his mind passed
and vision returned.

He lay on his belly in a patch of brush, staring down at a distant dusty road far below, at a clot of figures walking slowly
along the road. He let the captive mind expand until he could feel

its thoughts and emotions. Once again—hate and fear. This one had escaped from the city. He was huge and strong. He carried a stout club and he had killed three men in making his escape. Contempt and pity for the captives. Hate for their captors. Fear of discovery. This was a simpler, more brutal mind than the first one. Easier to control. He watched for a time, then slid out of the mind and thrust his way toward the remembered direction of the road.

The new entity was more elusive and control more difficult. He found that he had taken over the body of a young soldier. He walked apart from the others. The captives were at his right, laboring under the weight of the poles that kept them joined, like one large many-legged insect. Raul fingered the spirit of this young soldier and found there revulsion for the task, contempt for the calloused sensibilities of his comrades in arms, pity for the dirty prisoners. He regretted the choice of occupation he had made and wished with all his heart that this duty was over. It would be better in the city at dusk when he could wander among the bazaars, a soldier returned from the wars, stopping at the booths to buy the spiced foods he loved.

Raul forced a turn of the head and looked back at the line. After several moments he found the thin man with the pike wound in his upper arm. He had been in that man's mind. Inside his own mind he felt the flutter of panic of the young soldier who had made a motion without apparent purpose. "Why do I turn and stare at the thin old one? Why is he of more importance than the others? Is the sun too hot on this helmet?"

Raul turned and looked up into the hills, trying to locate the brush where the fugitive hid. This seemed to alarm the captive mind even more.

"Why am I acting so strangely?"

The haft of the pike was comforting in Raul's hand. He lifted it a trifle, realizing that the habit action patterns of the young soldier would serve him well should he wish to use the pike. For a time he contented himself with looking about at the landscape, picking out of the soldier's mind the names of the objects he saw. A bird, a quick blue flash against the sky. An ox cart loaded with husks of corn. They passed stone ruins of an unguessed antiquity.

He turned when he heard a harsh scream. The thin one, whose

mind he had inhabited, had fallen. A heavyset soldier, his face angry and shiny with sweat, jabbed again and again with the pike, making the red blood flow.

Raul thrust with the ease of long practice, the tip of his pike tearing through the profiled throat of the heavyset soldier, who turned, eyes bulging. He clawed at his throat with both hands, dropped to his knees, then toppled face down into the yellow dust of the road.

In his mind he felt the panicky thoughts of the young soldier. "I killed him! I must be mad! Now I'll be killed!"

The soldier in charge swaggered over, scowling. He took in the situation at a glance and drew the short broadsword that only he wore. The others, grinning in anticipation, kept the young soldier from fleeing by making a half-circle of leveled pikes.

Raul, infected by the panic in his mind, thrust again with the pike. The broadsword flickered and lopped off a two-foot section of the end of the pike, stinging his hands. He looked down and saw the thrust as the broadsword went deep into his belly. The leader twisted the blade and withdrew it. The spasm and cramp dropped Raul to his hands and knees. He gagged as his arms weakened and his face sank slowly toward the dust. From the corner of his eye he saw the broadsword flash up again. The bright pain across the back of his neck drove him out into the nothingness where there was neither sight, nor sound, nor sense of touch.

At dusk he was in the city, with life and motion brawling and clashing around him. He led a heavily laden burro and at intervals he cried out that he had water, cool water for dry throats. In the mind of the water vendor he found the location of the palace itself. More and more he was gaining control of the directional thrusts, gaining confidence in gauging the distance from mind to mind. He was a guard at the castle gates, then a man who carried a heavy load up endless stone steps.

At last he became Arrud the Elder, the man of power. To his astonishment, as he gained control of the king's mind, he found it as simple and brutal as the mind of the fugitive. He found hate and fear there. Hate of the distant kings who drained his manpower and wealth in unending wars. Fear of treachery within the palace walls. Fear of assassination.

Raul relaxed to Arrud's action patterns. Arrud buckled the heavy belt around his thick waist. It was of soft leather, studded with bits of precious metal. He flung the cape over his wide shoulders, tucked his thumbs under the belt and swaggered down the stone hallway, thrusting open the door at the end of the corridor. The woman had long hair, the color of flame. She lay back on the divan and looked at Raul-Arrud coldly. She had a harsh, cruel mouth.

"I await your pleasure," she said bitterly.

"Tonight we look at the prisoners. The first ones have arrived."

"This time, Arrud, pick some strong ones for the beasts, strong ones who will fight and make the game last."

"We need the strong ones for work on the walls," he said sulkily.

Her tone grew wheedling. "Please. For me, Arrud. For Nara."

Raul relinquished his hold and faded into grayness. Only the gentlest of motions was necessary. He seeped slowly and relentlessly into the mind of the woman and found that there was an elusive subtlety about it that defied his initial attempts at control. At last he had her mind trapped. Her thoughts were hard to filter through his own mind. They were fragmentary, full of flashes of brilliance and color. Only her contempt and hate for Arrud was constant, unvarying. He found that maintaining a delicate balance of control was far more difficult when handling the woman-mind. He would possess her mind so utterly that he would lose her language, her female identity, to become, foolishly, Raul in a woman-body. Then she would surge back until he clung to the last edge of control.

In a short time he knew her. Knew Nara, daughter of a foot soldier, dancer, mistress of a captain, and then a general, and at last mistress of Arrud. He knew her contemptuous acknowledgment of the power of hair like flame, body that was cat-sleek, vibrant, clever.

Arrud came near the divan. He pressed his knuckles to his forehead, said slowly, "For a time I felt odd, in my mind. As though a stranger were in my mind, calling me from a great distance."

"You have not given me your promise about the strong slaves, Arrud."

He looked down at her. He reached with a hard hand, fondled her breast, hurting her with his clumsiness. She pushed his hand away and his lips went tight. He reached again, tore the sheer fabric of her garment from throat to thigh.

Raul fingered through her thoughts and memories, found the knowledge of the ivory-hilted dagger wedged between the cushions of the divan. He forced the woman's mind back, quelling her anger, supplanting it with fear. She willed herself to speak and he would not permit her to speak. Arrud slid with bulky clumsiness onto the couch, seeking the woman's throat with his lips. Raul forced the woman's hand to grasp the dagger. She was rigid with fear and he sensed in her mind the frantic thought that this was not the way to kill Arrud. This way she would be discovered. The dagger tip touched Arrud's back. The needle blade slid into the thick muscles as though sliding through water as it reached for the heart. His heavy body pinned her to the couch as he died. As Raul slid away, sickened and weary, he heard her first maddened scream.

Raul awakened in the glass case of dreams. He lay still for a time, and there was a deep, slow, aimless lethargy within him, an exhaustion more of the spirit than of the mind or body. The ten-hour dream had ended as he left the body of the woman. It seemed as though he had been in the odd, alien world for months. He took the metal plate from his mouth. His jaw muscles were cramped and sore. He turned slowly and pushed the side panel up, turned and rested bare feet on the warm floor of the level of dreams.

A woman stood there, smiling at him. The habits of childhood were difficult to overcome. It shocked him that he should be noticed by one of the adult women. She was not an old one.

"You have dreamed," she said.

"A long dream and it tired me."

"The dreams are like that in the beginning. I shall never forget my first dream. You are Raul. Do you know my name?"

"I remember you from the games of the children. A long time ago you became a dreamer. Fedra, is it not?"

She smiled at him. "I am glad you remembered." It was flattering to be treated with such friendliness by an adult. Childhood was a lonely time. Fedra was different, in the same way that he and Leesa were different, but not as much. She merely had not quite the frailness of the others, and there was some lustre to her brown hair.

He reached for his garment in the case, but she said, "Have you forgotten?"

He looked at her. She held the toga of a man in one hand, the thongs in the other. His heart gave a leap. To think of all the times he had yearned for a man's toga. And now it was here. His. He reached for it. She pulled it back.

"Do you not know the custom, Raul? Were you not told?"

Her tone was teasing. He remembered then. The man's toga and thongs must be put on the first time by the woman who will partner the man in the first mating dance he is privileged to attend. He paused in confusion.

She drew back and her mouth became unpleasant. "Maybe you think, Raul Kinson, that you would prefer another. It will not be easy for you. You are not liked. Only two of us asked, and the other changed her mind before the drawing."

"Give those to me," he said, his anger matching hers.

She backed away. "It is not permitted. It is the law. If you refuse, you must wear child's clothing."

He stared at her and thought of Nara with the hair like flame, the dusky body. Compared to Nara this woman was mealy-white, soft. And he saw the unexpected sheen of tears in her eyes, tears that came from the hurt to her pride.

So he stood and closed the panel on his case of dreams and permitted her to drape the toga on his shoulders, fasten the belt, with the slow stylized motions of the custom. She knelt and wound a silver thong around his right ankle, bringing the two ends of the thong around his leg in opposite directions, each turn higher so that the thong made a diamond pattern. She knotted it firmly with the traditional knot just below his knee. He advanced his left leg and she placed the thong on it. She still knelt, staring up at him. He remembered, reached and took her hands, pulled her to her feet.

Together, with not another word, they rode down from the higher levels to the proper corridor. They went back to the room where the others waited. The fat old one who directed the games of the adults glanced at them with relief. He went to the music panel and touched the soft red disc which started the music. The other couples ceased chattering and lined up. Raul felt like a child who had stolen the toga and thongs of a man. His hands trembled and his knees felt weak as he took his place in line, facing Fedra. He watched the other men from the corner of his eye.

The fat old one played a sustained note on the silver tube he wore around his neck. Naked skulls gleamed in the amber glow of the walls. The cold, formal, intricate dance, substitute for urge and need, began. Raul felt that he moved in a dream. The quick harsh world he had visited seemed more to his taste than this stylized substitution. He sensed the amusement in the others, knew that they saw the awkwardness of his hands and feet, knew that this same awkwardness shamed Fedra. This dance was required, he knew, because it meant continuance of the world of the Watchers.

As the music slowly increased in tempo, Raul wished that he were hiding on one of the highest levels. He forced himself to smile like the others.

4

BARD LANE STOOD AT THE WINDOW OF HIS OFFICE STARING OUT across the compound toward a new barracks building that was being constructed between two older ones. The wire mesh had been stretched taut and a crew with spray guns were spreading the plastic on the wire with slow practised strokes.

General Sachson had not underestimated the pressure. It was coming from all directions. A Cal Tech group had published an alleged refutation of the Beatty Theories, and the news services had picked it up, simplified it. *Credo,* the new micro-magazine, was screaming about "billions being squandered in some crackpot experimentation in the mountains of northern New Mexico."

A group of lame-duck congressmen was sublimating political

frustration by taking a publicity-conscious hack at the top-heavy appropriations for space conquest. A spokesman for the JCS hinted at a complete reorganization of the top management of military-civilian space flight efforts.

Sensing the possibility of cancellation of Project Tempo, the administrative branches in Washington—finance, personnel, procurement—were pulling the reins tight by compounding the numbers of reports necessary.

Sharan Inly tapped at the door and came into Bard's office. He turned and gave her a weary smile. She wore her usual project costume, jeans and a man's white shirt with the sleeves rolled high, collar open.

She glanced with distaste at the mound of paper on his desk. "Bard, are you a clerk or a scientist?"

"I'm too busy learning to be the first to do anything about the second. I am beginning to learn something about government paper work, though. You know, I used to try to handle every report—at least set up reasonable procedure for it. Then I found out that before I can get a report in, the whole thing is changed around. Know what I do now?"

"Something drastic?"

"I had rubber stamps made. Take a look. See this one? HOLD FOR ACTION—COORDINATION GROUP. And this one. FOR REVIEW AND REPORT—STATISTICAL COMMITTEE. Here is a pretty one. SUSPENSE FILER—PROGRAMMING BOARD."

"What on earth are they for?"

"Oh, it's very simple. Now take this report request right here. See, it came in three copies. The Industrial Research Committee of the Planning Board of the Materials Allocation Group of the Defense Control Board wants a report. And I quote. 'It is requested that on the twelfth and twenty-seventh of each month, beginning with the month following receipt of this directive, that the planned utilization of the appended list of critical metals be reported for three months in the future, each month's utilization to be expressed as a percentage of total utilization during the six months period immediately preceeding each report.' And here is their appended list. Seventeen items. Did you see that new girl in my outer office, in the far corner?"

"The little brunette? Yes, I saw her."

"Well, I route this report to her. She cuts a stencil and mimeographs the directive, runs off a hundred copies. She's my Coordination Group, my Statistical Committee and my Programming Board. On the twelfth and twenty-seventh of each month she'll mail in a copy of the directive with one of the rubber stamp marks on it. She'll send one to the Defense Control Board and one to the Materials Allocation Group and one to the Planning Board and one to the Industrial Research Committee. I let her use any stamp she happens to feel like using at the moment. It seems to work just as well as making out the report. Probably better. I have her put a mysterious file number on the stencil."

"Oh, Bard, how terrible that your time has to be taken up with this sort of thing!"

"I don't mind most of them. But here's a rough one. No more personnel, Sharan. At least, they're making it so complicated to put on any new person that the delay will run into months. We'll have to make do with what we have. They're hamstringing me, very neatly. And I can't fight back. There's no one to fight. Just a big vague monster with carbon-paper tentacles, paper-clip teeth, and a hide made of layers of second sheets."

"Why, Bard? Why are they turning against the Project? They believed in it once."

"It's taking too long, I guess."

"Can't you go to Washington?"

"I'm no good at that sort of thing. I get a compulsion. I know what to say, how to butter them, but I can't quite manage to do it."

She went over to a heavy oak armchair near the window, dropped into it, hooked one slim leg over the arm. She frowned. He walked over and looked out the window, following her glance. "Well, Sharan, even if it never gets off the ground, they can't say that we didn't build a big one."

Even in the brightest sunshine, the light that shone down on the project area was diffused. Four gigantic steel towers of irregular size had been constructed in the form of an irregular oblong. A square mile of tough fabric, painted with all the art of camouflage, was suspended like a grotesque circus tent over the towers. From the air it would appear to be another barren irregular hill of rock and sage and sand. Bard Lane's office was near the cave-like lip of the south edge of the outsized tent. The Beatty One stood in the middle of the tent. Around the base of the Beatty One was the constant, ant-like activity that had been going on for over a year.

Some of the labs were set into the solid rock of the surrounding hills. All project buildings not under the protection of the vast tent were designed to look, from the air, like just another sleepy village in the Sangre de Cristo Mountains, a village where the flagellationists still whip-cut the back of the selected man who labored under the heavy cross at Easter time.

He looked down at her for a moment, and resisted the impulse to rest his hand on her crisp hair, to feel, under his strong fingers, the delicate configuration of skull, the clean bone-line.

Bard locked his hands behind him and looked out to where he could see the dull metal base of the Beatty One, almost exactly one hundred and seventy feet in diameter, and so tall the round snout almost touched the fabric of the enormous tent. A platform elevator inched upward, carrying men in work clothes. The elevator was built on heavy steel circular tracks so that the operator could raise it to any point on the outside skin of the great vehicle.

"Does anybody expect it to fly, Doc?" she asked.

"I personally guarantee to get it at least twelve inches off the ground."

She smiled up at him, the smile flavored with rue. "News good and bad," she said. "The good is about Bill Kornal. We took him apart, every reflex, every neurosis, every response to stimuli, and we reassembled him. There is a change, sure. But it measures out as exactly as much as one would expect as an aftereffect of what happened to him. He is as sound and solid as that mountain over there."

"Good. Put him on. I'll sign the confirmation in the morning."

"And the bad news is that I can't find any real good reason to wash out Major Tommy Leeber. I don't have to like him, but I can't wash him out. Once you dig down through a lot of apparent complexities, the whole thing becomes very simple. He has a mind like a brass hinge. It works in just one direction: What is the best thing for Tommy Leeber? Totally directional, and of course he has a top security rating. So he's all yours, Bard. I brought him over. He's waiting out there for the deluxe tour."

Bard Lane glanced at his watch. "There's time. See you at dinner. Thanks for all the nice things you do for me."

Major Leeber had the same reaction as did every other newcomer to the project when he was finally taken close enough to the Beatty One to really appreciate the size of it. After he had been walked all the way around it, he finally shook himself out of his stunned air of disbelief, smiled his lazy smile and said, "So . . . I *still* don't believe it."

Dr. Bard Lane had the elevator brought to ground level and signaled the operator to take it up to the nose. He stood and leaned against a stanchion and watched Leeber move to the exact center of the platform. At the ogive curve, close under the overhead camouflage, the elevator tipped toward the hull and followed the curve on up to the last port. Leeber did not look well as he leaned away from the direction of the tilt.

"Come along," Bard said as he stepped over the lip of the port. He lowered himself to the deck inside, and began his familiar indoctrination speech as he gave the major a hand. "This will be the entrance port for the crew. The ship is designed for a crew of six. No passengers. The forward tenth of the overall length contains the living quarters, life maintenance systems, supplies and main control panels. We are in the control room. The three chairs there are on gymbals mounted on hydraulic pedestals designed to compensate for sudden increments in acceleration. They are similar to, but an improvement over, the systems previously used. Impulse screen mounted, as you can see, but not yet tied into either manual or computer control."

Leeber studied the main control panel and said, "Looks like a king size A-six, and not too much different from the A-five. Where are the directional jets?"

"Eliminated in favor of a twenty-ton gyro that can be turned through a ten-degree arc. In free space it will turn her in any desired attitude. A lot of weight to boost, but not much less than standard attitude jet installation and the necessary fuel controls, and we save a lot by eliminating the initial lift-off with chemical fuels, so we have no booster stages to jettison on the way out."

"Initial lift on atomic drive? Poison the air?"

"With a very short-life emission. Launch site will be clean in ten hours. At half-diameter outbound, they switch to standard A fuel, and keep it on CA. That means that——"

"——at twelve thousand miles out they go right onto the same old A-six atomic propulsion fuel and stay in constant acceleration. I'm not a civilian, Doctor. So this marvelous ship is just one big son of a bitch of an oversized A-six with a flywheel gyro, a short-life mix for takeoff. Wonderful!" His smile was ironic, his eyes cold.

"With one more little change, Major. Eighty days of CA will put her clear of the system. Then they switch to Beatty Drive. Drive is an inaccurate word, but we haven't come up with a better one yet. I worked with Beatty and ran the team that completed his equations after he died two years ago. Do you have any background in theoretical physics?"

"Some exposure. Try me, Doctor."

"What does 'frames of reference' mean to you?"

"The old analogy about three elevators and one man in each one. Elevator A is going up at top speed, Elevator B is going down slowly and Elevator C is stuck between floors. Each one is moving at a different speed in relation to each of the other two."

"Very good. But you have one motionless elevator. Take it a step further. Your motionless one is at zero velocity. Okay, where is the motionless point in space? You can be hanging in space absolutely motionless in relation to one star, but moving at ten thousand miles per second in relation to a star in some other direction. On a theoretical basis you would find a motionless point in space by computing the velocity and direction of movement of all the stars in all the galaxies and finding that point from which all those velocities both toward you and away from you, on whatever angle of inclination or declination, would average out to zero. If we had the math to solve a problem with an infinite number of unknowns, we do not have all the knowns to feed into it, due to the temporal limits—and physical limits—of observation. Are you with it?"

"I think I . . . Well, keep going."

"Here is the heart of it. Beatty called that the space-frame—the problem of finding the zero point in space. So he made the assumption there must also be a time-frame. He pictured a universe curved in upon itself in the Einsteinian concept, but composed of not only varying velocities and directions, but also varying temporal relationships. From this he extrapolated the idea that an average of the time relationships would give you a zero place, a place where time does not exist, just as an average of speed-relationships would give you a zero place where movement does not exist. So he applied that theory to the paradox of the expanding universe, and his equations did what the red shift 'tired light' theories failed to do. He proved that the apparent expansion was in fact the interrelationship of the velocity of light with a varying time warp throughout the observable galaxies, with the effect more apparent the greater the warp—i.e., in the most distant galaxies. I think I've lost you."

"Afraid so."

"Try it this way then. Until Beatty's work we believed that maximum attainable velocity would always be a fractional percentage point under the speed of light itself, because according to the Fitzgerald equations, at the speed of light the contraction of mass is infinite. Beatty gave us a way to bypass that barrier by thrusting a ship into another frame of reference of time. Here is our standard simplistic analogy. You are driving from El Paso to New York. It will take you three days. You leave on Monday. You expect to get to New York on Wednesday. So as soon as you are outside the El Paso city limits you push a little button on the dashboard labeled 'Wednesday.' And there is the skyline of New York, right down the road."

"Didn't . . . the Fitzgerald equations say that time contracts along with mass in ratio to velocity?"

"Excellent, Major! Beatty's equations showed that the time gradient between different systems, instead of having to be traversed at nearly light speed, can be capsuled into an abrupt time shift, just as when you drive across from one time zone into the next."

"Your jumps would be a little bigger than Monday to Wednesday, I'd imagine."

"The increments are in standard segments of one hundred years. But don't think of it as a hundred years passing in a flash. It is more a distance measurement. You arrive in New York at the precise moment that you left El Paso."

"So when do you know when to make the jump, how far you'll jump, and where you'll be when you get there?"

Bard Lane shrugged and smiled. "That's what took seven months of programming and three months of integral and digital computer time. Then we built the control panels according to the results of the calculations."

"And that nut smashed them?"

"Do you mean Doctor Kornal? He did. He is back on the job. My decision to take him back will stand up, so don't step over the line you seem to be edging too close to."

"Me? Hell, let's be friends. Life is too short. It's your risk, not mine. What do we look at next?"

"Dinner. I'll take you through the labs tomorrow morning."

"Where do I find the action?"

"I'll point out the club on our way back down to the launch pad."

5

BARD LANE SAT ON THE EDGE OF HIS BED. IT WAS AFTER MID-night on the same day that he had taken Major Leeber on the tour of inspection.

He sat and little rivulets of fear ran through his mind the way that rain will trickle erratically down a windowpane. The night was cool and the wind that came through the screen touched his naked chest and shoulders, but it did not stop the perspiration that made an oiled sheen on his face.

It was like a return to childhood, to the long-dead nights of terror. The scream. "Mommy, Mommy! It was a moldy man and he was sitting on my bed!"

"It's all right. It was just a dream, dear."

"He was here! He was! I saw him, Mommy."

"Shh, you'll wake your father. I'll sit here and hold your hand until you get back to sleep."

Sleep voice. "Well he *was* here."

He shivered violently. Now there was no one to call. There was someone you *should* call, but that might mean . . . defeat.

You can fight all the outside enemies in the world, but what if the enemy is in your own mind? What then?

It was a decision to make. He made it. He dressed quickly, snatched a leather jacket from the closet hook, shouldered his way into it as he left his quarters. From the slope he looked down on the project buildings. A thin moon rode high, silvering the dark buildings. He knew that inside the darkness there were lights, hum of activity, night shifts in the labs in the caves.

Sharan Inly had a room in the women's barracks. He walked down the slope and across the street. The girl at the switchboard was reading a magazine. She glanced up and smiled, "Good evening, Dr. Lane."

"Good evening. Dr. Inly, please. Would you connect the call in the booth?"

He shut himself in. Her voice was sleepy. "Hello, Bard."

"Did I wake you up?"

"Ten seconds later and you would have. What is it, Bard?"

He glanced through the booth door. The girl had returned to her magazine. "Sharan, would you please get dressed and come down. I must talk to you."

"You sound . . . upset, Bard. I'll be down in five minutes."

She was better than her word. He was grateful for her promptness. She came out beside him, asking no questions, letting him choose time and place. He led her over to the porch of the club. It was after hours and the chairs had been stacked on the tables. He set two of them on their legs. A dog howled in the hills. Over near the labor barracks someone laughed loudly.

"I want to consult you about a patient, Sharan."

"Of course. Who are you worried about?"

"Me."

"That sounds . . . absurd. Go ahead."

He made his voice flat, emotionless. "Tonight I had dinner with Major Leeber. I went back to my office to finish up some of the paperwork. It took a bit longer than I expected. When I finished, I was tired. I turned out the light and sat there in the dark for a few moments, waiting for enough energy to get up and go back to my quarters. I turned my chair and looked out the window. Enough moonlight came through the screen so that I could just make out the shape of the Beatty One.

"Suddenly, and without any warning, I felt a . . . nudge at my mind. That's the only way I can describe it. A nudge, and then a faint, persistent pushing. I tried to resist it, but its strength increased. There was a certain horrid . . . confidence about it. An utterly alien pressure, Sharan. A calm pressure. Have you ever fainted?"

"Yes."

"Do you remember the way you tried to fight off the blackness, and it seemed to grow stronger? It was like that. I sat absolutely still, and even as I fought against it, one part of my mind was trying to find a reason for it. Tension, overwork, fear of failure. I used every device I could think of. I tried to focus my mind on nothing except the look of the corner of the screen. I dug my fingers into the chair arm and tried to focus on the pain. The thing in my mind increased the pressure and I had the feeling that it was *fitting* itself to my mind, turning as it entered, so as to find the easiest means of entrance. I lost the ability to control my own body. I could no longer dig at the chair arm with my fingers. I cannot describe how frightening that was. I have always felt . . . completely in control of myself, Sharan. Maybe I've been too confident. Possibly even contemptuous of the aberrations of others.

"My eyes were still focused at short range on the corner of the screen. My head lifted a bit and, without willing it, I found myself staring out at the Beatty One, trying to make out its outlines. It was in my mind, strongly, that I was seeing the ship for the first time. I was sensing the reaction of the thing that had entered my mind. The thing was perplexed, awed, wondrous. Sharan, in that state, I could have been forced to do . . . anything. Destroy the ship. Kill myself. My will and my desires would have had no part in action I might have undertaken."

As she touched his arm, and said softly, "Easy, mister," he realized that his voice had climbed into a higher register, threatening shrillness.

He took a deep breath. "Tell me, is there such a thing as a waking nightmare?"

"There are delusions, fantasies of the mind."

"I felt . . . possessed. There, I've said it. The thing in my mind seemed to be trying to tell me that it was not inimical, that it wished no harm. When the pressure reached its strongest point, the moonlight faded away. I looked into blackness and I felt that all my thoughts and memories were being . . . handled. Fingered, picked at.

"And now, Sharan, comes the part that's pure nightmare. The thing pressed its own thought images into my mind. It was as though it substituted its memories for mine. I looked down a long, wide corridor. The floors and walls had a muted glow. The people had an almost sexless look, frail, neuter, blue-white people, but human. It was very clear they were inbred. They walked with a tired timelessness, a semi-hypnotic sort of dedication, as though every movement was a portion of custom rather than habit. And suddenly I was looking out through a huge window, a window at an enormous distance from ground level. Six cigar-shaped, tail-finned objects that could only have been space ships pointed upward at a purple sky and a huge dying red sun that filled a quarter of the sky. I realized that I was seeing a dying world, an ancient world, and the people who were left in it. I got an impression of sadness, of a remote and weary sadness. Then the presence flicked out of my mind so quickly that it dizzied me. My own will, which seemed to have been crowded back into a tiny corner of my brain, re-expanded suddenly and I was myself again. I tried to treat it as a . . . as something of no importance. I went back to my quarters and undressed, as though I could go to bed with no further thought of it. But I had to come and tell you about this."

He waited. Sharan stood up, walked to a post set into the cement porch, leaned against it with her hands in her pockets, her back to him.

"Bard," she said, "we talked about the X factor in mental illness. In psychiatry we have a recurrent phenomenon. A mind, temporarily out of focus, will use as material for delusion something that has happened in the immediate past. Our sleeping dreams, as you know, are almost always based on some reference to the previous waking period. Recently we have talked of being possessed by devils. Silly darn phrase. Bill told us his symptoms. What is more natural than for you to borrow his symptoms and use them as your own. But, of course, you carried it a step further, due to your background and your ambition. You had to make the devils into representatives of some extra-solar superrace, because you are too practical to be satisfied with an illusion of devils. Bard, this is all due to the pressure mounting, the fear that they'll stop the project, the needling General Sachson gave you." She turned and faced him, hands still in the pockets of the jeans.

"Bard, go on back to bed. We'll stop at my place and I'll bring you down a little pink pill."

"I haven't made you understand, have I?"

"I think I understand."

"Dr. Inly, tomorrow I'll report to you for the usual tests. You will advise me if you find anything out of line. If so, I shall make my resignation effective at once."

"Don't be a child, Bard! Who else could carry Project Tempo on his back? Who else could get the loyalty you do out of fifteen hundred of us working out here in this Godforsaken spot on something not one in fifty of us can understand?"

"Suppose," he said harshly, "that the next time I have this little aberration, I get as destructive as Kornal did?"

She walked slowly to him, pulled her chair closer, sat down and took his left hand in both of hers. "You won't, Bard."

"I believe it's part of your job to be reassuring, isn't it?"

"And to wash out those who show signs of incipient mental instability. Don't forget that. Part of my job is to watch you. I have been watching you. I have a complete file on you, Bard. For one moment, look at yourself objectively. Thirty-four years old. Born in a small town in Ohio. Orphaned at eight. Raised by an uncle. Public school. At twelve you had your own ideas of the way to solve the problems in the geometry book. You were skeptical of the Euclidian solutions. You won a science scholarship based on the originality of an experiment you did in the high school physics lab. You worked for the other money you needed. Cal Tech, M.I.T. You got a reputation when you helped design the first practical application of atomic power for industrial use. Government service. Years of exhausting labor on the A-four, A-five and A-six. Now do you know why you had this little . . . lapse in your office?"

"What do you mean?"

"You have no ability to relax. You've never had time for a girl, for a lost weekend. You've never fallen asleep under a tree, or caught a trout. When you read for amusement, you read scientific papers and new texts. Your idea of a happy evening is either to cover fifteen pages of blank paper with little Greek chicken-tracks, or have a bull session with some men who are just as one-sided as you are."

"Does the doctor want to prescribe?" he asked gently.

She snatched her hand away and leaned back in the chair. The moon had slanted low enough so that under the porch overhang it touched the line of her cheek, made a faint highlight on her lower lip, left her eyes shadowed.

After a long silence she said, "The doctor will prescribe the doctor, Bard. I'll come back to your quarters with you, if . . . you'll have me."

He was aware of his own intense excitement. He let the seconds go by. He said, "I think we'd better be thoroughly honest with each other, Sharan. It's the best way. You've put us into a delicate spot. Emotions are pretty well exposed at this point. I know your personal loyalty to me, and to the project. I know your capacity for loyalty. Now answer this honestly, my dear. If I had not come to you with this . . . trouble, would you have made that sort of offer?"

"No," she whispered.

"And if I had asked you, in the casual way that seems to have become a custom these past few years?"

"I don't know. Probably no, Bard. I'm sorry."

"Then let's drop the subject, with no harm done. I'll settle for a pink pill and an appointment in the morning."

"And after you are tested, Bard, I am going to send you out into the hills with a scope rifle I can borrow from a friend of mine. You are going to spend a full day potting varmints and thinking of something beside this damnable project. That's an order."

"Yes, *sir!*" he said, standing up and saluting.

"Please, Bard. You must understand that it was just weakness which made you feel that you had the symptoms Bill Kornal described. A weakness born of tension and strain. It was auto-hypnosis, pure and simple. It can happen to any of us."

"Whatever it was, Sharan, I didn't like it. Come on. I'll walk you back."

They went slowly down the road. There was no need for conversation between them. She had partially comforted him. After he was in bed, waiting for the mild drug to take effect, he wondered why he had been so reluctant to permit her to sacrifice her own integrity for the sake of the project. He thought of the slim clean look of her in the moonlight, of her young breasts against the fabric of her jacket. He smiled at his own reservations, at his reluctance to accept such a gift. They had both sensed that they were almost—but not quite—right for each other. And "not quite" was not enough for either of them.

RAUL KINSON REALIZED THAT EIGHT YEARS HAD PROVED FEDRA correct. One never forgets those first few dreams, those first three dreams—one for each alien world demarked on the dial at the head of the dream case.

Fedra had borne his child during that first year of the dreams. Sometimes he watched the children at their games, and wondered which one was his. He looked in vain for any sign of resemblance. He wondered at this curiosity, which the others did not seem to share.

Yes, the first dreams could never be forgotten. Even after eight years he remembered every moment of the second dream.

In his second dream he had a new certainty of contact, a new assurance born of the practice during the first dream. He was eager to see this second world. In his initial eagerness he had grasped the first contact mind, had thrust with all the power of intellect, motivated by strong curiosity.

And at once he had found himself in an alien body which writhed in bright hot light on a hard surface. He could not control the muscles or the senses of the captive body. Vision was broken fragments. Muscle spasms could not be controlled. He tried to withdraw pressure, but the host mind would not take over the body again. The brain he touched was shattered, irrational, sending messages of spasm to uncontrolled muscles. At first he thought he had inhabited a mind already broken, and then he began to guess that perhaps the full, uncontrolled thrust of his own mind had broken the host mind. He gave up all efforts at control and slid out of the host, impelling himself very gently toward the nearest contact.

He slid with restraint into this new mind, never taking over control, merely waiting and watching and listening at a sufficiently high level so that the language became clear. The new host was a brawny man in a blue uniform. He was saying, "Move back there! You! Give the guy air! Give him a chance, folks."

A second man in uniform came over. "What you got, Al?"

"Fella with a fit or something. I sent in an ambulance call. You there, did I hear you say you're a doctor? Take a look at him, will you?"

A man in gray bent over and wedged a pencil between the teeth of the man who writhed on the sidewalk. He looked up at the policeman. "Epileptic, I think. Better send for an ambulance."

"Thanks, Doc. I already did."

Raul looked curiously through the eyes of the man who called himself Al, who thought of himself as a policeman, as the metal machine on four wheels came down the street, making shrill screamings. It backed up over the curbing. Men in white examined the figure on the sidewalk, lifted him onto a stretcher and put him in the vehicle. It screamed into the distance.

Al took a small box from his jacket pocket, pressed a button and spoke with it close to his lips. He made a report and finally said, "I don't feel so great. Like maybe a headache. If it gets worse I'm going to call in and ask off."

He put the speaker back into his pocket. Raul looked out through Al's eyes at a broad street full of hurrying people and

strange objects on wheels guided by other people. The people
were similar in form and coloring to the people of the first world.
But their clothing was different. He searched through Al's mind
for words of identification and found that this city was called
Syracuse, in a bigger area called New York State. The street was
South Salina.

Raul also learned that Al's feet hurt, that he was thirsty, and
that his "wife" had gone to visit in some faraway place. He
sensed that the "wife" was a mating partner, but it was unexpectedly more than that. It was a sharing of lives as well as a
mating, and a living together in a specific non-community structure called a "home." Soon he found a familiar relationship in another one of Al's random thoughts. He thought of "money," and
Raul was able to identify it as the same kind of mysterious and
apparently useless pieces of metal which had been pressed into
his hand when he had been a water vendor on the first world. He
learned that Al was given money in return for his services as a
policeman, and the money went to provide food, clothing and the
"home." He inserted into Al's mind the thought that no one
would ever again give him any money and he was shocked by the
strength of the wave of fear which followed the suggestion.

He looked through Al's eyes into the store windows, trying to
guess the possible uses for objects he had never seen in any of his
years in the rooms of learning. When Al looked at something of
his own accord, Raul could interpret the thoughts, identify the
object and learn what it was used for. A thin stick with a metal
spool at one end was used to trick a creature that lived under
water and was called "bass." When the hook was in the flesh of
"bass," it was reeled in and lifted into the boat and later eaten.
When he saw the mental picture of a bass in Al's mind, the
thought of eating it made him feel queasy. When he forced Al to
look at something, the man's shock and fear at finding himself
doing something without awareness or purpose was so great that
his mind would freeze and Raul would learn nothing.

He spent ten hours in the city, learning to more skillfully detach
himself from one host and move on to the next, learning the gra-
dations of control, from a total takeover down to that point where
he could rest in a corner of the host mind and be carried about,
watching and listening and comprehending, with the host unaware

of his presence. He drank beer, watched part of a motion picture, drove a car and a truck and a motorbike, watched television, typed letters, washed windows, broke into a locked car and stole a camera, tried on a wedding gown in a fitting room, drilled teeth, mated, swept a sidewalk, cooked meat, played a game with a ball. He learned that one must move into a child's mind slowly and carefully, as into a small room full of fragilities, and once there one would find magical things, bright dreams and wishings. He learned that the minds of the very old ones are blurred and misted, with only the oldest memories still sharp and clear. He discovered the knack of so delicately insinuating a thought into the host mind that much could be learned from the response. Inside the mind it became a communication much like an odd conversation wherein the host mind thought it was talking to itself. Many of their thoughts were a little like dreams, in that they were yearnings and wishes and pictures of those satisfactions they wanted and did not have. Satisfactions of money and flesh and power. These were a frightened, insecure, discontented people, for the most part. They had all the violent impulses of the people in the first world, but in all their mechanized orderliness they had no way of releasing that violence. It shimmered in their minds and tore at them. They were not devoured by lions, but by their own buildings and machines. And they lived under a tyranny of "money" which seemed to Raul as cruel an oppression as that of Arrud the Elder, and as pointless.

The ten-hour dream ended, and he had tasted the minds of uncounted scores of hosts. He had awakened drained and wearied by the experience, he remembered. And he remembered also that as he had descended from the twentieth level he had passed Leesa, heading upward, and knew from her sly glance that she was on her way up to the rooms of learning. She was, at fourteen, taller than the others, ripening more quickly, but still dressed in the metallic sash of all the children of the Watchers.

Again, as after the first dream, he ate with a hunger that surprised him. Later he learned that the dreams always brought on this fierce need to fill the belly. As with the first dream, he tried to remember some of the alien words he had been able to speak while dreaming, but they were gone from his mind.

He finished and slid the eating tray back into the wall slot, hearing, as the orifice closed itself, the roaring of steam that would cleanse it for the next one to sit at that place. Two women and a man approached him as he stood up and asked him to come and sit with them in one of the talking places and tell them his dream. He went, but was so shy of his new knowledge, so obviously afraid his dream would sound both uninteresting and poorly told, that one of the women guessed the reason for his discomfort and told of her own dream first.

"I wanted to experience beauty and pain," she said, "and I chose the first world, and searched for half the dreaming before I found her. She was locked in a room of stone, and she was very weak but very beautiful. She had very strong thoughts, full of pride and hate and passion. I could not understand what they wanted her to denounce. It was some belief that had no meaning to me. I learned there was very little time left to her, and I hoped I would not have to leave her before they ended her. The men who kept her locked there tried to break her. Always one watched while the others used her. Finally she was taken in her stained rags through narrow streets. They threw filth at her. She was tied to a post and they piled things around her and a man stood in front of her and spoke in a very loud voice recounting her crimes. Then something was thrown into the substance around her, and the pain came up around her body, crackling and spitting. It was the most terrible torment I have ever found on any world, the fullest and most delicious pain. Just before her mind went dark, it became all broken lights and images and things of no meaning. When it went dark I moved into one who stood so close the red pain warmed his face, and I looked at the black sagging thing still tied to the post, and it had once been beauty, but then you could not tell what it had been. Then the dream ended."

In the silence Raul looked at the woman, Bara, saw her run the sharp pink tip of her tongue along her lips. Her eyes were shiny under the heavy lids. The glowing walls made highlights on her naked polished scalp.

One of the men smiled sadly and shook his head. "She always seeks pain and enjoys the enduring of it. Why should one want to feel what the dream creatures feel? I like best the second world. I move into the creatures and push their thoughts away. I do not want to gobble in their strange tongues. I like their darkness. I find a young strong male usually and make him crouch and wait and leap out at the weaker ones, breaking them with strong hands, running them down. The dream machines are clever. One could almost believe their screaming is real. Then they come to hunt the body I have taken. The game is to remain free until the dream ends. Sometimes there are too many of them with lights and weapons, and they break the body. Sometimes they catch it and hold it, and then I call them idiots in our own language, and they look sick with fear. These are exciting dreams." He wore a secret smile and kneaded his fingers together and nodded and nodded.

"Did you have good dreams in the first two worlds? Did you dream well in the second world?" the other woman asked. They all stared at Raul expectantly.

He stood up. "I visited a great many in the second world. Some of them were . . . good to know, to be with in that way. And I wanted to help them and did not know how. I liked them . . . better than many I know here, among us."

The three looked astonished and then began to laugh. It was a shrill and unfamiliar sound. There was little laughter among the Watchers. "Oh, oh, oh," they cried in weakness, and the tears streamed. When at last the man could speak he stood also and rested his hand on Raul's shoulder. "We should not laugh at you. It is all new to you. The dreams seem very real the first time. But you must understand, you *dream* the creatures. You and the machine create the creatures inside your sleeping mind. When you awaken they cease to exist. It is very plain that they cease to exist, because if they did exist, they would be here, would they not? This is the only place. All else is nothingness without end."

Raul frowned at them. "There is one thing I do not know yet. Can one go back to the same world and find the same person again?"

"Yes. That is possible."

"And has he . . . lived during the time you were not dreaming of him?"

"Lived?" the other woman said. "The question does not mean anything."

"In one of my dreams can I ever dream of someone who has been in the dream of someone else?"

"It happens, but not often. It does not mean anything, Raul. It is only the cleverness of the machines turning fantastic and impossible things of the mind into three orderly worlds which seem to have chains of strange logic. But the proof is, of course, that life could not be sustained under those conditions. You will understand one day soon that it is all clever illusion, and it is there for you to enjoy now that you are no longer a child."

Bara stood, with an echo of the laughter still purring in her throat. She plucked at a metal fold of Raul's toga. Her lips were swollen and pulpy-looking, and her voice was soft-slurred. "Raul, this is the only world. This is the place where all things are right for us. Don't let the machines delude you. Their magic is clever. Some of our people have gone mad through believing that the dream worlds are real. At last, when they begin to believe that this, the real world, is a dream, they have to be thrust out of this world. I have many reasons why I don't want that to happen to you." She tugged at his arm. "Come with me to one of the small game rooms and alone I will play for you some of the parts that I have known in dreams. You'll find it interesting."

He pulled away from her. He shouldered the man aside and walked away. At the twentieth level he looked down the row of cases. On the twentieth level the corridor walls and the floors were always dim. The brightest lights shone inside the cases themselves. Either way he looked, the cases stretched off, lining both sides of the corridor, diminishing into the distance.

He walked slowly between the cases. Many were empty. In many were dreamers. He saw Jord Orlan, hands crossed on his blue-white chest. Some were on their backs. Some curled. One woman dreamed with her arms clasped around her knees, her knees against her chest. He walked until at last he saw nothing but the empty cases, on either side of the corridor, mouth plates unused, cables coiled and waiting. The corridor turned sharply and he stared down another vista of the machines for dreaming. He walked slowly onward.

An inhabited case startled him. And then he saw that its occupant was long dead, cheeks and closed eyes shrunken into the skull, skin dark and withered. The lips were stretched back away from yellowed teeth and the teeth still loosely held the plate. One who died while dreaming, forgotten among the machines too far from the moving track to be used. When finally someone noticed that he was gone, it was probably believed that he had been properly inserted in the oval tube to speed down into the darkness.

Raul stood for a long time and looked into the case. He thought of telling Orlan, but that would entail explaining why he found it necessary to wander in unused places. This one had been dead a long time. Possibly he would never be found. He never would be inserted, head first, into the oval tube. Women were placed in the tube feet first. It was the Law.

Above his head was the soft sigh of one of the grilled apertures through which the warm air rushed. He turned and walked back to the broken track and went up in search of Leesa.

He found Leesa on a high level watching the screen where an ancient war was being fought. Sounds of battle roared from the speakers. He called to her and she turned off the machine, ran quickly to him, her eyes glowing.

She grasped his arm. "Tell me quickly! Tell me about the dreams."

He sat down, scowled up at her eager face. "Somehow, I know they are all wrong. One day you will know it too. The dreams have more meaning than . . . what they say."

"You are being absurd, Raul. They are only dreams. And it is our *right* to dream."

"A child does not speak that way to a grown one. The dreams, I say, are reality. They are as real as this floor." He stamped his bare foot.

She drew back a bit. "Don't . . . say that, Raul. Don't say it, even to me! They could put you out of the world. Through the door you told me about. And that would leave me alone here. There would be no other ugly one like me, with this hateful hair and these hideous heavy arms and legs."

He smiled at her. "I won't say it to anyone else. And you shall enjoy the dreams, Leesa. The women who look as you will look when you are grown are considered very beautiful."

She stared at him. "Beautiful? Me? Raul, I am ugly like the women in these pictures I watch."

"You will see. I promise."

She sat on her heels beside his chair. She smiled up at him. "Come, now. Tell me. You promised you would. Tell me about the dreams."

"On one condition."

"You always make conditions," she said, pouting.

"You must promise that you will help me search through all of these rooms, all of these thousands on thousands of spools. It may take us years. I do not know. But somewhere, Leesa, we shall find answers to all this. This place did not grow. It was built. What are the dreams? Why do we call ourselves the Watchers? It had to have a beginning. And somewhere, here, we will find the story of creation. Who made this world?"

"It has always been here."

"Will you help me search?" She nodded. And as she kept her eyes on his face, her lips parted, he told her of the dreams of the first two worlds.

And on the following day, he told her of the third world, as soon as his dream had ended. He saw her directly after he had reported back to Jord Orlan and had been instructed in the single Law of those who dream. He was still shaken by the significance of Jord Orlan's instruction.

She sat as before, staring up at him, rapt.

"The third world," he said, "is entirely different. The first world is all blood and cruelty. The second world is a place of nervous fear and mechanisms and intricate social patterns based on an odd sort of fear. This third world . . . I am going to return there again. Many times. Their minds are full of power and subtlety. And I know that they know of us."

"But that sounds silly, Raul! It's only a dream. How can the creatures in a dream know of the dreamers? The other ones do not."

"With the first mind I invaded, I was too cautious. There was a moment of resistance, then none. I went in confidently. While I was still moving softly, the mind thrust me away with such a surge of power I was forced to leave it. It took some time before I could find it again. This time I entered more firmly. The pressure was enormous. At last, when I took over sensory control, I saw that I was sitting in front of a small structure. The landscape was

pleasant. Woods, trees, fields and flowers. There was no crude-
ness about the structure. The inner walls, which I could see,
glowed the way these corridor walls glow. The machines in the
house appeared to be automatic, much like the lower levels here.
When I tried to sift the captive mind, to find out what sort of
world this might be, I found nothingness. At first I thought the
thing might be brainless, and then I remembered the astonishing
power of the mind. I had full control of the body, but the mind itself seemed able to erect a barrier that shielded its thoughts. I
looked in all directions and saw men and women, simply dressed,
standing at a respectful distance and staring toward me. I stood
up.

"My host let one thought seep into my mind. He told me to attempt no violence or those who watched would kill him immediately. The thoughts he transmitted to me came slowly and clearly
and I had the impression he was speaking to an inferior, simpli-
fying his thoughts for the sake of contacting a less acute mind. He
told me it would be best to return to the place from whence I
came. If I attempted to move to another mind, the new host
would immediately be placed in the same position in which he
found himself. I formed, with his lips, our word for 'why.' He
said that they could read each other's thoughts and found it relatively simple to sense an alien presence. I could detect grim
humor. The others stood and watched and I began to feel that in
some odd way he was still in communication with them through a
channel I could not tap. I felt that he knew all about the dreams
and the dreamers. I tried to make it forcefully clear that I was
only curious about his world, that I intended no violence. I sat
down again and he asked, again with that touch of humor, what I
wanted to know."

"It sounds so dull!" Leesa said.

"It did not seem so. We spent the entire dream in talking. They
call the third world Ormazd. It seems to be named after some
principle of goodness. They each live alone, quite simply, and at
a considerable distance from one another. They give great care
and attention to training and teaching their young. He seemed to
'speak' to me as if I were a child. They live for the development
and progress of pure thought, thought independent of all emotion.

They have been progressing in that pattern for twenty thousand years. The reading of minds is part of that progress, and he told me that when they had at last eliminated all language and all words, they had eliminated all possible misunderstanding between people. They have no crime, no violence, no war."

"And you say it isn't dull?" Leesa asked.

"Here is what puzzles me the most. I know he knows about us. He told me to dream about other worlds rather than about his. But the mental word he used was not exactly 'dream.' It was more like scan, or measure or survey. I tried to question him and got that grim mental laughter. He said we are powerless to disturb them. When I said I was seeking knowledge, he said that it could do no possible good to give it to me. He said it was too late. Too late for us. He said it would be easier for me to stay away from their world. And then in that odd laughter-of-the-mind, there was sadness for a moment. I had the feeling he had not meant to let me see the sadness. It was very quick, and all I got was something about a great plan having failed. I could feel his pity. I was very glad when I woke up at last."

"The first two worlds sound *much* better," she said.

"I can dream of any world I please now that my first three dreams are done," he said. "I went to Jord Orlan and he told me the Law."

"Can you tell me?"

"It is forbidden. But of course I will tell you. We both know too many forbidden things already, Leesa. This is the Law as he told it to me. If ever the dream creatures on any world make machines which will take any of them from their own world to some other world where they can live, then the dreams will end."

"Why will they end?"

"I asked that. He said that it is the Law. He said that a long time ago the first world came dangerously close to building such machines, but the Watchers obeyed the Law and caused the people of the first world to destroy their own machines time and time again until there were great explosions and now the world is a long way from building such machines. The third world has no interest in building such machines. The danger is on the second world. He said that he is afraid that too many of us have forgotten the Law. In his lifetime he has destroyed, he said, three great ships on the second world. He said we should all be dreaming in the second world, but many will dream of nothing but the first world. Jord Orlan roams the second world in every dream, looking for the great machines that will end the dreaming."

"If it is the Law," Leesa said, "then it must be done."

"Why? You and I have learned to read and to write. Only you and I can read the old records, fit the old spools to the viewing machines. Jord Orlan is firm and kind, but he no longer questions anything. He did when he was young. Now he accepts. He does not ask for reasons. That is blindness. I will know *why,* and if the reason is good, I will obey. What is the meaning of my life? Why am I here?"

"To dream?"

He could never forget the first three dreams, not even after eight years of dreams had been superimposed on those first ones.

While others dreamed their idle amusements and mischiefs and sensations, Raul had made the dreams and the waking times all a part of the same search. On the silent upper levels he spent eight years going through forgotten spools and records of all the eternity of the Watchers.

And for eight years he spent every dream in the second world, and the early dreams were always wasted when they began in some primitive place of jungle or desert, because usually then the dream would end before he could move from mind to mind a sufficient distance to reach some city where there would be libraries and laboratories. Many of the dreams were wasted in small villages until he learned the knack of thrusting upward as strongly as he could, floating in blackness, then thrusting downward and reaching out for the sense of other presences. Then as he learned the geography of the second world, he learned how to identify the area where the dream first took him, and thrust in a chosen direction for an estimated distance. Then only the first hour of ten might be wasted, but for the remainder he would be reading, through skilled and professional minds, the texts and papers on astronomy, physics, mathematics, electronics, history. . . .

At last the answer came to him, shockingly, abruptly. He realized he had known it for some time but had not been able to accept it because it required such a total inversion, a turning inside out and outside in of all previous beliefs.

The answer was as blinding as a flash of intense light.

It was as unanswerable, as unarguable, as death itself.

7

RAUL KINSON KNEW THAT HE HAD TO SHARE HIS NEW KNOWLEDGE with Leesa. They had grown apart since she had been permitted to dream.

He found her with a group of the younger adults. He watched her from the doorway. She had achieved the popularity, the leadership, that had been denied him. Though all thought her ugly, she was a source of constant pleasure and amusement to them.

No one could match the diabolical cleverness and inventiveness of her mind once she had taken over the hapless body of some poor citizen of world one or two. And no one could tell the dream exploits more entertainingly.

Discontent, he knew, had driven her down the more obscure pathways of the dreams, had made her vie with the others in the excesses of the dreams. She had gathered around her a group that attempted to outdo her, and always failed.

Raul listened, feeling sick at heart. In their game, each member of the group gave a short summary of their latest dream. If the group shouted approval, they would tell it in detail.

A woman said, "On the second world I found a host body on a boat. A great brute of a man. It was a small boat. I threw everyone overboard and then jumped myself. The food was left on the table. The other dream creatures will be sadly confused."

The woman pouted as no one showed approval. A man said, "I became the one who guides one of the big machines which go through the air. I left the controls and locked the door and stood with my back against it and watched the faces of the passengers as the machine fell strongly to the ground."

They looked at Leesa for approval. Her smile was bitter and her laugh lifted harshly over the laughter of the others. She said, "Because in the last dream I caused a great accident, you all must try to do the same thing. This last dream of mine was a small thing, but it amused me greatly."

"Tell us, Leesa. Tell us!"

"I slipped very gently into the mind of a great man of world two. A very powerful man, full of years and dignity. Over the entire ten hours of my dream, I made him count all objects aloud. The vehicles on the street, the cracks in the sidewalk, the windows in buildings. I made him count aloud and did not permit him to do anything except count aloud. His friends, his family, his co-workers, they were all horrified. The man of dignity counted until his voice was a hoarse whisper. He crawled around on his ancient knees and counted the tiles in the floor. Doctors drugged him and I kept control of the old man's mind and kept him counting aloud. It was most amusing."

They screamed with laughter. During the next dream period Raul knew that all of them would seek variations of Leesa's latest game, but by the time they gathered to recount their dreams, Leesa would have gone on to something else.

Raul thought of the myriad lives she had broken in her attempts to prove to herself that the dreams were in no way real, but the twist of her mouth betrayed her. He knew that she still suspected that the dreams might be real, and each additional torment she inflicted on the dream creatures made more heavy the load of conscience.

In the life she led apart from the dreams and the telling of the dreams, she had nothing to do with other adults. She was aided in this by her appearance which, though it matched standards of beauty in worlds one and two, appealed in the world of the Watchers only to those who thought to stimulate jaded tastes with the unusual.

She looked across the heads of the others and met his glance boldly. He beckoned to her and she walked slowly toward him. He went out into the corridor and she followed him. "I wish to talk to you, Leesa. It is something important."

"The dreams are important."

"We will go up to one of the rooms of learning."

She stared at him coldly. "I have not been up there in over two years. I do not intend to go up there now. If you wish to talk to me, you can meet me on the second world. We talked there once before."

He agreed reluctantly. He had a sour memory of the last time they had talked on the second world. He arranged the place and the time with her, and the recognition signal. They ate together and went up to the corridor of dreams, entered their respective cases.

He had grown almost accustomed to the clamor of the traffic, the pushing, hurrying throngs on the streets of this, the greatest city of the second world. He was late, he knew. This time it had taken almost an hour to cover half a continent. Possibly Leesa had wearied of waiting for him. She had little patience these days.

Once near the hotel he selected a lean young male body, took over the mind with a casual brusqueness that bordered on the careless. He marched the captive body into the hotel. He had thrust the host-mind far back into a corner of the captive brain. Even in panic, the struggles were weak and far away, a faint fluttering that did not interest him. There were several young women in the lobby, obviously waiting. Near the clock he took a handful of objects from the pocket of the captive body, dropped them clumsily on the floor. He bent and gathered them up—knife, change, lighter.

When he straightened up, a tall girl in gray stood before him. He looked deeply into her eyes and said, in his own tongue, "Hello, Leesa."

"You're late, Raul."

"I'm glad you waited."

They stood together and talked in low tones.

To the bystanders it appeared that a nervous young man had just arrived to meet his date. They walked out of the hotel together. She said something in the tongue of this city. Through use he had learned a great deal of it, but it was easier to relax the pressure on the host-brain, to allow it to flow up to a point where its language became his. She smiled and repeated, "Now where?"

He turned down a quieter street. He looked up across the

street, saw a man and a woman standing together looking out the window of another hotel, looking down the street. "If they're alone in that room," he said, "it should be a good place."

As the gray nothingness closed around him, he made the practiced movement, slanting upward, reaching out ahead. Tendril-tips of prescience brushed another mind, tasted the blade-quick reaction of woman-mind, veered, found the other resistance point, flowed softly in.

He was standing, looking down five stories at the street. A young couple stood on the opposite side, talking excitedly. Leesa stood beside him, and she laughed. "Let them try to explain that to each other," she said.

He looked at the small room. He pushed the captive mind down to the very thin edge of the breaking point, holding it there by an effort of will that had become almost unconscious. The body was older than the previous one. And he sensed that it was not a healthy body. It carried too much soft white weight. The woman, however, inhabited by Leesa, was beautiful in a clear-lined way.

Leesa sat on the bed. "Now be interesting, Raul."

"I intend to be. Listen closely. For six months I have had almost all the answers, almost all of our history. Now I have the last pieces. I have gotten some of it from the rooms of learning, some of it through constant questioning of the best minds of world three. And the remainder from the science of this world. A very long time ago, Leesa, a longer time than you can visualize, our world was much like this one."

"Nonsense!"

"I can prove every part of this. Our race had vast numbers. We found the secrets of travel through space. Our home planet circles a dying red sun very near a star these people call Alpha Centauri. Twelve thousand years ago the Leaders, realizing that life could only be sustained on our home planet through a constant adjustment to the dwindling moisture and sinking temperature, directed a search for younger planets, planets suitable for migration. Three were found. This planet, also planet one, circling what these people call Delta Canis Minoris near Procyron, ten and a half light-years from here, and planet three, in the system of Beta Aquilae near Altair, sixteen light-years from this place, were found to be suitable."

"I hear the words you say, and I can find no meaning in them."

"Leesa, please listen. Twelve thousand years ago, our world was dying. The Leaders found three planets to which our people could migrate. The first world of the dreams, called Marith. This second world, Earth. The third world, Ormazd. For two thousand years the Great Migrations were the task of all our race. Ships were built which could cover the vast distances in a remarkably short time. Our race was ferried across space to the three inhabitable planets."

"But, Raul——"

"Be still until I finish. The Leaders were wise. They knew that there were three raw savage planets to be colonized, and in the colonization there would be a divergence of culture trends. They were afraid that our people, diverging in three separate directions, would become enemies. They had a choice. Either set up the colonization in such a way that there would be frequent contact between worlds, or else isolate the three colonies until such time as they had advanced to the point where contact could be reestablished without fear of conflict between them. This latter choice was selected because it was felt that by encouraging divergence, each planet would have something new to contribute to the race as a whole once contact was reestablished. In order to implement the second choice—in order to prevent premature contact between the colonial planets—the Watchers were established.

"We, Leesa, are remote descendants of the original Watchers. All the migration ships were destroyed except the six I showed you from the window. The place Jord Orlan calls our 'world' is merely a vast structure built over ten thousand years ago, when the Leaders used all the science at the disposal of our race to make it as completely automatic, as immune to time as possible. The original Watchers, five thousand in number, were selected from all the numbers of our race. They were the ones with the greatest emotional stability, the most freedom from hereditary disorders, the highest potentials of intelligence. Those original Watchers were indoctrinated with the importance of their duties, their debt to the future of the race. They were given the great building on a dying world, and six ships with which to make periodic patrols to the colonial worlds."

"But the ships are not——"

"Listen carefully. It was planned that there would be no contact between colonial worlds for five thousand years. Yet ten thousand have passed, and still it is the Law that we must prevent those 'dream' worlds from creating devices to enable them to leave their planets. Here is what happened. The structure Orlan calls our 'world' was too comfortable. Patrols were made for almost three thousand years. But those who made the patrols detested being taken out of the warmth and leisure of the structure. It had been built too well. The Watchers had not yet lost the science of the race. It took a thousand years to find a way to eliminate the physical patrols and still discharge the responsibilities given them. At last the Watchers, experimenting with the phenomenon of hypnotic control, with thought transference, with the mystery of the communication of human minds on the level of pure thought—a thing regarded as a superstition on Earth, yet practiced to the extent of near-atrophy of speech on Ormazd—devised a method of mechanically amplifying this latent ability in the human mind. The things we call dream machines are nothing more than devices which hook the massive power sources of our contrived world to the projection of thought, with three control settings so that the narrow, instantaneous beam is directed at whichever colonial world is chosen by the 'dreamer.' When we 'dream' we are but conducting a mental patrol of the actual colonial planets."

"That is absurd! You are mad!"

"For many, many years the dreams were sober, serious affairs, conducted as they were meant to be conducted. The ships sat idle. The outside world grew colder. No one left the building. The science was lost. The Watchers failed in their purpose. The genetic selection of the original Watchers was varied enough to prevent the inbreeding and resultant stagnation for five thousand years. But when the science behind the dream machines was lost, the machines themselves acquired a primitive religious significance. We have become a little colony, less than one fifth of the original number. We are blind to the true purpose of our existence. We have gone on for double the length of time originally intended. We are a curse and an affliction to the three colonial planets, merely because we believe that they do not exist, that they are something for our pleasure."

"Raul, you know that I am not here. You know that I am in the dream case which is mine for all my life, my hand under my cheek, and——"

He went on inexorably. "We deal with three colonial planets. Marith, our favorite playground, has been turned into chronic primitive barbarism. Four thousand years ago Marith was close to space flight. We smashed them, through the dreams. There, when we possess a person, we are known as devils, as demons.

"And five thousand years ago Earth was ready for space flight. We smashed that culture, completely. When we were through, we left behind us the Aztecs, with only remnants of what had been an atomic culture. We left them with the rudiments of brain surgery, with stone pyramids shaped like the space ships they had tried to build, with sacrifices to the sun god on top of the pyramids—sacrifices actually to the hydrogen-helium reaction which they had conquered and which we had destroyed as they attempted to use it. Now Earth culture has returned to an atomic culture. We shall smash it again, drive them back into savagery. When we take over an Earth body, they have many names for us. Temporary insanity. Epilepsy. Frenzy. Trance. There are over seven hundred of us who are permitted to dream. Seven hundred feckless children who can commit acts without fear of consequence.

"On Ormazd they know who we are, and what we are. Twice we have destroyed their attempts to cross space. They no longer have the urge to leave their planet. They have found vaster galaxies within the human mind than any that can be conquered by machines. All three colonial planets would be better rid of us, Leesa."

In a halting voice she said, "I have tried to believe you. But I cannot. Were I to believe you, it would mean that . . ."

"You might have to accept a moral responsibility for the acts you have committed, for death you have brought to people as real as you and I?"

"We are in the dream cases, Raul. The clever machines make this world for us."

"Then break that mirror. Tomorrow you can return to find it broken. Or dive from that window. Tomorrow you can return to find the broken body of the girl you are inhabiting."

"That is because of the cleverness of the machines."

"There are other proofs, Leesa. On Ormazd you can find the records of the original Migrations. On Marith, you can read their mythologies, and find reference to the ships that landed, belching fire. They think they came from the sun. On Earth here, a race believes themselves descended from the sun. And there are traces, in Earth mythology, of giants that walked the earth, of great ships and chariots that crossed the sky. All three planets were populated by manlike creatures before our remote ancestors arrived. On Earth, after a time, the two races could interbreed. On Marith and Ormazd the original races died out. You see, Leesa, there is too much proof to be ignored."

She was silent for a long time. "I cannot believe what you say. Tomorrow I shall enclose myself in the case. I shall become a naked savage girl in a jungle, or a woman leading a burro down a mountain path. Or I can meet with my friends on Marith and we can play the game of identification, or the game of killing, or the game of love, or the game of the chase. No, Raul. No. I cannot change what I believe."

"Leesa," he said softly, "you have always believed, in your heart, that these worlds are real. That is why you have been so wanton, so cruel, in your dreams, because you were trying to deny their existence. You and I are different. We are not like the others. We are stronger. You and I can change the——"

He stopped speaking as he saw the woman on the bed put her hand to her forehead and look at him oddly. She spoke so slowly that even without releasing the host, he understood her. "George, I feel so strange."

Leesa had gone. He knew not in what direction. She had ended the talk in such a way that he could not find her. He let the host-mind take over the maximum amount of control, right on the edge of the fading of vision and hearing which would mean a full release of the host.

"Something wrong with those drinks, maybe. That bartender had a funny look. Maybe it was a mickey. I feel funny too."

The woman lay back on the bed. Raul felt the slow beginning

of desire in the host-body. The woman smiled up at him. As the man moved toward the bed Raul released the last of his control, faded off into the familiar area where there was no color, no light. Nothing but the strange consciousness of direction. He slanted downward with a gentle impulse, drifting until he felt the nearby entity, orienting himself to it, gathering it in slowly. Vision came. He was in a taxi. He was late. The host-mind was fogged with alcohol, but the emotions were particularly vivid. Raul read the mind as one might turn the pages of a book. Despair and torment and the desire for death. Hate, fear and envy. But most of all an enormous longing for a sleep that would be endless. The man paid the driver, walked slowly into a lobby, took the small self-service elevator up to the eighth floor. He unlocked the door and went in. The woman came out of the bedroom with the shining weapon in her hand. She pointed it and shut her eyes. The little hot bits of lead bit warm liquid channels into the host-body—not pain. Just shock and warmness and a sort of melting. The host-brain faded quickly, and as Raul slid away, he caught the last impulse of consciousness. Not satisfaction with the surprise gift of the death that had been desired—but panic and fear and longing for the things of life as yet untasted.

Raul did not find ease of spirit until at last he entered the mind of a man, an old man, who sat in the park, half dozing in the sun. In that mind he waited for the dream to end.

8

IN THE PRIVATE ROOMS ASSIGNED TO HIM BECAUSE HE WAS Leader, Jord Orlan stared at the girl who sat facing him, hoping to disconcert her with his silence. This Leesa Kinson was too . . . alive. The heavy stands of black hair were unusual. Hair like that of the dream people, or like that of her brother, Raul. The planes of her face had strength and her lips were too red. Jord Orlan preferred the quieter, drabber, frailer women. With an effort he brought his memory back to the reason for summoning her to him.

"Leesa Kinson, it has been reported to me that you have had no child."

"That is right."

"It has been reported that you have favored no man among us."

She smiled as though it were of no consequence. "Perhaps no one finds me acceptable. I have been told that I am remarkably ugly."

"You smile. Have you forgotten the Law? Too many of the women are barren. All who can have a child must do so. It is the duty of all to have a child. You are as strong as a man. It is the Law that you must have many children. The weak ones too often die, and the child with them."

"You talk about the Law. Where is the Law? Can I handle it, read it?"

"Reading is a habit of the first and second worlds. Not here."

Her lip curled. "I can read. I learned when I was a child on the high levels. My brother taught me. I can read our language and I can write it. Show me the Law."

"The Law was told to me. It was told enough times so that I remember it and even now I am teaching it to others. I had hoped to teach it to Raul but——"

"He has no interest in being Leader. Is it against your Law to learn to read?"

"I find you impertinent. It is my Law and also yours, Leesa Kinson. To learn to read is not against the Law. It is merely pointless. What is the reason for reading? There are the dreams and the food and sleep and the rooms for games and healing. Why read?"

"It is good to know something that others do not know, Jord Orlan."

"If you persist in impertinence I shall punish you by denying you the right to dream for many many days."

She shrugged and regarded him steadily. Her gray eyes made him oddly uncomfortable. He said more gently, "The old ways are the best ways. Why are you not happy?"

"Who is?"

"Why, I am! All of us are. Life is full. You and Raul are the discontented ones. The strange ones. When I was small there was one like you two. In fact, I believe that he may have been the father of your mother. He, too, had a different appearance. He created much trouble, and was punished many times. He struck many of the men, and he was hated and feared. Then one day a woman saw him just as he climbed into the oval tube that leads down into the unending blackness. She had no wish to stop him. You see, that is the end of discontentment. You must learn to be contented."

Her eyelids grew heavy and she yawned. It angered him.

He learned forward. "Leesa Kinson, I believe that this attitude of yours is unnatural. I believe that it was caused by your brother. He has been a bad influence. He has nothing to do with any of the games. When he is not dreaming, it is impossible to find him."

An idea began to shape itself. He considered it carefully. "May I go?" she asked.

"No. I am curious about your brother. I have attempted to talk to him many times. No one knows of his dreams. He does not enter into any of the games. I suspect him of neglect of the prime responsibility of the dream. Has he talked to you of . . . of any matters which could be considered heresy?"

"Would I tell you?"

"I think you might be glad to. I am not vindictive. If his ideas are incorrect I shall attempt to change them. If you refuse to give me any information, I shall order you to favor a man of my own choosing, one who will follow orders. It is within my power to do that. And it is the Law that you shall bear children."

Her lips were compressed. "Orders can be disobeyed."

"And you can be taken to a place on the lowest level and thrust out of this world for failure to obey an order. I would not care to do that. So tell me what Raul has said to you."

She moved a bit in the chair, not meeting his glance. "He . . . he has said things that are not right."

"Go on."

"He has said that the three worlds of the dreams actually exist and that what we call dreams are just . . . a method for us to visit the three real worlds. He says that this world is just a big structure and that it rests on a planet that is like the other three, but colder and older."

Jord Orlan stood up quickly and began to pace back and forth. "It is more serious than I believed. He needs help. Badly. He must be made to see the Truth."

"The Truth as you see it?" she asked gently.

"Do not scoff. What did you say when Raul told you his absurd theories?"

"I told him that I didn't believe him."

"Very good, my child. But now you must go to him and you must pretend to believe what he says. You must encourage him to say more. You must find out what he does, in his dreams. And you must report everything back to me immediately. When we know the full extent of his heresy we will be in a better position to take his hand and lead him to the Truth." His voice grew more resonant. He faced her, his arms spread, his face glowing. "Once, when I was young, I doubted too. But as I grew wiser, I found the Truth. The entire universe is encompassed within these familiar walls. Outside is the end of all, an unthinkable emptiness. Our minds cannot comprehend utter emptiness. It is a thousand times less than the floating just before you enter the mind of a dream creature. In this universe, this totality, there are nearly one thousand souls. We are the static nub of the universe, the only small place of reality. It has been thus forever, and forever shall be. Now go and do as I say, Leesa."

As she went to the doorway she remembered what Raul had told her the day before she was first permitted to dream. "If a small living creature is put in a white box before its eyes are open, if it lives out its life in that box, if food and warmth are provided, and if it dies in that box—then, in the moment of death, the little creature can stare at the walls of the box and say 'This is the world.'"

His words had come back to her an uncomfortable number of times.

She found Raul on one of the highest levels. The micro-book page at which he stared was incomprehensible to her. He heard the soft sound of her bare feet against the floor and turned, startled.

He smiled. "A long time since you've come up here, Leesa. I haven't seen you since you interrupted our talk."

He clicked off the projector. "What were you looking at?" she asked.

He stood up and stretched. His expression was sour. "At something I'll never understand, I'm afraid. This box contains all of the texts used by the technicians who piloted the Migration ships. I only found them by accident. I could look for the rest of my life and not find the intermediary texts. The science is beyond me. In the old days it was beyond any individual man too. They were organized into work teams and research teams. Each man handled one part of a particular problem and all of the work was coordinated through the use of integral calculators. But maybe I can——" He stopped suddenly.

She sat in one of the other chairs. "Can what?"

"Maybe I can find out enough so that I can handle one of the patrol ships. I know the interior details of the ships now."

"What good would that be?"

"I could go to one of the three worlds. I could take some of them onto the ship and bring them back here and bring them into this tower and show them to Orlan and the others. Then they'd stop this childish babbling about the Law, and about this being the only true reality. There are men on Earth who could look at a patrol ship, one man in particular who could learn much from one, so that even if I were unable to return, he would be able to . . . I talk too much."

"Maybe I find it interesting."

"You didn't a short time ago."

"Couldn't I have thought it over?" she said, pouting.

There was excitement in his tone. "Leesa! Are you beginning to see what I've seen for so long?"

"Why not? Maybe I could . . . help you."

He frowned. "You might, at that. I'd about given up hope of ever . . . Never mind. I guess I should trust you." He looked directly into her eyes. "Do you understand now that you've spent six years smashing the lives of people who actually exist, who exist and go about their affairs while we're talking here? Do you believe that?"

She held the chair arms tightly. "Yes," she said, as calmly as she could.

"I told you that we've outlived our purpose. If nothing were done we'd eventually disappear, but we'd go on and on, striking like random lightning into the lives of men until the very end, making public figures do dangerous and incomprehensible things, making obscure little men and women commit acts that baffle their courts, confound their friends and ruin their lives. I am going to put an end to it."

"How, Raul?"

"Marith is too primitive for space travel—Ormazd too concerned with the human mind to be mechanistic. Earth is my hope. There is a man there who is in charge of a project to build a space ship which is quite like those I showed you from the window. Since so many odd accidents—which we can explain and they can't—have happened to all previous attempts, this one is being handled with the greatest secrecy. With eleven billion hostminds to choose from, roughly, the less than eight hundred Watchers are unlikely to find this project, even though it is in an area where we have ruined previous projects. I am trying to protect that project and I am trying to get into more direct contact with a man named Bard Lane who is in charge. I want to explain what has happened to previous projects and assure him of my desire to help, and warn him against what one of us might do while dreaming. Not long ago someone stumbled across the project, possessed one of the technicians and spoiled months of work. I haven't been able to find out who it was. They haven't been back, but they may come back. I can't go and talk to the others. It would arouse suspicion, because it would be something I haven't done in years. But you might be able to find out, Leesa."

"And if I should find out?"

"Tell the person who possessed the technician that you stumbled on the same project and destroyed it utterly. In order to do that convincingly, you should . . ."

"Why do you pause?"

"Can I trust you? Somehow, you do not seem sufficiently . . . shattered by the realization that in the dream worlds we are dealing with reality. The day when I was at last convinced, I thought for a time that I might go mad. I wanted to go up to the corridor of dreams and rip all the cables free, smash all the dials."

"You can trust me," she said evenly.

"Then, in order to convince the person who did the damage, you should take a look at the project. It is called Project Tempo. I will explain to you exactly how to find it. It is quite difficult because of the lack of contacts in the surrounding countryside. I have been most successful through using the drivers of vehicles, and it is a matter of luck to emerge near a road. The last time it took me so long that I had but a little more than an hour to . . . do what I planned."

"What are you doing when you go there?"

"Explaining to Bard Lane just what we are."

"How do you find it?"

"Before I tell you, I must have your solemn promise that you will do no damage to the project. Do you promise?"

"I will do no damage," she said, and in her thoughts she added, on the first visit, at least.

He opened a case on the floor. "Here," he said, "is a map I made here after committing it to memory on Earth."

She knelt beside him. She watched his finger trace the possible routes of entry to the project area.

9

DR. SHARAN INLY SAT AT HER DESK, HER HANDS PRESSED AGAINST her eyes, her fingernails digging into her forehead just below the hair line. She wished with all her heart that she had become a stenographer, or a housewife, or a welder.

You could deal with humans, and be interested in them as humans even when they were cases duplicating those in the texts. Yet, as you treated them, you kept a tiny bit of yourself in reserve. It was self-protection. And then you would run into a case that would break your heart, because somehow you had gotten too involved with the individual as a person, not as a case.

"I hope you've got an explanation," Bard Lane said coldly as he slammed into her office.

"Shut the door and sit down, Dr. Lane," she said with a tired smile.

He sat down. His face had a drawn look. "Dammit, Sharan, my desk is piled high. Adamson needs help. The fool committee that wants to administer the death kiss to this whole project is waiting. I know you can bring anyone here at any time, but I think you might have checked first. Just a little consideration for the amount of work I——"

"How did you sleep last night?"

He stared at her, stood up with determination. "Fine, and I eat well, too. I even take walks. Want me to make a muscle for you?"

"Sit down, Dr. Lane!" she said crisply. "I'm doing my job. Please cooperate."

He sat down slowly, a look of fear in his eyes, growing fear. "What is this, Sharan? I guess I slept well enough. I felt tired this morning, though."

"What time did you get to bed?"

"A little before midnight. I was up at seven."

"Thomas Bellinger, on the routine guard report, noted that you went into your office at ten minutes after two this morning."

Bard gasped. "The man's mad! No! Wait a minute. If somebody could plant a man who looks like me . . . Have you alerted all guards?"

She slowly shook her head. Her eyes were sad. "No, Bard. That won't work. You passed the full test series with flying colors just this week, but it still won't work. You noticed that Bess Reilly wasn't in your office this morning?"

He frowned. "She's sick today. She phoned from her quarters."

"She phoned from here, Bard. I asked her to. Bess was a little behind in her work. She went in early this morning. She went into your office and took yesterday's tape off the dictation machine and took it out to her desk to transcribe it. When she started to listen to it, she thought you were playing some sort of joke. She listened some more and it frightened her. She very properly brought it directly to me. I've been over it twice. Would you care to hear it?"

He said softly, "Dictation . . . a funny nightmare is coming back to me, Sharan. Silly thing, like most of them are. It seems I had something that I had to get down before it went out of my mind. And I dreamed I . . ."

"Then you walked in your sleep, Bard. Listen to what you said."

She moved the small speaker closer to his chair, depressed the switch on the playback machine.

It was unmistakably Bard Lane's voice. "Dr. Lane, I am taking this method of communicating with you. Do not be alarmed and do not doubt me. I am physically nearly four and a half light-years from you at this moment. But I have projected my thoughts into your mind and I have taken over your body to serve the purposes of the moment. My name is Raul Kinson and I have been watching your project for some time. I am anxious for it to succeed, as it is your world's only chance to free itself from those of us whose visitations are unprincipled, who only want to destroy. I do not want to destroy. I want to help you create. But there are dangers that I can warn you about, dangers which you do not, as yet, understand. Take warning from what happened when your technician, Kornal, was seized by one of us. We are the survivors on your parent planet. I do not wish to tell you too much at this moment. Be assured that my intentions are friendly. Do not be alarmed. Do not fall into the logical error of assuming that this is an indication of mental unbalance. I will attempt to communicate with you in a more direct manner a bit later. Hear me out when I do."

Sharan clicked the switch to the off position. "You see?" she said softly. "The same delusion as before. This is just a further refinement of it. I'm both glad and sorry that Miss Reilly brought it to me. But here it is, Bard. Now do you think I should have sent for you?"

"Of course," he whispered. "Of course."

"What am I to do?" Sharan asked.

"Do your job," he said. His mouth was a hard, bloodless line.

Her voice was dispassionate, but her hand trembled as she handed him the note previously prepared. "This will admit you for observation. I see no need to assign an orderly to you while you pack what you'll need. I'll advise Adamson that he's acting chief until you're replaced."

He took the note and left her office without a word. After he closed the door softly behind him, she buried her face in the crook of her arm, her shoulders hunched over the desk. She pounded gently on the desk top with her clenched left fist.

Bard Lane walked from the hospital lounge into his room at the end of the corridor. He wore the beltless bathrobe they had issued to him, the soft plastic slippers. He lay on the bed and tried to read the magazine he had carried in from the lounge. It was a news digest, and seemed to contain nothing except hollow-sounding absurdities.

New Navy sub successfully withstands the pressure at the deepest point of the Pacific. Mello Noonan, creamy-tressed star of video, lands her heli-cycle on the observation deck of the new Stanson Building, smilingly pays the forty-dollar fine. Russians, through careful research, prove that man first walked erect at a spot fourteen miles east of present-day Stalingrad. Teen-age girls in Houston set new fad by shaving their heads and painting them green. When they meet on the street, they doff shoes and 'shake hands' with their feet. Memphis musician brains girlfriend with tuba. Widow in Victoria, Texas, claims to be receiving spirit messages from long-dead Valentino. Georgia ax killer claims, at trial, that he was 'possessed'—accusing mother-in-law of putting the evil eye on him. Injunctions issued against further use of new Reno slot machines which provide divorce papers for a fifty-dollar fee. Doctors unable to bring nine-year-old twins in Daytona out of trance caused by forty-one hours spent in front of their home video screen. Vote fraud in North Dakota . . . dope ring indicted . . . gambling ship sunk . . . bride leaves third grade . . . multiple murder . . . drives car into shoppers . . . jumped from eighty-third floor . . . minister fires church . . . dresses four inches shorter next year . . . curb service vice . . . hate. . . fear . . . anger . . . envy . . . lust . . .

He lay back on the bed. The magazine slipped to the floor, landing with the dry sound of a dead winged thing. Madness in the world. Madness tolling in his mind like a huge cracked bell in a forgotten tower, a bell swayed by the unknown winds. He shut his hands hard, squeezed his eyes shut and felt his soul as a fading focal point of certainty in this alien body, in this body of webbed nerves and muscle fiber and convoluted brain. He knew that any idea of plan or order in this mad world was pure delusion, that man was a tiny creature, knotted with the most deadly instincts, that he could look at the stars, but never attain them. In the back of his mind he stood at the edge of a distorted cliff, and he leaned toward the darkness. So easy to fall, to drop downward with a scream so vast and so solid that it would be as a smooth silver column inserted slickly in his throat. He would fall with his head tilted back, his lips drawn wide, with white-rimmed iris, with long tortured spasm that . . .

The bed moved. He opened his eyes. The little blond nurse from the lounge sat on the end of his bed. The stiff starched uniform had a bold life of its own, as though, inside it, her tender body recoiled from any touch against its harshness. The temple veins were violet tracery against the luminescent skin. Her large eyes were blue-purple glass beads from a costume jewelry counter.

"As bad as that, Bard Lane?" she said.

He frowned. Nurses were not supposed to sit on patients' beds. Nurses did not speak with such casual informality. Possibly in the psych ward the nurses had special leniency from the rigid rules applying to those who nursed more obvious wounds.

"Maybe I can do a soft-shoe dance to show how gay I am," he said.

"He didn't tell me about you. I thought I'd take a look while he's getting you out of here. Of course, he might not approve."

"Who are you talking about, Nurse? And what didn't he tell you, whoever he is?"

"Nurse is so formal. My name is Leesa."

"Very odd name. And you seem like an odd girl. I don't follow you very well, Leesa."

"I don't imagine that you'll be able to, Bard Lane. Actually I was talking about Raul, my brother, if that means anything. Raul Kinson."

Lane sat up, his face flushed with anger. "Nurse, I'm not so far gone that I'm going to stand still for any half-baked experiments. Go on back to Sharan and tell her that it didn't work. I'm still rational."

The nurse tilted her blond head to one side and smiled. "I like you when you're angry, Bard Lane. So fierce! Anyway, Raul is sorry that he got you into this mess by being too anxious to get into communication with you. Now he's trying to straighten things out for you. Poor Raul! He thinks that you actually exist. All of you people are so obsessed with the idea of your own reality. It gets tiresome."

Bard stared at her. He said slowly, "Nurse, this is just friendly advice from a patient. Why don't you go to Dr. Inly and ask to have the standard series? You know, when a person works around . . . mental cases for a long enough time, it sometimes happens that——"

Her laugh was raw gold, and oddly sane. "Goodness! So solemn and so kindly! In a minute you'll be patting me on the head and kissing my forehead."

"If this approach of yours is supposed to help me, Nurse, I . . ."

She became serious. "Listen to me. You're just part of an unpleasant and rather dull dream as far as I'm concerned. Raul seems to get a certain amount of amusement out of fooling himself about you. I wanted to see what you looked like. He seems very impressed with you. But I don't have to be. I . . ."

A stocky woman in white appeared in the open doorway. She scowled. "Anderson! What is the meaning of this? Number seventeen has been signaling for the last ten minutes. And I've been trying to find you. You know better than to sit on a patient's bed. I'm sorry this happened, Dr. Lane, but——"

The little blond nurse gave the supervisor a solemn wink. She slid up toward the head of the bed, curled a soft arm around Lane's neck and kissed him firmly and warmly on the lips. The supervisor gasped.

The little blond nurse straightened up. Slowly a look of horror came over her face. She jumped to her feet, holding her hands at her breast, twisting her fingers until her knuckles cracked.

"I demand an explanation, Anderson," the supervisor said ominously.

"I . . . I . . ." Two tears spilled over her lower eyelids and ran down her cheeks. She backed away from the bed.

"I think Leesa is a little upset," Bard said. His tone was placating.

"Her name is Elinor," the supervisor said crisply.

The nurse turned and fled. The supervisor sighed. "More trouble. I'm shorthanded, and now I'll have to send her up for tests." She plodded out of the room.

Sharan Inly was staring at Major Tommy Leeber. His smooth, jocular voice was just the same, his oval face kindly, his eyes jet-hard. But his words made Sharan feel a distant thunder in her ears, a weakness that was like the lethargy that came before a dead faint.

"If this is some sort of stupid joke, Major——"

"I'll start from the beginning again, Dr. Inly. I made a mistake. But you made one also. My name is Raul Kinson. For the moment I am using the body of this man named Leeber. That shouldn't be too difficult to accept as a basic premise. I used Lane's body and sent him a message. Both you and Lane apparently jumped to the conclusion that he is mentally unsound."

"I think General Sachson would like to have Lane and myself off the project, Major Leeber. I don't care for your way of trying to eliminate me."

"Please, Dr. Inly. There must be some test we can make. If I could repeat the message that I left for Lane to find——"

"Bess Reilly could have told you the message."

"I don't know who she is, but please have her come in and ask her."

They waited. Bess Reilly arrived within a few moments. She was a very tall girl, angular and without beauty, except for her eyes, sea-green, long-lashed, expressive.

"Bess, have you spoken to anyone about that dictation tape on Dr. Lane's machine?"

Bess lifted her chin a fraction of an inch. "Dr. Inly, you told me not to tell anyone. And I didn't. I'm not the sort to——"

"Have you talked to Major Leeber today?"

"I saw him once yesterday for the first time. I've never spoken to him."

Sharan gave the girl a long, steady look. "Thank you, Bess. You can go."

The door closed behind her. She turned to Major Leeber. "Now tell me what the tape said."

Leeber repeated it. In two places he made minor changes in sentence structure, but the rest of it was completely accurate. There was a calmness and a confidence about him that disturbed her.

She said, "Major, or Raul Kinson, or whoever you are . . . I . . . this is something that I can't bring myself to believe. This idea of taking over other people. This idea of coming from some alien planet. There are cases on record where persons have repeated the contents of sealed envelopes. You'll have to do better."

"Bard Lane has to be put back in charge. I am going to have to frighten you, Dr. Inly. But it will be the best proof I can give you. Without attempting to explain how, I am going to vacate this host brain and enter your brain. In the process, Major Leeber will revert to complete consciousness. But he won't remember very much of what has gone on. I will use your voice to get rid of him."

Sharan's smile felt as though it had been painted across her lips with a stiff brush. "Oh, come now!"

She sat with her palms pressed flat and hard against the cool desk top. The idea, in spite of its preposterousness, gave her an odd feeling of shame, as though an alien invasion of her mind would be a violation more basic than any physical relationship could ever be. Her mind had been a temple, a place of refuge, a place of secret thoughts, some of them so abandoned as to cause, in someone without her knowledge of psychiatry, a sense of guilt. To have these secret places laid bare would be . . . like walking naked through the streets of a city.

She saw the shock on Leeber's face, his confused look around the office, the way he rubbed the back of his hand across his mouth. And then she had no more time to watch Leeber. She felt the probe of unseen tendrils. She felt their softness. She tried to resist. Memory fled back to a time years before. A slushy day in a northern city. She had been playing in the gutter with the boy from next door. The water from the melting snow ran swiftly down the slope. They had built dams out of snow to contain it. But it would not be contained. It snaked around the dams, ate through them, thrusting always forward with gentle inevitability.

She moved back and back, seeking a last defensive point. And suddenly there was the sensation of the entire entity within her brain, adjusting itself to the familiar neural patterns, settling itself in a way that was oddly like the manner in which a dog, before sleeping, will turn around and around.

Words had always been planned a few seconds in advance. Her lips parted and the knowledge of the meaning of her words was simultaneous with the utterance of the words themselves.

"The sun is bad here, Major. It has made you a little dizzy. Drink a lot of water today and take salt tablets. You can get them at the dispensary. Stay out of the sun and you'll be all right by morning."

Leeber stood up. "Uh . . . thanks," he said. He paused at the door, looked back at her with a puzzled expression, shook his head and went out.

The thought came to her. It was not written out inside her mind. It was not expressed in words, and yet the words formed to match the thought. "Now you understand? Now you believe? I will relax controls. To communicate with me, speak aloud."

"I've gone mad!"

"That is what the others think. No. No, you're not insane, Sharan. Watch your hand."

She looked down. Her hand reached out and took a pencil. It moved over toward the scratch pad. Without volition, she wrote her own name. "Sharan." And then the room dimmed and faded and she knew nothing. As sight came back she saw that she had written another word under her own name. At least she imagined that it was a word.

"Yes, a word, Sharan. Your name in my own writing. I had to force you far back away from the threshold of consciousness in order to write it."

It was written with bolder strokes than her own handwriting. It looked as Arabic might look if written with cursive style rather than individual word signs.

"Mad, mad, mad," she said aloud.

Anger in her mind. Alien anger. "No. Don't be a fool! Believe! Wait, Sharan. I'll find your thoughts and your beliefs. I'll learn all there is to know of you, Sharan."

"No," she said.

She sat rigid, and tiny soft combs moved through all parts of her mind. Memory came to her, days long passed, hopelessly cluttered and out of sequence. The music at her mother's funeral. A passage from her doctor's thesis. A man's insistent lips. The song she wrote once. Discontent. Pride in her profession. Endless minutes and she felt as though she were pinned flat on a vast specimen board . . .

"Now I know you, Sharan. I know you well. Now do you believe?"

"Mad."

No more anger. Resignation. Fading. Gone—dwindling slowly away, a song half heard in the far sweet dusk of summer.

She sat alone. She pulled open a drawer, took out one of the slips like the one she had given to Bard Lane. She started to fill it in. Name. Symptoms. Partial diagnosis. Prognosis.

The door opened and Jerry Delane, the young dispensary doctor, came in. She frowned at him and said, "Isn't it customary to knock, Dr. Delane?"

He sat down facing her across the desk. He said, "I told you that I would leave Leeber's mind and enter yours, and I did. Of course you can call me a fantasy your sick mind has dreamed up, so I'll give you physical proof." He pulled her dictating machine toward him, set the switch, smiled at her and spoke into it. "Fantasies cannot record their words, Sharan."

To Sharan, all light seemed to fade in the room with the exception of the light around his smiling mouth. It seemed to grow larger, rushing toward her, overpoweringly large. And then it was as though she were moving swiftly toward the smile. Roaring down a tunnel toward the white even teeth, the murderous redness of the lips . . .

She was on the leather couch and he was kneeling beside her. He held a cold wet compress against the left side of her forehead. His eyes were tender.

"What . . ."

"You fainted and fell. You toppled against the edge of the file cabinet."

She frowned. "I . . . I think I'm ill, Jerry. I had odd thoughts . . . delusions about——"

He stilled her words with a gentle finger against her lips.

"Sharan, please. I want you to believe me. I am Raul Kinson. You must believe me."

She stared at him. Slowly she pushed the hand away from her forehead. She walked to the desk, wavering slightly. She switched the dictation machine to play back, set it a fraction ahead. The voice, thin and metallic, said, "Fantasies cannot record their words, Sharan."

She turned and faced him. In a dead voice she said, "I believe you now. There is no choice, is there? No choice at all."

"No choice. Release Bard Lane. Get him over here. The three of us will talk."

They sat and waited for Bard Lane. Raul stared at her. He said softly, "Odd, odd."

"You can use that word?"

"I was thinking of your mind, Sharan. I have avoided the minds of women. They have all had a shifting, unfocused, intuitive pattern. Not your mind, Sharan. Every facet and phase seemed . . . familiar to me. As though I have always known you. As though your every emotional response to any situation would be the feminine parallel of my own reaction."

She looked away from him. "You haven't left me much privacy, you know."

"Is privacy necessary? I know of a world where words are not used. Where a man and a woman, mated, can dwell within each other's minds at will. They have true closeness, Sharan. In your mind I found . . . another reason for making certain that this project succeeds."

She felt annoyance as the flush made her cheeks feel warm. "This is a brand new approach," she said with acid tone. "Maybe you'd like to fingerprint me too."

Bess Reilly came in. She slammed the door, yawned, hitched her bony hips onto the edge of the desk. She grinned at Jerry and said lazily, "Time's running short, Raul. And I can't say I'm sorry. You don't have much fun in your dreams, do you? I've had to change hosts forty times to find you again."

"I felt you near a few moments ago," Raul said. He turned to Sharan. "I present my sister, Leesa Kinson."

Sharan looked blankly at Bess Reilly's familiar face. Bess stared at her. She said, "Does she believe you, Raul?"

"Yes, she does."

"It gives me a funny feeling to have one of them understand how it is with us. I never had it happen before. Once, for a gag, I tried to make a man understand who I was when I took over the body of his bride. It took him just about an hour and a half to go crazy. I haven't tried since. That is, until today. I took over a little blond nurse and tried to introduce myself to your friend, Bard Lane. He got a bit confused. Are you in any danger of going crazy, girl?"

"Yes," Sharan said. "If this keeps up."

Bess laughed. "Don't take yourself too seriously."

Bard Lane came in slowly and shut the door behind him. He glanced curiously at Jerry Delane and Bess Reilly. He addressed himself to Sharan. "You sent for me."

"This is your old friend, Leesa," Bess said. "How did the little nurse act after I moved away from her?"

Sharan saw the color leave Bard's face. She spoke hurriedly. "Bard, we were wrong. Just believe me. They've proven it to me. It is impossible, I know. But it's true. Some sort of long-range hypnosis, I guess. But there is a Raul Kinson. He had . . . he is using Jerry Delane's body. He wants to talk to us. And his sister, Leesa, is . . . Bess is Leesa. Jerry and Bess won't remember what has happened. That recording you made. Everything is true, Bard. I think one moment I've gone mad and the next moment I know it's the truth."

Bard Lane dropped heavily into a chair and held his hand across his eyes. No one spoke. When at last he looked up, his expression was bleak. He stared at Jerry. "What is this test you have to say to me?"

Speaking slowly, pausing at times, Raul Kinson told of the Watchers, the Leaders, the Migrations, the dream machines, and of the perversion, over fifty centuries, of what had once been a logical plan. He told of the one Law which governed all of those who dreamed.

Bess sat on the edge of the desk, a bored look on her face.

Bard looked down at the knuckles of his clenched fist. "And so," he said softly, "if we can believe you, you give us the answer to why, with most of the techniques under control, every attempt to conquer deep space has been a miserable failure."

There was no answer. He looked up. Jerry Delane stood with an odd expression on his face. "What am I doing in here? How did I get in here?"

Bess slid quickly off the desk. "Did you call me, Dr. Inly?" she asked in a shrill, frightened voice.

Sharan forced a smile. "The conference is over, kids. You can go. You will stay, Bard?"

Jerry and Bess left the office.

"Have we gone mad?" Bard asked.

"There is no such thing as shared delusion, mutual fantasy, Bard," Sharan said in a tired voice. "And either you are still in the ward and all this is taking place in your mind—or else I have gone off completely and I only imagine you are here. Or, what seems the most difficult of all—it is all true." She stood up. "Dammit, Bard! If I close my mind to this thing, it means that my mind is too little and too petty to encompass it. But try—just try —to swallow this tale of alien worlds, Leaders, Migrations. No, it won't wash. I have a better idea."

"Which I will be delighted to hear."

"Sabotage. A new and very clever variety. Some of our friends on the other side of this world have managed to develop hypnotic technique to a new level of efficiency. Maybe they use some form of mechanical amplification. They're trying to discredit us if they can't drive us mad. That has to be it."

Lane frowned. "If their technique is that good, why do it the hard way? Why not just take over Adamson and Bill Kornal and a few other key men and have them spend a few hours damaging the Beatty One?"

"You forget. They already took over Kornal. It gave them a few months of grace. Now they're experimenting. Maybe they will try to talk us into leaving here and going to another country. You can't tell what they have in mind. Bard, the one who calls himself Raul Kinson warned me that he was going to enter my mind. And then he did. It was . . . degrading and horrible. We've got to get in touch with our own people who might know something about this. Maybe some of the ESP men. And then there's Lurdorff. He's done some amazing things with hypnosis. Hemorrhage control. That sort of thing. Why are you looking at me like that?"

"I'm trying to picture just how you'd state the problem without ending up on the receiving end of some fancy shock therapy, Sharan."

She sat down slowly. "You're right," she said. "There's no way we can warn them. No way in the world."

10

LEESA, WALKING DOWN ONE OF THE LOWER LEVELS, SAW JORD Orlan step off the moving ramp, glance at her and look quickly away. She lengthened her stride to catch him.

"I have something to tell you," she said.

He looked nervously down the corridor.

"It's all right. Raul has gone up to the unused levels."

"Come then," he said. He led the way to his quarters, walked in ahead of her. When he turned around he saw that she was already seated. He frowned. The respectful ones waited to be asked.

"I have been expecting a report, Leesa Kinson."

"Raul trusts me. Perhaps, too much. It makes me feel uncomfortable."

"Remember, this is for his own good."

"I've had to pretend to be very contrite for all the damage I've caused in the dream worlds to all those precious little people he thinks are actually alive."

Jord Orlan forgot his annoyance with her. "Very good, child! And have you shared his dreams?"

"Yes. He explained how he found a space ship project by searching the mind of a certain colonel in Washington. He told me how to find the project. We met there, in host bodies. Raul seems very proud of the people who work there. He wants to protect the project against . . . us. Not long ago the project was damaged by one of us who came across it, probably by accident, and forced a technician to smash delicate equipment. Raul does not want that to happen again."

"How does he hope to prevent it?"

"He has told two of them about the Watchers, and he has managed to prove to them that we exist."

Jord Orlan gasped. "That is a paradox! To convince someone who does not exist of existence on the only true plane. Many of us have amused ourselves trying to tell the dream people about the Watchers. They invariably go mad."

"These two did not. Possibly because the woman is an expert on madness and the man is . . . strong."

He stared at her. "Do not fall into the trap in which your brother finds himself. When you spoke of the man you looked as though you might believe him to be real. He is merely a figment of the dream machine. That you know."

"Then isn't it pointless, Jord Orlan, to destroy what they build?"

"It is not pointless because it is the Law. You are absurd to argue. Come now. Tell me about the location. I shall organize a group. We will smash the project completely."

"No," she said, smiling. "That would spoil my game. I am beginning to find it amusing. Leesa reserves that pleasure for herself, thank you."

"I can make that an order."

"And I shall disobey it and you can thrust me out of this world and perhaps never find the project."

He thought for a few moments. "It would be better were we to do it, a group of us. Then we should dream-kill the dream creatures with the greatest skills so as to lessen the danger of a new project for many years."

"No!" she said sharply. Then her eyes widened with surprise at the force of her own objection. She raised her fingertips to her lips.

"Now I understand," Jord Orlan said comfortably. "You find one of the dream creatures amusing, and you do not wish your sport to be denied you. Very well, then, but make certain that the destruction is complete. Report back to me."

As she reached the doorway he spoke to her again. She turned and waited. He said, "Within the next few days, my dear, Ryd Talleth will seek you out. I have ordered him to. He is the one most inclined to favor you—but he will need encouragement."

"He is a weak fool," she said hotly. "Do you not remember your promise, Jord Orlan? If I did as you asked, you would not force me into any such——"

"No one is forcing you. It is merely a suggestion," he said.

She walked away without answering him. She was restless. She walked down to the corridor lined with the small rooms for games. She stood in the doorway of one of them. Three women, so young that their heads still bore the thinning shadow of their dusty hair, pursued a squat and agile old man who dodged with cat-quick reflexes. They shrieked with laughter. He wore a wide grin. She saw his game. He favored one and it was his purpose to allow her to make the capture, even though the others were quicker. At last she caught him, her hands fast on the shoulder piece of the toga. The others were disconsolate. As they filed out of the room, leaving the two alone, Leesa turned away also. Once again she touched her lips and she thought of a man's heavy hands, square and bronzed against the whiteness of a hospital bed.

The next few rooms were empty. The following room was one with light controls. A mixed group was performing a stylized dance. They had turned the lights to blood red. It was a slow dance, with measured pauses. She thought of joining, but she knew that in some inexplicable way, her entrance would set up a tension that would remove some of their pleasure.

Restlessness was in her like slow spreading rot. On the next level she heard the sound of the small ones crying. She went and looked at them. Always, before, she had found a small pleasure in watching their unformed movements. She looked at them and their faces were like so many identical ciphers—circles of emptiness, signifying nothing.

She rode up to where the tracks no longer moved. She went halfway up to the twenty-first level, then dropped and curled like a child. She covered her face with her hands and wept. She did not know why she was weeping.

||

BARD LANE HEARD HIS NAME CALLED. HE TURNED TO SEE MAJOR Tommy Leeber striding diagonally across the street from the mess hall to intercept him.

Major Leeber's smile sat a shade stiffly on his lips and his eyes were narrowed.

"I hope you have a minute, Dr. Lane."

"Not very much more than that, I'm afraid, Major. What seems to be the trouble?"

"According to the records, Dr. Lane, my loyalty check was tops. And my brain waves passed all Sharan's witch-doctor techniques. So what's with these two shadows I've picked up?" He jerked his thumb back over his shoulder toward the two guards who stood several paces behind him, obviously uncomfortable.

"Those men are assigned to you in accordance with new operating instructions, Major."

"If you think you can chase me out of here by making me so uncomfortable that——"

"Major, I don't care for your tone, and I can't say much for your powers of observation. Everyone with access to fabrication zones and lab areas is subject to the new orders. You will notice that I have a guard too. We are in a critical phase. If you start acting irrational, you'll be grabbed and held until you can be examined. Me too. As a matter of fact, you have it a bit easier than I do. Part of my job is to watch the guard while he watches me. We're using this method as a defense against any . . . temporary insanity where Dr. Inly did not detect the susceptibility of the employee."

"Look, how do I get rid of these boys?"

"Leave the project area, Major."

Leeber knuckled his chin. "Look, Doc. I happen to know that

you're not getting new help in here. So where do the extra guards come from?"

"Other occupational classifications."

"Which slows down the works plenty, doesn't it?"

"Yes, it does."

"Already you are in plenty of hot water because of being so far behind schedule, Dr. Lane. Doesn't delaying it further seem to be a funny thing to do right now?"

For a moment Bard wondered how his knuckles would feel against the dark military moustache, the full lips. It would be a pleasure to see Major Leeber on the seat of his pants in the street.

"You may report this new development to General Sachson, Major. You may tell him that if he cares to, he can reverse this security regulation of mine. But it will be made a matter of record. Then, if someone else should get as destructive as Kornal did, the blame will be in his lap."

"For my money, Doc, the old man won't be too upset. He has it figured that inside of sixty days there won't be anybody here but a survey and salvage outfit, making chalk marks on whatever is worth keeping."

"I don't think you should have said that, Major Leeber," Bard said in a low voice. "I don't think it was smart."

He watched Leeber carefully, saw the greased wheels turning over slickly. Leeber grinned in his most charming way. "Hell, Doc. Don't mind me. I'm being nasty because these two boys tailing me have fouled up an operation that was all briefed out."

"I don't expect loyalty from you, Leeber. Just a reasonable co-operation."

"Then I apologize. I'm all lined up with a little blond cookie who runs a computer in the chem lab. And all I could think of was these two boys looking over my shoulder."

"Then take her out of the area, Leeber. When you report back in at the gate they'll make you wait until guards can be assigned."

Leeber scuffed the dust with the edge of his shoe. "A noble suggestion, Doc. Will you join me for a quick one?"

"I can't spare the time, thanks."

"Okay, I guess I don't want these boys joining in on my date. Guess I better take her out of the area, eh?"

"Either that or there'll be four of you. Five, when you count the guard assigned to her. A female guard."

Leeber shrugged, gave a mock salute, and sauntered away.

Bard Lane went into the mess hall. He took one of the small tables against the wall where he could be alone. He was lifting the glass of tomato juice to his lips when he felt the familiar pressure against his mind. He made no attempt to fight it. He held the glass poised in mid-air, then raised it to his lips. The sensation in his mind made him remember the first science courses he had taken in college. A hot afternoon, when he stared into the microscope, delicately adjusting the binocular vision until the tiny creatures in the droplet of swamp water had seemed to leap up at him. There had been one with a fringe of long cilia. It had slowly enfolded a smaller, more globular organism, merging with it, digesting it as he watched. He had long remembered the silent, microscopic ferocity, the instinctive ruthlessness of that struggle.

And now his mind was slowly devoured while he sat calmly drinking the juice. He replaced the glass in the saucer. To the onlooker he was Dr. Bard Lane—the boss—the chief—the "old man." But he knew that as far as free will was concerned he had ceased to be Bard Lane.

The alien prescience was quickly interlaced through his engram structure, much as a bobbin might shuttle back and forth in a textile machine. He sensed the fingering of his thoughts.

His new familiarity with the reception of the thoughts of the alien made those thoughts as clear as though they had been softly whispered in his ear.

"No, Bard Lane. No. You and Sharan Inly have come to the wrong conclusion. We are not of this planet. This is not a clever device to trick you. We are friendly to your purpose. I am glad to see that you have taken the precautions that were suggested to you. Please make it very clear to all your trusted people that they must move quickly whenever there is the slightest doubt. Any faint peculiarity—any unexpected word or movement—will be the basis on which to move. Delay may be fatal."

Bard made his thoughts as clear as he could by mentally thinking each word, mentally underlining each syllable. "How do we know you *are* friendly?"

"You can't know. There's no way of proving it to you. All I can say is that our ancestors of twelve thousand years ago are mutual. I told you about the Plan. The Plan is failing because the people in my world have forgotten the original purpose. One world—Marith—lives in barbaric savagery. Another—Ormazd— has found the key to the search for happiness on their planet. We are inbred and decadent. Your project is hope for mankind."

"What are your motives?"

There was a silence in his mind. "If I am to be honest with you, Bard Lane, I must mention boredom, the desire for change, the wish to do important things. And now there is another reason."

"What?"

Their sympathetic emotional structure had been so carefully interleafed that Bard Lane was disconcerted to feel the hot blush on his cheeks and neck. "I want to be able to meet Sharan face to face. I want to touch her hand with mine, not with the hand of someone whom I could inhabit."

The thought broke hurriedly to other matters. "I have wondered if there is any way that I can give you technical help. I do not understand the formulas behind the operation of your ship. All I know is that propulsion is dependent on alternating frames of temporal reference. That is the same formula that was used for our ships long, long ago. As I told you, six of them stand outside our world. I have discovered micro-book operation manuals, but they are beyond me. I could memorize wiring charts and control panels and then, using your hand, draw them for you."

"There are problems we haven't licked yet. You could try to do that."

"What should I look for?"

"The manner in which astrogation charts were coordinated with the time jump. Our astronomers and mathematical physicists believe, at this point, that once the jump is made, it will take weeks to make observations and reorient the ship. They are working on some method which will extend the time jump as a hypothetical line through space from the starting point to the new time frame. Then the coordinates of that hypothetical line, using opposed star clusters for reference points, would eliminate starting from scratch on orientation in the new position. Can you follow that?"

"Yes. I will see if I can find out how it was done in the past."

The guard stepped closer and took a startlingly firm grasp of Bard Lane's arm just above the elbow. His expression was respectful, but his grasp was like iron.

"Sir, you have been talking aloud to yourself."

The alien prescience slid off to a spectator's cubicle within Bard's mind.

Bard smiled up at the guard. "Glad you're alert, Robinson. I'm doing some practice dictation on an important letter I have to write after lunch."

Robinson looked uncertain. Bard put his napkin beside his plate. "I'll be glad to go along to Dr. Inly's office, Robinson, but——"

"I think maybe you better, sir. The order was pretty strict."

Heads turned as they walked out of the mess hall, the bruising grip still punishing Bard's arm. He heard the buzz of conversation as the door swung shut behind them. The sunlight was a blow from a fist of gilt. They went down the street toward Sharan's office.

And the alarm sirens began to shrill.

Bard ripped away from Robinson's grasp and lifted his long legs into a hard run toward the communications center seventy yards away. The sirens died into a moan as he burst through the door. The man at the master switchboard, gray-pale with strain, glanced at Bard, cut in a wall baffle onto the circuit and said, "From the ship, sir. Go ahead. It'll be picked up."

"Who is this?" Bard demanded.

The answering voice was metallic. "Shellwand. On the ship. We've just found a guard on G level, near the shielding, laid out cold, sir. We're trying to get everyone out of the ship, sir."

"Who did it?"

"We won't know, sir, until we—— It's beginning to tremble, sir! The whole——"

The diaphragm in the baffle began to pick up resonance and bray. The man at the master board cut it off. They all heard it then. Once heard, it could never be forgotten. Bard Lane had heard it many times.

It was like the low roll of muted thunder behind distant hills, combined with a thousand roaring male voices, singing a sustained note in discord.

It was the song of men who try to reach the stars. It was the resonating fury of fission, held just short of instantaneous detonation. At Hiroshima it had been one thunderous whip-crack of fate that brought a new age to man. Now the whip-crack was harnessed, controlled, directed, guided.

Bard Lane turned and dived from the room. His shoulder caught the flimsy door and knocked it spinning from the torn hinges. He did not feel the pain. He ran out into an open space and stood with his feet planted, fists clenched, shoulders back, staring toward the Beatty One.

The thunder noise grew louder. Blue-white flame licked out around the fins. Heat cracked against his face and he turned his eyes from the unbearable glare. As the vast sound grew even greater the Beatty One nuzzled upward at the camouflage tent. It rose with painful slowness, with the ponderousness of some unthinkable prehistoric beast. It ripped up through the tent, slowly gaining speed, profiling the tent to its ogive nose, tearing the tent from the towers, slipping through it, igniting it with the fierce tail flame. Now the blue-white unbearable flame was twice as tall as the ship had been. It reached from tail to earth, as though the Beatty One balanced on it.

The base of one tower, softened by heat-lick, settled and the tower leaned slowly toward the north, not gathering speed in the fall, just slowly bending over to lie gently against the ground. The steel of the elevator frame was puddled at the base, but stood miraculously erect. A tiny figure toppled from the elevator platform, crisping to blackness before it neared the ground.

The white gouting stern of the Beatty One was now thrice as high as the towers still standing. The thunder was lifting up through octave after octave as the speed of the Beatty One increased. A great flap of burning fabric fluttered down. The rest of the fabric slid off and the silvery length of the ship, a mirror in the sun, was revealed. Even with the despair that filled his heart, the horror and the great shock of failure, Bard Lane felt and recognized the strong sense of awe at the sheer beauty of the ship.

A tiny figure toppled from the high open port. The ship had

moved just enough off the perpendicular so that the toy figure came down, not spinning, motionless in the sun-hot air, toward the street of the village. It hit in the dust, bursting work clothes, rebounding eighteen inches before lying still, a jellied, grotesque thing. The hard roar changed to shrillness and the Beatty One winked high in the sun. High and higher. Vapor trail. And higher. Then slowly canting over, as he knew it would do without the 20 Mohs stability plates which had not yet been installed in the A-six jet flow. It made a bright white line against the impossible blue of the sky, an arc, a parabola, as neat as any inscribed on graph paper. A line up to a peak and a line down. The shrillness was a scream that tore at the inner ear. A line down to the earth. He saw the flare and guessed the distance at fifteen to twenty miles, due south. The scream still continued after the explosion flare had filled half the sky, then stopped abruptly. The air pushed hard against them, then the earth shook as though a truck were going by. At last came the gutteral crack-boom of the explosion. And silence. Brown cloud lifting in mushroom shape toward the blue sky. A bit of the vapor trail was still high in the sky, wavering off in the prevailing wind.

Bard Lane took two steps to the curbing, sat down and held his face in his hands. Nearby, a wooden building crackled as the flames bit into it. The project fire engines screamed to a stop, sirens ridiculous in comparison to the memory of the scream of the dying Beatty One—a mosquito trying to outshout an eagle. Somebody rested a steady hand on Bard Lane's shoulder. He looked up and saw the stolid, seamed face of Adamson. Tears had cut channels in the dust on his cheeks.

"Nick, I . . . I . . ."

Adamson's voice was gruff. "I'll take an emergency crew down and see what she did when she hit. If we're lucky, she'll be five miles from the village. Better go get on the radio, Bard, and give the word. Then I think you ought to make an announcement over the PA." Adamson walked solidly away.

He walked to his office. The guard had voluntarily given up his assignment. The project personnel stood in the street. Not large groups. Two or three or four. Low voices. Long silences. They glanced quickly at him and then away. He went through the outer office. Bess Reilly sat at her desk. She sat with her forehead against the top of her typewriter. Her bony shoulders shook but she made no sound.

After he advised Sachson and Washington by coded radio, he obtained a clear circuit over the PA for every amplifier in the area.

He spoke slowly. "This is Lane. We don't know what happened. We may never know who or what was responsible. You will be wondering about your jobs. I doubt very much whether we will be given a second chance. By the day after tomorrow we'll have the checks ready for termination pay for most of you. Certain clerical, stock record, and lab employees will be retained for a time. A list of those who will be needed will be posted on the bulletin board tomorrow afternoon. One thing. Don't ever feel that because of what just happened, all of what we have done is wasted. We learned things. If we're not given a chance to use them, someone else will, sooner or later. They will learn from the mistakes we made. All employees will please proceed immediately to the time clocks and remove their time cards. Turn them in to Mr. Nolan. Mr. Nolan, after there has been time for all cards to be picked up, send someone to gather up the unclaimed ones. That's the only way, I'm afraid, that we'll ever learn who made the . . . first and last trip on the Beatty One. Dr. Inly, please report to my office. Benton, rope off the takeoff area, and advise me when the count is down to a one hour safety period. Those of you who lost personal possessions in the barracks fire, prepare the standard claim form. You can get forms and instructions from Miss Mees in the Accounting Office. Brainard, start your labor crews to work torch-cutting, for scrap, the tower that fell outside the radiation area. The club will be closed tonight. And . . . I don't know how to say this properly, but I want to thank every single individual for . . . devotion and loyalty beyond anything I ever experienced before. Thank you."

He released the switch and looked up. Sharan Inly was standing in the doorway. She walked to his desk. "You wanted to see me."

He grinned in a very tired way. "Thanks, Sharan."

"For what?"

"For being bright enough not to start commiserating with me, telling me how sorry you are and how it wasn't my fault and all that."

She sat down, hung one denimed leg over the arm of the chair. "There isn't anything to say. Our good pal who calls himself Raul got to one of the group and fixed us. On the other side of the world somebody feels very, very good, I imagine."

"What are you going to do, Sharan?"

"They'll find another slot to put me in. Maybe I'll be back in the Pentagon, testing the Oedipus complexes of quartermaster second lieutenants. Something frightfully thrilling along that line. But now I have a hobby."

"Hobby?"

"Finding out how they worked that long-range hypnosis. There are a few people I can trust not to think I've lost my mind when I give them the story."

"But you won't be taking off immediately, I'm afraid. There'll be an investigation. We'll have the star parts. You and I and Adamson and Leeber and Kornal and a few of the others. Stick around, Dr. Inly. See the big three-ring circus. Hear the tigers howl for meat. Pay your money and see the seven wonders of the world."

A storm front was moving in from the north. The day was unexpectedly and unusually muggy. Extra chairs had been brought into General Sachson's conference room. Two bored girls sat at a small table near the windows, supplementing the recording devices with the aid of two stenotype machines. They had covered several yards of the white tape with the staggered letters. The door was closed against the reporters and photographers who waited in the corridor.

Bard Lane sat at the witness table. His armpits were sodden and he had a dry, stained taste in his mouth.

Senator Leedry was a dry wisp of a man, tiny and withered, but with a plump and arrogant little paunch. He smiled as he spoke. His baritone voice was alternately scalpel, cutting torch, and caress.

"I appreciate, Dr. Lane, your attempts to explain technical data in a manner that we poor laymen can understand. Believe me, we *appreciate* it. But I guess we're not as bright as you imagine. At least, I'm not. Now, if it isn't too much trouble, would you explain once again to us, your *theory* about the accident."

"The A-six uses what they call, in Army slang, 'soft' radiation. The shielding also acts as an inhibitor. When actuated, the pellets are fed down to the CM chamber for combustion. The CM chamber utilizes the principles of the old shaped charge to achieve thrust. The controls had not been installed for the A-six drive. There is no possibility of an accidental transfer of pellets to the drive chamber."

The Secretary of War, Logan Brightling, cleared his throat to interrupt. Cartoons depicted him perfectly as a hairless Kodiak bear wearing a wing collar. "Why was the Beatty One equipped with the hot stuff for the A-six drive before the controls were installed?"

"In spite of the inhibitors, the pellets generate appreciable heat. The Beatty One had an efficient method of utilizing this heat for self-contained power. To use that power for the necessary welding and structural work was more efficient than attempting to bring outside power to the ship. You could say that once we had the internal power source working, the Beatty One was helping to build herself. To continue, I have explained that I do not feel that it could have been an accident. The wall chart shows a schematic cross section." Bard Lane walked over to the chart. "A man could enter here. It is the normal inspection procedure to check the shielding at regular intervals and take a careful count of all escaping radiation to determine whether or not it is well within safety limits. From this passage a man can work his way completely around the shielding and the drive chamber. At this point is a port that can only be used when the storage section contains no pellets. Beyond the port the radiation will kill a man in approximately twelve minutes. Once through that port it would take a person not more than three minutes to manually dislodge the pellets from their niches in the conveyor and drop them down onto the plate above the drive chamber. In a few minutes more the person could clamber down there, activate the motor on the plate and let the pellets drop into the drive chamber itself. Without the required inhibition, the CM would be instantaneously achieved and the ship would take off. Inspection of the area

where the Beatty One stood has shown us that there is more re-
sidual radiation than would normally be expected. Thus we assume that the drive chamber was fed with more pellets than
would normally have been carried there at one time by the conveyor, and thus we can assume that it was not an accidental ac-
tuation of the conveyor itself."

Leedry pursed his dry lips. "Then, Dr. Lane, you would have
us believe that someone went into that . . . that searing hell of
radiation and sabotaged the ship?"

Bard returned to his chair. "I can see no other answer. After
five seconds by the open port to the storage section, there would
be not the slightest hope of living more than twenty minutes no
matter what medical attention was given. The person sacrificed
his life. There were twelve technicians on the ship at the time,
along with twelve guards watching them under a new security bulletin I issued four days before the accident. Evidently the sabo-
teur overpowered his guard. The elevator operator and two laborers too close to the ship perished, bringing the total death toll
in the takeoff to twenty-seven. A large section of the burning
camouflage cover fell on a typist from the accounting office. She
died yesterday of her burns. So the total is twenty-eight."

General Sachson went over to Leedry, bent down and whispered in his ear. Leedry did not change expression. He said, "Dr.
Lane, would you please move over to the other table for a few
minutes. Dr. Inly, will you please come forward."

Leedry let the seconds mount up. Sharan concealed the thud of
her pulse, the sick nervousness that gave her mouth a metallic
taste.

"Dr. Inly, you have previously testified as to your duties and
the operating regulations which have covered those duties. As I
understand your regulations, once you have committed any project employee for detailed observation, the minimum length of
time in hospital is seven days. Yet, according to your records, we
find that Dr. Lane was sent in for observation and released after
only three days. I trust you have some explanation of this deviation from your stated regulations."

There was a buzz of conversation in the room. The chairman of
the investigating committee rapped for order.

Sharan bit her lip.

"Come, Dr. Inly. Surely you know why you ordered Dr. Lane's release!"

"I discovered that . . . the evidence on which I had committed Dr. Lane was not what . . . I had first thought."

"Is it true that you have been very friendly with Dr. Lane? Is it not true that you have often been alone together? Is it not true that there was a very strong rumor among the project employees that your relationship was—shall we say—a bit closer than a normal professional relationship would indicate?" Leedry leaned forward in his chair, as intent as a questing hawk.

"I resent your implication, Senator."

"Merely answer the questions, Dr. Inly."

"Dr. Lane is my very good friend. Nothing more. We were often together and we often discussed what courses of action would be best for the project."

"Indeed?" Leedry asked.

Bard stood up. "Senator, I consider this line of investigation as wholesome as scribbling on a lavatory wall."

"You're out of order!" the chairman snapped. "Sit down, please."

"Take the stand again, Dr. Lane," Leedry said. "We will need you again in a few moments, Dr. Inly."

Bard took the stand. Leedry again waited for his fellow committee members to stop their whispers. "Dr. Inly is quite attractive, don't you think?" he asked Bard in a jovial manner.

"She is a competent psychologist," Bard said.

"Ah, undoubtedly. Now then, Dr. Lane. Yesterday we took testimony from one of the hospital supervisors. Can you explain how it was that you were seen in the hospital making love to a young nurse named Anderson?"

"May I ask what you are trying to prove?" Bard asked. His voice was low.

"I'll be glad to tell you, Dr. Lane. I can best tell you by asking you one more question. Dr. Lane, you are quite a famous man, you know. You are quite young for the enormous responsibilities which were given you. You have spent a trifle more than one billion dollars of the taxpayers' money. Money that came from a great number of little people who work hard for a living. Surely you felt the weight of that responsibility. Now answer me this question, Dr. Lane. During the period of time since you permitted one William Kornal to return to his duties after having smashed key control equipment, have you at any time sincerely felt that you are and have been unsuited for the responsibilities which were given you?"

Bard Lane doubled his big brown fists. He glanced at Sharan Inly and saw that her eyes were misty. "Yes, I have."

"And yet you did not ask to be relieved?"

"No, sir."

"Dismissed. Wait in the anteroom. Please take the stand, Major Leeber. I understand that you have been in the position of an observer ever since the Kornal incident."

"That is correct." Major Leeber sat very straight in his chair. Each bit of brass on his uniform was a tiny golden mirror. His voice had lost the lazy tone. It was crisp. His mouth was a firm line.

"Will you give us your opinion of the quality of Dr. Lane's management?"

"I can best do that by giving the committee a verbatim quote from a report I sent to General Sachson, my commanding officer, three days before the 'accident' occurred. I am quoting paragraph three of my report. 'It appears that Dr. Lane is best suited to perform supervised technical work in the research field and that he has neither the temperament nor the training for administrative work that is required of the head of a project such as this one. The informality here is indicative of a lack of discipline. Dr. Lane goes to ridiculous lengths in his new security regulations, detailed above, yet permits fraternization between high-level personnel and CAF-two typists on the clerical staff. The undersigned officer strongly recommends that every attempt be made to bring this situation to the attention of those persons in Washington who are in a position to direct a full scale investigation of the project.'"

Leedry turned to Sachson. "General, don't bother taking the stand. Just tell us what you did with the major's report."

"I endorsed it, stating my approval of Leeber's conclusions and sent it by courier officer through the Chief of Ordnance to the Commanding General, Armed Forces. I assumed that it would be taken up with the Secretary of Defense."

The Secretary of Defense rumbled, "It was on my desk for my

personal attention when the flash came that the Beatty One had taken off prematurely. I compliment the General and Major Leeber on their handling of this matter. I shall see that it is made a matter of record for their two-oh-one files."

Sharan Inly laughed. The sound was out of place in the room. The laugh was as chill as the tinkling of crystal. "Gentlemen, you amuse me. The Army has resented Project Tempo from the beginning. The Army feels that space travel attempts are absurd unless carried on in an atmosphere of company formations, service ribbons and seventh endorsements. Dr. Lane is caught in the middle and he'll be disgraced. The sad truth is that he has more integrity in his little finger than Major Leeber is even capable of visualizing." She turned to Leeber and said mildly, "You really are a rather despicable little man, you know. Gentlemen, this whole affair makes me sick at heart and rather close to being ill in quite another manner. I am leaving and you can cite me for contempt or restrain me physically. I imagine the latter will be more your style. So nice to have known you."

She brushed by the sergeant at arms at the door. It closed gently behind her.

"Let her go," Leedry said. "I rather imagine that she'll have a long, long wait before Civil Service is able to place her in another government position. And she just told us all we need to know. Her infatuation with Lane, and the effect of that infatuation on her judgment is now a matter of record. I suggest that we consider arriving at a conclusion. My personal opinion is that Project Tempo failed due to the gross negligence and mental instability of Dr. Bard Lane. We should clear out the witnesses and poll the committee."

General Sachson, as he stood up, said, "If I could have the privilege of making one comment, Senator."

"Of course, General," Leedry said warmly.

"You will find in my record that two years ago when Project Tempo was being considered, I read the survey reports and filed a negative opinion. That girl—I should say Dr. Inly—inferred that the military has attempted to block Project Tempo. I wish to deny that allegation. I am a soldier. I follow orders. Once Project Tempo was approved, I gave it my wholehearted cooperation.

The minutes of my staff meetings in connection with Tempo are available as proof of this cooperation.

"However, in all honesty, I must confess that from the beginning I considered Tempo to be a wild scheme. I believe that with persistence, with the application of discipline and effort, we will succeed in conquering space in accordance with the plan outlined by General Roamer sixteen years ago. First we must beef up our moon base. The moon is the stepping stone to Mars and Venus. Gentlemen, it is sound military thought to consolidate your own area before advancing further. Project Tempo put the cart several miles ahead of the horse. The old ways are the best. The known methods are tried, and they will be true.

"Is this time-jump theory something you can see, feel, hold on to? No. It is a theory. I personally do not believe that there is any variation. I think time is a constant throughout all the galaxies and all the universe. Lane was a dreamer. I am a doer. You know my record. I do not want this fiasco to make you turn your backs on space flight. We need a vastly augmented moon base. From a moon base we can look down the throat of Pan-Asia. We must reinforce that base, and not dissipate our efforts in humoring the more lunatic fringe of our nation's physicists. Thank you, gentlemen."

Leedry led the round of polite but enthusiastic applause. Major Leeber rose quickly to his feet and clapped with the rest.

12

FOR AN UNCOUNTED NUMBER OF DAYS, RAUL KINSON SAT IN ONE of the rooms of learning, alone, many levels above the rest of the Watchers. Infrequently he went down to pick at the food on one of the trays. Once Leesa found him. He did not look at her, or hear what she said. He was vaguely aware of her presence and felt a mild distant relief when she went away.

Over and over and over again he saw, as he had seen it through

Bard Lane's eyes, the roaring ruin of the Beatty One, the ruin of his hopes, the clear cue to treachery. He wanted Leesa's throat between his fingers, yet knew that he could not kill her.

He did not dream. He did not wish to project himself back to Earth. He had been ashamed of the Watchers before. This was a new shame, more intense than ever before. And slowly he came back to life. Hour by hour. On Earth there had been one ship. Here there were six. Would a man die outside the building? If a man could live, could find his way into one of the six ships . . .

He knew where the door was. If he died outside the building, it did not matter.

He went down to the lowest level, hurried by the throb of the power rooms, glancing often over his shoulder. He made certain that he was not followed. The rooms that lined the corridor leading to the door contained things that the others no longer understood. Odd garments. Tools. Undisturbed for centuries.

At last he came to the door. The top of it was on a level with his eyes. Two spoked wheels projected from the door itself. He touched one. It turned easily. He spun it hard. It spun without sound, stopped with a soft click. He did the same with the other one. He glanced back up the corridor, then grasped both wheels. His breath came deep and hard and excitement fluttered along his spine. He pulled slowly. The door opened. He knew of wind and coldness, but always he had felt them in an alien body and now he knew that such sensations had been muted. The wind was a dull knife scraping his flesh and sand, heaped against the door, trickled in onto the corridor floor. He knew that he could not stand such cold. The sand prevented him from closing the door again. He dropped to his knees and shoveled the sand back out with his hands. At last he could close the door. As he leaned against it he began to stop shaking as the warmth seeped back into his body. It seemed incredible that beyond the door there was not another corridor, equally warm.

He found the garments in the third room. They were metallic, dark green. The inner lining was soft. He found a large one, put it on awkwardly. It felt strange against his legs, heavy. The fastening was difficult until he discovered that the two strips of metal down the front would cling together firmly of their own accord.

Thus clad against the cold, it was only as he returned to the door the second time that he thought of a more obvious danger. When shut the door would remain closed until he pushed against it from the outside. But if Jord Orlan or any one of the old ones should be following him, should come and spin the wheels——

"Raul!" she said, close behind him. It startled him badly. He turned and stared at Leesa, then turned his back to her.

"Raul, you must listen to me. You must!"

"There is nothing you can say to me."

"I know what you think of me. I betrayed you, Raul. I gave you my word and betrayed you. You know that I smashed that ship." She laughed in a strange and brittle way. "But you see, I didn't realize that I was betraying myself too."

He did not turn. He stood stolidly, staring at the burnished metal of the door.

"I have dreamed many times, Raul, trying to find him. I have found Sharan Inly. I told her what I had done. She hated me, Raul. And after a long time I made her understand. She is . . . kind, Raul. But she cannot find him. No one knows where he has gone. And I must find him and tell him . . . why I did that to him."

Behind him he heard an odd sound. A small sound. He turned. She had dropped to her knees, and sat on her heels, shoulders slumped, face in her hands.

"Never before have I seen you weep, Leesa."

"Help me find him, Raul. Please help me."

"I want you to find him, Leesa. I want you to see, in his mind, precisely what you did to him."

"I know what I did to him. I was in his mind once, Raul, after it happened," she said, lifting her tear-tracked face. "It was . . . horrid."

"How can that be, Leesa? Remember? They are only dream creatures. They don't exist. The machines are clever. The dream machines manufactured Bard Lane for your special amusement."

"Don't. Please don't."

"Don't tell me, my sister, that you have come to believe those creatures exist," he said mockingly. "What could have changed your mind?"

Her eyes were grave on his. There was an odd dignity about her. "I cannot think it out the way you do. I was in his mind. I know his thoughts, his memories and his dreams. I know him better than I know myself. It is just that I cannot go on living in a universe where he does not exist. And if he exists, then all the others do. You have been right. All the others have been wrong, as wrong as I have been."

"I should trust you now?"

"Is there any reason for distrusting me . . . now?"

He took her hands and lifted her to her feet, and he smiled. "I shall trust you again. If you help me, maybe we can find him again. I know how you feel, Leesa, because I cannot . . . stop thinking, remembering. She was . . ."

"Sharan Inly?"

He turned away from her. "Yes, and a cruel trap for both of us, Leesa."

"How can I help you?"

"I am going out to the ships. I am going to try to board one. I have learned some of the operating instructions. Our lifetimes will be long over before Earth builds another ship like the one you destroyed. Those ships out there have the same principle. I shall board one and I shall take it to Earth."

Her eyes grew wide, shocked. "But . . ."

"It may be too cold out there. I may die. There may not be enough oxygen left on this planet. If I fail, you will go in that second room. Select a tool that cuts cables. Take it up to the dream cases by stealth. Start with the unused cases. Cut the cables on every one. Every one. Do you understand?"

"Then I will never find him."

"That would be a good thing. I do not want to go to Sharan Inly in some other body. I want to go and touch her with this hand, look at her with these eyes. Nothing else is any good."

"One of those ships . . . after so many years . . . it is incredible, Raul."

"I've had the door open. I think I can live out there. Help me. Wait for me here. I must be able to get back inside. If anyone should come, you must keep them from touching those wheels on the door. Do you understand?"

"Yes."

He went to the door and pulled it open. He saw her shrink away from the shrill wind. He lowered his head and plunged out.

She pushed the door shut. He stood for a moment, turning his back to the wind, finding out if he could breathe the air. He had to breathe fast and deep. The cold bit into his bones and the sand scoured the naked backs of his hands and his cheeks. He turned and squinted across the dim plain toward the six ships. With the position determined, he walked toward them, leaning into the wind, shielding his eyes with his hand, holding the other hand in his armpit for warmth. As the unprotected hand began to grow numb, he changed hands. He looked again and saw that his hundred steps had carried him off to the left. He corrected his direction and continued on. A hundred steps more. The ships seemed no closer. The next time he looked they were closer. And then, panting with the exertion, he saw new details of their construction. He turned his back to the wind and cried out as he saw his known world far behind him. Taller than the ships, yet dwarfed by the ragged hills behind it, it reached white levels up toward the purpled sky. Blank featureless walls, each level recessed a bit, reaching up to a dizzy height above him.

He fought the desire to return. He went on. Behind him, the wind erased his tracks. The ships grew larger. Their fluted sterns rested on the sand. One of them was canted at a slight angle. Never had he realized their true size, nor their distance from each other. The last hundred feet was the easiest because the nearest ship cut the force of the harsh, steady wind. The sand was piled high in long sharp ridges extending out on either side of the ship. Above him, the bulge of the ship was a dizzy overhang. The surface, though still of shining metal, was pitted and scarred and worn. And there was no way to get into the ship. No way at all. He circled it, almost weeping in frustration. Shining and unclimbable metal. He steadied himself with one hand against it as he clambered awkwardly over the drifts. Both hands were so numb that he could not feel the texture of the metal against his fingers. He made two complete circuits of the ship. Across the plain the tall white world seemed to watch with silent amusement.

He tripped and fell heavily. His face struck against the side of the ship, half stunning him. He lay, trying to summon up the energy he would need to get back to his feet. The ship was inches from his eyes. He tensed. An angular crack showed in the metal, too straight to be accidental. He sat with spread legs, like a child in a sand pile, and dug with hands that were like clubs. The crack grew, turned into the right angle of what could be a square port. He began to laugh as he dug, chuckling deep in his throat, over the wind-scream.

He stopped digging and patted the ship affectionately, called it words of endearment. And now he felt much warmer. Pleasantly warm.

He fumbled up onto his feet with drunken dignity. Pretty ship. Take him to Earth. See Sharan.

Raul turned. No need to go to Earth after all. There was Sharan, standing there, smiling. She didn't mind the wind. She was warm too. He advanced toward her and she backed away, teasingly. His feet made no tracks in the sand.

"Sharan!" he bawled hoarsely, his voice lost in the constant wind-shriek. "Sharan!" He lifted his unfeeling legs in a stumbling run. She was still elusive, backing toward the white warm world he had left. He hoped Leesa was watching, so that she could see Sharan too. Now Sharan was gone. He couldn't find her. He ran on and tripped and fell headlong. He was far too comfortable to get up. Too warm. The sand piled quickly up along his left side, and at last spilled across the back of his neck with a gentle touch that was like a caress.

13

SHARAN INLY LOOKED WITH DISTASTE AT THE NARROW STREET. The man from the agency pulled up at the curb and stopped. It was dusk and neon was beginning to flicker.

The agency man pointed toward the place called Joe's Alibi.

"He'll be in there, miss. Want me to go yank him out? It's no place for a girl, and he won't be in any shape to come willingly."

"I'll go in," she said.

"I better come with you then. You'll need help with him."

"If you wish," she said.

The agency man looked at the grubby children nearby, carefully locked the car before crossing the street with her.

They heard hoarse laughter as they crossed the sidewalk. The laughter and the rumble of conversation stopped as Sharan pushed the screen open and walked in. She walked into the room and then turned to the agency man.

"He's not here," she said with sinking heart.

"Take a second look, miss," he said.

She looked at the man at the table. His chair was tilted back against the wall. His chin was on his chest and he was asleep. His gaunt gray face was stubbled with beard and his open collar was soiled.

Sharan went quickly to the table. "Bard!" she cried softly. "Bard!"

"That his name?" the bartender said in the silence. "We call him the perfessor. He's what you might call a mascot around here. You want him woke up?"

The heavy-shouldered bartender came around the corner of the bar, tilted Bard's chair forward, caught him on the front of the stained suit, lifted him effortlessly and slapped his cheek with a full arm swing. It resounded like a pistol shot.

"Take it easy, friend," the agency man said softly.

Bard opened his eyes owlishly. "Now listen to his act," the bartender said. "Perfessor! Can you hear me, Perfessor? Tell us about them Martians."

In a hollow, whisky-hoarse tone, Bard said, "They come to us from a distant planet and take over our souls. They fill our minds with evil and lead us to dark deeds. You never know when they are coming. No one ever knows. We should be on guard."

"Cute, ain't he?" the bartender said, grinning.

Sharan curled her fingers and took a half step toward the bartender. "Get away from him," she whispered.

"Sure, lady. Sure thing. No harm intended."

Bard found her with his eyes. He frowned. "What do you want?"

"Come with me, Bard."

"I like it here. Sorry," he mumbled.

The agency man stepped around her. He caught Bard's wrist, brought it around and up into the small of Bard's back. Bard made feeble struggles. The agency man marched him to the door as Sharan followed.

"Take good care of the perfessor, sweetheart," one of the customers said. Sharan flushed. The room was once again filled with laughter.

She unlocked the car and the agency man edged Bard in onto the seat. As soon as Bard was sitting, he fell asleep again. He was between them as the agency man started the car. "Smells a little strong, don't he?" the agency man said.

Sharan didn't answer. The rooming house was in the next block. It was a scabrous building, full of the memories of evil, of the wry ghosts of orgy.

"Second floor front," the agency man said. He woke Bard up. Bard Lane seemed dazed. There was no more protest in him. Sharan followed them up the stairs, the agency man supporting Bard with an arm around his waist. The door was unlocked. The room was tiny, shabby, and the hall was sour and dim.

"You want I should stay and help you, lady?" the man asked.

"Thank you. I'll take it from here on," she said. "And thank you."

"All in the day's work. Be careful. Some of them go a little nutty when you start to wring them out."

He had collapsed on the narrow bed. He snored. She locked the door behind her and took the key. In an hour she was back with a complete set of new clothes that would fit him. She turned on the single light, cleaned up some of the litter in the room. The bath was across the hall. No shower. Just a tub.

His shoes were cracked and broken things that could have come from a trash barrel. He wore no socks. His ankles were grubby. She laid out his shaving things, the new clothes, in the bathroom.

Then came the nightmare of waking him, of seeing the eyes open vague in the gray face. He no longer seemed to know her. She supported more than half his weight getting him across the hall. He could not help himself. He sat on the stool with his back against the wall and let himself be undressed, like a child. Getting him into the tub was a major engineering project, and then she had to wait until the cold water revived him enough so that she could be sure he did not drown. She went out and brought back a quart of hot coffee. He drank it and looked at her with a bit more comprehension.

"Bard! Listen to me. Clean up and get dressed."

"Sure, sure," he mumbled.

From time to time she went back to the bathroom door and listened. She heard him splashing, moving around. Later she heard the scrape of a razor. She bundled his old clothes in the plastex wrapper that had been around the new clothes.

At last he came slowly into the room. He sat down quickly, cupped trembling hands over his eyes. "How do you feel?" she asked.

"Rotten, Sharan."

"There's some coffee beside you. Better have some." Even with the container held in both hands, some of the hot coffee spilled out onto the back of his hand.

"You didn't find a very good answer, did you?" she said.

"Is any answer a good one?"

"Giving up isn't a good answer."

"Please. Spare me the violin music. I was discarded. It seemed necessary to act the part."

"Everybody has a streak of martyr, Bard."

He stared at her. His eyes were hollow, lifeless. "They fixed me good. They tied the can to me, baby. No lab in the country would touch me. You know that. I had some money saved. I was going to show everybody. I interviewed some accident victims—the ones where I suspected Raul and his gang had a part in it. I took a tape recorder. Know the most common expression? 'I don't know what came over me,' they said. I tried to get a newspaper interested. They talked very pleasantly while they sent for the little men with the nets."

"I read about it, Bard," she said softly.

"Good article, wasn't it? Funny as hell."

"You haven't been in the news for a month. The public has a short memory. They've forgotten you."

"That's a comfort."

"Feel better now?"

He stared at her. "Dr. Inly, the patient refuses treatment. Why don't you go excise a few prefrontal lobes or something?"

She smiled at him. "Don't be childish. Finish the coffee. We're going to get you a haircut and a steak—in that order."

His smile was mild acid. "And why do I merit all this attention?"

"Because you are needed. Don't be defensive, Bard. Just do as I say. I'll explain later."

Dusk was over the city and they were in an oak booth at the back of a quiet restaurant. His eyes were brighter and some of the shakiness had gone out of his hands. He pushed his coffee cup aside, lit her cigarette and his own. "Now it's time to talk, Sharan."

"We'll talk about a mistaken premise, Bard. We assumed that a hypnotic device operated from the other side of this world destroyed the Beatty One. After they delicately told me that I was all through and that I'd be called if there was a vacancy for anyone with my rating, I . . . contacted again. With the Beatty One gone, there didn't seem to be much point in it. I jeered at their fantasy of an alien world. I jeered at our friend, Raul, and at his sister. It took them a long time. I brought Lurdorff in on it. He's too egocentric to ever doubt his own sanity. And now he believes, too. They're what they say they are."

He stared at her without expression. "Go on."

"Everything he told us appeared to be true. It was the girl who destroyed the ship. She took over the A-six technician named Machielson. She had him overpower the guard. The rest of it went just the way you guessed. Bard, do you remember the time I told you that I wished I could fall in love with you?"

"I remember."

"Someone else did. The sister. She found out too late. She thought we were figments of her dreams. Now she, like Raul, is convinced that we are reality. The logical processes of most women are rather odd. She and her brother have been helping me look for you. I explained about investigation agencies and how expensive they were. The next day a man stopped me in the street and gave me all of the money out of his wallet and walked on. A second and a third man did the same. That's the way Raul fixed the money angle. And now we've found you."

Bard stubbed out his cigarette. He laughed softly. "Sort of a long range affair, isn't it? Raul identified their planet as being near Alpha Centauri. If he gave me a picture of what is actually their world, my lady love has a bald and gleaming skull, the body of a twelve year old child. I can hardly wait."

"Don't make a joke out of it, Bard!" she said with some heat. "We need you. If we're ever going to live up to the promise that we had in the Beatty One, you have to help us."

"I see. Raul gets one billion people to each hand us a dollar and then we start from scratch."

She stood up quickly and stubbed out her cigarette. "All right, Bard. I thought you might want to help. I'm sorry. I was wrong. It was good to see you again. Good luck." She turned away.

"Come back and sit down, Sharan. I'm sorry."

She hesitated, came back. "Then listen. Of all men on this planet, you have the best overall grasp of the problems involved in the actual utilization of Beatty's formulas. Some forgotten man on Raul's planet perfected those formulas roughly thirteen thousand years before Beatty did. Raul has gotten to the ships he told you about. He nearly died in the attempt. When he was gone too long the first time, Leesa went out after him and managed to get him back before he froze to death. He has been in one of the ships a dozen times. He thinks that it is still in working condition. He has activated certain parts of it—the air supply, internal heating. But as far as the controls are concerned, you are the only one who can help. He is baffled."

"How can I help?"

"We discussed that. He can use your hand to draw, from memory, the exact position of every knob and switch, along with a translation of the symbols that appear on them. If the principle is the same, which he is almost certain that it is, then you should be able to figure out the most logical purpose of each control."

"But . . . look, Sharan, the odds against my being right. They're tremendous. And the smallest mistake will leave him lost in space, or aflame on the takeoff. Or suppose he does find us. Suppose he barrels into our atmosphere at ten thousand miles per second and makes his landing in Central Park or the Chicago Loop district?"

"He's willing to take the chance."

She let him think without interruption. He drew aimless lines on the tablecloth with his thumbnail. "What would be gained?"

"What would the Beatty One have gained? And you do read the papers, don't you? Mysterious crash of stratoliner. Father slays family of six. Bank embezzler throws two millions into Lake Erie. Novelist's girlfriend buried alive. Auto charges noon crowds on busy street corner. We've always considered that sort of thing inexplicable, Bard. We've made big talk about irrational spells, about temporary insanity, about the way the human mind is prone to go off balance without warning. Isn't that sort of thing worth stopping, even at a billion to one chance? Religions have been born out of the fantasies the Watchers have planted in the minds of men. Wars have been started for the sake of amusing those who have considered us to be merely images given the appearance of reality by a strange machine."

Again the silence. He smiled. "How do we start?"

"We've worked out a coordinated time system. Their 'days' are longer than ours. We'll have to go to my place. They expect me to bring you there so that contact can be made. It is quicker than searching each time. We have an hour before we have to get there."

She had a hotel suite. Bedroom and sitting room. Physically there were two people in the room. Mentally there were four. Bard sat in a deep chair, the floor lamp shining down on the pad he held against his knee. Sharan stood by the window.

Through Bard's lips, Raul said, "We'll have to make this a four-way discussion, and so all thoughts will have to be vocalized. How will we make identification?"

Sharan said, "This is Leesa speaking. Raul, when you or I speak, we'll hold up the right hand. That should serve."

It was agreed. Bard felt the uncanny lifting of his right hand without his own conscious volition. "In Dr. Lane's mind, Sharan and Leesa, I still find considerable doubt. He seems willing to go along with us, but he is still skeptical." The hand dropped.

Bard said, "I can't help it. And I admit to certain animosity, too. Leesa, as I understand it, ruined Project Tempo."

Sharan lifted her right hand. "Only because I didn't understand, then. Believe me, Bard. Please. You have to believe me. You see, I——"

Bard's right hand lifted and Raul said, "Leesa, we haven't time for that sort of thing. Don't interrupt for a moment. I want to draw the instrument panel for Dr. Lane."

Bard Lane felt the pressure that forced him further back from the threshold of volition. His hand grasped the pencil. Quickly a drawing of an odd instrument panel began to take shape. Across the top were what appeared to be ten square dials. Each one was calibrated vertically, with a zero at the middle, plus values above, minus values below the zero point. The indicator was a straight line across the dial resting on the zero point. Below each dial were what appeared to be two push buttons, one above the other. Raul murmured, "This is the part that I cannot understand. I have figured out the rest of the controls. The simplest one is directional. A tiny replica of the ship is mounted on a rod at the end of a universal joint. The ship can be turned manually. From what I have gathered from the instruction manuals, the replica is turned to the desired position. The ship itself follows suit, and as it does so, the replica slowly moves back to the neutral position. Above the ten dials is a three-dimensional screen. Once a planet is approached, both planet and ship show on the screen. As the ship gets closer to the surface, the scale becomes smaller so that actual terrain details appear. Landing consists of setting the ship image gently against the image of the planet surface. Such maneuvering is apparently on the same basis as the Beatty One. But there is no hand control for it. There are diaphragms to strap on either side of the larynx and velocity is achieved through the intensity with which a certain vowel is uttered. I tested that portion of the ship by making the vowel sound as softly as I could. The ship trembled. I imagine that the purpose is to enable the pilot to control the ship even when pressure keeps him from lifting a finger. I feel capable of taking the ship up and landing it again. But unless I can understand the ten dials below the three-dimensional screen, it is obvious that no extended voyage can be made."

The pressure faded. Bard said, "Have you tried to discover the wiring details behind the dials?"

"Yes. I cannot understand it. And it is so complicated that by memorizing one portion at a time and transmitting that portion to you, I feel that it would take at least one of your years before it would be complete, and then I would have no real assurance that it was entirely accurate."

"Plus and minus values, eh? How good is your translation of the figures? Is your math equivalent to ours?"

"No. Your interval is ten. Ours is nine. The roughest possible comparison would be to say that your value for twenty is the second digit in our third series."

"Then the nine plus and nine minus values above and below the zero cover a full simple series. I am always wary of snap judgments, but those dials remind me, unmistakably, of the answer column in any computing device. With ten dials and only plus values alone, you could arrive at our equivalent of one billion. Adding in the minus values, you can achieve a really tremendous series of values. The available numbers could be computed as one billion multiplied by nine hundred and ninety-nine million, nine hundred and ninety-nine thousand, nine hundred and ninety-nine. Navigation always assumes known coordinates. Assume, for a moment, that the basic future-past relationship is expressed as plus and minus. Assume further that utilizing the varying frames of temporal reference, it is necessary to cross, at the very most, ten time lines to arrive at the most distant star—the star that, from your position, is equidistant no matter in which direction you start out. Now, for any nearer star, there will be a preferred route. There will be an assumed direction. You will intersect the frames of reference at an assumed point. Thus, your controls should be so set as to take advantage, at the proper fractional part of a second, of your plus-minus, or, more accurately, your future-past distortions. This would mean an index number, starting from your position, for each star—not a fixed index number, but a number which, adjusted by a formula to allow for orbital movement and galactic movement, will give you the setting for the controls. One of the unknowns to fit into the equation before using it is your present value for time on your planet. No. Wait a minute. If I were designing the controls I would use a radiation timing device for accuracy, and have the controls work the formula themselves so that the standard star reference number could always be used."

"It will have to be that way. It has been centuries since we have maintained any record of elapsed time."

"The buttons under the dials should be the setting device. The upper button should, with each time you push it, lift your indicator one plus notch. The lower button should drop it, one notch at a time, into the minus values. The final number, placed on the dials, should take you across space to the star for that specific setting. It would be the simplest possible type of control which could be used with the Beatty formulas—far simpler than the one on which we were working. But to use it, you must find somewhere, probably on the ship, a manual which will give you a listing of the values for the stars."

Bard Lane felt the excitement in Raul Kinson's thoughts. "A long time ago. Three of your years. Possibly more. I found books printed on thin metallic plates. They did not mean anything to me. Long bi-colored numbers. They were awkward to read compared with the micro-books. I remember the cover design—a stylized pattern of a star and planet system."

"That could be what you need. But let me make one thing clear. If I'm correct about the controls, and if you should use the wrong setting, you will, in all probability, never be able to find either Earth or your home planet again. You could spend forty lifetimes searching, with the same chance of finding either as of finding two specific motes of dust in the atmosphere of this planet. Make certain that you are quite willing to take the risk."

Leesa said softly, "Quite willing, Bard."

"Then find these books again. Study the numbers. See if they will fit the dials. See if you can determine our index number beyond doubt. And then contact me again."

Pressure on his mind faded quickly. Before it was entirely gone, Bard caught the faint thought: "This dream is ending."

The two of them were alone in the room. Sharan said softly, "Can he do it? Can he come here?"

He stood up and walked over to the windows. Across the street a couple walked hand in hand under the lights. A line had formed, waiting to get into the video studio.

"What is she like? What are her thoughts like?"

"Like a woman's."

"When will they be back?"

"Midnight tomorrow."

"I'll be here."

Ten of the older men were gathered in Jord Orlan's quarters. They sat stiffly and their eyes glowed. It had taken a long time for Jord Orlan to slowly bring them up to the proper pitch.

"Our world is good," he chanted.

"Our world is good," they responded in unison, the half-forgotten instincts rising up within them, hoarsening voices.

"The dreams are good."

"The dreams are good."

"And we are the Watchers and we know the Law."

"Yes, we know the Law."

Orlan held his arms straight out, his fists clenched. "And they would put an end to the dreams."

". . . an end to the dreams." The words had a sad sound.

"But they will be stopped. The two of them. The black-haired ones who are strange."

"They will be stopped."

"I have tried, my brothers, to show them the errors of their ways. I have tried to lead them into the ways of Truth. But they claim the three worlds are reality."

"Orlan has tried."

"I am not a vindictive man. I am a just man. I know the Law and the Truth. They have gone out into the nothingness, out into the emptiness that surrounds us, to look for the worlds of which we dream. Death will be a kindness."

"A kindness."

"Seek them out, my brothers. Put them in the tube of death. Let them slide down into the darkness and fall forever through the blackness. I have tried and I have failed. There is nothing else we can do."

"Nothing else."

They moved slowly toward the door, then faster. Faster. Jord Orlan stood and heard the pad of their feet against the warm floor, the growling in their throats. And they were gone. He sat down heavily. He was very tired. And he did not know if he had done the right thing. It was too late for doubts. And yet . . . He frowned. There was a basic flaw in the entire thought process. If outside was a nothingness, how could the two of them go outside and return? To have them do so would indicate that the nothingness was a "somethingness." And if that were true, then Raul Kinson's fanatic beliefs had to be given certain credence.

But once Raul Kinson was credited with any correctness, the entire structure of his own beliefs faded and dimmed. Jord Orlan's head hurt. It was a sad thing to have lived so long in perfect comfort with one's thoughts and then to have this tiny bitter arrow of doubt festering in his soul. He yearned to pluck it out. Possibly the spy had been mistaken. Possibly they did not go out into the nothingness.

He found himself descending toward the lowest level in great haste. He found the door. It did not take him long to remember the secrets of the twin wheels. He pulled the door open. And this time he dared to keep his eyes open. The wind whipped his cheeks. He squinted into it. The six ships stood tall against the huge red sun. Sand drifted in at his feet. He picked up a handful of it. He closed the door against the wind and leaned his forehead against the metal. He did not move for a long time. He turned and hurried back the way he had come.

Six of them were holding Raul. Raul's face was twisted with fury and, above the grunting of the captors, Jord Orlan heard the popping and crackling of Raul's shoulder muscles as he struggled, sometimes lifting his captors off their feet. Four of them were having an equally difficult time with the girl. They held her horizontally, two at her feet and two at her head. Her robe had been flung aside. As Jord Orlan neared them, they rushed with her toward the tube, toward the black oval mouth of it. But she twisted one foot free, planted it against the wall near the mouth of the tube and thrust with all her strength. They staggered and fell with her.

"Stop!" Orlan shouted.

"No!" the captors cried.

"Do you want their death to be easy? The tube is an easy death. Their sin is enormous. They should be thrust out into the emptiness outside to die there."

He saw doubt on their faces. "I order it!" he said firmly.

And, with Orlan leading, with the two captives no longer struggling, clad once more in robe and toga, the procession left the silent bystanders and went down to the door.

Orlan stopped the captors at the angle in the corridor. "Let them go on to the doorway alone. I shall go with them. If you look on nothingness it will forever blast your eyes and your mind. I will rejoin you when they have left."

They felt fear and anger, but fear was the stronger. They waited out of sight. Jord Orlan walked with Raul and Leesa.

He said, in a low tone, "I saw the odd garments. You need them to venture outside."

"What are you trying to tell us?" Raul demanded.

"That . . . there are things in our world that I do not understand. And before I die, I want to understand . . . everything. I did not believe the ships were there until I saw them with my own eyes. Now I share your sin. My belief has grown weak. If you could reach another world, then. . . ." He turned away. "Please hurry."

"Come with us," Leesa said.

"No. I'm needed here. If your heresies turn out to be true, my people will need someone to explain it to them. My place is here."

They left and he closed the door, retaining for a moment the image of the two figures leaning against the wind, the six ships in the background. He went back to those who waited and told them very calmly that it was all over.

14

THE LIGHT PLATES SET INTO THE CONTROL ROOM WALLS MADE A soft glow. Air came through the tiny grills in a sound like an endless sigh.

The entire control room was mounted on a shining piston that went straight down through the heart of the ship. The partitioned space along one wall, forty feet by ten, held the row of beds. Beyond the opposite partition were food stores, water tanks, sanitary equipment.

Leesa lay on the bunk and he folded the web straps across her body, drawing them tight. The last strap circled her forehead.

She looked up into his eyes. "Are we really ready?"

"We have to be. And I'll make a confession. If all this hadn't happened, I was going to try it alone, without you."

"Maybe," she said softly, "this is all just another dream, Raul. A more clever dream. Can you find Earth?"

"I know the number for Earth. I'll set it the way Bard Lane explained. And then, quite soon, we'll know."

"Promise me one thing."

He looked down at her. "What is it?"

"If we are wrong. If there are no worlds out there. Or if we lose our way, I want to die. Quickly. Promise?"

"I promise."

He slid the partition shut and went to the control panel. His pilot's couch was on rails so that, once he was in place, he could slide it forward under the vertical panel and lock himself in place. He strapped his ankles and his waist and pushed himself under to lie looking up at the controls. He activated the three-dimensional screen. There were the six ships, the tall white world, the sandy plain and the hills. He opened the book and took a last look at the reference number for Earth even though it had long since been memorized. He set the ten-digit number, six plus values and four minus ones, on the ten dials, checked it again. The replica ship was in neutral position. Only then did he strap the diaphragms firmly to his throat. He pulled the headband up and tightened it, slid his arms down into the straps.

And softly as he could, he made the vowel sound. The ship shuddered, trembled. On the screen the tiny image moved slowly upward, upward. Now the stern was as high as the bows of the other ships. He strengthened the vowel tone and the replica ship remained in the middle of the screen, the planet moving away below it, the curvature beginning to show, the white tower world dwindling.

He rashly strengthened his tone once more. A vast weight pressed his jaw open, punched down on his belly, blinded him by pressing his eyes back into his head. He heard, from a great distance, Leesa's scream of pain. He ceased all sound. The pressure slowly left him. He was dizzy with weightlessness. His home planet had shrunk to the size of a fist. It appeared in the lower right-hand corner of the screen and the image of the ship had dwindled until it was a bright mote against the darkening screen.

He took a weightless arm out of the strap, thumbed the knurled knob at the side of the screen. His planet slid off the screen and, by experimentation, he made the ship image grow larger. He moved close to it. The opposite knob seemed to rotate the ship itself end for end, but he realized that it merely shifted the point of vision. He adjusted it until he was looking forward from dead astern of the ship. The vast disc of the sun was straight ahead. He moved his hand to the replica ship and turned it through a ninety-degree arc to the right. As the sun slid off the screen, the replica ship moved slowly back to neutral. The screen showed distant spots of light against the utter blackness. He began to make the vowel sound again, cautiously at first, running it each time up to the limits of endurance, then resting in silence as the ship rushed, without noise, through the void. He understood that each time he made the sound he gave it another increment of speed. At last, no matter how loudly he made the sound, he could feel no answering downward thrust and he knew that the top limit had been reached.

Somewhere, ahead, the time setting would take effect. He did not know where. He did not know how long it would be.

15

FOUR MIDNIGHTS PASSED. BARD AND SHARAN WAITED THREE hours each time. The appointment was not kept. No thrusting fingers of thought entered their minds, singing gladly of reunion. For the first three midnights, Bard and Sharan were gay with each other, laughing too easily.

After the three tense hours of waiting had passed on the fourth night, Bard looked across the room at Sharan.

"He told me that their attitude was heresy in his world, Sharan."

"Why haven't they come? Why?"

"Logically we can make either of two assumptions. One, that they have been punished, perhaps put to death by their own people. Two, that they have started the voyage."

There were lines of strain around her mouth. "And the third possibility?"

"That it was a game they got tired of? That they have no ability to follow through on a course of action? Do you believe that, actually?"

Her smile was weak. "I guess not. Isn't it odd to feel that you know them so well, never seeing them?"

"Not so odd. Not with shared thoughts. Not with two . . . souls, if I can use that word, sharing the same brain tissue. Sharan, we owe them something. We owe them the assumption that they were forced, somehow, to start the trip. I don't know how long it will take. A month, possibly. Now just imagine what would happen if a ship of that description started to land here, or in Pan-Asia. Interceptor rockets would scream up. Shoot first and ask questions later. Our friends would be, within seconds, a large blue-white flash and a rain of radioactive particles. Have you thought of that?"

She put her hand slowly to her throat. "No! They wouldn't!"

"Look, Sharan. According to Raul and Leesa, the rest of the Watchers believe, even when they can visit three other planets through the dream machines, that they are alone in the universe. What is the primary egoism of man? That his planet is the only inhabited planet, his race the life-apex of the universe. Thus any unknown ship can *only* be the ship of an enemy nation on this same planet."

"Then they have no chance!"

"We are their chance, Sharan. We've got to let Earth know, somehow, that they are coming. They'll laugh at us. But even so, if Raul and Leesa are in transit, it might mean that at the crucial moment, someone may decide not to push the button. I wish they had come to us once more. I intended to warn them, tell them how to go into orbit outside the reach of the rockets and make identification. The way it stands they'll come directly in."

"If they never come, Bard?"

"We'll be the prize laughingstock of the century. Do you care?"

"Not really."

"We must start by giving the true story of the end of Project Tempo. We'll have to tell Bill Kornal first. Dr. Lurdorff will help us convince Bill. We've got to plant the story where it will get the maximum play from the press, radio, video, and everything else. That means that the four of us will have to put our cards, face up, in front of someone who not only can swing some weight around, but who has the sort of mind which might be receptive to this sort of thing. And Mr. X will have to have something to gain by carrying the ball. Any ideas?"

"It sounds like it ought to be somebody in government."

"Or how about a columnist with a big following. Let me see. Pelton won't do. I don't think we could sell it to Trimball."

"Say! How about Walter Howard Path? He has his column and the newscast on video. And he's the one that revived that ancient flying saucer business several years ago and claimed that the Air Force had never released the true data. He interviewed me, you know, after I walked out of that conference. He seemed nice, and the interview he published was at least a little bit friendly."

"I think he sounds like our boy, Sharan. There's the phone."

"So . . . so quickly?"

"How much time have we got to waste? Do you know?"

Sharan placed the call. It was almost four in the morning. Ten minutes later Walter Howard Path was on the line, speaking from his office-apartment in New York.

"Dr. Inly? Oh, yes. I remember you very well, Doctor."

"Mr. Path, would you care to have the exclusive story of what happened to Project Tempo?"

There was a long silence. "Dr. Inly, I wouldn't be terribly in-terested in it if it turns out to be some fairly tawdry little intrigue. The story wouldn't be good enough, and Tempo has been dead too long."

"Suppose I can show proof that Tempo was sabotaged by enti-ties from another planet, Mr. Path?"

"Oh, come now, Dr. Inly!"

"Please hold the line. There is someone else here who wishes to speak to you."

Bard took the phone quickly. "Mr. Path, this is Bard Lane speaking. If you want to gamble on this story, I suggest you fly out here. We haven't too much time to waste. I know that superlatives are sometimes distasteful. But this, Mr. Path, is the biggest story of this or any other century."

"What is your address there?"

Walter Howard Path was a lean, enormously tall man with stooped shoulders, seamed cheeks and restless eyes. With his hands jammed in his hip pockets, he slouched over to the windows of the suite and looked down into the street. The four of them watched his motionless back. The conference lasted for five hours. Walter Howard Path had been angry at what he suspected was a ruse for one hour, incredulous for two more hours, grudgingly intrigued for the fourth hour, and obscurely frightened from then on.

Without turning he said, "It's a hell of a gamble, folks. Even when the fit is so good. Even when it answers so many questions about this crazy, violent planet of ours. Dammit, people won't *want* to believe a thing like that. And the ones who will jump into line will be the faddists, the cultists, the chronic end-of-the-world kids."

The tape recorder had been switched off. Walter Howard Path ambled back to the small table, fiddled with the tape reel.

He gave them all a weary smile. "So I guess I've got to hold my nose and go off the high board. Today is Wednesday. I'll blow it in the Sunday column and on the Sunday night program. We better dig us a hole and crawl in and hold our ears."

"This is Melvin C. Lynn, reporting the news for Wilkins' Mead and the Wilkins Laboratories, where the secret of your happiness was developed.

"Tonight, listeners, I am going to give you a different sort of news program. Today a colleague, Walter Howard Path, broke a rather astonishing story. It is considered ethical in this newscasting field never to run down a competitor directly. However, your

Wilkins' Mead reporter feels that it is high time somebody took a lusty kick at Mr. Path's little red wagon.

"I have attempted to report the news to you honestly and sincerely. Sometimes I have fallen for a hoax. All of us have. But I have never been guilty of perpetrating one. Mr. Path has an enormous audience, far larger than mine. His responsibility to that audience is equally enormous. However, straight news reporting does not seem to satisfy our Mr. Path. You will remember his disinterment of the flying saucer hoax a few years ago. Possibly that sensationalism added a few more readers, a few more listeners.

"This time, however, Walter Howard Path has overreached himself. You all remember the scandal of Project Tempo. A Dr. Bard Lane, physicist, was dismissed for incompetence. He had shielded a technician, a William Kornal, who had committed sabotage on the project. There was a rumored intrigue between Dr. Lane and Dr. Sharan Inly, a sexy young psychiatrist on the project. In the finale debacle, twenty-eight persons died in the premature takeoff of the project ship. For honest reporters, there was no more news to be reported.

"Now let us examine what Walter Howard Path has done. He has gathered around himself a very unwholesome little group. Dr. Bard Lane, discredited physicist. Dr. Sharan Inly, sexy psychiatrist. Mr. William Kornal, unpunished technician guilty of criminal sabotage. Dr. Heintz Lurdorff, hypnotist and alleged psychiatrist. Remember that with the possible exception of Lurdorff, the other three have every reason to find some sort of excuse for their previous actions.

"These five persons have cooked up the most fantastic story that ever hit these tired old ears. Long-range hypnosis from another planet! People like us who can come here on thought waves, or something, and make us do whatever they wish! Remind me to use those Martians or whatever they are as an excuse to my wife the next time I stay out too late. Now see how neatly it all fits. This is a wonderful country, listeners. No matter how crazy your story is, you can find somebody to believe you.

"Let us check and see the possible results, if Walter Howard Path is permitted to use the power of the press, radio and video to spread this new yarn of his. Dr. Bard Lane will, in the minds of fools, be acquitted of mismanagement, negligence and preoccupation with pretty Sharan instead of his job. Sharan Inly will become the high priestess of the new cult, and probably do very well indeed, financially. Dr. Heintz Lurdorff will get some publicity to trade on. William Kornal will be able to say, 'See? I didn't do it. Them Martians did it.'

"And how about Walter Howard Path? Priceless publicity on a story none of the rest of us would touch. Here is his master touch, though. He says that two of the alien people who grab us and make us do tricks are coming here in person, on a space ship, for goodness sake! A couple. Brother and sister. Raul and Leesa Kinson. Your Wilkins' Mead reporter wonders how long it took our Mr. Path to think up those names. Ever play anagrams? Take that name. Leesa Kinson. Use the letters in it. You can make two words. 'No sense.' With four letters left over, a-l-k-i, a practically prehistoric slang word for alcohol. How long is Walter Howard Path going to feed us delusions out of the bottom of a bottle? How brazen can his hoaxes become?

"Your Wilkins' Mead reporter leaves you with this one thought. How can a responsible video network or a responsible publisher give house room to an irresponsible man like Walter Howard Path and still claim to function in the public interest?"

"From the wires of the Associated Press. Yesterday morning one person was killed and three injured in a riot at Benson, Georgia. The clash was between the new cult which spends hours on hilltops watching for Walter Howard Path's mythical spaceships, and a detachment of the Georgia State Police. The new cult calls itself Kinsonians."

Excerpt from an address given at the annual dinner of the American Medical Association: "It is not altogether strange that the mass hallucination of the late nineteen forties involving 'flying saucers' should now be duplicated by a similar mass hallucination involving 'space ships.' Even the most cursory study of the history of mass hysterias shows clearly a cyclical pattern, with the outbreaks averaging twenty to forty years between peaks of intensity. At the latest count the 'space ship' which we are to play host to, according to the Kinsonians, has been reported landing at twenty-six different places. It is no accident that the locations of the 'landings' correlate most amusingly with the activity of the Kinsonian groups in those places."

POLICY DIRECTIVE 7112
PUBLIC RELATIONS SECTION, ARMED FORCES

1. As there is no desire to give special attention to unfounded charges regarding Project Tempo through any formal statement in rebuttal, all personnel are directed to refrain from commenting to representatives of the press.
2. All military personnel directly connected with Project Tempo have been given changes of station to take them immediately outside the continental limits of the United States to new posts where the possibility of such interviews is lessened.
3. Official position on this matter, to be announced later, is that in the light of current world tension it is of dubious value to the national effort that mass hysteria should be whipped to such a peak that industrial absenteeism is at an unprecedented rate.
4. All officers and EM who profess publicly any degree of belief in Kinsonianism and, when warned, shall persist in such belief, will be considered unfit for duty.

"And now, ladies and gentlemen of the video audience, we bring you that lint-headed wonder of the stratosphere, that little man who *didn't* arrive in a space ship, that Yum-Bubble (Chew it, it's good for you) comic, Willy Wise! Hey, Willy! What's the matter, Willy? The cameras are over here, not up there on the ceiling."

"Don't bother me, Harry. I'm watching for that space ship. You want to make a million bucks, Harry?"

"That's the difference between you and me, Willy. I need a million bucks."

"Get another laugh and you'll need a job. Know what we ought to do? Put out some gunk to rub on your neck. I bet there are more cricks in more necks in this country than there are neckties."

"Willy, please look at the cameras. You've got a guest tonight. It's a she."

"Somebody else can watch for that ship. Hello, honey. What's your name?"

"Sharan Riley, Mr. Wise."

"Nice name, Sharan. I played Sharon, Pennsylvania, once. I killed 'em in Sharon. You got an aunt or a half sister or something named Sharan Inly?"

"Gee, no. She's famous."

"Say, I just got a theory, folks. How about this? You ever see a good picture of that Sharan Inly? Here's how it all happened. She meets up with that Lane guy, see. She likes him. She wraps those lovely arms around his neck and . . . Bingo! Ever since that moment, folks, Dr. Lane has been seeing space ships, Martians and little green men. Who can blame the guy? Up until that point he probably never had his nose out of a Bunsen burner, or whatever they use in those labs."

"Today in Albany, at the request of Governor LePage, a bill was rushed through the state legislature making it illegal for anyone to make public speeches in favor of Kinsonianism. Critics claim that the bill is an infringement of the right of free speech. The governor defended his action on the grounds that the State of New York is suffering a curtailment of the supply of food, power and other necessary items, arising from the absenteeism of the Kinsonians. The governor claims that the Kinsonians seem to feel that the arrival of the alien space ship will somehow be synonymous with the end of the world. Other states will await, with interest, the decision of the courts on the legality of the new measure."

THE SUNDAY DUSK SLOWLY DARKENED THE STREET. BARD LANE turned from the window. The one suite had grown to two connecting suites. Bess Reilly had been found, and it did not take much encouragement to bring her back to work for Dr. Lane.

The phone on her desk rang constantly. Sharan and Lurdorff, using the octagonal cards, played quad-bridge on a lamp table.

Kornal lay on the couch, his fingers laced over his stomach, peacefully asleep.

"What's the matter with them?" Bard demanded. "They stand down there in the street and just stare up at the windows!"

Heintz Lurdorff grinned. "You must aggustom yourself to being the high briest of what is bractically a new religion."

"It makes me nervous," Bard said. "And those phone calls make me nervous. That woman who called up this afternoon and called me the Anti-Christ. What was she talking about?"

"You are either the most honored or most detested man in America, Bard," Sharan said. "I'll bid eleven spades, Heintz."

"Always she geds all the gards," Heintz said dolefully.

"Anyway," Bard said. "We're doing it. We're doing what we set out to do. I almost hate to think of what will happen when and if that ship does set down. I don't know why all this . . . took the public fancy so strongly. Do you know, Heintz?"

"Of gorse. Mangind has always wanted a whipping boy. You gave them one. They love it. That governor of Nevada, he has helped."

"Investigating the senseless murder cases and pardoning people. I wonder."

Kornal yawned as he awakened. He looked at his watch. "Nearly time for our favorite man, isn't it?"

Bard turned on the video. The screen brightened at once. He turned off the sound while the commercial was on, then turned the dial up as Walter Howard Path's announcer appeared on the screen.

". . . regret to announce that Walter Howard Path will be unable to appear as usual. Mr. Path has suffered a breakdown due to overwork and has been given an indefinite leave of absence. This program is being taken over by Kinsey Hallmaster, distinguished reporter and journalist. Mr. Hallmaster."

Mr. Hallmaster sat behind a vast desk and smiled importantly at the video audience. With his twinkling eyes and projecting front teeth he looked like a happy beaver.

"I am honored to be asked to take over this weekly newscast. I am sorry, however, that Mr. Path cannot be with you as usual. He has my every hope for a speedy recovery.

"My first duty is to read you a statement prepared by Mr. Path.

" 'This is Walter Howard Path telling you that I have just received additional information regarding the space ship which has been alleged to——' "

"Alleged!" Bard shouted angrily. The others shushed him.

" '——and these investigators, hired by me out of my own pocket, have brought me additional information which now leads me to believe that I, as well as many of the public, have been misled by Lane, Inly, Lurdorff and Kornal. I have before me the notarized statement, among other things, of a tavern owner which states that for a period of three weeks Dr. Lane, in a consistently drunken condition, gave speeches in his tavern regarding so-called mental visitations from space. I sincerely regret that I was taken in. There is no space ship. There are no Watchers. The alien brother and sister are figments of the overripe imaginations of Lane, Inly, Lurdorff and Kornal. I say to all of you who through an honest mistake have become Kinsonians, just mark it all up to the rather unusual gullibility of your reporter, Walter Howard Path.' "

Hallmaster put the document aside, folded his hands on the edge of the desk. "There you have it," he said. "Mr. Path's health was broken by the discovery that he had been misled. I have a few other words to say about this entire matter, however. From an official and informed source high in Washington, I have it on good authority that there is something far more sinister involved than the efforts of a little clique of greedy people to make money out of being in the public eye.

"We know, for an absolute fact, that Inly, Lane, Lurdorff and Kornal were . . . shall we say, financially embarrassed at a time two weeks before Mr. Path's unfortunate backing of their wild tale. Now they are well enough off to spend money freely, living in expensive hotel suites, employing stenographic help. This money did not come from Mr. Path. Where did it come from?

"Now bear with me a moment. Suppose this nation were to be attacked. Interceptor rockets would flash up at the first target. But suppose that in advance we as a nation had been led to expect the arrival of some mythical space ship. Maybe the Kinsons will arrive in twenty simultaneous space ships which land in twenty industrial cities. Maybe their point of origin will not be some far planet, but rather the heartland of Pan-Asia. What then?

"Need I go further?"

For a jolly moment he let the implications settle into the minds of the vast audience. "And now for the more serious side of the news. We find that——"

Bard snapped off the set. The room was silent. The phone rang. Bess lifted it off the cradle and set it aside without answering it.

"That . . . low . . . dirty . . ."

"In five minutes," Sharan said softly, "he destroyed the whole thing, everything we've done. Every last thing."

"Maybe enough of them will still believe," Kornal said.

"After that?" Heintz Lurdorff said with a mild, dignified contempt. "I think now I go. I am sorry. There is nothing more we can do."

"The kiss of death, neatly administered," Sharan said. "Kissed off by a Wilkins' Mead culture. We need a new symbol. A monkey with six arms, like Vishnu, so he can simultaneously cover his eyes, ears and mouth."

"Give him one more hand, honey, so he can hold his nose," Kornal said.

After an hour on the phone, Bard Lane found out that Walter Howard Path was in a private sanitarium, committed by his wife, for an indefinite stay.

AS CLOSELY AS RAUL COULD ESTIMATE, IT WAS TEN DAYS BEFORE the keening whine of a warning device startled them into immobility. They had been eating at the moment it sounded.

Leesa, startled, lost her grip on the wall railing and floated out beyond any chance of grasping it again. She writhed in the air, but could not appreciably change her position.

Raul calculated, pushed against the wall with his hand as he let go of the railing. As he passed Leesa he grasped her ankle and the two of them made one slow pinwheel in the air before touching the high railing on the opposite side of the cabin. He strapped her in, then made a slow shallow dive toward his own position. He arranged his own straps, slid forward into proper position, staring up at the panel.

Five long minutes passed before there was any change.

And then came an indescribable twisting. It was as though in one microsecond, vast hands had grasped him, turning as though wringing moisture from a bit of cloth, releasing him. Dimly he heard Leesa's startled cry. His vision cleared at once and he saw that the value of the first dial had returned to zero. A softer bell-note sounded, and he guessed that it meant an end to the warning period. Adjusting the screen he looked at strange star patterns.

Days later, when the warning sound came again, they strapped themselves in. The second time jump was like the first, but easier to bear because it was expected.

For the third, one day later, they did not go to position. They waited near the rail, and as the twisting came, her fingernails dug into his arm. He watched the convulsed look fade from her face as they smiled at each other.

An hour later the warning sound was more shrill. Again they went to their positions. One twisting, wrenching sensation followed closely on the heels of the next. When at last he was able to look at the dials, he saw that all of them had returned to zero. With a weakened hand he adjusted the image screen.

"Is . . . it over?" Leesa called.

"I think so."

"What do you see? Quickly!"

"Wait. I must turn the ship. Now I see a sun. Blazing white, Leesa."

"Their sun, Raul."

"I've seen their sun from Earth. It is yellow, Leesa."

"Look for the planet."

He turned the ship. A tiny distant planet was ghostly in the reflected sun glow.

"I see a planet!" he called.

"Take us there, Raul. Quickly. Oh, very quickly."

Cautiously he made the sound that drove the ship ahead, gave them weight after so many days. He felt the slick movement of the great cylinder which compensated in part for the force of the acceleration on their bodies. He made the sound again and the planet began to grow. He watched it grow, and it did not seem that he could breathe deeply enough.

And then he knew. He did not speak for a long time. He called to her and his voice was old.

"What is it, Raul?"

"The planet has nine moons, Leesa. Theirs has but one."

In the long silence he heard the muffled sound of her weeping. The planet grew steadily.

"Raul, are we still heading toward it?"

"Yes."

"Do you remember your promise?"

"I remember."

"Close your eyes, Raul. Do not touch the controls. It will be quick, Raul." Her voice had a curiously haunting quality, as though she were already dead.

He closed his eyes. Resignation. An end of struggle and rebellion. It would have been better to accept, to force belief in the warm, slow world of the Watchers. He thought of Earth. Possibly he had misread the metallic sheets, selected the wrong index. Out of so many millions of numbers, it could easily have been the wrong one.

Bard Lane and Sharan Inly would never be able to convince Earth that the Watchers existed. Just as he could not convince the Watchers that Earth was another reality, as true as their own.

He opened his eyes. The planet was alarmingly close. They were diving toward it. He closed his eyes again.

Someday maybe Earth would build such ships as this one. First they would go to the other planets of their own . . .

As the thought came he opened his eyes wide. He gave the replica ship a brutal twist and in the same instant the vowel sound. As the acceleration hammered him into unconsciousness he kept the thin impression of the face of the planet sweeping slowly off the screen.

In Bard Lane's dream he was back at Tempo watching the Beatty One rise into the arc of destruction. But this time the drive impetus was not steady. It came in hard flaring jolts that made the ship rise erratically on her suicide course. The dream faded and the jolting sounds turned to a heavy knocking at the door. He rubbed sleep-stuck eyes, rose painfully from his cramped position in the chair in which he had fallen asleep after Sharan had gone to bed.

"Coming, coming," he called with annoyance. He stretched and looked at his watch. Ten in the morning. The windows were gray, patterned with rain flung against them by a gusty wind. For a moment he could not remember why he felt so thoroughly depressed. And then he remembered Hallmaster's talk the night before.

He was in a completely foul mood when he yanked the suite door open. "Why didn't you just batter it down?" he said.

A thick-jowled man mouthing a cigar stub stood planted in front of the door, two uniformed policemen behind him.

"Another minute and that's just what we would have done, friend," the man said. He walked flatfooted toward Bard, forcing Bard to step aside. The two policemen followed him into the suite.

"Maybe it would help if you tell me what you want," Bard said.

The jowled man knuckled his hat back off his forehead. "You're Lane." It was a statement of fact rather than a question.

"Nice of you to come and let me know so early on Monday," Bard said.

"I could learn to dislike you, friend." The stocky man turned and nodded at one of the two policemen. The uniformed man walked casually over and trod heavily on Bard's foot.

"Gee, excuse me," he said. He took his weight away, trod heavily on the other foot. Bard's fist swung automatically, all the strain and heartache and disappointments of months erupting into a rage that was like ice.

The policeman partially blocked the blow, but it slipped off his forearm and landed on the heavy cheekbone with a satisfying crack.

The two policemen moved in with deft efficiency and pinned both of Bard's arms. The jowled man took the cigar from his mouth and rolled it between his fingers.

"It was reported to me, Dr. Lane, by the management of this

hotel, that you were acting strangely. I am Hemstrait, the health officer. I came here to investigate the report and find that it was true. You attacked Patrolman Quinn without provocation."

"Just what do you want?"

"I don't want anything. I'm committing you to the state hospital for sixty days of observation and treatment. Nuts like you can't run around loose."

"Whose orders are you following, Hemstrait?"

The man had the grace to blush. "Hell, Lane. They'll do you some good out there. Where's the Inly woman?"

"You don't need her too."

"The hotel says that she's crazy too. I got a job to do. I got to investigate all reports."

At that moment Sharan, flushed with sleep, a white robe belted around her, opened the bedroom door and came out. "Bard, what is——" She stopped and her eyes widened as she saw Bard being held.

"You let him go!" she said.

"Lady, you're irrational," Hemstrait said.

"Don't say or do anything," Bard said quickly.

Hemstrait gave Bard a look of annoyance. He moved close to Sharan, rested a beefy hand on her shoulder. She shrugged it off. He replaced it. She moved away. He followed her, grinning. She cracked her palm off his thick cheek. He grinned and grabbed her. "Lady, as health officer I'm committing you to the state hospital for sixty days of observation and treatment. You ought to know better than to attack the health officer."

"It's no good, Sharan," Bard said in a bleak tone. "Somebody gave him his orders. The same people who took care of Path, probably. And gave Hallmaster that paper to read. We're a disturbing influence."

"Shut up, friend," Hemstrait said jovially. "Come on, lady. They'll be good to you out there. We picked up Lurdorff and Kornal in the lobby this morning. Kornal made such a fuss we had to put him in a jacket. Now you people are going to be more sensible than that."

On the following Wednesday morning, Sharan Inly, clad in the gray shapeless hospital garment, was taken by a matron-attendant to the office of the young state psychiatrist. The matron waited behind Sharan's chair. The psychiatrist was a thin-faced young man with an earnest, dedicated look.

"Dr. Inly, I'm very happy to meet you. I had hoped that when we did meet, it would be under . . . more pleasant circumstances. I particularly remember some of your papers that appeared in the Review."

"Thank you."

"I know that you must be interested in your own case. An unusually persistent delusion and, what is more startling, a shared delusion. Most unusual. And, as you may be aware, an unfavorable prognosis." He hitched himself uncomfortably in the chair. His smile was wan. "Usually I have to explain to the patient the implications of deep shock. Of course, you worked with Belter when he was perfecting the technique. . . ."

His voice trailed off.

Sharan fought the fear back. She made her voice calm. "Isn't that treatment a bit extreme in this case, Doctor? Memory patterns never return. That means complete reeducation from mindlessness, and sufficient damage so that on the Belter Scale, intelligence never goes beyond the DD level."

"Frankly," he said, "it makes me feel uncomfortable to prescribe it in the case of this delusion the four of you share. Dr. Lurdorff grew quite violent. He will be treated this afternoon. A shame, actually. So brilliant a mind . . . but misdirected, of course. All of you can be turned into productive members of society. You'll be quite capable of leading a satisfying life, of doing routine work. And you know how we've speeded up reeducation. Speech is adequate in a month. Incontinence ends in a week."

"May I ask if a consulting psychiatrist can be called in, Doctor?"

"Oh, this treatment is the result of consultation, Dr. Inly. Very good men. Now, outside the delusionary cycle, you are quite capable of making decisions. With the nonviolent cases it is policy here to give you time to write letters, make wills, dispose of property, that sort of thing. We'll give you false memory of a different life, a new name, a slightly altered face. You'll be sent, of course, to one of the critical labor areas, and a competent social worker will get you started."

"Actually, it's death, isn't it?"

"Now let us not be emotional, Dr. Inly. I had hoped that as a psychiatrist and a neuro-surgeon, you would——"

Sharan forced a smile. "I guess it's time for confession, Doctor. We all thought up this Watcher business as a publicity thing. We all needed money."

He shook his head sadly. "Surely you know better than that! Such a perfectly standard reaction, Dr. Inly. Under induced hypnosis you all clung to every single phase of the shared delusion."

"A question then. If a delusion can be shared, possibly it isn't a delusion."

He chuckled, at ease for the first time in the interview. "You people! Don't you see that basically it's a desire for escape? The world as you know it has become unbearable for the four of you. Too bad you didn't recede into a catatonic state. We could have treated that. Instead you invent a delusionary race on a far planet on which you can blame your own inadequacies. Dr. Inly, we are the only race in the universe. Anything else is a dream. The only reality is here. And we must accustom ourselves to live with it, unpleasant as it may be, or else be treated by someone who can make the world bearable to you by some artificial means."

"And you, Doctor, are a blind, simpering, egocentric fool."

He flushed. "I have too much sympathy for you, Dr. Inly, to permit you to anger me. Use a long view. You are a healthy young woman. Dr. Lane is a sturdy man. Your validity from now on will be in work units for society and in the bearing of children. I was prepared to reeducate the two of you as a family unit. It would be interesting to see what degree of devotion could be induced. That choice, of course, is up to you and Dr. Lane. I shall see him next."

"It doesn't matter," Sharan said tonelessly. "It won't be . . . me. I shall be dead. You forget, Doctor, that I worked with deep shock techniques. I have seen that . . . mindlessness."

"Then I shall tell Dr. Lane that you are willing. We'll be ready for the two of you tomorrow morning. The attendant will arrange legal help for you, and see that you have writing materials."

Sharan turned at the door and tried to speak to him again. The young doctor was making notations on her file. He did not look up. The attendant urged her into the hall with gentle force.

Bard Lane stood in the hall with two guards, waiting. His face was gray. He looked at her and did not seem to recognize her. Sharan did not speak to him. Sharan Inly would never speak to Bard Lane again. Two strangers would speak to each other, and that was no longer important.

18

IT IS A PLEASANT THURSDAY MORNING IN OCTOBER OVER MOST of the country. One high is static over most of the Gulf Coast. Another is apparently anchored in the Chicago area. The Secretary of Weather is conferring with Agriculture on the advisability of securing Canadian permission to dissipate the front building up in the northwest.

An Atlanta hostess decides to continue the party that started Wednesday afternoon. She stirs guests out of their stupor, smilingly hands them the amphetamine cocktails which will bring the gaiety back to life.

A bemused broker shivers in the web seat of his heli-cycle as he laboriously forces it above its operational ceiling, hoping that the Air Police won't intercept him until he is quite ready to loosen the strap and take the long, long drop into the corduroy canyons of the city far below.

Timber Mulloy, sullen and hung over, leads his protesting musicians through an early-morning practice session for a new visitape album which may bring in enough royalties to catch up on back alimony payments.

At Fonda Electric seven hundred girls are waiting for the ten A.M. cigarette break.

A teen-age heiress in Grosse Point stands nude before her full-length mirror and cuts her throat with a hard, ripping pull of her right hand and wrist.

In an isolated radar station, Major Tommy Leeber stares at his tarnished major's leaf and curses the day he was selected as aide by General Sachson. Sachson, a continent away, stands in front of a steel mirror and carefully clips gray nostril hairs while he thinks of the two years before he can retire.

Sharan Inly lies face down on her cot, waiting for them to come for her. On the other side of the building Bard Lane sits on his cot, slowly leafing through the memories that will be taken from him.

It is a pleasant morning.

In Connecticut a sanitarium attendant is being cursed by his superior for not finding Walter Howard Path in time to save his life.

It is thirty seconds after ten o'clock. Seven hundred girls are striking matches and clicking lighters.

Twelve miles from Omaha, a radar-radak technician frowns as he studies the pip on his screen. He adjusts for a new focus, and, as he puts the track on automatic, he runs his eye down the list of EXP flights. On automatic track the height, speed, and direction appear below the screen.

Speed is a constant. Direction almost due south. Altitude decreasing at the rate of a half mile a second.

His next moves are deft and quick. He punches the station alarm button, then throwns open the switch which sounds the alarm instantaneously in twelve interceptor stations and puts them in direct communication with his board.

A nurse lays out the salve to be applied to temples and electrodes. The technician checks the dials on the shock equipment. The young state psychiatrist shuts the door of his room behind him and walks down the hall without haste.

Alert is flashed to interception points. Five more screens pick up the image and tie in the interception stations. Rocket tubes, six hundred of them, ten at each interceptor station, are so tied in with the automatic track on the screens that they point, unerringly, at the proper interception point in the predicted track of the screen pip. If the pip had been shown as coming straight down, manual control of firing would have been automatically cut out. No human hand could have moved quickly enough.

At the master control station SW, outside El Paso, a hard-faced colonel cuts out all manual control at the interceptor points, and takes over the decision. There are six buttons under his fingers. Each one discharges one full ten-round from the designated interceptor point.

The mike is close to his lips. He watches the screen. "Course change," he says in a flat tone. His words boom loudly in a small room in Washington. The small room is beginning to fill rapidly. "Velocity down one half. Target now heading straight up. Continuing loss of velocity. Either unmanned with defective controls, or manned incompetently."

The speaker above the colonel's head says, metallically, "Intercept when we get a predicted course toward any critical area."

A major standing near the colonel says, "This will give the Kinsonians a bang."

The colonel doesn't answer. He is thinking of his son, of the eruption of crazy, bloody, irrational violence that had ruined his son's life. His iron face does not change. He remembers the voice of Walter Howard Path.

"New direction north-northwest. Altitude three hundred thirty miles. Within range. Velocity down to five hundred miles per hour. Altitude three hundred, velocity four seventy."

"Intercept," the speaker says.

Taut fingers poise over the buttons.

"Intercept," the speaker says. "Acknowledge."

Twenty-five years of discipline balanced against the memory of the stunned, uncomprehending look on the face of a boy.

"Recommend stranger be permitted to land."

He hears the major's taut gasp, sees the major's hand reaching to punch the buttons. He turns and smashes his fist against the major's jaw.

Flat, emotionless voice. "Believe stranger preparing to land Muroc."

∨ Video in the lounge at Fonda Electric. Radio in the room where amphetamine is working its frantic magic in Atlanta. Music from the pocket pack in the broker's pocket, faint against the hard roar of the wind as he tumbles over and over, down and down. Timber Mulloy, taking a breather, tuning in to hear one of his own records. Bedside radio in Grosse Point singing softly to something at the base of a full-length mirror. Radio playing soothingly on the desk of the floor nurse as a young psychiatrist walks toward the shock room, passing the desk . . .

". . . We interrupt this program to inform America that, at this moment, a space ship of unknown origin is attempting a landing at Muroc. The ship answers the description given by Lane to

Walter Howard Path in what was believed to be a hoax. Word has just been received that the first attempt at landing was unsuccessful. Further news will be reported as soon as received. We now return you to the network programs in process."

Jord Orlan left the case of dreams and returned to his chambers. He had bitten through his lower lip and the taste of blood sickened him.

He sat alone and tried to rebuild something in which he could no longer believe. A structure had collapsed in his mind, and the shards of it were useless.

He saw, in memory, the great ship, its ancient hide pocked by space fragments, sitting on the surface of an alien world. Outside, where there had been six ships, there were now five.

He had slid into the mind of a spectator, and he had seen Raul and Leesa taken in a vehicle from the side of the ship to a distant building. He had seen them, in one of the dreams, thinner than they had been when they left. At one point he had moved close enough to hear Raul speak, his voice thin with strain, yet exultant, speaking the Earth language awkwardly, clumsily because he was speaking from memory alone.

"The Doctor Inly and Doctor Lane. It is them we must see quickly."

There was nothing left to believe. And he remembered the Law. Such travel meant an end to the dreams. He saw, ahead of him, the long empty years, full of nothing but the games that were now pointless.

He knew what he had to do. He found a heavy tool in the lowest level. By the time he had finished what he had to do, his hands were raw and blistered.

And he went down to his people to tell them that the dreams had come to an end.

SHARAN STOOD BESIDE BARD LANE. THEY STOOD CLOSE TOGETHER
and looked through the glass wall of the studio. Raul and Leesa
sat behind a table, the cameras focused on them, the interviewer
at the end of the table. With the help of Bard and Sharan, Raul
and Leesa had won the right to dress as the people around them,
rather than in the conspicuous style of the Watcher colony.

"How long is this going to go on?" Sharan asked wearily.

"It will go on just as long as they are the only two outsiders on
this planet. That sort of novelty will never wear off."

"So you better hurry with Tempo Two, my friend, and go grab
off some people from Marith and Ormazd. How is it going?"

"Good, now that the Pan-Asia group decided to come in on it.
They're still a little wary of our generosity in giving them access
to the whole works."

Sharan looked at Leesa through the glass. "She's very patient,
isn't she?"

"She explained that to me. It's sort of . . . penance, you might
say. For what she has done in the past, what her people have
done. How do you like her English?"

"Not anywhere near as quaint as it was, at least." Sharan
giggled. "Know what I remember, Bard? The time you described
her as probably being bald and built like a twelve-year-old child."

Bard Lane remembered too. He looked at the slim, delicate,
dark-haired girl. She met his glance and made a small shrug of
patience. He said, "She told me that on her world she was considered some sort of a brute-woman. Here she's just a pretty girl
who looks a bit more fragile than the average. And your Raul
could lose himself in any crowd."

"He could not!"

Bard grinned. They listened to the closing minutes of the program. "Now, Mr. Kinson, you say that the Watchers have not

contacted you or your sister in any way during the weeks you have been here with us."

Raul frowned. "I do not understand that. I do not see why they have not done so. It would be so easy."

"Now I have something that may come as a surprise to both of you. We have just received tabulated data from all law enforcement agencies covering the time you have been here. There has been an unprecedented drop in crimes of violence. Violence is still with us, of course. Until we learn the secrets of that other world you told us about, it will probably always be with us. But motiveless violence, inexplicable actions—they seem to have gone way down."

Bard saw Leesa and Raul stare at each other, say a few swift words in their own tongue.

Leesa said, "It would seem then, that either they know and understand now, or they are not using the dream machines. We do not know which. We will only know when someone goes . . . back."

"Would you like to go back?"

She turned her head slowly so that she looked directly at Bard. Her chin lifted a bit and her eyes softened. "In my life, sir, I go nowhere without the Doctor Lane."

Sharan said, "My, my! How you can blush!"

"Hush."

"And you, Mr. Kinson? Will you go back if you have a chance?"

Raul frowned. "I do not know if I can say this well. It is a plan, and a part of the big Plan I told you about. Now the dreamers are not destroying. The three planets my ancestors colonized can join together. This Earth can give Marith much. But Earth and Marith can get most from Ormazd. We are three children, going different ways, now grown to strength with which each can help all.

"Now with my plan, and I mean for me as a person, as you know I have taken to wife the Doctor Inly in line with your customs, the same as my sister and Doctor Lane in that ceremony you made us do before cameras so all could see. Now I am saying too blunt, which goes against your custom. None of you watching this can know each other, in your hearts. Even now I do not know well the Doctor Inly, though married. Not as well as when, with the dream machines, I entered her mind to know it as my own. It is the same with my sister. We have talked. We are not as happy as we could be, because of the barrier between us.

"In dreams of Ormazd I learned that they can use the minds at close range the way the dream machines did over vast distances. It is there that I would go and my sister would go, with the two we have married. And there Ormazd can teach us this thing which is necessary if a person is not to be . . . forever a little apart and a little bit lonely.

"When it is learned by the four of us, we wish to come back and teach others. That way the rest of that violence which you told me can be also taken away from this planet. It is . . . a dream and a good one this time. For a long time the three planets of the children of the Leaders of long ago have waited for the time of reuniting, for the time of progress that is to come.

"All of this will be slow, I think. The biggest changes will not come in the life of any of us who are here or you who listen. But for myself, I want that small change which gives mind freedom to enter mind as soon as I can have. See, I do not speak well yet.

"To have this come about, I wish to be with my wife. I wish to work with the Doctor Lane. There are things I can learn and things I can do. I wish no longer to be an animal to be looked at with those camera things. My sister does not like this camera thing either. Now we wish to go to work on that very great ship which, we hope, will carry part of the name of a man who was good and wise and very brave."

He smiled into Sharan's eyes.

"That ship, it is to be called Pathfinder," he said softly.

the Girl, the Gold Watch, & Everything

Dear Fred,

   You didn't tell me it was going to be easy. But you didn't tell me it was going to be like this. Find Kirby Winter. Bring him back. Spare no expense. And you assigned me a good man to help out. At least Huddleston **used** to be a good man. Today you wouldn't know him. He stares into space and he sighs, and all I can get out of him is sometimes an aimless giggle.

   We found Kirby Winter, boss. We found him twice. And if you want him found a third time, you better send somebody else. But it will be a waste of money.

   In fact, Fred, I think you better tell the client to give up. If this Kirby Winter **did** hold out a couple of million bucks from his Uncle Omar's estate, nobody is going to get it away from him.

   I know what you're thinking. You're thinking Kirby Winter bought me off, and Huddleston too. I wish to God he had. I'd sleep better.

   All I can do is tell you just what happened. The tip-off was absolutely correct. We found him right here in a big suite in the Del Prado, and he'd been right here in Mexico City registered under his own name for two weeks. He's not trying to hide, at least not very much, Fred. Kirby Winter and party. The party is a party of one, exactly the same broad that was with him in Sao Paulo three months ago, that gorgeous hillbilly broad that looks sweet as angels; but don't let that fool you a minute.

What I can't understand, Fred, is how both you and the client got the feeling this Kirby Winter is sort of innocent and helpless. Maybe that's his past history, but he got over it. This is a very self-confident guy, believe me. And as far as style and dash are concerned, Onassis should have it so rich. He and his hillbilly broad, they have a very fine time. If he's scared of having somebody show up and take some of that money away from him, he doesn't show it a bit.

Well, once we had them located, we figured out how to get them back into the States. I had to do most of the arrangements myself because ever since all those funny things happened in Sao Paulo, Huddleston has been a little unsure of himself.

I set up a private plane, big enough for the four of us and the pilot, with enough range to get us over the border. As you suggested, it seemed best to bring the girl along too. Then the problem was get them from the hotel to the airport. I decided we'd make it fast and simple. Bust in, hold a gun on them, give them each a big enough shot to keep them very, very quiet and humble and eager to please. In that condition we could walk them down to a car and be off. And I'd let you know where to arrange to have us met.

I bought a passkey. They went out about nine last night, and Huddleston and I decided we'd wait and welcome them when they got back. So we let ourselves in and settled down to wait. We both had guns. I had the hypo all ready. I had a man ready to pull up out in front as soon as I gave the word. And the pilot was standing by.

They came in about midnight, laughing and talking. As soon as they were far enough into the room, we stepped out and covered them. I ask you, Fred, how could anything go wrong? I am not a careless guy.

But it went wrong, Fred. All you can do is try to believe what I'm going to tell you. They jumped a little and stared at us, and then they started acting as if it was the biggest joke in the world. It reminded me so much of Sao Paulo, I felt very nervous. And Huddleston's color wasn't very good. I told them that if they co-operated, nobody was going to get hurt. This Kirby Winter—and he is sort of a mild-looking guy—stared at me and shook his head sort of sadly and said that after Sao Paulo, they thought we'd give up, so that meant they hadn't made their point clear enough, so they'd make it a lot clearer this time. Huddleston told him to shut up. I went toward them with the hypo, figuring to take care of him first. Fred, I was being **very** careful.

Suddenly the hypo was gone. I stopped and looked at my empty hand. Kirby Winter and that tow-headed hillbilly girl were smiling at me. I looked at Huddleston. Fred, I swear, in the twinkling of an eye he had taken off every stitch and he was wearing a big blue sash tied with a bow around his waist, and printed on his chest in lipstick it said "Surprise!"

Remembering Sao Paulo, I decided that if things started to go wrong, I'd even them up by shooting Kirby Winter in the leg. As you know, I am fast and accurate, and I probably would have hit him just where I wanted to, except that when I tried to fire, I had a perfume atomizer in my hand instead of a gun.

Just as I stared at Kirby Winter, in that very same instant, Fred, without any warning at all, I was in the elevator and the door was closing. There was an elevator operator and three middle-aged tourist ladies and Huddleston in there with me. The door closed and we started down and the ladies started screaming and fainting. It was a mess in that elevator, Fred. Just like Huddleston, the only thing I had on was a sash, only mine was pink. And on my chest it was printed "Adios, amigo!" And we were both shaved absolutely bald and soaked in perfume, Fred. And that hysterical elevator operator ran us right down to the main lobby and opened the door. And Huddleston was so shook up, he tried to run.

Anyway, the wheels are turning, and if everything goes well, and if you send the money I wired for, they may let us out of here by tomorrow. Our lawyer says there aren't any major charges, but there sure are a lot of small ones. And he checked and found out that Kirby Winter and party checked out about noon today.

Personally, I don't think Huddleston is going to be of much use to anybody from now on. And I can't vouch for myself. If you think we were bought off, you'll have to admit it was a pretty strange way of covering up.

As I said, if your client wants Kirby Winter found again, you can send somebody else. I have been trying to examine what happened to us with a completely open mind. The easiest answer is to say that it is hypnosis. But Fred, I think it is just plain old-fashioned magic like we used to read about when we were kids. Why not? If there's magic in the world still going on, the ones who can do it won't let it get into the papers, will they?

And that uncle of Winter's, that Omar Krepps. Wasn't he supposed to be a very mysterious guy? A wizard, sort of? Maybe before he died he taught Kirby Winter how to use the spells or rub the lamp or whatever the hell he does.

And look at Sao Paulo. Winter and that nifty litttle broad of his took six of the biggest casinos for about seventy grand apiece while they were there. And if that isn't magic, Fred, tell me what it is? An invention they're using?

Honest to God, Fred, the way I feel right now, if that little hillbilly girl should suddenly appear right in this cell and turn into a purple kangaroo, it wouldn't shock me a bit. You take so much and you come to the end of being shocked. You know what I mean?

Maybe the client believes and maybe you believe that this Kirby Winter used to be sort of a goof. But, believe me, something changed him. And unless you find out what it was and how it happened, there's no use sending anybody else after him. The way they looked at us, Fred, honest, it was like they were a pair of Martians. Or the way you and I would laugh at a puppy that growls at you. Fondly, you know. And superior.

I hope the money is on the way, because if it isn't, we might be in here a long, long time. No matter when we get out, I'm thinking I might go into some other line of work. I've sort of lost my confidence.

Very truly yours,

Sam Giotti

SLOWLY, WITH A DEDICATED EFFORT, KIRBY TIPPED THE UNI-
verse back into focus. He heard the after-image of his voice going
on and on, a tiresome encyclical of complaint, a paean to the
scuffed spirit. The woman across the table from him was in
silhouette against the window—a window big as a tennis court on
edge—and through the window was an ocean, rosy with dusk or
dawn. It made a peach gleam on her bare tanned shoulders and
backlighted a creamy weight of blondness.

Atlantic, he thought. Once he had established the ocean, he
found the time relationship simplified. Looking from Florida, it
had to be dawn.

"You are Charla," he said carefully.

"Of course, dear Kirby," she said, amused, slightly guttural, almost laughing. "Your good new friend, Charla."

The man sat at Kirby's left, a solid, polished man, tailored,
clipped, manicured. He made a soft sound of amusement. "A
Spanish verb," he said. "Charlar. To chat. To make meaningless
talk. An irony because her great talent is not in talking, but in listening."

"My great talent, Joseph?" she said with mock astonishment.

"Your most unusual one, my dear. But we have both enjoyed
listening to Kirby."

Kirby nailed it all to a wall inside his head, like small signs.
Charla, Joseph, Atlantic, dawn. He sought other clues. It could
be Saturday morning. The burial service had been on Friday at

eleven. The conference with the lawyers had been at two in the afternoon. And he had begun drinking at three.

He turned his head with care and looked at the empty lounge. A barman in white jacket stood under prism lights paled by the dawn, arms folded, chin on his chest.

"Do they keep these places open all night?" Kirby asked.

"Hardly ever," Joseph said. "But they respond nicely to any small gift of money. A gesture of friendship. At the official closing time, Kirby, you still had much to say."

It was brighter in the lounge. They looked at him fondly. They were mature, handsome people. They were the finest two people he had ever met. They had slight accents, an international flavor, and they looked at him with warmth and with love.

Suddenly he had a horrid suspicion. "Are you—are you some kind of journalists—or anything like that?"

They both laughed aloud. "Oh no, my sweet," Charla said.

He felt ashamed of himself. "Uncle Omar is—was—death on any kind of publicity. We always had to be so careful. He paid a firm in New York thirty thousand dollars a year to keep him out of the papers. But people were always prying. They'd get some tiny little rumor about Omar Krepps and make a great big story out of it, and Uncle Omar would be absolutely furious."

Charla put her hand over his, a warm pressure. "But dear Kirby, it does not matter now, does it?"

"I guess not."

"My brother and I are not journalists, of course, but you could speak to journalists, you know. You could let the world know what a vile thing he did to you, what a horrid way he repaid your years of selfless devotion."

She was so understanding, Kirby wanted to weep. But he felt an uncomfortable twinge of honesty. "Not so selfless. I mean, you have an uncle worth fifty million dollars, there's an ulterior motive."

"But you told us how you had quit many times," Joseph said. The warmth of Charla's hand was removed. Kirby missed it.

"But I always went back," Kirby admitted. "He'd tell me I was his favorite nephew. He'd tell me he needed me. For what? All he ever did was keep me on the run. No chance to have a life of my own. Crazy errands all over the world. Eleven years of it, ever since I got out of college. Even there, he told me the courses to take. That old man ran my whole life."

"You told us, my dear," Charla said, her voice breaking. "All those years of devotion."

"And then," Joseph said sternly, "not a penny."

The brightness of the dawn was beginning to hurt Kirby's eyes. He yawned. When he opened his eyes, Joseph and Charla were standing. Joseph went over to the barman. Charla touched his shoulder. "Come, dear. You're exhausted."

He went with her without question, out through glass doors, across a vast and unfamiliar lobby. When they were a dozen feet from the elevators he stopped. She looked up at him in question. Her face was so flawless, the eyes huge, gray-green, the parted lips moist, the honeyed skin darker than her hair, that for the moment he forgot what he was going to say.

"Darling?" she said.

"I'm not staying here, am I?"

"Joseph thought it would be better."

"Where is he?"

"We said good night to him, Kirby dear."

"Did we?"

"Come, dear."

The elevator climbed through a fragrant silken silence. He drifted down a long corridor. She took a key from a jeweled purse and let them into the suite. She closed the blinds against the dawn sunlight and took him to a bedroom. The bed was turned down. New pyjamas and an assortment of new toilet articles were laid out for him.

"Joseph thinks of everything," she said. "Once he owned some hotels, but when they began to bore him, he sold them. Kirby, dear, you must have a hot shower. Then you will sleep."

When he came back to the bedroom in the new pyjamas, she was waiting for him. She had changed to a robe of some soft fabric in a shade of gold. She had brushed her hair. She stood up and seemed very small to him without her high heels. The fitted robe sheathed and revealed a figure to fog the lenses of the little men who take pictures for the centerfolds of the more forthright magazines. It curved and cushioned into all the right dimensions and then, implausibly, curved just a little bit more. Though he felt, with thunderous pulse, as though someone were thumping him lightly on the top of the head with a padded stick, and though he felt appallingly winsome, like a boy groom, he also felt a solemn sense of responsibility. Here was a totally first-class woman, mature, fragrant, expensive, sophisticated, silken and immaculate. And one could not sidle up to her, dragging one foot and saying shucks. Heartening himself with a thousand memories of Cary Grant, he tried to saunter up to the woman, wearing a smile that was tender, knowing and suitably ravenous.

But he sauntered his bare toes into the cruel narrow leg of a small table. With a whine of anguish he lunged, off balance, at the woman—clutching at her with more the idea of breaking his fall than with any sense of improper purpose. The flailing leap alarmed her and she darted to one side emitting a small hiss of dismay. One frantic hand caught the strong golden fabric at the throat of her fitted robe. For one full half-turn, the durable fabric sustained them in the beginning of a skater's whirl, but then there was a ripping sound, and as he tumbled into a far corner he caught a glimpse of her as she plummeted out of the robe, spinning, struck the edge of the bed, bounced once and disappeared over the far edge with a soft padded thud.

He sat up, pushed the ruined robe aside, clasped his toes in both hands and made small comforting sounds.

Her tousled head appeared slowly, warily, looking at him from beyond the bed, her eyes wide. "Darling!" she said. "You are so impulsive!"

He stared at her with his face of pain. "Kindly shut up. This has been happening ever since I can remember, and I can do without the funny jokes."

"You always do this!"

"I always do something. Usually I merely run away. In the summer of 1958 I went with a beautiful woman to her suite on the seventh floor of the Continental Hilton in Mexico City. Three minutes after I closed the door, an earthquake began. Plaster fell. The hotel cracked open. We had to feel our way down the stairs in the dark. The lobby was full of broken glass. So please shut up, Charla."

"Throw me my robe, dear."

He balled it up and threw it to her. He got up and hobbled to

the bed and sat down. She came around the foot of the bed and
sat beside him. The robe, belted in a new way, covered her.

"Poor Kirby," she said.

"Sure."

She patted his arm. She chuckled. "I've never been undressed
quite that fast before."

"Very hilarious," he said.

She touched his chin, turned his head so that he looked down
into her eyes. For the moment she looked very sad. "You do
tempt me, dear. Because you are so very sweet and nice. Too
many charades these days. And too many men who are not like
you in any respect."

"If they were all like me, the survival of the race would be in
doubt."

She pulled him closer. He kissed her, abashedly at first and
then with mounting enthusiasm. When he toppled her back, she
wiggled free and shook her head and made a face at him. "No,
dear. Joseph and I are very fond of you. And you have had a
ghastly time. And Joseph told me to care for you. Now hop into
bed like a sweet lamb, and take off the top of the pretty pyjamas
and lay face down and I shall make you feel very, very good."

"But—"

"Darling, don't be a bore, please. I don't want to change our
friendship so soon, do you?"

"If you're asking me—"

"Hush. Some day, soon maybe, you will become my lover.
Who can tell? Is it not more fun to guess? Be a good boy."

He stretched out as instructed. She came back after turning out
all the lights but one. She poured something cool and aromatic
onto his back and began to knead the muscles of his back and
shoulders and the nape of his neck with clever fingers.

"My word, you have lovely muscles, dear," she said.

"Dynamic tension."

"What?"

"Exercises anyone can do."

"Oh. Now just let everything fall away. Slide down into the
darkness, sweet Kirby. Abandon yourself to pure sensation."

"Um."

"Rest, my dear. Rest."

Her soothing hands stroked the tension out of him. He was so completely exhausted he could have fallen into sleep like falling ten thousand feet into a midnight swamp. But her touch, her gentle teasing voice, the awareness of her fragrant and erotic presence kept him suspended, floating on the surface of sleep. She hummed and the tune seemed familiar, as though he had heard it in a foreign movie.

He reached back through time to the previous Wednesday, at midnight. Fifty-seven hours ago? That was when the word had reached him at his hotel in Montevideo. The old man was dead. Omar Krepps. Uncle Omar. It was shocking to think that even death itself had the power to reach out and take that strange, invulnerable little man.

As he thought of the return trip he sank deeper in the pool of sleep and his images became confused, changed by Charla. The breast-nosed jet took off down a pale silken runway of tenderest flesh while the nude and shadowy hostesses gathered close around him, humming to him. In the midst of this half-sleep he was vaguely aware of Charla turning him, helping him into the pyjama top. Her mouth came down upon his, sweet, deft and heavy, and as he tried to lift leaden arms to hold her close, she was gone. He thought he heard her say, "I'm so sorry, dear." He wondered what she felt sorry about. The other light went off. The latch clicked. He fell off the edge of the world.

2

KIRBY WAS HAULED UP OUT OF SLEEP BY A RANGY YOUNG GIRL HE had never seen before. She shook him awake. All the lights in the room were on. He braced himself up on his elbows. She was pacing around the bed so rapidly it was difficult to keep her in focus. She was yelling at him, and the words made no sense. She had a wildly cropped mop of palomino hair, fierce green eyes bulging with fury, a lean face dark with rage. She wore a coral shirt, striped stretch pants, and waved a straw purse the size of a snare drum.

It took him long dull seconds to realize she was yelling in a language he did not understand.

When she paused for breath, he said faintly, "No comprendo, Señorita."

She switched immediately into a torrent of fluent Spanish. He spoke it reasonably well, but not that well. He caught just enough to realize it was idiomatic, graphic and probably would have sent a Mexico City cab driver running for shelter, his hands clapped over his ears.

"Mas despacio, por favor," he pleaded when she paused for the next breath.

She looked at him narrowly. "Will English do?"

"Do what?"

"Where is my goddam aunt, and what the hell right does she think she has pulling one of her cute tricks and getting me thrown the hell off the first decent television script I've seen in a year? She can't call me down here like I'm some kind of a slave. Where's that spooky Joseph, buddy? Don't you *dare* try to cover for either one of them, buster. I've handled her sniveling little secretarial types before. I want the facts, and I want them right now!"

She put a small nose with abruptly flared nostrils five inches from his and glared directly into his eyes. "Well?" she said.

"Facts?"

"Facts, fellow."

She had an almost imperceptible accent, but there was an illusive familiarity about it.

"I think you're in the wrong room."

"I *know* I'm in the wrong room. The other rooms in the suite are empty. That's why I'm in this room. Don't stall."

"The suite?"

She stamped her foot. "The suite! Yes, the suite! My God, start tracking, fellow. Hook up with reality. This big lush suite in the Hotel Elise, eighth floor, Miami Beach, ten o'clock on this gaudy Saturday night in April, in this suite registered in the name of Charla Maria Markopoulo O'Rourke, buster, my unsainted aunt, this suite it cost me a twenty-buck bribe to get into after steaming all the way from the Coast on a jet."

"Charla!" he said. And knew where he was, and why the girl's accent, though less than Charla's, had seemed familiar. Up until that moment he had thought himself in Montevideo. "Uncle Omar is dead," he said.

"Don't waste those sick codes on me, buster. I unjoined Charla's wolf pack ages ago. Little Filiatra changed her name and her outlook and her habits because she got sick up to here of all the cute, dirty, sick little tricks. I'm Betsy Alden now, by choice, and I'm a citizen and a good actress, and she gets me reinstated fast or I'm going to belt her loose from her cunning little brain."

"If you'd back away a little, I could think better."

She went to the foot of the bed and glowered at him. "Where is she?"

"Look. You seem to have the idea I work for her."

"Please don't try to be cute, friend."

"Honest to God, my name is Kirby Winter. I had a terrible day yesterday. I got drunk. I never met Charla until late yesterday some time. I didn't even know the rest of her name. I don't know who you are. I don't know where she is. I don't have the slightest idea of what you're talking about."

The girl stared at him, biting her lip. He saw the suspicion and the anger slowly fade away. And then she looked at him with cold, mocking contempt.

"So terribly, terribly sorry, Mr. Winter. I guess I just wasn't thinking. I should have guessed you wouldn't be on the team. You don't look bright enough. You do look more the fun and games type. Muscled and clean and earnest. But not even knowing her right name? My word! Charla must be getting really hasty and desperate. Isn't she a little elderly for you?"

Contempt was more distressing than her inexplicable anger.

"But I was only—"

"Check the bureau before you leave, Mr. Winter. She tips very generously, I've been told."

The girl whirled and left the room, slamming the door behind her. The slam re-echoed through all the brassy corridors of his hangover, and made his stomach lurch. Suddenly he was covered with icy sweat. He lay back and closed his eyes, wrestling the furry Angel Nausea. He wished the damned girl, in spite of her moral judgments, had had the grace to turn the lights off. He wondered if one could perish of thirst while being wracked with nausea. In a little while—in just a little while—he would get up and turn off the lights. . . .

There was daylight beyond the closed blinds. The room lights were off. He got up and found his way to the bathroom. He looked at his self-winding watch. It had stopped. He felt weak, rested, thirsty and ravenous. He looked into the mirror and saw his own mild and fatuous smile, blurred by a gingery stubble of beard. He wondered if he had merely dreamed the angry girl. And Montevideo. And the funeral. He was certain he hadn't dreamed Charla. He was totally certain of that. He remembered his inheritance and immediately felt chagrined and depressed. But he felt too good to stay depressed.

After the long shower, a shave with the new razor, and a minty scrubbing with an unfamiliar toothpaste, he knotted a big towel around his waist and went back to the bedroom. Someone had opened the blinds. Golden sunlight poured in. There was a huge glass of iced orange juice on the bedside table, and a note written in violet ink in a bold yet feminine hand on heavy blue-gray stationery embossed with the initials C. M. M. O'R. It looked like some odd abbreviation of Commodore, and he knew that the angry girl had not been something dreamt. Charla Maria Marko-something O'Rourke.

"Kirby, dear. I heard the shower and took steps. You must have been at the very end of your rope, poor thing. Little men are hurrying to you with a sort of care package. Your clothes have been bundled off, pockets empty, look on the dressing stand. Packages in the chair. I bought them by guess alone last evening before the lower level shops closed. When the animal has been clothed and fed, you'll find me on the sun balcony. I need not ask you if you slept well. Good morning, darling. Your Charla."

He looked out his windows. They faced east. The sun was more than halfway up the sky. The door to the main part of the suite was ajar. He picked up the phone and asked what time it was. "Twelve minutes after ten on a beautiful Sunday morning in Florida," the girl said pertly.

Twenty-seven hours in the sack, he estimated. He went to the chair where the packages were stacked. White nylon tricot boxer shorts, waist thirty-two. Correct. Rope sandals, marked L. Comfortable. Gray dacron slacks, cuffed. Perfect at the waist. Possibly one-half inch shorter in the inseam than he usually wore them. Close enough. One short-sleeved sports shirt with a button-down collar. Fine for size and styling. But the colors—narrow vertical stripes in gray, pale blue, coral and light yellow, each narrow stripe divided from the next one by a narrow black line, and the fabric was a light-weight silk. As he was buttoning the shirt there was a knock at the corridor door. Two uniformed waiters, deft, smiling, courteous, came in with a large clinking cart and quickly set up his vast breakfast, hot in the tureens, on the snowy linen. They had a Sunday paper for him. He tried to hide the fact he was salivating like a wolf. Everything has been taken care of, sir. Thank you, sir. If you need anything else, sir. He wanted them to go before he grabbed the eggs barehanded.

"Shall I open the champagne now, sir?"

"The what!"

"The champagne, sir."

"Oh. Of course. The champagne. Just leave it the way it is."

Not until he had nothing left but a second cup of coffee was he able to even pretend to look at the newspaper. And then he could not keep his mind on it. Too many other mysteries were unsolved. He turned and lifted the champagne out of the crushed ice. It was not a split. It was a full and elegant bottle. He was wrapping it in a fresh napkin when he noticed the two champagne glasses on the nearby tray-table.

How big a hint does a man need, he thought. He took the bottle and the glasses, and, feeling incomparably elegant, went off in search of Charla O'Rourke. He found one empty bedroom without a sun balcony. He found a second and much larger bedroom with open French doors facing the east. He walked, smiling, squinting, trying to think of some suave opening statement, into the hot bright glare. Charla was stretched out on her back on a wide long sun-cot of aluminum and white plastic webbing, her arms over her head. Sun had reddened the gold of her body. She was agleam with oil and perspiration. He stood and boggled at her, all suave statements forgotten. He tightened his grip on the champagne bottle just in time. She seemed to be asleep. At least she was breathing deeply and slowly. She wore three items—a ridiculous wisp of white G-string, white plastic cups on her eyes, and a blue towel worn as a turban. He stood in an awed, oafish silence, aware of the sound of the ocean surf far below, of a drone of traffic on Collins Avenue, of faint music from somewhere. Not plump at all, he thought. Where did I get that impression? Firm as an acrobat, but just with more curves than there's room for. More than anybody should have.

She plucked the plastic cups from her eyes and sat up. She smiled at him. "Poor dear, you must have been exhausted!"

"Gahr," he said in a wispy voice.

"And you brought the champagne. How dear of you! Is something the matter? Oh, of course. The puritan syndrome." She reached for a short white terry jacket and put it on without haste. He found himself wishing she would button it and wishing she wouldn't. She didn't. "We spend so much time at Cannes, I forget your odd taboos. Now you may stop boggling at me, dear boy. Do you think I've had enough?"

"Gahr?"

She pressed a firm thumb into the honey-pink round top of her thigh. They both watched the white mark fade slowly. They watched it intently. "Quite enough, I would say," she said. "Some people find a dark tan quite attractive, but it does change the texture of the skin, you know. It becomes quite rough, comparatively." She rose lithely and walked by him and into the relative gloom of the big bedroom, saying, "Come on in, dear." He followed her, carrying the bottle and the glasses, his mind absolutely blank.

He did not see her stop abruptly when she was three steps inside the room. He did not see her stop and turn. His eyes had not compensated. He walked into her, and in the instantaneous impression of heat and oil and perfume of that impact, he dropped the bottle onto his foot. He saw her floundering backward, grabbed at her with the hand which had held the bottle, misjudged his distance, struck her rather solidly on a terried shoulder and knocked her over a footstool. She lit solidly and said something in a language he did not understand. Somehow he was glad he did not understand it.

She crawled over and retrieved the unbroken bottle and stood up. "If you'll stop hopping up and down on one foot, Mr. Winter, you can pour me a glass of champagne."

"I'm sorry."

"Thank God you didn't get playful until we got off that balcony, Kirby."

"Charla, I just—"

"I know, dear." She worked the wire loose, deftly popped the cork. The champagne, after the thump, foamed abundantly as she filled the two glasses. She put down the bottle, took one glass from him, looked speculatively at him as she sipped. "Instead of perfume, dear, bring me liniment, instead of jewels, bandages. Now fill my glass again and be patient while I tub this oil away. Could I trust you to scrub my back?"

"Gahr."

"No, we had best not risk that. Here's to caution, Kirby dear. Champagne is dripping off your chin. Wait for me in the next room, please."

He carried the bottle and his glass into the large sitting room of the suite, walking on knees as reliable as wet yarn. He sat down with care, emptied his glass and filled it again. He felt as if he had a permanent double exposure on the sensitive retinas. No matter where he looked, he saw Charla supine, foreshortened, in deathless Kodachrome, in an incomparable clarity of focus, a vividness of the great, round, firm, self-sustaining weight of breasts, with their buttery tan, the skin without grain or sag or flaw, the nipples a darker hue, large but not gross, aimed, slightly divergent, at the tropic-blue morning sky.

When he shook his head violently, the pervasive image blurred. When he shook his head again, the image slipped back and down into the cluttered warehouse of memory. It lay atop the rest of the debris, instantaneously available.

He heard the end of the metallic thunder of the water roaring into her tub, and as he fancied her stepping into it, he groaned aloud. O thank you, Uncle Omar. Thank you for instilling a helpless youth with such grave suspicions of women and all their works, that here and now, in my maturity, in my thirty-second year, I cannot confront a lovely and half-naked lady without getting cramps in my toes and saying gahr.

But he had the dim suspicion that such were the obvious riches of Charla that even a far more worldly man might have experienced a visceral tremor or two.

Considering the wretched paucity of his experience and the extent of his carefully concealed shyness, he marveled that when he had come upon her there, he had not merely given a mad cackle of laughter and vaulted the cement railing a hundred feet above the gaudy roofs of the beach cabanas.

He knew well the forlorn pattern of his increasingly compulsive search for sexual self-confidence. In this world that Hugh Heffner had made, he alone seemed forever bunnyless. And it was becoming less a matter of hunger than of pride.

He knew that women found him reasonably attractive. And he had laboriously developed that brand of semi-insinuating small talk which gave women the impression he was as accustomed to the casual diversion as the next fellow. But there was the damnable shyness to contend with. Where do you start? How to start? In situations where unattached women were abundant, he had developed into a fine art the knack of making each of them believe he was intimately concerned with one of the others.

Once in a great while he would finally overcome the shyness, turn into the final pattern for the attack on target, and then have the situation blow up in his face. He knew he was not a clownish man. It depressed him to look back on too many slapstick situations. One would think it possible for a man of dignity to approach a woman like Charla without suddenly, inadvertently, peeling her like a grape and hurling her over a bed. His face grew hot as he remembered.

It was, he suspected, because he tightened up in the clutch. With the bases loaded, two out, and a three-nothing count on the clean-up hitter, the rookie comes in, steps on the rubber, glares sternly at the batter—and drops the ball.

Sometimes nature intervened. As in the case of the earthquake. A man could begin to believe he was hexed.

Sometimes, as with Andrea last year in Rome, it seemed pure accident. He had rescued her from a yelping throng which had confused her with Elizabeth Taylor. The talk had been amusing. They were staying in the same hotel, on the same floor. She was alone, trying to recover her morale after a bad marriage and a messy divorce. It was understood, without words, that he would walk a dozen feet down the corridor and tap at her door and she would let him in.

The prospect terrified him. He had presented too glib and sophisticated a front. She would expect a suave continental competence, a complete and masterful experience. And it was rather much to expect of a fellow whose most recent—in fact, whose only affair—had taken place twelve years earlier in the back seat of a 1947 Hudson in Johnstown, Pennsylvania, in a public park during a rainstorm with a noisy, pock-marked girl named Hazel Broochuk, and had lasted for about twelve incomparably clumsy minutes.

Though these were hardly the experience factors one would bring to an assignation with a woman who could be mistaken for Liz, he steeled himself to carry out the impersonation to the best of his ability. After a scalding bath, he donned his wool robe and marched up and down his room, fists clenched, jaw set. To the sound of trumpets, he turned toward his door, marched out into the corridor and firmly yanked the door shut. He yanked the door shut on a substantial hunk of the hem of the robe. The door locked itself. The keys were inside, on the bureau. Maybe in the world there were men of sufficient aplomb to go tap on the door sans robe. It certainly would reduce any areas of confusion as to the purpose of the small-hours' visit. But Kirby Winter was not one of them.

And the worst time of all, perhaps, was when, emboldened by brandy, hand in hand with a sweet laughing little darling of a girl, they had run like the wind from the big house in Nassau down toward the beach cabana in the moonlight. And halfway there the wire clothesline had caught him just under the chin.

But for each opportunity denied him by the fates, there had been twice that number he had run away from, in sweaty terror. He sneered at himself and sipped the champagne. You are a clown and a coward, Kirby Winter—a lousy, neurotic, mixed-up coward, and yet you go around making women believe you're a gay dog. Gahr, indeed.

Charla came into the room. She planted herself in the corner of the couch near him before he could begin to stand up. She was barefoot. She wore short pink shorts and a candy-striped halter and a pink ribbon in her hair. He realized that if he focused beyond her instead of right at her, she looked about fifteen. Startlingly precocious perhaps, but no more than fifteen. Only the direct gaze detected the webbed flesh under her eyes, the lines bracketing the mouth, the slight sag of tissue under her chin.

"Again, dear," she said, holding her empty glass toward him. He filled it and his own and put the bottle back on the ice. "That shirt is really handsome."

"Thank you. It's very nice. The other things are nice too. But I really can't accept—"

She made a face at him. "So grim and stuffy all of a sudden? Are you cross when you wake up? I am. That's why I left you alone, Kirby dear."

"No. Not cross, I guess. It's just—"

"Pressing wasn't enough for your suit. It'll be back this afternoon. With your tie and socks and so on, dear. Really, I threw your shirt away. I hope it didn't have some sort of sentimental value. It was actually shabby. Please tell me you *do* feel better. I mean, when one makes a special effort to—"

"I feel a lot better, Charla."

She pulled her knees onto the couch and sat crosswise, wrinkling her eyes at him as she sipped her drink. She was long-waisted, he saw. The weight of hips and breasts made her waist look smaller than it was. Her glossy legs were short and rather heavy, but seemed exactly suitable for her.

"Mad with me?" she asked.

"Should I be?"

"Oh, because I teased you a little. Do you remember?"

"Yes."

"Such a cruel thing a woman can do, isn't it?"

"I guess so."

"I may tease some more, you know."

He shifted uneasily. "I guess you might."

"But some time I might not be teasing at all." She stared at him, her eyes wide and innocent. "Poor little man. How will you be able to tell when the time comes when I don't tease?"

He cast about for a change of subject. "That girl."

"Oh, yes. She disturbed you. My niece. Now she calls herself Betsy Alden. I was very cross with her, Kirby. I still am."

"She made quite a fuss."

Charla shrugged. "I seem to have done some horrible, damaging thing to her career. I didn't realize. I wanted her to come here to see me. After all, I am her only aunt. She wouldn't come. She had some silly idea of her play-acting being more important. So —I remembered an old friend and called him up. He called a good friend of his. Suddenly they didn't need her. Is this so terrible?"

"Only if she can't find another job."

"She says she'll have trouble. She cursed me. She was very noisy and vulgar. Once upon a time she was a very sweet child. It's hard to believe."

"Did she leave?"

"Oh, no! She has to stay here. Because she will now have to beg me to undo the terrible damage she thinks I've done. After she becomes sweet enough to me, then I shall phone my friend again, and then she will be in demand again for those idiotic television things. It's what she seems to want, poor child."

"At first she thought I worked for you. And then she got another idea about me, and that wasn't right either."

Charla's smile was curiously unpleasant. "She mentioned that. I admit it is not accurate. But it could have been, so easily, don't you think?"

"I guess so."

"You seem so solemn today, Kirby. Even, forgive me, a little bit stuffy. You talked so much on Friday night, and were so charming and hurt."

"I must have been a nuisance. I want to thank you for—giving me a chance to sleep it off. And I really must be going."

"Oh, not until Joseph comes and we tell you our idea."

"Idea?"

"Come, dear. We know you have no specific plans. You told us that."

"Did I? I'll have to find something—"

"Maybe you've found it, Kirby. You have certain attributes Joseph and I could use, you know. You make a good impression, dear. You look very decent and earnest and reliable and trustworthy. Many people look like that, but it is a false front. You are what you seem to be, dear."

"I beg your pardon?"

"And you have such a great capacity for loyalty. I'm certain your Uncle Omar was pleased with you, and made wonderful use of you. He trained you. And really good people are so hard to find these days. And you're at home in so many countries. We have little problems you could help us with."

"What sort of problems?"

She shrugged. "Here's one at random. We have one nice little ship. The *Princess Markopoulo,* Panamanian registry. We think the captain and the agent are conspiring against us. The profits are so tiny. You could go aboard as my special representative and find out what is wrong. There are always problems. And we don't want to give up the way we live and handle them ourselves. It would be too dull. You would be busy. It would be amusing. And we would pay you well. Between assignments you could be with us. We would pay you twice what your Uncle Omar paid you."

"Do you know what he paid me?"

"You told us, dear. And you've saved a veritable fortune! Eight thousand dollars. Dear Kirby, that would last me perhaps one month. And you will have to find work."

"I must have done a lot of talking."

"You told us your inheritance from your dear dead uncle. A pocket watch and a letter."

"And I don't even get the letter until a year from now," he said, and divided the small amount of champagne left.

She hitched closer to him, touched her glass against his, looked into his eyes. "So why not have the amusing life? It is good fortune for all of us we met the other night. We are very good friends, no? Here is what we shall do, Kirby Winter. You settle what must be settled here. By then the *Glorianna* will be here. And we shall have a cruise."

"The *Glorianna?*"

"My dear toy yacht, dearest. Holland built. Lovely staterooms and a crew of five. We always have charming guests aboard. Much fun, much wine, maybe a little love. My crew is bringing her down from Bermuda now. The best food in the world, my dear. We insist on that. Spend a month as our guest and then we shall decide your future. Why do you look so troubled?"

He shrugged. "Superstitious, maybe. Things like this just don't fall into my lap, Charla."

She put her empty glass aside and moved closer to him. She took his hand and lifted it to her lips. It made him feel curiously girlish and awkward. She looked at him with a sweet gravity. "You do make me like you—too much, perhaps. We should have met another time. When there were no jobs to offer, when you were not troubled and disappointed. When we could both be honest."

"What do you mean?"

"I meant nothing. A woman's chatter." There was a knock at the door and she asked him to let in Joseph. With great enthusiasm Charla told Joseph that Kirby had agreed to come cruising on the *Glorianna* and then he would take the job they had decided to offer him. Kirby found himself shaking Joseph's hand and being effusively congratulated. Things seemed to be moving too fast. He tried to find the right opening to tell Joseph it was not that definite, and suddenly realized he was being instructed to move out of his own hotel and move here, to the Hotel Elise.

"But I—but I—"

Joseph put a fatherly hand on Kirby's shoulder. Charla was on Kirby's other side. She slid her arm around his waist, hugged herself close to him. In the arctic reaches of his mind, walls of ice toppled into the sea.

"Nonsense, my boy," Joseph said. "The hotel is not full. I happen to own a certain percentage of it. When you return with your luggage you will be all registered. Because I am busy on small matters, Charla is often lonesome. We would be grateful, both of us. You will be doing us a favor."

"Well, I guess I could—"

"Splendid!" they cried simultaneously, and Charla gave him a heartier little hug, full of rounded dizzying pleasures. Her glowing face was upturned toward his, her eyes full of warm promise. Joseph had taken a gold cigarette case from his pocket. It slipped from his hand. Both men stooped simultaneously and cracked skulls. Kirby straightened up, off balance, half-blinded by the white burst of shock and pain. He swung his arm up to catch his balance and caught Charla smartly under the point of the chin with his elbow. Her teeth made a chopping sound and her eyes glazed and she wobbled momentarily.

She looked at him fearfully and made a curious gesture and spoke in a foreign language. It sounded like an incantation, and in the middle of it he thought he heard her say, "Omar Krepps."

"Shut up!" Joseph said to her in a deadly tone. He was holding a palm against his brow.

"I'm sorry," Kirby said miserably. "I just seem to—"

"It was an accident," Charla said. "Are you hurt, dear Kirby?"

"I—I'd better be on my way, I guess."

3

AS KIRBY OPENED THE REAR DOOR OF THE CAB TO GET IN, A GIRL eeled by him and took the cab.

"Hey!" he said indignantly.

Betsy Alden glowered at him. "Just shut up and get in, stupid!"

He hesitated, got in beside her and said, "But what are—"

"Driver! Go north on Collins, please. I'll tell you where."

"But I want to go—"

"Will you shut up!"

They rode a dozen blocks in silence. He looked at her rigid profile, thinking she would be quite a pretty girl if she wasn't always mad. The taxi was caught by a light. "Right here," she said and quickly handed the money to the driver and got out. When Kirby caught up with her, she was walking south, carefully examining the oncoming traffic.

"Will you kindly tell me—"

"In here, I guess," she said, caught at his arm and swung him along with her into a narrow walkway leading to the side entrance of one of the smaller beach hotels. Once in the lobby she looked around like a questing cat, then headed for a short flight of stairs to the mezzanine. He followed her up the stairs. She wore a green skirt and a white blouse. She had changed to a smaller purse. Her toffee hair was more orderly. Following her up the stairs he realized she was singularly expressive. Even in the flex of lean haunches under the swing of the skirt she seemed to project both stealth and indignation.

"Sit over there," she said, indicating a fake Victorian couch upholstered in shiny plastic under a fake Utrillo upon an imitation driftwood wall. He sat on the couch. She stood by the railing, looking down into the lobby for what seemed to be a long time, then shrugged and came slowly over and sat beside him.

"I'll tell you one thing and you remember it, Winter," she said. "No matter how careful you are, it might not be enough." She gave him a very direct green stare.

"Are you all right?"

"How are you reacting to my dear Aunt Charla? How's your pulse?"

"Miss Alden, I have the feeling we aren't communicating."

"When she wants to really set the hook, she can make any Gabor look like Apple Annie. There's fine steam coming off you, Winter."

"She's an unusual woman."

"And she takes no chances. She had to have me here on standby. Just in case you'd rather settle for something younger, taller and not quite so meaty. But I told her a long time ago I'm through playing her games. She can take care of her own pigeons without any help from me. I got off her merry-go-round when I was twenty years old. And I was a very old twenty. Charla would be all right—she might even be fun—if she weren't so damned greedy."

"What is that about a pigeon?"

"What else do you think you are? Do you think she's smitten by your charm?"

"She got smitten a few times."

"What?"

"Miss Alden. Just for laughs. What are we talking about?"

She frowned at him. A strand of the tan-gold hair fell across her forehead and she pushed it back. "I checked the newspapers. Omar Krepps was your uncle. That's what we're talking about."

"I don't understand."

"When I was fifteen years old she yanked me out of school in Switzerland and began lugging me around the world with her. She and Joseph are operators, Winter. Canadian gold, African oil, Indian opium, Brazilian girls—you name it, and they've bought it and sold it. They aren't the biggest and they aren't the shrewdest, but they keep getting richer, and it's never fast enough to suit them. They are in and out of cartel and syndicate operations with other chums of the same ilk, and their happiest little game is trying to cheat each other. I was only fifteen, but I soon learned that in their circles, the name Omar Krepps terrified them. Almost a superstitious terror. Too many times Krepps would suddenly appear, skim the cream off a deal and leave with the money. I believe they and some of their friends tried to have him killed, but it never worked."

"Kill Uncle Omar?"

"Shut up and listen. And believe. That fat little old man seemed able to be nine places at once. One time he skinned them good, intercepted cash on its way to a number account in Zurich somehow, and just took it, and they could do nothing about it because they'd in effect stolen it first—Joseph and Charla and some of their thieving pals. At that time Charla was wearing a ring that opened up. A poison ring, I guess, with an emerald. She opened it idly one day and there was a little wad of paper in it. She unfolded it. It said, 'Thanks, O. Krepps.' When she came out of her faint she had the wildest case of hysterics you ever saw, and she had to go into a hospital for a week. You see, the ring hadn't been off her finger since before the money was taken."

"I can't really believe Uncle Omar would—"

"Let me finish. Krepps died last Wednesday. They were in Bermuda. They flew here Thursday morning. You arrived at dawn on Friday, and by dawn on Saturday you're in bed in Charla's suite. How much accident is involved in that?"

"I thought I met them by accident."

"That pair doesn't cotton to the random stranger. There's always a reason for every move. What do they want from you?"

"They've invited me on a cruise."

"Tell me all of it, Winter. Every word you can remember."

He told her an edited version of it.

She scowled. "And your Uncle Omar left you practically nothing? I guess they must want to pick your brains and find out how he operated."

"But I didn't have anything to do with—making money. I don't know anything about the business end of it. He told me what courses to take in college. When I got out I went to work for him, doing the very same thing right from the beginning."

"Doing what?"

"Giving money away."

"What!"

"Just that," he said helplessly. "He had some sort of clipping service and translation service and I would go and make investigations and give the money away if in my opinion everything was on the level—and if it could be kept quiet."

"Much money?"

"I think it averages out somewhere around three million a year."

"To charities?"

"Sometimes. Sometimes to individuals trying to get something started, or small companies in trouble."

"Why did he want to give it away?"

"He never seemed very serious about anything. He never explained. He just said he did it to keep his luck good. He was a jolly little man. He didn't like to talk seriously. He liked to tell long jokes and do card tricks and show you how he could take his vest off without taking his coat off."

"Did you see much of him?"

"About once a year. He was always going off alone. It made people nervous. He had apartments and houses here and there, and it was hard to tell just where he'd be. But I never ran out of work, no matter how long he was out of touch. And he hated publicity of any kind."

"You are not lying to me," she said. It was more statement than question.

"No. While he was alive I wasn't supposed to tell anybody what I did for him. Now I guess it doesn't matter too much. The notoriety he got in the very beginning—I guess it made him secretive."

"What notoriety?"

"A long time ago. My parents were drowned in a boating accident when I was seven, and I went to live with Uncle Omar and Aunt Thelma. She was his older sister. She was good to me, but she certainly made Uncle Omar's life miserable. We lived in an old house in Pittsburgh. Uncle Omar taught high school chemistry and physics. He had a workshop in the basement where he tried to invent things. I guess it was the only place in the house where he was happy. Aunt Thelma was always crabbing about the money he spent on tools and equipment and supplies, and complaining about the electric bills. When I was eleven years old he quit right in the middle of a school term and went out to Reno and won a hundred and twenty-six thousand dollars. It was in all the papers. They called him a mathematical genius. They hounded him. Every nut in the country made his life miserable. He put money in the bank for us and disappeared. He was gone almost a year. He reappeared in Reno and lost a hundred thousand dollars there, and then nobody was very interested in him any more. After that he took us down to Texas where he'd built a house on an island in the Gulf off Brownsville. He set up a trust fund for Aunt Thelma and sent her back to Pittsburgh. I stayed there with him for a little while before I went back. By then he had a lot of business interests all over the world. He supported me and paid for my education and gave me my job when I graduated. But—he didn't leave me anything, and I don't know anything about his business interests. In fact, I didn't know him very well. The papers say it's a fifty-million-dollar estate. He left me his watch and a letter to be handed to me one year from last Wednesday."

"And you told Charla that?"

"Yes."

"And told her what you've been doing for a living?"

"I guess I did."

"And you've gone all these years without even trying to make any guesses about your uncle?"

At the moment Betsy Alden irritated him. "I may act like an idiot, but I have average intelligence, Miss Alden. My uncle left that cellar all of a sudden. And how many high school teachers become international financiers?"

"So he found something that gave him an edge."

"An edge over other people, so he gave a lot of the money away. Maybe it was conscience. At least it made him feel better."

She nodded rather smugly. "And so Charla is terribly interested in that letter. Isn't it obvious?"

"But she can't—I can't get it for a year."

"Mr. Winter, any explanation of how one little man could terrorize Charla and her group, fleece them, and end up worth fifty-million dollars is worth a year of effort. And by the end of the year she can have you in such captivity, you'll turn the letter over to her without even opening it, and whinnying with delight at the chance to please her in some small way."

"You have a dandy opinion of me."

"I know Charla. I've seen her at work."

"Where do you come in? What do you want? Do you want the letter?"

"All I want, believe me, is some leverage. I don't care how or where I get it, but I want to be able to pressure Charla into fixing it so I can go back to work where I belong. She brought pressure down on me." She stabbed Kirby in the chest with her finger. "And if I can use you to get her off my back forever, I would be a very happy girl. And at the same time I might be doing you a favor, like keeping you from sinking into a swamp."

"Do you hate her that much?"

"Hate is complex. This is a simple emotion. Contempt. She's really quite easy to understand. Her only motivation is greed. Greed for money, power, pretty things, admiration, sensual pleasure. She likes to use power, Winter. So does Joseph, but she's captain of that team."

"He's your uncle?"

"Hardly. She calls him her brother, but he's more a sort of half brother-in-law. And not what you'd want to call a wholesome relationship. But they do seem so charming, don't they? It makes them a deadly team."

"I keep feeling that you are dramatizing this. I just can't believe they—"

"Wait a minute. I just thought of something. You are his only living blood relation. And it was in the papers, so Charla must know that. So in addition to whatever is in the will, won't you get his personal papers and records?"

"I guess so. I hadn't thought about it."

"Believe me, Charla will. And Charla has. Now don't you dare turn anything over to her."

"What do you think I am?"

"Don't be angry. We know there's something she wants, badly. So we have to find out just what it is she wants. Once we find out what it is, then you can decide whether you want to sell it to her, whatever it is. If you do, let me be your agent. I'll get you more than anybody else could."

"People keep moving too fast lately."

"I'm essentially rougher than you are, Kirby Winter. I'm a graduate student of the school of Charla. You move into the Elise. If you start dragging your feet now, they may change tactics." She scribbled an address and a phone number and handed him the piece of paper. "When you find out anything definite, get in touch with me here. It's a little apartment I've borrowed from a hokey friend. He's on one of his annual tours of duty in New York. He goes up there and does commercials so he can afford to live down here and write plays. He's sick with love for me. Look, Kirby. You don't have to like me and you don't have to trust me. What are you losing so far? And call me Betsy."

"Losing nothing, so far. Possibly my mind. Nothing important though."

"Play along and play it very cozy, and when you do find out what they're after, then you can decide whether or not to get in touch with me. Okay?"

"Okay, Betsy."

Her eyes changed. "When people don't push me around, I'm nicer than this, really."

"And I'm less confused, as a rule."

"I don't know anything about your tastes—or your opportunities, but the less you give away to Charla, the more you'll get of her." She looked slightly uncomfortable. "Just don't let it dazzle you, Kirby. Just keep remembering she's one of the world's great experts on—horizontal persuasion. Keep your head, and we can make her pay and pay and pay."

"If there's anything to sell."

"If she wasn't convinced there is, she wouldn't be here." She patted his arm and stood up quickly. "I'll be waiting to hear from you. Wait five minutes before you leave."

4

THERE WERE NINE MESSAGES IN HIS BOX AT THE HOTEL BIRDLINE in downtown Miami. They all requested that he return the phone calls of Mr. D. LeRoy Wintermore, of Wintermore, Stabile, Schamway and Mertz, the law firm which handled Uncle Omar's personal matters—as opposed to the captive attorneys who handled the corporate affairs of Krepps Enterprises and all the other interlocking corporations.

Wintermore was a fragile snow-crested old man with, as Kirby had once heard his Uncle Omar say, a skeptical attitude toward all established institutions, including the law.

Kirby packed his two suitcases of personal gear before phoning Wintermore. It took him seven minutes. He phoned the number on the most recent slip and found he had reached D. LeRoy Wintermore at his home. It was Sunday, of course, but it did not feel like Sunday.

"Dear boy!" Wintermore said. "I was fretful about you. When you found what—uh—dispensation Omar had made, you seemed a shade surly."

"I wasn't exactly ecstatic. I don't think I'm greedy especially, but after all, there is supposed to be fifty-million kicking around some place."

"Possibly it was his intention to improve your character, Kirby."

"I have more than I can use now."

"At any rate, there seem to be a few minor difficulties to be ironed out. They want you at a high level conference at the Krepps offices tomorrow morning at ten."

"They?"

"Your uncle's elite corps of earnest executives. I shall be there too, by request, and if it appears that you need legal representation, I shall be ready to stand at your side. Fearlessly."

"What's up?"

"I have no idea, but they seem to have the impression there was some sort of collusion going on between you and Omar. Hidden assets. Something idiotic. They seem agitated. And something else has disturbed them. Since last Wednesday, every one of Omar's houses and apartments has been thoroughly ransacked."

"Really?"

"And they seem to want to connect it all up with whatever mysterious services you performed for Omar."

"Did he ever tell you what my work was?"

"Dear boy, I never asked."

"Mr. Wintermore, even though the only things mentioned in the will are the watch and the letter, won't I get all Uncle Omar's personal records and papers?"

"In the normal course of events, you would."

"But now I won't?"

"Omar had a rather serious warning of his heart condition three months ago. He came to my office and took personal material from our files and left us just the basic essential documents. I asked him what he was going to do with the papers he took. He said he was going to burn them. He smiled rather broadly and said he was going to burn everything. And then he took a silver dollar out of my left ear. He was extremely clever with his magic tricks. It is my understanding he did burn everything, except for one case of documents now in the main vault at Krepps Enterprises. A lovely man, dear boy. Lovely. But with a secrecy fetish. And the executive staff over there seem to find you infected by the same disease."

"I was following orders. I'll be there at ten, Mr. Wintermore."

He hung up and looked around the room and wondered if he would ever find reason to check into the Hotel Birdline again. It was centrally located, but sometimes the nights were made hideous by people hammering on the wrong doors and cawing in the hallways and striking one another with the damp sounds of expert impact until the sirens came. But it was cheap and reasonably clean and he could always get a room in or out of season, and the management stored, free of charge, that small store of personal possessions he did not take along with him on his world-wide errands of mercy, support and investment.

Now he carried his suitcases down to the desk, experiencing stomach pains which reminded him he'd forgotten lunch. Hoover Hess, the owner, was working the desk. He was a loose, asthmatic, scurfy man with the habitual expression of someone having his leg removed without anesthetic. His smile was a special agony. He had gone as high as a seventh mortgage and been down as low as a second. He averaged out at about four.

He smiled. "Hey, Kirb, this thing with your uncle. I'm sorry as hell. It happens like that sometimes. Bam! You're gone before you got time to fall down. How old was he?"

"Just turned seventy, Hoover."

"Well, I guess now you're set, hey?"

"Not exactly. I want to check out. I'll be over at the Elise on the Beach."

"Like I said, set. Taking a suite? Why not? Live it up, Kirb. Order up some broads. Order up some tailors. Drink that stuff from the good years."

"Well, I'll be sort of a guest over there, Hoover."

"Sure. Until the legal thing clears and they give you the bundle. I understand. And I'm sorry to lose a good customer. What I want you should do, Kirb, when you get the bundle, we'll sit down some place and let me show you the books on this thing. What I figure, consolidate the mortgages. It would be just the right kind of investment for you."

"I really won't have anything to invest, Hoover."

"I know how it goes. You got to have an answer. Every clown in the world comes around with hot deals, but you know me a long time, right? You don't have to give Hoover Hess any brushoff. I know you good too, Kirb. You play it just right. Nice and smooth and quiet. No fuss from any broad you bring here, right?"

"But I didn't—"

Hoover Hess waved a pale freckled hand. "Sure. Be cute. That's the way you play it. The one I see those times, she was a lady. The glasses is always good, the flat heels, the outfit like a school teacher. Some guy hasn't been around, he gets fooled, right? But you been around, you watch her walk, and you know it's class stuff, chin up, swinging that little round can only one sweet little inch side to side walking through here to the crummy elevator."

Kirby suddenly realized Hess was talking about Miss Farnham, Wilma Farnham, the only other staff member of Uncle Omar's secret give-away program, the one-woman clipping service, keeper of the files, translator of foreign news items, totally devoted to Uncle Omar's hidden program. She had been on the job six years, working out of a small office in a building far from the main offices of Krepps Enterprises. His field reports went to that office. The money was arranged through that office. Uncle Omar had assigned rough priorities to the projects she dug up. Then the two of them, Kirby and Miss Farnham, had worked out the schedules. When he was in town they often had evening conferences over work in progress and future missions in his room at the Birdline. She always pushed hard for the health things, the bush hospitals, the village ambulance services, the child nutrition programs. She was consistently dubious about the struggling little entrepreneurs, and always made Kirby feel she thought him too gullible for the job. She had worshipped Uncle Omar. He felt guilty, realizing this was the first time since returning he had wondered what would become of her now. But there stood Hoover Hess, leering at him.

Feeling that he was betraying and degrading Miss Farnham, he gave Hess a broad, knowing, conspiratorial wink.

"Out of them glasses," Hess said, "and out of them old-lady clothes, with her hair mussed and a drink in her, I bet she's a pistol, Kirb."

"How much do I owe you this time?"

"You're past checkout, but I won't charge you for today. You come in dawn Friday. Make it three nights, plus two phone calls. Comes to eighteen eighty-four. No credit card?"

"I had to turn them in."

"So who needs cards with so much cash coming? You can just sign if you want."

"I'll pay cash, Hoover. Thanks."

When he had his change, he walked to the lobby booth. No

point in trying the office to get Wilma Farnham. It was listed
under O.K. Devices. O.K. for Omar Krepps. He looked up Miss
Farnham's private number. After the phone rang eight times he
gave up and took a cab back out to the Beach and checked into
the Hotel Elise. The desk clerks were extraordinarily cordial.
Room 840 was ready for Mr. Winter. It was approximately six
times the size of his room at the Birdline, with chaises, tables,
gentle music, six shower controls, a sun deck, an ocean view,
vases of cut flowers, bowls of fruit, his dry-cleaned suit hanging in
the closet, the other laundry on a low chest of drawers. When he
was alone, he went out onto the sun deck. He could not see the
deck where he had walked out to be confronted by Charla supine,
but he estimated it was perhaps forty feet to his right, screened by
an architectural concession to privacy. He looked down. Little
brown people were stretched out on the bright sun cots near the
cabanas, looking like doll bodies awaiting the attentions of the
costumer. He went back into the room and over to the biggest
bowl of fruit. When he looked at it, it made him think of Charla.
He selected a pear, and it turned out to be such a superior pear,
he had to eat it over the bathroom sink, a deep oval of stainless
steel set into a long countertop covered with cherry-colored tile.
He looked at the rounded shape of the sink and thought of
Charla. He bit into the pear and thought of Charla. He glared
into his own mirrored eyes and thought of Charla. Finally he had
to dry his sweaty face on a hand towel and go stand in front of
the nearest air-conditioning vent.

  He went down into the ornate maze of bars and shops and din-
ing rooms in the bowels of the hotel and found a grill room that
would serve him a steak sandwich and coffee. It was after four.
He tried to sort things out logically. He wasn't very good at it.
Miss Farnham had always seemed skeptical of his attempts at orderly analysis. Uncle Omar had never seemed to mind when he
reached conclusions he could not justify through any exercise of
logic.

  Betsy Alden presented too many possibilities. He did not even
want to think about her. Thinking about her was like having a
dull headache. She could be a neurotic having hallucinations. She
could be absolutely accurate. Or she could be at any point between those two extremes.

I am not, he thought, so remarkable, so enchanting, so superior, that Joseph and Charla lay all this on because they can't help themselves. All over the world, whenever they found out I might come up with funds, I've been hustled, but never so good, never so completely. So they do want something. And it isn't the way you hustle a potential employee. As far as I know, I haven't got anything they want. But they think I have it or will have it. There is something somebody wants. It did well by Uncle Omar. Well enough, so that all the outposts have been ransacked, but according to Mr. Wintermore, there would have been nothing in any one of them, not even at the island.

I told them I have nothing. I'm still being hustled. I was too drunk to lie, so they must think I have something I don't know I have, or will get something later that I don't know about. The letter. As good a guess as any. Or maybe, as Betsy suggested, the personal papers.

So what are the ethics? Go along with it? Tell Betsy when I get a clue? Do I owe her anything? Maybe. It depends on how accurate she was. A little free ride shouldn't corrode the soul.

But how much corrosion is implicit in Charla Maria Markopoulo O'Rourke? Suddenly he realized he could readily check it out, indirectly at least. If Charla and Joseph were as influential as they seemed to be, and as powerful as Betsy implied, the Miami papers would have something about them in the morgue.

"Darling!" Charla said, sliding into the booth to sit facing him, reaching across to take his hand in hers. "Wherever have you been?" She wore a blue and white cotton print cut alarmingly low, and a totally frivolous hat. He felt the heat of her hands through white gloves. She stared at him so earnestly, so glowingly, so heatedly, he almost turned around to see who she could be looking at directly behind him. It was a dark corner of the grill, a paneled booth, a lamp with an orange shade. The impact of her made her seem larger than life, a face seen by courtesy of Eastman color when you sit too close to the screen. The nose was snubbed, the cheeks broad, the gray-green eyes slightly Asiatic, the hair milky, heavy, the shade of old ivory, mouth broad, lips heavy and slightly parted and delicately moist, disclosing the small, white, even teeth.

"Just—uh—errands," he said.

She released his hands, pouted at him. "I've been forlorn. I've missed you terribly. I even wondered if you'd been waylaid by my poor little confused niece."

"Uh—no."

"That's good, dear. She may try to tell you some of her mad nonsense. I should warn you in advance, I guess. I feel disloyal telling you these things about her because, after all, she is the daughter of one of my half-sisters. I guess we should have realized we'd have a problem with her when she was expelled from that nice school in Switzerland. But she did seem so sweet, at fifteen. We did our best by her, Kirby, but she has—a very weak grasp on reality. Possibly we should have institutionalized her. But—family, you know—one keeps trying. Actually, that's why I had her come here this time. More bad reports. But it might not do any good. She seems totally rebellious."

"Bad reports?"

"We try to keep track of her, discreetly. Darling Kirby, I don't want to bore you with family problems. But she is really terribly —unstable. She acts out her own fantasies."

"Oh?"

"She has accused me and Joseph of truly horrible behavior, and I haven't known whether to laugh or cry. Unscrupulous men have taken advantage of the way she seems compelled to act out the dreams in her strange mind."

"I beg your pardon?"

"She seems very erratic this time. She may approach you, Kirby. And she may try to make you a key figure in one of her fantasies. And when she does, she will probably throw herself at you."

"Throw herself at me?"

"It will just be another little drama she is constantly writing for herself in her mind. If it should happen, I can't tell you what to do. You seem like a most decent person, Kirby. If you refuse to play the male lead opposite her paranoid heroine, she'll probably find someone who will. She's reasonably attractive. Maybe it would be best if you—humored her. You would be gentle, wouldn't you?"

"B-But—"

"Thank you so much, dear. Just indulge her. Say what she wants to hear. I'll be trying to find another opening for her. I have some good friends in the entertainment world. Don't you think it is better for her to be free than to be shut away somewhere?"

"I guess so."

"One doctor suggested that it is a sublimation of something she does not want to face. By accusing me of vicious, horrible, incredible things she seems to ease her own feelings of guilt. To her I am some sort of dream figure living amidst monstrous conspiracies. Joseph and I joke about it sometimes, but it is a heartbreaking kind of humor. We're really not complicated. Perhaps we like to live too well, but we can afford it—even though we are always being cheated somehow. And maybe you will be taking that worry off our minds, dear."

"I haven't really—"

"They gave you an impossible room and I made them change it. Tomorrow you and I are going shopping. I know exactly the sort of clothing you should be wearing. And that haircut is really tiresome if I may say so. It's as if you are trying to sneak through life without being noticed, Kirby. And you have *so* much possibility. When I'm through with you, you'll walk through the world as if you own it and women will turn to stare at you and their eyes will go wide and their little hands will get moist and they'll make sly little plots to meet you."

"I don't think I exactly want that kind of—"

"You'll *relish* it, believe me. Come on now, dear. Joseph will be waiting for us in the suite. We'll have some drinks there, and the limousine will pick us up at seven-thirty and take us to a perfectly fabulous restaurant."

By ten-thirty that evening, Kirby Winter found himself taking particular pains to enunciate clearly. And sometimes, if he closed one eye, he could keep Joseph in better focus.

"Nice of you to invite me on a cruise," he said. "But I don't want to feel—"

"Obligated?" Joseph cried. "Nonsense! It is our pleasure!"

Kirby carefully turned his head and said, "Where'd she go?"

"To freshen her make-up perhaps."

"I don't dance often, Joe. I didn't mean to come down on her foot like that."

"She forgave you."

"But I keep remembering that scream."

"She is just unusually sensitive to pain, Kirby. Her nerves are closer to the surface than most. But since she is equivalently sensitized to pleasure, I imagine it is a characteristic she would not willingly give up."

"'Mazing woman," Kirby said solemnly. "'Mazing."

"I was just thinking, my boy, if you should feel you might be leading a parasitic life on the *Glorianna,* if it would offend your instincts, there is one project you might take on. And a worthwhile one I would say."

"Like what?"

"You were close to Omar Krepps. A fantastic man, fantastic career. But the world knows little about him. He saw to that. I think it would be a rather nice gesture of devotion and respect, dear boy, if you busied yourself with a biography of him. Later we could get some professional to put it in proper shape for publication. Just think of all his quiet charities which will never be recorded unless you do it. And there might be a kind of poetic justice in it. It might make you a bit of money."

"Interesting," Kirby said.

"I imagine that for a project like that, you could gather up his personal papers, documents and records."

"And bring them aboard, huh?"

"You'd be working aboard, would you not?"

"The mystery of Omar Krepps."

"Might make rather a nice title, that."

"Sometimes you sound English."

"I did have some schooling in England."

"You know, I bet you'd like to help me sort out those cases of personal records."

"Is there that much!"

"Hell, yes."

"I'd be happy to help, of course, if you need me."

Kirby felt shrewd as a fox. "All in storage under my name at the Hotel Birdline. Cases of crud. Diaries."

"I had no idea you had all that. You didn't mention it the other night."

"Forgot it."

"When the *Glorianna* gets in, we can have it all brought aboard."

"Oh sure."

"Aren't you acting a little strange, Kirby?"

"Me? Strange?" As he grinned the room tilted and then came slowly back. He felt reckless. "Joseph, old buddy, we're all strange, each in our own little way. You, me, Charla and Betsy."

"Betsy?"

He grinned broadly and drained his Irish coffee. "She's maybe the weirdest one of all. She can tell what's going to happen before it even happens. She's a witch, maybe."

Joseph's big, bronzed, glossy face was suddenly like something on a coin. "Just what did she predict, Kirby?"

Suddenly, too late, the alarms rang. The fox became a rabbit and ran under a bush.

"Who predict what, Joseph?"

"Has Betsy been talking to you?"

"Excuse. I think maybe I might be going to be a little bit sick."

He went into the men's room, leaned close to the mirror, and made strange savage faces at himself until somebody else came in. . . .

"Naughty boy," the gentle, chiding, loving voice said, husky-sweet in the night. "Oh, yes indeed, a very naughty boy." Fingers stroked his forehead. He opened his eyes cautiously. He saw a dark edge of building overhead, and half a sky full of stars. A head, bending over him, blocked out some of the stars. The face was in dark shadow, but light came from somewhere behind her, silvering the outline of her head.

"Dear God," he whispered.

"Oh yes, darling boy, you drank much too much. And such a waste, really. Such a waste of all manner of good things."

He moved his head slightly. There was a smooth, rounded, pneumatic warmth under the nape of his neck. As he began to wonder just what it was, a stir of the warm night breeze ran along his body and he felt as if he was entirely naked. He moved one hand cautiously. He was naked. He sat up abruptly in spite of the pain which split his head in two. He got his head up into the light for a moment before Charla took him by the shoulders and yanked him back down so firmly his head bounced once off the resilience of her thigh then settled into its previous position. At least he had gathered some information. He was on a sun deck, on a sun cot, and from the micro-glimpse of the room beyond, he guessed it was his own. Charla sat at the end of the cot, his head on her lap. And at least there was a reassuring layer of fabric over the rubbery convexity of his fleshy pillow.

"Don't leap like that, dear one," she said.

"I was just—"

"So naughty," she crooned. "Getting so squiffed. Lying to me. You shouldn't lie to me. You did see Betsy."

"For a minute." He hesitated. "Where my clothes?"

"Right here on the floor, sweet. After we got you up here and you passed out out here on the deck, you felt so sweaty and hot and miserable, I took them off."

"Oh."

"I'm really very angry with you. You don't know who your real friends are, do you?"

"I don't feel very good."

"Of course you don't! And you haven't acted very well. Just rest now. You've spoiled it all for us, for tonight. Didn't you know you were spoiling things for your Charla?"

"I didn't know it was—"

"Did you think I'd be so vulgar as to make an appointment? I'm a woman, darling. Maybe there'll be another night. Maybe not. Who can say?"

"The liquor hit me."

The fingertips closed his eyelids, then moved gently across his lips. "Maybe you were exhausted, dear. Maybe poor, stringy, little Betsy used all your resources."

"No! We just sat in a hotel and talked."

"Her hotel?"

"No. Just a hotel. In the lobby."

"And you listened to that poor crazed mind and began to doubt us. Where is she staying, dear?"

"An apartment."

"Do you know the address?"

"She didn't tell me."

"Don't you think you've done enough lying for one night?"

"Really, she didn't tell me. She said she'd get in touch."

"She knows you've moved here?"

"Yes."

"And when she does get in touch with you, you'll let me know, won't you, lover. Immediately."

"Oh yes. I'll do that, Charla."

She sighed. He felt the perfumed warmth of her exhalation against his face. "You have put me off, you know. Just a little. I told you, I have to be a little more than half in love. I think I was. But not now."

"I'm sorry. Please forgive me."

She held his head, eased herself out from under him and lowered his head to the woven plastic of the sun cot. She stood beside the cot for a moment looking down at him. Because of the darkness of the night, he was just able to keep from making some violent, ludicrous concession to modesty.

"I'll try to forgive you, darling. But you really must be very good from now on. I must leave you now."

The remembered mouth came slowly down upon his, flexing, changing, with soft heated movements. His arms went around her without volition, holding her with an increasing strength until suddenly he made a great Hoo-Aah sound and leaped like a stung horse, galvanized by the sudden, shocking, forceful, momentary grasp. She pulled free and, from the doorway into the room, laughed in a gentle mocking way, and was gone.

He lay quivering under the stars, then went in and had an icy shower, and left a call for nine o'clock. It was a few minutes before three. He found a switch for the deck light and picked up his clothes. After he sorted them out and hung them up, he turned off the deck light and went out again into the April night to sit on the wide concrete wall at the end of the deck, sit naked on the abrasive texture, his back against the solidity of the hotel, knees flexed, forearms on his knees, hands slack, cigarette in the corner of his mouth. He could look to his left and straight down, down past architectural solutions, straight down through an obscured and dizzy vista to a tiled death below. He could look straight out at a night-dark sea and sense the slow pulse of the swells and the tides. He could look to his right and see the few highlights of the aseptic sun cot, a prop in a play now over. The wind was fresher, almost cool enough to be uncomfortable. His heart rapped a little too fast, and he had a dull headache. But these physical stigmata were minor compared with his emotional trauma. Charla, with a single vulgar tweak, had reduced him to clownishness, had turned consternation into farce, had shown, symbolically, her ability to destroy his pride, dignity and manhood at her option.

He thought sourly of all the should-have-done things. Another man, a real man, might well have burst from the couch with a roar of rage at such playful violation of privacy, grasped her, swung her onto the couch and ravished her there, under the stars, a fitting punishment for impertinence. (But maybe that was really what she was asking of him!)

He wondered what, long ago, had created this incapacity to deal with people like Charla. He looked out at the sea and wondered why he should be afraid of anything, of anyone. The sea went on, and the shore people changed, but there were stars so lasting that the sea itself was smaller than the life of one man in comparison. Compared to the sea, compared to the stars, of what moment was one snatch of the fishwife hand, one small humiliation, on one night, for one man?

He thought of her hands, small, strong, quite square-looking, beautifully kept, the nails long and curving, the pads of the palms prominent.

He groaned and snapped his cigarette toward the sea and went to bed.

THE EXECUTIVE CONFERENCE ROOM WAS SIXTEEN STORIES ABOVE the street, with a huge window framing the bay, a segment of causeway and distant pastel confections of hotels out on the

Beach. The decor was lime and white, and the big round table and the captains' chairs were lusterless black.

There were eight men at the table. D. LeRoy Wintermore sat at Kirby's left. At his right was a square, pale, motionless fellow named Hilton Hibber, representing the trust department of the bank named executor in Omar Krepps' will. The other five men were Krepps Enterprises executives. They depressed Kirby. They always had. He could not tell them apart. They all had names like Grumby and Groombaw and Gorman. They all had snowy linen, gold accessories and an air of reverence. And they all had big fleshy faces weathered to a look of distinction, perfect governors on television dramas.

And he had always found their general attitude tiresome. They seemed to resent the frivolity of the decision to have the main offices in Miami. And somehow they had pigeonholed Omar Krepps as being a rather ludicrous eccentric, a little man who complicated their grave chores by hopping around picking up odd bits and pieces of businesses which they then had to fit into the measured structure of empire. And they had never tired of trying to tuck O.K. Devices into the fold. In far countries Kirby had always been getting little multicolored forms with small holes in them and blanks for him to fill out. Uncle Omar had told him to ignore them and he did. But they kept trying, and sometimes they would write him sad scolding letters.

The middle one called the meeting to order and said, "Let me recap the terms of Mr. Krepps' will, gentlemen. All the assets of the estate are to be turned over to the Omar Krepps Foundation. Krepps Enterprises will be slowly liquidated over a period of time as its holdings in other corporations are transferred. We five executives of K.E. become officers and directors of the Foundation, in addition to our continuing corporate duties. It has occurred to us, Mr. Winter, that it would be fitting that you should be connected with the Foundation in some active capacity. We are mindful of the fact that Mr. Krepps left you no money in his will. We shall need an executive secretary for the Foundation, and we are prepared to offer you a salary of twenty-five thousand dollars a year."

"I haven't asked for anything," Kirby said.

The five looked sternly at him. "You are unemployed, are you not?" the spokesman asked.

"At the moment."

"Gentlemen!" said D. LeRoy Wintermore suavely. "You are giving me and my client here the impression some deal is underway. But we cannot properly assess its merits until we know what you expect of him."

"Your client?" the spokesman asked. "Isn't that a conflict of interest?"

"No indeed," the old man said.

Hilton Hibber cleared his throat. "Perhaps I can shed some light. In going over the summary records for tax purposes, I find that over the past eleven years, some twenty-seven million dollars in cash and liquid assets have been drained from the asset structure of K.E. and turned over to O.K. Devices. Inasmuch as all taxes were paid on this money, Internal Revenue took no particular interest in it. But O.K. Devices was entirely owned by Omar Krepps. And now they wish to consider that twenty-seven million part of the estate. If they do, scraping up the tax money on that amount would gut the structure of K.E. and reduce the scope of the Foundation seriously. The current books of O.K. Devices were turned over to me. They were maintained by Miss Wilma Farnham, who, aside from Mr. Winter, was the only other employee of O.K. Devices. The books show a current asset value of four hundred dollars. There are no notes payable or receivable, no accounts payable or receivable." He hesitated and took out a white handkerchief and wiped his face, though the conference room was cool. "In fact, there are no records at all, aside from the depreciation account on office equipment."

"And we know why there are no records," the spokesman said in a strangled tone. "Miss Farnham claims she was following Mr. Krepps' instructions. She hired a truck and helpers, and on the day following the death of Mr. Krepps, she took all the files and records to a remote area and burned them. She stacked them, poured kerosene on them, and burned them, by God!"

"Most unfortunate," Mr. Wintermore murmured.

"Furthermore," Mr. Hibber said, "the Revenue people will assume this was done to conceal the location of the hidden assets.

Obviously they will eventually subpoena both Miss Farnham and Mr. Winter in an attempt to extract information regarding these assets. So I suggest that—uh—co-operation at this point on the part of Mr. Winter might be beneficial to all."

Everyone looked at Kirby Winter. "Let me understand this," he said. "You're in a tax jam. You don't know what I've been doing for the past eleven years, and you are dying to know. If I explain what I've been doing and what happened to the twenty-seven million dollars, then I get a nice reward of an undemanding job for life."

The spokesman smiled. "Badly stated, of course. But if you should refuse the offer, you can't blame us for suspecting that some of this missing money might be—diverted to your private account."

"That statement is slanderous, sir," Wintermore said tartly.

The spokesman shrugged. "Perhaps. But we're all realists here. We have to protect ourselves."

Kirby leaned back in his chair and studied the intent faces. "You just want to know where all that money is, huh?"

He saw six eager nods, six pairs of glittering eyes.

He smiled at them. "It's gone."

"Gone!" It was a sound of anguish.

"Sure. I gave it all away."

Consternation turned immediately to indignation. The spokesman said, "This is hardly the time for frivolous responses, Winter. Mr. Krepps was eccentric. But not that eccentric." He leaned forward and struck the table with his fist. "Where is that money?"

"I gave it away," Kirby said. "You asked me. I told you. I gave it away."

"My client has given you his answer," Wintermore said.

"In view of Mr. Winter's attitude, I see little point in continuing this meeting," the spokesman said. "His attitude is not unlike Miss Farnham's attitude. Obviously they are agreed not to co-operate with us. May I ask your plans, Mr. Winter?"

"I might go on a cruise."

"With twenty-seven million dollars?" Hibber asked in a cold voice.

"I never carry more than fifty dollars in cash."

"Where do you keep the rest of it?"

"I gave it all away." He leaned to his right and whispered to the elderly attorney.

Wintermore straightened up and said, "As the only living relative, my client is entitled to whatever personal papers and documents Mr. Krepps left here."

All five executives looked uncomfortable. "He left a case of documents in the vault here," the spokesman explained. "When we were faced with—this problem, we examined them. It would seem to be—some sort of a joke. The case contains fifty or so pounds of texts and pamphlets on jokes and magic. Decks of marked cards. Handkerchief tricks. Interlocking rings. The old man was—rather strange you know. The case is back in the vault —any time you care to send for it."

On the taxi ride back to Wintermore's office, the old man was silent and thoughtful. When they were in his private office, he began to make a strange sound. Kirby looked at him with alarm. Wintermore's face was dark. Suddenly Kirby realized the old lawyer was laughing.

"Oh dear, oh dear," Wintermore said. "Forgive me. I have added up all the little clues in a long friendship. Oh dear. Yes indeed. There is no other answer. You did give the money away."

"That's what I told them."

"But you see, they can never believe it. It is a concept so monstrous, they rebel at it. Omar delighted in practical jokes. And this is the biggest practical joke in financial history. Wherever he is, he is laughing as helplessly as I am. Those p-poor earnest fellows! And I am sure Miss Farnham was following his instructions when she burned the records." Wintermore blew his nose and stood up and said, "I'll get your watch."

"Doesn't the will have to be probated or something first?"

"Not for keepsakes, Kirby."

Wintermore came back in a few moments with a fat, old-fashioned, gold pocket watch on a worn chain. The watch was running and on time. On the other end of the chain was a charm in the shape of a little gold telescope. Kirby looked at the watch and then he looked through the telescope, turning it toward the windows. The light illuminated a little interior scene done with photographic realism. Kirby gasped and stared and then looked questioningly at Wintermore.

"My dear fellow, your uncle did not care to live with a woman. But that does not mean he found them entirely useless. He was a man, even as you and I."

"I feel as if I never knew him at all."

"He was not an easy man to know."

"He always seemed—impatient with me, as if I was a disappointment."

Wintermore leaned back in his leather armchair. "He didn't say much about you, Kirby, but when he did I detected a certain amount of anxiety. It was as if he was terribly anxious that you should be ready. As if some great trial or task would eventually be given you. I wouldn't say he faulted you for diligence or imagination. But he seemed to be waiting, with decreasing patience, for you to stand on your own two feet."

"God knows I tried to quit often enough."

"Quit and go crawl into a hole was the way he put it, I believe. Once he wondered aloud in my presence if you were going to be a ninny all your life. Forgive me, but the quote is exact."

"I don't feel hurt. I've wondered the same thing."

"If Omar could have seen you this morning, he would have been heartened."

"Would he?"

"You were splendid, my boy. Skeptical, indignant, indifferent. I would have expected you to apologize to those five impressive gentlemen for any inconvenience you had caused them, make a full statement of what your duties have been, and gladly accept the position they offered."

"You know, I'm surprised I didn't. But people have been pushing me around ever since I got back here."

"You baffled them, Kirby. You gave them no leverage, no handle, no button to push. So naturally they think you were speaking with the independence of hidden millions."

"So Uncle would have been heartened. So what? It came a little late, didn't it?"

"It would seem so."

Kirby looked again through the telescope, sighed and put the watch in his pocket. "Let them squirm for a while. I'll take them off the hook when I'm ready. Or maybe I won't. I don't know."

"They won't just sit there wringing their hands, you know. Expect some sort of counterattack."

"When it comes, you can tell me what to do. You're my attorney."

"It would be interesting to know what Omar had in mind. I do wish we could open that letter he left for you. But I have had a long and ethical career, young man, because I have had the good judgment never to trust myself. We have a Mr. Vitts in this office, a man of truly psychotic dependability. I had him put that letter in his personal safety deposit box. Mr. Vitts delights in sacred trusts. Boiling him in oil would not give anyone access to that letter one day sooner."

"Before the year is up, I may have a better idea of what's in it."

"If you ever have a plausible guess please tell me. Omar was a strange fellow. He made no wrong moves. I've often wondered at the secret of his success, and the only answer that seems even halfway reasonable is that, long ago, he devised certain mathematical procedures which enabled him to predict future events. I keep wondering if those formulae are in that letter. It would account for his anxiety about you. The ability to predict would be a terrifying responsibility."

Kirby frowned and nodded. "It would account for those gambling winnings when I was a kid. And then he lost them back on purpose, so people would leave him alone."

"I intend to live through this year, too. Just to learn what is in the letter."

Kirby walked from Wintermore's office to a neighborhood drugstore for a sandwich and coffee. One little word kept rebounding from the cerebral walls. Ninny. It was a nineteenth-century word, yet he could not find a modern equivalent with the same shade of meaning. Probably it was a corruption of nincompoop. Ninny—that soft, smiling, self-effacing, apologetic fellow, the type who is terribly sorry when you happen to step on his foot, the kind you can borrow money from in the certainty he will never demand you repay it. And if he was a little brown dog, he'd wear his tail tucked slightly under, and wag it nervously, end-lessly.

He wondered at his own degree of ninnyism. How severe was it? How incurable was it? Could a man walk through life in a constant readiness to duck? On the other hand, were not the op-posite traits rather unpleasant? Arrogance, belligerence, domina-tion. Yet the arrogant man seemed to have considerably less difficulty with one primary aspect of existence.

"Girls," he said aloud. A fat woman on the adjoining stool turned and gave him a long cold stare. Kirby felt himself flush and felt his mouth begin to stretch into a meek smile of apology. As he began to hunch over, he straightened his shoulders, lifted his chin and said, "Madame, I was talking to myself, not to you. If you feel you're in the presence of a dangerous nut, I suggest you move to another stool."

"Whaddaya? Some wise guy?"

"You glared at me, so I responded."

"All kinda nuts in Miami," she muttered and hunched herself over her tuna fish.

Kirby felt a small glow of pride. Perhaps not completely a ninny. But one had to start in small ways. One had to emerge, step by step, from ninnyism, acquiring confidence at each small victory.

Actually, at the conference, he hadn't given a true ninny reac-tion. Ninnyism would require making a detailed statement of what he had been doing for O.K. Devices, and making them be-lieve it. He had told the truth, but as a gesture of revolt, had made it sound like an evasion. In all honesty he had to admit that it was the intransigence of Miss Wilma Farnham which had back-stopped his moments of rebellion. Let the executives sweat.

When a chunky girl came to take his money he braced himself and said, "The coffee is lousy."

"Huh?"

"The coffee is lousy."

She gave him a melting smile. "Boy! It sure is."

He went to the phone booths and called Wilma Farnham at her apartment. She answered on the second ring, her voice cool and precise.

"Kirby Winter. I tried to get you yesterday," he said.

"Yes?"

"Well, I thought we ought to talk."

"You did?"

"What's the matter with you?"

"Nothing's the matter with me, Mr. Winter. The office has been closed. I've turned the books over to the attorneys. I'm seeking other employment. Mr. Krepps left me a generous bequest, but I shan't receive it for some months they tell me. The relationship is over, I would say. Good-by, Mr. Winter."

He called her back. "What could you possibly have to say to me, Mr. Winter?"

"Listen, Miss Farnham. Wilma. I heard you burned all the records."

"That is correct."

"So it looks as if the tax people might subpoena us—"

"Mr. Winter! I knew you would call me. I knew that the instant Mr. Krepps died you'd forget your word of honor to him. I intend to *keep* my word, Mr. Winter. I would rot in prison rather than break my word to that great man. But I knew you would immediately start currying favor with everybody by telling them everything you know. Believe me, there is no longer any documentation for anything you have told them or will tell them. And you cannot wheedle me into breaking my word, or frighten me into breaking my word. You are a miserable, sycophantic weakling, Mr. Winter, and I would say your uncle overestimated you all your life. Don't bother me again, please."

And once again the line was dead.

Twenty minutes later he was pressing the bell for her apartment. When she answered over the communicator and he told her who he was, there was a silence. The lock was not released. He pressed other bells at random. The door buzzed and he pushed it open and went into the tiny lobby. The elevator was in use. He went up two flights of stairs, found her apartment in the rear and beat upon the door with his fist.

"Go away!" she yelled.

He kept hammering. A door down the hall opened. A woman stared at him. He gave her a maniac grin and she ducked back into her apartment.

Finally the door swung open. Wilma Farnham tried to block the way, but he pushed roughly by her, turned and shut the door.

"How dare you!"

"Now *there's* a great line. It swings, Wilma."

"You're stinking drunk!"

"I'm stinking indignant. Now you sit down, shut up and listen." He took her by the shoulders, walked her backward into the couch and let go. She fell back with a gasp of shock and anger.

"Nothing you can say to me—"

"Shut up!" He stared at her. She wore a burly, shapeless, terry-cloth robe in a distinctly unpleasant shade of brown. Her brown hair fell to her shoulders. She was not wearing her glasses. Her small face was wrinkled with distaste, and she squinted at him myopically. "What the hell gives you the impression you've got this monopoly on loyalty and virtue and honor, Wilma? What makes you so damn quick to judge everybody else, on no evidence at all? What gives you the right to assume you know the slightest damn thing about me, or how I'd react to anything?"

"B-but you always just sort of drift with—"

"Shut up! You did as you were told. That's fine. My congratulations. But it doesn't make you unique. I did as I was told, too. I did not tell them one damn thing."

She stared at him. "You're trying to trick me somehow."

"For God's sake, call any of the brass. Ask them."

She looked at him dubiously. "Not a thing?"

"Nothing."

"But those lawyers told me you would tell everything. They said it was the only way you'd get a dime out of the estate."

"They made just as bad a guess as you did."

"Did you just say—nothing? Just refuse to talk?"

"I did better than that. I told them something they couldn't possibly accept—something they couldn't possibly believe."

"What?"

"I told them I gave it all away."

Her eyes were suddenly too round for squinting. "But—that's—"

Suddenly she began to giggle. He would not have thought her capable of any sound so girlish. Then she began to guffaw. He laughed with her. Her hoots and shouts of laughter became wilder, and the tears were running down her small face, and suddenly he realized her laughter had turned into great sobs, great wrenching spasms of grief and pain.

He went to her, sat with her. She lunged gratefully into his arms, ramming her head into the side of his throat, snorting, snuffling, bellowing, her narrow body making little spasmed leapings with her sobs, and he could make out a few words here and there. "Sorry—so alone—ashamed—didn't mean—"

He held her and patted her and said, "There, there, there."

At last she began to quiet down. He became conscious of the fresh clean smell of her hair, and of the soft warmth of her against him, and of a hint of pleasant contour under the dreary robe. She gave a single great hiccup from time to time. Abruptly, she stiffened in his arms, thrust herself away and scrambled to the far end of the couch.

"Don't come near me! Don't touch me, you son of a bitch!"

"Wilma!"

"I know all about you. Maybe the rest of them roll right over on their back, but you better not get the idea I'm going to."

"What the hell!"

"Hah! A wonderful imitation of innocence, Kirby Winter. I'm glad you're loyal to your uncle, but that doesn't mean I have to respect the *other* things you stand for.

"I knew what you had in mind, setting up those little conferences in that sordid hotel room. We both knew what you were after, didn't we? That's why I was on guard every single moment. I knew that if I gave you the slightest opportunity, you would have been after me like a madman."

"What?"

"I was on guard every single minute. I had no intention of becoming your Miami plaything, Mr. Winter. You got enough of that, all over the world. I used to go to that room in absolute terror. I knew how you looked at me. And I thanked God, Mr. Winter, I thanked God for being so plain you weren't likely to lose control of yourself. And I made myself plainer when I came to that room. Now that it's all over, I can tell you another thing too, something that makes me sick with shame. Sometimes, Mr. Winter, in all my fear and all my contempt, I found myself wanting you to hurl yourself at me."

"Hurl myself!"

"It was the devil in my heart, Mr. Winter. It was a sickness of the flesh, a crazy need to degrade myself. But I never gave way to it. I never gave you the slightest hint."

"All we did was sit in that room and go over the reports and—"

"That's what it *looked* like, yes. Ah, but how about the things unsaid, Mr. Winter, the turmoil and the tension underneath. What about that, Mr. Winter?"

He raised his right hand. "Miss Farnham, I swear before God that I never, for the slightest moment, felt the smallest twinge of desire for—"

He stopped abruptly. He saw anew the neat sterility of the apartment, the plain girl, the look on her face of sudden realization, hinting at the horrible blow to her pride that would soon be evident. And he knew that even if she was slightly mad, he could not do that to her.

He dropped his hand abruptly and gave her a wicked wink. "I guess I can't get away with that, can I?"

"Beg pardon?"

He winked again. "Hell, baby, I used to see you walking, swinging that little round can one sweet inch from side to side and I used to think—uh—if I could just get you out of those glasses and those old-lady clothes and muss your hair up a little and get a drink into you, you'd be a pistol."

"Y-you filthy animal!"

He shrugged. "But, like you said, cutie, you never gave me an opening. You never made the slightest move."

She seemed to cover the distance from the couch to a doorway across the room in a single bound. She whirled and stared at him. Her face was pale. Her mouth worked. "Th-then," she whispered, "if I didn't—why in God's name didn't you?"

In the trembling silence he reached for the right response, but all he could find was his own terrible moment of truth. He felt impelled to meet it. "Because—I'm scared of women. I try to hide it. Women terrify me."

She wore an expression of absolute incredulity. She took a half-step toward him. "But you're so—so suave and so—"

"I'm a lousy fake, Wilma. I run like a rabbit, all the time."

She bit her lip. "I—haven't had many chances to run. But I always have. Like a rabbit. But you!"

"You're the first person I've ever told."

Suddenly she began to laugh again, but he could not laugh with her. He heard the laughter climbing toward hysteria.

"No," he said. "Not again! Please."

She whooped, whirled, bounded through the doorway and slammed the door. He could hear her in there, sounding like a small stampede heading through swamp country. He slowly paced back and forth until the sound diminished and finally died away. He sat in a chair, his back toward the bedroom door.

"Wilma!" he called.

"In a minute," she answered, her voice husky from weeping.

He took the gold watch out. He looked cautiously through the little telescope and shivered. He was studying the intricate monogram on the back of the watch when the bedroom door opened.

"He always carried that," she said. "Always."

"I guess I will. I'll have to wear a vest or get some kind of a belt clip arrangement."

She was behind him, looking over his shoulder. Suddenly he was inundated by an almost strangling cloud of perfume.

"Sometimes he'd look through that little telescope and then he'd chuckle."

"I bet."

"I asked him about it once. He wouldn't let me look through it. He said I didn't speak the language. I didn't understand. Will you let me look through it?"

"I—uh—maybe when—uh—"

She came around the chair. She made a wide circle around it and stood where he could see her for the first time, some eight feet away. He tried to swallow but could manage only half the process. "Bought it two years ago," she said in a grave whisper. "Tried it on once."

She had brushed the brown hair until it gleamed, and for the first time he saw the reddish highlights in it. She was facing him squarely, but she had her face turned away from him. She stood like a recruit who had just been chewed out for bad posture. She was not trembling. Rather she seemed to be vibrating in some galvanic cycle too fast for the eye to perceive. He had the feeling that if he snapped his fingers all the circuits would overload and she'd disappear in a crackle of blue flame and a hot smell of insulation. He slowly began to strangle on the half-completed swallow. She wore a single garment. He could not guess at what possible utility it might have. There was an inch-wide ruffle of black lace around her throat. There were similar visible ruffles around her wrists. There was a third circling her hips, apparently floating in air several inches away from the pale and slender thighs. The three visible bands of black seemed joined together by some incredible substance as intangible as a fine layer of city soot on a windshield. Miraculously affixed to this evanescence, and perfectly umbilically centered, was the pink, bloated, leering face, on some sturdier fabric, of the most degenerate looking rabbit he had ever seen.

He completed the swallow with such an effort, it felt as if he were swallowing a handful of carpet tacks. For a tenth of a second he marveled at the uncanny insight of one Hoover Hess, and with a sobbing sound of guilt, inadequacy and despair, he roared out of the apartment and down the corridor toward the stairs. He heard a howl of frustration, and a long, hoarse, broken cry of, "Oh you baaaaaaastaaaarddd!" As he clumped down the stairs the corridor fire door swung slowly shut, and he heard those hoots of laughter again, heard them begin to soar upward, and then the door closed and he could hear no more.

Two blocks from the apartment building he suddenly heard himself saying, "For God's sake, Wilma!" and realized he had been saying the same thing over and over for some time. The gold watch was still clutched in his hand. Two old ladies were staring at him with strange expressions. He slowed his headlong stride, put the watch in his pocket and gave them an ingratiating smile. One old lady smiled back. The other one tilted her chin at the sky, braced herself, and with a volume that made every car in that block give a startled swerve, screamed, "Stop thief!"

It panicked him into a dead run, but as soon as he was around the next corner he slowed down, his legs trembling. He stood staring blindly into a bookstore window until his breathing was normal. He oriented himself and discovered he was seven or eight blocks from the Hotel Birdline. Suddenly, for the first time since telling it, he remembered the lie about Uncle Omar's personal records. He remembered how crafty he had felt when telling it. Sober, he knew it was a blundering stupidity.

He went to the Birdline. The one without any space between his eyes was at the desk, the one with the volcanic acne. The clerk leaned into the small office beyond the switchboard and yelled to Hoover Hess. Hess came out, rubbing his hands, projecting the smile of agony.

"Kirb, buddy, you ready to talk business? You can't make a better—"

"Not right now, Hoover. I'm a little too rushed. I was wondering about my stuff you've got here. I thought I'd—"

"Understand, I'm a guy appreciates a sweet gesture, but I told you so long as I got the room down there, the storage was on the house, right?"

"Yes."

"And I'm the kind of a guy wouldn't change the deal on account of you inheriting big, right?"

"But—"

"So what I mean is, I'm touched by the fifty bucks, Kirb. It was a nice thing to do, believe me."

"Fifty?"

Hess looked shocked. "Was it more? Did those slimy bastards take a clip out of it on the way over here?"

"Uh—no. It wasn't any more."

"Rest easy, Kirb. They come and got the trunk and the big wooden case along about eleven this morning."

"Who?" he said weakly.

"The guys from the Elise! In the truck from the Elise! Chrissake, don't you even remember who you sent after it? Look, if you could come in and sit down for just five minutes, Kirb, I could fill you in on the whole picture. The way I figure, in exchange for consolidating the mortgages and bringing it down to an interest rate that makes sense, instead of the cannibal rates I got to pay, what you should have is a piece of it. I even got an inspiration about your name, to go with the place. The Winter House. How about that!"

"Some other time, Hoover."

"Any time you say. I'll drop everything. Everything."

Kirby headed across the lobby toward the pay phone. He had

to skid to a stop to let a sailor by. The sailor had considerable ve-locity. He was skidding across the tile floor, revolving slowly, his eyes closed. He was smiling. He carried on into three short wide men in tense argument over a racing form, catapulted the three of them into a couch and went on over with them as the couch went over backwards.

He dialed Betsy's memorized phone number.

"Kirby! I was about to come looking for you. I tried the hotel a thousand times. Are you there now?"

"No. Look, I think you were right, at least a little bit right any-how."

"Thanks a lot!"

"Don't be so sarcastic. The way things are going, how am I ex-pected to trust anybody?"

"Why Kirby, dear! Your teeth are showing."

"I think I did a stupid thing. I mean I thought it was shrewd, but I was drunk at the time."

"It's a poor week for it."

"I know. But it worked, sort of. But I've got the idea they're going to be awfully damned mad. And I was supposed to meet her at two o'clock over there. She was going to take me shop-ping."

"Standard procedure. She has a wonderful way of getting all her men to end up looking exactly alike. They all end up looking like fairy ski instructors. I think it's the tan, the sideburns and the ascot that does it. She's mad for ascots. And it's a long way after two, Kirby."

"I have the feeling it wouldn't be too smart to go over there now. Let me tell you just what—"

"Come on over here. We can talk. I hate phones."

"I'd rather tell you over the phone."

"Come on over here. I'm alone. We can thrash it all out."

"But—but—but—"

"Get over here on the double, you clown!" She hung up.

A little word started bounding about in the back of his mind. It was made of fat little letters, fabric letters, stuffed. NINNY. The fabric, curiously, was the same shade of pink as the face of the lecher rabbit centered on Miss Farnham's gossamer funsuit. He squared his shoulders. He walked carefully around the broiling brutal confusion of cops, sailors and horse players in the front of the lobby, deaf to the resonant tock of hickory against bone, and took the single cab in front.

As they pulled away, the driver said, "Like they got Saturday night on Monday afternoon in there, huh?"

"What?"

"The riot, man!"

"Sorry, I didn't notice it particularly."

After a long silence the driver said, "I don't know what the hell kind of date you got, mister. All I know is I wisht I had it."

He had trouble finding the address. It was a crooked little bayfront street, more alley than street. The building had been added onto in random fashion over the years, and each segment of it seemed to sag in a different direction. Apartment Four, when he finally found it, was one flight up, via an open iron stairway bolted to the side of the building. The door was painted an orange so bright it seemed deafening. Over the bell was lettered *b. sabbith*. He was tempted to press the doorframe with his thumb an inch below the bell, wait ten seconds, then flee down the staircase. "Ninny," he whispered and pressed the bell. There was a tiny porthole in the door. A green eye looked out at him. The door swung open.

"Come in and look at this creepy place," she said. She was in stretch pants again. Plaid. And a sleeveless blue blouse. Barefoot. Cigarette in the corner of her mouth. Toffee hair in harsh disarray.

Most of the apartment was a big studio room. He saw a kitchen alcove and a single door which had to lead to a bath. Glass doors opened out onto a tiny breakfast porch.

She stood, hipshot, and included the whole decor in one wave of her arm. "Observe. Rugs to your ankles. Strategic lighting. Cutie little hearth with, for God's sake, a dynel tiger skin in front of it. Any chair you sit in, you need a helping hand to get out of. That damned bed is nine by nine, and twenty inches high. I measured it. The little library is all erotica. Seventeen mirrors. I counted. Thirty-one pillows. Counted them, too. In the way of groceries, one-half box of stale crackers, one-half box of stale puffed wheat, twenty-one cans of cocktail goodies, two bottles gin, fourteen bottles wine. Make a wild guess, Winter. What is Bernie's hobby?"

"Uh—philately?"

She spun and grinned at him. "You come on slow, but sort of nice, Kirby. I figured you for a fatal case of the dulls. Maybe not. I recommend this couch over here. It's the only thing you can get out of without a hoist. It must have come with the place." She sat down, patted the place beside her and said, "The detailed report, friend."

He told her all, with a little editing here and there. She seemed quieter, more thoughtful than the last time he had talked to her. "What's the stuff you had stored?"

"Just personal junk. Books, records, photographs. Tennis stuff. Hunting stuff. Even a pair of ice skates."

"That's a nice touch. Ice skates. That'll make them very happy. But we are forwarder. Now you know for sure they want something. Uncle's personal records. The clue to the edge he had over the competition. And you say there aren't any records at all. Are you sure?"

"Pretty sure."

"Could the Farnham broad have something tucked away? She sounds desperately loyal."

"I doubt it."

"Charla and Joseph are going to be very irritable, Kirby. But I think they'll think you're still the best link to what they want. And I don't think they know exactly what they do want. But they want it bad. Badly enough so they shouldn't treat you too badly. You sure you didn't give them my address? While drunk?"

"If I had, they wouldn't be trying to find out."

"They don't want us to get together on this. They'd rather deal with a goof, not somebody I've toughened up for them."

"I don't care much for that word, Betsy."

"Oh, for goodness sake, be honest with yourself. If I hadn't planted the seeds of suspicion, Charla'd have you on a leash by now, trotting you around, scratching you behind the ears, tying your new ascots, and giving you the slow strip and tease routine, until you wouldn't be able to remember your name if somebody asked you quick."

"I'm not so sure."

"You just don't know Aunt Charla. Hell, where are we? I think you ought to trudge on back there and play cute. Make out you know what they're after. Admit you tricked them. Say you'll listen to an offer. Maybe then we'll get a better clue as to what they really want, if they know."

"I don't think I'm very good at this sort of thing."

"I *know* you're not very good at it. But hang in there. I think we might get some volunteer help. Bernie's coming down soon with a crew and some models and so on to do some commercials here. Mad ones all. Maybe they'll help us add a little more confusion to the deal."

"Do we need more?"

"Poor Kirby."

"The thing is, in eleven years you get sick of dealing with people you know you'll never see again. I kept wanting to get out. I had this idea of maybe finding a town way off a main road with maybe twenty-eight people in it, so I would know them and they would know me, tomorrow, next year, ten years from now. I could stop trying to remember names and faces. And I'd know where I was before I woke up in the morning, instead of figuring it out afterward."

"With me," she said, "it's a dream of being back in that school. I was there for six years, you know. From nine to fifteen, the longest I've ever been anywhere. And I dream a class is leaving and I have to leave too, and I'm crying. But then they take me out of the line and I know I can stay, and it's the most wonderful thing. All the others are marching away, but they're going to keep me."

"But they didn't."

"Charla came in a car big as a freight engine, with a driver in uniform and an English Lady Something with her who made a horrible snorting sound when she laughed. I was supposed to be in a play at school, but they didn't give a damn. They drove me to Paris and bought me a lot of clothes. We met some other people there, and then we all flew to Cairo."

"Sometimes you have more accent."

"I can get rid of every trace of it when I have to."

"Could Charla have arranged to have my uncle's places—robbed?"

"Why not? It isn't her usual style. It's a bit crude, and probably quite expensive. But she has the pragmatic approach."

"They won't be able to get that letter."

"They can afford to wait a year. And all you got was a keepsake."

He took the watch from his pocket. She reached over and took it from him. "A real grandpa kind of watch." Before he could stop her, she looked through the little gold telescope.

"Happy days," she said in a tired voice. "Don't let Bernie see this. It's all this apartment needs. There's room on that wall for a mural." She took another look. "They make this junk in Japan. A girl in school had a candybox full. Hers were all set in rings." She handed the watch back to him. Just as he put it back into his pocket, she leaned toward him, reached toward him. Because of his humiliating flight from Wilma's apartment, he had resolved to fight fire with fire. He reached toward Betsy. His aim was defective. His palm slid into and across an abrupt nubbin of breast, frank and firm under the blue blouse as an apple in the sun. And he saw a glimpse of teeth in something not a smile, and something flashed and smashed against the left side of his face. The sudden pain filled his eyes with tears. She was a blur. As vision cleared he saw her looking gravely at him as she sucked her knuckles. With the tip of his tongue he isolated the metallic crumb in his mouth, moved it out to his lips, plucked it out and stared at it. It was a piece of filling. It made a small clinking sound as he dropped it into the ashtray.

In the silence she reached for him again, took his cigarettes from his shirt pocket, took one out of the pack and put the pack back.

"Get carried away by the decor?" she asked.

"I just thought—"

"Maybe Charla has warped your values, pal. Maybe with her it's a social gesture, like passing the butter. Or asking for the next dance. Not with me, Winter. I put a higher value on myself."

"She said it was the other way around," he said miserably.

"How many lies are you going to believe?"

"From now on—not very many."

"I didn't mean to hit quite that hard, Kirby."

"I've had better days than this one, I guess."

She got up and moved across the room. Again he marveled at her talent for expression. The stretch pants projected demureness, regret and impregnability. She fiddled with a panel board on the far wall. Suddenly he heard a rising, hissing scream and knew a jet was diving into the building. As he sprang to his feet, the great sound turned into an infantry barrage. She twisted the volume down and it suddenly was Latin music, bongos, strings, a muted trumpet.

"High fidelity is part of the treatment, too. Two hundred watts, maybe, with tweeters and woofers hidden all over the place."

"Loud, wasn't it?"

"The records are down here. There's no activity you can think of that he hasn't got music to do it by. But I've got it on FM radio now." She moved restlessly across the room, moving to the rhythm, half-dance, half-stroll. "If we just knew exactly what they're after."

"Well—I better go back there and see if I can find out."

"Don't let them know where they can find me."

"I won't. But what would they do?"

"Find a way to keep us apart. It might be something unpleasant."

He tried to think of Charla doing something unpleasant. But when he thought of Charla, the air seemed to get too thin. He saw her, vividly, wearing Wilma's smoky wisp, smiling at him, and the image was combined with the tactile memory of Betsy's small firm breast against his hand. Betsy came over and stared at him. "Do you have some kind of seizures?"

"Me?"

"Try cold showers, deep breathing and clean thoughts, Winter. Now take off, so I can take a nap."

6

HE ARRIVED AT THE ELISE AT QUARTER TO FIVE, AND THOUGH HE went directly to his room without stopping at the desk, the phone began to ring ten seconds after he had closed the door. It rang and it also flashed an imperative red light at him.

"Couldn't you have let me know you'd be delayed, dear?" Charla asked.

"I'm sorry about that."

"Do you have anyone with you?"

"No."

"That seems very odd."

"What's odd about it?"

"Don't public figures usually have a swarm of people around them, eh?"

"Public figures?"

"Kirby dear, you're so lovably obtuse. You better scoot right down here before the sky falls on you. Down the hall, dear. To the suite. I guess we're lucky we didn't try to do any shopping. We'll be lucky if we can make it to the *Glorianna,* dear. She got in this morning."

"What are you talking about?"

"Dear God, don't you really know?"

"No."

"Didn't you stop at the desk?"

"No."

"Then you better hustle down here and let me tell you about it."

She hung up. As soon as he hung up the phone began ringing again. He answered it. A tense male voice said, "Kirby Winter?"

"Yes?"

"Look, fella. I won't horse around. If nobody's got to you, twenty-five hundred bucks on the line for a twenty-four-hour ex-

clusive. This is Joe Hooper. Remember that name, hey? And I'll
see you get protection from everybody else until this time tomorrow. Is it a deal?"

"I don't know what you're talking about."

"Don't be coy, sweetie. You got to move fast. You sneaked by
pretty good, but word got around and they're on their way up
there now."

"Who?"

"Are you Kirby Winter, for Chrissake?"

He heard a commotion in the hall, and people began pounding
on his door. "Excuse me, but there seems to be somebody at the
door."

"That's *them,* you nut! Is it a deal?"

Kirby sighed and hung up. He started toward the door and
hesitated. It sounded like a big crowd out there. Suddenly there
was a sharp rapping on the locked interconnecting door at the
other end of his room, and a muffled voice. "Kirby?" He recognized Charla's voice. He went over to the door and answered her.
"Open the latch, dear," she said.

He opened the door. She smiled at him and tilted her head and
listened to the commotion in the hall. "My word, they gather
quickly don't they?" She wore a yellow mandarin coat over white
Bermuda shorts, and she was wearing huge opaque sunglasses.

"Who?"

"All the news people, lover. All jostling and pushing and
despising themselves and each other and you, their nasty little
strobe lights and pencils and tape machines all aimed and ready. I
thought it might be like this, so just in case, I had Joseph pick up
this room in between you and the suite. These interconnect so this
whole oceanside can be turned into a big suite. Joseph had to get
a dear little honeymoon couple moved out of this room to arrange it."

"What do those people want?"

"Don't stand there like a ninny, dear. They sound as if they
might actually break the door down."

He went with her through the extra bedroom and into the suite.
She closed the interconnecting door behind them. In the suite she
handed him an afternoon edition of the Miami *News.* They had a

two-column picture of him on page one. It was an old picture. The head said, MYSTERY NEPHEW IN KREPPS TAX DODGE. He sat down very abruptly.

"At noon today Walton Grumby, Executive Vice President of Krepps Enterprises revealed that serious estate tax problems are anticipated in the Omar Krepps estate because of the refusal by Kirby Winter, nephew of the late Krepps, to reveal the whereabouts of approximately $27,000,000 diverted over an eleven-year period from Krepps Enterprises into a mystery company known as O.K. Devices, entirely owned by Krepps.

"Grumby told reporters that O.K. Devices occupied a small rental office in the Fowler Building, employing only a Miss Wilma Farnham of Miami, and Kirby Winter. The day after the death of Krepps, Miss Farnham, either on her own initiative, or on the advice of Winter, destroyed all the files and records of O.K. Devices and closed the rental office. Grumby stated that Krepps was always highly secretive about the operations of O.K. Devices, and it seems possible that the company was merely a device for draining off the liquid assets of Krepps' other ventures and placing them out of the reach of the Internal Revenue Service.

"Grumby stated that Winter traveled to all parts of the world on confidential orders from Krepps, returning infrequently to Miami. Earlier today, Winter refused to disclose his confidential activities to Krepps Enterprises executives or to state what had happened to the $27 million. The Farnham woman also refused to reveal any details of the operations of O.K. Devices or to state on whose instructions she had burned all the records.

"Grumby told reporters that in view of these indications of conspiracy, it seemed possible that Winter and the Farnham woman may attempt to flee the country. At press time neither Winter nor the Farnham woman had been located for comment."

"Good Lord," Kirby said, staring blankly at Charla.

She came and sat close beside him and took off the sunglasses.

"Do you see all the implications, dearest?" she asked.

"I guess they're anxious to talk to me."

"That figure has a horrid fascination. A million dreary little people are absolutely vibrating with the vision of all that money hidden away in the romantic corners of the world. They hate you for having it. And they have a sneaking admiration for you for grabbing it all as soon as your uncle died."

"But it wasn't that way!"

"Does that make any difference, really?"

"But if I explain the whole operation in detail—"

"Without any documentation at all? And you *did* tuck a little bit away here and there for yourself, didn't you? Don't look so indignant. If you didn't, you are an idiot, of course. Didn't Miss Farnham intercept a little? How can you be sure? But it isn't the news people you have to worry about."

"What do you mean?"

"Dear Kirby, the world is jammed with animals who would happily put you and your Miss Farnham on a double spit and roast you over coals for just one per cent of that much money. All of a sudden, dear, you two are very tasty animals in the wrong part of the jungle. And I think you might find out how sharp the teeth are if you walk out that door." She had been edging close to him and he had been trying to move away, inconspicuously. Now he was at the end of the couch and the satin weight of one breast was on his arm.

"You need us more than ever," she said.

"Huh?"

"The *Glorianna*, dear. Don't be so dense. Either we smuggle you away, or the world tears you to pieces, believe me. And I really don't know why we should even dream of helping you, after that nasty trick you pulled on us. Ice skates, indeed!"

"I was just checking."

"Joseph was livid with rage, but I told him it served us right for underestimating you. It was quite clever, really. But I imagine you wouldn't have been so wary if Betsy hadn't given you a lot of wrong impressions about us."

"But—I guess you do want something."

"Of course, dear! Isn't it refreshing to have it out in the open? We can all stop playing games, can't we?"

"I guess so."

"No secrets?"

"I guess—that depends."

"On what? Darling, if you're thinking of being so crude as to require some sort of agreement, you might spoil things for us, don't you think? I couldn't promise to be your absolute slave. But it might turn out that way, once we're at sea. I wouldn't really strike a whore's bargain, no matter what is at stake. It would make it all so terribly ordinary. And we want it to be extraordinary, don't we?"

Thinking of Betsy, he chose his words carefully. "I think, instead, I'm thinking in terms of a different kind of bargain. How my end of it will come out. And what the safeguards are."

She was so close he could see a tiny amber wedge in the gray-green iris of her left eye, and see the exquisite detail of her lashes and brows, the individual hairs like gold wire.

The eyes narrowed and she took a deep breath and held it. "Then you have it!"

"Have what?"

"Just don't get too bloody clever, Mr. Winter. You could bitch it for yourself, you know."

"How could I?"

"All of a sudden, pet, your dead uncle has put more pressure on you than we ever could. Now I think you're going to have to make a deal. Maybe you won't have any choice."

He was feeling his way. This was a new and rather deadly Charla, a confirmation of Betsy's description. "Just suppose, even with all that pressure, I don't need you."

"Indeed?"

"Just suppose a goodly chunk of that money did get stashed. Where I can get to it. And suppose I have the idea you people are a little crude."

"Crude?" she said thinly, shocked.

"Ransacking all Uncle Omar's little hideouts."

She studied him for a long time. "So you're a good actor too. I think that makes you twice as dangerous as cleverness alone, you know. When the stakes are high enough, it's worth making a direct move sometimes. It could have worked. Then who would need you?"

"But it turns out you do."

She tilted her head. "And why the aw shucks, gee whiz, Huckleberry Finn reactions to my little—attentions, Kirby?"

"I like to be disarming."

"Dear Jesus, you *are!* So what makes you immune? Is Farnham that good?"

"Probably."

She got up to pace slowly, frowning. He noticed she had lost some of her accent in the past few minutes. "Very nice," she said. "Set the mark up and when you get to the kill, he second-cards you to death. I suppose you are thinking in terms of a partnership."

"Not particularly."

"Is it in the same place the money is?"

"Is what?"

She stamped her foot. "Don't be so damned coy! Certainly you know we could have done it the other way at any time. You drank whatever I handed you. And we could have gotten you to a place where screaming wouldn't matter. Joseph hasn't got the stomach for it, but I have, friend. I have. I find it very interesting."

He swallowed a sudden obstruction in his throat. "So I guess that must mean it wouldn't have done you any good."

"It wouldn't do *you* any good, dear."

"I guess you have to assume I know what I'm doing."

She nodded, reluctantly. "I'm beginning to think so. But what the hell was your uncle thinking of? He must have realized this would happen."

"If this is the way he planned it."

She gestured toward the newspaper. "If you brought this down on yourself, you must have a lot of confidence, Kirby."

"I didn't make any public statement." He went over to the phone. He looked at his watch. "I want to see if I can get Grumby at home by now."

"Better let me place the call for you. Knowing where you are would be worth money to the girl on the switchboard."

He looked up the number. Charla placed the call. When she had Grumby on the line, she handed the phone to Kirby.

"Interesting press conference you held, Mr. Grumby."

"Ah, Winter! You must understand that we have to protect ourselves."

"Then you'll understand my statement when I make it."

"I don't think I follow."

"All I can say is that I was an underling. Uncle Omar certainly didn't leave me anything. All I can say is that O.K. Devices was some sort of tricky corporate thing I never quite understood. It never made sense to me, using all that money to buy property and securities abroad and then putting the deeds and certificates and a lot of cash into Swiss banks in your name and the names of your associates. But I did it because I was paid to do it. And I can tell them that Miss Farnham is baffled too, because she burned the records at your request."

There was a long silence. In a rather rusty voice, Grumby asked, "What is the purpose of all this, Mr. Winter?"

"I am going to try to avoid making any statement at all."

"A statement like that—fictitious one might destroy us all."

"In the absence of any documentation, it could get sticky for everybody. I'm just suggesting that you don't try to get any cuter."

"We may have seriously underestimated you, Mr. Winter."

"You can't retract the statement. But you can avoid making any more. I have all the trouble I need right now." He hung up.

Charla looked at him approvingly. "You can be quite a serpent."

"At heart I'm a ninny."

✓ "It's an effective disguise. Omar did look like such a sweet, baffled old man. We should have assumed you'd take after him."

The phone rang and she answered it. "Who? Oh, yes, of course. What is that? Oh, no, my dear. My brother and I hardly know the young man. Seen with him? You must be mistaken. Not that I would mind, you understand. It's really quite exciting being in the same hotel, actually. Even the same floor, I understand. He must be a *very* interesting chap. All that money. My word! I'm sorry my brother and I have to leave this evening. It would be amusing to stay here and watch the fun. No, of course not. You're very welcome."

She hung up. "A bright girl, that one. Playing percentages, bribing the help, I imagine. Possibly the bellhops who carried you upstairs last night. I tried to stay well out of it, but those boys are quite observant. Well, darling, you might as well bring your suitcases in here and we'll leave it up to Joseph to plan a good way to get you out of here tonight and onto the *Glorianna*. She'll be refueled by now. And it's just what you need, you know. The dramatic, mysterious disappearance."

"That's all I need."

"We'll do our bargaining at sea, Kirby."

"Will we?"

"Dear boy, give me credit for *some* intelligence. If you weren't interested in making a deal, you wouldn't be hanging about, would you?"

"I guess not. I—uh—think I'll shower and change."

"Take your time, dear. We won't be out of this for hours and hours. Want your back scrubbed?"

"No thanks."

"Don't look so severe. Any other little service you can think of?"

"Not right now. I'll let you know."

"I'm sure you will, you lovely serpent."

When he was back in his room with the door bolted, he went and listened at the corridor door. He could hear a murmur of voices in the hall, and some laughter. He walked back and forth, biting his lip, smacking his fist into his palm. He remembered her words, "a place where screaming wouldn't matter." It made him feel sweaty and chilled.

At seven-thirty he stood on the exposed landing with the green eye looking out of the porthole in the bright door at him, shadowed by the dusk.

"It's me," he said in a squeaky, muffled, breathless voice. "Me!"

Betsy opened the door and let him in. "Dear Lord," she said softly. "Anybody follow you here? No, I guess they wouldn't."

He undid the jacket and belt of the hotel uniform and took the hotel pillow out. He pulled the wads of tissue out of his cheeks. He collapsed into a chair and said, "They sent up a fat one."

"A fat what?"

"A fat waiter. I called from the honeymooner's room."

"From the whose room?"

"I haven't hit anybody since I was thirteen years old. He put the tray down and turned around and—Pow. I left a fifty-dollar bill in his hand. Then I walked right through all of them."

"All of who?"

"Why would they have uniforms this color? Salmon and emerald?"

"Kirby, I heard all about you on television, on the six o'clock news, and I could guess that the thundering herd is after you, but really, you'd better start at the beginning. Unless you start somewhere near the beginning, I am going to all of a sudden start screaming."

"She said something about screaming, and it was very nasty."

"Kirby!"

"All right. All right." And he told her. There was, for once, no need for in-process editing. She listened carefully, thoughtfully.

"So she finally showed her teeth, did she?"

"My God, the last place I ever want to be is on that yacht. And it's a damn strain to talk to somebody and not really know what you're talking about."

"I think you are a sweet lamb and I think you did very well. But where are we? Now she thinks you know what it is she's after. But you have no idea what it is?"

"Absolutely none."

"But now she knows she's either got to be awfully damn cute to get it away from you, or awfully rough, or pay your full price, or come in as a partner. What does it sound like, whatever it is?"

"All I can think of, I swear, is some sort of an invention."

She nodded gravely. "That's where I've been going too. Years and years ago, he *did* try to invent things. And suddenly he became rich and powerful. He got an edge, a gimmick, something that works. I think that Charla and Joseph reasoned it all out by inference. Maybe they don't even know exactly what it is. But they could guess it could be written in his personal papers."

"And they think I know exactly what it is."

"Maybe it would be awfully useful right about now if you could lay your hands on it, Kirby."

He closed his eyes. "You know, I'm just about whipped. Everybody in the world thinks I've got twenty-seven million dollars squirreled away and they all want it. Just six people know I gave it all away. You, me, Wilma, Wintermore, Charla and Joseph. And I gave Charla the idea I'd kept some. But they want something else, and I don't know what it is, and you don't, and you seen to think they don't either."

"Leaves Wilma, doesn't it?"

He opened his eyes. "Could she know?"

"Maybe she could know without knowing she knows. Maybe she could have it without knowing she has it."

"Guess I better phone her."

He phoned Wilma. A man answered. He had a precise, high-pitched voice. "Who wishes to speak to her, please?"

He hesitated. Betsy was listening too. She nodded. "Kirby Winter."

"You wouldn't mind proving you're Mr. Winter?"

"How do you expect me to—"

"Just a moment, please. I must get the questions she wrote down. You can prove you are Mr. Winter by answering them correctly." He was gone for twenty seconds. "Are you there? Good. First, please give me the name of the man you were dealing with at the time of your uncle's death."

"Uh—Manuel Hernandez y Gomez."

"And the name of the man in Rangoon in December?"

"Oh. Dr. Na Dan Boala."

"Thank you, Mr. Winter. I suggested this precaution to my sister. She was in such a state of horrible emotional shock, she wasn't thinking with—her customary precision. I am Roger Farnham. She hoped you might call. Now, thank God, I shall be able to leave also. The harassment is sickening, as I guess you must have learned by this time. I must say, it is a grim reward for my sister's years of loyal faithful service to your uncle."

"I didn't have anything to—"

"I realize that, of course. And there is much about this I can't pretend to understand, sir. Wilma will tell me very little. But I do know, of course, she is—uh—incapable of hanky-panky."

"Yes. Of course."

"I'll doubtless be followed when I leave here, but I'll have the satisfaction of knowing I won't be leading them to Wilma. Do you know that the reporters actually badgered her into hysterics?"

"That's too bad."

"It took considerable guile to get her hidden safely away."

"I can imagine."

"And it would be a shame if you led the world to her hiding place."

"I'll certainly try not to."

"She's too delicate for this sort of thing. I'm leaving it up to you to do the right thing, and find some way out of this for her. Someone should be sued for the filthy hints they put in that interview."

"I don't think they'll be doing any more hinting."

"The damage is done, apparently. At any rate, sir, I have a home, a family and a profession to return to. Please tell her I cannot be expected to damage my own life in some vain attempt to assist her."

"Where is she?"

"You will be careful about contacting her? She does want to see you."

"I'll be very careful, Mr. Farnham."

"I smuggled her to the house of one of my associates, Mr. Winter. He is on a sabbatical leave in France, and he left the key with me. Unfortunately the phone is disconnected. Have you a pencil? Two-ten Sunset Way, Hallandale. It has considerable privacy due to the plantings Professor Wellerly arranged with that in mind. A small pink house. She has food and water, and she should be quite safe there, from the rabble and the curiosity seekers. But she is upset, naturally. Give a long ring then a short and then a long, and she will know it is either you or me, sir. She will open the door to no one else. And I believe I am right in saying we are both depending on you to do something to clear up this unfortunate situation."

"Thank you."

"Not at all, sir. It's my duty to my sister. Good evening."

"Well now!" Betsy said as he hung up. "How cozy you'll be! In your wittle pink housey."

"So how do I get there?"

"I can't say that I really care how you get to Hallandale, friend."

"In this uniform?"

"Bernie Sabbith is almost your size, and there is a whole closet loaded with stuff. Be his guest."

"She wouldn't think of letting me stay in that house with her."

"You're kidding!"

"I mean it. She's a very—she's sort of an odd girl. Uh—very proper."

"Even under emergency conditions like this?"

"I wouldn't want to risk it. Really, it would be a terrible risk for me to leave here. Any cab driver might recognize me."

"Well, my friend, you can't stay here. I'm a very odd girl too."

"Is it or is it not important to you to help me?"

"Indeed it is, but there are some kinds of help—"

"I was thinking, Betsy, I could write a note to her telling her to trust you. You know, she really doesn't think much of my judgment. Then you could go out there and stay there with her tonight and talk the whole thing out and maybe you and she can figure out what it is that Charla is after. I can reduce the risks by staying here alone. Then you can come back tomorrow and if you've learned anything we'll know what to do, and if you haven't, then we can try to figure out the next step."

At first Betsy was reluctant, but at last she agreed the idea had some merit. She made drinks while he wrote the note. Then, having laid in some stores during the day, she cooked ham and eggs in the tiny kitchen corner. Just before she left, a little before nine, she showed him where the television set was. She crawled on her hands and knees to the intricate headboard of the enormous bed, flipped the switch that moved a ceiling panel aside exposing the picture tube built into the ceiling. The other controls were next to the switch.

"If Charla locates the place, ask her to watch TV with you, Kirby."

"If I can arrange my life properly, I'll never see that woman again."

"What's the matter. Scared of her?"

"Totally."

Betsy gave him a wan smile. "Frankly, so am I."

7

AFTER CHECKING AGAIN TO BE CERTAIN THE DOOR WAS LOCKED, and after a lengthy hunt for the final elusive light switch, Kirby Winter crawled to the middle of the giant bed. There was a troublesome fragrance of Betsy about the pillow. It was a warm night, with a murmurous traffic sound, a ripped-silk sound of far off jets, the adenoidal honk of boat traffic. The ten-o'clock news had displayed other pictures of him, still shots, grinning like an insurance salesman. And there was one picture of Wilma Farnham, looking severe. The newscast made them sound like the master criminals of the century. Informed sources believed that Winter and the Farnham woman had already fled the country. They had both made mysterious disappearances under the very noses of the ladies and gentlemen of the press. One could see them chummed up on Air France, snickering, tickling, getting bagged on champagne, heading for that stashed fortune and a simple life of servants, castles, jewels, furs and tireless lechery.

He wondered about Betsy and Wilma. By now they would be deep in all their long talking, and he blushed to think of Wilma, distrait, uttering all her shy girlish confidences. "And all the time he really was terrified of women. You should have seen him run from me in absolute horror."

He was physically exhausted, but he could not slow his mind down. He knew he would not sleep, but suddenly he was down in the jungly world of nightmare. Wilma, giggling, opened zipper compartments in long cool pale thighs to show him how solidly stuffed they were with thousand-dollar bills. Charla had little gold scissors, and she smirked and cooed as she cut the ears from little pink rabbits which screamed every time. She was bare and golden, oiled and steaming, and when she turned he saw the vulgar placement of the little tattoo which read "Ninny." He walked into the scene in the little gold telescope and found Uncle Omar there, off to one side, chuckling. Uncle Omar thrust a deck of cards toward him and told him to take any card, but when he took the card it was warm and heavy and moving, and suddenly he was back in an old car in a heavy rain of long ago, and he found the dream blending into a reality of some warm, solid, busy, rubbery creature burrowing against him, snuffling and giggling and snorting, raking him with small claws. In a few moments of night fright, he tried to dislodge it, thrust it away from him, but the very act of clutching at it, the agile roundnesses under his hands, turned fright into a sweet aggression, his mind— standing aside—awed, wringing its hands, finding no way to intercede.

In a vague and troubled way, as he became aware of the helpless inevitability of it, he felt all the responsibilities of literary allusion, of equating it with fireworks, ocean surf, earthquakes or planetary phenomena. At the same time he was remotely, fretfully concerned with identity, wondering if it were Charla, Betsy, Wilma—but soon realizing that particular problem was, as of the moment, entirely academic. He just did not have time to give a damn.

So it transpired without benefit of analogy, or time to create one, aside from the hurried thought it was rather like some sort of absurd, stylized conflict, like a sword fight to music where you duck in time and in relation to the imposed necessities of tempo. As the fight was both won and lost, in a white blindness, he sensed, from a long way off, her vast tensions, some spaced yippings, then a buttery melting of the creature quelled.

And then there was a head beside him, wedged into his neck, tickling him, and a breath making long slow hot whooshings against his throat, and a hand that came up to idly roam his indifferent cheek.

"Hoooo—boy!" she whispered. "Hooooo, *Bernie!* Oh, you the doll of all times. The livin' most."

"Um," he said, pleased that his heart had decided not to hammer its way out of his chest.

"Suh-prize, suh-prize, huh, sweetie? Nice suh-prize?"

"Um."

"Couldn't make the damn key work for hell. Figured on you changed the lock, and I would truly kill you dead, you'd done that to Bonny Lee one time. Then it worked and I come a-mous-ing in, felt the bed, looking for two pair of feet. I find two pair, Bernie-boy, there be the gawddamnedest fracas around here you heard ever."

"Uh."

"You doan talk much to a gal missed you so bad, honey. Don't you get the idea now I could be hustling you for any piece of that TV crud, on account of you just use them sick-looking broads you brang down here like always. I come here because you're just the most there is anywhere, and I love you something terrible, and it was real wild and nice, hey now?"

"Um."

She ran her fingertips across his upper lip. "Hey! You gone and shaved it off! Now what in the world you look like, I wonder."

She scrambled away from him. She fumbled with the head-board control panel for a few seconds and then a bright overhead spot blinded him. He shut his eyes tightly, opened them a little bit and squinted at the girl.

She was kneeling, staring down at him, a deeply browned leggy girl. Her brown eyes were huge and round. Her mouth was shaped into a round shocked circle. She had big round brown breasts with a startling white stripe across them. She had a flat tummy, smooth muscles of a swimmer, and under a tight tangled cap of white curls, a lovely, delicate, angelic face, bronzed and in-nocent.

"Who you, you tow-head son of a bitch!" she yelled. "What kinda smart-ass trick you pulling anyways? I'm gonna rip the face right offen you!" Her fingers curled dangerously.

"Now hold it!"

"For what? What do you think I am anyhow? Where's Bernie?"

"I don't know."

"You were supposed to be him, gawddamn it!"

"I don't know about that."

"Anybody pull what you pulled, mister, somebody ought to take a rusty knife to em and plain—"

He sat up and glared at her. "What the hell is the matter with you?" he roared. "I was sound asleep! I didn't know who you were, and I don't know who you are. I was so sound asleep I didn't know even *what* you were."

A corner of her mouth twitched. "You could have got the general idea I was a girl."

"That occurred to me!"

"Don't you roar at me, you sneaky bassar! You woke up, all right, soon enough, and you could have figured it out, being in Bernie's bed, maybe some mistake was happening. But did you say a damn word?"

He stared at her. "When? And what was I supposed to say? My God, girl, it's like a man falling off a building; you'd expect him to tie his shoes and wind his watch on the way down."

Her mouth twitched again. "Real something, wasn't it?" Without warning her eyes filled and she put her hands over her face and began to sob like a child. She toppled sideways and lay curled up, shivering and weeping.

"Now what?" he said with exasperation.

"S-S-Sneaky b-b-bassar!"

"Why are you crying?"

"What you d-done to me. In my whole l-life I never had no affair with s-somebody I din even know. Makin' me feel like a slut girl. Makin' me feel all cheap and r-r-r-rotten. Oh, oh, oh."

"You hush, whatever your name is."

"Doan even know my *name!*" she wailed. "Bonny Lee Beaumont, gawddamn you!"

"My name is—" He hesitated. "Uh—Kirk Winner." He pulled her right hand away from her face and grasped it and shook it. "Now we're introduced. For God's sake, stop blubbering."

"But I din know you *then!*"

"But if you'd known you didn't know me, then it wouldn't have happened would it?"

She stopped abruptly and looked up at him, sidelong and wary. "Huh? How does that go?"

"As far as you were concerned, I was Bernie. Right? So there's no reason to blame yourself, is there?"

She was silent for a moment. Then she sat up, snuffled once, nodded at him. "I guess I got to think on it the way you say. But I broken a secret vow to myself, made when I was fourteen, how never in my whole life would I sack out with no man I din feel love for. Even it's an accident, it still counts, sort of. I even feel funny you lookin' at me, and it never bothers me with no man I love. But I get dressed, that's funnier yet. I doan know what the *hell* to do, mister. What's your name again?"

"Kirk Winner."

"Friend of Bernie's?"

"A friend of a friend."

"You down on the television thing?"

"No."

"Married?"

"No."

She tilted her head. "You're not such a bad *looking* fella anyways."

"Thanks so much."

She wrinkled her clear young forehead into a thoughtful scowl. "What bothers me, it was so real *fine,* Kirk. I mean I had the idea there had to be love, so when it's fine with a stranger, it makes me out some kind of animal like."

"You were expressing the love you feel for Bernie. That's what made it right, Bonny Lee."

She grinned. "You talk things out good for me. You'll be having me coming around with all kinds of problems, hey?"

"Any time."

"I keep wondering now how Bernie would look without the mustache. Gawddamn it, I thought I was going to get to see."

"How old are you, Bonny Lee?"

"Twenny, practically."

"Dear God. You live with your folks?"

"My folks! You some kind of a nut or something? My folks, they're farmin' on shares, South Carolina, and I was fourteen, went into a beauty contest you were supposed to be sixteen, and I sure God looked sixteen or better. I didn't do good on the talent part, but the prize I got was one of the judges taken me to New Orleans and I never been back since. Married one time and it was a mess and I shucked him fast, man played clarinet and drank shine. Then I got to singing around, and now I'm working a place, Rio's, up North Miami, singing and sort of stripping some, but not down to raw, and a bongo thing I do too. But what's coming on for me good now is a career, and that one marriage was plenty I can tell you, and Bernie he's been good to me, starting last year. So I have a ball, it saying on my work card I'm twenny-two, and my own little car and all, and friends enough, but Jesus I didn't count on walking into nothing like this here. I tell you true, it has plain upset the hell out of me, Kirk."

She swiveled and moved off the bed in a leggy stride, moved out of the bright area of the light. She was in a shadow area then, where the only visible things were the bright hair and the two pale areas of bikini.

"Folks!" she said and snorted. "I swang that hoe enough under that hot sun, and I stayed, I'd be wore down with nakedy kids by now, cause there you don't have your first young by fifteen, you got to be looking like a toad frog, and I sure didn't. And don't."

"No, you don't."

"Took that little judge's wife seven weeks to hunt him down, and then she bust every dish in the apartment. On him, and me going out the back way with the little bit of money he had left by then. That taking the money is the only thing I ever did shamed me until this night, Kirk."

Moving slowly, she picked her clothes off the floor, shook them, hung them over an arm of a chair. She came back toward the bed, picked up a white purse and sat on the edge of the bed, toward the foot of the bed, just out of the cone of light, facing him.

"Glaring on you," she said. She got up and switched on a low lamp in a far corner, turned off the overhead prism and sat on the bed again. She took a small brush out of her purse and brushed the fitted cap of white curls. She was partially silhouetted against the light. She lit two cigarettes and stretched toward him and handed him one.

"Well, hell," she said wistfully. "You can't win 'em all."

He had begun to realize how remarkably good he felt. He wanted to ride a chrome bike down Main Street, no hands, waving all the flags of the Americas. He wanted to get a reasonably good start and run right up the side of a few tall buildings. He could do a tireless handstand and twirl batons with his toes. This was indeed a splendid girl. He was very fond of her.

"What's so gawddamn funny?" she demanded.

"Sorry. I didn't realize I was laughing."

"What you do for a living, sugar?"

"I—I'm sort of between jobs."

"What's your trade?"

"Sort of—investments."

"And the investment was three kings against a lousy little full house. That's how it goes, sugar."

"Uh—Bonny Lee?"

"Yay?"

"You—uh, you said it was—pretty fine?"

"You were there, weren't you, brother? You weren't all that much sound asleep, and that's for sure. You want a medal of honor or something? I swear to God, some day I hope to meet a man doesn't want to be told he's the best there is. What is it with men anyhow? A girl, she just wants to be lovin' and wanted, and a damn man, every time, it's like he wonders if he can make the Olympics. You all scared you haven't got it? Y'all go round provin' it often enough, then swaggering around like you'd done something special, like as if it was something any mink couldn't do quicker and oftener. Big deal. I give you a passing grade. Okay?"

"Sorry I mentioned it."

"So am I, sugar. So am I. There's one thing bores me damn near to death, it's talking about it. Folks get hungry and have a fine steak, they sit over the bones and talk about it? They get thirsty and have a big cold drink, they sit around peerin' down into the glass a-wonderin' what temperature it was, for Gawd's sweet sake. The way I figure—"

"I said I'm sorry I brought it up!"

"Shees marie, you don't have to beller at me, sugar! You know, you got a temper onto you?"

"I'm a very mild guy! I always have been! I *never* lose my temper! Get off my back, will you?"

"Kirk, sugar, you're real edgy. There anything to eat?"

"Some cold ham. Rye bread."

"I'll just whomp up sanwiches, make us both feel better. You know it's three in the morning?"

She went into the kitchen corner and turned on the bright overhead fluorescence. He propped himself on the pillows so he could watch her. Her long legs were so tanned they looked carved out of redwood, shaped lovingly, sanded to sleekness, polished. As she bent and moved and worked, he admired the smooth clench and slither of the young muscles of haunch and back and shoulders. And he felt the vast contentment of what he knew could be no more than a momentary ownership, and he wanted to find a heavy stone and chunk himself in the head with it for having deprived himself for so long of this kind of fatuous, arrogant smugness he had not realized existed.

She began to hum and then to sing. Her singing voice was an octave deeper than her speaking voice. Both the song and the phrasing were tantalizingly familiar.

"Billie!" he said suddenly.

She turned and grinned at him. "God rest her soul. Played all them records til nothing left but a scratchy hiss, then boughten some more and played those out too. Withouten Lady Day, I'd have hardly no career at all, sugar. There any one of hers you like special?"

"God Bless the Chile."

She clapped her hands with delight. "Damn *all,* Kirk honey, that there is *my* song. Seven thousand times I sung that, all alone and for the people, and not one time it wasn't like my heart turning over slow. I can *cry* to that song, thinking of that poor lost broad and how the world broke her down. After this here ham, I'll sing it to you good, and you shuten your eyes, you'll think she's come on back for sure. Say, here is some of that burgundy red wine all fizzed like a sof'drink, like I had here one time before. You want some tall with ice?"

"I'd like that, Bonny Lee."

She brought the wine in tall glasses, and thick sandwiches on white napkins, all on a teak tray. Nothing had ever tasted better to him. "I'm night people," she said, chewing busily. "Three o'clock, four o'clock, I could gnaw the ears off a gallopin' horse."

"But you get out in the sun."

"Set my alarm for noon, usually. Swim fifty lengths, five at a time, bake myself in between. Keeps me tightened up nice, you think so?"

"Very nice, Bonny Lee."

She took the tray out and brought back more wine. When it was gone she put the glasses aside and said, "Now close your eyes and hear Billie."

She did it beautifully, her tone smoky, gentle. Midway he

opened his eyes. She was singing with her eyes closed, swaying slightly. "—rich relations give crust of bread and such. You can h'ep youself, but doan take too much. . . ."

After the last note was gone into the silence of the room, she opened her eyes and they were shiny.

"You liking that, Kirk sugar, knowing about Billie and all, asking for that one—it's somehow something starting out all dead wrong and swinging around right. You feel that?"

"Yes, Bonny Lee."

"And it could set that first time all the way right if I was to know it was you, maybe. But I don't want you thinking wrong, this being the first time in my whole life knowing a gentleman friend such a short little time. But time got messed up kind of for us."

"I wouldn't think wrong."

She went over and turned out the light and came back. In a little while she said, "Kirk sugar, what for you shaking so?" In another little while she said, "You know, you're hands are like *ice!*" And in another little while she said, "Sugar, is it really meanin' all this much to you, honest?" And when she knew it did, she whispered, "Then it's meaning ten times as much to me too. Which I am now to let you know. Shees marie, here I am tumblin' into love again, and a damn tow-head, cold-hand, eviltemper yankee, a gamblin' out-a-work man, and so gentle-sweet I can start crying any minute, and nobody does any more talking from here on in."

THERE WAS A HORNET BIG AS A SEA GULL PERCHED ON SOMEthing right in front of his face. It had a wide nasty little face, graygreen eyes, long heavy milky hair, a puffy mouth heavily lipsticked. It smacked its evil little mouth and swung its stinger back and forth. It had big veined wings which looked as rigid as plate glass. At intervals the wings would vibrate for several seconds, becoming almost invisible, making a harsh resonant burring sound.

The hornet was gone. A phone was ringing. He sat up, lost in space and time, still half wary of the hornet. He was in a huge vague bed in a shadowy room, with a dawn slant of sun coming in from the breakfast porch. As an orderly part of his mind picked up the count on the ringing of the phone, he turned and saw a tousle of curls sunk into a pillow at the far edge of the bed, four feet away, and a brown nape of tender neck, a silky V of white hair against it, and a deep brown shoulder, and a pale blue sheet, draped, molding the long girl-shape of the rest of her—incredible ornamentation to an unknown morning. Memory was suddenly an avalanche, pouring into the dry arroyo of the stunned and empty mind. He felt a stab of delight so unexpected it was more like pain than joy. He felt as if somebody had suddenly thrust a hollow needle into his heart and pumped it full of spiced molasses.

. . . thirteen, fourteen, fifteen, and the phone went on and on. By the simplest deduction, it had to be Betsy Alden. Anybody else would have given up. By letting it ring and ring, she was letting him know who it was.

. . . nineteen, twenty, twenty-one . . .

He found the phone on the shelf to the left of the headboard.

"Yes?"

"Good *morning*, Kirby," Joseph said, the rich voice almost gelatinous in its baritone flexibility.

"Uh—how—"

"You've really been *very* tiresome lately, Kirby. But all will be forgiven if you can give us a little co-operation now. You are really in all kinds of trouble, now, you know. The vicious assault on that poor waiter was a stupid mistake. But you seem to be reasonably ingenious, so we think you can probably devise some way of getting from that apartment to the *Glorianna* without incident. Listen carefully, my boy. She is tied up at the Biscayne Marina, E Dock. Please be aboard by ten at the latest."

"What time is it?"

"Twenty after seven. It should give you ample time."

"But I don't—"

"Filiatr—Betsy, rather, is a very silly, stubborn, emotional child. She tried to be clever. Let's just say it isn't wise to attempt a fool's mate against the queen's gambit. Perhaps she was counting upon a sentimentality which doesn't really exist. Or trying to play us against you. It's rather hard to tell at the moment. She's no longer very coherent. I must congratulate you upon not confiding in her completely. Because she really became very eager to confide in us. We did learn you two young people have become quite fond of each other in a very short time. And, of course, where to get in touch with you. And with Miss Farnham. Charla is wonderfully eager to talk with Miss Farnham too, and they should be bringing her here any moment. But we won't start asking her tiresome questions until, say, ten o'clock."

"What are you trying to—"

"I'm urging you to join us, old boy. I'm counting on your sense of responsibility for Betsy. And your sentimentality, I suppose. She's really too high strung for this sort of treatment, you know. Also, unless you've suddenly become irrational, you must realize that with the way things have developed, you need us quite badly. We'll be expecting you, Kirby."

The line was dead. He hung up and looked at his hand and noted that his fingers were trembling. He got up and put on his shorts and went around to the other side of the bed. He sat on his heels and looked at Bonny Lee's dear sleeping face and thought his heart would burst with the wonder of it. It was dark against the pillow, lips parted, a face of absolute innocence. Her hand rested near her face. It was a lean, tanned, muscular hand, very like the hand of an active boy in his early teens. In the reflected glow of the early sunlight he saw the white hairline outline of a scar on the back of her hand shaped like an L. He wondered where she had gotten it.

He put his hand on the warmth of the bare shoulder and shook her gently. "Bonny Lee, darling. Hey! Bonny Lee!" Aside from a faint frown that disappeared immediately, there was no response.

He shook her more violently, spoke more forcefully.

"Wurrow!" she said, a small, irritable squalling sound, and flounced over onto her other side. He rolled her back over and shook her.

Finally she opened her eyes and slowly focused on him. She

glowered at him. "Middla ni'," she mumbled. "Middla ni'. Lemmilone." And she was gone again. He pulled the sheet off her, pulled her legs out of bed, took her by the shoulders and sat her up. She sat with her chin on her chest, shoulders slumped, mumbling and growling at him. When he took his hands from her shoulders, she toppled onto her side and gave a small, purring snore. He sat her up again, took her wrists and started to pull her into a standing position. When he realized he would merely be pulling her off the bed onto her face, he reached and took her around the waist and stood her on her feet about two feet from the bed. She started to sag, then braced her legs. She peered at him, her eyes slightly crossed. As soon as he let go of her, she made a slow half-turn, took one step and dived face down across the bed. He stood her on her feet again and began to walk her. She leaned heavily against him, staggering, cussing him, groaning. He released her suddenly, ready to catch her if she fell. She wobbled around, caught her balance, shuddered violently, combed her fingers back through her curls and focused on him.

"So what the *hell* you doing, Kirk? Gawd!"

"Please wake up, Bonny Lee."

She squinted toward the porch. "Dawn!" she said despairingly. "Sonuvabitch!"

"I would have let you sleep, but I need your help."

She looked at him with venomous suspicion. "I tell you, sugar, it better be important."

"It is."

She shuddered again. She turned and blundered toward the bathroom. He heard the shower begin. He went over and examined her clothing. Lime slacks, a white blouse with a yellow figure, a little yellow jacket, white sandals, two blue-green wisps of nylon. He put her clothing on a chair just outside the bathroom door. The shower stopped. The door opened wide enough for her wet brown arm. "Fetch m'purse, sugar!" she called. He put it into her hand. He checked Bernie's wardrobe, laid out a gray sports shirt and dark blue slacks.

In a little while she stuck her head out, started to say something, saw her clothing, smiled at him and took her clothes into the bathroom. The protocol was slightly confusing. Apparently one could move about as unself-consciously naked as a tenpin until morning ablutions began, at which time modesty set in.

She came striding out, brushed and lipsticked, giving a little hitch at the waistband of the lime slacks, tossing her jacket and purse on a chair, smiling at him. "Once you're up I guess it isn't too terrible. I been told I'm a little hard to wake up."

"You bounced out of bed the first time I whispered your name."

"You're next in there. I'll neaten up some. What you staring it?"

He realized his expression was probably rather strange. Looking at her, he had been reminded of something a teammate had said about Mickey Mantle. "The more he takes off, the bigger he looks."

Clothes changed Bonny Lee. She looked taller and thinner. It did not seem plausible that all of that well-remembered abundance of breast and hip, all the fecundities, the armsful and handsful of sweet sighing weight could have disappeared into such a compacted trimness, into the tailored litheness of a clothed and pretty stranger.

Her smile disappeared and her brown eyes widened. "Oh, Gawd, you never seen me in clothes afore!" She blushed violently, deepening her tan to redness and making her face look moist. "I wanna fall right smack through the floor, sugar."

"It's all right. We understand how it happened."

"Sure enough, but I'm thinking on how it would *sound* to somebody. Shees marie, how the hell would you explain it?"

"We don't have to try."

"You rushing me out of here on account of somebody coming?"

"No."

"Just who is this friend of Bernie's that's a friend of yours?"

"She's an actress."

"Oh, great!"

"Uh—Bernie's in love with her, I think."

"Anything in a skirt, Bernie's in love with it. Take your shower."

When he came back out in the gray shirt—too snug across the

shoulders—and the blue slacks—too high above the shoes—rubbing a jaw made raw by the only razor blade he could find, he smelled coffee. She'd made the bed. She moved slowly toward him, her jaw belligerent, her fists on her hips, her brown eyes narrowed. The waiter's colorful uniform was behind her, on the foot of the bed.

"You wearin' Bernie's stuff, Kirk. You maybe been a waiter at the Elise? Just what the hell is going on?"

"Bonny Lee, I just can't explain right now—"

"Right now is when you do, mister, or it's going to be like you was wrapped in bob wire and spun like a top toy."

He made two forlorn beginnings, then said, "My name is really Kirby Winter."

She tilted her head. "You say it like it meant something."

"I thought it might."

"Kirby Winter? Sounds like I know of you somehow. You talk nice. School educated. Some kind of actor?"

"I'm—sort of in the news. Starting yesterday."

"I don't pay much attention to—" She stopped abruptly and put her hand to her throat. She peered at him, shocked and incredulous. "Sugar, you *him!* Twenny-seven million bucks! You the one stole and hid all that money!"

"I didn't steal it. I haven't got it."

She shook her head wonderingly. "You kin to that Kroops."

"Krepps. Uncle Omar."

She moved back to the bed and sat down limply and stared up at him. "You and some little old school-teacher-lookin' gal tooken it, and like the whole world looking for you all over hell and gone, and you cozied up in bed here with Bonny Lee Beaumont, herself."

"I didn't take a dime."

She studied him for a few moments. "Kirk, sugar. I mean Kirby. I surely know you didn't. I know the rough kind and I know the sly kind, and once in ever' long while, the sweet kind, which you are and which there's not enough of, and I wouldn't say you tooken it at all, so why don't you go turn yourself in and say how it came about?"

"I can't. There's so many reasons, there isn't time to tell you, but I just can't. I just hope—you'll be willing to help me, even though you know who I am."

"Even though? Don't you make me cross now, sugar. On this here big crazy old bed you learned me who you are, and what you want of me, I will do. But let's put a cigarette and coffee with it," she said and got up.

They took the coffee out onto the breakfast porch. There was a sun-glare on the bay. "You said you've got a little car?"

"Down in the alley. A little old yalla Sunbeam thing."

"Do you know where the Biscayne Marina is?"

"Sure thing. I knew a boy kept his boat there one time."

"I'd like you to drive me there, Bonny Lee."

"Then what?"

"Just leave me off there."

"That's all? Not much favor to that, Kirby."

"A lot of people know my face. A lot of people are looking. It could turn into a mess."

"You running away by boat?"

"I—I expect so."

"Can't put the top up on the car on account it doesn't have a top any more. You could kind of scrunch down, I expect. Let me see what I can find." She went into the apartment. He heard her opening and closing drawers. Music began to play. She came back out with a wide-brimmed planter's hat and a pair of dark sunglasses. "Should be news any time now. Here, you try these."

The hat was a little small, but he could pull it down far enough.

She nodded. "You look like anybody and ever'body. Camera a-hangin' round your neck, you'd be invisible any place in Florida entire. No need of scrunching."

"Aren't you going to ask if taking me there is going to implicate you in anything?"

"Implicate? That mean messed up in? I love a somebody, Kirby, I do like he asks me."

He took the glasses and hat off and stared at her. "Love?"

"You weren't listening in the bed, sugar?"

"Well, yes, I was, but I thought it—was sort of a manner of speaking."

"Hell yes it was, and I'm speaking it again. You got something against it?"

"No. I just mean that—well, I mean you seem to accept the fact I'll go off in a boat—and you don't know if we'll see each other again, and you don't seem to—well, to really care very much—and I thought—"

"You know, you could be, like they say, over-educated."

She wiped her lipstick onto the paper napkin, came smiling around the table and bent over him, put her hand on the nape of his neck and began to kiss him with considerable skill and energy. He groped for her and turned her and brought her into his lap. Within minutes they were trembling and gasping and giddy. She pushed his hands away from her and sat bolt upright, her hands on his shoulders, head tilted, smiling. Her eyes looked drowsy.

"I love you good, Kirby. And love is a pretty thing. See how fast all worked up we gettin'? That's the good of it, sugar. Going to bed is happy and it's fun. It's the way you get the good of it with none of the bad. It's like everybody has forgot that's all it is and all it was ever meant to be. People got to mess it up, it seems. Cryin', moanin', clingin' onto one another, all jealous and selfish and hateful. We love each other on account of we give each other a lot of happy fun, and if it comes round again, we'll take some more, and if it doesn't, we got this much already anyhow. But no vows and pledges and crap like that, hear? That's what people do because they got the funny idea it's the right thing to do. And before they know it, the fun part is gone, gotten itself strangled on the fine print, like it was a deed to some land. I live free and simple, Kirby, and I look on myself in the mirror and say hello to a friend I like. The day I stop liking her, I change my ways. So this is who loves you, and that's what the word means, and I got friends would die for me and me for them. What I say, you run onto a hell of a girl."

"I did," he said. "I did indeed."

"Any man *using* me," she said intently, "he gets a kick turns him soprano. I'm eager, but I'm no gawddamn free lunch counter for any bassar prowling for kicks, hear?"

"I'm not."

"Don't ever get to be. Hey! That's the news starting."

They went inside and sat on a couch. After the national news, Kirby was the first item on the local news.

"State, Federal and local authorities have joined in the hunt for mystery man Kirby Winter and his accomplice, Wilma Farnham. Last night Arturo Vara, room service waiter at a Miami Beach hotel, swore out an assault warrant against Winter. As the police reconstruct it, Winter, hemmed in by reporters in the corridor outside his hotel room yesterday, broke into an adjoining room, placed a call for room service, then, when Vara arrived, slugged him, donned his uniform and made his way through the reporters to the elevators and escaped from the hotel. He has not yet been apprehended."

Bonny Lee turned and stared at Kirby and raised one eyebrow in question. He nodded, guiltily.

"Dr. Roger Farnham, Associate Professor at Florida Eastern, elder brother of Wilma Farnham, disclosed that after a brief unfruitful interview with the press yesterday, Miss Farnham left the apartment where she lived alone, taking a few personal possessions, and has not been seen since. Police have established that Miss Farnham and Winter held clandestine meetings at a Miami hotel during his infrequent returns to this area from various foreign countries.

"The question which is on everyone's lips is what could have happened to the missing twenty-seven million dollars turned over to O.K. Devices by Krepps Enterprises at the direct order of Omar Krepps, international financier, who died suddenly last week. It is believed that Winter and the Farnham woman carefully planned the huge embezzlement over a period of time, including the destruction of the files and records and, according to police theory, including plans to leave the country, plans they may have consummated last night.

"In addition to the assault charge, Winter and the Farnham woman face embezzlement charges lodged by Krepps Enterprises. At midnight last night K.E. posted a reward of ten thousand dollars for any information leading to the apprehension of either or both of the fugitives. They are also bringing civil suit against both Winter and the Farnham woman. Both the tax and immigration authorities are anxious to serve summonses on both Winter and the woman.

"Winter is described as being six feet, one-half inch tall, weight about one-ninety, sandy hair, dark blue eyes, age thirty-two, small crescent scar on left cheekbone, clean-shaven, polite, soft-spoken, highly intelligent, disarming."

Bonny Lee went over and turned off the radio. She came back to him, shaking her head. "You now a celebrity, man." She touched his cheek. "Where'd you get the scar?"

"A little girl hit me with a rock when I was about six years old." He grasped her hand, touched the scar he had seen. "How about this one?"

"I swang back-handed at a little old buck-tooth boy pinched me when I was about eleven."

"You need ten thousand dollars?"

"Hope to God I never do need it so bad, sugar. Can you think of anything at all they *don't* want you for?"

"Armed robbery."

"Keep trying. Maybe you'll get lucky. Sugar, I better get you onto that boat before anybody tracks you right to here."

"Or before I get too scared to walk out the door."

He put on the hat and the glasses and checked his pockets. He went and got the gold watch off the shelf near the phone. Thanks for everything, Uncle Omar, he thought.

"How far to that Marina?"

"Ten minutes, about."

√ Before they went out, he kissed her. They held each other tightly for a few moments. She looked up at him. "Fun?"

"More than I can say."

"I could get a little weepy over you, Kirby. Let's go."

The Sunbeam roadster was, he guessed, about three years old, dinged, dirty and beginning to rust out. But the engine roared immediately, and she yanked it around a corner like a toy on the end of a string. He clapped his hat back on just in time. It was almost nine o'clock. She drove with her brown hands high on the wheel, chin up, eyes slitted, cigarette in the corner of her mouth. She shifted up and shifted down, and danced in and out of the lines of morning traffic with what at first seemed like terrifying abandon, but he soon recognized as such skill that he felt entirely safe in the noisy little yellow car.

She cut through to the waterfront, turned north and went three blocks, and when she began to downshift he saw the big Marina sign and all the pleasure craft at the wide docks. Suddenly she gunned it and went on by, and he saw the prowl cars at the curb and saw the uniformed men on the dock. She turned the next corner, braked, and tucked the little car into a parking slot.

"That door there is shut and locked," she said.

"I don't know what the hell to do!"

"Just sit tight and let Bonny Lee find out for sure. What's the boat?"

"The *Glorianna*."

She found a newspaper under the seat and handed it to him. "Hide behind this, sugar. Be right on back."

She was gone for a full fifteen unbearable minutes. Then she piled into the car and drove away from there. She headed west, found a shopping center, parked amid the other cars.

"It took me a time, Kirby, to single me out a cute cop and get him a-coming over to me to show off how big he is. That *Glorianna*, she took off twenty minutes ago and those cops got there ten minutes too late. Now as near as I can tell, what happened is they found out a lot of your stuff was moved out of some cruddy hotel, and it took time to track it down, and they found it got took to that Marina and put aboard the *Glorianna*. So they figure you're on it and they got you nailed good, because they got the Coast Guard looking already and they'll pick it up any time. It's a big old son of a gun the man there said. You know, they got the idea that twenty-seven million got put aboard, and they're all standing around so sweaty they can't hardly stand it. It wouldn't hurt me a bit to know what did get moved onto it, sugar."

"Personal junk. Total cash value, maybe two hundred tops. There's even a pair of ice skates."

Her eyes looked startled. "Shees marie. *Ice* skates!

"I've got no place to turn, Bonny Lee."

"I should truly like to hear from the beginning. Should we go back to Bernie's?"

"I'd rather not go back there."

"All we need is a place to talk, for now. And the last place they'd look I'd say is a public beach. Okay?"

"Okay, Bonny Lee."

The noise of the little car eliminated any chance of conversation. She drove over to the beach and headed north. By ten o'clock they were on a cement bench in a small open pavilion, looking out across a wide beach toward the curl and thud of the blue Atlantic waves. Though it was a Tuesday morning in April, there were hundreds of people on the beach. He was beginning to feel depressed and helpless.

"You load it all onto me, sugar, and then you get a new opinion."

He told her. He droned a leaden parade of facts, without color or hope. And in the telling of them, he disheartened himself even more. He took it from the first legal conference after the funeral right up to the morning phone call from Joseph.

He stared woodenly at her. "Think I should go try to explain?"

"Who the hell would believe you? Gawddammit, Kirby, they'd start looking for the needle marks in your arm."

"Do you believe it?"

"I'm this girl loves you. Remember? I do. But it is sure God an effort. Not loving you. That's right easy. Believing all this stuff comes hard. Charla. What the hell kind of name is that? Sugar, after those three broads, you sure got a change when I hopped into bed."

"What should I do?"

"You ever get a cake with a hacksaw in it?"

"I was afraid you'd say something like that."

"If both them girls were on that boat, the Coast Guard got them by now for sure. And that Charla and Joseph are maybe jammed up as bad as you."

"I doubt it."

He took Uncle Omar's gold watch out of his pocket. He fiddled with it, absently. He wound it, pulled the stem out, set it to correspond with his wrist watch. It had an hour hand, a minute hand and a sweep second hand. It had a fourth hand motionless at twelve o'clock, silver instead of the gold of the other hands. He wondered what it was for. He pushed the stem in again, and suddenly discovered that by pushing it in and turning it, he could turn the silver hand back to a new position.

In the instant he did so, the world turned silent and his vision clouded. His first thought was that he was having a heart attack. There was such an utter silence he could hear the murmurous sound of his own blood in his ears. Any speculation as to what might have happened was drowned in a total, primitive, unreasoned terror. To known hazards, the human animal can react with fear bleached with reason. The unknown drops him back into the cave nights, into the sabered terror, awash in adrenaline, the sphincter precarious, muscles knotted for the sideways leap, the head-down whimpering run.

He sprang to his feet, gasping, trembling, and yanked the sunglasses from his eyes. He felt a strange resistance as he jumped up, as though a wind he had not felt or heard pressed against him. All the world was still. With the sunglasses off, the world was a pale, unpleasant red. He had seen the world look like that before, when he had looked through the prism of a single lense reflex camera with a red filter on the taking lense. But through the camera he had seen the normal unending movement of the world. Now he was in a pink desert, or a garden of savage sculpture, or inside a painting by Dali filled with the horror of a timeless motionlessness.

A single wave, the length of the beach, curled and did not fall. The gulls of pink stone hung from invisible wires. He turned and looked down at the girl. The color of her face was unpleasant, and her lips looked black. She was caught in that eternity, hand half-raised in gesture, lips parted, tongue touching the edge of her front teeth. She had the merciless stillness of a body in a casket.

He closed his eyes tightly, opened them again. Nothing had changed. He looked at the gold watch. The gold hand that marked the seconds was motionless. He looked at his wrist watch. It, too, had stopped. He looked at the gold watch carefully, looked at the silver hand and at last was able to detect the tiny movement of it as it crept up toward twelve. He held the watch to his ear and thought he could hear a tiny sound, a faint, sustained musical note. He had set the silver hand back to ten. It was at seven minutes to twelve. It seemed a fair assumption he had been in the red world of silence for three minutes.

He took two experimental strides. Again he felt the odd resistance against his body. And his shoes felt as if they weighed twenty pounds each. It was difficult to lift them, to move them forward through the air and then to push them back down again. They had a strange weight and inertia, as though he walked through glue. And the pressure against his body seemed caused by an equivalent inertia in his clothing. He bent down and picked up a discarded paper cup. It was like lifting a cup made of lead. He felt the weight and resistance of it when lifting it, but when movement stopped, it seemed weightless. All the normal muscle-to-brain signals were distorted. Cautiously he released the cup. It remained suspended in the air, exactly where he had released it. He reached out and pushed it. He could move it through the air, but its motion stopped the instant he stopped exerting pressure against it. In this red world a body in motion did not tend to stay in motion. He grasped the cup and squeezed it. He could crumple it, but it was like crumpling a cup made of heavy lead foil rather than thin cardboard.

He looked at the watch again. Three minutes to twelve. He looked down the beach at the hundreds of motionless people. He looked toward the drive and saw the frozen river of traffic. Far over the city a jet was pasted against the sky. Fifty feet away was a small boy halted in the act of running, horridly balanced on the ball of one bare foot.

Cautiously he pressed the stem of the watch in, thinking he might turn the silver hand back to twelve, trying to believe that if he did so the world would be the same again, knowing he could not endure another three minutes of the red silence.

When he pushed the stem in, the silver hand, like the hand of a stop watch, snapped back to twelve. The noise of the world crashed in around him and the redness was gone instantaneously. The wave struck, the cup fell, the boy ran, the flying things flew.

"Think you could—" Bonny Lee said and stopped, stared at him, stared at the bench, looked at him again, swallowed, and said, "You can sure God move fast, sugar! Wow! You're in better shape than I thought."

He looked at her and laughed. He laughed until the tears ran down his cheeks, and until he began to hear an edge of hysteria in his own voice. She tried to laugh with him and then stopped, staring at him with concern.

"Kirby! Kirby, dammit!"

"I'm in great shape," he said, gasping. "I've never been in better shape!"

"You losing your damn mind, sugar?"

He dialed the gold watch back to the red world. He wanted time to think, time to control the helpless laughter. But laughter was easy to control. It sounded too hollow, too ghastly in the silence. She was again frozen, this time looking directly into his eyes.

He shuddered, shaking himself like a wet dog. He looked at the watch. He had set the silver hand at quarter of twelve. Fifteen minutes, if he wanted all of it. Or just depress the stem and let the world snap back to life. No. That was a distorted version of reality, an invitation to insanity. The world was the same. It was continuing. He had merely stepped out of it. Everything had stopped but the vibrations of light itself. And the dingy red look of the world might mean that light itself had slowed in relation to him. More logically, he had changed his objective relationship to time, so that perhaps one hour of red time would be a fractional part of a second of real time. Of course, that could lead you into conjecture as to which one was "real" time, a philosophical route to the same goal—insanity.

Using that premise, he considered the phenomenon of the paper cup. The feeling of weight would, in that event, be the product of its natural inertia multiplied by the extraordinary speed, the "real" world speed with which he had lifted it. And when he had released it, it had dropped back to the speed of the real world, which in the red world was an objective motionlessness. When he had crumpled it, he had stopped the invisible upward motion. It had begun to fall, imperceptibly, and when the world had returned to normal he had seen, out of the corner of his eye, the rest of the fall.

Suddenly he knew why Uncle Omar had been so extraordinarily deft at amateur magic. And he knew what had happened at Reno. He could see the plump, nervous little highschool teacher with the shabby clothing, with the tense smile, watching the dice coming to rest on the green table and, at the very instant they stopped, moving into the red world, circling the table, reaching through the silence to turn one die to the proper winning number, returning to his place, and instantaneously catapulting himself back into the "real" world.

And he could guess where all the rest of the money had come from, and why so much had been given away. And he knew he had received his inheritance. It was as if he had been looking through a kaleidoscope, turning it aimlessly, looking at the meaningless patterns of the fragments, then had by accident turned it just so and had the bright bits form a realistic image. He marveled at the control, the caution, the life-long guile of Omar Krepps.

He reached out and touched the girl's cheek with his fingertips. Her cheek felt neither warm nor cool. It seemed to have no discernable temperature. And it felt unhumanly firm, as though fashioned of some dense but very slightly resilient plastic. He touched the pale curls and they had the texture of iron wire. When he bent them, they stayed in that position.

Again he found himself in danger of making the subjective error of assuming the world had changed. He found himself glad he had been forced, by Uncle Omar, to take the courses in Logic. Bonny Lee was in "real" time. Through her eyes he was merely movement far too fast to leave any retinal image, his touch on cheek and hair, too brief to leave any sensory impression.

He suddenly perceived one of the rules Uncle Omar must have followed all his life. You must return to the real world in the exact space where you left it. Otherwise you can drive men mad. In spite of all the caution of Omar Krepps, he had been considered most odd and most eccentric by the rest of the world. Perhaps there had been some carelessness from time to time. Now he knew the reason why Charla and Joseph thought of him with an almost superstitious awe. In international financial intrigue, the gold watch would give Uncle Omar the insuperable advantage of a one-eyed man in a world of the blind.

This was the edge! This was what they wanted, yet could not specifically describe. It made him feel cold to think of this device in the hands of Charla.

Ten minutes more. He resolved he would let the time run out and see if, when the silver hand reached twelve, the result would be the same. He started to walk, but the inertia of the shoes made it a slow and difficult effort. He took them off. When he dropped one, it remained in the air. He started to push it down to the sand, then realized it made no difference to leave it there. He could walk more easily, but he had to press against the inertia of his clothing, and knew that if he was naked he could walk freely.

His feet did not sink into the sand as far as he would normally expect, but he did leave curiously perfect shallow footprints. He wondered about it and realized that the soft sand had begun to fall back into the prints but, in the red world, the motion was too slow to be visible. He walked by the eeriness of the red statues, all the way to the water's edge. He stepped into the water. It offered resistance, but his foot sank into it. It was like stepping into firm jello. When he pulled his foot out, the impression, inches deep, remained. Drops of sea water hung in the air, perfect spheres, pink in the red light of the world. One was as high as his face and, on impulse, he leaned and took it into his mouth. It was like a firm little blob of gelatine. He chewed down on it and swallowed it. It left a salty taste in his mouth.

Five minutes.

He walked back through the people. He made himself stop and look into their faces. He came upon a little girl feeding gulls. The hurled morsel of stale bread was a few inches from her fingertips. The gulls were poised. A yard from the back of the little girl's head there was an object frozen in the silent air. It was a toy sand shovel. He looked and saw a fat boy several years older than the girl, his face bloated with hate and rage, ten feet behind the little girl, frozen in somewhat the attitude of a big league pitcher when the ball is halfway to the plate.

Kirby reached out and put his hand against the tin shovel and pushed. He moved it several feet to the side. The fat boy wore swim trunks and a baggy T shirt. Kirby walked in front of the little girl and reached up and put his hand around the body of one of the gulls and pulled gently. He pulled it down and walked it over to the fat boy. He pulled the boy's T shirt away from his bare stomach. It was like bending metallic mesh. He pushed the gull up under the T shirt and bent the bottom edge of the shirt back in.

Two minutes.

He hurried up the beach to the pavilion. He put his shoes on and positioned himself as before, and discovered he had time to spare. On playful impulse he took a cigarette out and placed it carefully between her parted lips. The silver hand moved closer and closer. . . .

The bright morning was like a light turned on.

She gave a great leap of surprise and took the cigarette out of her mouth. "What the *hell!*"

"A trick my uncle taught me," he said. He turned and looked down the slope of the beach. Gulls dipped. A bright shovel had spun harmlessly into the sand. A fat boy had gone mad, howling, leaping, whirling, until a gull, crying alarm, darted up, leaving some white feathers floating down. The perfection of his footprints was gone, and the footprint in the water.

Bonny Lee's face looked strained. "Tricks are fun, but I din like that one worth a damn, Kirby. Make me all cold and queasy."

He sat on the cement bench beside her. "I'm sorry."

"Honess, Kirby, first you act like the end of the world is here, then you're laughing like a nut, then you do some spooky trick. I thought I had you figured, but now I—"

"Something important—suddenly happened, Bonny Lee."

"I don't get it."

"I want to do—a sort of experiment. Look right at this spot here on the bench between us. Look at it very carefully. Then tell me what happens and tell me how you feel about what happens."

"You know, I'm getting terrible nervous about you, sugar."

"Please, Bonny Lee."

He twisted himself back into the red world, this time turning the silver hand further than before. He turned it all the way around to twelve again and there it stopped and would not go further. This, then, was the limit of the red world, one hour of subjective time. He put the watch down and carefully, cautiously let go of it. Nothing changed. So it was not necessary for actual contact to be made throughout the red time interval. He saw a piece of broken shell a few feet away. He picked it up and placed it down on the cement right in Bonny Lee's line of vision. He picked the watch up and pressed the stem with his thumb. The silver hand snapped all the way around back to twelve, and he was back in the bright movements of her world.

She started. She looked gray under her tan. She closed her eyes and swallowed and then reached and touched the fragment of shell. She moved it a few inches and shivered. She stared at him, and sounded close to tears as she said, "You gotta stop this kinda tricks, Kirby. Please."

"What happened?"

"You saw it! Gawddamn it, you *did* it! All of a sudden, a hunk of shell is there. It didn't grow or fall from any place or—it was just *there!*"

"How did you feel?"

"Terrible!"

"I mean, what did you feel?"

"Whattaya mean, sugar, *what* did I feel? I'm just looking where you say and then—" She stopped and peered at him and looked angry. "I get it now, you spooky bassar! You're hypnotizing me! You're not supposed to be able to do it to anybody doesn't want it done. And I don't like it. So cut it out, hear?"

"I'm *not* hypnotizing you, and stop getting sore. Now I want to try something else. If it works, it might frighten you at first, but—"

"No more, Kirby!"

"Didn't you say you wanted to help me?"

"Sure, but—"

"And you love me?"

"I guess so, but—"

"Then let me try this, and I swear it won't hurt you in any way, and I'll explain it to you if it does work."

She looked at him sullenly, dubiously, and then gave a nod of agreement. He moved over close to her and put his arm around her. He held the watch in both hands in front of her. "Put your hands over mine."

She did so and said, "What has that old gold turnip watch g—"

The world was red and she was frozen, unyielding. Maybe you couldn't take another person into the red world, take someone out of "real" time. He snapped the silver hand back.

"—ot to do with it?" she said.

"Try touching the watch this time."

"Make up your mind," she said. Again she was a statue in the redness.

He came back to reality. "This time, get your fingers like this, your thumb right against the stem, and now as I press down, you press down too and give a little turn and—"

He was alone on the bench, his arms holding a girl no longer there. The watch was gone also.

He had the immediate memory of closeness, of the lithe

warmth of her. She had winked away into nothingness, and in its own special way, it was a nastier, more gut-wrenching shock than his initial foray into the red and silent world.

No, two could not go.

Kirby sat stunned with the realization of what he had done to her. She had neither the maturity nor the background to cope with the silent horror of that other world. He stared into distance and did not see her. Her primitive mind, shrewd though it was, would shatter under such an impact. He had a horrible thought. Perhaps, believing the watch to blame, she would hurl it into the sea. It would stop, and leave her forever trapped in that red time, where no one could see her or hear her, where all the rest of her life might pass within, perhaps, a half-hour of real time.

He sat dazed by guilt, by the enormity of what he had inadvertently, stupidly done to Bonny Lee Beaumont.

9

NOT UNTIL KIRBY STOOD UP DID HE SEE, BEYOND THE END OF THE concrete bench, a little pile of clothing—a pair of lime slacks, white sandals, a white blouse with a yellow figure, a yellow jacket, a white purse. He picked them up and put them on the bench. The items missing were the blue-green nylon bra, the matching panties.

Her voice came from ten feet behind him. "Hey! Hey, sugar, this is more damn fun!"

He spun and saw her there in the sunlight, brown and beautiful, winded, glowing with excitement. The sun glinted on the gold watch in her hand. She put her fingers on the stem of the watch. "Give it to me!" he yelled, but she was gone before he could say the last word.

He heard thin cries, almost but not quite like the yelping of the gulls. He looked far down the beach to the north where the crowd was the thickest and it seemed to him that all the people down here had gone mad simultaneously.

He squinted against the glare and thought he saw Bonny Lee appear and disappear again in the middle distance, but he could not be certain.

He began to realize that he had made a poor estimate of her response to the red world. Bonny Lee had a totally pragmatic mind. She would not give a damn for theory. All that would concern her was that it worked, and he had given her the clue as to how to make it work. Though—from the viewpoint of his limited experience—she had given him ample, skillful and luxurious proof that she was a woman grown, and even though she had devised a philosophy of existence which seemed to suit her and seemed to work for her, he remembered that she was but "twenny, practically," that there was a child inside the woman, and the child had never had much chance for the games of childhood, and that she was a hoyden, reckless, irreverent, comical and inventive. He remembered, too, that she was in bursting health, firm, fleet and tireless.

He squinted at the people running to and fro in the distance, yelping, and he wondered if he had not inadvertently loosed upon them on this pleasant Tuesday morning something just as fearful as a playful tiger. He remembered the mischief and the satisfaction of tucking the gull under the fat boy's shirt. He had astonished himself with that act. Surely Bonny Lee would go a good deal further than that before astonishing herself.

He wondered if he should walk down the beach and see what was happening. But Bonny Lee would expect to find him at the bench.

He saw two figures coming up the beach at a dead run. They seemed more energetic than fleet. He stared at them as they went by. First one would hold the lead and then the other would overtake her and pass her. They seemed to be heading for the parking lot. They were a pair of young women of rather generous construction, naked as a pair of eggs.

An elderly tourist who had been walking by came to a dead stop near the bench and stared at the running women. He wore a Truman shirt, Bahama hat, Bermuda shorts, blue sneakers. He watched them make the sweeping curve toward the parking lot and disappear. He turned and stared questioningly at Kirby.

"'Til this very minute, son, I prided myself on twenty-twenty vision."

"Sir?"

"Mind telling me what just run by?"

"Uh—two young women."

The man moved closer. "Son, what would you say they were wearing?"

"They didn't seem to be wearing anything."

The old man peered at him. "If I was your age, son, I'd be right with 'em, running like a deer. You don't seem even interested. You sick?"

"I—was thinking of something else."

"I got down here from Michigan day before yesterday. Maybe I got the wrong idea. Maybe that ain't so unusual a sight around here."

"Well, I wouldn't—"

"Good day in the morning, here comes another one!"

She was a small sunburned redhead, with a transistor radio in one hand and a thermos bottle in the other. She was near the end of her endurance, wobbling from side to side as she cantered along.

After she, too, was out of sight, the old man sighed heavily. "One thing I give you, son. You picked the right place to set. Is it a new fad, you think?"

"I don't know."

"I hope it catches on." He shaded his eyes and peered up the beach.

Suddenly Bonny Lee was close enough to touch and there was a pile of paper money on Kirby's lap. It spilled onto the bench and onto the sand. She laughed once and was gone.

The old man whirled around. "Son, you got a high laugh on— ain't you spilling something?"

"Oh, this?"

"Money, ain't it?"

"Yes," Kirby said heartily. "It certainly is." He grabbed at the bills that started to blow away.

"I think the sun has got to me," the old man said. "I think I better get the hell out of it." He plodded away.

Some other people had moved near, staring curiously at the money. Kirby gathered it up quickly. She hadn't bothered with one-dollar bills and there were only a few fives. It made a wad so thick that after he had folded it once, he had difficulty putting it in the side pocket of the borrowed slacks. He picked up Bonny Lee's clothes and walked away from the bench, north along the beach, knowing that she could always find him. While she was in the red world, he would be motionless to her. He became aware of a vast traffic jam in the drive behind him. He heard sirens in the distance. He came upon a man walking in a slow thoughtful circle, hitting himself in the forehead with his clenched fist.

Suddenly Kirby had a new pipe in his mouth, a bouquet of roses tucked under his arm, a gold ring with a big yellow diamond on the little finger of his left hand, and Bonny Lee in her pretty undies striding along with him, chuckling. He made a frantic grab for her, but she danced back, fiddled with the watch and flicked out of his world. He looked at the place where she had disappeared and saw blurred shallow footprints heading north. The fact that they were blurred and not perfect meant she had already reappeared somewhere else. He realized that inasmuch as his world was static to her, in relation to his time, she had to reappear somewhere else the instant she disappeared in front of him.

Later he was to learn that, during the fifteen minutes she was on the loose, she spent, as near as she could remember, about four subjective hours in the red world, four hours until she tired of the games and could think of no more.

Later he was to learn, in more detail, of the bewildering calamities which befell all those unfortunates among the thousand and a half people enjoying that stretch of Atlantic beach.

As Bonny Lee told him, "There they were, all them broads, naked as the law allows, strutting it around to work up the guys, and I figured it would be a lot more honest they should unwrap the merchandise entire and see how the guys reacted then. That's before I was working it so good, before I learned you can do it okay one-handed, just push down with your thumb and give it a little bitty twist. So all the ones in the right positions so I could get at their suits and halters and stuff, I went to work, where they were gathered thickest, and honess, sugar, I worked like a horse, maybe a half-hour, peeling that stuff off them and carrying it down and tossing it out over the water—pushing it out. When everything is red, you can't throw anything. It kind of stops."

"I know."

"Nine outa ten, I swear, they looked a hell of a lot better with the suits on. A lot of those guys got a bad shock. Anyhow in that one patch of beach I got maybe forty stripped entire, and got the top half off I guess twenty more. And what good is a joke you can't see it, hey? So, seeing how I was dressed, I thought I should sort of hide, then I realized compared to them sixty broads, I was *overdressed*. So I just went to a spot where nobody was looking right at me and pressed the dingus."

"How did you find out about doing that?"

"Anybody smart enough to make a cute thing like that is going to make it so you can use it and not be waiting around for the time to run out. So I tried turning it and tried pushing it and found out how."

"Oh."

"Shees marie, Kirby, you shoulda seen! Out of sixty, maybe three or four took it cool. The rest went straight up in the air, screeched like to bust your ears, scrabbled around for towels, but I'd got rid of them too. Then they tried to find something to hide behind or under. But a beach is damn empty, you know. Those guys had their mouths hanging open and their eyes bugged out, and the broads milled around, yelping, and then all the ones could swim, like those lemming things somebody told me about once, they went into the ocean on the dead run, maybe seven guys with good reaction time right after them. And the ones couldn't swim, they headed every which way, the smart ones heading toward where I hadn't gathered the towels and stealing them from other folks. I laughed until I had the hiccups, and then two guys started closing in on me so I went back into the red place, put two big sand buckets over their heads and took off."

"How about the money?"

"The money?"

"The money you dumped in my lap."

"Oh. That. Oh, that's from when I went over into all those stores over there. Ever' time I went by a cash drawer, I took some. But carrying stuff is a drag. You gotta kind of push it or pull it along. In the department store I found a hell of a thing, you know? An old lady had tripped or something right at the top of the escalator and there she was, tilted way out, her hands out in front of her, her face all screwed up. That's when I found out you can move people, too. I went behind her and got her around the waist and braced myself and first I thought I couldn't. But if you give a real steady pull, they come along. I pulled her back and straightened her up and there she was, about eight inches off the floor. So I got in front of her and pushed her about six feet, and pulled her back down onto the floor. Then I picked her packages out of the air over the stairs and put them in her arms. I had her holding them funny, but I didn't want to try bending her arms. I was afraid I'd break something. So then I went to the racks and got a dress and put it on and went back and stood by her and turned the world back on. She gave a big jump and dropped all her packages. She wore the damnedest expression, sugar. She stared at the escalator and then she picked the packages up and stared at the escalator again and dropped them again. Then she picked them up and shook her head and started walking toward the elevator. It was right after that I found out something else funny."

"What was that?"

"In the sports part—I was still wearing the dress off the rack—there was a little bit of a boy throwing a basketball to a clerk. It was in the air. The clerk had his hands out, grinning. The ball was in the air and in my way, so I just shoved it toward the clerk as I went by. A second later time ran out on me. I forget all about time in a store anyhow. And I heard this thud and this horrible gagging sound and something falling. I looked around and the clerk was rolling around on the floor hugging his stomach, and making them sounds, and the little boy staring down at him, and the little boy's mother."

" 'Honey, you threw it too hard,' she said to the little boy. They helped the clerk up and his face was a terrible color. The woman said she was sorry her little boy had thrown it so hard. The clerk told her she was missing a great opportunity. He said she should take the little jerk out to spring training and by October he'd be in the series, making big money. The woman started yammering and the little boy started crying and the clerk started yelling, so I turned the whole thing off and got out of the damn dress and got rid of the purse I took to carry your money in, and came back. I think it was right after that I got into the softball game."

"The softball game?"

"No. First I took car keys. Gawd, sugar, it's funny walking in those cars knowing if you push the dingus, they're suddenly going like hell. I was going to reach into those and take the keys, but I didn't rightly want I should get nobody killed, so I took the keys out of the cars stacked up for the red light. There was a big convertible so I climbed into the back and turned the world on, after I pushed all the keys into the trash basket on the corner. Every yuk in the world starts blowing his horn and nobody can move. The guy at the wheel looked around and saw me and I smiled pretty at him and he shut his eyes and turned pale white. So before he could open them, I turned everything off again and went and got all the keys out of the cars stacked up the other way, since the light had changed. Everybody in such a damn hurry, sugar, it's good for them to take a little time out."

"I'm sure they enjoyed it."

"Then I got into the softball game, way down the beach. A big old muscly lunk was showing off for his girl, busted into a ball game of little kids, smacking that ball way down the beach. So I found me a girl way off and took her cute little short shorts and her little halter and come back and practiced some until I could stop everything when that ball was just out in front of the plate, and then I'd go out and push it up six inches or down six inches, and the little boy pitching turned out having the biggest-breaking curve strike you ever see, and the big bassar—he like to sprained his back swinging, his girl laughing at him—got so mad he slang the bat at the little pitcher. But I stopped it in time, pushed it back toward him too hard I reckon, and he hadn't ducked would have whomped his head clean off whistling by. He shaky like an old man, his girl leading him away."

"You kept busy."

"I would have said it got to be way late in the middle of the afternoon, but a little bit of time here goes a long way there. Took food I wanted offen a picnic, taken it to a quiet place and ate fast. Found me a brute man cuffin' his little wife around, and I sure God played hell with him." She smiled in fond reminiscence. "Park fellas painting a restroom close by. Ended that brute man up buck naked, painted bright green, mouth packed full of sand, sobbing like a big old fat baby."

"Good Lord!"

"Found me a big-jaw, mean-eye wife blasting her little husband for staring at girls, him lying on a woolly blanket nearby looking heartsick, so I give her something to work on for sure. Towed over a mess of pretty little girls, one at a time, and like to clean covered him up. Turned the world back on and that woolly blanket was like onto a bucket of worms afore they could all get untangled and take off ever' which way. She screamed for sure, but I don't think he heard a word, just sat there wearing a funny little smile. Got up and walked clean away from her, still smiling. Never had so much fun in my whole life entire."

But all that came later. At the time she gifted him with the pipe, the ring and the roses, he wasn't certain he'd ever see her again. And that very probably wasn't what Uncle Omar had planned for him—if, indeed, the old man had arranged things in some pattern he had yet to discern. He put the ring in his pocket, flipped the pipe into some plantings and jettisoned the roses in a trash basket. The continuous blare of horns from the expanding traffic jam was making the day hideous. There seemed to be a lot of women in swimming, screaming instructions to people on the shore. Suddenly he realized that an impressive number of police had begun to appear on the scene, blowing whistles, yelling at each other and expressing confusion.

As a tall young officer came hurrying by, Kirby turned away too quickly. The cop stopped abruptly and came toward him, staring at him intently. "Take off them glasses, buddy," he said.

"But I'm only—"

An ugly-looking revolver was suddenly poised, aimed at the middle of his chest. "Hand over some identification, real slow and easy. Make me nervous and I twitch. My whole hand twitches something awful. Trigger finger and all."

Kirby placed his wallet in the cop's hand, very, very gently.

The cop flipped it open, took one quick glance at it and began to grin and bounce up and down on his toes. "Oh, you fine hand-some ten thousand bucks! Oh, you pretty package, you! What you say is that Corporal Tannenbaumer collared you. You keep men-tioning that, hah? Promise me now, or I bust those teeth off at the gum line. Can you remember the name?"

"Corporal Tannenbaumer."

"Now grab the back of your neck with both hands. That's nice. Harry! Hey, Harry! Come see what *I* got!"

Harry, too, was lean and bronzed, with that look of eagles marred only slightly, as was Tannenbaumer, by a minor look of adenoidal vacuity.

Harry glanced at the wallet identification and said, "Honest to God, Tanny, you could fall in a sewer and come up wearing a gold bridge. Want I should go get the Sergeant?"

"No, Harry. For one grand you ignore the Sergeant. For one grand we take him in all by ourselves, and let the Sergeant worry about all this other crap."

"For two, Tanny."

"One and a half tops."

"We got to walk him a hell of a ways, Tanny."

"So cuff him to me."

"Why not to me?"

"Because for ten grand, Harry, you would sap me and leave me face down here in the cruddy sand, so don't squirrel around with me. What's going on down the beach there anyhow?"

"The report said there was a lot of naked broads, Tanny, and there are a lot of naked broads. And the other report said like forty guys lost their car keys in traffic, and the tow trucks are working on it. And there is one guy painted green they're still try-ing to catch. But the way it figures, some smart-ass crowd set up all the confusion so as they could clean out them stores across the way. The hell with it, Tanny. We got a good day's work right here."

"I got a good day's work. You got one and a half, after I get mine. Hustle them cuffs, Harry."

Tannenbaumer moved beside Kirby and held out his left wrist. Kirby, by instruction, held out his right wrist. Harry got the cuffs out and looked at Bonny Lee's clothing on the sand. "What's that stuff?"

√ "Girl clothes, for God's sake. So what? Maybe he was figuring on disguising himself. Are you stalling for the Sergeant to get into the act? He'll take the full ten and give us a couple cigars and a day off. Hurry!"

Harry made as though to snap the cuffs on the two wrists and suddenly he was standing there with both his own wrists handcuffed. Tannenbaumer stared at him. "How the hell! Harry, you cruddy thief, you're stalling!"

"What are you arresting him for?" Bonny Lee demanded.

Harry and Tannenbaumer turned and stared at her. Tannenbaumer said, "We got an ordinance underwear ain't allowed on any public beach in Dade County. You go get some clothes on, kid, or you get took in."

"Get these off me, Tanny," Harry said plaintively. "The key's in my shirt pocket."

"You run while I'm busy, Winter, and I blow one of your knees into a bag of pebbles."

Tannenbaumer unlocked one of the cuffs, and then it was on his own wrist. "My hand musta slipped," he said apologetically. "Where's the key?"

"You got the key, Tanny."

"I had the key."

"It musta fell in the sand, huh?"

"Harry, I think the Sergeant is headed this way. You, kid, you got to go get out of that underwear."

"I'm not bothering anybody," Bonny Lee said.

"I wasn't so busy, Tanny, she'd be bothering *me*. How about you?"

"Shut up. Look, Harry. What we do now is, we cuff him to my other wrist, and we go in like this."

"Won't it look a little funny, Tanny?"

"We can't help that."

"How will we drive the car, Tanny?"

"We'll all sit in the front. Hold your wrist out, Winter. Harry, I hand you my gun?"

"You didn't hand it to me, Tanny. Hey, girl, you see him hand me the gun?"

"Leave her out of this. Give me your gun, Harry."

"Hell, they musta both fell in the sand. Tanny, we're not making this arrest very good, you know?"

"If they fell in the sand, where are they?"

"We been moving around, Tanny. Maybe we kicked sand over them."

As they were both looking behind them at the sand, Bonny Lee sidled quickly over to Kirby, put the watch and chain into his hand and said swiftly, "Carry me outa here, sugar. I can't carry you."

Tannenbaumer turned around and yelled, "Get away from—" And was suddenly a red statue in the eerie light of a dying sun. Kirby looked at the watch. He had flipped the silver hand back twenty minutes. He was impelled by a feeling of haste until, by an effort of logic, he realized he was occupying an instant of no-time, and thus had all the time wanted to take. He stuffed the watch into his pocket and bent the pocket back around it. He put his arms around Bonny Lee's waist. She felt like a stone statue covered with a layer of tough rubber. With a slow and steady effort he was able to lift her off the ground. He lifted her a couple of feet into the air and released her. He went around behind her, braced both hands against the rounded rigidities under the blue-green nylon and, his feet digging into the sand, moved her a dozen feet away. He was gratified to know he could get her away from there, but it was a rather disheartening effort.

He left her there and reviewed the situation. A natural caution made him wary of leaving a nothingness for the two cops to stare at. There might be a reduction of future trouble and future questions if he could give them a chance to talk each other into it being a case of mistaken identity. He walked to where red statues stood by a red refreshment stand and walked among them and selected a girl first. She was Bonny Lee's size, and blonde, and would have been very lovely except for her deplorable lack of chin. The less inertia, he decided, the easier she would be to manage. She had on a wraparound skirt, and taking it off was like unwinding sheet tin from around a fence post. The halter top was a little more complicated. She had been caught in a frozen toothy smile. The underthings were lacy black below, uplift white above. By the time he had covered the fifty yards with her, he had, by trial and error, discovered the easiest way—to arrange her horizontally, hug her feet into his armpits and tow her. He stood her where Bonny Lee had been, rewarding Harry and Tannenbaumer with her dental smile. He remembered to leave his shoes behind when he went and selected a man. The effort was like pulling something which was being simultaneously pulled from the other direction. The moment effort stopped, the forward motion stopped. By the time he'd reached the scene with the stranger who resembled him in size only, his breath was creaking and his legs were weak with effort. He rotated the man and positioned him. He went wearily over to Bonny Lee and turned her into a horizontal position, ready for transit. He rested and reviewed the details. He recovered his wallet from Tannenbaumer's shirt pocket, inserted one of his cards in the stranger's wallet and put it in Tannenbaumer's pocket. He picked up Bonny Lee's clothing and wedged it under her arm. He shoved her purse and shoes and his shoes into the front of his shirt. He grasped her feet, hugging them under his right arm, and, leaning far forward, began to tow her toward the parking lot, two hundred yards away. He rested several times. Finally he tried to make the job easier. He pulled her feet apart, carefully bent her legs at the knees, then hooked her legs over the tops of his shoulders, plodded on, holding her wooden ankles in his hands.

Suddenly the world went bright. Bonny Lee slammed him with a tremendous impact, seat first, right against his shoulders, and banged him headlong into the sand and went tumbling end over end beyond him, with a yelp of pain and fright and a welter of flying garments. He sat up, spitting sand, and looked back. The chinless girl stood screaming, and the manacled cops were in tandem, chasing the substitute.

"Whyn't you watch it!" Bonny Lee shrilled at him.

"Are you hurt?"

"You didn't do me any good, you silly bassar! What the hell are you—"

He spun her into red silence. He got up, saw that he had given himself a half-hour, arranged her for transit again, and took her to the parking lot. He found a small maintenance building with a wall screening it from the road. The building itself stood between them and the beach. He straightened her legs and stood her against the wall. The look of indignation and anger was frozen on her face. He tried to brush the sand out of her hair, but the small particles remained in the air near her head. He looked in all directions to be certain they were safe, then pushed the watch stem.

"—trying to do?" she said, catching her balance. She looked around. "Oh."

"The time ran out on me."

"You shoulda checked, Kirby. You could get somebody hurt. You move something and then turn the world on, and it goes like hell. I seen a fella comes to Rio's and gives me a bad time, just walking out of the ocean, so I give him a good lift up and back, like to sprain a gut, then pushed that dingus and he went on up like out of a cannon, roaring and going end over end and landing back in the water fifty feet out."

"Are you hurt?"

She fingered her shoulder and her hip. "You like to brushburn half the hide off me, sugar. What do we do now?"

"Let's start by you putting your clothes on."

"Fair enough. Shees marie, I'm pooped for sure. Where's the cops?"

"Chasing the wrong guy."

"You put another guy there?"

"And a girl."

"Lot of work, wasn't it?"

"Yes, but we shouldn't be careless with it, Bonny Lee. If too many things happen which can't be explained, somebody is going to figure out that—"

She buttoned her blouse and slapped the rest of the sand out of her hair. "What you don't know about people, Kirby, anything they can't explain, they make up something suits them. If suddenly a guy can fly just like a bird, he'd know for sure it was clean living and deep breathing." She opened her purse and fixed her mouth. "Sugar, let me have that big old watch a minute."

"Sorry. We're getting into the car and getting out of here."

"Getting bossy, hey?"

They got into the little Sunbeam. The parking lot did not exit on the same street as the traffic tie-up. She stopped at the exit to the lot, the motor running. She frowned at him.

"What's the matter, Bonny Lee?"

"I was figuring out something. Don't mess with that watch while we're moving, sugar. The car would stop cold dead and you'd keep on going. I'd have to clean you off the dash and the windshield with a sponge."

"Uh—thanks. What were you doing that was making all that confusion?"

"Lots of things. Tell you later."

"Where are we going?"

"We need a safe place, don't we? I'm busting my biggest rule. No man was ever going to set foot in my place. Ever'body knows about it, and you can sure get in without being seen."

"How?"

"Sugar, sometimes you're right stupid."

"Oh. Of course. Sorry."

"What time is it?"

"Twenty after eleven."

"In the *morning!*"

"In the morning, Bonny Lee."

She had a garage apartment in an old part of the city, behind a stately old house of Spanish-Moorish design which, she told him, had been cut up into small apartments and was occupied almost exclusively by old ladies with small incomes. "Coming and going at all hours, and the kind of work I do, I give 'em something to cluck over," she said. "But it keeps the men scared off from bothering me here, and I get along with them, most of them. And they bring me cakes and stuff."

She explained how he could get in, and dropped him off a block away. He gave her ten minutes and spent the time strolling along the narrow quiet street on a shady, overgrown sidewalk. He leaned against an iron fence and, when he was not observed, he stepped into the red world. It was easier to carry shoes than to wear them. He went back to the house she had pointed out. In a lawn across the street a sprinkler made a static pattern of shining pink droplets hanging in the silent air. A small dog paused for its moment of forever, staring intently up into a tree, ears forward.

He walked along the driveway. Three old ladies sat at a metal table in the back yard in the shade of a beach umbrella, mouths ajar, knitting needles rigid. He went into the open door of the garage and turned to the right as she had told him, and up the stairs. Pulling the screen door open at the top of the stairs was like opening the weighty door of a vault. Indoors, the redness seemed more oppressive, but he could see that by normal light it would be a tiny cheerful place with bright draperies, straw furniture, gay rugs and pillows. There were framed publicity pictures of her on one wall and he peered at them with approval through the bloody murk.

She was in the small bedroom, sitting on the dressing table bench. She had pulled her blouse down from her right shoulder and was stopped in the moment of rubbing something into the abrasion from her fall. The room had a three-quarter bed, ornamental iron bars on the window, a deep window seat, a bamboo chaise, a vase of wilted flowers. He stood behind her and started to pop into her world and then hesitated. He had almost fifteen minutes left. And too much had been happening too fast. Her head was turned sharply so she could see her shoulder. He kissed the side of her throat. In this world it had the rigid somewhat waxy texture of polished wood. He went over and sat on the bed. The unyielding rigidity of it startled him for a moment before he remembered that in the redness everything was fibrous, toughened, yielding reluctantly to forces and pressures.

He looked at her, sitting erect, six feet away. Her back was arched, her shoulders good, the waist slender, the lime slacks plumped to the pleasant tensions of her ripeness. There was a tantalizing familiarity in the back of his mind and after a moment he identified it. He had seen a television play—two years ago?—a fantasy about a department store dummy, played by a blonde actress—Ann Francis?—and after she had been free for a little while, they had forced her back into the store, and in the final scene she had become rigid and waxen again, frozen in position, displaying a summer frock.

Bonny Lee seemed just as unreal, just as unalive, but he could move his thumb a quarter of an inch and bring her to glowing life. He had not had time to think about her, actually. But now he could take time which was no time at all, because it was time the world was not using. He felt toward her a vast and tender gratitude. She had cut briskly through a thousand dreads and fears and mysteries and had brought him joyously to his delayed maturity. It would be all too easy, he sensed, out of his new-found confidence and arrogance to devaluate the gift, to use cheap and easy words—shallow, ignorant, amoral, much as the swaggering adolescent feels obligated to jeer at the girl he so clumsily seduces.

The revelations of Bonny Lee gave him a new perspective on himself and on the world. Having thought himself uniquely inadequate, he now wondered how many other Kirby Winters there were, milling about in the world, winking at the right times, laughing at the punch lines, handling the little flirtations very well indeed, but poised to run in terror if it appeared the lady was trying to say yes.

He remembered the sound of the rain on the tin roof of the old Hudson, and the feral graspings and gabblings of Hazel Broochuk, and how weeks of plotting and importunings all came to a ghastly inconclusive end in the incredible clumsiness of those few minutes. He could have gotten as much excitement and almost as much pleasure by falling into a hay baler. And he remembered her thin pocked face in the faint light, twisted with contempt as she wriggled back into her skirt, and remembered the dreadful words which had remained forever in his mind, written in a puckering of scar tissue. "You not worth a goddamn, boy. You done me no good. Owning a hammer don't make nobody a carpenter, boy, so you better leave me off down in the middle of town. I'll say where."

And there had been no one to hustle the crashed pilot into another aircraft, and the nerve was gone, and he spent thirteen years on the ground—until Bonny Lee erased the myths, peeled the scars away, showed him the bed was a picnic shared, rather than a lonely stage, where instinct was the only value and the only necessity.

Five minutes remaining.

He hefted the watch in his hand. It was the only object in the red world which did not have that odd sticky drag of inertia. And he felt an overwhelming awe at all the things it represented, at all the temptations implicit in its ownership. Here was absolute power, and total corruption. Here was a freedom so complete it became not freedom at all, but enthrallment to the witchery of being able to dislocate time itself. Here was invisibility, voyeurism, invincibility, wealth—in fact, all the night dreamings of adolescence, in one-hour subjective packages. Here was, in a specialized sense, immunity.

The possibilities of it gave him a sense of reckless, dizzy elation, yet at the same time made him distrust himself. The obligations implicit in the possession of such a device were severe. Use of it had to be related to some responsible ethical structure. And a good part of the responsibility was to conceal the power and the purpose of the device from the world.

Suppose, he thought, there were fifty of these in the world, or five hundred? Chaos, anarchy, confusion and fear. It would be as though a new mutation had occurred in mankind, a time of the superman, making privacy meaningless, making all ownership conditional.

Suddenly he was filled with an awed respect for Omar Krepps. For twenty years he'd had this edge, this advantage, and he had kept it as quiet as possible. Had he displayed the abilities this gave him, other men might have conducted research in this same direction. Apparently Uncle Omar had decided that this device would turn the world to a shambles were it released. He could see a pattern in the things Omar had done. He had quieted the publicity about his gambling winnings by returning and purposely losing an amount almost as great as the amount he had first won. He had made amateur magic his hobby—to help cover any slip he might make. He had avoided all personal publicity. And he had hidden behind great wealth, acquired quickly—yet so short was public memory, it was as though Omar Krepps and his ancestors had been rich since an earlier century.

The noise and brightness and movement of reality came into the room, and within the first two seconds he turned the silver hand back, halting reality. Bonny Lee's hand had moved higher on her shoulder. Her head had turned slightly. He had sunk into a sudden softness of the bed and then it became rigid again, but in a more comfortable contour.

How then, had Uncle Omar acquired the money? Wealth, he realized, is a strange abstraction concerned with the exchange of bits of paper, signing them, filing them, recording them at the right times, in the right places. Stock manipulation would not be too difficult, once the procedures were understood. He could imagine Uncle Omar trotting busily through a red hour, inserting the proper orders in the proper files, using the red time to give him the same advantage as hindsight. Once acquisitions had been made, control could be turned over to Krepps Enterprises, and money had a knack of multiplying, when there was enough of it.

But if Omar Krepps had been so aware of the potential menace of the device he had created, why hadn't he let it die with him?

The reason, possibly, was a kind of egotism. Someone had to know. And, long ago, Uncle Omar had apparently selected Kirby as the inheritor of this fantastic power, had judged him capable of using it well, had seen to it that Kirby acquired the academic background which would enhance a judicious use of the device. The courses which his uncle had insisted he take, and which had seemed so impractical at the time now made increasing sense. Sociology, psychology, philosophy, ancient history, comparative religions, ethics and logic, anthropology, archeology, languages, semantics, aesthetics. And then eleven years of the exercise of judgment in a context which required no competitive instinct, and made secrecy, reserve, evasion and rootlessness a habit of life.

He now sensed that it was an ideal background for the new owner of such absolute power. It created a minimum risk of the device being used for violent, random, frivolous, acquisitive purposes. It directed the new owner to use it for the maximum good of mankind.

But, in that case, why had Uncle Omar not explained the whole situation long ago? Perhaps because Uncle Omar had thought him lacking in strength and resolution, had been impatient with him, had even told Mr. Wintermore that his nephew was a ninny. And then, after the warning attack, Uncle Omar had apparently prepared for death by setting up a curiously random situation. The watch first and—a year later—the letter. He knew the letter would relate to the watch. What if he had put it in a drawer and forgotten it? What if he had been in a moving vehicle, a car, train or plane when he had fiddled with the silver hand? Why had Uncle Omar so instructed both Kirby and Wilma Farnham that immediately after his death they would be in grave difficulty? Surely Uncle Omar could have anticipated what would happen.

It all seemed to be some kind of a test, but he could not see any consistent pattern in it.

For the first time he examined the watch with great care. The ornate initials OLK on the back were worn thin. There was a catch near the stem so the back could be opened. He hesitated, put his thumbnail against the catch and snapped it open. There was a second case inside, of smooth gray metal, with absolutely no way to open it. On the interior concavity of the gold back was engraved something else, almost as ornate as the initials, unworn. He translated, with some difficulty, the Latin words. "Time waits for one man." It had that ring of slightly sour humor so typical of Omar Krepps. He snapped the case shut and for the first time he began to wonder about the power source. It would seem plausible to assume that distortions of space, time and energy could be achieved only through expenditures of vast power. The watch seemed to be permanently sealed. It had an old-fashioned bulkiness. Certainly the distortion of time could not be achieved through purely mechanical means. He held it to his ear and again thought he heard the faint musical note, in a minor key, like a faraway wind in high tension wires. And he wondered if its capacities could be used up, if it would work only for so long, or for so many times. That sort of information would probably be in the letter.

What if Wintermore had fiddled with the extra hand?

He felt exasperated at his uncle. It did not seem possible Omar would have left so many things to chance.

What next? The watch, properly and carefully used, with sufficient advance planning, would enable him to solve the problems of the various criminal actions and civil actions. But it would have to be done in a way which would quiet public interest rather than enhance it. A total notoriety—as Uncle Omar had realized—would make life impossible. One would be sought at the ends of the earth by nuts, monsters, shysters, maniacs, fanatics, reporters.

He knew he had started badly. Letting it get into the hands of Bonny Lee had been an inadvertent violation of the implied trust and responsibility. It should be treated with as much gravity, care and respect as a cobalt bomb. Four times he had tried to escape from Uncle Omar's control into a life of normality, of the small goals and pleasures of the average life. He knew that chance was gone, unless he denied the responsibility by smashing the watch, or dropping it into the sea. That was one possible decision, but he could not make it until he had used the watch to remove all pressures, regain anonymity.

Again there were five minutes left. He looked at Bonny Lee and felt a great galloping rush of desire for her. But electric as the urge was, there was a strange placidity about it, an assured and comforting smugness. In Rome last year he had desired the woman named Andy just as much, but there had been no flavor of happiness to it. And because it had made him wretched, it had distorted desire into too significant a thing. So now something new had been discovered. Frustration bloated the role of sex, kept it in the center of the stage and gave it all the lines. It had stunted the other aspects of his life through its false importance. Release had suddenly put it in proper context. It was dwindled, and could now share the lines with the other actors—essential to the play but not obsessional, suitably dramatic but linked to reality, capable of comedy as well.

I was a legless man, he thought, and watched everyone in the world walking and running and climbing, and the attribute of leglessness colored every reaction to some degree. I pretended I had legs, so no one would notice. Now I have legs, and though walking is a joy, legs are now just a part of living, and the awareness of them comes and goes. I accept the fact of having legs.

He went over to Bonny Lee, bent and put his lips against the rigidity of her mouth and pressed the world back to life. The warmth and softness came in a twinkling and she gave a convulsive leap of fright, a small squeak of dismay. The brown eyes narrowed.

"That's right sneaky," she whispered. "Like to jump clean outa my skin, you bassar. It's not a kind of thing anybody is ever going to get used to, sugar."

She wiped her fingers on a tissue and went into the other room and closed the heavy plank door and bolted it. She moved casually into his arms, kissing him lightly on the chin and gave a huge, shuddering yawn. "I'm pooped entire, Kirby." She trudged over and sat heavily on the bed and yawned again and knuckled her eyes. "Don't you go near the window so any of those biddies can see you."

"I've got a lot of problems to think about, Bonny Lee."

She kicked her sandals off and stretched out on the bed. "Can't think of a thing until I get some sleep. Aren't you bushed too?"

"Yes, I guess I am." He went over and sat on the edge of the bed and leaned over her and kissed her with considerable and lengthy emphasis.

She chuckled. "Man, you're not as sprung as I am."

"Bonny Lee?"

"No, sugar. It would be a waste of talent for sure. Please let me sleep, sugar, and then we'll see. You oughta sleep too. Whyn't you go on out on the couch where you can quieten down nice?"

"I shouldn't waste time sleeping, with all that—"

She silenced him with a sudden gesture, bit her lip and said, "Gimme the watch, sugar."

"I really don't think you ought to—"

"I wanta try something, stupid! I'm not going to get cute, I'm too gawddamn tired to get cute. You gotta trust me, or we are going absolutely no place at no time. Hand it over."

He hesitated, gave it to her reluctantly. She grasped the stem of the watch. In something that seemed like a flicker of movement just a little too fast to be visible, she was in an entirely different position, the watch on the bed a few inches from her slack hand, her eyes closed, breathing slowly, deeply, audibly through her parted lips. He spoke to her and she did not answer. He shook her and she whined. When he shook her again she reached for the watch. An instant later she had flickered into a slightly different position, and she was completely bare. One instant she was wearing her clothes. The next instant they were in midair beside the bed, falling to the floor. He woke her again and she mumbled and growled and took the watch and flickered into a different position. He touched her shoulder and she came awake quite easily. Her eyes were slightly puffy with sleep. She yawned and stretched luxuriously. With the awakenings, the entire procedure had taken just a couple of minutes.

She smiled at him and said, her voice soft and husky, "Three whole hours. Mmmmm. Now you." She wriggled over to the wall.

"Get comfortable first, sugar, cause the damn bed and pillow get hard as a stone. Better strip on account of clothes feel sorta like cement."

He stretched out and turned the world red. He made the full twist, turning it back the maximum of one hour. She was sculptured of smooth dark red wood, propped on one elbow, smiling at him. He was in the rigid hollow in the bed his weight had made. He tried to go to sleep, but the clothing was oppressive. He got up and tried to take it off, but it was as stubborn as thick lead foil, so he clicked back into the world and stripped rapidly, his back to her, his face hot with the confusion of modesty, of a daylight intimacy he had never known before. In haste and an awkward confusion he stretched out again and flipped into redness and soon drifted into sleep. Suddenly he was awakened and her head was on the pillow, facing him, a few inches away.

"Take another hour, sugar," she whispered. "Take two. I can wait."

He went back into redness and into sleep, and was awakened with her smiling at him as before. "Doesn't it work good?" she whispered.

He yawned, marveling at her quick instinct for the utility of the device. It was something he would never have thought of—or at least not for a long time.

"That was one strange thing about Uncle Omar. Sometimes he seemed to be able to get along on no sleep at all. We wondered about it sometimes."

"That old man had it made, Kirby. It's like only a couple of minutes since I woke up for the last time. You want a little more sleep?"

"N-Not at the moment."

"You know, I din think so, somehow," she whispered. "This must be my day for breaking all the rules there are." She moved closer. She hooked a warm firm silky leg over his. She was so close all he could see was the single huge brown eye, moist and bright, feel the heat and weight of her breath. "It's so nice to love you," she sighed. "Because you're sorta shaky and scared, kinda. And sweet. What you do, you make it *important,* Kirby. And that makes me go all funny, like marshmallows and warm soup, and my heart is way up here going chunk chunk chunk, and I almost wanta cry, and let's make this time all slow and sweet and dreamy and gentle and closer than anybody ever got to either one of us, and be talking to me. Be saying the nice things, and I shall say them back, ever' one."

10

KIRBY WINTER AND BONNY LEE BEAUMONT MADE LOVE, TOOK naps in the red world, showered together with a playfulness, with small mischiefs and burlesques, bawdy comedies over soap and shared towels—a playtime so alien to his own estimates of himself that he felt as if he had become another person. He had strode in lonesome severity past all the fiestas, thinking them flavored with evil and depravity to be righteously condemned. But suddenly he had been invited in, where all the warmth and the music was, and had found himself caught up—not in depravity, not in decadence, not in wickedness—but in a holiday flavor of a curious innocence, a wholesome and forthright and friendly pursuit of quite evident pleasures.

In any plausible use of aesthetic theorizings, she had contours, textures and colorings which made her, as an object at rest or in motion, highly pleasing to sight, touch, taste, and hearing. Through the very process of appraising her as not only an individual, but also an object of aesthetic value, pleasing to him, he was able to achieve an inversion of that logic and assume that he, in kind, was also, to her, an individual as well as an object which pleased her. And this brought him to an objectivity which altered his prior attitude toward his body, changing it from something ludicrous, something so grotesque as to merit concealment, to an object meriting that pride which was a reflection of her pleasure.

He was pleased to be tall, grateful for a muscularity in part inherited and in part developed, perhaps, as a byproduct of many sublimations, distressed at a roll of softness around his middle, particularly after Bonny Lee's soapy, derisive, painful pinch, and was resolved to become as taut as she, knowing it would please her. Though at first the physiological mechanisms of desire had a distressing obviousness, targeting him for saucy jokes, he achieved acceptance of the inevitable and then progressed to a degree of self-satisfaction bordering upon the fatuous.

Yet throughout the whispered soapy games, in spite of his years of inadvertent continence, he could guess she was a rare one, precisely suited to bring him back into the race of men with minimal delay. He sensed that had there been any trace or trick of self-consciousness about her, any contrived modesties or measured reservations, had she in fact struck any other attitude other than that of a happy, exuberant, exhibitionistic, inventive, gamboling, young, coltish creature, he would have tumbled back into awkwardness, irrational shame, dismay and the puritan persuasion that anything so delicious must, of necessity, be evil.

There was a pattern in the love play, little times of promising to stop all this nonsense, and then an instinctive awareness of whose turn it was to become the aggressor, to be repulsed playfully, or with mock solemnity, or with wicked reprisals, and sometimes the sweet and momentary acceptance, abandoned quickly by one or the other before it went on beyond any chance of stopping it.

She sat on the edge of the blue tub and he scoured her hair dry with a big maroon towel and watched it spring back to damp tight ringlets. Suddenly the games were over, with no need to explain it to each other, with only the need to carry her to the bed and, with all the accumulated tensions, quickly, strongly, boisterously, strenuously, joyously take it so quickly over the edge that in her completion she made sounds like a slow, strange laughter while, with an astonishing strength, she held him absolutely motionless.

They listened to the two o'clock news with astonishment and incredulity. After the fifteen minutes ended, there was a special fifteen-minute bulletin on Kirby Winter—the adventures of.

When the final commercial came, she turned off the little transistor radio and placed it on the night stand beside the bed.

"Even crazier than the news, sugar, is it being the two o'clock news. My head is out of joint. All these naps. It should be tomorrow, almost. No more naps, Kirby, because you know what'll happen for sure. Get all rested and want each other again and take more naps and—hell, we keep this up the only way you'll leave is on a stretcher, or float out the window."

"I can't understand how Betsy Alden—"

She sat up and frowned at him. "Say, did your Uncle Omar look a lot older than he was?"

"What?"

"A day is got to have twenny-four hours, sugar. Lemme see. You know I stuck maybe an extra eleven onto this one? Time and a half, like. I bet if I had the same kinda day every day for ten years, I'd all of a sudden be thirty-five insteada thirty. Was he old-lookin'?"

"I guess he was. I guess he looked older than his age."

She lifted a long brown leg and flexed it. "Hefting them people around on the beach and all, I wore myself down. So there's wear and tear, but now there's just a little sore, like the day *after* you do too much."

"Didn't you hear the broadcast?"

"What kind of a smart-ass question is that? Surely I heard it. They've all gone nuttier than ever."

"So they made a positive identification and so then I overpowered two policemen, disarmed them, handcuffed them and lost myself in the crowd. So now I'm armed and considered dangerous."

She giggled at him. "Eliot Ness'll be coming after you, sugar. Anyways, what could those cops say? You know, I'm about to starve, sugar. I got some steaks. How you want yours?"

"Medium."

"You want it medium, but you get it rare, sugar. I'm to be taken care of you, hear?"

He remembered the money, the confusion on the beach, the pipe, the ring and the roses, and asked her what she'd done. She put the steaks on and came back and told him some of it, went and turned them over and came back and told him more, then went and brought in a tray, with the steaks and glasses of milk and a big stack of French bread and a bowl of sweet butter. As they ate she told him all the rest of it.

He went and got the wad of money and the ring out of the bor-
rowed slacks. She watched him silently as he counted the money.
He stared at her and said, "Sixty-six hundred and twenty dollars,
Bonny Lee!"

She shrugged. "Geezel, sugar, it din seem like stealing it, but I
guess it was. Nothing I did seemed real. You know. But you
heard what the radio said. Twenny thousand. Hell, they're all
adding it all on for the insurance."

"How about the ring?"

"Oh, that. Over near the bathhouses I see a fat ugly bassar with
two of his buddies, got a guy backed against a wall looking for
some way to run. I din like three against one, so I froze them still
and wrapped the belt off one of them round his ankles, tied a
necktie on the ankles of another one and gave the littlest one a
big push. I guess I only tilted him over an inch. I worked the ring
off the pinkie on the fat one, and I went fifty feet off, sorta behind
a bush. The little one went ass over teacup into a cactus patch
and the fat one went down backwards and the other one went
down sideways, and the little guy against the wall took off like he
was a deer." She took the ring from him and scratched her empty
milk glass with it. "Diamond, all right," she said. "Big sonuvabitch, huh?"

She glanced at him quickly enough to catch his fleeting gri-
mace.

"Don't talk so sweet and pretty, do I?"

Her perception startled him. "I don't mind, Bonny Lee."

She tossed the ring onto the tray. "Maybe you do. Maybe I do,
too. But maybe there isn't a gawddamn thing neither of us can do
about it, sugar. I got to be a woman entire afore I learned up on
being a lady. I had four year of schooling, all told. You want you
a tea party lady, you just go get yourself one, hear? Go grab one
offa the P.T. and A. You and she can talk up a storm on art and
culture and such, Kirby, then you try taking a shower with her
and hustling her into the sack and see how things work out, see if
you don't have to sign contract papers forever with a guarantee
income afore she'll even step down offa her high heels."

"Bonny Lee!"

"Oh, don't look at me so gawddamn pitiful, you sonuvabitch! I get along fine and I don't need you nor anybody." She hurled herself face down on the bed and began to sob, making sounds like a small boy punished. He patted her and soothed her and held her.

Finally she got up and went in and bathed her face and came out, grinning somewhat shamefacedly, snuffling from time to time. "All a damn lie," she said, "and you know it. You being schooled makes me feel funny. I want to do better, but what the hell chance have I got? Shees marie, I work six nights a week and that's when they got night schools, even if I could get in. Sorry, sugar. I don't crack up so much. It's on account of this being such a goofed up day, maybe. I'm just a share-cropper girl outa Carolina, cheap, ignorant and fun-lovin'."

"You low rate yourself too much. You're bright and quick."

"So is a she-fox. Let's drop the whole thing."

"You're the same age as a college kid."

"Compared to a college kid, I'm a hunnerd n'ten."

He picked up the wad of money and dropped it beside her. "You took it. So use it, if you mean what you say. Use it until it runs out, then go back to work."

She looked thoughtful for a few moments, then looked sidelong at him. "Say, didn't you hear that broadcast? First things first, Kirby."

The news had been peculiarly distressing. The *Glorianna* had been intercepted down near Dinner Key and had put in there and tied up while the Metro police had made an investigation. On the yacht had been a skeleton crew of three, Mr. Joseph Locordolos, a Spanish national and a developer and speculator in hotel and resort properties, his sister, Mrs. Charla O'Rourke, a Greek national and member of the international set, and Miss Betsy Alden, Mrs. O'Rourke's niece, a naturalized citizen of the United States who had worked in New York and Hollywood as a bit-part actress on television. The yacht was registered in Panama. Mr. Locordolos was very agitated at being halted in such a peremptory fashion. All the papers were in order. He explained that they were taking a short shake-down cruise of several hours to see whether the newly installed radar was working properly. Both he and his sister explained that, while staying at the Hotel Elise, an establishment partially owned by Mr. Locordolos, they had made the acquaintance of Mr. Kirby Winter, nephew of Omar Krepps whom they had known slightly over the years. They said Mr. Winter seemed quite depressed and, because the boat was roomy enough, they had suggested he come along with them to Nassau, and he could then fly back from there. Mr. Winter had said he would think about it, and they had assumed he would not be joining them until the trunk and the crate arrived aboard. They had been unable to contact Mr. Winter to ask him about it, but they assumed it was his intention to go with them to Nassau, perhaps for a longer stay than he had indicated would be possible. Perhaps, as soon as they heard of the huge embezzlement, Mr. Locordolos admitted, they should have contacted the police. Instead, as he explained, he investigated the contents of the two containers and found nothing of any importance in them. He had given up, of course, any idea of permitting Mr. Winter to accompany them, and had merely been waiting until Mr. Winter put in an appearance, at which time he was going to have the containers moved onto the dock at the Biscayne Marina and wash his hands of the whole matter. Though the police had a search warrant, Mr. Locordolos felt that it might not be properly applicable to a vessel of foreign registry; however he volunteered to overlook the legal considerations and asked for a complete search on a voluntary basis. The police impounded the items Mr. Winter had shipped to the yacht, and found nothing else of any pertinence to the Winter case. They had previously impounded the suitcases discovered in Winter's temporary quarters at the Hotel Elise.

During the search of the boat they had an opportunity to interrogate Miss Alden. She was in bed in one of the staterooms. Mr. Locordolos and Mrs. O'Rourke had explained that the young actress had suffered a minor breakdown from overwork and they were taking her on a restful cruise. Miss Alden, in a weak voice, had confirmed all aspects of the explanation given to the police.

In the meanwhile, Winter having been definitely identified as being still in the area as of eleven that morning, all exits from the city were being watched. So many pictures and descriptions had been circulated, it was not believed he could remain long at liberty. It was entirely possible the Farnham woman had already departed for some planned rendezvous with her co-conspirator, and once Winter was picked up, it was entirely possible he would disclose where the Farnham woman could be found. With both of them in custody it seemed possible that recovery of the secreted millions might be undertaken.

Grumby, in yet another public statement, had warned all authorities involved in this complex matter that Kirby Winter, once apprehended, might very possibly attempt to confuse the picture by falsely implicating others. He asserted that despite periodic pleas, Mr. Krepps had never revealed the use that was being made of the twenty-seven millions diverted from Krepps Enterprises to O.K. Devices. He stated under oath that they had never seen a dime of this money, had no idea what had become of it, and assumed that it was properly covered in the Krepps will in that portion which spoke of the bulk of the estate which should be established as the Krepps Foundation. In an accompanying statement, the District Director of Internal Revenue stated that all appropriate income and gains taxes had been paid on the twenty-seven millions prior to their disappearance into the mysterious operations of O.K. Devices. He said that in the absence of any other records, the twenty-seven million could now be considered a part of the estate and taxed as such. If during the interim period additional values had accrued, then doubtless capital gains taxes would be due and payable in the event the assets of O.K. Devices were found and liquidated. However, in view of the unusual aspects of this situation, he was prepared to wait and find out what had happened. If the executives of K.E. were indeed blameless in this situation, as they appeared to be, then possibly some adjustment might be made to avoid punishing them financially for the wrongdoing of another.

Mr. D. LeRoy Wintermore, of Wintermore, Stabile, Schamway and Mertz, made yet another statement, saying that in view of the cluttered situation, he was exercising the option of delaying the assessment of the total estate until one year from the time of death. He hoped that things would be more orderly by then. He said it would delay the establishment of the Foundation, but it might well make the tax computations easier for all concerned. In closing he said that he felt that Kirby Winter had neither the cleverness nor the resolve to engineer such a vast malappropriation of funds, and wondered aloud if the whole thing might have been more logically planned and executed by the Farnham woman.

Winter, meanwhile, was wanted for assault, resisting arrest, theft of police weapons and carrying concealed weapons without a license—all this in addition to the summonses, the subpoenas, and the formal charges of embezzlement, tax evasion, conspiracy and fraud.

The morning disturbance on the beach was neatly accounted for. It seems that a large rowdy band of teen-agers had run amuck on and near the public beach, yanking the beach costumes off women, snatching the keys from parked cars, racing through the stores and grabbing money, and playing other cruel and grotesque tricks upon the innocent. County officials believed them to be under the influence of some sort of narcotic which had turned them into a large pack of reckless animals, and said it was possible they might be part of the spring college group down from Jacksonville, Daytona or Lauderdale, or even on their way back to school from the Bahamas.

"I am a large, rowdy band of teen-agers," Bonny Lee said happily.

"They have a description of one of the gang. You heard him. Several people reported her. A short-haired, deeply-tanned blonde in pale blue underwear."

"Aqua."

"The same one Tanny and Harry saw, you know."

"Uh-huh. I know."

"I replaced her with an item in black panties and a white bra."

"Stacked?"

"Best I could find on short notice."

"Blonde?"

"Natural."

"Beautiful?"

"Completely."

"You tryna be a bassar?"

"Except she had an unfortunate profile. An almost perfectly straight line from the edge of her upper teeth right down to the base of her throat."

"That's better. Enjoy the undressing bit?"

"I was too nervous to notice."

"That's good too, sugar. That's right sweet of you."

"I'm damned worried about Wilma."

"Who? Oh, the one looks like a priss. From what he said on the phone, that Joseph guy, they were bringing her to the boat. So was she hid someplace aboard?"

"I don't think so. Charla told me they had a crew of five. The news account said there was a crew of three. So I think it's a safe bet two were sent after Wilma and didn't get back in time. Joseph got some news flash about the cops checking on my things that were moved out of the hotel, and he got nervous and took off. Maybe they got to the dock with Wilma in time to see the boat chugging away."

"Or maybe they came and saw the cops like we did."

"So what would they do?"

She shrugged. "That's an easy one, isn't it? She was in a safe place, until Betsy told Joseph about it. So they can't walk the streets, and I suppose a crew would live on a boat, so why not take her on back where they got her and stay there with her until Joseph gets in touch, huh?"

"It's logical, I guess. But it might be a long wait, you know. If they didn't buy what he said all the way, they'll be watching him."

"You said there's no phone there. Where is it?"

"Ah—two-ten Sunset Way, Hallandale."

"We could find it, you know."

"But the big straw hat and the glasses didn't work so well, Bonny Lee. That cop wasn't fooled."

"Because you flinched. Remember? You tried to ask him what was going on, he'd never looked twice, believe me. You be okay, sugar, just head up and ready to spit in their damn eye. I'll get me some clothes on."

It was a quiet street of small ugly stucco houses on the sizable plots of pre-war Florida, their ugliness softened by the tropic plantings which had grown up in almost vulgar profusion. Professor Wellerly's house, tinted a faded pink, was more obscured than the others on the street. It was a hot, sleepy afternoon. A power mower made an angry snorting sound several houses away. Birds were yelping, raiding a fresh store of berries on the tall bushes lining Wellerly's driveway.

A laundry truck passed them. Bonny Lee slowed and, when the truck was out of sight, she turned into the weedy shell driveway of a boarded-up house.

She turned toward him. She had changed to a black and white checked shirt, a white crisp skirt. "Sugar, I don't wanna be no nuisance woman, but how about you show up right here? I mean so I'll know nothing is messed up."

He nodded, gave himself the full hour just in case. It seemed odd to him that it was easier to get used to the redness than to the silence. The abrupt silence was so absolute it was like being enclosed in a padded vault. He slapped his thigh just to assure himself he had not lost the power to hear. He took off his shoes and walked back three houses to the Wellerly house. After he got beyond the screen of plantings he saw the blinds were closed. When he went around the corner of the house a mockingbird startled him. It hung there motionless at the same height as his face. He circled it and saw the back bumper of a car parked behind the house. He realized Bonny Lee's guess might be absolutely correct. He looked at the car. It was a newish cheap dark sedan, and might logically be a rental car. There was a dark blue baseball cap on the front seat.

He circled the house and found it was completely closed up. He tried several ways to gain entrance and was stymied by the leaden inertia of all objects in the red world. Remembering what Bonny Lee had told him of the odd behavior of objects, he picked polished stones out of a big planting pot. They were the size of plums and lifting them was like pulling them up through heavy glue. He released nine of them in midair, properly positioned, five in front of the back door, four in front of a back window. He then gave each of them a lusty push toward target, aiming them at latches and hinges and frames and locks. They stopped the moment pressure was taken off them. He remembered his promise and hurried back to the car where she sat, looking up at him with the unchanged expression of concern he had seen on her face in the instant of departure.

He clicked back to normal time, and heard a distant thudding, crashing, splintering, tinkling of glass.

"What in the world are you—"

"Back in a minute," he said and turned her off along with the rest of the discovered universe.

He hurried back and hid behind the car and turned the world on, then thought better and turned it off immediately. The shattered door hung from one hinge. The window was completely gone. He went into the kitchen and discovered that the stones had gone through the door and window and across the kitchen and into the dish cabinets and cupboards, and he suddenly felt ill to think of what could have happened had Wilma been standing there. A new lesson learned.

They were in the living room. Two beefy young men were stopped in the middle of a card game. The room lights were on. Apparently, back in the normal world it was hot in the room. They were shiny with sweat. The big one with light hair had his shirt off and a hand towel draped around his neck. He had intricate faded tattooing on his forearms and biceps. The other was shorter and wider, and burned dark by the sea. Both of them had long sideburns, coarse, thickened features, that impenetrable look which is a combination of slyness and animal hungers and a taste for brutality.

The dark one held a card poised. Both of them were looking toward the kitchen with startled expressions. Wilma Farnham stood by a book-lined wall near the small coquina rock fireplace, books from floor to ceiling. Her brown hair, in an unkempt cascade of wispy strings made her small face look smaller. Her glasses were crooked, her blouse half out of her skirt, her mouth oddly slack with surprise as she too stared beyond him toward the kitchen. The drink in her hand was tilted and, as she stood off balance, a dollop of it was stopped halfway to the floor.

He went to work. It was difficult work, but in its special way, enjoyable. Within fifteen subjective minutes he had the tattooed one and the dark one neatly arranged. He had found it easier to work on them when they were suspended horizontally in the air a yard above the figured rug, but it had taken every ounce of his strength to bend them, straighten them, hoist them into that position. He'd wrapped their wrists and ankles with heavy twine which, in the red world, reacted like thick copper wire. He'd stuffed their mouths with toweling and tied it in place. Finally he had sheathed them in bedsheets, wrapping it like foil, then wound them from ankle to shoulder in clothesline. Bending it around them was like wrapping them in copper tubing. He had to grasp the rope at some distance from them in order to get that leverage which made the task easier.

He hurried back to the car. Bonny Lee looked startled when he reappeared.

"What's this little delay, hah?"

"Sorry. Look, I got to get back there in a hurry, but you can come in there now. Through the back door. Bring the car in and turn it around, facing out."

"Okay."

He twisted the stem and walked back through the deadness of the silence. Wilma had used the several seconds to move closer to the two mummies, and again she was spilling as she stared at them. Kirby felt mild regret at missing the chance of seeing them fall simultaneously, side by side. At first he was going to appear, carelessly, thoughtlessly, in front of her. Just in time, he went back to the doorway off to one side and slightly behind her. He stepped into normal time and normal space and said, "Wilma!"

Suspended liquid fell onto her bare instep. She swung around, took one uncertain step and peered at him. She pushed her glasses into place and said, "Loanbeehole, Sir Lanschlot, as I live and bree!"

"Are you drunk!"

She tottered toward him, smirking. "Za skunk, cutie bug. Bessa my life in selfless devotion a duty, 'n you know what I get? Pleece looking for me. An that Bessy girl asking me things I don't know'nything about. Ol' Omar's stone cold dead, 'ny got no job, 'na hole thing's giving my dear brother a nervous stomach, 'n you, you silly man, I popo—propozizhun you, firse timin my lousy wretched choked-up life I gotnuff guts. 'N whattayou do?" She put her nose inches from his chin and looked up at him cross-eyed. He could hear the Sunbeam snoring into the drive. "Whattayou do? Run! An then—" She backed off slightly. "An then here I am, poor incent girl at the mercy of those two sailors an all they want to do is play cards. *Course* I'm drunk, fren! Firse time." She burped herself slightly off balance, recovered, beamed at him and said, "I like it!" She turned vaguely and stared at the shrouded figures. They were both making small helpless spasms and smothered grunting sounds. "What happened alluva secon to Rene and Raoul?" she asked plaintively.

Bonny Lee came in and stared at Wilma. Wilma swung around again and held Bonny Lee in an inquisitive squint, pushing her glasses back against the bridge of her nose. "Who you, pretty fren?" Wilma asked.

"Wow!" Bonny Lee said. "I figured in your picture you looked like a school teacher. Excuse me all to hell."

Wilma peered at Bonny Lee, pulled herself together with precarious effort and said, attempting precision, "Ektually, my dear, I yam more the cerebral type."

Bonny Lee sighed. "You want to talk to her, I guess, don't you, sugar?"

"If possible."

"Who's in the packages?"

"Rene and Raoul, seafaring men."

"They look like they'd keep. See what you can do about some coffee, Kirby." Bonny Lee gave a hitch at her skirt and marched toward Wilma. It was as though she had rolled up her sleeves and spit on her hand. She marched Wilma, wailing protests, sputtering with indignation, into the bedroom wing.

All Kirby was able to find was some instant coffee of an unfamiliar brand. But it looked dark and smelled strong, and the label said nothing about how it would improve sleep. In the other end of the small house were the distant sounds of conflict, yelpings and the roar of water. He went in and checked Rene and Raoul. They were still until he checked their bonds, and then they began thumping and grunting again. He could hardly blame them. It must be very uncomfortable in there, he thought. The sheets were getting wet with sweat and beginning to cling. It was very muggy inside the house.

He filled a big pottery mug with strong steaming coffee and took it into the bedroom. The bathroom door was ajar. Wilma's clothes and Bonny Lee's clothes were on the bed. He put the mug on a table and walked back out. Bonny Lee seemed to be winning. All he had heard was the rushing roar of the shower mingled with a heartbroken whimpering. He fixed the knots more se-

curely and went over and studied the bookshelves. Professor
Wellerly apparently acquired books in every field of human
knowledge, providing the title was dull enough and the binding
sedate. He gathered up the spilled cards, shuffled them and dealt
random poker hands. The gold watch would considerably simplify poker. He evolved various methods and decided the most
useful one would be to freeze the scene in the instant the dealer
was reaching to pick up the deck which had just been cut. Take
the cards and arrange for three or four strong hands, and give the
others nothing so they would fold. Give yourself the best hand,
by a narrow margin. Like four little threes against three pat
hands, a flush, a full house—aces up, and a high straight. Put the
sorted deck back under the reaching hand, sit back and wait for
the action.

"Kirby, sugar!" Bonny Lee called. He went in. Bonny Lee was
dressed again. Wilma sat huddled on the edge of the bed wearing
a man's summer robe that was like a tent on her. Her hair was
darkened and flattened and she looked sullen and drowned. She
stared down at the floor.

"Sip the nice coffee, sweetie," Bonny Lee ordered.

"No thank you," Wilma said in a precise but muted voice. "I
think I might be going to be ill."

"Sip the pretty coffee, sweetie, or we strip again and I trot you
in and wedge you under that cold water and I take that big brush
and I scrub off all the hide you've got left."

Wilma hunched slightly and humbly sipped her coffee.

"You know, she's not really so bad, except how she don't even
try, for God's sake. She's got a real cute figger."

"Figure."

"Figure," she said carefully.

"Hell, I'm sorry, Bonny Lee."

"I'm not. Not at all. You keep it up. Anyhow, she *has* got a
real cute—figure, sorta like boyish, but not enough so anybody's
going to get confused. But geezel, them wire glasses and that ratty
hairdo and them Salvation Army clothes—"

"I have no urge to be cheap and obvious," Wilma said.

"Stay snotty and I'll stomp your spectacles, sweetie. You're not
obvious for sure. All the men in the world are in a big candy

store, and you're out there in the dark knocking on the window with a sponge. You ever hear a whistle in your life? Ever get pinched?"

"Thank you, no."

"Do you some good, sis. Makes you stick out on top and swing on the bottom. I'd put bright green contacts on you, give you a Cleopatra beehive, put you in something too tight to sit down in, and four inch heels, and learn you to be walken slow, with your shoulders back and your belly in and your butt stuck out, dangle earrings and musky perfume. Not my style, but in gear like that, sis, you'd make strong men cry."

"Cleopatra beehive?" Wilma asked shyly.

"Not exactly beehive. The Egypt bit, like Liz."

"Liz?"

"Oh for God's sake," Bonny Lee said. "You talk to her."

"Betsy brought you my note?"

"Yes, Kirby."

"And you talked to her?"

"All night, just about. She kept trying to make me remember things about your uncle. She thinks there's something special hidden. I don't have it. I don't even know what it is. Your uncle was a very unusual man. He was so smart, Kirby, he didn't need any special kind of thing. His great mind was enough. I did just as he told me to do, and no matter what they do to me, I'll never, never—"

"I understand your loyalty, Wilma. Out of that loyalty could you be denying the existence of something you know exists somewhere?"

"I swear I'm not, Kirby. I swear it. She told me where you were. Why would you hide in the apartment of a cheap person like that, Kirby?"

"As I don't know the man, I'm not ready to pass judgment."

"Would that be how you met this trashy girl? Who is this girl, Kirby?"

"Bonny Lee is a good fr—excuse me. Bonny Lee is a girl I am in love with."

"Oh dear," Wilma said.

Bonny Lee winked at Kirby. "Y'almost flunked out, friend."

"That was a lie, wasn't it?" Wilma asked in an almost inaudible tone, "When you told me you were frightened of women. You were saving my face, weren't you? How you must have laughed after you got away from me!"

"I told you the truth. I ran in pure panic, Wilma."

"But right now you seem—different. You don't seem scared of anything in the world—anything."

"I'm scared of a lot of things."

"But he's gettin' right brassy around the broads lately," Bonny Lee said and giggled at Kirby's look of annoyance. "I hear tell he undressed one right on a public beach. Din' even know her name."

Wilma looked horrified. "Kirby! Are you well?"

"I'm perfectly all right," he said angrily.

"Didn't she struggle?"

"Poor dear little thang couldn' move a muscle," Bonny Lee said.

"*Please,* Bonny Lee! Please."

"Sure, sugar. I'll be good."

"Wilma, have you been keeping track of the news reports?"

"I think I heard it all, but parts of it I can't remember very clearly. About that yacht and your things being on it, and about you escaping from those policemen this morning, and taking their guns. It just—didn't sound like you."

"When did Betsy leave here?"

"Very early. She said she was going to go race a bluff. That doesn't sound quite right. Run a bluff? Yes, that was it. But the expression is unfamiliar."

"I guess you must realize her bluff didn't work."

"I don't understand what happened. I guess it was almost three hours later when those sailors got here. They rang the bell properly, so I assumed it was Roger or you or even Betsy coming back. They forced their way in. They seemed quite—cordial in a rather unpleasant way. When I started to be severe with them, Rene, he's the big one, but I didn't know his name then, smiled and took my wrist and turned it slowly until I was finally down on my knees with my face against the carpet. It was absolute agony. My arm still feels odd, you know. Then I knew I had better go along quietly. I couldn't understand who they were. I was afraid they were some thieves who had hurt Roger and made him tell where they could find me, and then they were going to force me to reveal the location of that money, that absurd money that's all gone. But I gathered they were taking me to a yacht, the yacht they worked on, and that Betsy was there waiting for me. They made me sit on the floor in front with my head back under the dash. It was very hot and dirty and uncomfortable. Then suddenly something was very wrong. They became cross with me and with each other, and they argued about what to do and then they came back here. From what they said, I gathered the boat had left without them. They were most surly and rather apprehensive until at last we heard the news about the yacht. But they said Betsy had been taken ill. She seemed a very tense and excitable person, but I did not guess she was close to having a breakdown."

"Sis," Bonny Lee said, "you kill me. You really do. Those bassars grabbed that Betsy girl and took her onto that boat and hurt her until she said where they could find you and find Kirby here, and made Kirby promise to come on account of being maybe able to help Betsy and to keep them from doing you like they done her. This thing you don't know what it is, they want it bad."

Wilma stared solemnly at Bonny Lee. *"Hurt* her?"

"Sweetie, of a Saturday night in the wrong part of New Orleans, you can get you crippled for a lifetime for a cruddy seven bucks, so why should this make you bug your eyes? Where you been livin'?"

"This is terrible!" Wilma said. "Your uncle would have agreed, Kirby. We must find out what it is they want and see that they get it, or prove to them no such thing exists."

Bonny Lee gave a laugh of derision. "We know what they want, and they don't get it."

"What is it?" Wilma demanded.

"Bonny Lee!" Kirby said warningly.

"No sweat, sugar. Even if I wanted to tell her, she just isn't ready yet and I can lay odds she never will be. What'll we do now?"

"Get her out of here."

"But where? Oh. My place. Hells bells. At least it's the one address those people don't know already."

Wilma stared at Kirby, her unpainted lips parted. "Did you— overpower those two sailors, Kirby?"

"Watch it, Winter," Bonny Lee said. She turned to Wilma. "Sweetie, you don't drink so good."

Wilma flushed. "It seems that I just—I just stopped giving a damn about anything. Life had become too confusing to be endurable."

"Surprise hell out of you, sis, how much more complicated life can get for a drunky broad. Get out of here, Kirby, and I'll find some damn thing to put on her."

"I have clothes."

"I know, sweetie. And glasses. And your picture in the papers."

Kirby got up and walked out of the bedroom. As he took the first step into the living room, the side of his head blew up. As the floor came toward him, he seemed able to observe the phenomenon with a remote, clinical interest. It was the way they blew up a cliff. First you saw the flash and then the dust and the rumble and tumble of boulders. He heard a remote screaming of women as he fell into velvet.

KIRBY CAME UP FROM FAR PLACES, LIKE BLUNDERING UP CELLAR stairs in the dark toward the edge of light at the kitchen sill. He opened his eyes and the light was like a spray of acid. There was a slow regular pulsation over his ear, like a child trying to get a balloon started.

Somebody took hold of his chin and shook his head roughly, and he marveled that it did not come loose and fall off.

He squinted up into the oversized face of the big one, Rene.

"Look at some good knots, buddy," Rene said jovially.

Kirby was sitting in an armchair. He looked down. There was a single strand of clothesline lashing both arms together, just above the elbows, pulling his elbows tightly together, making him hunch his back awkwardly. His hands, slightly numbed, were not restrained, but the arc of their movement was limited. A second strand lashed his knees together, just above the knees. Both lines were fastened with a single, competent square knot.

"Learn something every day, buddy. Never tie wrists. Never tie ankles. See them knots? You can't get anywhere near either of them with your fingers or your teeth, and you got no way to wiggle out. You don't know a thing about knots."

"I guess you got loose," Kirby said dispiritedly.

"And got Raoul loose. He was nearly loose anyway. So I got by the door and pow!"

"Yes indeed," Kirby said. "Pow." He looked around the empty room. "Where's Miss Beaumont? And Miss Farnham?"

"Beaumont? That was the blonde, huh? She decided not to hang around." Rene looked and sounded annoyed. He had a makeshift bandage on his wrist and long deep scratches on his throat. "When we tried to grab her, she went off like a bomb. Bit hell out of me. Scratched like a tiger. Kicked Raoul good, belted him one in the eye and went out the back, through the door you busted all to hell."

Kirby struggled to force his mind into paths of logic. Rene sat on the couch. He seemed perfectly relaxed.

"Aren't you afraid Miss Beaumont might summon the police?"

"Her? Nah. She won't. She run right into the boss and a couple boys he picked up local. One good thump on top of the head settled her right down."

Kirby moved his arms and was able to see his wrist watch. It was twenty minutes of five. "What's going to happen now?"

Rene shrugged. "We just wait. The boss is figuring some kind of deal to get you and Wilma onto the *Glorianna*. Maybe they'll take off with all the right clearances, then anchor off someplace, and we'll get out to her in a small boat."

"Oh."

"It made the boss real happy to see you, Winter. I guess you're the jackpot in this thing. The boss thinks everything is going to work out just fine from here in. It got pretty messed up for a while. Too much publicity. The boss hates publicity on a business deal. If, like they say, you got twenty-seven million hidden away someplace, I guess you're worth a lot of effort."

"Where would they take Miss Beaumont?"

"I don't know. I don't know if too many people are still interested in the boat. They'd have to take her someplace else, and if the boss has gotten some more help lined up, maybe there's another place lined up too. How about that twenty-seven million, Winter?"

"What about it?"

"That's what the boss is after, hah?"

"I wouldn't have any idea."

"Anybody steals that much, they're a pigeon for the first people that can get to him. Money like that isn't any good unless you can keep it a secret."

"I'm happy to have the benefit of your expert advice."

Rene came slowly to his feet, walked over, leaned, reached and with calloused thumb and finger gave the end of Kirby's nose a forceful quarter turn. It was contemptuous, degrading and astonishingly painful. The tears ran down Kirby's cheeks.

"Talk nicer when you talk to me," Rene said. "We got a long wait. You can make it easy and you can make it rough."

Rene went back and sat down and began to pare his ridged nails with a pocket knife. After a few minutes had passed, Kirby said, "Excuse me, but did Joseph say when we might be taken away from here?"

"Who?"

"Mr. Locordolos."

"I ain't seen him. Just the boss was here. Mrs. O'Rourke."

"Oh."

Rene shook his head sadly. "And that Wilma got very snotty with the boss. That wasn't so smart. The boss gave her a shot. A Syrette thing like out of an aid kit. Thirty seconds and she was snoring like a bugle."

Raoul came wandering in from the direction of the kitchen. His left eye was puffed. He was spooning something into his mouth out of a can held in a big brown fist.

"What you got now?" Rene asked disgustedly.

"Beans."

"More beans for God's sake?"

"Good."

Raoul sat in a chair and finished the beans. He set the can aside, wiped his mouth on his forearm, stared blandly at Kirby for a few moments, then turned to Rene and began to speak in a language Kirby was able to identify after a few moments as the vulgar French of North Africa, larded with Spanish, Italian and Arabic words. Though he could follow it very imperfectly, he suddenly realized Raoul was suggesting to Rene that he be permitted to go into the bedroom and cure his boredom by amusing himself with the scrawny little sleeping chicken. Raoul accompanied this request with winkings so convulsive they distorted half his face.

To Kirby's horror, Rene did not react with appropriate violence. In fact, he seemed bored. He asked some casual question Kirby did not catch. Raoul said something about who was to find out, in any case. And what harm could it do? It would pass the time.

As it seemed that Rene would shrug and nod approval, there was a curiously muscular convulsion in Kirby's mind, like a gagging in the throat. The fat watch—the golden edge—had pulled reality too thin, had made it too easy to think of the submissive world as a stage for low comedy, for tricky effects, for narrow triumphs of virtue over the brute. The watch had dislocated the world, had made temptingly feasible all the traditions of fantasy, but here would be no slender triumph of virtue. Here, for Wilma Farnham, all the games could end, and he would be powerless to stop these two. For Kirby Winter the world settled suddenly back into its ancient grind of blood and pain, of small lonely disasters in the hearts of men.

He caught the sense of Rene's next remark, something about waiting, something about how, if they had to stay here the whole night, then, orders or no orders, they would share the chicken, wait until she wakened and could be suitably instructed in obedience, and then cut cards for her.

Raoul shrugged and yawned and said that inasmuch as he had already lost money at cards, maybe now they could play again and this time make the chicken part of the stakes. For later.

Kirby's eyes had finally stopped watering. The end of his nose felt as big as a biscuit.

The two men moved over to the coffee table. As Rene shuffled the pack he stared at Kirby and said, "How'd you put us out and tie us up?"

"I had help," Kirby said.

"That figures. Did you use some kind of a gas, maybe?"

"Something like that."

"The boss wondered. She'll want you to tell her all about it. Anything she can use, she wants to know about."

"Deal," said Raoul.

The cards made small flapping sounds in the humid silence of the room. From all evidences, Kirby felt that it was a reasonably good guess that the watch might still be in the right hand pocket of the borrowed slacks. He bent his cramped back further, shoved his lashed elbows down beside his right thigh and ran his left elbow along his thigh. He felt the round bulk of the watch and thought he heard a tink of the heavy chain against the case.

"Don't get smart," Rene said, suddenly alert.

"Just trying to work a cramp out of my shoulder," Kirby said humbly.

Raoul spoke in the crude patois of the African port cities. Kirby missed much of it, but he caught the essence. Don't exercise yourself about the clerk type, my friend. He is too weak and scared and helpless to make problems for us.

The helplessness, Kirby realized, was the greatest danger. The gold watch could as easily have been a mile away, for all the good it could do him. Helplessness froze the mind, preventing any kind of creative scheming. It made one believe that Charla would manage to arrange everything just as she wanted it, in spite of the police search, in spite of all the alarms and publicity and public fascination with an amount of money beyond any rational comprehension. And in spite of anything he might do, he would find himself on the *Glorianna* with the crew of five and the three shattered young women. Or perhaps, all impudence gone, Bonny Lee was at this moment falling all over herself in her eagerness to tell Charla about the mysterious powers of the inherited watch. Soon they would come for it, test it, and perhaps quietly and efficiently crack the skulls of everyone connected with the venture and drop them off at the edge of the Gulf Stream, with suitable wires and weights.

The awareness of defeat, the anticipation of defeat, was like a sickness. He had only pride to fight it. This is the time, he thought, when I must become whatever Uncle Omar thought I could become, hoped I could become—or give up completely.

He wondered if Bonny Lee's little car was still out there. It would seem logical that they would leave it behind. It was rather conspicuous. For Charla, Bonny Lee would be a new factor in the equation. But he sensed that Charla adjusted with maximum speed and efficiency to all new factors. He was doubly grateful he had told Bonny Lee about the whole mess he was in. She would be in a better position to anticipate Charla's moves. He hoped Bonny Lee had the good sense to play absolutely dumb. If there was the slightest hint she knew anything of value, Charla would not rest until she had found out what it was—as unpleasantly as possible.

If Bonny Lee's little car was out there, one could assume the keys were in it, as Bonny Lee had known the probable necessity for leaving quickly.

Rene and Raoul were arguing over the play of one hand. Raoul seemed to feel he had been cheated.

"About that twenty-seven million," Kirby said.

They both stared at him. "Yes?"

"It's very boring and uncomfortable just sitting here. Maybe there's some game three could play. For some of the money."

"You've got no money," Rene said. "We took it. We split it. Twelve hundred." The rest of it, Kirby remembered, was tucked under Bonny Lee's mattress.

"I could give you an I.O.U. against the other money."

Rene looked contemptuous. "And the boss would pay us off on your I.O.U. Winter?"

"She wouldn't. I would."

"You won't be doing anything."

Here was the special moment of truth. Defeat was implicit in the length of clothesline around his arms, biting into his flesh. He smiled at the two men. "Don't you wonder a little bit why I'm taking all this so calmly?"

Rene looked mildly uncertain. "You're not like a lot of the jokers the boss has clobbered. I figured you'd try to make a deal with me. I wouldn't buy, even if you did. But maybe I wonder why you don't."

"Deal," said Raoul.

"Shut up. Winter, I don't see how you got any edge at all.

Three days aboard and you'd sign over your sister, if she asks you. She'll pick you clean and then she'll keep you for kicks or throw you away, and there isn't a damn thing you can do about it."

"Deal," Raoul said again.

"The best Mrs. O'Rourke can get from me is a partnership deal."

"That's going to surprise hell out of her."

"I expect it to. I've got it all tucked away in photo and thumbprint accounts."

Rene stared at him dubiously. "Thumbprint?"

"They're number accounts, of course, but there's no draw against them except on personal application. Six hundred different accounts in nine different countries, all set up the same way."

Rene thought for a minute. "So if you dropped dead, what's the deal to get it out then?"

"There isn't any. Any time five years passes with no activity in any account, it's automatically closed and the net is delivered to whoever I nominated, whichever person or organization in each case. So I'm no good dead to your boss, and there's nothing she can force out of me that'll give her access to what she wants."

"But she doesn't know this?"

"Not yet. And when she finds out, she's going to have to treat us nicely, me and Miss Farnham and Miss Beaumont, and even Miss Alden."

"What if they haven't been treated so nice already?"

"Then I'll reduce Mrs. O'Rourke's participation, as a sort of penalty for greed and bad manners. You see, my friend, I'm going to end up in pretty good shape—assuming Mrs. O'Rourke is a logical woman."

Rene stared at him with a corrugated brow. "So why hassle with her the way you been doing?"

"Why should I split with anybody? But now that she's won this round, I might as well cut her in. There's enough to go around, I'd say, wouldn't you?"

Rene grinned like a yawning dog. "One half of one twenty-seventh would do me good for the rest of my life."

"I wouldn't gamble for that much. But whatever I did gamble for, I guess you can see I'd be in a position to pay off, if I should lose."

"She say keep tied," Raoul said. "Deal."

"We can keep him tied, Raoul, and still bring him into the game."

"Don't like it," Raoul said.

Rene switched to the rough argot, and reminded Raoul of what he had said about Kirby being no cause for worry, and reminded Raoul that they would be playing the stranger only for money, that they would keep a separate record of winnings and losses to determine who would have the little chicken first. Raoul shrugged his acceptance.

Rene came over and picked Kirby up, chair and all. It was a shocking demonstration of raw power. He set the chair in front of the coffee table. With a flick of the seaman's knife he severed the line around Kirby's arms. With more line he deftly lashed Kirby's left arm to the arm of the chair, put a fairly snug loop around Kirby's throat and tied that to the back of the chair. Though it was pleasant to be released from the previous cramped position, Kirby realized he had gained less than he thought. His right arm was free, but it would be awkward, obvious and too slow to stick his right hand in the trouser pocket and hope to manipulate the watch in time. And even if he did, he would be almost as helpless in the red world. He had learned enough of the behavior of inanimate objects to know that the rope would become like stiff cables.

"All you need is one hand loose," Rene said. He put two hundred dollars in front of Kirby. "You owe me two hundred, pal."

"Want it in writing?"

"I can make you remember it."

"I'd rather put it in writing. Have you got a piece of paper? I think I've got a pen right here." With difficulty he put his hand in the side pocket of his borrowed slacks.

"Hold it!" Rene yelled.

His fingers touched the watch stem and he pressed and turned. The world was a murkey red. They were caught in the cessation of time, staring at him. He took the gold watch out. He placed it on the table and tried to undo the knots binding his left arm, but knew he could not budge them. It was a strange impasse. Even if he could get hold of a knife, he doubted that he could saw his way through the rope. Objects had an obdurate toughness in this subjective space where time stood still. The silver hand moved. The gold hands of the watch were motionless at quarter to six.

He knew he would have to set himself up for a better opportunity, but did not know how he could manage it. But the watch would have to be in a more convenient and accessible place, yet without any impression of any blur of movement which would make them suspicious. He suddenly had a reasonable idea, and tucked the watch under his thigh, chain out of sight, stem pointing out. He put his right hand back in his pocket and, through the fabric, reached the stem of the watch with his middle finger and pressed it.

"I thought I had a pen but I guess I don't," he said and slowly took his hand out of his pocket and showed them it was empty.

"We don't need it in writing. Stay away from pockets," Rene said.

"He got nothing on him," Raoul said.

"Neither did that guy had a razor in his hat brim, and he cut you up pretty good," Rene said.

"Shut up and deal."

They agreed on five card stud. Kirby held his own. Raoul lost steadily. He was the eternal optimist, confident the last card would solve all his problems.

"Your friend is very lucky," Kirby said to Raoul.

"Deal."

Kirby licked his lips and said, "And he has very quick hands."

Raoul tensed. He leaned toward Rene, and spoke the argot with a speed Kirby could not hope to follow. Kirby let his right hand fall casually near the watch. He could hope for some small change, some small opening, but did not know what it might be. At the end of his gunfire warning, Raoul slapped a knife down on the table beside him, not within Kirby's reach. Kirby had not seen him take it out or open the blade.

As Rene began protestations of innocence, Kirby thumbed them to murky stillness. He remembered what he had learned from Bonny Lee regarding the behavior of objects in motion. He leaned forward as far as he could. The loop bit painfully into his throat. He could not reach the knife. He took a playing card by one corner and found that by extending it, he could touch the knife. He began to scratch at the knife with the edge of the card, bringing it a millimeter closer each time, pausing to lean back from time to time to take a breath. At last he could grasp it. He released the card and it remained in the air. He took the knife and worried it, point first, blade up, under the double strand that held his left arm to the arm of the chair. When it was in position, he pulled up on it as hard as he could. It made no impression on the strands of line. He brought the watch over and put it in the fingers of his left hand where he could manipulate it as quickly as possible. He pressed, and when the silver hand jumped back to twelve, he turned the stem back immediately. In the instant of reality he heard a loud fragment of one word from Rene and felt a tug at his left arm. Now the knife was two feet above the level of his head. The strands had been sliced and were slightly apart. He peeled them back and freed his left arm. He put the watch in his lap and worked the stiffness out of his left arm. He pushed the loop out and was able to slump in the chair and work it up over his head, not without some further attrition to his bruised nose. He reached up, recaptured the knife and used the same procedure on the line around his legs just above his knees. Before he thumbed the watch stem, he looked at Rene and Raoul. Their glance had swiveled toward him and the first faint indication of astonishment was beginning to change their brute faces.

He worked it more quickly than before, freezing the knife at eye level this time. He peeled the rope back and got up and paced around the room, feeling the familiar drag of the inertia of his clothing, slipping his shoes off after tiring of the effort of moving them about. There were two heavy masonry pots on either side of the fireplace. Whatever had been growing in them had died and withered to naked sticks. With great effort and by degrees he positioned the two pots in midair, and, after estimates of the forces involved, about seven inches above the heads of the two men.

It would not do, he realized, to give the impression of having suddenly disappeared, not in front of two witnesses. So he got back into the chair right in their line of vision, before thumbing the watch stem. His discarded shoes clumped to the floor. The card fluttered down. The knife chunked deeply into a cypress beam overhead. The pots fell, thudded against thick skulls, smashed on the floor. Rene slumped sideways on the couch. Raoul bent slowly forward and bounced his forehead off the coffee table.

As soon as he ascertained they were both breathing, Kirby, profiting by experience, tied them precisely as he had been tied, finding it easier to operate in the brightness of real time, where materials were not as stubborn. Realizing they might untie each other, he added the refinement of the rope loop about the throat, fastening Raoul to an iron eye in the front of the fireplace, and Rene to a sturdy catch at the base of a window across the room.

Wilma was still in the oversized robe, face down across the bed, her head hanging over the edge. She snored rhythmically, insistently, beautifully. After ten minutes of proddings, slappings, pinchings, and an attempt to walk her, he knew that all he could hope to achieve was a temporary interruption of the snoring sound. She was a limp, warm, loose-jointed doll, and the most infuriating thing about the whole procedure was that she seemed to be smiling.

But, with or without her co-operation, he knew he had to get her out of the house. He had already given up more hostages than he could afford. He felt less regard for Wilma, but more responsibility. He pulled the robe off her and tried not to stare at her more than was necessary as he dressed her. Compared with Bonny Lee, as well as the girl on the beach, Wilma seemed to wear extraordinarily practical underthings, opaque and designed for long wear. She kept slipping away, toppling over and picking up the rhythm of the snoring again.

After a few attempts to brush her wild brown hair, he looked in bureau drawers until he found a bright scarf. He put it around her head and knotted it under her chin. He noticed that someone had stepped on her glasses, bending the frames and powdering both lenses. This place was not safe, but he could not think of a place which might be. In any case, he would need money.

Rene stirred as Kirby was recovering the money from his pockets. He opened blurred eyes, shook his head, winced.

"How the hell'd you do that?" he asked weakly.

"I had help."

Rene closed his eyes. "You seem to get it when you need it."

Kirby found the rest of the money and the keys to the rental car in Raoul's pockets. Raoul kept sleeping. Kirby found his pulse. It felt solid and steady. He thumbed Raoul's eyes open. They were crossed. He wondered if that had any special clinical significance.

He went in and picked up Wilma and hung her over his left shoulder, his arm around her legs. As he walked back into the living room, he thought he heard a sound outside. He darted his hand into his pocket and made the world red, made it safe for a quick reconnaissance. He eased out from under Wilma's folded figure and made a quick tour of the area and found nothing amiss. The Sunbeam was in the drive. The keys were in it. He was hidden from the world by all the Wellerly's tropical shrubbery. Just as he was about to bring reality back so he could move the car out of the way, he remembered Wilma. He hurried back in. It would have made a strange and awkward fall for a sleeping girl. He fitted his shoulder into her middle and once again brought the untinged world back.

"Mrs. O'Rourke isn't going to like this at all," Rene said.

"My friends sneaked up on you. What could you do?"

"She'll think of something we could have done."

He took Wilma out and put her on the floor in the back of the rental sedan. He backed the Sunbeam around the sedan, out of the way. He got into the rental car, put on the sunglasses and the baseball hat and drove out. He drove swiftly east to Route 1, a half-mile away, and parked at the first convenient motel.

There was an old man at the desk. He had a ground floor vacancy.

"You and the missus, aye?" He peered beyond Kirby. "Whare is she?"

"Taking a nap in the back. She's very tired."

Kirby signed the register and paid cash for the night. He drove to the unit, parked close, unlocked the door and went back and lifted Wilma out. When he got her into his arms and turned, the old man was standing there. "She sure God *is* tired, mister. Wouldn't be sick, would she?"

"She's just a heavy sleeper."

"I don't want nothing funny going on. I run a nice place here. Where at's your luggage, mister?"

"In the back end."

"Now I just want to see you got some luggage."

"Let me take her in first."

"Better set her down, because you got no luggage, you're not bringing her into my place."

Kirby propped Wilma on the seat. He had to admit that the look of her didn't inspire confidence. She looked drugged. And was.

He went to the trunk and unlocked it and, as with his left hand he began to raise it, he twisted himself out of normal time. Forty feet away a man was unloading his car. He had put a row of suit-cases on the paved parking surface in preparation for carrying them inside. Kirby went over and took two of the smaller items. He pushed them back to the sedan, shoved them into the trunk. He took the same position as before, lifted the trunk lid the rest of the way.

"I like for everybody to have luggage," the old man said in apology.

"Sure," Kirby said. He went to pick the girl up again. This time she slipped her arms around his neck.

"Soooo sleepy," she mumbled. "Sooo terr'ble sleepy."

The old man carried the bags in. Kirby plumped Wilma onto the nearest bed. She began to snore immediately.

"Sure a sleeper," the old man said.

After he was gone, Kirby held the door open and turned the world red and silent and took the small suitcases back. The man stood in an attitude of perplexity, finger pointing, obviously counting the items of luggage. Kirby pressed them against the ground behind him and went back into the room. When he thumbed the stem of the watch, the door swung shut. He took off Wilma's shoes. He wrote a short note to her. "You are safe here. I'll come back when I can. Don't leave the room and don't phone anyone under any circumstances. Put the chain on the door. I'll knock five—pause—three, rapidly."

He brought the room key with him, and made certain the door was locked. He drove to a public phone booth in a shopping cen-ter parking lot, phoned the police number in the front of the book and reported that it sounded as if somebody was trying to break into 210 Sunset Way, at the rear, and the Wellerly's were out of the country. When the first question was asked, he hung up.

He drove south toward Miami. It was quarter of seven. He had the feeling he was wasting too much time. And he felt guilty about the time he spent in the real world. When the world was red, time was stopped, and then, if bad things were happening to Bonny Lee, they stopped too. He could keep time at a standstill by walking the entire way, but he had to measure his own energies on the scale also. The sun was almost down. He could not afford to let the day end, because he could not be certain he would be able to see well enough in the combination of darkness and faint red light.

In his haste, he made a miscalculation. The woman ahead of him spurted ahead as though to make a red light before it changed, then changed her mind and jammed her brakes on. He piled the rental into the back of her plum-gray Continental, in a scream of rubber and expensive metallic clangor. As he sat dazed, she came yawping out of her car, her face red and ugly with anger. His door had sprung open. Off to the right he saw a cop striding toward the scene.

He grabbed the watch and stopped all the noise and motion. It took an effort of will to remember that, when the world was red, there was no need for haste. The rear end collision had happened in the center lane of three lanes of southbound traffic. Other cars had stopped all around them. He got out and checked the other cars. The first car in the left lane was a convertible. A conveniently small man sat behind the wheel. He had his fingertips on the wheel, and he was staring over at the accident, at the tall woman, stopped in the middle of a yelp. Kirby climbed in and levered the small man up and out from under the wheel. He shoved him out beyond the car, climbed down, took his ankles and towed him back to the rental and, with the increasing ease of experience in such matters, worked him into proper position, his fingertips on the steering wheel, his head still looking back over his right shoulder. He knew that maximum confusion would serve his purposes. He put his baseball cap on the small man, and wedged the man's tweed hat on his own head. As a final touch, he removed the policeman's service revolver, worked it snugly into the hand of the irate woman, pointed it up into the air, and gave a final solid pressure to the trigger finger. He clambered into the convertible, slid under the wheel, and turned the city back on, looking toward the little group as he did so. The woman fired into the air, hauled her hand down and stared at it. The cop started at the sound of the shot and began pawing his empty holster. The little man snapped his head around, stared with utter disbelief at the crumpled car, the cop, the woman with the gun, leaped out and began to run. The light changed and Kirby drove on, reasonably confident it was a matter that would never be completely straightened out.

As soon as he realized he was within reasonable walking distance of the Marina, he pulled over to the curb and stopped and then stopped the final slant of sunlight. He shoved his shoes inside his shirt, took the dark glasses off, and headed toward the Marina. Walking among the pink silent people was like walking through a stone orchard. Sometimes, in his haste, he brushed against them. They were rigid, unreal. A man stood lighting a pipe. The flame looked fashioned of pinkish brass. A woman huffed cigarette smoke from her mouth and it was unmoving in the air, like some strange semi-transparent plastic plume.

He went through the Marina gates and out onto the large central dock. The bay ripples were stilled, molten lead that had set and been oiled and polished and was touched with the red reflections of sunset.

The *Glorianna* was there, at the end of the T, not quite as large as he had expected her to be. Eighty feet, perhaps. A bald, mustachioed man stood forward, looking toward the city, stopped in the act of coiling a heavy line. The *Glorianna* had so much cabin space in ratio to deck space, she looked slightly ungainly, but she seemed to have enough beam and freeboard to be a good sea boat. He went up the gangway and onto the deck. She was pale and trim, spotless, luxurious, comfortable. He could find no one else topsides. All hatches were closed, so he assumed she was air-conditioned. He tried to get in, but in the red world he was insubstantial in relation to the objects in stasis. He was like a mouse trying to open a refrigerator.

When he had determined which was the most plausible entrance to the stateroom, he spent just long enough out of the red world to work the latch and pull the door halfway open.

He went in, leaving it open behind him. He went down the several steps of the short ladderway to the narrow passageway between the port and starboard staterooms. The master stateroom seemed to be forward, dead ahead. The door was ajar. By putting his shoulder against it he was able to slowly force it far enough open to be able to sidle in. Charla stood in the burgundy murk, in quarter profile, a glass in her left hand, gesticulating at Joseph with her right. She wore a short loose robe and her hair hung glossy to her shoulders. Joseph leaned against the paneled wall near the bed, his arms folded, his expression skeptical. He wore a dark business suit, white shirt, figured tie.

Kirby walked over and stared at Charla from close range. It startled him that he could have forgotten how perfect in texture, how remarkable and how sensuous her face was. It shook him slightly. He had thought he had gained enough sweet insulation from Bonny Lee to be immune to this older woman. But being this close to her made his knees feel loose and uncertain. He felt compelled to proclaim his newfound freedom from the obsession she had so quickly established, and so he leered at her and said, "Hi, sweetheart," and reached a hand toward her and fondled her. It was an unsuccessful performance. The leer didn't fit his mouth. The words were dead, as though he had spoken them directly into a wad of insulation. And the remarkable breasts felt like plastic bowls behind chain mesh.

He was about to turn and go in search of Bonny Lee and Betsy when he realized that something might be gained by listening to them. If they were here alone, it was unlikely either of the girls were being harmed. He searched the luxurious cabin for a suitable hiding place. On a less roomy craft, the area under the bed would have been used for stowage. But it was empty under there, and there was room enough. With the watch in hand, he could halt the scene if suddenly there was any hint of danger. He wiggled into the constricted area and, once he was concealed, bent the edge of the hanging spread back the way it had been.

The instant he depressed the stem of the watch he heard a great staccato torrent of a language he could not understand. The sound stopped abruptly. She said something in the rising inflection of a question, and walked over and slammed the door. She said something in the firm voice of command.

He answered casually, indifferently.

"If I say we speak English, Joseph, we shall speak English. Why did the door swing open? Rene is the only one with fluent English and he's ashore. I didn't get where I am by trusting anyone."

"Even yourself," Joseph said.

"We can't be too careful in this matter. Please don't make bad jokes. We tried the utmost care with Krepps, and failed miserably, several times. I must have whatever it is which gave him such strength, Joseph."

The bed creaked as Joseph sat on it. With his cheek against the rug, Kirby could look out and see Charla's bare feet. They moved over to stand in front of Joseph, as Joseph said in an ironic tone, "What do you expect? A device to read minds? A cloak of invisibility?"

"He read our minds, Joseph. He guessed our plans. He was a devil! Winter has whatever it is. But he is less of a man than the old one was. Now we can get it before he learns to use it well."

"Whatever it is. And if he knows what it is."

"I'm convinced he does. I told you the things he said."

"He could have been bluffing."

"But it will be nice to be certain, one way or the other."

Joseph sighed audibly. "It is still a most delicate matter. I would feel much better if that damned girl hadn't been so quick and so clever. What if she informs the police? That will complicate matters."

Charla laughed and sat beside Joseph. Kirby could have reached and touched her bare heel. "That one is not interested in the police. The way it was done, I was reminded of myself, long ago. Naturally those idiots you hired were not expert, but even if they had been competent she might still have—"

"Just how did she manage it?"

"One of them had a place he thought would be safe, to keep her there until we could bring her here, or at least prepare her to be brought here so she would be quiet and humble and answer properly if she were asked questions. He told me about the place. It seemed adequate. I should have been warned by the way she eluded Rene and Raoul, but I was concerned for her. She seemed totally unconscious. When I held a cigarette near her hand, there was no movement. I was planning how best to handle it if she were seriously hurt. The apartment we would use was over on the beach. It is on a canal. We could park behind it, out of sight, so no questions would be asked. I had them use care lifting her out of the car. Suddenly there was a veritable explosion, and I sat down rather painfully, and one of your idiots was rolling around groaning and hugging himself and the other was blinded by blood from his clawed forehead running into his eyes. The girl was running. She ran forty feet and dived over a low wall into the canal. By the time I reached the wall she was almost around a bend, swimming very strongly, leaving me with her cheap purse and a bruised seat. No, Joseph, that one will not go to the police. She knows who Winter is. She has the smell of money in her nostrils now, and when she has composed herself, she will think of some way to make the money come true. The police won't assist her in that. I do not know if Winter has known her long, but I would say she has possibilities, that one, hah? We could find her useful, I think. More than poor Betsy ever was. With Winter as a lure, possibly we can trap her. I found her address in the purse, so I sent your idiots to watch it and intercept her should she return to her place."

"And bring her here?"

"Of course not! Take her to that beach apartment and phone us here that they have her."

"But what if she goes back to the house?"

"Rene has been instructed. They will hold her there."

"This is a tiresome country, Charla," Joseph said. "In any reasonably well-managed country all of this would be restricted to a few officials, and you would know the price of the officials in matters of this sort. Here they scream delicate matters over the air and spread them all over their vulgar newspapers, and every moron on the street becomes a potential problem. We should never attempt any sort of business matter here. It was always better elsewhere, particularly in Spain, when Juan March would help with the arrangements."

"Don't whine, darling. We had no choice. Now Winter and the Farnham woman are in our custody. And Betsy will be given no further chance to become a problem. And even if we fail to pick up that Beaumont girl, who will believe her? And even if they should, we'll be well out of reach. We'll have all the time in the world to find out everything, and plan how to make use of it. Believe me, it will work just as smoothly as it would have the way we first planned it, before all this dreadful hue and cry began. Kirby Winter was troublesome for a time, but that is ended."

"I do not care for this business of the packing cases," Joseph said.

"Then how else can we bring them aboard so easily? Daniel will drive the truck out there at eleven, and we'll have them stowed aboard a little after midnight, sleeping sweetly. If that police search completely overlooked that hull compartment, darling, why do you think the customs people will find it tomorrow? And we can show them the packing cases, filled with completely innocent supplies, to prove what came aboard in the night. Darling Joseph, when those two innocents awaken, they'll be in cozy beds, far at sea, without any idea how it was done or where they are being taken. And after all business details have been attended to, I think Miss Farnham might find the crew's quarters educational. Unless you have any amusing ideas."

"Her picture didn't enchant me, Charla dear."

"She's a bloodless, stilted, self-important little wretch, dear, with a quick temper and a natural talent for virginity, but she did appear slender and seemed to move well. I rather doubt that even with your talents you could debauch her."

"Is that a challenge, my dear?"

"I could, of course, but it would be a different sort of venture entirely."

"I'll decide after I have had a look at her."

"You're losing your sense of adventure, Joseph."

There was a low laugh, a rustle of moment, and Charla's heels were swung up and out of sight. "It is much more likely, my dear," he said, his voice slightly muffled, "that as I grow older I find it increasingly difficult to settle for anything less than the best the world can provide."

"Yet you continue to make comparisons."

"To reassure us both. Just as you do."

"How sweet! How very sweet!"

Kirby, with sweaty fingers, put a halt to whatever was going on, as well as to the rest of all concurrent cultural phenomena.

He wormed his way out from under the bed. Charla had emerged from the robe. She had her head thrown back, her eyes closed, her lips smiling and parted. Her attitude made the business suit look particularly incongruous. He went over to the door and turned and looked at them again. He decided he could risk a fraction of a second to get the door open, without being noticed. He managed it and then, in the redness, pushed the door open far enough to slide out. Once he was in the corridor he braced himself and pushed it shut again. He could not latch it, but he could shut it almost all the way. He used other seconds of real time to test the doors of the other four staterooms. Three were empty. One was locked.

He considered the problem, and then spent five nervous moments in real time, ready to turn it off if he heard anyone approaching. When five minutes were up, he turned back to red. The master stateroom door had not been latched. He pulled it open. The business suit was not on the floor. It was arranged on a chair with a meticulous neatness. After one electrified glance at the bed, he decided he was cured of all lingering fragments of the Charla obsession. He had been uneasily apprehensive of making his invisible intrusion upon some scene of an evil so unspeakable it would fry his brain like grease on a skillet. But of all possible visions the one he had not expected had been that look of low comedy, like clowns belaboring each other with inflated bladders, like Harpo honking his cane, like a massive pratfall in a still shot from a Keystone Komedy. And what made it even more intensely ludicrous was the obvious air of deadly seriousness of the participants.

As he manipulated the soft lead sheathing that was Joseph Locordolo's sedate business suit, he realized that all reports to the contrary, as a spectator sport this activity was not even likely to replace tournament chess. As he pried pockets open, groping for keys, his tendency toward a howl of helpless laughter was smothered by a shocking thought. Suppose when he and Bonny Lee—would it have appeared as—

And, with a certain wry despair he realized it might seem the same. Thus he took another step toward joining the human race, the sweaty, ridiculous, pretentious, self-deluding, aspiring, flesh-trapped march of man.

The keys, six of them, were on a gold ring. He hung them in midair while he kneaded the suit back into orderliness, flattening it by leaning on it with open palms. He took the keys and swung the dead weight of the door open and shut again, without looking directly toward the sportive Charla and fun-loving Joseph.

It had to be a small key, and the second one he tried worked. He swung the door open. Betsy stared at him in complete astonishment. She had evidently been standing, looking out through the heavy glass of the sealed porthole. Her tan hair was rumpled, her face pale and without make-up. She wore a pale orange corduroy coverall arrangement, with short sleeves, a zipper down the front and a big silver buckle. It was a bad color for her and did not fit her properly.

"What in the world—"

He touched his fingers to his lips, closed the door and started to lock it with the key and then saw the oblong bolt and slid it into its socket. When he looked at her again she was trying to smile at him, and the tears were streaming out of her eyes. She came to him and he held her in his arms. She trembled and held him tightly, but made no sound of crying. She had a faintly sour smell and he wondered if it was the odor of pain and fear.

Finally she turned away and took a lurching step toward the deep bunk, turned and sat heavily, bent over and put her head between her knees. In a few moments she straightened up, smiling almost shyly. "Sorry. I almost fainted. I never faint." Her face twisted. "I guess it took a lot out of me. She—hurt me so."

He sat with her on the bunk, half facing her. "It was my fault."

"No," she said flatly. "Mine. I had to get cute. I had to try all the angles. I thought I could con her. I couldn't believe she'd ever really—do anything to me. And when I realized she was, I was going to be terribly brave. Joan at the stake. But in such a shamefully short time I was begging and babbling and betraying everybody. I'm so sorry, Kirby. I'm so ashamed. I told them where to find you and Wilma. Please forgive me."

"You should have told before she hurt you."

"And I would, the next time. It's such a simple way she does it, too. Just one of those damned electric reducing machines. She just ties those pad things on where you want them least, and revs the current up until you feel your own muscles beginning to tear you up. And not a mark, afterward. She's monstrous, Kirby. How did you get here? Where are they?"

"Keep your voice down, Betsy. They're just down the corridor, in the big stateroom. I think everything is going to be all right."

"Wilma didn't have a clue. My God, Kirby, she's a dreadful little prig. Terribly loyal. But she doesn't believe there really is any special thing they're after, unless she has it and doesn't know it. Where is she?"

"In a safe place for now, for a while, anyway. They had her for a time. Two of the men from the crew. Rene and Raoul."

"I remember Rene. Raoul is a new one, I guess. Rene is tough and quick and powerful and completely loyal to Charla. I never liked the way he'd look at me."

"They had both of us, in that house where Wilma was, but we —got away from them."

She looked startled. "Got away from them and—you got aboard and got into this cabin? That's very good indeed, Kirby. Maybe I made a low estimate."

"Joseph and Charla don't know I got away from them yet. They were going to bring me and Wilma aboard tonight in packing cases."

"Are you sure you didn't save them half the trouble?"

"I don't think so. I think it's going to be all right. You see—I found out what they're after."

"You did?"

"And I haven't any good ideas about how I can solve a lot of these damn legal problems, but I think I can get you off this boat."

"What is it? A handy dandy thought control machine? Or does it just melt big holes in the sides of boats?"

"You're sounding more like yourself."

"So I'm a little skeptical. Show me."

"It has—certain limitations, and I don't know how it works, and maybe I don't know how to get maximum use out of it yet. But I'll demonstrate it. It—it may frighten you, Betsy. It may frighten you quite badly because it—offends all reason. You'll try not to get hysterical if—it frightens you?"

"That's a luxury I don't think I can afford, Kirby Winter."

"All you need to know is the objective results."

"You mean it has something to do with that old—"

He stopped the flow of rational time, wondered whether he should get her used to it by degrees, then decided she was mentally strong enough to cope. He slowly pulled her rigid body out of the bunk, forced her over to a chair, leaned his weight on her thighs and pushed her down into it. Then he went over and stood by the door and picked time up where he had left it.

"—watch?" she said. She gave a leap of violent surprise, turned deathly pale, shut her eyes tightly and opened them again and stared at him. "My word," she whispered. "I didn't know what to expect, but this is—" She frowned. "Did I black out somehow?"

"No time passed at all. It was instantaneous."

"You moved me to here, and you to over there. What is the range?"

"Let's say it's about as far as I can carry a kitchen stove."

"You carried me somehow?"

"With difficulty."

"While time took time out?"

"Exactly."

"You could carry me past someone and they wouldn't notice?"

"No more than you would."

She nodded her head, quite slowly. "Your revered uncle, my friend, had quite an edge. An edge, in fact, so filled with interesting possibilities, it makes that twenty-seven million you gave away look like candy for the children. Why didn't he use it to— make himself king of the world? He could have managed it. Like a man with a rifle in the dawn of history."

"Maybe being king would have bored him. Being Santa Claus was more his style. Or maybe he had to keep what he had from being too obvious, or other men would have started looking in the same direction."

She nodded again. "Charla was convinced there was something to look for." She lost her thoughtful expression and stared across the room at him with a look of fearful intensity. "One thing we do know, Kirby Winter. A thing like that must never belong to my aunt. Never. She's bought every kind of immunity they sell, and she uses it all without mercy."

Suddenly there was a hurried sound in the corridor, a mutter of voices, and then a sound of heavy hammering.

Above the bunk there was a hiss and click of electronic circuits, and then Charla's voice came into the room, the low purring tones vastly amplified.

"My darlings!" she said. "How terribly fortunate I left that circuit open! And how glad I am we had the patience to listen. Dear Joseph even had the presence of mind to begin taping it after the first few words. We can play it back for clues, you know, but possibly we have enough. How did you put it, dear? A way to make time take time out. I have suddenly lost my respect for Omar Krepps. With that ability, he did very little with it, comparatively. While I'm talking I can't hear you, of course. That sound you must have heard was a timber being wedged between your door and the opposite side of the corridor. Apparently your miracle will not melt prison walls. I hope not. So at least we have created an impasse, have we not? And it will give us all time to think."

Kirby shuddered and looked at Betsy. Her eyes were closed and she was biting down on a bloodless lip. "I didn't know," she whispered. "I didn't know. But, knowing her, I should have guessed."

He went over to her and put his lips close to her ear. "All we have to do is get them to open that door."

"It is really quite amusing," Charla said, "that what I should have been looking for is actually that old gold watch you showed me, Kirby dear. The little telescope is a rather nice disarming touch. Really, I expected some sort of procedural thing, notes and formulae, something like that. But this really seems far more practical, a portable, useful, innocent-appearing device. What did you say, Joseph? Excuse me a moment, darlings."

"Damned witch," Betsy said distinctly.

Charla spoke through the concealed speaker again. "Joseph has had a fruitful idea. We shall have a hole burnt in your steel door, darlings, just large enough for the watch, and then you can pass it out through the hole. Otherwise I think you might find things becoming highly unpleasant."

When the hiss of the circuit stopped, Kirby said, "Before I'll do that, Charla, I'll take the end of the chain and I'll slam it against the inside of this steel door until I'm damned well certain it's unusable, unidentifiable junk."

"Dog in the manger?" Charla asked.

"Precisely."

"You bluff well, Kirby."

"No bluff, Charla. I'm infected by a chronic disease called a sense of responsibility. I'm a very noble fellow. I'd rather destroy it than have you have it to use."

"Nobility confuses me," Charla said. "Isn't it the traditional disease of adolescence? Aren't you rather old for it, Kirby?"

"I'm having a delayed adolescence, Mrs. O'Rourke. But you can check it out, if you don't believe me. Cut the hole in the door. The minute the chunk falls out, I start battering this gizmo to bits."

There was no answer, no faint hiss that preceded each speech.

"You've got her worried," Betsy whispered.

"She should be worried," Kirby said in a normal tone. "I mean every damn word of it. I can't get out of here. Okay. So nobody gets to use it."

Charla spoke again. "It would make me terribly angry, Kirby," she said with a tone of gentle regret. "I think both of you would have to die in the most unimaginable agony. You see, Betsy would have to share your heroics. And Miss Farnham. And Miss Beaumont. It's quite a heavy responsibility upon you, dear Kirby. I know it will trouble you."

When the hiss stopped Betsy asked in a thin and shaking voice, "What if he gives it to you, Charla?"

"Freedom, my dear. And a generous gift of money. I shan't be small about it."

He whispered to Betsy. "She won't want anybody around to tell what she has." Betsy sat quite still, then gave a nod of dreadful comprehension.

Charla laughed softly. "Or, if that seems to be too good to be true, I can at least promise something so quick and so painless you'll never know what happened. We have a lot of time for you to think it over, dears. No one will come aboard until we ask for clearance. So do talk it over for a bit."

"Charla?" Betsy called. "Charla!"

The speaker remained silent.

12

BETSY ALDEN LAY IN THE BUNK ON HER BACK, HER EYES WIDE open, her face expressionless, while Kirby Winter prowled the stateroom. It was fifteen feet long by eleven feet wide. There was an alcove with a sliding door containing a head, a small stainless steel lavatory, and a medicine cabinet. He inspected the two sealed portholes, too small for escape even if he could find something to shatter the heavy glass. He located the air-conditioning inlet and the exhaust vent. Twice he put himself into the red world of stasis.

One idea began to seem more and more feasible. He sat on the bunk and said, "I think I've got something."

"Nothing will work," she said listlessly.

"Listen to it, at least."

"We're whipped, Kirby."

He yanked her up and slapped her face sharply. "Damn you, Betsy. At least listen!"

She listened. She thought the plan was madness. But she could think of nothing better. Once she had accepted it, her help was efficient. They soaked blankets in water, getting them as saturated as possible. They spread them in one corner. She helped him heap all the other bedding and combustibles near the door. The fire started slowly at first, but when they were certain it had caught, they crawled under the sodden blankets, and had wet towels ready to wrap around their faces. Smoke became thick in the cabin.

Suddenly Charla spoke, with anger in her tone. "Very clever, dears, but it won't work, you know. Are you holding rags by the outlet?"

When the hiss stopped, Kirby began to cough, trying to sound as if he were choking to death. The furniture was beginning to crackle, and he hoped she could hear that. He felt heat on his face. He prodded Betsy. She was ready for her cue. She gave a scream of such convincing agony he wondered for a moment if the fire had somehow reached her. "Help!" she screamed. "Help me! Let me out!" She screamed again, and faded it off into a grisly bubbling sound.

He heard the commotion in the corridor. He knew what would happen next. They would feel the steel door, and feel the heat coming through it. The blankets were beginning to steam. There were shouts and a sound of hammering and then the door which he had unlatched was burst open, and just as he worked the watch to stop it all, he saw something aimed toward him in the murk, heard a sharp cracking sound. The flame stopped. The steam was motionless. The heat was gone. The blankets felt like slabs of molded oak. He worked his way out. Joseph stood just inside the door, almost in the static flames, aiming a long-barreled pistol with a rigid little tongue of flame protruding from the muzzle. Staying below the layer of smoke, Kirby searched the air between himself and the muzzle, and found the small slug suspended at the midway point. Assuming, he thought with a hollow feeling in his belly, a velocity of a thousand feet per second, and it had another seven feet to go before catching me squarely in the face, had I been seven one thousandths of a second slower—

Suddenly, to his astonishment, he saw that the bullet had a perceptible movement. He glanced at the gold watch and saw he had given himself a little over a half hour. It was the first thing he had seen move in the red world. He went close to it and timed its velocity, and it seemed to him that as he counted off ten seconds, it moved almost one full inch. It was a clue to the ratio between the two worlds. Two minutes per foot. Or a ratio of two minutes to one one thousandth of a second. Thus, one full hour of red time equalled three hundredths of a second of objective time. Suddenly he stirred out of his speculative trance. When he moved his face into smoke it felt like thick rubbery cobwebs. He pulled the girl up to a convenient height and, crouched below the smoke, pulled her past Joseph and into the corridor. Charla stood beyond the door, her expression anxious. The emotion he felt toward her was not fear or hate or anger, but merely a vast impatience, an irritability. He left Betsy suspended and went back in and plucked the lead snail out of the air and took it out into the corridor, aimed it at Charla's bland honeyed forehead and pushed it as forcefully as he could, releasing it an inch from the center of her forehead. He went back toward the flames, slowly bent Joseph's golden arm until the muzzle was directly under Joseph's chin, aimed upward, the silent tongue of blue flame a half inch from the jowl. He gave the trigger finger a forceful tug. He towed the girl along the corridor to the steps up to the cockpit hatch. It was ajar. He pushed it open and went back and got her and forced her out into the night. The sun had set over the land and the sky was like a banked fire but it was not as difficult to see as he had anticipated.

As he towed her along the dock he staggered with his weariness. He did not know how long he could continue. He had to find a safe place. He moved off the dock and into deep shadows and set her upright and leaned her against a tree. He peered at the dial of the gold watch and found there were a few minutes left. He put his thumb on the watch stem and he knew it was a trigger. They deserved to die. Yet he had the curious feeling that he would also be destroyed if he pressed it. Why should he pass ultimate judgment?

Suddenly, in all his weariness, he had a feeling of antic pleasure, of a wild exhilaration. Bonny Lee was free. Wilma was safe. Betsy was safe. The world was new again, and there was nothing able to stop him. He turned and ran through the bloody twilight as fast as he could. He went back into the yacht. The lead slug was touching her smooth forehead. He pulled it away, pushed it toward the flames. He pulled the muzzle away from Joseph's chin. He stepped back just as the red time ended. The pistol cracked, the flames crackled, Charla's face was changed by a look of vast alarm. He spun the world red again, stilling the flames. He looked at them as he now knew his uncle must have looked at them in times past. Ridiculous people. Fair game. A mildly interesting irritant in a greedy world. Death had too much stature, too much dignity, to be awarded them now. The watch could provide more suitable punishments. But at the moment he was too exhausted to follow through. He found a cabin and stretched out, set the watch to a full hour, suspended a heavy ashtray a few inches over his chest and went peacefully to sleep.

He awoke much refreshed, stopped objective time again and

went to see what he could do about Charla and Joseph. He took Charla off the yacht. When he was near where he had left Betsy, he took a breathing space and walked over and looked at her. She had taken three steps away from the tree, and she looked terribly confused.

He tugged the stubborn burden of Charla all the way to the nearest intersection, stopping frequently to look around for something suitable. He found it at the intersection, waiting for the light to change. It was a big gray truck with Navy markings. He peered in over the tailgate. About thirty men sat on the benches that ran along either side of the truck. They were not recruits. They had that bronzed competent look of career men, who, when faced with any unusual situation, would not be at a loss.

Sadly, slowly, he bent the short robe off the suspended figure of Charla. After the fevered dreams of performing this very act, it seemed wasteful that it had to be done with so little emotion. Regretfully he admired the exquisite structure and texture of her. He pushed her into a handy position, clambered over the tailgate and hauled her inside. He stretched her out across five military laps, pressed her down solidly, and climbed back out of the truck. It would give her, he thought, some unforgettable moments. He looked into the truck at the tableau in red marble, the bored male faces unaware of the rich burden. If he had gauged their reactions properly, the very first response would be the firm clasp of a bronzed hairy hand, right over her startled mouth.

It had taken twenty minutes to dispose of Charla. He went back after Joseph. He was not only a more difficult burden, but it was troublesome to think of some situation which would be as memorable to him as Charla's awakening would be to her. He pushed and tugged and floated Joseph all the way to the intersection, then left him suspended in air while he scouted a nearby cocktail lounge. It was doing an excellent business. He walked through to the back beyond the rest rooms and found a storeroom. The door was ajar. The key was in the lock. He went back among the throng and selected three women. He picked three mature ones without wedding rings, three who looked glossy and competent and somewhat virulent. They had style, prominent jaw lines and a few well-concealed traces of erosion. He trudged them back to the hallway outside the storeroom, one at a time. As he undressed them, one at a time, in midair, and levered them into the small dark room, it occurred to him that he was becoming so adept at it he could apply for a position fixing department store windows. The third one gave him pause. She had a truly astonishing tattoo.

By the time he plodded in with Joseph, time was growing short. He stripped him hastily, shouldered him in with his new acquaintances and slowly pulled the door shut. Clothing was suspended in the air all around him. He tried to turn the key, but he could not. Time had almost run out anyway. He switched the watch to normal time, turned the key and took it out of the lock and immediately switched back to enough red time to leave and get back to Betsy. The second touch on the watch stem cut short the very beginning of a scream. The clothing had fallen to the hallway floor.

He walked back to Betsy. He stood beyond her line of vision and turned the world on. She turned and saw him and gasped. "This—this is something nobody could ever get used to! But the damned thing works!"

He looked toward the intersection. The light changed. The Navy truck started up and moved slowly away through the dusk. He looked over and saw the billowing of smoke against the dark sky. He heard a distant sound of sirens approaching.

"It worked," he said.

"We came within an inch of getting murdered or fried and you stand there grinning like a moron! What's the matter with you?"

"Murdered, fried or shot."

"Shot?"

"You missed that part of it, Betsy dear."

She looked at him with a haggard, accusing face. "And you carried me right past them?"

"Yes indeed."

"And they just—stood there?"

"Like statues."

She moved closer to him. "Could you have killed them?"

"Yes."

"And you didn't?"

He thought her mouth had an exceptionally ugly look. They were in a small park area sheltered from the flow of headlights and the blue glare of the mercury vapor lights on the avenue. Her damp stained orange coveralls smelled of smoke. Her hair was tangled and her face was smudged.

"I had that idea, to tell you the truth."

"You fool! You do it again, you hear? Make everything stop. Go back aboard and kill them. Who could ever prove anything? Go kill both of them. They'll never give up. They'll never give up until they're dead."

He studied her. And he remembered how close he had come to doing just what she now suggested. Nothing would have ever been the same again. The watch, Bonny Lee, all would have been changed. And he would have lost one of the most precious attributes of this unique ability to make time stand still—the additive of wry mischief, of ironic joy. Bonny Lee had understood that instinctively. Murder would have turned the watch into a perpetual solemnity and a perpetual guilt—because, regardless of provocation, the owner of the watch was beyond the need to kill.

"Betsy dear, Charla and Joseph are too busy right now."

"Busy!"

"Aunt Charla is sort of riding around enjoying the evening. And Joseph is making some new friends."

"You act as if this is all some kind of a joke!" she said furiously.

He heard men shouting on the dock. The fire trucks arrived. He took Betsy by the arm and walked her away from there, staying in the shadows and on the darker sides of the streets. When they came to a shopping area where a cut-rate department store was open late, he left her in a shadowy place and went into the frozen silence and stillness of the store and found fresh clothing for himself, taking care to select the lightest weight sandals he could find. He changed, selected clothing for her, packed it into a lightweight suitcase and towed it on out. He realized he had been careful not to take anything that anyone was looking directly at. He was acquiring the habit of a basic ethic of using the time-stop. Do not frighten the innocent unnecessarily. With Charla and Joseph he had violated this concept. The sailors were the innocents, and he did not imagine they would seriously question the origin of the gift. And there was enough subjective phenomena in cocktail lounges to make objective magic almost unnoticeable.

When he returned to Betsy he did not bother to reappear in the same place and position. She started violently. They walked further into a small park. He opened the suitcase on a bench. She went behind bushes and changed to the cotton dress and Orlon cardigan he had brought her, and stuffed Charla's sodden playsuit under a bush. At a drinking fountain under a street lamp he held the mirror he had brought her while she wiped the smudges from her face and used the hair brush he had brought her, and used the stolen lipstick.

He risked a cruising cab and had the driver stop a block away from the Hotel Birdline. She went in with the money he gave her and rented a room, using a name they had agreed upon. He loafed in the shadows for ten minutes, and then halted time and went into the hotel. He looked at the register and saw they had given her room 303. He went up the stairs. She had left the door ajar as agreed. When he materialized instantaneously in front of her, her leap of surprise was smaller than before. He closed the door and said, "You're doing better, Miss Betsy."

"I think I'm just too tired to react. What is the world like when you're—doing that?"

"Absolutely silent. Red light. No motion anywhere. It's like being in a strange kind of a dream."

"Does it seem evil? Or is that a silly question?"

"It could be evil. I don't think it's a silly question. I guess it would depend on the person using it. I guess it would sort of— multiply whatever you are by ten. Because it's absolute freedom. You can make your fantasies come true. And if your fantasies are —sick, then that's the way you'll use it. Maybe it's just like any other kind of power. I haven't really had time to think about the implications. And not much time now. You'll be safe here and I have a girl to find."

"Just any girl?"

"Not exactly."

"Your face is dirty."

"I'll use guest rights on the shower."

"Of course. Go ahead."

He showered and put the stolen clothing back on. He reached into his pocket and found the watch gone. He ran out of the bathroom. She was sitting huddled on the edge of the bed. She held the watch out to him at arm's length. Her eyes looked haunted. "I didn't have the guts," she whispered.

"What did you have in mind?"

"Please don't be angry. I just wanted to try. But I couldn't. Maybe—I was afraid of my own fantasies. They aren't—particularly nice." She lifted her chin with a kind of tired defiance. "I would have killed them."

"I know."

"For many many reasons. But you didn't. So maybe you have the right to use that magic, and I don't."

"You had the sense not to try. That's something."

She stood up and sighed and moved into his arms. She turned her mouth up to him and he kissed her without passion.

"Will you come back here?" she asked.

"I don't know. I'll leave money in case I can't. I'll phone at least."

When she looked up at him her eyes seemed softer, more gray than green. There was a faint smell of smoke caught in that palomino hair. Her back was hard and slender under his hands. "I owe you lots," she said. "And I think you are quite a guy. If you can make any use at all of a sort of neurotic but very grateful girl, and you want to come back here, feel free." She pushed herself away. "Have I said something so terribly amusing?"

"I'm sorry. It isn't you. It's me. I was thinking of all the other nights I spent in this pleasure palace. It was just sort of ironic for the moment. Betsy, you are very tired and very sweet and very desirable."

"Desirable in general. Nothing specific."

"I'm sorry. Nothing specific."

"Then I'm sorry too, because I do feel sort of specific." She sighed and smiled and touched his cheek. "Go find your girl."

Two blocks from the hotel he suddenly came upon a disguise which would render him completely invisible in nighttime Miami. It was a little past nine o'clock. He removed the disguise from a man who was in no condition to realize he was being robbed. Kirby donned the disguise and looked at his reflection in a store window. A comedy derby, a bright red plastic cane and a big round beribboned badge on which was printed "Eddie Beeler—

Lubbock, Texas." He lurched slightly, faked a soft hiccup and nodded at himself with satisfaction.

He hailed a cab and asked to be taken to Rio's in North Miami.

The driver said, "You wanta go where the action is, you don't wanta go there, sport."

"Going to meet some buddies there."

"Okay, so what you do, you go in and bring them out and I'll take you where the action is."

The driver started up. He had the news on. Kirby asked him to turn up the volume. ". . . were involved in the search for Kirby Winter and Wilma Farnham when police traced a shipment of Winter's personal possessions to the yacht. Prompt action by area firefighting units prevented serious damage to the luxury vessel. The scene of the fire looked like attempted arson, but the three crew members aboard at the time can shed no light on the matter. The stateroom was occupied by Betsy Alden, actress niece of Mrs. O'Rourke, and as yet the police have been unable to locate either Miss Alden or Mrs. O'Rourke. While the fire was being brought under control, Joseph Locordolos, owner of the *Glorianna,* was being apprehended in a nearby cocktail lounge. Locordolos, severely battered and lacerated by the women upon whom he was forcing his attentions, and in a semi-hysterical condition, was booked for assault, exposure and lewd behavior, and is reported as not yet being in condition to be questioned regarding the two women who were aboard or the origin of the fire.

"A further element of mystery concerns the other two members of the crew of the *Glorianna,* Rene Bichat and Raoul Feron who were apprehended earlier today in the Hallandale home of Professor Wellerly of Florida Eastern. When Metro police went to the house in response to an anonymous phone tip, they found considerable damage to the house and found the two seamen in the shuttered living room, bound hand and foot. The two men have refused to explain their presence there and are being held.

"Evidence collected on the scene indicates Wilma Farnham may have been hiding out in the Wellerly home. Professor Wellerly and his family are in Europe, and he is a friend of Roger Farnham, Miss Farnham's brother, who denies any knowledge of his sister's whereabouts.

"Another factor, as yet unexplained, was the presence of a sports car behind the Wellerly residence, registered in the name of Bonny Lee Beaumont, a night club entertainer now working in the Greater Miami area. As yet police have been unable to contact Miss Beaumont.

"It is now believed that there was a closer connection between the people aboard the *Glorianna* and Kirby Winter and the Farnham woman than was first presumed. But an aura of mystery thickens around the millions embezzled from the estate of the late Omar Krepps."

The news ended. The driver turned the radio down and said, "Why the hell do they have to make it sound so hard? This Winter had it all set up for his buddies to bring that Glory Annie here and take him off with his broad and the money. But it's so much money and so much heat, everybody wants a bigger cut, so they start fighting among themselves and they screw up the whole deal for everybody. Why is that so hard to figure?"

"So where are they now?"

"Who knows, sport? This town has a million transient rooms, and there's so many ways to get out of it, you can't seal it off. Right? And there's enough confusion going on, how can anybody find anybody? It's like the whole town is going nuts. Beach riots, crazy traffic jams, people all over claiming they're seeing spooks. What it is, it's the humidity. It gets just to the right place and this town always starts to unravel. I seen it before."

When they reached Rio's, Kirby told the driver there would be no point in his waiting. The structure looked as though a pagoda had been mated with Mount Vernon, then boarded up and used as a proving ground for neon tubes. It sat in the middle of an asphalt field half full of cars. At intervals, a little worm of blue neon would appear way over on the left, out of total blackness. It would start to move across, picking up speed, picking up more width, additional colors until, when it reached the far right it occupied the whole height of the building. Then it turned into a huge white waterfall. Then it said RIO'S—in red—big enough to drive a truck through the O. And, as it was shouting RIO'S, three banks of floodlights flicked on, one after the other, illuminating three plywood girls, thirty feet tall. The first one was a brunette labeled Perry Meson. The middle one was Bonny Lee. The third was a redhead disastrously named Pooty-Tat O'Shaugnessy. They were all smiling. They were bare, except for the strategic placement of their name signs. They were all of a height, standing elbow to elbow, reproduced by some color photomural process, and the six breasts aligned, big as bushel baskets, had a fearsome implausibility which induced, rather than lust, a feeling of inadequacy. This peculiar vision of his love gave Kirby a feeling of petulance and indignation, like a small boy discovering he is expected to share his candied apple with the entire first grade. It was but a minor compensation to note that the incredible Pooty-Tat made the other two look immature. RIO'S flickered off and the lighted cutouts lingered another two seconds. The building was in total darkness for a moment and then the little blue worm reappeared.

When he hauled the heavy door open, he was assailed by a blast of noise so tangible he wondered that it did not push him back out. He went through the hat check foyer without relinquishing funny hat or cane, and moved into the smoky gloom. Waiters pounced, scurried, slid through tiny spaces between the shadowy tables. Everyone seemed to be yelling to be heard over the brass din of a small and exceptionally noisy group of musicians on a cantilevered shelf playing an accelerated version of "Smoke Gets in Your Eyes," with the compulsive, crashing beat of a twist number. A lot of people seemed to be yelling "Go!" in time to the beat. At the far end of the large room, on a small platform stage, bathed in a hot pink spotlight stood Miss Pooty-Tat O'Shaugnessy wearing nought but a drowsy smile, a sequined G-string and two little silk tassels. She had her fingers laced at the nape of her neck and seemed totally relaxed, except that one little red tassel was revolving clockwise, the other counterclockwise, each completing one revolution exactly on the smashing beat.

"Parm me!" a waiter snarled and shoved Kirby out of his trance. He went to the crowded bar and found a four-inch space between two beefy men. The service was fast, the drink small, weak and expensive. When the harried bartender brought his change, Kirby tried to ask when Bonny Lee would be on, but the barman was gone before he could get the words out. At the final thump of the last bar, Pooty-Tat added a bump to the other activities, and the pink spot went off.

"She ain't on tonight," one of the beefy men said.

"Cop trouble, somebody said," the other man said.

"How come?" the first man said.

"Her car got used on a B and E that went sour and they made her through the plates, but she should have showed and said it was borrowed. You fade and they nail you every time, like accessory."

When the bartender started to snatch Kirby's empty glass, Kirby grabbed him by the wrist and said, "How can I get in touch with Bonny Lee?"

The man yanked himself free and said, "Try a classified ad, doll."

Five minutes later, as Kirby was wondering what to try next, there was a tap on his shoulder. He turned and saw an old waiter with a face like a tired bulldog. The waiter moved away, giving a little jerk of his head for Kirby to follow him. Ten feet from the bar the waiter stopped.

"I play a little game, okay? Like I say a front name and you give me the rest of it, okay? Bernie?"

Kirby stared at him blankly. As the waiter shrugged and started to turn away, Kirby said, "Sabbith?"

"Slow thinker, huh. Come on with me."

Kirby followed him along the side of the big room, through a door, down a corridor and past a noisy kitchen to other doors. He knocked on one of them. "Yes?" a high clear voice called.

"It's Raymond. I got with me maybe the guy you wannit."

"Let him in, love. And thank you so much."

Raymond opened the door and let him in. It was a small, incredibly cluttered room, harshly and unpleasantly lighted. Pooty-Tat sat on a ratty couch eating a steak sandwich, sharing the couch with a precarious pile of clothes, cartons, magazines, empty Coke bottles, paper editions, phonograph records and other debris. She wore a blue denim smock.

"Do sit down," she said. The dressing table bench was the only place available. She had a high voice, a rather chilly and precise English accent, with that special clarity of tone English girls often have.

"Actually, love, I hardly expected such a festive look. But the little scar is just where she said it would be, so you must be the one. Do take off that insane hat, Mr. Winter."

"Is she all right?"

"You do ask that rather nicely. Concern, anxiety. As far as I know, she is perfectly all right."

"Where is she?"

"In due time, Mr. Winter. I have been wondering about you. We are all terribly fond of Bonny Lee. A limited background of course, but marvelous instincts. Sometimes her instincts fail her, though, and she does become involved with some horrid sod. Then we do what we can, you see."

"I would like to know where—"

"Are you quite certain you are good for her, Mr. Winter? You do seem to have involved her in some sort of stickiness. And you're even more of a fugitive than she at the moment. I can't pretend to know much about it, but haven't you made off with rather a lot of money? Don't look so alarmed, love. I trust her completely, and she trusts me. I wouldn't turn you in."

"I didn't mean to get her into any trouble or danger."

"You certainly *seem* harmless enough. You have quite an earnest look. You see, I was just getting up when she rang me up, and I had to scurry over to the Beach and pick her up. She'd cadged a dime to phone me, and she was in a drugstore, absolutely sopping wet, terribly busy fending off a randy little clerk. But she would not take time to change. She was frantic with worry about you. I couldn't even drive fast enough to suit her. We went to the health school and picked up three of my friends. I have this ridiculous letch for horribly muscular men. They're invariably dumb as oxen and sexually not very enterprising, but sometimes they are useful if one anticipates a brawl. So then we went scooting to Hallandale, with Bonny Lee on the edge of the seat using rather bad language, but the place was crawling with police officers. We parked a block away and I sent my brightest oaf to go find out what was up. No sign of you, he said, or of some girl Bonny Lee was asking about. Just two rather bitter and surly fellows, low types apparently, being led into a police vehicle. So then we took my fellows back to their muscle flexing. Bonny Lee was wondering what she should do about her poor little abandoned car. She had stopped fretting about you. In fact she seemed awfully amused about something, but wouldn't give me a clue. I took her to that horrid nest amongst those squadrons of tireless old ladies, but quite suddenly she scrooched down and hissed at me to go right on by. It seems two unsavory types were parked on her street, the two she had apparently eluded by plunging into a canal. She was all for our gathering up my friends once more and returning to give them a bashing about, but I must say I had begun to have quite enough of this darting about, and I became a bit cross, so I took her back to my place where at last she had a chance to get out of that dank clothing and rinse the salt out of her hair."

"Is she there now?"

"You are an impatient fellow. She was going to come to work until we heard over the radio that the police wanted a chat with her. She had a perfectly reasonable impulse to turn herself in and explain, but the more she thought about how she would explain things, the less she wanted to try. And she thought that if they did happen to hold her for questioning, you might hear about it and do some utterly idiotic thing like dashing to her rescue. She seemed to assume you would be searching for her, and when I expressed small reasonable doubt, she became quite ugly about it. She was afraid you might go to her place, and there was no way to warn you. We made arrangements about how I might contact you and identify you should you come here."

There was a muffled roar, a concerted shout. Miss O'Shaugnessy tilted her head. "Dear Perry. She always gets that same response to that part of her act. The child is incredibly flexible."

"I'm anxious to see Bonny Lee."

"Of *course* you are, and I would have sent you dashing to my place if you'd arrived earlier. But it is after eleven, you know. And I had a dear friend arriving at my place at eleven to nap and wait for me, an absolute bronzed giant of an airlines pilot, with the most astonishing external voluntary muscle structure I've ever seen. The deltoideus, triceps brachia, latissimus dorsi and trapezius are like great marvelous wads of brown weathered stone. The poor lamb has just enough awareness to push all his little buttons and levers to get his aircraft from here to there and back, and he crinkles charmingly when he smiles, but it would be too confusing to him to find Bonny Lee at my place. He wouldn't know how to react, and it would upset him. So it was arranged that she would leave before eleven. She has my little car and she is wearing some of my clothing, and she will be at Bernie Sabbith's apartment at midnight. She hopes you will meet her there, but in the event you don't, she'd planned to enlist the help of Bernie and his friends in whatever gruesome difficulties you two seem to have gotten into. Actually, I think all Bernie can contribute to any situation is additional confusion, but perhaps some use can be made of that. So, you see, you have time to spare. And you've been watching every morsel of this sandwich, you know."

She went to the kitchen. A few minutes after she returned, a sandwich and coffee was brought to her little dressing room.

"Does—uh—Bonny Lee do the same sort of act you do, Miss O'Shaugnessy?"

"My name is Lizbeth, love. Lizbeth Perkins, actually. You are a rather stuffy fellow, aren't you? What if she did exactly the same routines? Would it make her unworthy of you?"

"I just wondered," he said, miserably.

"Have no fear, love. The degree one is required to strip is in inverse ratio to one's other talents. Your darling has a lovely voice, and she's getting better all the time with those bongos. And she moves about well. I suspect the pictures outside upset you? Bonny Lee was upset too, and if you look closely, you'll see that though Perry and I are as nature made us, some clever wretch with an airbrush removed Bonny Lee's little frivolous bandeau. But she wasn't agitated about the exposure, love. She was jealous of her category—entertainer rather than stripper. You men are such dismal creatures, really, beset with Edwardian scruples. I can't sing a note, and as a child I trained for ballet, but whoever heard of a prima ballerina measuring forty-one, twenty-five, thirty-seven? What those slack-jawed idiots out there fail to realize is how many hundreds and hundreds of sweaty hours of brute labor it has taken for me to develop the skill to flex all the muscles of my body, singly or in any desired sequence. It's not what one could call a skill of any historic significance, Mr. Winter, but it pleases the fools, supports me well, and keeps me in a condition of astonishing health. Is it somehow more reprehensible than being able to bash a small ball a long distance with a club? Dear me, I do hope Bonny Lee hasn't become emotionally involved with a dingy little moralist."

"I didn't mean to—"

"Hush, love. I'm merely educating you to a proper level to appreciate Bonny Lee. She is a dear child, loving and honest and gay. And you must enjoy her for exactly what she is, the way one enjoys sunshine and gardens. If you try to confine her or restrict her or change her into what you think is a more suitable image, she will very probably break your heart. She's terribly young, you know. Old in some ways, young in others. In time she might well become very famous, if clods like you can keep from making her feel coarse and insecure."

"I think I see what you mean."

"I hope you do, love. If I didn't suspect you have possiblities, I wouldn't have wasted the time and the words."

"I'm not very—deft about girls, Lizbeth."

"So much the better. Deft men fall into dim patterns. And the dreadful clue to all of them is that they seem to feel they are doing the girl some enormous favor. I like a man to feel grateful, and bloody few of them do. And the worldly ones seem to feel obligated to prove their skill by showing off a whole arsenal of nasty little tricks which they seem to feel should induce an absolute frenzy. My word, I've had it up to here with being compared to a cello or a sports car. I'm a rather direct woman, Mr. Winter, and I like love to be direct and pleasant and on the cozy side, and as comfortable as one can make it. So don't fret about being unaccustomed to girls. I suspect Bonny Lee finds it all rather sweet. And don't you dare brood about her other affairs. You'll merely poison your own mind and spoil it for both of you. She will be totally, absolutely faithful to you for as long as the game will last, and that is all you can expect or should hope for."

He finished the last of the coffee and put the cup aside. "This is all very interesting, and I suppose you are an unusual woman, and maybe you can't help being so damned defensive, but I am getting Goddamned well tired of listening to a lot of little lectures from women. I am tired of having my head patted, and I am sick of a lot of over-simplified little bite-sized pieces of philosophy about life and love. I just happen to think the world is a little more complex than that. And with your kind indulgence, Lizbeth,

I shall go right on making my own stuffy and sentimental and un-reasonable mistakes in my own way. I have had a very long day, Lizbeth. The mind of man cannot comprehend the kind of a day I have had. Mentally and emotionally, I am right at the frayed end of the last bit of string there is. I do not defend or attack your right to flex muscles I never heard of. I make no attempt to typecast you, so please do me the same favor. I appreciate your assistance to Bonny Lee, and your concern for her. But my atti-tudes and responses, are, I am afraid, my personal business. If I have annoyed you, I'm sorry. But I do have to be leaving."

She looked at him very thoughtfully. She nodded. "Now didn't she just come up with something! Possibly the hat and the cane and the badge warped my judgment, love. You might come back one day, Mr. Winter. If you're free. But spend some time on the weights and bars first. No more lectures. Not a word of advice. You do seem quite able to cope. All I can do is wish you luck."

She put out her hand. It was a small hand, rather plump, but implicit in the quick squeeze she gave him was the warning that with an effortless twist she could probably sail him over her shoulder like a quoit.

13

SOME VERY FREEHAND PARKING HAD OCCURRED IN THE ALLEY BY Bernie Sabbith's apartment. As Kirby climbed the outside stair-case he heard guffaws and breaking glass. The door was open a few inches. He knocked, but after he realized no one could hear him, he pushed the door open and went in.

All the tricky lights were on, and the big music system was throwing a mighty wattage into all the built-in speakers. A table bar had been set up and a man in a white jacket was mixing drinks as fast as he could. At first glance there seemed to be fifty people in the apartment, but he soon realized the mirrors had doubled the apparent number.

There seemed to be a group of curiously identical young men, all dark, all spankingly clean, all wearing dark narrow suits, knit ties, white button down shirts, all smiling with a certain ironic tilt to one eyebrow, all holding chunky glasses containing ice and dark whisky. The rest of the young men seemed as young, but they looked as if they cut each other's hair, got their clothes out of mission barrels and bathed on bank holidays.

The girls seemed divided into two groups, too—a pack of languid starved ones in high fashion clothes, and a bouncy, racy, noisy batch in odds and ends of this and that. A fat little girl in a ratty red leotard came bounding toward him with yelps of delight lost in the general confusion.

"Let me guess!" she yelled. "You are a conventioneer! Your name is—uh—Eddie Beeler! You heard the sounds of action, O Conventioneer, and you have traced it with incredible instinct to the very fount of *all* action! I, Gretchen Firethorn myself, shall be your guide and mentor, O Eddie."

"Which one is Bernie Sabbith, please?"

"Oh shoot!" she said. "You spoil everything. Couldn't you have just wandered in, for God's sake? That's Bernie, over there in the khakis and the white jacket, not the little one making drinks. Further. The one plastering the blonde against that mirror."

As Kirby hesitated, the fat girl took the funny hat, the cane and the badge, in what seemed to be one swift motion and bounded off, whooping. He worked his way between the twisters to where Sabbith was mumbling to the semi-smothered blonde. Bernie was a tall and angular man, seemingly constructed entirely of elbows and knuckles.

When Kirby finally got the man's attention, he swung around and stuck his hand out and said, "Glad you could make it, pal. The bar's right over there. Glad you could show." He turned back to the blonde.

"Have you seen Bonny Lee Beaumont?"

Bernie turned around again. "Bonny Lee! Where is she? You bring her, pal?"

"No. I'm looking for her."

"She isn't here tonight, pal. There's the bar. Get yourself a—"

"She's supposed to arrive at midnight."

The blonde started to slide sideways. Bernie grabbed her and straightened her up again. "Pal, some day I'd like to have a nice long chat, but right now you're a drag. Noonan!" One of the dark-suited ones presented himself. "Noonan, get this conversationalist out of my hair, like a pal."

Noonan gently led Kirby away. "Mr. Sabbith seems to be busy at the moment. What is the angle of impact, sir? Chamber of Commerce? Press, radio, television, talent?"

"I'm supposed to meet a girl here."

"Sir, if that was the guarantee, that you shall have. With a few spoken-for exceptions, I can offer you your choice of any member of our happy crew, our tight little ship. I would suggest one of the ragamuffin types, one of our off-camera laborers in the vineyard. If, on the other hand, you want the model type, I suggest you take two. Their energy level is so low, sir, they save their tiny sparkle for the deathless moment when they hold up the product."

"I'm supposed to meet a specific girl here!" Kirby shouted over the music. "I know her." As he made a helpless gesture, somebody put a drink in his hand.

"Can't you remember her name?"

"I *know* her name!"

"But you don't know what she looks like?"

"She's going to *arrive!* I want to *wait* for her!"

"Sir, you seem too solemn about all this. This is an epocal night in the short brilliant history of Parmalon."

"Of what?"

Noonan staggered and clutched his heart. "Don't do that to me, fellow. Parmalon! Seven shades, seven lotions, seven secret ingredients, the seven lovely lives of a beautiful woman. And we are down here, sir, bankrolled to do ten tropical commercials which will tear the living hearts right out of all the frump housewives in America." He tapped Kirby solidly on the chest. "Do you know who Bernie Sabbith is?"

"I think so."

"He is Guts. He is shining Brass. We are surrounded by the Loyal Ones, on and off camera. Shrewd agency minds. Fantastic technicians. Talent, beauty, dignity and greed." He thumped Kirby again. "Sabbith went in there as the writer. Do you know what he is now? He is the writer, *and* the director, *and* the producer, with twenty-eight grand apiece in hand for each and every message. That is what we celebrate, fellow. And we tolerate no solemnity, no groaning of the bored. Gather a damsel, grasp the wine, howl and prance, fellow. Let us see a little forthright debauchery. What is your trade, fellow?"

Kirby looked him squarely in the eye. "Philanthropy."

"Good God, another agency man?"

More glasses broke. A spindly girl did a comedy trampoline act on the giant bed, to mild applause. The next record was Cuban, from the time when Cubans were cheerful, flexible folk.

A vision floated over to Noonan and Kirby. She was the young Ingrid, a younger Greta, a juvenile Marlena, drifting, pensive, faintly confused as though she had just been awakened, or had just been given a good one behind the ear. She had great sad tilted dreamy gray-blue eyes, oval shadowed hollows in her cheeks, a golden drift of cobweb hair, a white length of throat. She seemed to be on the edge of tears, and in her dusky voice was a throb of heartbreak.

"Noony," she said, "this one come down with the scurds?"

Noonan was most gentle with her, as though she were the only survivor of some inconceivable disaster. "No, dear. I'm sorry."

"Diddly bring the scurds?"

Noonan patted her thin shoulder gently. "Some one else is bringing them, dear. Don't you fret. What did you say your name is, sir?"

"Eddie. Eddie Beeler."

"Eddie, may I present Minta Burleigh. Minta, dear. Show Eddie what you do. Minta?"

She looked at Noonan, at the floor and at her empty hands and said mournfully, "Whaddle I use?" Noonan gave her his cigarette case. She turned slowly and focused on Kirby. She held the cigarette case up. She tilted her head. She smiled at Kirby, and suddenly she was specific, obvious, glowing, direct—like something that emerges from the fog and bears down upon you. "For that seventh loveliness," she said in a throbbing, dramatic contralto, "Parmalon! In the jeweled decorator case, for the woman who cares so much." Her lights went out like an unplugged Christmas tree and she listlessly handed the case back to Noonan.

"She's worried about some skirts," Noonan explained. "There's a color matching problem in a medium shot where she walks toward camera."

"Fugging scurds," Minta murmured.

"Be nice to Eddie, dear," Noonan said. "I got to go calm Harry down again."

Minta tottered slightly and looked at Kirby. The vast eyes seemed to cross slightly for a moment. She turned her hand out, held her wrist up where Kirby could read what someone had printed with a ball-point pen on the tender, transparent, blue-veined skin. "Worm I sacked?" she asked.

"Sultana. Seven-twenty," he read.

She swayed toward him, hooked her weight on his belt and laid her gentle cheek against his chest. "Sokay," she sighed. "Just no messing the hair, no bruise the mouth."

Bonny Lee appeared just beyond Minta, looking at Kirby with an odd expression. "Having fun?"

Kirby made gentle efforts to disentangle Minta. He was afraid of fracturing or dislocating something. "I've been waiting for you," he explained.

"Sorta killin' time, sweetie? Where'd you get the disaster case?"

Minta swayed around and looked at Bonny Lee. "Where are all the peasants coming from?"

Bonny Lee slowly drew back a clenched right fist. Kirby spotted one of the dark-suited ones standing a little to one side, his eyes closed, swaying in time to the Latin beat. He put his hands on Minta's narrow waist, picked her up and set her down against the man with the closed eyes. She had been as easy to lift as a child. She immediately hooked her weight onto the man's belt and laid her gentle cheek against his chest. The man didn't open his eyes. In a few seconds they began to dance, moving slightly to every fourth bar of the music.

"It was just like that, Bonny Lee," Kirby said.

She gave him a narrow look. "Sure. Just in case I never showed, huh?"

"Bonny Lee, we've got too much to talk about to get started off this way. I've been terribly worried about you. I've got to tell you what happened. We've got to figure out what to do next."

"Look like you already knew." She looked around at the party.

"Man, we're going to get no help out of this outfit. They gone past the point. Let me say hi to Bernie and we'll take off."

"I see no reason why you have to say anything to him."

"Oh, you don't!"

"No, I don't!"

"So you rove free as a bird and I can't even say hello! Is that it?"

"You got the wrong idea about that girl, Bonny Lee. But I don't have any wrong ideas about Bernie Sabbith."

She moved closer and glowered at him. "The only idea you got about Bernie is he's a friend, and right now no more than a friend, and I say hello to friends."

"Never more than a friend. Get that clear!"

Suddenly she looked amused. "Just listen to us, hey? Sure, Kirby. Never more than a friend. And that's all you have, too. Friends."

He saw her wend her way through the confusions to Bernie's side. When he hugged her, Kirby glowered at them. He turned and went off in pursuit of the fat girl. She was forlorn at giving up the hat, the cane and the badge. Bonny Lee came back to Kirby, near the door, and she seemed to stumble against him, put her arm around him. He felt her hand in the side pocket of the cord jacket. Suddenly she appeared in a new place two feet to the right of where she had been. She handed him the watch, and she was smiling cheerfully.

In the middle of the big room, Minta Burleigh went mad. All eyes were on her as she leaped, yelped, spun, flailed in a frenzy of the dance. Her Slav eyes were crazed, and the cords in her pale throat stood out. Her partner got in the way and got a crack across the chops which staggered him. As the dance began to diminish, Bonny Lee urged Kirby toward the door. The door closed behind them, cutting the major part of the din, and Kirby could hear Bonny Lee chuckling as they went down the stairs to the alley.

"What did you do?" he demanded.

"Packed her pants with shaved ice, lover. Guess there's life left in her. But, gawddamn, she's built scrawny."

Lizbeth's car, an English Ford sedan, was parked at the mouth of the alley. They got in and as soon as they'd closed the doors, Bonny Lee made a small furry sound in her throat and came into his arms, filled with a ready warmth and kisses and strength of round arms, and at long last said, "How come I could get to miss you so dang much? And you a city type fella."

"What has that got to—"

"Trouble is, you think too much. By the time you through walking around something, thinking at it, it like to take off. I just couldn't figure how you'd try to find me, but I guess you finally decided trying Rio's. How'd you like Lizbeth? You catch her act?"

"Yes, I—"

"And I went round and round with that Charla friend of yours. There's a woman mean as a snake, Kirby. And she had those two hoodlum boys to quieten me, but they weren't enough, not for a girl who one time when she was thirteen got run into the piney woods from a tent meeting by seven old boys full of shine, twicet as tough, each one, as those boys Charla had trying to keep holt of me. In those moony woods, I chunked two of them with rocks, tipped one into a crick, kicked one ontill he screamed like a girl and plain outrun the other three. They picked them the wrong gal, just like that Charla did. No man has ever forced me, nor ever will."

"I want to tell you—"

"So things can get ordered out for you, a little at a time, if you go at it direct, and I took something else off you tonight, that waiter you slugged."

"What?"

"By now he's told the police he's taking back the complaint on you, and even if he hasn't, you got this paper I brang you, sweetheart."

He looked at the paper in the flame of a match. On it was written, "The man hitting me taking my cloths, he was short fat bald maybe sixty year. I say it Mr. Winter so my name is on newspaper, for important." It was signed by the waiter and by two witnesses.

"How did you get this?"

"I was at Lizbeth's place and getting restless, so when I heard about the fire I thought maybe those two boys wouldn't be waiting at my place any more, so I went to see and they were gone. And I wanted my own clothes on account of in the top half of Lizbeth's there's room enough for me and a set of drums. I got into some of my own clothes and took money from under the mattress and went to the Elise. That waiter and I had a little talk. Somewhere while I was talking he got the idea he better settle small and get out, or somebody might float him away on the tide. So he took five hundred, and his signature is a little bit wiggly, but it's good enough I think. It was a just a little favor, lover. If I could get to talk personal to them two hungry cops, I bet you I could fix that up too."

"I'm beginning to think you could."

"Anyhow, when we got back to that little pink house with those muscly fellas of Lizbeth's, I knew you'd got hold of that golden watch and used it good, and taken that Wilma girl away with you, so I stopped being so fretful about you, but I sure wish you'd taken my car so we'd have one less trouble. Sugar, you better tell me all of what happened, every dang bit of it, and you better be real complete, because I have it in my mind you went off with Wilma and here it is after midnight. There's time in there to burn a boat and do too much else too."

They were turned, facing each other in the small car. He held her hands and told her all that had happened. When he came to the situation with Joseph and Charla, the way he had left them when he had carried Betsy off the boat, her fingers dug into his hands. When he told her about how he had changed his mind and gotten back to them barely in time, her grip softened.

"Hold me some," she said in a low voice. He held her.

"How much difference would it have made if I didn't get back?"

"Maybe none, to us," she whispered. "We could make us up some reasons why it was a thing to do. But it would have been a dirty thing."

"I sense that. But why?"

"Why a dirty thing? Because they'd be bugs with you stomping them. And people aren't bugs. Not even those people. Anyways, if you'd used it to kill folks, I couldn't ever use it again to do something happy, like packing ice in around that ol' scrawny girl up there."

She bounced back away from him and said, "Sweetie, you got a tendency to treat that watch too solemn. Afore you know it, we'll be bowing down to that darn thing, and then it will be the watch in charge instead of us. I say if there isn't fun in something, the hell with it."

"You think I should use it more—frivolously?"

"It would be good for you."

"What should I have done to Charla then? What would you have done?"

"Hmmm. I'd want to scare that mean ol' gal and unfancy her a little."

"Like, for example, stripping her and stuffing her into a truck full of sailors?"

She kissed him quickly. "If you can even think up something like that, honey, it means you're coming along just fine. Just fine."

"That's what I did."

"What!"

"And the truck drove slowly away."

She whooped, yelped, bounced, pounded his chest with her fist and laughed until she cried. And he got almost as much reaction from Joseph's untidy fate.

Suddenly she sobered, and her eyes narrowed. She leaned toward him in the faint glow of street light. "Speaking of you a-takin' the clothes off that fat little blonde woman, just how good did you get along with that Wilma girl and that Betsy?"

"I told you Wilma is in that motel in Hallandale. And I left Betsy at the Birdline."

"Gals stashed all over town, huh?"

"It's either feast or famine."

"I'm all the feast you need, Yankee. I'm a banquet all day long, so when we go check on those gals, we *both* go. Wilma first, I guess. We have to make sure they stay put before they go wandering around messing things up."

"And then what?"

"I was thinking about that," she said quietly.

"We can run. You and me. A long, long way."

"And leave a mess like this? The law would never give up."

"What else is there to do?"

"That old uncle of yours left you in a real good mess. And I keep thinking maybe he had a reason. And maybe the reason is in that letter he left."

"But I can't get that for a year."

"Maybe he left you a way to get it a lot sooner."

Suddenly he realized what she meant. "Of course!"

"And he could have meant for you to get hold of it sooner than a year, Kirby."

He pulled her close and said, "You're a very bright girl, Bonny Lee Beaumont."

Unreckoned minutes later she began to make languid efforts to untangle herself. "First," she said regretfully, "let's go check on all your other women."

14

ON WEDNESDAY MORNING, YOUNG MR. VITTS, OF WINTERMORE, Stabile, Schamway and Mertz received the anonymous, puzzling phone call. It preyed on his mind as the morning wore on. He knew it had to be nonsense, yet he knew he would not feel easy until he had assured himself that the packet entrusted to him was exactly where he had placed it, exactly where it belonged. At eleven, canceling his other appointments, he went to the bank. He signed the vault card, went with the attendant and operated his half of the double lock and took the japanned metal box to a private cubicle.

He opened the lid and saw the labeled packet Mr. Wintermore had entrusted to him, and felt like a fool at having wasted time coming to the bank to stare at it, just because some crackpot had told him it was gone.

And suddenly it was gone.

He shut his eyes tightly and opened them again and looked into the box. The packet was gone. He put a trembling hand into the box and fingered the emptiness. He slumped onto the small bench and closed his eyes. He knew he was overworked. A man who could not trust the evidence of his own senses had no business accepting fiduciary responsibilities. He knew he would have to go at once to Mr. Wintermore and confess that the Krepps packet had disappeared, and he had no idea where it had gone. He would ask for some leave, and consider himself fortunate if he was not forced to resign.

When he stood up, he moved like a very old man. The packet was back in the lock box. Had it been a cobra, he could not have recoiled more swiftly. It took him a few moments to acquire the courage to touch it, then lift it out of the lock box. At first it seemed to him to be of slightly different weight and dimension than he remembered, and it looked as if it had been resealed, but then logic came to his rescue. No one could possibly have touched it. He'd had a mild hallucination based on nervous tension and overwork. There was no need to tell Mr. Wintermore about it. Everything was entirely in order. He would try to get a little more rest in the future, a little more exercise and sunshine. He returned the box to the vault and walked back to his office, consciously breathing more deeply than was his custom.

Most of the documentation within the packet consisted of a detailed, witnessed, notarized certification of where the twenty-seven million had gone, affirming that O.K. Devices was primarily an eleemosynary operation, and because taxes had been paid on monies diverted to O.K.D., no claims for deductions had been in order.

Bonny Lee knelt on the bed behind Kirby and read over his shoulder as he read Uncle Omar's personal letter to him.

"My dear Nephew: It is entirely possible that you will never be able to comprehend this letter. You will think it evidence of senility, unless you have discovered *It,* and made use of *It* to gain access to this letter—a matter you should find rather simple —well in advance of schedule.

"I have taken elaborate safeguards. One, of course, was my attempt to shape your mind and character so you would be capable of properly using It, but at no time did I feel that you had reached the point of development where I could merely hand It over to you, as though giving you the world and all that is in it. I decided to make it all so difficult for you, the very act of discovering the capacities and making use of them would be sufficient trial by fire to solidify those aspects of your personality which I felt too indefinite to make you worthy of such a strange trust.

"The other safeguards are technical, and I fear so complete that the odds are against It ever being used by anyone after my death. The first device was extremely cumbersome, created nausea in the user, and was operative for but three minutes at a time. Over the years I simplified and perfected it. All technical notes regarding it have been destroyed. All you need know, if you have discovered Its capacities, is that it is permanently sealed, and uses cosmic radiation as a power source, accumulating it and storing it with such rapidity, no use is so excessive as to weaken It. Yet should any fifty-day period pass without its being used, the accumulation will overburden the storage capacity and fuse the basically simple device beyond all possibility of constructive analysis. This is one safeguard. In addition, should any attempt be made to open the sealed mechanism, the same result will be obtained. Lastly, due to a microscopic diminution of the essential element of the device, through use, I estimate that it will last no less than twenty and no more than twenty-five years from the date of this letter.

"I might add here that I took into account one psychological safeguard. I have directed Wintermore to hand it to you personally, and he is the least likely man I know to either let it out of his hands prematurely, or to fiddle with it and thus accidentally learn its properties.

"If you have waited a full year to read this letter, my boy, you will have no idea what I am talking about.

"If, on the other hand, you have learned the properties of the object, and have used it to solve certain problems I set up for you, then you will realize why I have surrounded it with these safeguards. Morally, perhaps I should have destroyed it when I knew I had not long to live. But possibly it was vanity which kept me from doing so. If you know what it will do, you can perceive the horrid burden of responsibility in having discovered the phenomenon, in having made selfish use of it, in having, I hope, partially atoned for such use, and having faced the dreadful image of a world where such a thing would be available to unscrupulous men.

"I even face the fact that some other person may be reading this letter, and you will never see it. In that event, it is possible I have indeed loosed a demon on the world.

"But if you have it, know what it is, and understand this letter, my boy, I need not charge you with any special duties and responsibilities. What you are will determine how you use it, and I have tried to shape you to that end. If the burden seems too great, all you need do is set it aside for fifty days.

"In these, my last words to you, I caution you about one thing, and one thing only. Keep it to yourself. Do not share its use with anyone. The man who owns it and can use it is the most powerful man the world has ever seen. It is not a power which can be safely shared."

Wilma Farnham, with sufficient advance notice to attract the widest possible coverage by the news media, and the maximum attendance by the executive personnel of Krepps Enterprises, governmental authorities and assorted attorneys of all parties at interest, made the first public appearance, with hair, make-up and clothing selected by Bonny Lee Beaumont.

Wilma, carefully coached by Kirby and Bonny Lee, made an intricate deal with the opposition. Once it was agreed that, if she could present satisfactory documentation as to the disposition of the twenty-seven millions, all criminal charges against Kirby Winter would be dropped, and all civil charges would be limited to those which could be established on the basis of the documentation she would present, she calmly produced the detailed statements.

KREPPS GAVE IT ALL AWAY, the headlines said.

The incident of Bonny Lee's little car was readily solved. Wilma swore she had borrowed it.

Betsy Alden was the next one to turn herself in. She had walked off the *Glorianna* an hour before the fire and had been for a time at the apartment of one Bernard Sabbith (verified by Mr. Sabbith) and had then gone to a downtown hotel and registered under a pseudonym (there was no law against it) and had remained there until she had discovered, at this late date, that the police wanted to talk to her.

ACTRESS CLEARED, smaller headlines said.

By the time Kirby Winter made his public appearance, the public imagination had gone bounding on ahead to new phenomena, as always—in this particular instance eleven young men in Coral Gables, insurance agents, store managers, stock salesmen and the like, whose discreet little wife-swapping club had worked like a charm for over two years until it had been discovered that one of them had been rigging the basis of selection by using a marked deck. They became suspicious of him when they noted that he was the only one who never ended up with his own wife. After having been disciplined with more enthusiasm than good judgment, he made full confession from his hospital bed.

The only residue of public opinion regarding Kirby Winter was a feeling of dull indignation that he had not, after all, stolen millions. He did not help matters by projecting a public image of a mild and rather wordy and tiresome man who wanted to talk of nothing but the Good Works of the late Omar Krepps. And the public has a minimum interest in Good Works. KREPPS HEIR TELLS OF GIVEAWAY, the very small headlines said.

Betsy Alden disappeared without further publicity. Sabbith took her back to New York with him. She has since been seen on major networks, telling why her clothes are fluffier, her drains are spotless and her nasal passages are open.

Wilma Farnham, after a few lessons from Bonny Lee, became a demure little ivoried odalisque with a weighty hairdo, bright blue contact lenses, a whispery voice and dresses which looked too tight to sit down in. Walton Grumby kept asking her to come to the K.E. offices and explain over and over what her duties had been with O.K. Devices. When he decided to go to Paris, Cairo and Rangoon to spot check the reported disbursement of cash, he took her along, just in case he happened to think of any additional questions.

After a partial recovery from a wide spectrum of traumatic nervous disorders, Joseph Locordolos was permitted to return to the *Glorianna*. Criminal charges were dropped and he settled civil actions out of court at considerable expense. His visa was cancelled, as were the visas of the five crew members. They were ordered to remain aboard the *Glorianna* until repairs had been completed. Joseph did all in his power to delay the repairs, hoping that Charla would reappear before he would be forced to leave port. He was very worried about her. He kept wondering what horrid thing Winter could have done to her, if perhaps he had killed her and hidden the body. When he thought of Charla dead, it made tears come to his eyes.

On the eighth day after the fire, Charla came calmly aboard. It was mid-morning. She walked into the main lounge and said, "Hello, Joseph." She sat down. He had jumped to his feet. He looked at her with consternation. She was perhaps fifteen pounds lighter. Her cheeks were hollow. Her eyes looked enormous. Her lovely flaxen hair had been cropped quite short. She wore a cheap little blouse and a cheap little skirt and she carried a big vulgar red purse.

He ran to her, knelt beside her chair and flung his arms around her and sobbed into her neck. "Oh, my poor darling, what has happened to you!"

"How are you, Joseph?" she asked. Her voice had a formless, faraway quality.

"How am I?" he cried. "I am *terrible!*" He sprang to his feet, and, pacing back and forth, he described the outrage that had been perpetrated upon him. "They were like tigers! Veritable tigers!" he declared. "And he did it with that devil's device, the same thing his uncle used upon all of us, but never so—exuberantly. My God, the expense it has been! I still can't sleep. I keep waking up. In my sleep I see that tattoo." He knelt beside her again. "We must have that device, Charla. We must have it. That soft fool should have killed us when he had the chance. Listen, my dearest. I have purchased information. He went from here to New York. He is with Bonny Lee Beaumont, the girl who escaped from you. An entertainer. They plan to go to Paris." He stopped and looked at her closely. She seemed dazed. "Darling, you are not listening!"

She was staring at the paneled wall of the lounge. "Do you know what AWOL means, dear?" she asked.

"How should I know what that means?"

"Absent without official leave. Oh, they were very disturbed, you know. To have thirty-three of them go AWOL all at once, with an official vehicle." She turned her head and looked mildly at him. "The vehicle was the truck, you see. They were on their way from Port Everglades to Key West. That's where their destroyer is. Key West."

Joseph struck himself in the head with his fist. "What are you talking about? Where have you been?"

"Suddenly I was in a truck, with a lot of sailors."

"How hideous!"

"A destroyer is the smallest seagoing combat ship. It is generally from three hundred to four hundred feet long and displaces from two thousand to three thousand tons. Destroyers are used mainly to screen other ships, to picket certain areas and to escort ships."

"Charla!"

"Destroyers are long-range, high-speed, hard-hitting ships. For protection they rely on watertight compartments and speed. Sailors call destroyers 'tin cans' because of their thin metal hulls."

He grabbed her and shook her until her teeth chattered, but the moment he released her, the sing-song recital was resumed.

"The most common type of destroyer in the U. S. Navy is known as the 692 Class or 'long hull', developed during World War II. They have two main engine groups of high-pressure steam turbines that total over sixty thousand horsepower. Engines, boilers and other machinery for propulsion occupy nearly three-fourths of their length below the main deck."

He bent over in front of her and looked into her eyes. He saw for the first time a horrid benignity there, a calmness, a curious smugness—as though all searches were ended, all fires quenched.

"Listen to me, my dear. We shall leave tomorrow. We shall go to Nassau, Charla, and from there we shall fly to Paris. And there we will find this Kirby Winter and we—"

"No, dear," she said calmly, sweetly.

"What?"

She stood up and yawned and stretched. He noticed that in spite of the way she had leaned down, her color was excellent. She started toward the hatch. "I just came aboard to get some clothes and some money."

He followed her. "But where are you going?" he pleaded.

She turned and gave him a blank stare. In a tone of voice which indicated she thought it an incomparably stupid question, she said, "Back to Key West, of course."

"But Charla!"

"They're waiting for me, dear. Destroyers are armed with torpedoes in tubes on deck, multipurpose five-inch guns, and depth charges."

She went into the stateroom. He heard her in there, humming. He could not remember the name of the song. It had something to do with anchors. He stood in the doorway. She started to change her clothes. But as soon as she was undressed, Joseph had to turn abruptly away and go to his stateroom, and lie down. When he heard her leaving, he called, "I'll wait for you in Nassau!"

After she left, he wondered how long it would be before she turned up. He hoped it would be a reasonable length of time— long enough for him to adjust to her brand-new tattoo.

And at the moment Charla was clambering expertly into the waiting gray jeep, Kirby Winter, thirty-five thousand feet over the Atlantic, was lifting a glass of champagne to the angel lips of his white-headed wench and drowning quite happily in her rogue eyes.

Ballroom of the Skies

No question is so difficult to answer
as that to which the answer is obvious.
—GEORGE BERNARD SHAW

1

THE WORLD, BRANSON THOUGHT, IS LIKE THAT CIRCUS ACT OF
long ago, back in the sweet-colored days of childhood, when the
big top was as high as the sky, and gigantic horses marched the
earth.

He remembered the act. The ragged clown teetering on the high
wire, clutching his misshapen hat, reeling toward destruction,
catching himself in that last throat-thickening instant to flounder
some more. You believed in him then. That poor dazed clown,
petrified by height, yet trying with pathetic and humble courage to
please the crowd, taking from the baggy clothes the white dinner
plates and, fighting his fear and his constant losses of balance,
managing somehow to juggle the plates. Oh, how white they had
shined in the spotlights!

You could see how the awkward body would plummet to the
hard earth, and you wanted to stop looking, yet could not stop.
And then suddenly his balance became sure and certain. He
stripped off the baggy clothes to reveal himself, taut and muscular
in the spangled tights, bowing to applause. You laughed aloud
into Daddy's eyes, knowing how close you had been to tears.

Now all the men of the world watched the humble clown on
the high wire. He juggled atomics, and napalm and all the hundred ways to separate the soul from the body, either quickly or
very slowly. He wavered up there in the spotlights and all the
eyes watched, knowing that when at last he fell, it would all be
gone—the tent and the music and the elephant girls, forever and
ever. He had remained up there too long. The nerves of men were
ground thin and fine. You waited for him to strip off the baggy

clown clothes and bow to the applause of the world. But he never did. He was caught up there, impaled for eternity on the bright shafts of the spotlights.

Once he had seen a revival of a Harold Lloyd picture. He had seen it when he was a child, at the Museum of Modern Art, and the picture, even then, had been fifty years old. The bespectacled man had been blindfolded and he was walking about in the steel beams of a building under construction, a skyscraper, back in the days when buildings stretched upward toward the sun, rather than downward into the warm safe earth.

The comedian had not known he was a dizzy height in the air. He wandered about aimlessly, arms outstretched. When he stepped off into space a girder, being hoisted up from below, would always present itself just in time to take his weight. It had been one of those Saturday showings. He remembered how all the children had screamed at the tension of that old silent film.

Maybe it was a truer analogy, because the clown was aware of his danger, and the comedian walked in an absurd innocence.

Now the Museum of Modern Art was gone, and the dwindling radiation of the area was so slight that the lead sheaths on the buses were more to impress the tourists than from any real necessity.

That had been the time, in the early seventies, when you had been certain that the clown would fall, that the beam would not arrive in time. But they had pocked one another's cities with the new ugliness, hurled the dwindling wealth of the planet at each other for a time. Ostensibly the democracies had won. The armies had hammered their way back and forth across Europe for the third and last time. Now, as had been predicted so many times before, Europe was wasteland, physically and spiritually incapable of rising again from her knees. Vassal states, with marginal resources, struggling for meager existence.

Somehow, insanely, the world had caught itself once more— saved itself on the very brink of destruction. Of all the industrial economies left, only Pak-India, reunited, was capable of trying again. And India wasn't interested. The astonishing effect on her standard of living as a result of the ruthless years of compulsory sterilization had given her the vigor to absorb Burma, Thailand, Ceylon, the Malay Peninsula and a rich slice of South China.

Reclamation of jungle and desert gave her the most solid basis of raw materials in the world, with the exception, perhaps, of Brazil, which had but recently moved her seat of government to Buenos Aires.

It wasn't, Branson thought, the line-up that anyone could have guessed back in the days before the war. Communism, both as a religion and as a political theory, had failed when its pie in the sky hadn't materialized. It had failed when it had run up against man's peculiarly basic desire to do as he damn pleased.

Each time the world tottered on the high wire, it recovered its balance in a weird and wonderful way. Now Pak-India was the king-pin democracy, with the United States trying to assure itself that it was a full partner, rather than, as was obvious to any objective person, a junior partner. Huddled together under India's skirts were all of the nations of Europe except Spain—all the nations, including those new nations which were the result of a partitioned Russia. Also, under the same skirt, was Australia, Canada.

But the clock had turned backward and the new enemy was the old enemy all over again. Fascism—a strong triple coalition of Brazil, which had taken over three quarters of the South American continent, marching and singing under the silver banners of Garva, and North China, singing the same songs, though with oriental dissonance, under a man called Stephen Chu, and Irania, which included Arabia, Egypt, most of North Africa marching with burnoose and iron heels under the guidance of that renegade Anglo-Egyptian, George Fahdi.

The crazy years since the war had passed, and now all the strong new lines were drawn. Don't step over my line. Look at my armies, my bomber fleets, my missile stations. Don't step over my line.

Malthus would have called the war a failure. It killed only seven millions. And each day, Branson knew, eighty thousand new souls and mouths were added to the world. Eighty thousand net. Nearly thirty millions a year. The old ant-heap pressure, leaning on us again. The eighty thousand increment each day was a jackstraw to be placed carefully on a precarious structure. Use steady hands, there. You aren't building it right. Build it my way. Build it my way, or else. . . .

The Fourth World War coming in from the deeps, rolling up in an oily way, ready to crest and smash on what was left of the world. And now, each time, it had to be the last one. Yet, somehow, it never was.

The clown world fought for balance. The comedian stepped off into space.

Branson left his desk and walked over to the window. Rent cheaply and in fear, and you get a window to look out of. An expensive office would have a clever diorama where the window would be. The psychologists had become important to underground architecture. If a man must live and work underground, it must be made to look like above-ground, because man is not a mole.

In the bright noisy dusk of New Times Square, ten stories below, the crowds moved slowly. American cars wheezed and clattered through the streets, their turbines laboring under the low-grade fuels. Here and there he could see a long glittering Taj or a Brahma, cars whose cost and upkeep were far beyond the purse of anyone who worked for wages. The Indians made the best automobiles in the world. Tata Automotive designed cars for looks and power, while what was left of Detroit had to concentrate on substitute materials, on fuel economy, on standardization of design from year to year. Some of the foreign cars, he knew, would be driven by tourists from Pak-India. It was sometimes difficult to stomach their arrogance, their conscious certainty that everything in India was better than here in the States. Far better. They had, somehow, become the brash new nation, the young giant born in ashes, rising to strength.

But, Branson knew, they had to be dealt with delicately. Their tourist rupees were sadly needed. And their embassies were powerful. Odd how, if you didn't speak either Hindi or Tamil, they thought they could make you understand by yelling at you. Their President, Gondohl Lahl, had that same arrogance. The only product of America which India seemed to approve of wholeheartedly was the beauty of its longlegged girls.

Some of the weariness of the past year left Darwin Branson as he thought that it was barely conceivable that now, through his own efforts, the war-tide might be halted, the drums and bugles stilled. His mission had been a secret one, entrusted to him by that wise, farsighted President of the United States, Robert Enfield. From the practical point of view, it had merely been a piece of horsetrading. Enfield, and the other leaders, had known that the economy could not stand another war. India could get nowhere by demanding, and she refused to plead. The triple coalition would not deal with India directly on these matters. The United States became the *sub rosa* contact between them.

What Darwin Branson had seen in Buenos Aires, in Alexandria, in Shanghai, in Bombay, had convinced him, all over again, that the nature of man is good, rather than evil. There was fear all over the world. Now, at last, the era of the man of good will could be initiated.

It had been a hole and corner affair. Meetings in furtive places, in cheap offices such as this one. Two more meetings and the deal could be made. A new mutual assistance pact for the world at large. Something, at last, with meaning. Something that would unwind the hard strands of fear and give mankind breathing space again, give him time to look around.

He looked at his watch. Another twenty minutes of thought, of solitude, and they would join him. Young Dake Lorin who had been his assistant, his husky right arm during the long year of cautious dickering. And that strange Englishman, Smith, who was empowered by his Leader, George Fahdi, to make a deal. Once all the offers were in, President Gondohl Lahl could be contacted. See the concessions the others will make? And this is all they want from you. The net result will be a bettering of the standard of living in every nation involved. And that will mean an easing of the tension. He had it on good authority that Gondohl Lahl would go along with it, and he knew that Smith would be cooperative.

He stood at the window, a small tired man with white hair and a furrowed face, eyes with a look of kindness. Midwife to peace. That was what Robert had called him.

Fifteen more minutes. He heard footsteps in the empty corridor. Thinking they had arrived earlier than planned, he went to the door and opened it. The young couple seemed unremarkable. They had better than average looks, and a disconcertingly assured way.

"I'm afraid you have the wrong office," Darwin Branson said politely.

"I'm afraid we have the right one, sir," the young man said, almost regretfully. There was always the danger of assassination by fanatics. Yet this couple did not have that special look, unmistakable once seen.

Darwin Branson was still pondering that point when the young man killed him, so quickly, with such an astounding speed that there was no interval between life and death, no period wherein Darwin Branson was permitted to be aware that life had gone and the great darkness had begun.

The girl caught the body, carried it lightly and easily into the alcove. She stood, holding the body, her face expressionless, while her companion made quick preparations. The hand tool made a faint electronic whirr. She placed the body on the screen he had unfolded. She walked out of the alcove and stood waiting. She heard the water running in the alcove sink. After a time the whirring stopped, and then the sound of water. Her companion came out, refolding the screen. He nodded and she went to the office door, opened it. Darwin Branson stood outside, his face as empty as death. She motioned to him. He walked in woodenly and took his seat behind the desk. The man leaned over and whispered one word into Darwin Branson's ear. He nodded to the girl and they went out of the office, closed the door.

"Thirty seconds," the girl said. The man knocked on the office door. Darwin Branson came to the door.

"I'm afraid you have the wrong office," Darwin Branson said politely.

The young man smiled. "Sorry, sir. I guess I have. Pardon me for bothering you."

"Perfectly all right," Branson said. The couple walked to the stairs. They went down five stairs and waited. They heard the elevator come up, stop. The door clanged open. Two men walked toward Branson's office.

The man nodded at the girl. She responded with a quick, almost shy smile. It was full night. He opened the stairwell window and they stepped easily out onto the narrow sill above the street. He closed the window behind them. They reappeared in the same instant on the high cornice of a building across the square. They looked down into the lighted office below, where three men were talking earnestly. Then the couple played a wild game, flickering like black flames from one high stone shoulder to the next, until at last he seemed to guess her intent and appeared at the same instant she did on the splintered stub of the Statue of Liberty in the harbor, touched her shoulder before she could escape. They laughed silently. It had been like the crazy game of children who had finished a hard lesson. They clasped hands and were gone.

Back in the office Darwin Branson talked to Smith. He instinctively did not like the man, did not trust him. Smith had . . . an oily look, a slippery look. Perhaps it would not be wise to trust him with the whole picture. He looked as though he could twist it this way and that, turn it inside out and find there some advantage for himself.

Dake Lorin sat, apparently taken in by Smith. Darwin Branson felt a bit contemptuous toward Dake Lorin. That young man was so . . . excessively noble. So naive and gullible. Dake would have you believe that the world could become a Garden of Eden once again. Sitting there, the whole preposterous six feet six inches of him, with that harsh black hair, and the dumb shelf of brow over the shadowed eyes, giving his face a simian look, as though Dake were some great sad ape trying mournfully to rectify the errors of mankind. Dake was just the type to be taken in by this oily Smith person.

As Darwin Branson talked he wondered why he had wasted the past year on this chase of the wild goose. A few compromises would make no difference. The world was war bound, and Robert Enfield should stop kidding himself, stop thinking that the United States could step in with *sub rosa* mediation and stave off disaster. The crucial point, rather, was to select the winning side while there was still time to make a selection.

He saw that Smith was aware of his contempt, and he was amused.

2

SMITH HAD BEEN AWKWARDLY SKEPTICAL. HE WAS A MOON-faced man with nail-head eyes, fat babyish hands. Dake Lorin had exerted himself to be charming, to make a friend of this Smith. It had been most difficult. He kept thinking that Smith was a complicated mechanical doll. And if you tripped the wrong reflex, you would be inundated by the standard line. Irania is strong. Irania is quick. Irania is brave. Our leader, George Fahdi, is farsighted.

Smith was in the country on a forged passport, arranged with the oblique assistance of one of the Under Secretaries of State. Dake had picked him up in Boston to drive him down to the conference with Darwin Branson.

The trick was to get under the automatic pseudo-patriotic reflex, and get down to the man himself.

Dake drove the small nondescript car at a sedate sixty-five, slowing for the stretches of neglected shattered slabs. The car, like most of the works of man, was a shade too small for Dake Lorin. His knees and elbows seemed always to be in the way.

"I understand your Leader was impressed with Mr. Branson."

Smith shrugged. "He told me later that he felt Mr. Branson was a great rarity. A good man. There are not many good men."

"I've worked with Mr. Branson for a year."

Smith turned in the seat. "So? You are . . . by trade, a government employee?"

"Not by trade. By trade I guess I'm a newspaperman. I was filling in in the Washington Bureau a couple of years ago. I interviewed Branson. He . . . stuck with me. The guy has quite an effect."

"You intrigue me," Smith said in his toneless voice.

Dake made a small decision. In order to disarm this Smith he would have to do a bit of a striptease, let his soul show a bit.

"I've always been a lone wolf type, Mr. Smith. Maybe a bit of a visionary. That state of mind always had a cause, I suppose. When I was twelve, a wide-eyed kid, the police picked up my Dad. He was a small-time politician. And a thief. He would have been safe all his life, but there was a change of administration and they threw him to the wolves. It was a deal. He was supposed to get eighteen months. But the judge crossed them up and Dad got ten years. When he found out that his old pal, the governor, wasn't going to pardon him, he hung himself in his cell. My mother pulled herself together and we got along, somehow. I had a lot of schoolyard scraps. It made a mark on me, I guess. I grew up with a chip on my shoulder, and a fat urge to change the world so that things like that couldn't happen."

"Quite a dream to have."

"I suppose so. Anyway, it gave me a drive. I learned the hard way that I couldn't change the world by punching it in the mouth. So I decided to instruct the world. I became a two-bit messiah in the newspaper game. But that's like knocking down stone walls with your head. What you tell them on Tuesday they can't remember on Wednesday. Then I interviewed Darwin Branson and later it seemed as if he'd been interviewing me. For the first time I'd found a man I could talk to. A man who believed—just as I believe—in the innate decency of mankind. I talked my fool head off. And went back, unofficially, to talk some more. Then, when I heard he was going to retire, I felt lost. As though the one sane man left in the world had given up. He got in touch with me and put his new assignment on the line. I got out of newspaper work right then. And we've been working on it for a year."

"And it's still a dream, Mr. Lorin?"

"I'll have to let Mr. Branson tell you about that."

"It has been my experience, Mr. Lorin, that visionary tactics do not fit the world of practical international politics."

"Look at it this way, Mr. Smith. We've been carrying a double load of fear ever since Hiroshima. Every one of us. It has an effect on every joint human action, from marriage to treaties. Fear makes each nation, each combination of nations, aggressive. And that aggressive outlook adds to the increment of fear. Each power group has established 'talking points.' Thus, everyone has demands to make, demands that will apparently not be met."

"We demand that Pak-India cease acts of aggression on their northwest frontier."

"Precisely. And it seems that all the demands balance out. In other words, if, through one vast treaty agreement, all the 'talking points' could be eliminated, it would give us the breathing space we need and . . . it might lead to the habit of similar world treaties in the future, once a new set of demands and 'talking points' have been set up. The result may be visionary. The method is practical, Mr. Smith."

"We will not make concessions," Smith said firmly.

"Stop talking like your Leader, Mr. Smith. Forgive my bluntness. Talk as a man. A living, thinking organism. You have ambition. Otherwise you would not have reached such a high place under George Fahdi. Being in a high place, you sense the precariousness of your position. What would you give to be able to look ten years into the future and see yourself still important, still trusted, still . . . safe?"

"Life is not that certain."

"Yet we all want it to be that certain. We want to know that we will be free to live, and love, and be happy. Yet, as nations, we act in such a way that it increases rather than reduces our uncertainty. As though we were under some compulsion. Like lemmings, racing to the sea to drown themselves. Mr. Branson does not believe that it is necessary that, through our acts as nations, we must live in fear. He believes that, acting as nations, acting in good will, we can make this world as good a place to live as it was during the first fourteen years of this century. Your Leader is a man, just as you are. As I am. He does not need aggression to consolidate his position. He needs a constantly increasing standard of living to make his place secure. Proper treaties, proper utilization of world resources, can make that possible."

"You sound like a free trader from the history books."

"Perhaps. I am not as convincing as Mr. Branson."

"War, Mr. Lorin, is a cyclical phenomenon."

"That's been our traditional excuse. It's a cycle. Who can stop cycles? It's sunspots. Who can change the sun? Mr. Branson calls that statistical rationalization."

"Your Mr. Branson sounds like an impressive man."

"He is. Believe me, he is."

Dake parked the car in a garage near New Times Square and they walked through the last faint grayness of dusk toward the rented office. Dake was dismally aware that if Smith wished to apply the trite fascist tag of decadent democracy, New Times Square gave him overpowering opportunity. There was no use telling a man like Smith that what he was seeing was a fringe world, a place of fetid lunacies, not at all typical of the heartland of the country where stubborn, dogged men were working in lab and field and mine to recreate, through substitution, the lost wealth of a great nation. The problem of the world, as Branson had said so many times, was in the field of bionomics. Man has made his environment precarious for himself, by denuding it of what he needs. This problem of mankind, the great and pressing problem, is to readjust that environment to make it once more a place where man can exist. Human nature, Branson maintained stoutly, does not have to be changed. It is basically good. Evil acts are the products of fear, uncertainty, insecurity.

The war of the seventies had caused a further moral deterioration. Man sought escape in orgy, in soul-deadening drugs, in curious sadisms. Along 165th Street the fleng joints were in full cry. In the mouth of an alley three women, loaded to the gills with prono, were mercilessly beating a Japanese sailor. Giggling couples pushed their way into a dingy triditorium to rent the shoddy private rooms where the three gleaming curved walls were three-dimensional screens for a life-size, third-rate showing of one of the obscene feature shows turned out in the listless Hollywood mill. Censorship restricted such public showings to heterosexual motifs, but further uptown, private triditoriums showed imported specialties that would gag a gnu.

The land was full of sects which, in revulsion at the metropolitan moralities, had founded new religions that insisted on complete celibacy among the fanatic congregations, each member pledged never to reproduce his kind. A chanting line wearing purple neon halos picketed the triditorium. A child lay dead in the gutter and a haughty Indian stood beside his glistening Taj answering the questions of a servile traffic policeman in a bored and impatient voice.

"In here, Mr. Smith," Dake said, glad to get the man off the street.

They rode up in the groaning elevator, and walked down the hall to the office. Darwin Branson got up quickly from behind his desk. Dake felt a warm assurance at seeing the man, felt an end to his own doubts.

The conference began. Dake was so accustomed to hearing the gentle assurance with which Branson wheedled that he listened with half an ear. He suddenly focused his full, shocked attention on Darwin Branson when he heard him say, a bit coldly, "Naturally, if all the arrangements please your Leader, President Enfield wishes your Leader to . . . ah . . . remember us with friendliness."

Dake said, "Darwin! Good Lord, that implies that we're . . ."

"Please!" Branson said with soft authority. Dake became reluctantly silent, telling himself that Branson had some good motive for handling this interview on a different tone and level than all the others.

Smith smiled. "I was afraid, after listening to your young friend, Mr. Branson, that I would find myself dealing with a saint. I am glad to detect a . . . shall we say . . . practical approach."

"This country, Mr. Smith, can't afford *not* to make friends, particularly with a coalition as powerful as yours."

"Could I safely say then, that those concessions we make shall be more . . . ah . . . spectacular than effective?"

Dake had never seen quite that smile on Darwin Branson's face before. "Please, Mr. Smith. You must remember that we are gentlemen of sincerity and integrity. Think how President Gondohl Lahl would be annoyed should he begin to think that whereas his concessions were made honestly, yours were made with a view to appearances."

Smith nodded. "I see what you mean. We must, above all else, be sincere. Now I am wondering if . . . your other dealings, with Garva and with Chu, have been made with this same degree of sincerity. I think that is a fair question."

"Of course, Mr. Smith. I will say this. They are all hoping that it is not . . . too good to be true."

"I believe," said Smith, "that I shall offer an alternate concession to the one you ask for. I believe we shall surrender Gibraltar to Spain."

"Eyewash," Dake said hotly. "That means nothing. You can have missile stations zeroed in on it to immunize it any instant you feel like it."

Smith looked at Branson and raised one eyebrow. Branson said, "Don't underestimate his offer, Dake."

"But it's so obvious. You've said a hundred times, Darwin, that each concession has to be real and honest, or the whole thing will fall down. When everyone else sees that Irania is just making a . . . pointless gesture instead of a real concession, they'll withdraw their promises and we'll be back where we were."

"Your young man seems to be filled with childish faith, Mr. Branson."

"An attribute of most young men, I'm afraid. I'll relay your offer to the others, Mr. Smith."

"And spoil a year's work, Darwin," Dake said dully. "I . . . just don't understand."

Branson stood up. "Can we assist you further, Mr. Smith?"

"No thank you. Arrangements have been made for me. I'll be in Alexandria in the morning. And, I assure you, the Leader will not forget your . . . cooperation."

Smith bowed first to Branson and then, a bit mockingly, to Dake Lorin. He left quietly.

The moment the door shut, Dake said, "You've blown it, Darwin. You've blown it sky-high."

Branson leaned back. He looked weary, but satisfied. "I think I've handled it in the only possible way, Dake. It has become increasingly obvious to me that we couldn't ever bring them all together."

"But yesterday you said . . ."

"Things have happened between yesterday and now. Things I can't explain to you. We've had to lower our sights, Dake. That Smith is an oily specimen, isn't he? But he's the representative of Irania. Oil reserves, Dake. A tremendous backlog of manpower. And influence gradually extending down into Africa, down into vast resources. They'll be good friends, Dake. Good friends to have."

"Now slow up just a minute. That is the kind of thinking, Darwin, we have both openly said we detest. Opportunistic, blind thinking. Lining up with the outfit which seems to have the biggest muscles. Damn it all, this is an about-face which I can't comprehend."

"When one plan looks as if it will fail, you pick the next best. That's mature thinking, Dake."

"Nuts, my friend. It's an evidence of a desire to commit suicide. You, of all the people in the world, to suddenly turn out to be . . ."

"Watch it, Dake!"

"I won't watch it. I gave a year of my life to this, and now I find that all along you've been giving me the big one-world yak, and the brotherhood of man yak, while without letting me know you've been setting us up for a power deal."

"A power deal, my young friend, is the best that an indigent nation can hope for. We have to line up with the people who can hit the quickest and the hardest. I . . . think we've managed it."

"You've managed it. Leave me out of it. I'm through, Darwin. You've tried your best to drag me into it, to assume that somehow—merely through being here with you—I become some kind of . . . partner. It was more than a dream, for God's sake!"

"Remember how the British survived for so long, Dake, after they'd lost their muscles? Always creating that delicate balance of power and . . ."

"Ending in hell, Darwin, when the Indians threw them out of Fiji, when all the throats in the Solomons were cut. I can't seem to get through to you. We weren't doing this for us. We were doing it for the world at large, Darwin."

"Sometimes it is wise to accept half a loaf."

Dake Lorin felt the tingling tension in all his muscles, felt the uprush of the black crazy anger that was his greatest curse. The blindness came, and he was unaware of his movements, unaware of time—aware only that he had somehow reached across the desk to grab the front of Branson's neat dark suit in one huge fist, had lifted the smaller man up out of the chair. He shook him until the face was blurred in his vision.

"Dake!" the man yelled. "Dake!"

The anger slowly receded. He dropped Branson back into the chair. He felt weak and he was sweating.

"Sorry," he said.

"You're a madman, Lorin!"

"You're a cheap little man, Branson. I have a hunch. I have the feeling there are people who'll understand exactly how you sold out the human race on this deal. And I'm going to put the case before them. All of it. Every part of it. Then let the world judge you, Branson."

"Now just a moment. This involves a question of security, Lorin. I can have you classified as potentially subversive, have you sent to labor camp until you cool off. You know that."

"I don't think you can stop me."

"You've been engaged in secret negotiations. Any violation of security will be evidence of your disloyalty."

Dake said softly, "And you're the man who called those regulations, called the labor camps, the new barbarism, government by aboriginal decree. You changed overnight, Darwin. You're not the same man. I'll do what I can, and you can kindly go to hell."

"While you're doing it, examine your own motives again, Dake. Maybe you've spent your life looking for martyrdom, and this is your best opportunity."

"That's a low blow."

"You're upset, Dake. In a way I don't blame you. Disappointment is hard to take. But you are my friend. I don't want to see you hurt."

Dake stared at him for long seconds. There was nothing else to say. He turned on his heel and left the office, slamming the door violently behind him, taking wry pleasure in the childishness of the gesture.

IN THE STATELY CATHEDRAL HUSH OF THE AUSTERE TIMES-NEWS offices the following morning, Dake Lorin was slowly and uneasily passed up the ladder from managing editor to assistant publisher, to publisher. He sat in paneled waiting rooms, eyed by myriad horse-teethed young ladies, by deftly innocuous young men. This was not the newspaper world with which Dake was familiar. The war, with its wood pulp starvation, had brought about the combine of the last two competing dailies, and during the darkest hours the paper had been down to four half-size sheets, with the ubiquitous "shrdlu" appearing in almost every story.

Now the paper was back to a respectable bulk, photoprinted on the tan grainy paper made of weeds and grasses. Here was no muted thud and rumble of presses, no bellows for "Boy!" Here was an air of sanctimonious hush.

"He will see you now, Mr. Lorin," a slat-thin female announced.

Dake went into the inner office. The window dioramas were of wooded hills, blue mountain lakes. The publisher was a small round man with matronly shoulders and a dimpled chin.

"Sit down, Mr. Lorin," he said. He held a card between thumb and forefinger, as though it were something nasty.

"I refreshed my mind, Mr. Lorin. The morgue typed me a summary. Your name, of course, was familiar to me the moment I heard it. Let me see now. Combat correspondent. Wounded. Married while on leave in '73. Wife killed by bombing of Buffalo when the suicide task force was repulsed. Returned to job as reporter on Philadelphia *Bulletin*. Did a good job of covering convention in '75 and became a political columnist. Syndicated in sixty-two papers at peak. Quite a bit of influence. Frequently under fire as a 'visionary,' a dreamer. Columns collected into two books, reasonably successful. Advocated Second U.N., until India withdrew and it collapsed. Took a sudden leave of absence a year ago. Activities during the past year unknown. Suspected to hold some ex-officio position in current administration, State Department side."

"Age thirty-two, twenty-nine teeth, scimitar-shaped scar on left buttock. Very undignified wound, you know," Lorin said.

"Eh?"

"Never mind. Has anyone told you my reason for seeing you?"

"Mr. Lorin, I am terribly afraid that the . . . ah . . . philosophy behind your political theorizing of the past would not be in accord with our . . ."

"I don't want a job. I have one exclusive I want to give to you. I want to write it and I want the best and biggest splash you can give it. I came here because you have world readership."

"An exclusive? Our people dig, Mr. Lorin. We insist on that. I seriously doubt whether there could be any new development in . . . ah . . . your field which has not already been——"

Dake interrupted bluntly, hitching his chair closer, lowering his voice. "How about this sort of an exclusive, Mr. Haggins? Darwin Branson did not retire. He was given a very delicate mission by President Enfield. I worked on it with him for a year. The idea was to act as a middleman, to ease off world tension by getting all sides to do a little horse-trading. It was to be done in secrecy, and in the strictest honesty. All sides but Irania have agreed to make honest concessions. Irania was the last one. If Branson had dealt with Irania firmly and honestly, we could have had a chance to see at least five years of peace ahead of us. But I was present when Branson blew the whole scheme sky high by trying to make a second-level deal with the Iranian representative. Irania will make a token concession, of no value. Then the others will water down their concessions, and the net result will be more world tension instead of less. I doubt whether your . . . diggers have uncovered that, Mr. Haggins. I want you to make a big splash so that the world can know how close it came to temporary nirvana. It might do some good. It might be like a nice clean wind blowing through some very dusty parliamentary sessions. Your sheet is influential. I feel that your cooperation is in the public service."

Haggins looked flustered. He got up and walked to the nearest diorama as though he were staring out a window. He had a curious habit of walking on his toes. He clasped his hands behind him, wriggling his thumbs.

"You . . . ah . . . hand us a very hot potato, Mr. Lorin."

"Any good story is likely to be, isn't it?"

"As you know, in exposing corruption, venality, we are absolutely fearless."

"So I've heard," Dake said dryly.

"However, there is one consideration here which we must examine . . . ah . . . rather closely."

"And that is?"

"The possibility that our motives might be misinterpreted, Mr. Lorin. You have stated that this was all . . . secret negotiation. I refer now, of course, to the Public Disservice Act of '75. It would not give us recourse to any court of law, or any chance to state our own case. The Board might arbitrarily consider our publication of your story a Disservice to the State. You know the answer to that. Confiscatory fines."

"I feel that it is worth the risk."

Haggins turned toward him. "Risk is in direct ratio to what you have to lose, is it not?"

"That Act itself is the result of fear. If there were less fear in the world, Mr. Haggins, that Act might be repealed."

Haggins came back to the desk. Dake could see that he had reached a decision. He was more at ease. He said, "A bit visionary, Mr. Lorin?" He smiled. "We do our best, Mr. Lorin. We feel that we improve the world, improve our environment, in many modest, but effective ways. Now you would have us take something that I can only consider as a vast gamble. If we should win, the gain is rather questionable. Should we lose, the loss is definite. By losing we would forfeit our chance to continue to do good in our own way."

"In other words, it's a lack of courage, Mr. Haggins?"

Haggins flushed, stood up, his hand outstretched. "Good luck to you, sir. I trust you will find a publisher who will be a bit more . . . rash, shall we say." He coughed. "And naturally, I will not mention this to anyone. I would not care to be accused of a personal Disservice. I am a bit too old to work on the oil shale."

Dake looked at the pink, neatly manicured hand. After a few moments Haggins withdrew it, rubbed it nervously on the side of his trousers. Dake nodded abruptly and left the office, took the elevator up the reinforced concrete shaft to ground level. Fear was a tangible thing in the world. Fear, on the government level, the business level, the personal level. Live out your neat little life and hope for the best. Fools took chances. Men carried weapons when they walked the night streets. Dake did not. His very size protected him adequately, his size and his look of dark, compressed fury.

He ate soybean steak in a small dismal restaurant and continued his search. At *Life-Look* and at *Time-Week* the brushoff was less delicate, but just as effective.

At dusk he managed an interview in a rattletrap building in Jersey City, an interview with a vast brick-red Irishman with a whisky rasp and a smell of barbershop.

The Irishman interrupted him. "Fleng the theories, Lorin. All that prono soup is over my head. You want to reach people. I've got a circulation. So let's get down to it. How about the stash, the dinero, the rupees, the happy old dollars?"

"How do you mean?"

"I'm used to fighting. Hell, I've got the most pornographic set of comic strips this side of Capetown. They're always trying to shut me down. I got a half million press run. So I do this. I put a banner head. Paid Advertising, it says. Not the opinion of the publisher, it says. I give you inside page one, and you write it and sign it. Thirty thousand rupees it costs you. Sixty thousand bucks. Lay it on the line and you can use that page for any damn thing you want. You can use it to challenge Gondohl Lahl to a personal fistfight if you want to. You'll do a labor camp stretch if that Enfield crowd doesn't like it, and Kelly will still be here, operating at the old stand. That's the deal, and take it or leave it."

"How much down?"

"The whole thing down. They'll confiscate anything you got before they ship you out. I can't take chances."

"It's a lot of money, Kelly."

"You look like a guy with a lot of money."

"I'll have to . . . check with some friends. I'll make a decision and come in tomorrow and tell you."

"If the answer is no, don't bother to come in. I won't dicker. That's the price. It stands. What are you doing tonight? I got a couple cute little Singhalese tourists lined up, and four freebees to a new private tridi way uptown."

"No thanks. See you tomorrow."

"Not too early. I expect to have a hangover."

Dake went back to the city and bought passage to Philadelphia on one of the feeder lines maintained by Calcutta International Jetways. CIJ used all Indian personnel for their major schedules, but hired U.S. personnel for the feeder lines, entrusting to them the creaking, outmoded aircraft. Once U.S.-owned airlines had linked the entire world. But, in the exhaustion following the war, with the regimentation and labor allocations that had cut travel so severely, the airlines, starved for freight and passengers, had slid inevitably toward bankruptcy, in spite of the subsidies of an impoverished federal government. Thus, when CIJ had made a reasonable offer for all lines and franchises, the airlines had taken it gladly, the investors receiving CIJ stock in return for their holdings. CIJ service was quick, impersonal, efficient. There were only two other passengers on the sixty-seat aircraft. Dake knew that CIJ took a continual loss on the New York-Philadelphia run, but maintained the frequent schedule for the convenience of the Indian nationals who supervised their investments in both cities. He leaned back in the seat for the short run. The spattered lights of the city wheeled under one wing. The other two passengers were a pair of Madrassi businessmen. They conversed in Hindi and Dake could catch words now and then, enough to know that they were talking about the Philadelphia branch of the Bank of India.

He could never quite become accustomed to being considered by the Pak-Indians a second-class citizen. Toynbee had coldly outlined the ecology of civilizations. The great wheel had turned slowly, and the East was once again the new fountainhead of vitality. Their discrimination was subtle, but implacable. In major cities Indian clubs had been established. Americans could be taken there as guests, but were forbidden membership. There had been a fad when American women had begun to wear saris, to make imitation caste marks on their foreheads. The Pak-Indian Ambassador had called on the President. Saris disappeared from the shops. Fashion magazines hinted that caste marks were crude, even rude. Everyone was happy again. For a time it had been possible to emigrate to India, that new land of opportunity. But so many had taken advantage of it that restrictions became very tight, and it was still possible, but very very difficult to manage, involving a large cash bond. Though the war of the seventies had done much to alleviate racial tension in the States, there had still been small though influential Negro groups who had joyously welcomed the dominance of a dark-skinned race in world affairs. They had soon found, to their dismay, that the Pak-Indians were supremely conscious of being, in truth, an Aryan race, and brought to any dealings with the Negro that vast legacy of hatred from the years of tension in Fiji, culminating in the interracial wars. Of Pak-India proper, only Ceylon had any percentage mixture of Negro blood, due to the African invasions of ancient years, but Ceylon was to Pak-India much as Puerto Rico had been to the United States prior to Brazilian annexation.

Indians would treat you with courtesy, even with affability, but in any conversation with them you could detect, running like a symphonic theme through the orchestration of words, their conviction that you were a citizen of a decadent nation, one that had gone beyond its peak of influence in world affairs, one that was doomed to the inevitable status of a supplicant nation, free in name only.

We had it, he thought, and we threw it away. We ripped our iron and coal and oil out of the warm earth, used our copper and our forests and the rich topsoil, and hurled it all at our enemies, and conquered them, and were left at last with the empty ravaged land. How could it have been avoided? What could we have done that we did not do? Should we have used that great moment of momentum in 1945, well over thirty years ago, and gone on to take over the planet? Should we have dropped the sword, misered our resources, and succumbed meekly during the increasing pressures of the middle sixties? How did it come about that any step we could take was wrong, that every course open to us was but a different road to a different classification of disaster? England had been dying too—just a few scant years ahead of us in the inexorable schedule, yet we had been unable to learn from her defeats, unable to cut a new channel. It was almost, he thought, as though there was some unanswerable paradox against which every world power must inevitably run and collapse. Some cold and alien influence in the world, breaking the hearts of men.

Or perhaps it is all merely our own stupidity. Our blindnesses. Our inability to see and comprehend the obvious. Perhaps we are all like Darwin Branson. Able for a time—even for a sustained length of time—to influence our environment for good, yet always failing somehow in that last crucial moment. As Branson had failed when the blindness came over him.

He wondered what Patrice would say. He dreaded seeing her.

Her love was a contradiction. She seemed capable of loving every aspect of him as a human being except his final, innermost motivation.

Unscathed Philadelphia had its standard joke about itself. When, during the war, many of the executive branches of government had to be evacuated to Philadelphia, and when the city itself was not bombed, the Philadelphians proclaimed that the enemy had been smart enough to realize that by obliterating all the red tape, they would be helping the U.S. instead of hurting it. The air of immunity had carried over into the present time of fear. There was less underground construction here than elsewhere. It was a prim, old-lady city, walking through the mud with its skirts carefully held up, not too daringly, and with a wise and knowing air as though that old lady, in her almost forgotten youth, had raised a bit of forbidden hell.

Deceleration thrust him forward against the straps, and ten minutes later he was in a wheezing, clattering taxi headed toward Patrice's unexpectedly modest home near Upper Darby. Patrice's father had died in '71 just one week and two days before the passage of the hundred percent inheritance tax bill. His fortune had its beginnings back when the original Gundar Togelson had been pirating oil land from Mellon. Each Togelson since then had increased it until the late sixties when the capital gains tax was revised to take seventy percent of all capital gains. After inheritance taxes, Patrice, in addition to maximum gifts each year her father was alive, inherited about five and a half millions. At the present time it was nearly the last fortune left relatively intact, inside the country. Under the impact of the confiscatory taxes many people had managed to emigrate with their funds to economically sunnier lands, just as the socialist government in England had driven many private fortunes to Bermuda and elsewhere.

Patrice Togelson, a tall, warmly built Viking girl, had brought to Dake a deep, earthy, physical need. Yet he knew that in the management of her money she was like flint, and like quicksilver. Like flint in her calculating hardness. Like quicksilver in her ability to detect the tiniest loopholes, slide through them. They had met after he had taken a casual swipe at her in his column, criticizing her for buying into an Indian land deal to take advantage of the tax concessions Washington had given the investment of Indian capital.

Patrice had appeared in his office at the *Bulletin* the next morning, blue eyes like ice, jaw set, hair a bright flow of autumn barley. She had leaned both fists on his desk, breasts lifting with the deep breathing of her controlled anger.

"You, my friend, are out of your depth this time," she said.

"And you, lady, are an anachronism. You are a female pirate. You are a con artist."

"You cost me more money yesterday than you'll make in your whole life."

"Then the least I can do is buy your lunch."

They glared at each other, grinned suddenly, laughed aloud and went out together. It had been at first a good friendship, even though their personal philosophies were poles apart. For two basically aloof people, it had been a warmth of friendship that had quite astonished them. They found they laughed more often when they were together. One night, in front of the November fireplace in her small home, he had kissed her, expecting it to be casual, finding it to be shockingly hungry.

They were friends, and they became lovers without losing all of friendship. She was almost six feet tall, yet built in perfect feminine scale. They laughed about being in a world too small for them. They did not use the word "love" or the word "marriage." They were faithful to each other without perceptible effort. They were discreet in an age that jeered at discretion. For a time their physical preoccupation with each other became obsessive, but when they recognized the danger of that, recognized the weakness of it, they fought free of it into a relationship which was rather like that of two semi-alcoholics who would excuse themselves for an infrequent three-day bender.

Together they acquired a sixth sense about what subjects to avoid. They knew that they were two proud, strong, dominant people, who happened to believe in different things. There was too much artillery they could bring to bear on each other. It was enough for him to see the morning sun in the warmth of her hair, hear fond laughter in her throat, hold her through her quickened times of completion.

The inevitable blowup came when he told her why he was taking a "leave of absence." It had been an unpleasant scene. Even as they fought, neither of them retreating a step, he guessed that she too was aware of the loneliness to come, the empty aching nights.

The taxi driver examined the tip, grunting something that could have been thanks, and clattered off. Dake went up the walk, knowing that no fortress was ever as well protected as this house, this small tidy house, knowing that by breaking the infra-red beams he had become target. He stood on the porch, waiting. The door was suddenly opened by the pretty Japanese maid, who gave him a gold-toothed smile and said, as though he had visited there yesterday, "Good evening, Mr. Lorin."

"Evening. Does . . ."

"She knows you are here, sir. She will be right down. A brandy, sir? I'll bring it to you in the study."

He was amused. The study was for business transactions. The lounge-living room was for friends. He wondered if Patrice were prescient. Simpler than that, perhaps. She knew him well. She knew his inflexibility. And so she would know that this was not a personal call. He sat in one of the deep leather chairs. The maid brought the brandy, an ancient bottle, and two bell glasses on a black tray. She put them on the small table beside his chair, and left without a sound.

When he heard Patrice's distinctive step he stood up quickly and smiled at her as she came into the study. Her smile was warmer than he expected. As always, she had that remembered look of being larger than life size, more vital. She wore dark red tailored slacks, a matching halter.

"Quite a tan, Patrice," he said.

"I got back from Acapulco yesterday."

"Pleasure trip?" he asked wryly, her hands warm and firm in his.

She made a face. "A good buy. Hotel property."

"With your Indian pals?"

"Uh uh. Some Brazilian pals this time."

"Both ends against the middle, Patrice?"

"Of course. How else does a girl get along?" She inspected him, her head tilted to one side. "You look gaunter, darling. Hollow-eyed. I bet your ribs show."

"The strain of being a do-gooder."

"Aren't we being just a little bit too nasty nice to each other?" She held her hand up, thumb and forefinger an inch apart. "Just that much brandy, please. Would I look too severe if I sat at the desk?"

"Not if it's where your checkbook is."

✓ She bit her lip. "This could be interesting, couldn't it?" She seated herself behind the desk. He took her the brandy, went back to the deep chair.

She sipped, watching him over the rim. She set the glass down and said, "I have a feeling we're going to spar, and it might be nasty, and before we spoil each other's dispositions, I want to say something. I've had a year to plan just exactly how I should say it. Just this, Dake. I've missed you. Quite horribly. I wanted, and tried, to buy you and put you in stock. It didn't work. I've been going around rationalizing it, telling myself that if you *could* be purchased, I wouldn't want you. But I'm not that way. I wish you *could* be. I wish you had sense enough to be. Life has plenty of meaning without you. It had more when you were around. I miss that increment. I'm a selfish, hard-fisted, dominating woman, and if there's any way I can acquire you permanently, I'm going to do it."

"Okay, Patrice. Equal candor. I've missed you. I've wished that either you or I could bend a little without breaking. But I know that's like wishing for the moon. We were fine until we got into a scrap about pretty basic things. Things like selfishness, like human dignity."

"My world, Dake, is a pig pen. The smartest greediest pig gets the most corn."

"My world is a place where there's hope."

"But we both seem to be living in my world, don't we? Now tell me why you look haunted, and miserable, and . . . sick at heart, Dake."

He told her. She had the knack of listening with an absolute stillness, of applying her intense awareness to the problem at hand. He told her all of it, up to and including Kelly.

"And so you came to me."

"Asking for sixty thousand dollars. Maybe you can write it off as a charity."

"I don't believe in what you're trying to do."

"I don't expect you to. I'm begging."

"For old time's sake. Isn't that the tritest phrase in the world?" She opened a drawer, selected a checkbook, scrawled a check, tore it out. She sat, her chin balanced on her fist, waving the check slowly back and forth.

"I don't make gifts, Dake. I make deals."

"I had a hunch it wasn't going to be that simple."

"You can have this check. Once that stuff hits the streets, you're going to think a building fell on you. It is going to cost me half as much again to argue the Board into letting you run around loose. Then I'll give you thirty days' wait for the impact of what you write. If nothing happens, and I am certain nothing will, you will be the one to bend a little. You will try to accept the world on its own terms. And accept me along with it, Dake."

"Then it is a purchase, after all?"

"How much pride do you leave a lady?"

"How much pride do you leave me?" he asked harshly. "Okay. Accept the fact that I'm a monomaniac. If what I want to do fails, I'll try something else."

"Little boy with a tin bugle, waking up all the forces of decency in the world. Look, people! The cow's in the meadow, the sheep's in the corn!"

"I don't know how to say this. A man does . . . what he has to do."

"And if it's an obsession? If it's something with its roots inbedded in a childhood catastrophe? Should he continue to destroy himself? Or try to effect a cure?"

"That's almost what Branson said to me."

"You told me very emphatically that he was a god walking the earth. It looks as if he remained a god to you until he questioned your . . . sanity. And then he became a monster. Personally I like his angle of snuggling up to Irania. India has been moving too fast. It balances things off a bit."

"And gives us more tension, a bigger load of fear."

"Gives mankind as a whole more fear. I'm an individual. I take my own pride in being able to take care of myself."

"Anarchy?"

"Why not? That is, if you are faster and have bigger teeth than your neighbor?"

"We can't talk at all. We never could. We never will."

Her face softened. "Oh, Dake. We *did* talk. Lots."

He sighed. "I know. Sometimes it seems as if we're . . . such a damn miserable waste of each other."

She put the check on the corner of the desk within his reach. "It's on a rupee account in a branch of the Bank of India. Need it certified?"

"No. I can cash it. No deal then? No bargain?"

She looked down at her folded hands. A strand of the soft hair swung forward, shining gold in the lamplight. "No deal, Dake. I guess it's for . . . old time's sake."

He put the check in his wallet. "Thanks, Patrice. I thought you'd be . . . a lot tougher."

She lifted her head. "I was going to be."

"Anyway, I appreciate it."

She stood up quickly, came to him, sat on the arm of the deep leather chair, leaned against him, her arm around his shoulders.

Her smile was crooked, and looked as though it hurt a bit. "I'm like your Darwin Branson," she whispered.

He looked up at her. "What do you mean?" She turned away, oddly shy.

"I'm practical. I, too, am willing to settle for . . . half a loaf."

He took her shoulders, turned her, pulled her back into his lap. Her hair had a clean spicy scent. Her lips were on holiday, from the long year apart. She kissed him with her eyes wide, blue, and terribly near in the lamplight.

4

KELLY LICKED HIS THUMB AGAIN, WINKED AT DAKE, AND CON-tinued to count. "Twenty-seven, twenty-eight, twenty-nine, thirty. Thirty thousand happy rupees. The page is yours. Got it with you?"

"I want to borrow an office and a typewriter, Kelly. I'll work the rest of the day and have it for you sometime tomorrow afternoon."

"It will be in Thursday's edition, then."

"I want a proof drawn on it, and a chance to check it before you lock it up."

"At the moment you are my favorite man in all the world. Anything you say."

"And I want a receipt, Kelly."

The man scrubbed his red chin with a big knuckle. "My boy, you bring up a fascinating point. Indeed you do. Now we're both men of the world. How would it be if I give you a receipt for fifteen thousand? It would ease my tax picture considerable."

"Thirty thousand."

"Let's split the difference. I'll give you back . . . say, two thousand, and a receipt for twenty. We both gain that way."

"Suit yourself," Dake said wearily. "Just show me where I can work."

"I knew you were a sensible man when I laid eyes on you. Let me see. I can't give you Carter's place. The murals would keep your mind off your work. Come on. I know where I can put you."

The office was small, and it hadn't been dusted in a long time. The typewriter looked adequate. Dake tried it, using his gunfire four-finger technique. Kelly walked out, whistling. Dake shucked his coat, tossed it on the couch. He poked his hat back onto the back of his head, laid his cigarettes beside the machine, and pondered a lead. He tried a few and tore them up. Finally he found one he was satisfied with:

"This week humanity booted the ball again. It was an infield error. The shadows stretch long across the diamond. The long game is drawing to a close. Death is on the mound. He threw one that President Enfield got a piece of. Enfield's hit put Darwin Branson on third. He had a chance to come home. He ran nicely most of the way to the plate, and then faltered. They put the tag on him. 'Yerrout!' yelled the celestial umpire.

"Now we're waiting for another decision. We're waiting to find out whether that was the third and last out, retiring the side. We stand in the long shadows, in the hopelessness of an emptying park, waiting to find out if our long game is over. To find out if, maybe, it is being called on account of darkness."

He looked at the lines. He had a sense of destiny in him. Once in every age, man and moment meet. And the man brings to that moment some ability that sets the world afire, that brings it lurching back from that last brink of destruction. The typewriter clattered in the dusty office. He worked on at white heat, working with the sure and certain knowledge that what he was writing would lift up the hearts and hopes of men everywhere. The year of leave seemed to have heightened his facility. There was no rustiness, no groping for words, or for effect. He had it, and he was using it with the pride and assurance of a man at the peak of his abilities.

He ripped a sheet out, rolled a fresh one into the machine. He hit the tab set and . . . came to a shocked standstill on the shoulder of a dusty country road. He could see the countryside clearly, hear the faraway bawling of cattle. And shimmering through it, directly in front of him, he could see the keyboard of the typewriter. It was as though he coexisted in two realities, one superimposed over the other. Standing in one, sitting in the other, visions overlapping. He managed to stand up blindly and move away from the typewriter. The countryside faded and was gone.

He stood at the window of the small office for a time. The experience had made him feel faint and dizzy. He grunted with disgust. This would be a hell of a time to have the strain of the past year pile up on him and destroy his ability to work. This was, perhaps, the ultimate gamble. Lay it on the line for them. Get it all down. Dates, names, people, the delicate machinery of deals and counterdeals. Show all the men of good will how close they had come to the political and economic equivalent of the Kingdom of Heaven. Raise the old war cry of "throw the bastards out!"—but this time on a global scale. Pray that copies of the article would be pirated, smuggled through the fine mesh nets of censorship. Patrice, with her "me for me" philosophy could never understand how a man could stake his life on one turn of the card, if he believed in the card. A man could have a sense of destiny—believe in his heart that he could manufacture a pivot-point for the world to turn on. Let us have no more double vision. No time to go mad.

He went back and sat down at the typewriter again, reread his lead, and found it good. He raised his hands a bit above the keys and stopped, shut his eyes hard. Each key had turned into a tiny reproduction of Patrice's face. With his eyes still shut he put his fingers on the keys, felt the softness of tiny faces under the pads of his fingers. He opened his eyes and looked at the paper in the machine. He began to type and stopped, as horror welled up to the point of nausea. His fingers were bloodied and the little faces were smashed, and he had heard the tiny cries, the rending of tissue. Sweating, he wiped his hands on his thighs as he stood up, knocking the chair over.

He stood with his back to the machine and tightened his muscles until his shoulders ached. He looked cautiously at his fingertips. The blood was gone. Hallucination, then. A minor madness. He thought it out objectively. Self-preservation, probably. Trying to save the organism from disaster. A glandular revolt against dissolution. He looked cautiously over his shoulder. The typewriter was sane, normal, familiar.

He sat down and began to type. His thoughts were fluent. His fingers could hardly keep up. He tore the second sheet out of the machine and read it.

"And so it is a baseball game and game and never the over of the now and the then and given. Tender and mathew and meatloaf the underside twisteth of the die and the perish now. All ye who enter can frenzied the window savior . . ."

The whole page was like that. Gibberish. Insanity. The stream of consciousness of an idiot who remembers words but has lost their meaning.

He tried again, writing more slowly. It was no good. He found a pencil in the table drawer. He took one of the copy sheets and tried to write. The pencil became too hot to hold. He examined blisters on his hand which faded even as he looked at them. The paper curled into flame, and he slapped it out. A moment later it was unscorched. He could no longer repress a primitive panic. He ran from the office and down the corridor, heart pumping, hands sweaty.

He did not quiet down until he was on the street. And suddenly he felt like an utter damn fool. Take a break and then go back and get it written. He walked to a small restaurant and sat at the counter and ordered coffee. The waitress was gray and surly with a prono hangover. A tiny radio yipped like a terrier. He listened with half his mind.

". . . and late last night Darwin Branson, retired statesman and political philosopher was committed to Bronx Psychiatric Hos——" The waitress had flipped the dial as she walked by.

"Would you mind getting that station back, miss?"

"Yes, I'd mind. He already gave all the news."

She stood braced, ready to blow up completely if he insisted. You couldn't argue with a prono hangover. He paid for his coffee, left the cup untouched and spent ten minutes on the corner before he could find a cab willing to take the long trip.

He reached the hospital at noon. He was suspected of being a reporter and the desk tried to bar him. He produced the confidential credentials Darwin had given him. The desk reluctantly put him in contact with the resident doctor assigned to the case.

The doctor was young, unimaginative, and delighted with the case.

"Lorin you said? Worked for him, eh? Well, I suppose you can take a look. We've been checking him most of the morning. Come on."

They had Branson in a private room. A nurse was in attendance. She stood up as they came in. "Respiration is ten now, Doctor. Heart forty-four. Temperature eight-six point six."

"Damndest thing I ever saw," the doctor said in a pleased tone. "Cops brought him in last night. Found him sitting in the middle of the sidewalk. Thought it was a pronie first. We checked him. He was apparently conscious. But no reaction to anything. Couldn't make the pupil contract. Couldn't find a single damn reflex."

Dake stared at the silent waxy face on the pillow.

The doctor said, holding out a clipboard, "Just take a look at this chart. This is one that's going to be written up. Pulse, respiration, temperature—every one heading down in a line so straight it could have been drawn by a ruler. This man is just like a machine running down."

"Heart forty-two, Doctor," the nurse said softly, releasing the slack wrist.

"Tried every stimulant in the books, Mr. Lorin. No dice."

"What's your prognosis?"

"He just doesn't react to anything. Thought of encephaloma at first. Doesn't check out. It looks like he's just going to keep slowing down until he . . . stops. And there's no key in the back to wind him up. Damn unprofessional opinion, I guess, but that's the best I can do. Everybody in the place has seen him and suggested things. None of them work."

"Do you mind if I stay with him?"

"How about family? We've been unable to locate any."

"There isn't any."

"You can stay around if you want. I'll send an orderly in with another chair. From the way it looks, I don't think you'll have a long wait."

"You've never seen anything like it before, or heard of it?"

The young doctor frowned. "I've never seen one before. But I've heard rumors of others. Usually important people, come to think of it. They just seem to get . . . tired."

The doctor went out. An orderly brought another chair. Dake sat on the other side of the high bed from the nurse. He was on Darwin Branson's left side. He looked at the slack hand resting on the white sheet. Time now to forget the quarrel, and remember the better things—the good talks, the flexibility and dexterity of that wise brain.

"In my gullible years, Dake, back when I used to believe in statistics, I made a personal survey of the quality of major decisions and charted them. Of course, on the quality angle, I was being a Monday morning quarterback. I came up with a neat graph which alarmed me. Men of influence all over the world, men in high places, make wise decisions and the world improves. Then, all at once, their quality of judgment becomes impaired and the world suffers for it. They move in a vast confused flock, like sack-suited lemmings. Horrors, I was face to face with a cycle. Sun spots, addling the brains of men. Some alien virus in the air. Or God, perhaps, assuring his children of their suffering on earth."

"Did you find an answer?"

"Only in myself, where perhaps each man must find his answers. I resolved to so codify my beliefs that should I ever find myself tempted to betray my own philosophy, I would merely have to refer to my mental outline and make the decision which I would have made were I not subject to the cycle. I decided to risk Emerson's indictment of small minds."

And yet, thought Dake, you turned your back on your own beliefs only yesterday. You destroyed the labor of a full year. Horrid timing. You became ill a day too late, Darwin.

No more of those long good talks, no more of the knowledge of working for the greatest good of mankind.

"Dake, we seem to supply ourselves with destructive dreams. Chief among these is the Space Dream. It goes like this: We have made such a mess of our world that it is of no use to attempt to bring order out of our chaos. So save our best efforts for the next green world. Tomorrow the moon, next week the planets, next year the galaxy. We'll spread through the heavens, and our seed will be the bronzed, steel-eyed pioneers, and their fertile women, making green wonderlands for us in the sky. That dream, Dake, eases the conscience of those who are doing less than their best. Thus it saps our energies. 'This is man's world. We must live here. We will never reach the stars.' I would like to see every man believe that. And then if, in a thousand years, we break free, it will be pure profit—and we will have something besides hate and conflict to take along with us on the gleaming ships."

Dake thought how incredible it was that Darwin Branson should, on the last day of his life, make his first venture into opportunism.

He looked at the left hand, and then looked more closely, his breath catching in his throat. He remembered the scene just before he had left to meet Smith. Branson, being left-handed, had been trying awkwardly to snip off a hangnail on the middle finger of his left hand. Dake had volunteered help, which was gratefully received. The nail had been split a bit, and so he had pared it down carefully. That was the day before yesterday. Yet right now the nail was fully as long as the others. It could not possibly grow that fast. Dake knew he had not imagined the incident. It *had* been the left hand. He reached out and took the cool slack hand.

"Please don't touch the patient," the nurse said sharply.

He released the hand, stood up and bent over to stare more closely. He looked at the slack face, comatose, dying.

"What's the matter?" the nurse demanded.

Dake glanced at her. He knew at once how far he'd get if he tried to tell her this was not Darwin Branson. They'd have him in the next room down the hall. He sat down slowly, hoping that his emotions did not show on his face.

"Dake, I believe a fiddle-playing gentleman once commented that after you have ruled out all the impossibilities, that which remains is the solution. By the same token, if after all of the impossibilities have been ruled out, you have nothing left, then you have made a mistake in classification. You have overlooked a possibility by labeling it impossible. Like a man with a pocket lighter captured by aborigines. The wise man of the tribe says that it is impossible that there is lightning captured in that silver box. He says it is impossible that there is a tiny man in there, rubbing sticks together. He says it is impossible that fire can be made by any other than those two methods. So he falls down and worships, because he finds himself in the presence of the impossible. It was his third supposition that needed reclassification."

"Darwin, how about wrongly classifying the impossible as possible?"

"Men have tried to trisect the angle because that is an impossibility that *looks* possible. Conversely, man has never tried teleportation seriously. How do we know that may not merely be a possibility which happens to *seem* impossible, and would yield to sustained attack?"

"Pulse thirty-eight," the nurse said softly.

Dake looked at the yellow-gray face. "God help me to think this out as you would have, Darwin," he said to himself.

He had classified as "possible" Branson's sellout. But, knowing the man, it could more correctly be classified as impossible. Branson had been the man who said good-bye to him when he went to collect Smith. So the man to whom he brought Smith back was not Branson. And, if the charts were right, not even human. A doll. A toy. A clever thing wound up and set in motion at a critical juncture in history for the purpose of substituting—or more correctly, sustaining—chaos in the place of possible peace and order.

Next step: Was any world power capable of creating this manthing?

No. Reasoning: If so, the technique would have been used for greater selfish gain, and were this the first trial attempt it would have been highly unlikely that Branson would be selected.

If the pseudo-physiology of this man-thing is beyond human abilities, then the only place of origin is extraterrestrial.

But, to assume that means also to assume that there is some valid reason for the maintenance of world disorder. He caught the error in his own logic. He was trying to judge the validity of extraterrestrial motivations on a human basis. He could almost imagine his skull swelling with the pressure of new concepts, new modes of thought.

Okay then. Assume that interference isn't in the form of a mile-high spaceship that sits down in the front yard. Assume it is something that comes delicately, insidiously. Unnoticed. What about duration? New, or has it been always with us?

He had an answer to that which was more instinctive than logical. More Fortian than objective. Because it solved, with one swift answer, the great dismal riddle of how man—basically a creature capable of love—had been unable to live in peace in his world.

Dake could hear the soft, even voice. "Evil is not within man, Dake. Evil is man's response to outward things—to hunger, disease, pain, fear, envy, hate. Maybe it is man's answer to insecurity. Take the common denominators that are not evil. Songbirds, flowers, motherhood. All times, all nations, all men have held them in esteem. We seem to have lost our way. Yet I cannot believe that we have turned our back on God, Buddha, Mohammed, Vishnu. Rather we have been denied them in some curious way."

The answer to the riddle of the world—lying here on this hospital bed. If it could only be proven. Prove it and then you could cry to the skies, "'We have been led! We have been tortured and twisted and set against each other! We have been a culture dish into which some agency has continually dropped acid—not enough to sterilize, but just enough to make us writhe."

How would you go about it. Autopsy? He looked at the grain of the skin, the ridged nails, the gray beard stubble. Clever, clever. They could cut the body and never find a soul. But, then, they had never found one and so could not recognize the absence.

As he became more certain, he slowly became aware of his great and dangerous knowledge. Any agency powerful enough and clever enough to effect this substitution would have a quick answer ready for any human who became suspicious, who tried to broadcast his knowledge.

Where was the real Darwin Branson?

"Pulse thirty-two," the nurse said.

The young doctor entered the room again, checked the chart, talked softly with the nurse. He thumbed an eyelid back, focused a light on the pupil. Another nurse brought in a tray. The doctor pulled the sheet back, swabbed a place over the heart, injected a needle deeply, pushed the plunger, emptying the hypodermic. He took the limp wrist and counted the pulse.

"Can't kick it up one beat a minute," he said, his voice too loud for the room.

Dake barely heard him. He sat, slowly compounding his own dilemma. There was an alternative he had overlooked. The reactions in the office Kelly had loaned him had been irrational. A sign of collapse. This whole new and startling train of thought could be another sign of collapse. No hangnail. No substitution. No extraterrestrials.

Before you could even think of proving something to the world, you had first to prove it to yourself. Either the aberrations in the office were evidences of "interference," as was the substitution, or both factors were indicative of imminent mental collapse—a collapse due to strain, overwork, tension.

He massaged the back of his neck. Funny feeling of tension there. Had it for a week. Almost a feeling of being watched. It would come and go. A feeling of a great eye focused on you. A big lens, and you were a bug on a slide.

Either one of two things happened at five minutes past three. Either Darwin Branson died, or the man-thing ran down and stopped, its function finished. Dake left the hospital. The death watch of reporters in the main lounge converged on him. He shouldered his way through, savage and silent. They cursed him as he left. He had no heart to go back to Kelly's place. The significance of the article he had wanted to write had dwindled. Either there was a vastly bigger article—or no article at all. He thought vaguely of trying to get back the thirty thousand and decided there would be time enough the next day. He walked for blocks and caught a bus over to the island. A girl with brown hair and curiously pale gray eyes took the seat beside him.

5

THE GIRL WITH THE BROWN HAIR AND THE PALE AND LUMINOUS gray eyes had watched the tall figure of Dake Lorin as he boarded the bus. She stood on the corner as the bus lumbered down the block. She fished in her blouse pocket for a cigarette, drew it out of the pack between two fingers, and hung it in the corner of her mouth, lit it with a casual, vulgar snap of the cheap lighter. Smoke drifted up along the smooth brown cheek. She stood there in her cheap tight yellow dress. Chippy on the make. As good a cover as Miguel Larner had been able to devise for her.

And he had been thorough, in his remote, time-tested way, making her open her innermost screens for the hypno-fix of the cover story. You're Karen Voss. You're twenty-four.

Miguel had taped the fix from the fading brain of the actual Karen Voss. Thorough Miguel. A year back he had taken a job as a night orderly in a big hospital, smuggled the recorder in, and taken tapes off the ones on the way out of life. Better, he claimed, than inventing the cover. And it was better. It steamed the facts indelibly onto your brain patterns. No problem of learning how to stand, talk, walk or spit. And it gave Miguel a library of cover stories to apply when needed. Miguel's efficiency kept the staff down. And it overburdened the existing personnel, she thought bitterly.

She gave a drifter the cold eye, and wrinkled her nose at the reek of prono that followed him down the street. Observation first. She looked along the street slowly and found only three probables. Chances were they'd use only one Stage Two agent on this. And if the hospital was hot to get at the autopsy, he'd be jackrabbit busy making the technicians see brain convolutions where there were none. Lorin would be out from under until they picked him up again.

Observation first, and then, with screens drawn tight, a quick probe at the possibles. She tried the old lady first, the dawdling window-shopper. The probe sank deep, with none of that almost metallic ping of probe against agent screen. The old lady winced and rubbed her temple. Same with the taxi driver fiddling with the motor. That was a soft mind. Babyfood mush. She hit it almost too hard. The man dropped the wrench with a clang and his knees sagged. He straightened up slowly and rubbed his eyes. She hit the third one, the man leafing through the magazine on the far corner. A good firm mind, that one. But no ping. No screens. The impact gave him a quick frown. The man took off his glasses and held them up to the light, put them back on again.

Karen Voss didn't like the next step. This was the moment when they could punish you, knock you frothing and epileptic to the sidewalk, crunching your own bones with the muscle spasms that were the penalty for carelessness.

She lifted the outer screen, with all the caution of a kid peeking under a circus tent. With it up, you had a receptivity, but not enough. You had to get all four up, one after the other, and stand there naked. The time lag in receptivity of the potential gave them time to hit you with a full broadside.

One . . . two . . . three . . . four. All up. Naked in the daylight. Naked brain-stuff itching at the thought of the plunge. She attuned herself slowly up through the bands. She began receiving in the middle range. As she suspected, a Stage Two. But distant. A good hundred yards away. And only one. She brought him into closer focus, yet remaining too remote for detection. No need. He had his hands full. She could tell by the rhythm that he was producing illusion for three, or possibly four earthlings. Get any more on the scene and he might yelp for help, and as the help might come in the form of a Stage Three, Karen decided she'd better move.

Fourthreetwoone. Clack. All back and down and tight and trim. All armor in place. Now the bus. Three blocks away. Four. She dropped her cigarette, stamped daintily on it, and walked with chippy hip-switch to the corner, bland-eyed and arrogant.

She wore the Pack B on the inside of her wide stiff belt. It was handiest there. She could casually hook one thumb inside the belt and work the three tiny knurled wheels. Same Senarian principle as the space cubes and the parent web, limited by the speed of thought. But even the Senarians couldn't give you anything but a primer version. Any more than they could repair anything beyond the simplest circuits in that huge satellite brain that circled their old home planet, and was such a shrine to the heart planets. And that brain, built by the Senarians' remotest ancestors had given them the parent web and the Pack B too many thousand years ago to count.

She could remember the manual you got at Training T when they broke you in on the Pack B. "The Pack B must be considered as a device to focus and concentrate the power of thought. Practice in visualization is highly important in utilization of Pack B. The student will carefully examine each detail of a selected portion of the game field. The student will then walk one hundred paces from that spot. The student will imagine himself standing on that selected spot with all the power of concentration and visualization. The first wheel, marked (1) in the illustration, reduces the effective value of the mass of the student to a minus power. The second wheel, marked (2), must be set for the desired range. Set the second wheel first. Visualize. Turn the first wheel one-half revolution clockwise. Turn the third wheel, marked (3), one click. If visualization is strong enough the third, or selector wheel, will reinstate effective mass at the point of visualization. After practice this can become an almost instantaneous factor. The effective range is ten thousand yards. This same principle activates the parent web and the space cubes, though in that instance, the visualization, being generated by the parent web, is of such a high order, and the power source is so great, that there are no effective limits to the range. The speed of thought is the final barrier. Beyond that any further acceleration would be contra-temporal."

But of course one could not go about among the earthlings appearing and disappearing. It would upset them. Miguel became furious if you didn't use the utmost caution. Get away from prying eyes when you make the jump. You have two seconds of relative invisibility at the new location. So use those two seconds to make certain you are not observed, and if there's a chance, click it again to select the departure point and try again.

She moved into a sheltering doorway, made certain no one could see her, and then visualized herself standing on a corner watching the bus lumbering toward her a half block away. She brought into sharp focus the details of the bus.

Two, one, three. A twisty little wrench in the head, and there's the bus, heading for you. She looked around quickly. One man in range. To him she would be the faintest silvery shimmer. She stepped behind a post, felt the quick flooding weight. She patted her brown hair, favored the man with an insolent look of appraisal. Stuffy Miguel would have frowned at that post routine. The man looked faintly startled at not having noticed her before, probably.

She pulled herself up onto the bus, dropped her fare in the box and went back, pleased to see that Lorin was sitting by himself. She eased down beside him with a pleased little sigh. Poor bewildered earthling. A good somber strength in that face. Good level mouth on him. Suddenly she remembered a very ordinary trick that she had almost overlooked. She probed quickly and lightly, felt no screen. She sighed again.

Illusions for the big man. It would take illusions to get him back to Miguel without risk of interception. Too bad direct control was so readily detectable, so obvious that anyone could catch it with just the first screen down, and catch it a mile away or more.

Trouble with illusions, they made the earthlings crack so easily. And Miguel wanted him intact. The bus speakers droned their inevitable commercials. And this lad had already had a liberal dosage of illusion.

She cast about for a reasonable idea, something that wouldn't disrupt the other passengers. She saw a vast fat man pull himself aboard, come down the aisle sweating and puffing. The sudden hard jolt against her outermost screen shocked her. The brain made its lightning calculation of probability. She pulled all screens tight, probed the fat man. In the same split second as the hard expected "ping" occurred, she slid the stud on the catch of her handbag—a fraction of a second too late. He had blanketed her, and she retaliated quickly. Deadlock. Neither of them could yell for help now. She turned casually. He had taken the seat behind them. She looked into his bland eyes.

This time, she realized with sinking heart, they had miscalculated badly. Miguel Larner, in spite of the Branson fiasco, had thought he could retrieve it with the assignment of two Stage Two agents. So far she could count five that Shard had assigned.

The fat man tried a probe again. Apparently he thought she was a Stage One, who could be broken down. It reduced her respect for him, but that respect returned immediately as she realized he had used it as a feint, that he was busy on an illusion. A very respectable illusion. A uniformed policeman angrily waving the bus into a side street. It was almost real enough to deceive her. She thought quickly. Block the side street with something.

A blow crashed against the back of her head. As she fell forward off the seat, she cursed her own stupidity in not thinking of a definite physical attack, the most elementary move, and therefore one of the cleverest. Though consciousness slipped a bit, she held the screens tight, recovered. Lorin was helping her up.

"That fat guy hit me in the back of the head, mister!"

Lorin turned. "What's the idea, friend?"

This time Karen Voss was ready with the illusion. The fat fist struck Dake Lorin in the face so quickly that Karen guessed Dake had no chance to notice that the fat man's arms had stayed at his sides. She was pleased to note that Lorin had beautiful reflexes. The fat man's head snapped back and he crumpled in the seat. She probed deeply and viciously, realizing with satisfaction that Shard would be minus one Stage Two agent until probe wounds healed, in six months. She had broken through the first two screens.

She saw a chance to simplify things. Illusion made the fat man's head flop over at a crazy angle. This could be done with artistry. She gave the passengers a loud male voice. "Hey, you killed him!"

She took the stunned Lorin by the arm. "Come on, let's get off this thing. There's going to be trouble."

She yanked the cord and pushed at Lorin, followed him to the front of the bus. He got off blindly. She took his wrist. "Come on." People yelled at them. No one pursued. They would quiet down when they saw the fat man was all right.

Karen hurried down the block with him and around a corner. She stopped and leaned against the side of a scabrous building, dipped again into her blouse pocket to bring out a cigarette and hang it on her lower lip. Lorin lit the cigarette for her with a hand that trembled. She could sense his emotions. Distaste for her, annoyance with the situation, a vague shame that he had run. She knew that he was a troubled man, as who wouldn't be with the illusions Shard's agent had provided for him to block the newspaper article. Yet she was slightly uneasy. She had studied Branson and Lorin. She knew them well. And now Lorin seemed a bit *too* upset. She wished she dared take him under full control. He might be hard to handle.

"I cert'ny want to thank you, mister."

"That's all right. I hope I didn't get us in trouble, miss."

"Karen. Karen Voss. I bet I know you. I bet you're Dake Lorin. I used to see your picture next to your column all the time."

He looked mildly pleased. "Don't tell me you used to read it."

"Sure. Maybe you wouldn't think so. I go for that stuff. Politics, economics, international relations. I got a friend. He's got money. Lots of money. He was saying just the other day he'd like to see you back in business. He says you used to make a lot of sense. Maybe he'd back you—buy space in a paper or something."

"The Public Disservice Act keeps anyone from saying anything very critical, Miss Voss. I don't think your friend would want to join me on a shale pile."

She snorted. "Nobody touches him. Not twice anyway. I guess you heard of him. Miguel Larner."

"The racketeer? Certainly I've heard of him. He's got his hands in every filthy . . ."

"Don't go Christer, Mr. Lorin. Mig has got . . . well, two sides to his nature. He might be a lot of help to you." She was secretly amused at her words. "He's a good friend of mine. Want to see him?"

"I don't think so."

"Maybe you're in some kind of trouble. He likes helping people. You wouldn't think so, would you? But he does."

"I don't think there's anything he can do for me."

"You in a rush? You got an appointment or something? It isn't far."

She could sense his indecision. She urged him gently. At last he agreed reluctantly. She broke the connection by sliding the stud on the catch of her bag. Miguel would have heard Lorin agree. He'd be ready. She walked beside the tall man, alert for any form of interception. She hailed a cab, settled back in the seat beside Lorin, giving him a mechanical sultry smile, crossing her round brown legs.

By the time they reached 215th Street he said, accusingly, "Not far?"

"Just a couple more blocks, honey."

The cab let them out. Lorin paid the fare. She saw his quick curious glance at the sleek above-ground lobby. As they passed through the doorway Karen felt the barrier break, fold shut again behind them. She gave the traditional sigh of relief that came up from the stubbed toes of her shabby pumps. Nothing could touch her in here. Nothing could reach into the warm security of the egg-shaped barrier. The pointed end of the egg was above-ground, making a small dome over the entrance. The rest of the egg encircled all of the levels below-ground. Here Miguel Larner, Stage Three, presided over the agent teams, routed the field operations, maintained the communications network. Usually, the moment she was inside, she could erase the Karen Voss hypno-fix temporarily and revert to her own identity. But with Lorin in tow she had to keep her makeup on.

The Stage One at the desk had been alerted.

"We want to go down and see Mr. Larner, Johnny." *How did I do?*

"I guess you can go right on down, Miss Voss." *Nice going, lady.*

"Thanks, Johnny." *And scratch one Stage Two.*

"You're welcome, Miss Voss." *Don't get too many credits. We'll miss having you around.*

She led the way back to the elevator. As it slid silently down the shaft she gratefully let the rest of the screens slip. She had released the first one to permit communication with the Stage One at the desk. She felt warmly proud of herself, knowing that she had come out of this with a credit. One step closer to the heart worlds, my girl. One step closer to Training T to become a Stage Three, and then one more tour and you're out of it, and you can go to work. Next time, by God, they'll have to do better than this chippy cover. The fix went a little too deep. You had to watch your reflexes.

"Have you known Larner long?"

"A pretty long time. Here we are." The door slid back and they walked directly from the elevator into the main room of Larner's suite. It was a garish room, furnished with the best that Bombay supply houses could offer. One whole wall was a vast and intricate diorama, portraying a walled garden with a pool. Miguel spent a lot of his time by the pool, and the perspective was so cleverly done that it gave the impression of being a vast open space, rather than a twenty by twenty cube cut into bedrock. Miguel kept the controls set in such a way that the diorama changed through each hour of the twenty-four, from cloudless days to full-moon nights.

Miguel was sitting out by the pool in the four o'clock sunlight, a chunky sun-browned man with very little forehead and eyes like oiled anthracite. He wore lemon-yellow bathing trunks, and had a glass in his hand.

He waved casually. "How's it going, Karen? Come on out. Who's your friend?"

They went out by the pool. "Don't you recognize him, Mig? It's Dake Lorin." *Is this going to be one or two credits? I broke down a Stage Two.*

Miguel reached up with a languid hand. "Nice to know you, Mr. Lorin." *I suppose you were too busy congratulating yourself to scan properly. Take another look and see why it's only one credit for not seeing the obvious.*

"I was telling Dake how you always liked his stuff, Mig." *All right, so I missed it. But when you assign two and they assign five, it keeps you busy. I see what you mean. Carelessness. Something about a fingernail.*

"I've missed your column, Mr. Lorin. Used to get a charge out of it, the way you hacked at everybody." *Yes, they should have had somebody there ready with an illusion, checking to see if Lorin accepted the doll.* "Have a drink, folks? Sit down."

They took poolside chairs. "Gee, I'd go for a collins. How

about you, Dake?" *Are you getting what I'm getting, Miguel? He's balanced on the edge. It's a little beyond his credibility, and he is wondering about his own sanity.*

Miguel pushed a button. The servant appeared almost at once. He gave the orders. *So we must be very careful, girl. A little push might send him over the edge. Once we use him, maybe we can run a check and see. But I don't think he'd make it. Rigidity there. Father image. Streak of the Puritan. Somber messiah. They seldom check through. Too dependent on the nature of reality.*

"Hasn't Mig got a nice place here, Dake?" *Don't forget the quota. He might do very nicely.*

"I guess I could be classified as unemployed right now, Mr. Larner," Dake said. "Ive been working for the government for a year. And today my . . . superior died. A bit suddenly. It was sort of unofficial employment, so I guess that ends it."

"Weren't you working for Branson?" Miguel asked.

"Why, yes! How did you know that?"

"I got sources. I have to keep in touch. Anything Branson did might effect imports and exports. And anything that effects those, changes my income. You got any plans, Mr. Lorin?"

"I'm writing a newspaper article for Thursday publication."

"Hot?"

"It would have been hotter if Mr. Branson hadn't died. It will probably be classified as a Disservice to the State."

"Putting your head in the noose, eh?"

"I suppose you could call it that. It just seems . . . more important than what can happen to me. Trouble, though, is that it's critical of Darwin Branson. He's the man who died today."

"You need a place to work?"

"Thanks, no. A man is letting me use an office."

"If it doesn't work out, I got a place here you can use. A nice setup." *Do you want to fix Kelly, girl? Now that we have him here I want him to stay.*

"This would be a nice quiet place to work, Dake," Karen said. *Let Dale do it. I've been outside too long. It made hash of my nerves, Miguel. See how restless he is getting? He wants to leave.*

"I changed my mind, Karen," Miguel said. "This is easier. I just put him under full control."

She looked quickly at Lorin, saw the automaton rigidity of his posture, the eyes in trance. *But how can you . . .*

"Aloud, please. Para-voice is an insidious habit on tour. The easiest way to keep him here is to take full control. Let him believe he went back to Kelly and Kelly changed his mind and gave him a refund of his money, and backed out. Then we'll release him up above in the lobby with the idea he has come here to take up my offer. It just seems simpler. Ready now, and I'll turn him over to you. Take him to one of the rooms upstairs and give him the complete memory pattern of seeing Kelly and coming back here at, say, nine this evening. Leave him in stasis up there and then you can rest and take him up to the lobby at nine."

Karen waited. When Miguel released Lorin she caught him deftly. There was a split second of release in which Lorin stirred and made a faint sigh, almost a moan. Then she had him. As she went through the wide doors into the main room and toward the elevator, she looked back and saw him following her with that odd walking-on-eggs stride of the controlled. There was always a pathetic vulnerability about the controlled which touched her. It seemed particularly poignant in this case, all the tall hard strength of the man following as docile as a lamb.

She took the elevator up two levels and walked him down a corridor to an empty room. Lorin sat on the edge of the bed, turned stiffly, lifted his feet up, and lay back, eyes open and staring, arms rigid at his side.

Karen sat on the edge of the bed and quickly took him through all the mechanical actions of returning to New Jersey, talking to Kelly, listening to the man's protestations, accepting the refund, returning to the city. She took him on an aimless walk, had him eat a solitary meal, decide to take Miguel's offer, and return to the apartment. She stopped the visualization the moment he stepped through the door, through the barrier. It was the work of but five minutes to give him the entire visualization, and it took another few seconds to push consciousness even further back so that he would remain in stasis until she called to get him.

With an impulse that surprised her a bit, she bent over and kissed his unconscious lips lightly. Poor big oaf. Poor bewildered earthling, torn this way and that. Pawn in a game he'd never know. She kissed her fingertip, touched the middle of his forehead, smiled down at him, and left the room, shutting the door quietly, even though it would have made no difference at all if she had slammed it.

6

KELLY STUBBORNLY PUSHED THE MONEY BACK ACROSS THE DESK. He said, "Now take it, Mr. Lorin. I already told you. I've reconsidered. I don't think that disclaiming the article would give me enough immunity. They'd wonder why I accepted it."

Dake wearily pocketed the money, stood up. "I guess there's nothing I can do but look for someone else."

Kelly leaned back in his chair. "Now if you'd come to me with a little better backing. Say with a note from Mig Larner, or somebody like that . . ."

"What made you mention his name?"

"I was just using him as an example. If Mig says you won't get in trouble, you won't. He keeps all the right wheels greased, that lad does."

Dake left Kelly's place. It was after six. He had a long search for a cab. Once he was back in Manhattan he got off at New Times Square. Strange day. Darwin . . . or what was supposed to be Darwin . . . dying like that. He felt strange. Almost unreal. It was an odd sensation, as though his side vision were impaired, as though he could only see straight ahead, and everything else was a grayness, a nothingness. It was the same with sounds. He kept hearing sharp individual sounds, but the background noise of the city seemed to be missing. It seemed to him as though there were some serious impairment of all his senses. Yet, oddly, he could not seem to bring himself to stop and check that impairment—to turn his head quickly, to listen consciously for all the background noise. And those people he did see, those normal characters of the streets were subtly altered. Colors had slightly different values. And his instinctive and automatic appraisals seemed distorted.

He saw a lovely girl looking into a cluttered shoddy store window, examining the ersatz fabrics. He found himself looking at her with a peculiar feeling of envy and jealousy. And he was conscious of the breadth of shoulder of the men. He could not be certain, or even investigate the fact, but he had the wry idea that he was mincing along rather than walking. The world had a dream-like aspect, and it seemed to him that, almost on an unconscious level, he was trying to tell himself that he was dreaming, yet not being able to force the thought up to the level of action.

He found a quiet restaurant where he had never been before. He ordered a sweet drink which normally he despised. And found it surprisingly good. He ordered a very light meal, and yet it seemed to satisfy him completely. The world was a bit out of focus, and yet he could not capture his wandering attention and apply his intelligence to a thorough appraisal of exactly where and why it was out of focus.

After he finished the meal he decided that the next step was definitely to return to see Miguel Larner. He decided to work it from a different angle this time. Complete the article, and then find someone willing to print it, either free or for a fee. Let the article speak for itself. Let the public learn exactly what Stephen Chu and Garva had been willing to do. Let them learn about the trade concessions Gondohl Lahl had promised. Let them learn that the enemy coalitions were, behind their brave front, pathetically eager to effect a compromise, achieve a period of stability. And show them all how the conversation with Smith had destroyed this chance.

He was surprised at how quickly time had gone. He stepped out of the cab in front of Larner's place at nine o'clock, paid the man and walked into the lobby. He walked in and stumbled on the smooth floor for no reason at all, caught himself. There had been an odd little twist, or click, and now side vision had returned, he could hear the full range of sound, colors had their former values.

That odd girl from the bus was leaning on the clerk's desk. Voss. Karen Voss. He wondered why he hadn't wasted a single thought on the fat man in the bus since leaving Larner's place that afternoon. Pretty damn callous to kill a stranger and forget it.

"Hi there, Dake," Karen said. "Just talking about you. Remember the fat man on the bus?"

"I certainly do."

"I guess it looked worse than it was. You just knocked him out. Heard that he's okay. I had Mig check on it."

"I still can't understand why he hit you. I'm damn glad to hear he's okay."

"Maybe I reminded him of somebody who picked his pocket once. And maybe I did. I've got a lousy memory. How do you like the dress?"

She whirled the full skirt. He said, "I guess I like it. Little daring, though. That style is older than you know. The women of Crete started it a long, long time ago."

"All I know is that Mig had it flown over from Madras." She took his arm. "Mig is psychic. He told me you'd be back. I'll go down with you. 'Bye, Johnny." *I'm starting to like this big lug. Did you see him blush? That's a lost art.*

"Come back, Miss Voss." *Don't get the geef over any earthling, lamb. There's no future in it.*

Poo.

On the way down in the elevator, Dake felt his cheeks grow hot again. He said, "Are you a . . . uh . . . special friend of Mr. Larner?"

She squeezed his arm. "I guess I give him a few laughs. That's all."

He was embarrassed at his own show of interest. There was something pleasingly childlike about this Karen Voss, but he knew that she was one cheap, tough, hard little article. It was in her stance, her eyes, the shape of her mouth. That opaque quality of sexual arrogance of one of those little girls who have learned too much too fast.

"Does Mr. Larner ever go out?"

"Why do you ask that?"

"I just had the strong feeling that he didn't. That maybe he wouldn't be safe on the outside."

He looked down into speculative luminous gray eyes. She was standing so close to him that he could see the little amber flecks that ringed the pupil. He decided that it was the high quality of the intelligence of those eyes which was so startlingly at odds with the chippy walk, the too-tight clothes, the insolent curve of lip.

"Not as bright as all that," she said.

He stared at her. "How did you know what I was thinking?"

For a moment she looked genuinely disconcerted. Then she threw her head back and her throat pulsed in a raw vulgar bellow of laughter. "Jesus H. Gawd," she gasped. "Now I'm getting psychic yet. Or maybe we're soulmates, sugar. Ever think of that?"

Miguel Larner was in his diorama garden, in the long sweet dusk of a midsummer evening which contrasted with the October night in the city above. Sound tracks gave to scrupulous perfection the muted night-cries of insects, the fluid silver of a distant nightingale, the garrump of a conclave of frogs in a bog on the far side of the meadow.

"Hey, Mig! He came back like you said." *And he caught me off guard in the elevator. I could swear he was sending on the paravoice band, and doing it perfectly.*

"Sit down, people. Glad you came back, Lorin. Especially if it means I can help you." *I noticed how clear he was this afternoon. A latent, perhaps.*

Dake sat down as soon as Karen was seated. "As a matter of fact, the man who was going to print the article backed out. And returned my money. That didn't seem in character. I've got it here. I thought perhaps you could——That's damn funny! I put it right here in this pocket."

Girl, you seem to be making a habit of being careless with this one.

Karen laughed. "A demonstration, Dake. I wanted to show you how an expert picks a pocket. I did it on the elevator." *Decent recovery, Miguel?*

Thirty thousand rupees, girl. Let's see the illusion.

Dake took the money Karen handed him. He handed it to Miguel. "Here's thirty thousand rupees, Mr. Larner. I wonder if you could use it to get me a spot where the article will get a decent readership."

If he's a latent, Miguel, wouldn't that help?

Screens raised, eh. Afraid I'll see the sudden emotional interest in this one.

Let me give him a strong primary impulse and see if he's latent receptive too.

All this will wait until we've used him as a countermove against Shard. In another moment I might get impatient with you, girl.

Miguel took the money, shoved it casually into his shirt pocket. "Lorin, you're not hiring me with this. I'm just keeping it for you. You go ahead and write the article. I'll find a spot for it. And give you the change. Why don't you stay right here? One of my secretaries is on vacation. Complete apartment with no one in it."

"I wouldn't be in the way?"

"Not a damn bit. Give me your local address and I'll send somebody over for your stuff."

"Just a hotel room. I've been living in hotel rooms ever since going with Branson."

"I'll have you checked out then."

Dake gave Miguel the name of the hotel. Miguel said, "Show him where he hangs his hat, Karen. Next floor above, Dake. End of the hall. Give Johnny a ring, Karen, and tell him Mr. Lorin is in 7 C, for an indefinite stay."

They left the diorama garden. Dusk had faded into night. Karen took him up in the elevator and down to 7 C. The door was unlocked. Karen went in first, flipping the light switches, activating the diorama. It was a moonlit seascape with a sound track of waves against the beach.

"Very luxurious," Dake said.

What?

"I said it's very luxurious." He glanced at her, wondered why she wore such a smug look, as though she had proved something to herself.

"It's got a liquor cupboard too, Dake. Build you a drink?"

"If you'd like. I think I need a drink. This has been . . . one of the craziest days of my life."

She had her back to him, sitting on her heels, looking into the liquor cabinet. *Scotch okay for you?*

"Are you a ventriloquist or something, Karen?"

She turned toward him. "Why?"

"Your voice had the funniest quality right then. It seemed to come from all corners of the room at once."

"Used to sing a little. Maybe that's it. Why has this been a crazy day, Dake?"

"I ought to talk to somebody. Just let me ramble, even if it doesn't make sense to you. That sounded pretty superior, didn't it?"

"Not too. You couldn't expect me to follow everything you could say."

She brought him a tall drink. "Kashmiri Dew. Eight years old." She perched on the arm of his chair, rather disturbingly warm against his arm. "Mind?"

"N-no. I guess what's troubling me the most is wondering if I'm losing my mind."

"Don't they say that if you're wondering about it, you aren't?"

"I don't have much faith in that. I've always been a sort of functional pragmatist."

"Don't make the words too big, Professor."

"If I could see something, feel it, touch it, smell it, hit it with my fist, then it existed. And my actions were based on thought which in turn was based on realities."

"I sort of get it, sugar."

"So today reality began to go sour on me. Typewriter keys don't bleed. A man's fingernail doesn't grow a quarter of an inch in two days. And ever since I left here this afternoon, until I got back, everything was curiously unreal. Like I was walking and talking in a dream. When I couldn't find that money in my pocket, I began to think it *was* a dream."

"What's this typewriter keys and fingernails routine?"

"Little things where my senses didn't send the right messages to my brain. As if I suddenly saw you walk across the ceiling."

"Shall I?"

"Don't look at me like that. I begin to think you can. Anyway, what has a man got to hold onto except reality?"

"Okay, sugar. I rise to ask a question. I'll name a list. Faith, hope, love, honor. Can you touch them, smell them, hit them with your fist?"

"Those items are the result of thought regarding other concrete items which can be detected with the senses."

She turned and kissed him suddenly. Her eyes danced. "I'm beginning to get it, Professor. You could feel that, couldn't you. But if it ended up in you loving me, you would only get that from . . . from inference."

"I get the damndest feeling that you're way ahead of me. And don't do that again."

"If you don't like it, I won't. Let's continue the discussion, Professor. Let's play suppose. Like that guy Midas. Everything he touched turned to gold. Okay. According to you he should have gone nuts. But he didn't. He starved to death. What was that? Strong brain? Suppose an ordinary guy. A guy like you. His world starts to frazzle on the edges. Wouldn't he have enough pride to keep telling himself that he was okay? That something was doing it to him, on purpose?"

"Persecution complex, eh. So he's crazy anyway."

"Suppose another thing. Suppose this precious reality of yours that you like so well, suppose all that is fiction, and when you begin to see crazy things, you're seeing the real reality."

"You have a very unique mind, Karen."

"The adjective has been used on me before. But not that way, sugar."

"You should have done more with yourself. That quality of imagination is rare."

"You know, Dake, you're a little on the stuffy side. How about if I like me the way I am? How about that?"

He grinned. "My reformer instinct always crops out. Forgive me."

"You said it was funny this afternoon after you left here. How?"

"Colors looked odd. People looked odd. I had the feeling that I wasn't seeing or hearing as much as I should."

"So this style started in Crete. How veddy veddy interesting!"

He quickly averted his eyes and felt his face get hot again. She laughed at him. "It's no trick to read your mind sometimes, Lorin, man."

"Look, I don't want to be too stuffy, but . . ."

"I have the idea Patrice wouldn't care."

He frowned at her. "Dammit, that's about enough. I know I didn't mention her to you. You've got a lot of extra-sensory perception or something."

"I read the gossip columns. Sort of a cold dish, isn't she?"

"Miss Voss, you pry. Now, out! I'm going to try to do some work."

She slid off the arm of the chair, winked blandly at him. "All right, dear. Use the phone for food. They bring it down. All the office stuff is through that door. Your clothes and things ought to be over soon."

She went to the door, burlesquing her normally provacative walk. She winked again, over her shoulder, and left. He sat for a time thinking of what she said about reality. What if all the "normal" things were illusionary, and all the things that went bump in the night were fragments of reality, seen through the mist of illusion? He shrugged off the idea. Maybe a table top *is* a matrix of whirling bits of energy. Maybe all the true matter that makes up a man, once you eliminate the spaces between nucleus and perimeter electrons, *is* no bigger than the head of a pin. But you can beat on a table with your fist, and the wood hurts your hand. And you can break a man's jaw and hear the bone go.

He found that the small office was beautifully equipped, and as clean as an operating room. He worked on the article, regaining the free flow of words which he had experienced in the office borrowed from Kelly. He used the same lead, tightening it a bit, altering it to include the death of Branson.

After an hour of work he went out to phone for food. He was famished again. His clothes had been brought, neatly unpacked in the bedroom. The food was brought. He worked for another hour and then went to bed. He sat on the edge of the bed in his pajamas. He put his feet up and lay back. A funny example of *déjà vu*, he thought. As though he *had* been in this room before. Or a room very like it. With Karen. She had sat on the edge of the bed. Later she had kissed his lips. She had told him something. Something about Kelly. It was so difficult to . . .

Sleep came quickly. The dream was as crazy as the day. Myriad voices echoing inside his skull. He couldn't get them out. They were little people, trudging around in there. Pinching and prodding his brain. Nibbling at the edges with tiny rodent teeth. Yelling at each other. All talking at once. Commenting on him. Hey, look at this. And this over here! What do you know? Pinch and prod and nibble, and all the voices going like too many records playing at once. Definitely latent. And a receptive. But a fracture line here, and here. Father image. Won't do. Won't do at all. But look at this!

He woke up, sitting up, hearing his own roar of "Get out!" still lingering in the silent air-conditioned room. He was sweaty and chilled. He pulled the blanket up over him. He could hear faint music. Very odd music. He couldn't recognize the instruments. Probably some new Pak-Indian fad, he decided. Damn stupid to accept Miguel Larner's hospitality. Well, use any means if the end is good. Damn destructive philosophy, however, if you overdid it. Question. Who was using who, whom?

————IT WAS A FINE SUMMER MORNING ON MANARR. THE SUN beamed hot on the shallow placid seas, on the green rolling traces of the one-time mountains. The fi-birds dipped over the game fields, teetering on membranous green wings, yelping like the excited children. Picnic day. Picnic day. Everyone was coming, as everyone had always come. Hurrying from the warm pastels of the small houses that dotted the wide plains, hurrying by the food stations, the power boxes. Hooray for picnic day. The smallest ones set their tiny jump-sticks at the widest settings and did crazy clumsy leaps in the warm air, floating, sprawling, nickering. The maidens had practiced the jump-stick formations and groups of them played towering floating games of leapfrog on the way to the game fields, spreading wide their skirts, swimming through the perfect air of this day. The young men watched and bounded and set their jump-sticks narrow to do the hard quick tricks. Picnic day. Today there would be water sculpture, and sky dancing, and clowns. Day of laughter, evening of the long songs, night of mating. Time for work tomorrow. The hard work that cramped the brain and so often brought tears, under the unforgiving eye, the cold trim face of the earthling. Someone had said that today the earthling would judge the water sculpture, lead the sky dance. Few believed it.

————Ten parsecs beyond the outermost star system the great ship rested. It had been built in space. No planet crust could withstand its weight, and thus it had never felt the full tug of gravity at close range. It was the flagship for a full division. On the master control cube, three dimensional diagram of a galaxy, tiny red spheres showed the placement of each ship of the division. In this hour it was a nervous ship. Quick flick of eyes. Lick of tongue tip across dry lips. Silence. The launch had arrived an hour ago. At last the bell called all officers. They hurried to central assembly, stood in formation at attention.

After five minutes the earthling arrived, with his cold and bitter eyes, the flat iron slab of a face, wearing his symbols of command. The prisoner was taken to the vast open space in the middle of the hollow square of the formation.

They said he could give you a writhing agony with a mere glance, read your most secret thoughts, turn you to a mindless thing. The officers stood like statues.

The harsh voice of the earthling filled the huge room. "Officers. Observe the prisoner. He commanded a ship. He forgot the need for endless vigilance." The prisoner stood with a face like death.

"They came once. They came out of the blackness between the galaxies. They would not communicate. They were merely a patrol. Yet it took the total strength of the galaxy to hurl them back. They will come again, in strength. We are stronger now, yet not strong enough. The prisoner grew bored with vigilance. For two thousand years there has not been one second of relaxation. Nor will there be until they return, as they inevitably will. Remove the prisoner."

He was marched away, head bowed.

The earthling said, in a quieter tone, "Defense cannot remain static. Every ship in this division is obsolete." There was a stir and murmur in the ranks of officers.

"The first ship of the new class is being assembled. It has better shields, heavier weapons, a new and more effective hyper-drive. This crew has been selected for immediate return and training. I shall transfer command headquarters to one of your sister ships. On your return with the new ship I will once again command the division from your ship. Within five years complete replacement of the ships of this division will be effected. Obsolete ships will be placed in reserve. Patrol areas will be twice as far from the galactic rim as we are now. I have recommended brief leave for each of you on his or her home planet. Dismissed."

————At Bionomic Research they had all been uneasily aware of the new earthling who had replaced gentle, easygoing The'dran. But the long days drifted by and they slowly became used to his habit of roaming through the low gray buildings. They prepared the metal tapes which listed, in minute detail, the almost infinite ecological factors of the unbalanced planets and fed them through the whispering calculators, getting the slow results that so often looked like utter nonsense. It was very slow work, but who could hasten it? Nature moved slowly. If the answer was to eliminate one certain type of shrub on such and such a planet, who was to hasten it? In perhaps fifty of the planet years in question, elimination of the shrub would have caused the extinction of a certain class of insect which in turn was the food source for a specific class of lizard which restricted the natural watershed by tunneling too indiscreetly among tree roots and stunted growth.

So they began to accept the earthling as a symbol, and nothing more.

Until one day, in a cold flat voice, and with unfriendly eyes, he called them parasites and time-wasters and fools. He revised all the old ways, formed them into research teams, assigned one field team to each research team, demanded synchronized recommendations, with a target date for putting them into effect. The old ways were gone. The slow warm days. Now it was hurry, hurry. Planets must be bionomically balanced, with resources utilized toward the setting of an optimum population level. Transportation of necessities between planets is a waste. Hurry, hurry, hurry. It should have been done yesterday, the day before yesterday. Please the earthling with your energy, or end up at Center with your technical qualification erased and your number changed to manual labor.

————On Training T, far from the power webs, far from the intricate geometric pattern of the space cubes, gleaming on the vast metallic plain, far from the black training buildings and the instruction beams, a Stage Two wept. The mind, seemingly strong, flexible, elastic, had not been able to take the Stage Three instruction. A hidden fracture line. They would not go on with it. Another attempt would result in mindlessness. He was a strong, bitter, powerful man, graduate of the Irish slums of New Orleans. With fists and teeth and grinding ambition he had fought his way up. And he wept because here, so very clearly, so very precisely, was the end of the line. Yet a young girl—linguist, dreamer, poet —had made it, knew what her assignment would eventually be.

———In Madrid, behind the egg-shaped barrier that enclosed and concealed the luxuries of the sun-bleached castle, Shard checked the agent credits, made out his requisition for personnel. Forty Ones, sixteen Twos, two Threes. No Stage Three could keep track of his own credits. He realized sourly that the filling of the requisition in total would be his only indication that he had served well in this, his third tour. He yearned to be rid of the stinking, brawling, sniveling billions, to be clear of the miasmic stench of fear and hate. Endless battle for a world. An endless stirring of the pot.

He asked that the Gypsy girl be brought in. She had a boldness he liked, a boldness stronger than her fear. He produced illusions for her, watching her mind closely, always slanting the illusions more and more closely toward the secret focus of all her fears. Knives and worms and things with claws that crawled. Nineteen, she was, yet through her man she had been leading her tribe of *gitanos* for over two years, and leading them with an iron will, leading them well.

He turned her breasts to lizard heads and her fingers to tentacles and she fainted, blood on her mouth. Yet when she revived, she spat at him and cursed him, with *flamenca* fury. She would do. One of the unbreakable ones. One of the precious bitter ones.

Shard took her down the slanting tunnel to the small space station. He took her personally. A signal honor. He touched the stud and the orifice slit in the gray cube opened. He thrust her in, reached in and touched the guide stud for Training T, stepped back. The cube shimmered, iridescent. Projected thought of the power web of the parent planets, caught here in plus mass stasis. It changed from pink to a watery greenish silver, and then, achieving minus mass, it disappeared at once, the air filling the vacuum with pistol shot sound. Little Gypsy, who now would age one year in ten. Shard stood, wishing somberly that they had enlisted him at nineteen, rather than at forty. Yet, at nineteen, he hadn't been ready, as she was ready. At nineteen he would have broken, utterly. She might break, under training. He doubted it. He had seen too many. He walked back up the tunnel, denying himself the ease of the Pack B, trying, as he walked, to anticipate Larner's next strategem, to plan for it, to nullify it.

8

MIGUEL LARNER SAT ON THE APRON OF HIS DIORAMA POOL, DAN-gling his legs in the water. The Stage Three who was to be his eventual replacement lounged in a chair nearby. His name was Martin Merman and he was a bland-faced young man who, in prior life, had been an exceptionally successful guerrilla leader. His very successes had brought him to the attention of one of Miguel's predecessors.

The two men had a warm relationship, based primarily on the essential loneliness of all Stage Threes. Miguel made a point of keeping Martin Merman well versed on all current operations. Not only did it train Merman, but he often came up with quite acceptable alterations in established programs. Para-voice between them was reserved for those situations when speed of communication was essential. When there was no pressure they preferred the leisure of actual conversation.

"The Branson operation has been one of the subtler ones," Miguel said. "We couldn't handle it openly because of the possibility of interference by Shard. That's why I stepped in over a year ago and steered Enfield and Branson into handling it as a secret mission. Looked like a better chance of getting it all wound up before Shard realized it."

"How did he get onto it? Do you know?"

"When he blocked the assassination of George Fahdi, and I still insist it wasn't your fault it didn't work, he left an agent close to Smith, unfortunately a Stage Two who caught in Smith's mind the details of the pending trip to see Branson. They found they couldn't control Branson properly. That's when they made the substitution. Lorin could still snatch our fat from the fire. They tried to block him with illusions. We lost him and picked him up again at the hospital and Karen brought him here. I can get his account of the conferences published. Fahdi is the trouble point. World indignation might be just enough to tip him over."

"Won't Shard's people be hunting for this Lorin?"

"Obviously, but I suspect they know he's here where they can't touch him."

"What are you going to do then, Miguel?"

"He's finished the article. Damn good, too. As soon as I place it, I'm going to turn him loose."

"And let Shard's people pick him up and force a repudiation?"

"Exactly."

"Then what's the point of the whole thing? What is gained?"

"It's a feint, Martin. The real target is Smith."

Merman frowned and then grinned. "I see what you mean. Let Smith see his opportunity. Let him give George Fahdi a false account of the talk with Branson, now that Branson is dead, and then use his own knowledge of the *sub rosa* deal to ride into power and . . ."

"He has already given Fahdi the false account. He was quick to see the advantage after a little . . . gentle suggestion. Too bad he's a psychopathic personality. Be good material otherwise. Tough enough. Ambitious enough. Keep Shard concentrating on Lorin and maybe Fahdi can go the way of most dictators. If he's tipped over, that will put the fear of God into Stephen Chu and Garva for a time. Will of the people. All that sort of thing."

"So this Lorin becomes your stalking horse."

"Which won't please the fair Karen. Bit of an emotional set there."

"Really? It does happen sometimes. I remember a girl, back when I was a Stage Two. Talked myself into believing she could make it. Cracked up in no time at all."

"Lorin has some good latent abilities. But he won't survive

Shard's gentle attentions. He's already had just about as much as he could take. There was a flaw in the substitution and he noticed it. And he can't quite bring himself to look squarely at all the inferences."

"Fahdi is prime target?"

"Like Hitler, back when I was a Stage One, Martin. That was a wild and merry chase. The Stage Three in charge arranged three assassination attempts, and each one was blocked, barely in time. Good Lord, that was nearly forty years ago."

"When you were nearly four years younger, Miguel?" Martin Merman asked gently.

"When you are a Stage One you believe in too many things. Fahdi is prime. I have three people building up the student revolt in the Argentine, several lobbying on the trade agreements at New Delhi, one teaching Garva some new and more destructive pleasures of the flesh. Those are top order. Except for this Branson thing, Shard seems to depend on those old trustworthy 'border incidents.' They're effective, but only in a limited way. Stability, unity, must come from within. That's why I've assigned so many of our people to the routine job of agricultural research—helping the actual researchers see old things in a new way. But I have a hedge against defeat, too."

"That's a nice trick if you can manage it."

"Back to the oldest continent, Martin. Back to the newest power rising in the heart of Africa in another forty, fifty years. We're stirring them up there. Making them think. Making them come alive. Like all the years of labor in India."

Martin frowned. "What would happen, Miguel, if . . . one side or the other achieved a victory so sweeping that . . . there was no turning back."

"You mean if the pot boiled over? It won't. It can't."

The soda hissed into the glass as Miguel made a drink for Dake Lorin. He handed the tall man the glass.

"Drink a toast to yourself, Dake. You get it on the front page of the *Times-News*. Bylined. Wire services all over the world."

Dake stared at him. "They wouldn't touch it when I took it to them."

"You couldn't tell them those Disservice people wouldn't raise a stink. I can. Old friends I got down there. Here's your money back. Didn't need it."

"What's your object in helping me, Mr. Larner?"

Miguel shrugged his thick shoulders. "The way I work. I do you a favor. You do me a favor. That makes the world go around. Got any plans?"

"Not yet. I thought I'd see if I can't get back into the same sort of thing I was doing working for Darwin Branson. I want to see if I can get an appointment with Enfield."

"Want me to fix that?"

Dake smiled. "I guess you could, all right. I guess there isn't much you can't do. But I think I better try this on my own."

"He isn't going to be too happy when that paper hits the streets. And that ought to be in . . . about two hours."

"Think the article will do any good, Mr. Larner?"

"That kind of thing is over my head, Dake. I see it this way. Nothing will keep that dope from filtering into Brazil, North China, Irania. Of course nobody will try to keep it out of Pak-India. So the world gets to know that all the big boys were right on the verge of making a deal, and didn't quite do it. Enough people yelling and maybe it will go through anyway. Public opinion might scare the big shots. Then we'd have that free exchange of information, reopening of frontiers to air travel, cooperative use of the canals, a few disputed boundary lines redrawn to satisfy both parties. As I see it, it could work. Lloyds of Calcutta is giving seven to three on war within the next year. Maybe your article will change hell out of those odds."

"I don't think any part of it is over your head."

"I stick to my own line. Prono, and supplying the fleng joints, and the tridi franchises. Hell, so long as I can keep making a fast rupee, I should sweat up the world? I should live so long? Nice having you around, Dake. Let me know how you make out."

"You sound like a friend of mine. She has the same approximate philosophy. She calls me a do-gooder. Patrice Togelson."

"I know about her. She and me, we'd make a good team. Bring her around some time."

"She thinks she's a team all by herself. I've got to take this money back to her. She loaned it to me. To make a damn fool of myself with."

"Good luck, boy. Don't take any wooden rupees."

Dake went up and picked up his suitcase, went the rest of the way up to the lobby. He nodded at Johnny, the desk clerk, told him he was leaving for good. As he turned toward the door he heard his name called.

He turned. Karen was running toward him from the elevators. Her eyes were wide with alarm. "You're not going?"

"Yes, I am. And thanks for everything."

"But you haven't seen Miguel! He doesn't know you're going."

"I just said good-bye to him, Karen."

She half turned away from him. There was an odd expression on her face, as though she were listening for a sound that was just beyond his hearing range. Her face changed then, screwed up like the face of a child about to cry.

"Good-bye, Dake." She held her hand out. He took it.

"Good-bye, Karen."

When he was outside the door he glanced back. She stood inside, watching him through the glass. She was not standing in the casual, slumped, hoyden posture of Karen Voss. She stood slim and straight, with a sort of forlorn dignity on her face. He walked to the corner, turning once to wave. She did not respond. A charcoal-burning cab picked him up and clattered its desolate way toward the CIJ terminal. He had a twenty-minute wait for the next Philadelphia shuttle jet. The newspapers arrived barely in time. He bought two copies and took them onto the aircraft with him. Aside from two typos, the article was exactly as he had written it. And they had bannered it SECRET DEALS REVEALED, with the subhead BRANSON'S DEPUTY IN FOUR-POWER AGREEMENT CLAIMS IRANIAN DOUBLE-CROSS SHAPING UP.

The coin was up in the air, he thought. It could land heads or tails. Heads would be a new agreement, a lessening of international tension. Tails would merely quicken the war which more than half of the world now called "inevitable."

He read it through twice, quickly, and then glanced at the rest of the news. Massacre in a religious encampment in Iowa. Fire razes abandoned plant of Youngstown Sheet and Tube. Gurkha Airforce takes long-term lease on Drew Field in Florida, in conjunction with the missile launching stations at Cocoa. Maharani kidnap attempt foiled. Skyrocketing murder statistics blamed on prono addiction, yet growers' lobby thwarts legislative control. Bigamy legalized in California after Supreme Court review. Tridi starlet found dead in bed. New North China conscription planned. Brazil develops deadly virus mutation. New soil deficiency isolated at Kansas lab. Texas again threatens secession. Enfield Key Westing.

Dake frowned as he read the last item. With the publication of his article, he would be poison to anyone except Enfield himself, and perhaps with him too, but at least it was a chance. There were a few more minutes of the flight left. During the last two days he had come to avoid all introspective moments, to busy his mind with activity—any kind of activity—just so it kept him from thinking.

Stream of thought was like a swift river that ran smoothly down a channel and then broke suddenly against a rock. That rock was the flaw he had seen in Branson, and the manner of his "death." After striking the rock, the current boiled into an eddy, circling aimlessly. A thousand times he had tried to dismiss it by telling himself that he was mistaken. Auto-hypnosis. A tiny flaw in the mind, a wrinkle resulting from strain. For the first time in many days he thought consciously of his wife. The dull feeling of loss lingered always in his subconscious, ready to be brought to the surface. A quiet, bright-eyed girl who had loved him. There had been for a long time an inability to believe that she was dead. He would meet her around the next corner. Maybe the strain had started when he had at last faced the fact that she was utterly and incredibly gone. Wife and father—and both, somehow, killed by different aspects of the same thing. Father killed by a small corruption, and wife by a vaster one—yet the difference was only in degree.

These, he thought, were poor years for a constructive idealist. The dream was always the same. Do a little bit, to the limit of your strength, and it will become a better world, after you have gone. If each man does a little bit . . . Maybe, back in the eighteen hundreds that dream had a little validity. Men could believe, back there, that the world became a little bit better each year. But then, following the first two world wars, the dream had somehow become reversed. Men of good will began to believe that the world was getting worse. Thought became nihilistic, or existentialistic. Praise the gods of nothingness.

Yet somehow there had been more vitality in thinking the world was getting worse than in the tepid philosophizings of the middle sixties when it was believed that the world never gets better or worse—it remains always on an even keel of disorder, Christ played off against Dachau, with the game always ending in a draw. A bad time for functional idealism. Patrice and Miguel were the inevitable products of the culture. Let me get mine—fast.

How much simpler to fall into their way of life. The devil take my grandchildren. Corruption is always with us. The game always ends in a draw, and all the efforts of one man cannot affect that immutable decision.

Patrice provided the easy doorway. She had always urged him to come in with her. "There are so many things you could do, darling. I need someone to handle public relations, to deal with some of my compadres who seen to resent dealing with a woman. Some of the Indians look at me as though they thought I should be in purdah. I could pay you well, but it wouldn't be charity or a gift or anything, because I *do* need you."

Not quite yet, Patrice. Not until I can recognize the inevitability of defeat. And maybe I'll never recognize that.

As the aircraft dipped over Philadelphia he saw that there had been another one of the power failures which seemed to become more frequent each year. Angular sections of the city were blacked out. Nobody screamed with outraged indignation any more. With enough technicians, money and standby equipment, there would be no power failures. But Philadelphia, as all other cities, lacked all three factors. Standard correctional procedure was to appoint a committee to look into the findings of the committee which had been appointed to make a survey. The answer was always the same. We lack oil and coal and ore and copper and zinc and tin and timber and men.

He caught a cab, had to transfer to another when the first one broke down. He felt uneasy riding through the dark streets with the money in his wallet. Philadelphia was infested with child gangs. The dissolution and decay of the school system had put them on the streets. They had the utter, unthinking ruthlessness of children in all ages. The guerrilla days had filled the land with weapons. Put an antique zip gun in the hands of an eleven-year-old child from a prono-saturated home, and you had an entity which thought only in terms of the pleasing clatter of the gun itself, with imagination so undeveloped as yet that the adults who were ripped by the slugs were not creatures capable of feeling pain, but merely exciting symbols of an alien race. They were like the children he had read about who had lived in caves in the rubble of Berlin after the Second World War.

He got out of the cab in front of Patrice's house, saw the lights and felt secure again. The cab drove away as he started up the walk. The faint movement of a shadow among shadows startled him. He saw it from the corner of his eye. He turned quickly, saw nothing. He waited for a few moments and then turned toward the house. The pretty Japanese maid opened the door and gave him her usual welcoming smile, glinting with gold.

"Good evening, Mr. Lor——"

He had stepped into the hall. She stared at him and her face changed, grotesquely. She put one hand to her throat. She took a step backward and her eyes bulged in a glassy way as though, at last, after years of nightmare, she now faced the ultimate horror.

"What's wrong with you?"

She took another step and suddenly crumpled, to lie still on the hall rug. He leaned over her. Patrice came out into the hall.

"Dake! What on earth happened to Molly?"

"I don't know. She just stared at me and looked horrified and fainted. I guess it's a faint."

Patrice knelt by the small frail figure, began to rub her wrist, pat her wan cheek. "Molly! Molly dear!"

She frowned and then glanced up at Dake. "I don't know what ——" She stopped and stared at him intently, and her face suddenly looked like chalk. "God," she whispered softly. "God!" She shut her eyes tightly, squinching up her face. She swayed on her knees as though she would topple over the figure of the maid.

"What's wrong!" Dake demanded. "What is it?"

She kept her eyes shut. "I don't want to . . . look. It's . . . your face."

Dake instinctively lifted his hand to touch his face. He rubbed

his left cheek with his right hand. It felt completely normal. He
ran his hand across his mouth and suddenly stopped, his heart
thudding. He gingerly touched his right cheek, his fingertips making a whispering sound against the hard polished bone. He slid
his fingertips up to touch the empty ivory eye socket.

He reached the big hall mirror in three strides and stared at
himself. Had a polished skull-head stared back at him it would
not have been anywhere near as horrible as to see the face evenly
divided between life and death. One side flushed, warm, alive. On
the other side the naked teeth.

Impossibility!

Face to face with all the myriad logical answers. None of them
logical. Take half a man's face off and he bleeds to death. He
looked into the mirror and saw, behind him, the reflected image
of Patrice, her face in her hands, kneeling beside the still form of
Molly—the little maid who had been so proud of learning the syllable L that she had changed her name.

He saw a cliff in the back of his mind, and sanity clung,
scrabbling with bleeding fingers, to the sheer edge. Easier to drop
into nothingness, turning over and over through the endless fall.
Easier to scream and giggle and destroy the two women with
murderous fear.

He walked slowly to a position behind Patrice, looked down on
her shining head.

His voice sounded rusty. "Would you ever try to tell anyone
about this?"

"No. No!"

"Then how many others have seen things . . . like this, and
knew they dared not speak of them, Patrice?"

"What are you trying to say?"

"Are we dreaming this? Is it happening? Are you the Patrice of
my dreams?"

"You're . . . in my dream, Dake. In my nightmare."

"How do we go about waking up?"

"You know we're awake," she whispered. "What . . . are
you?"

"A beastie? A demon? I'm Dake. I don't understand it any better than you do. Look at me."

"No."

He took the shining hair in his fist and wrenched her head back. "Look at me!" She moaned, but kept her eyes tight shut. With his free hand he thumbed back her eyelid, even as she clawed at his wrist. She did not move or breathe. The wide eye stared at him. She screamed then. A scream that tore his nerves. That final utter scream of the last panic. She jumped and spun away, staring at him, still screaming, pausing only to fill her lungs and scream again. And stopped. And stood in the echoing silence and began to laugh, bending and twisting and holding herself with laughter, running then, doubling over with laughter, running against the door and rebounding to run again and at last tearing it open, running out into the night, laughing, tripping, falling, lying there in the diagonal of light from the open door, her legs still making spasmodic running motions, her laughter sounding as though her throat were slowly filling with blood. . . .

He understood. Her bold proud mind had been full of arrogance, of certainty, of the knowledge of infallibility. Faced with the hideous and inexplicable, the mind had been unable to bend, unable to accept impossibility. And so, under strain, it had broken clearly, cleanly. Her example oddly gave him an understanding of how close he was to the same fracture line, gave him that necessary increment of pliability that kept him from breaking.

He knew that they would bring her back, quickly perhaps, to a relative sanity. But that new sanity would be a weak patch on the broken mind. She would walk in uncertainty, with the morbid expectation that around the very next corner she might find . . . a new inexplicable horror.

Molly, the Japanese maid, was a different case. Here was no proud and rigid mind, dependent on an explicable world. Here was a willingness to accept the unknown on its own terms. It would give her bad night dreams. It would give her delicious chills from time to time. But she would not break through the necessity of having to find a reason for something that was without reason.

They came, the obsequious and silken little doctors of the very rich, murmuring their concern, manicured fingers timing the flutter of pulse, phoning in subdued voices for the very best of hospital suites, the most accomplished of private nurses, and making the deft quieting injections, cautioning the attendants who levered the still Viking body into the chrome and gold of the huge Taj ambulance for the hushed flight through the night streets of the city.

One doctor rode with the sleeping woman, and the other, with many nervous glances at his watch, questioned Dake and Molly. Dake had known from the vaguely irritable glances the doctors had given him that his face was no longer horror. He had furtively fingered his cheek to make certain.

Molly sat in a straight chair, her fists propped rigid atop her thighs, her ankles neatly together, the black hair drawn back tightly, sheening oiled blue and green in the lamplight. Her eyes would flick toward Dake, slide uneasily away.

"It seems," the doctor said, "to be a form of hysteria. It may help the diagnosis, Mr. Lorin, if you would tell me the apparent cause."

"I was only here a few moments before it happened, Doctor. I flew down from New York this evening, and taxied out here."

"When you first saw her did she seem upset in any way?"

Dake was laughing inwardly. It was unpleasant laughter. Try to tell this neat fussy little man the truth and he would have you wrapped up and labeled for delivery to one of the state institutions, despite the shortage of beds and treatment for the insane. The spiraling curve of psychosis during the past fifteen years had altered the admission requirements. Potential violence seemed to be the only remaining criterion. The milder species of manic-depressive, psychopathic personalities, schizos, paranoids—all roamed the streets, lost in their ritualistic fantasies. There had been a rebirth of that dark ages belief that to give money to the mad is one of the doorways to grace. Membership in the most marginal cults was, to many, an accepted release for obsession.

"She did not seem upset," Dake said. "It seemed to happen quickly."

The doctor turned to Molly. "Has she been herself lately?"

"Yes, sir." Soft voice that trembled.

He looked at the maid and knew she would say nothing. The doctor sighed and looked at his watch again. "You aren't much help, either of you. Miss Togelson has always impressed me as a very strong personality. This is rather . . . shocking, from a personal point of view. Neither of you know what she meant with all that babbling about skulls?"

Dake saw the maid shudder. He said, "Sorry, no."

"I'll be off then."

"Could you give me a lift, Doctor, if you're heading downtown?"

"Come along."

As they went onto the porch Dake heard the maid slide the locks on the big door. As they got into the car he saw the lights coming on in room after room. Molly would want a lot of light around her. She would want the night to be like day.

The doctor drove with reckless casual impatience. "Where are you going, Mr. Lorin?"

"I checked luggage at the CIJ downtown terminal."

"I'll drop you at the door."

"Can I phone you tomorrow to find out about Miss Togelson?"

"In the afternoon."

The doctor let him out and started up almost before Dake had slammed the car door. He went into the brightly lighted terminal. Two large groups of Indian tourists were chatting, laughing. Their women wore saris heavily worked with gold and silver. They gave him a quick incurious glance. They came from a hard, driving, ambitious and wealthy land. It was fashionable to tour the bungling rattle-trap Western world. So quaint, my dear. But the people! So incredibly lethargic. And so excitingly vulgar. Naturally we owe them a debt—I mean this is the country where modern mass production methods originated, you know. In fact, we used to import their technicians, send our young people to their engineering schools. Think of it! But of course we've improved tremendously on all of their techniques. Tata set up the first completely automated steel mill. I suppose the war *did* exhaust these people terribly. We don't know how lucky we are that Pak-India has never been a bomb target. And we're strong enough so that it never will be. You heard President Lahl's latest speech, of course. Any overt act will be punished a thousandfold. That made Garva and Chu and Fahdi sit up and take notice.

9

DAKE TOOK HIS LUGGAGE TO A NEARBY HOTEL, REGISTERED, HAD a late supper and went up to his room. He was unpacking his toilet articles when the bellhop arrived with the typewriter.

"It doesn't look like much, sir, but the assistant manager says it's in good shape." He carried it over to the desk by the window and set it down.

"I didn't order a typewriter sent up."

The bellhop was a chinless and earnest young man. He gave Dake an uneasy smile. "I suppose that's some kind of a joke, Mr. Lorin. I guess I don't get it."

"What do you mean?"

"Well, I was in here ten minutes ago when you sent for a boy, and you told me you wanted a typewriter. I mean, if it's a gag, I don't get it."

Before the episode with Patrice, Dake knew he would have objected strenuously. He would have phoned the manager and asked if this was a new method of gouging the guests. He would have demanded that the typewriter be taken away.

But the world was altering in some obscure way. A brassy little wench had talked imaginatively of the delusion of reality. Half a death's head in a mirror. A woman mad from fright. A fingernail. Fundamentally he was a man of curiosity. A reporter. He could not ignore the objective questions triggered by subjective experience.

He tipped the boy. "Not a very good joke, I guess."

The boy sighed. "Thanks, sir. You had me worried there for a minute. I wondered if I was going nuts. Good night, sir."

The boy closed the door after him. Dake stood in the middle of the room, rubbing his chin. This, like every other damnable thing that had happened, had two aspects. The other side of the coin was that he *had* requested a typewriter. Insanity. Delusion. But

Molly and Patrice had seen something. Could that be objective proof? Only, he thought, if he could prove to himself that he had gone to her house and what he imagined had happened had actually happened. He went quickly to the phone. It took twenty minutes to get the hospital. Phone service had changed over the years from a convenience to an annoying irritant.

The girl at the hospital switchboard answered at last.

"Do you have a patient there, recently admitted? A Miss Patrice Togelson?"

"Just a moment, sir. I'll check."

He waited. She came back on the line and said, "Yes, sir. She was admitted about three hours ago. She is resting comfortably, sir."

"Thank you."

He hung up, sat on the edge of the bed, lit a cigarette. All right. Take it another step. How do I prove I made that call, and prove I talked to the girl at the hospital switchboard? The call will appear on my bill. Yet, when I see it noted on the bill, how do I know I am actually seeing it?

There was a stabbing pain centered behind his eyes, a pain so sudden and intense that it blinded him. He closed his eyes and opened them again, aware of an abrupt transition, aware that time had passed. Instead of being seated on the bed, he was seated in front of the desk. A dingy sheet of hotel stationery was rolled into the typewriter. Several lines had been typed.

Dake read them mechanically. "To whom it may concern: When Darwin Branson died I saw that I could use his death to my own advantage. I saw a way I could put myself back in the public eye. I had worked for Darwin Branson for a full year, but his assigned task had been to make a detailed survey of State Department policy decisions. He was not engaged in any way in secret negotiations.

"The article I wrote for the *Times-News* was a ruse. No such agreements were made. I had the plan of writing the article in order to help promote world unity. I realize now that it was a delusion of grandeur. I realize now that the article will have the reverse effect from what I had planned. I feel that at the time I wrote the article I was not responsible for my actions.

"The only way I can make amends is to write this full confession and then proceed to . . ."

It stopped there. The sudden time transition seemed to leave him numbed, unable to comprehend. The words seemed meaningless. He moved his lips as he read it again, much like a child trying to comprehend an obscure lesson in a textbook.

"No!" he said thickly.

The pain again focused behind his eyes, but not as intensely as before. It was almost as though it were coming to him through some shielding substance. It made his vision swim, but it did not black him out entirely. There was a pulsating quality to it, a strength that increased and diminished, as though in conflict.

He tried to keep his hands at his sides, but they lifted irresistibly to the keys of the typewriter. A new word. ". . . take . . ."

He held his hands rigid. Sweat ran down the side of his throat. Two hard clacks as his fingers hit the keys. ". . . my . . ."

The feeling of combat in his mind, of entities battling for control, was sharp and clear. He did not feel that he was fighting with any strength. He was something limp, helpless, being pushed and pulled at the same time.

". . . own . . ."

His hands flexed, the knuckles crackling.

". . . life."

And again, without temporal hiatus, his pen was in his hand, his signature already scrawled at the foot of the sheet, the sheet out of the typewriter. Blackout, and he was at the window, one long leg over the sill, the window flung high, sharp October night breathing against his face, an enclosed court far below, a few lighted windows across from him, like watchful eyes.

Conflict crescendoed in his mind and was suddenly gone. Emptiness. He straddled the sill, motionless. No more pushing and pulling. Easy now to let go. Easier than trying to find answers to problems. Easier than fighting insanity. Let go and spin slowly down through the whispering night, down by the lighted windows, down to that final answer. He heard himself make a sniggling sound, a drunken giggle. He sensed the impending rupture of his brain. A bursting of tissues. His hand tightened on the sill. Come

now, God of darkness. Take your tired child. Find the dark land
father, hanging in the stone cell of eternity, turning slowly with
blackened face. Find the wife who one instant was warmth, and
now lives forever in the heart of the whiteness hotter than the
sun.

But . . . WHY?

Drop with question unanswered? Fall to the smash of bone on
stone and never know why?

His mind wheeled for one insane instant and focused on WHY.
Big letters, the color of flame, written on the black night. Never
knowing was more horrid than continuing the conflict, the distortion of reality.

He released his hold and fell into the room, fell with a slack-
muscled helplessness, his head thudding on the rug. He lay on his
back and grasped his hard thighs with long-fingered hands, sensing the fibrous nerves, meaty tissues, churn of blood. He tasted
his aliveness with his hands, content not to think for a little while.
The drapery moved with the night wind. The wind cooled the
sweat on his face. He heard the faraway city sound. Not like the
roaring burly sounds of the old days. The cities had thinner
sounds now. A lost and lonely scream was a part of each night.

Dake sat up slowly, feeling as though hallucination had drained
his strength. He hitched closer to the window, wanting to close it.
The sash was out of his reach, yet he did not quite dare stand to
reach it. He hitched over, stood up, leaning against the wall. He
reached one hand over, blindly, slid the sash down with a shatter-
ing bang. He turned his heavy shoulders against the wall.

In front of him was an evanescence, the faintest silvery
shimmer. It was much like that first warning flicker of migraine,
dread shining blindness.

And Karen Voss stood there, brown hair tousled, thumb tucked
pertly in the wide belt, luminous gray eyes full of pale concern
and sassy arrogance. He drew his lips back flat against his teeth
and made a small sick sound in his throat and tried to reassure
himself by passing his hard arm through the vision. His wrist
struck the warm roundness of her shoulder, staggering her.

"Don't try to explain things to yourself," she said quickly. Her
voice was tense. "Got to get you out of here." She stepped

quickly to the desk, snatched up the typed confession, ripped it quickly. She looked over her shoulder at him. "I hate to think of how many credits I'm losing. Start drooling and babbling and prove I'm wrong."

Dake straightened his shoulders. "Go straight to hell," he said thickly.

She studied him for a moment, head tilted to one side. She took his wrist, warm fingers tightening, pulling him toward the door. "I remember how you must feel. I'll break some more rules, now that I've started. You're expected to go mad, my friend. Just keep remembering that. And don't."

At the door she paused. "Now do exactly as I say. Without question. I kept you from going out that window."

"What do you want?"

"We're going to try to get out of here. The competition is temporarily . . . kaput. If we get separated, go to Miguel. You understand? As quickly as you can."

He felt her tenseness as they went down all the flights of stairs to the lobby, went out into the night. "Now walk fast," she said.

Down the block, around the corner, over to Market. She pulled him into a dark shallow doorway.

"What are we . . ."

"Be still." She stood very quietly. In the faint light of a distant streetlamp he could see that her eyes were half shut.

Suddenly she sighed. "The competition is no longer kaput, Dake. They've got an idea of direction."

An ancient car meandered down the potholed street, springs banging, engine making panting sounds. It swerved suddenly and came over to the curb and stopped. A gaunt, raw-looking man stepped out, moving like a puppet with an amateur handling the strings. He went off down the sidewalk, lifting his feet high with each step.

"Get in and drive it," Karen said, pushing impatiently at him. He cramped his long legs under the wheel. She got in beside him. He drove down the street, hearing behind them the frantic yawp of the dispossessed driver.

She called the turns. They entered an area of power failure, as dark as one of the abandoned cities.

"Stop here and we'll leave the car," she said.

They walked down the dark street. She stepped into an almost invisible alley mouth. "Wait," she said.

Once again she was still. He heard her long sigh. "Nothing in range, Dake. Come on. North Seventh is a couple of blocks over. Bright lights. Crowds. That's the best place."

"It's a bad place to go. For a couple."

"We're safe, Dake."

"What did you do to that man in the car?"

She didn't answer. Her high heels clacked busily in double time to his long stride. They came to streetlights again. Brown hair bounced against the nape of her neck as she walked.

"What did you people do to Branson?"

Again she refused to answer.

"If you *are* people," he said with surly emphasis. "I don't care about your . . . motivations. I won't forgive what was done to Patrice."

"Please shut up. Stop grumbling."

Two men appeared suddenly out of the shadows, a dozen paces ahead. Dake stopped at once, turned and glanced quickly behind them, saw the others there, heard the odd whinnying giggle of a mind steeped in prono, anticipating the sadist fury. Karen had kept on walking. He caught her in two strides, hand yanking on her shoulder.

She spun out of his grasp. He gasped and stared at the two men. They had turned into absurd dolls, leaping stiff-legged in grotesque dance, bellowing in fright and pain. One rebounded off the front of a building, caught crazy balance and rebounded again. The other pitched headlong into the gutter and rolled onto his back and began banging his heels against the pavement, arching his back. Dake could think of nothing but insects which had blundered into a cone of light which had blinded them, bewildered them, driven them frantic with heat and pain. Behind them the other men bounded and bucked and sprawled. Karen did not change her pace. He caught up with her. She gave him a sidelong gamin grin, a squint of ribald humor in the glow of streelights.

"Dance of the pronies," she said.

"And there is no point, I suppose, in asking you . . . what did that?"

"Why not? A headache. A rather severe one. It gave them something to think about. Like this."

He staggered and clapped his palm hard over the lance of pure flame that ran from temple to temple, a rivulet of fire. It stopped his breath for a moment. And it was gone as quickly as it had come. There was no lingering pain. But the memory of pain was almost as hurtful as the pain itself.

She took his hand. "You'd be much more difficult, Dake. Prono makes mush of them. Soft, sticky little brains. Like wet glue. We'll go over there to that place. A breathing spell. I've got to think how I can get us back to New York."

The fleng joint was a slow cauldron of mass desperation. Prono and fice, and fleng strip routines, and the gut-roil of the kimba music, and the rubbery walls like white wet flesh. During the Great Plague in London, man, obsessed by dissolution, had made an earnest attempt to rejoin the slime from which he had once come. Now the plague was of the spirit, and the effect was the same. They pushed their way through to a lounging table, and waved away the house clowns, refused a cubicle ticket, managed to order native whisky. She put her lips, with their heavy make-up, close to his ear.

"We're going to separate here, Dake. That will be the best way. I could try to help you get to Miguel, but they can find me easier than they can you. I'll be more harm than help."

"And if I don't want to get to Miguel?"

"Don't be such a fool. It isn't a case of wanting. If you don't get there, you'll die. Maybe you want to do that. If you want to die, then I'm wrong about you."

He turned toward her and saw the sudden panic change her face. Though her lips did not move, and he was certain she had not spoken, her words were clear in his mind, coming with a rapidity that speech could not have duplicated.

"I didn't do as well as I thought: A Stage Three picked us up. Coming in the door over there. The man with the long red hair. I'm going to distract him. Leave as quickly as you can and don't pay any attention to anything. Understand? Anything! No matter how crazy it looks to you. Go to Miguel as quickly as you can and . . . be careful when you get there. You'll be safe once you're in the lobby. But the street out in front will be dangerous. Be very careful. Go now. Hurry!"

He slid from the table and plunged toward the door. A small man with a wooden look on his face hopped up onto one of the show platforms and dived at the sick-looking man with the long red hair. A woman screeched and raced at the red-haired man. Dake felt a surge of terror so strong that he knew, somehow, that it had been induced in his brain by Karen to give him more speed, more energy.

The red-haired man was twisting in a knot of people who oddly fell away from him, as though all interest in him were suddenly lost. Dake burst through the door and found himself running with others. Running with a pack of others. And he saw that they were all himself. He saw a dozen Dake Lorins bursting from the door, running in all directions, and he screamed as he ran, screamed and looked back over his shoulder as he screamed, saw the red-haired one stand on the sidewalk and then topple as someone dived against his legs. He ran silently then, lifting his long legs, running until white pain burned his side and scorched his lungs. He slowed and walked, struggling for breath, his knees fluttering, sweat cold on his body.

The cabdriver was reluctant. He said he didn't make trips like that. He yielded to two arguments—Dake's strangling arm across his throat and the thousand-rupee note in front of his eyes. Dake took the man's gun and shoved it inside his belt. Dawn wasn't far away as they turned into the only tunnel to Manhattan that had not become flooded and unusable through neglect. In the city the white police trucks were collecting the bodies of those who had died violently in the night. Dake felt caked and dull and old, worn dry with emotional hangover. They went through the dark streets in those predawn hours when life is at its lowest ebb—the hours of aimless regrets, of the sense of waste, of the knowledge of death. The October stars wheeled in a corrosive indifference to all the works of man. The city slept . . . restlessly.

MINDFUL OF KAREN'S LAST WARNING, HE HAD THE DRIVER STOP two blocks from the above-ground lobby of the apartment dwelling where Miguel lived. He gave the man the thousand-rupee note, returned his gun. The man gave him a surly nod, made a screeching U-turn, reckless of his precious tires, drove back downtown, single red eye blinking as the rough road surface joggled a loose connection.

Dake moved with instinctive animal caution, staying on the darker side of the street, stepping lightly and quickly through patches of faint radiance. The above-ground lobby was lighted. He could see the head of the desk clerk bent over a book on the high desk. The soft light of the lobby made a semicircle of radiance that reached almost to the midpoint of the road.

Dake waited for a time in the shadows, oddly restless, and then walked out boldly, heading directly across the street for the doors. His heels were loud on the asphalt. He heard a faint scuffing noise in the shadows behind him and to his left. He did not turn, but lengthened his stride. The area of light was two steps away. He took another long stride and was caught there, motionless. Something had clamped down on volition, something that held him as though, in an instant, he had been turned to ice, or stone. He could not change even the direction of his sight. The clerk was just off his center of vision. He saw the head lift abruptly. He moved then, taking a long step backward with infinite unwilled stealth. Another step.

Miguel Larner appeared suddenly, just inside the doors. Dake had not seen where he had come from, or how. The man wore a pair of florid pajamas. He stood very still. A stranger appeared behind him, another beside him, and a tall woman appeared over near the desk. The five persons inside the bright lobby stood and watched him. They were fifty feet away. He could see no expression on their faces, but their eyes seemed bright, feral. He was aware of how alien they were. They emanated a tangible coldness.

Something behind him was frightened. He could taste fright that nibbled at the edges of his mind. A hard compression of force erupted into his brain. It sucked him forward, running with a vast awkwardness, a shamble-legged, slack-armed lunge that took him stumbling across the sidewalk, diving for the doors that flicked open barely in time, to let him slide and roll on the slick floor, to thud against the base of the desk as the woman stepped lightly out of the way. He sat up. They had all moved closer to the door. They filed out and stood in a row on the sidewalk. On the far side of the street something flounced and rolled and made guttural sounds in the darkness. They all came back in. Miguel Larner came over to Dake. His eyes were vast and hung in pure velvet blackness, unsupported. There was nothing else in the world but the eyes of Miguel Larner. Little fingers pried under the edge of Dake's soul and flipped him. He fell off the edge into blackness.

It was a cloudless spring morning by Miguel's dioramic pool. Dake shut his eyes again. He remembered a time long ago. Eight years old. He had seen the overhead lights of the operating room. Then heard a hollow echoing voice in his head, saying, as though in a long tunnel, "mmmm-*gas!* mmmmm-*gas!* mmmmm-*GAS!*"

And then the bleary awakening—the over-large faces of his parents looking down at him on the bed—big faces suspended at odd angles. "How do you feel?" A voice that echoed down a long empty tunnel.

He opened his eyes again. He was on a gay beach chair by the pool. Miguel and a stranger looked at him with that cold sobriety, that extra-human speculation he had seen in the lobby— how long ago? A year, or a minute.

Miguel's lips moved. "Mr. Lorin. Mr. Merman."

"How do you do." Dake wanted to let loose crazy laughter at the quaintness of the formality. He trapped the laughter in his throat.

Merman had a boy's face, an old man's eyes.

"You did well," Miguel said, "to get in range of Johnny. Otherwise Karen's rather pathetic little exhibition of stubbornness would have been quite pointless. They've brought her in. She wants to see you. I'll call her. Don't speak to her."

No answer seemed necessary. Miguel gave Merman a quick sharp look and nodded. Dake had the idea they were communicating with each other. Karen came out to the pool, stood on the apron at the far side of the pool and looked at Dake. He was shocked at the change in her. Her face was wan and pinched, and her eyes were enormous. Her mouth had a trembling, old-lady uncertainty about it, and her fingers plucked at the edges of her grubby skirt. Two things seemed mingled inextricably in her eyes. A keen, warm, personal interest in him, and also a look of confused dullness—the look sometimes seen in the eyes of a dog beaten once too often.

Miguel nodded at her and she turned and left, walking aimlessly, shaking her head, saying something to herself that Dake could not understand.

"What happened to her?" Dake asked.

"I'll tell you, but just remember it, don't try to understand it. Later . . . if you are more than I think you are, understanding will catch up with you. Remember this. Two screens badly torn. The third screen bruised. She'll be a long time healing, relearning, readjusting. She'll be a long time here, Dake Lorin."

"What is this all about?" Dake asked. He had a sense of futility as he asked the question. Miguel Larner went over to the pool, sat and dangled his legs in the water, his bare brown back toward Dake. Dake looked toward the young-old face of Merman. His eyes veered suddenly toward something that had moved on the stones of the terrace. A tiny column of little naked savage figures snake-danced their way toward his ankles. Four-inch figures with animal faces. Their tiny cries were like the cries of insects. He instinctively snatched his feet up into the chair. They swarmed up the chair legs.

The memory of Karen's voice came to him across present horror. "You're expected to go mad, my friend. Just keep remembering that. And don't."

He shut his eyes and slowly lowered his feet to the floor. He felt them running across his clothing, plucking at him, prodding, pinching. They clambered up his chest, up his face, entangled tiny fists in his hair and swung themselves up. He opened his eyes and he was in utter blackness. He was naked. A long cold something coiled its way slowly across his foot. He set his teeth in his lower lip and did not cry out or move. He fell to hot bright yellow sand. Fat spiders skittered across the sand. He looked more closely and saw that they were dismembered human hands, standing tall and agile on plump fingers, circling him with quick darts of movement. Two of them struggled toward him, dragging something, dragging, he saw, Karen's head, the spider fingers scrubbling in the sand with the effort. A shadow crossed him. He turned and looked up, squinting at a featureless sky. Something hung there. A figure so huge that it reduced him to the size of an insect. A rope encircled its neck, extending out of sight into the sky. The huge figure turned slowly. He looked up into the purpling bloated face of his father. He turned, ready to run whooping through all the yellow sand of eternity, ready to run with bulged eyes until blood burst his throat. He dropped to his knees on the sand. He covered his eyes. He sensed the ancient brain scar, felt it swell and tear slightly and then knit itself, fiber clasping fiber, compacting into strength. He stood up and turned and looked calmly up at the vast naked face. Spiders scuttled off into the sand waste. Coils moved off into darkness. The bitter little insect squeakings faded into an utter silence.

Miguel's bare brown back appeared and the sand faded around it, faded into terrace and pool and the still spring morning of the diorama.

Miguel turned and looked at him over the brown shoulder, smiled. "It seems I must be proven wrong occasionally."

"I'll never break," Dake said, not knowing why he had selected those words.

"Merman will show you the way."

He followed Merman. The rock slid aside. The glowing tunnel shafted down through bedrock. Three cubes of a fatty gray that was no color at all stood in a rough cavern hollowed out of the rock. The radiance in the cavern had an almost radioactive look.

Merman turned to Dake. The boyish lips did not move. "You are going to a place where you will be trained. You will accept training eagerly, because you want to turn it against us. That is to be expected. You wonder what we are. You will not learn that until you are skilled."

An orifice slit opened in the side of one of the ten-foot cubes. He edged through the opening. The cube, except for a small triple row of studs near the opening, was featureless. Merman reached through the opening, touched a stud, stepped back quickly. The slit closed. Light came through the cube walls. He looked at Merman as though looking through water. Long ago, in his mother's kitchen, he had delighted in using an object called an egg slicer. Place a hardboiled egg in the cupped place, and pull the handle down slowly. Tiny wires sliced through the egg.

This was that egg slicer, and it happened in the space of a tenth of a heartbeat. A billion wires. Each one sliced neatly through his body. The pain Karen had given him was, by comparison, a tiny pinch, a nip of the flesh.

And the pain was gone, the orifice partially open. His one desire was to get out of that cube as quickly as humanly possible. He was caught in the yielding slit for a moment, and then tumbled free, thinking he was on the floor of the cavern. A sky of such a pallid blue as to be almost white burned overhead, deepening in color toward the horizons. He was on hands and knees on a featureless metallic plain. Around him was a matrix of the gray cubes arranged in painfully perfect geometric design, all joined by gleaming metal tubes. His cube was joined to its neighbors, as were the others. He stood up, and his feet left the metallic surface in an awkward little jump. Here and there cubes were missing from the pattern, leaving the tube ends raw and naked. It was oddly disturbing to see the design incomplete, as though looking at a lovely woman with several front teeth missing.

Low against the horizon off to his right two small moons hung clear in the sky, one slightly larger than the other. The sun overhead had a redness about it that altered the shadows of the cubes and tubes, giving them a burned look.

Far across the metallic plain rose the gigantic trees of childhood, and near the bases of them, dwarfed by their size, he could see the low black buildings to which he must walk. He knew he had to go there. He did not know how he knew. It had the inevitability of a dream compulsion. Strangely, he felt acceptance in him. This was not his world. This was not his planet or his system. He knew that if night came he would see unthinkable constellations. He threaded his way through the geometric maze of cubes, stepping over the low tubes that joined them. He came to the open plain and walked toward the buildings. He tried to hurry and found that the best pace was a long gliding step. There was no rebellion, no questioning of reality. He was *here* and it was very necessary to get to the black buildings, and very necessary to learn what had to be learned, and acquire the skills that must be acquired. There would be only one chance.

They came out of the buildings and he was but mildly aware of his own odd lack of curiosity about them. There was merely a sense that some of them were learning, as he would learn, and some of them taught, and some of them ran the machines for teaching.

All of them, men and women, and the odd-looking non-men, and non-women, wore only heavy skirt-like garments that extended to mid-thigh. They chattered in strange tongues, and some spoke awkward English, and some spoke good English. He was herded quickly into a room, stripped, scorched with a harsh spray of some astringent liquid, given a garment and hurried along into another place where he was measured by a pair of violet-eyed non-women, whose faces were subtly wrong, whose movements were curiously articulated in a quite unexpected fashion. He knew, somehow, that it was measurement that they did. As they swung the little burring heads of the glowing equipment down over his body, as he felt the chitter and nibbling, and saw the smooth gray plates dropping into the trough near the wall, he sensed that every grain, fiber and atom of him was being measured and remembered and recorded. He cooperated like an automaton. Like a man who has gone to the same barber for so many years that he has learned to move his head to exactly the right angle at exactly the right time. He suffered the wheel and blackout of the ribbands that encircled his head, the electronic cluckings of the little plates that sucked against his temples.

Cleaned and dressed and measured and recorded and remembered, he was sent alone down a corridor. He turned in at an open doorway, knowing that it was the right doorway. The door banged down behind him like a guillotine, and automatonism left him at once. He guessed that it was a feeling of suddenly being released from post-hypnotic influence. There was the same fear, the same uncertainty.

The girl stared at him. She had dark tangled hair, broken fingernails, a hard bold bright light in her eyes. Her garment was a livid orange that went well with the slender brown of her dusky body. The room walls were cocoa brown, rounded at the corners, featureless. There was light, without visible light source.

She spoke to him in a harsh tongue, her voice rising at the end of the phrase in a question.

He shook his head. "I don't understand." She tried again, slowly. He shrugged. She made an obscene gesture with her hands, spat on the floor toward his feet, turned her back.

He stared at the simple furnishings of the sealed room, the rigid cots, the two chairs, the single table.

"You have been placed together because you cannot understand each other's language."

The voice seemed to have its origin inside his head. He saw the girl wheel, look for the source of the voice, and he knew that she heard it too.

"This room is so constructed that it aids the projection and reception of thought. When you have learned to give your thoughts to each other, you will find that together you can open the door."

The voice stopped. They looked speculatively at each other. He looked into her eyes and tried to will her to go to the table and sit at one of the chairs. He made the command clear in his mind. She was staring hard at him. She suddenly shrugged and turned away, and he guessed that she had been trying to will some message into his brain. He had neither projected nor received. It was going to be far more difficult than he had imagined. He tried to think of some simple way they could experiment.

At last he took her arm and pulled her over to one of the chairs. She sat down, scowling at him, obviously disliking being touched. He sat in the other chair so that they faced each other across the table. He bit off a sizable fragment of fingernail, showed it to her. She looked puzzled. He put his hands behind him, transferred it to his left hand, and then placed both fists on the table.

"Left," he thought. "Left hand."

She reached out and tentatively touched his left hand. He showed her the bit of nail and she beamed at him, clapped her hands. Then, after many more attempts, they both became depressed. She was correct six out of ten times, then seven out of twelve, and then eleven out of twenty. He tried each time to push the thought into her mind. It was much like being under water and trying to push against a huge stone. One could kick weakly, but there was no pivot place. No place to brace the feet. No way to put force behind the effort.

He was pleased to see that she had a determination and tenacity that matched his own. Her small jaw was set hard with the effort. She took the fragment of nail and tried. He strained to hear her thoughts, found that he was only guessing, operating solely on hunches. They worked at it with stubborn energy until they were exhausted. His despair was transformed into anger at her. He could not succeed because they had given him this fool girl. Anyone else but this ignorant wench with the hot eyes and the gypsy manners.

He looked into her dark eyes and glowered at her. He backed slowly within his mind until he had a place where he could seem to brace himself. As though he had his shoulders against a thin hard membrane an inch in back of his eyes.

You're too stupid.

Her hard brown hand flashed and caught him across the mouth. She half stood up with blazing eyes and then slowly sank back into the chair, looking a bit awed.

He found the same place within his mind to brace himself and tried this time, forcibly, yet without anger. *Nod your head if you can understand me.*

She nodded her head violently, white teeth gleaming in the dusky face.

Stand up and then sit down again. She obeyed like a chastened child, demure and obedient. He found that even that short practice enabled him to do it with more ease.

You must learn, too. I found it by accident. He touched his temple. *Imagine a thin hard wall in here. You must back against it to . . . be braced. And then you must . . . throw your thought from that position, thinking of each word.*

She frowned at him. She raised her eyebrows in question.

I heard nothing. Try again.

There was a black flame in the depths of her eyes. *You are a big arrogant clown.*

I got that clearly. Try again.

She flushed. *It was anger. Anger made it easier.*

I should have told you that. How did you come here?

A man took me to a large villa. There were other men. I saw frightful visions. They tortured my mind. I was put in a big gray box. It brought me here.

Do you know why you are here?

I am aware that there are things which must be learned. This is one of them. There will be others. This way of talking makes one weary. There is the matter of the door. It was said to us that together we could open it. Yet there is no latch.

When I snap my fingers we will both speak to the door the way we have spoken to each other, as strongly as possible, saying but one word. Open.

They both looked toward the door. He snapped his fingers. He could feel her projected thought blending with his own. The door slid slowly up out of sight into the groove overhead.

She reached the door first, ran through, and then turned and walked, docile and mild, down the corridor.

As soon as he reached the corridor, he felt the automaton will overcome his own. It turned him in the opposite direction.

A huge man who reminded him of a brown bear stepped out of a doorway to bar the hallway.

My congratulations. That was very rapid. You are a latent. Some have remained in that room for a thousand hours. Project to me. It is called para-voice.

Dake found it much harder to manage outside the room. The rigidity against which he tried to brace himself was softer, more yielding.

It was easier in the room.

"It always is. But I could receive you. We will use normal voice now. Para-voice is tiring. You will be given practice hours from time to time."

The big man took Dake's arm. Dake willed himself to pull away, but could not. He allowed himself to be led down the corridor.

"This place is called Training T. I have been here for twice your lifetime. It is work that pleases me best. Now we have our little surprise for you. The technicians found your best memory, my boy. It is ready now. You have not slept in years, you know. Not really slept. Too much conflict in your mind. Here you must sleep. Drugs are not effective. Only true sleep will heal your mind, my boy."

They came to a big door that was oddly familiar, ringing a tiny chime in the back of his weary mind.

The big brown man turned the old-fashioned knob and the door swung inward, as Dake had known it would. Dake walked into his room and the man closed the door softly behind him.

It was his room. His bed. The lamp was on over his bed. It had been a plain parchment shade, and one day he had found the silhouette of a sailing ship in a magazine. His mother had helped him cut out the hard parts. The room was in perfect scale to him. Perfect scale for an eight-year-old boy. Familiar pattern of the rag rug. The stain where he had spilled the grape juice. Place where he had crayoned the wall through the bars of the crib. No crib now. The big soft bed, with the pillows starched and white. The bed was turned down, and the flannel pajamas were laid out, where Mother always put them. Faded blue pajamas with a faint white stripe. Slippers with the heels all broken down and a lot of the lamb's wool worn off.

He undressed and put his clothes on the same chair as always and put on the pajamas and pulled the string tight at his waist and tied it. He shoved his feet into the slippers and went through the other door to the bathroom. He had to reach high to get his battered toothbrush with the chipped pink handle. The big tub had feet like white claws that clasped white porcelain spheres. Those tub feet had always fascinated him. He scrubbed his knuckles because there probably wouldn't be much time in the morning before school. The mirror was too high. He couldn't see his face unless he pulled the stool over and stood on it. But he was too sleepy for the interesting game of making horrid faces at yourself. The worst one was when you put your fingers in the corners of your mouth and pulled.

He padded back into his bedroom, closing the bathroom door behind him. He looked at his books and ran his fingers over the backs of the bindings. He opened a cigar box and looked at the shells he'd collected at Marblehead last summer. He turned out the light and went over to the window and opened it. He knelt for a time with his chin on the sill and looked out. Boston lighted the sky. He could see the familiar single streetlight across the backyards. It was haloed with soft snow. Snow was falling in Chelsea, sticking to the bare branches of the big elm in the back yard.

Somebody in the neighborhood had Christmas carols on the radio. He wondered if he'd get the bike. They said it was too dangerous in the street, and the police wouldn't let you ride on the sidewalk. Heck, you could be careful, couldn't you?

He crossed the dark room, knelt for the barest minimum of prayer, and scrambled up between the crisp sheets, nestling down, pulling the blankets up over him. A red bike. Joey's was blue.

He yawned and turned onto his side, warm and certain in the knowledge that after he was asleep his mother would look in, tuck the blankets in, kiss him. He could hear Daddy down in the kitchen with some of his friends. He heard the low voices and then the rich explosion of baritone laughter, suddenly hushed. He guessed Mother was telling them not to make so much noise.

He banged at the pillow, turned onto his other side, and gently coasted down the long velvet slope on the magical red bike, into the deep sweet shadows of sleep.

He came vaguely awake when she came in, and he stirred at the touch of her lips. "You think I'll get it?"

"Get what, dear?"

Irritation at such density. "The bike. The red bike."

"We'll have to wait and see, won't we? Now go to sleep, dear."

Firm hand fixing the blankets. He was faintly aware of the tallness of her standing over him, the faint sweet scent of her. The floor creaked as she crossed to the window, closed it a little. Somewhere people were laughing in the night. She closed his door behind her as she left the room. She hummed to herself as she headed toward the stairs.

II

SCHOOL WAS GETTING HARDER ALL THE TIME. THAT DARN MISS Crowe. Always making it tough just before vacation. All the kids were excited about the Chinese invading Korea. He wished he'd been a Marine in Korea. Patrols. Fire fights.

That darn Miss Crowe. "Children, we are going to study projection." She wrote it on the board, spelling it as she wrote. "Now you all know what electricity is." She stepped to the front seats and tapped Joey on the head. She made that funny smile, like when she thinks her jokes are funny, and said, "Joseph's head is full of electricity. It's what he thinks with." The whole class laughed and Joey got red as a beet.

"But Joseph's electrical field is unorganized. Think of one of those big signs overlooking the Common. Now those signs spell out words. All the light bulbs light at once to spell out a word. If all those little light bulbs were flickering, going on and off without any order at all, we couldn't read the word, could we? Sometimes Joseph, by accident, makes all the little bulbs light at once, usually when he's very excited or upset, and then we can sometimes see his thoughts, not clearly of course, but enough to know for a split second what he is thinking. It happens so seldom, however, that we never recognize it as true projection. We call it a hunch, or a good guess. In projection we will all learn first how to make the words clear. And after we have made the words clear, then we will learn how to project real images. We'll project dogs and cats and new toys and everything we can imagine."

"A red bike?" Dake said without thinking.

Miss Crowe looked at him. "Yes, a red bike, Dake. But I shouldn't advise you to try and ride it." Everybody laughed at him and he got as red as Joey had been.

Maralyn, who was always asking questions and bringing junk to Miss Crowe, stuck her hand up.

"Yes, dear?"

"Miss Crowe, if all that goes on in somebody's head, how can somebody else see it?"

"It isn't exactly seeing, Maralyn. Joseph has energy in his brain. Projection is a case of learning to focus that energy. And because each of us uses the same sort of energy to do our thinking, Joseph can learn to focus it so strongly that he actually does our thinking for us."

"Suppose I don't want *him* doing my thinking for *me*," Maralyn said with contempt.

"As we are learning projection, dear, we will also learn how to close our minds against it."

Maralyn sat down, flouncing a little in the seat. Dake hated her.

Miss Crowe went back to her desk. Joey looked happy to have her stop tapping his head. It seemed to make him nervous.

"Now, class, this will be a little demonstration to show you what we will be able to do, every one of us, before summer vacation."

Dake liked that part. She just sat there looking at the class, and, gosh, she put songs in your head, and band music, and she made some poems, and then a whole lot of puppies came running in through the closed doors, and bright-colored birds flew around and made a heck of a racket. It was really keen the way she could do that.

But after that first day, the fun was all gone. It got dull and hard. Standing up there like a goof and trying to give the whole class some dopey word. Miss Crowe would write it on a piece of paper, write a lot of things on pieces of paper and you drew out your piece and it was always some dopey word. House, farm, cow, seashell, road, lamp, doctor. Never good words like bike, pirate, sloop, robber, pistol.

You had to practice at home, too, and Mother and Daddy could do it so much easier and better than you could that you felt like you'd never learn anything. He guessed it was important stuff, all right. Miss Crowe had cut out all the other subjects, and it was nothing but that projection, projection, all day long. She kept saying you had to learn it when your mind was young, or something.

Christmas came, and no red bike because it was too dangerous. There were skis, but it turned warm and there wasn't any snow. He horsed around with Joey most of the vacation and they projected stuff at each other, and he worked at trying to make a bike he could see, even if he couldn't ride it, like Miss Crowe said.

He got so he could make some stuff, but not a good bike. One afternoon he made a real sharp red bike, right in his room, but he couldn't hold on to it. It got shimmery and went away and he couldn't bring it back.

When school started again the whole class got so they could do the words loud and clear. Then there were little sentences. Kid stuff. I see the horse. The horse sees me. My uncle owns a cat. It has kittens. It sleeps in the barn. That Maralyn was a pain. She projected words so sharp they hurt your head and you wished there was some way you could put your fingers in your ears to stop the racket.

Next they got hard words. You want to do *cat* and you can think of a cat all right, but a word like *thought* or *religion* or *doubt*—it was tough to think of ways to put it across. But finally they all got that. And then they had to take turns going further and further down the hall and doing the hard sentences. Maralyn was the only one who could go way out in the school yard by the swings and still make you hear. It was pretty faint and you had to strain for it, but she could do it.

Next came learning how to shut it out. In order to push out the words you had to sort of brace yourself against a sort of imaginary membrane in your mind. Miss Crowe called that the "first screen." Finally they all got the trick of being able to sort of get that membrane around in front of your thoughts. You had to kind of slide through it and then hold it up in the way, and it blocked out all the projection. It sure was a relief to be able to stop hearing that screamy noise Maralyn could put in your head.

Miss Crowe said that because her mind was stronger, she could project right through your screen if she really poured on the coal, but that would hurt you and the screen would have to heal up before you could project or receive or anything. She said that she had four screens she could put up, one behind the other. She said that with all of them down, she could catch projections even when the person wasn't trying to project, provided they didn't have any screen up. She said that when they had all learned how to project and receive selectively, and could make images, and knew how to use the second screen, then they could all be called Stage One. To get to be a Stage Two like her and use all screens you had to really work at it. Gee, it looked as if school would last the rest of his life.

But it got to be sort of fun when they got so they could make the images. Illusions, Miss Crowe sometimes called them. It turned out Joey was better at it than Maralyn, and that sure scalded Maralyn. Joey had an animal book home, and one day he about startled Miss Crowe out of her wits by having a giant sloth hanging from the transom over the door to the classroom. Dake worked on the red bike until he could make it with no trouble. After a while it got dull, making the bike, so he made other things. But working on the bike had helped. He could make things almost as good as Joey could. Joey got in bad trouble, though, with Miss Crowe. He got his hands on a medical book with illustrations, and he kept making little tiny naked women running around when Miss Crowe wasn't looking, and Maralyn told on him. Miss Crowe said if he kept acting up, she'd burst his first screen and give him a long rest until he learned how to use his new skill. Her nose always got white when she got mad.

Dake made a great big dog that followed him around and only disappeared when he forgot it. Once in his room he made a boy that looked just like him, exactly, and that scared him a little. But it gave him new ideas. Once on the way home with Joey, he saw Maralyn and so he made a duplicate of her standing right in front of her, only Maralyn had her head under her arm. Maralyn went screaming into her house and told Miss Crowe the next day, and he got the word, just as Joey had. Then she gave the whole class a big dull lecture about misusing your talents and all that sort of thing. He and Joey could talk easy to each other in that para-voice, but it was funny how it seemed quieter and nicer to really talk, and say the words.

The big test came right before summer vacation, and each one of them had to go all alone up to the principal's office. A lot of funny-looking people were sitting around. Dake was pretty nervous. He had to talk in para-voice to each one of them separately, and then to the whole group and then to any two of them. Then he was told to screen himself and they pushed at the screen. They pushed so hard it hurt badly, but he didn't yell, and they didn't break the screen. He guessed they were just testing to see how strong it was. He had the feeling they could bust through in a minute if they wanted to. Next they made him lift the first screen and they pushed on the second one. He wasn't so sure of how to use the second one, and it was a different kind of pain, not quite as sharp, but worse somehow. Then he had to illusion up a bunch of stuff. From a list. It was pretty hard stuff. A little full moon the size of an apple, and a life-size army jeep, and his father and mother. They gave him a chance to fix up the illusions a little when they didn't look quite right. The jeep was the worst, because he couldn't remember how the front end was supposed to look, so it stayed a little bit misty until he put a Chevy front end on it.

They told him he'd passed and the big brown-looking man shook hands with him and he walked out to go back to the class. But he walked out into a long shining black corridor that he'd never seen before.

There was a funny twisty feeling in his brain and suddenly he remembered where he was. The room, the shell collection, the red bike he didn't get. They were all twenty-six long years ago. Joey had been dead for years. Maralyn had married Vic Hudson and gone to live in Australia. He desperately resented being drawn back up into life, out of the best years, the long golden endless years.

The big brown man took his arm.

"You did as well as I expected you to, Dake."

"Was it all . . ."

"Illusion? Of course. We find that if we regress the student to the happiest time of his life, before the world began to disappoint him, it increases his speed of receptivity. You've spent a great many weeks meeting each day with one of our better instructors and illusionists."

Dake felt as though the illusion of the lost years had somehow healed him, made him stronger and more certain.

"And now I have the abilities of a Stage One?"

"Just the mental abilities. There are some physical skills to learn."

"It seems to me like a crazy contradiction. You teach me something that, if you taught it to . . . everyone on earth, all the bad things would be erased. Hate, fear. No more conflict."

The man continued to walk him down the featureless corridor. "Quite true," he said mildly.

"Why isn't this knowledge used for good?"

"This answer may seem very indirect to you. But it is an answer. I am a failure. Too mild. Too sympathetic. I bleed from the heart too often, Dake. So I'm better off here."

"Indirect? It doesn't mean anything."

"Don't be impatient. You've graduated to one of the huts near the game fields. We've seen the last of you here . . . until next time."

"Where do I go?"

"Just go out that door. The instruction beam will pick you up. You'll find that you'll walk to exactly where you are supposed to go."

Dake walked across a field of spongy aqua-colored grass. He turned and looked back, saw the low black buildings, the grotesquely enormous trees, the metallic plain beyond with its intensely orderly arrangement of cubes. The brown man stood in the black doorway.

Good luck!

Dake lifted an arm, turned and went on, feeling only a complete certainty that he was headed in the right direction.

The huts ringed the enormous game fields. They were of the same featureless black of the larger buildings so far away that the big trees over them were on the far horizon. The huts were set far apart. There was a single communal building. The guiding influence led him directly to the communal building. On the far side of the game fields was a small group, too far away for him to see what they were doing. There were more of the violet-eyed non-human clerks in the communal building. They had a grotesque and peculiar grace of their own. The influence over him was not as strong as when he had first reported. His acceptance was not as automatic. And their attitude was different. They seemed servile, humble, overcourteous as several small objects were handed to him.

If it would please you, these objects should be taken to your hut. We cannot approach the huts or we would take them.

Which hut?

They all made thin sounds of pain, cringing before him.

Too strong, too strong. The words were sweet-singing in his brain. One of them moved carefully around him to the door, pointed. *That one, Earthling. Then you must join the others.*

He crossed to the hut, carrying the odd objects in his hands. The interior was stark. Bed, table, chair. He placed the objects on the table, fingered them curiously, joined the group at the far side of the game fields.

He counted them as he approached. Eleven. Some turned and looked toward him. He stopped abruptly as a stone-faced middle-aged woman appeared directly in front of him. Her expression was wise, sardonic, half-amused.

"Lorin, I see. Consider yourself a straggler. No one seems to organize things properly any more. Where is the Gypsy girl?"

"I haven't any idea."

"Meet your fellow sufferers."

She gave the names quickly as Dake faced the group. His glance moved across one lean tough masculine face, moved quickly back to it. "Tommy! Good Lord, I . . ." He took two steps toward the familiar man and then stopped suddenly, wary. He glanced toward the stone-faced woman who had called herself Marina.

"No, I'm not an illusion," Tommy said in his slow familiar drawl. He approached Dake, gripped his hand strongly. "Satisfy you?"

Marina said, "You may take a break, Watkins. Go off and gabble with your long-lost Dake Lorin."

They walked apart from the others. Dake covered his confusion by saying, "How long? Not since the war, is it? Last I heard you left the city desk and went to Florida to run some jerkwater newspaper, Tommy. I envied you. It seemed to be a good answer."

Are you thinking I have any answers to . . . all this?

Dake stared at him. *I was hoping as much.*

*And I'm hoping you have some answers. I don't know where
we are, how we got here, or whether you happen to be a figment
of my diseased imagination.*

Tommy dropped to the springy odd-colored grass and spoke
aloud. "Nobody else in the . . . ah . . . class has the vaguest
idea. See, we've got a couple of Chinese, and a Malay, and a pair
of Austrians. But no language problems, chum, in para-voice.
Sentence construction comes through a little strange sometimes.
We do a lot of chatting. So I can tell you just what happened to
you, Dake. You got mixed up in something-or-other, and so many
weird things were beginning to happen you thought you were
going off your rocker. So finally you found yourself in New York
or Madrid where they slapped you in a gray box and you tumbled
out here, and these characters began to teach you stuff that's patently impossible. Oh, we have long discussions. Many of them
about reality. Big question. Are we really here?"

Dake sat near him. "How did you get here?"

"Started to do a series on a guy doing some fantastic work in
agriculture. I began to get the weird idea somebody was guiding
him. Steering his mind for him. Clues led to a racketeer named
Miguel Larner in New York. Went to see Larner. He nearly
drove me crazy. Almost, but not quite. So here I am."

"Mine is about the same. I'll tell you about it later. Right now,
Tommy, what do we know? Somehow we got onto a different
planet. We've run into a culture and a technology far superior to
ours. They're training us to raise hell on earth."

"I go along with that, Dake. On the surface, an evil pitch. Underneath, I . . . don't know. There is something . . . terribly important that we don't know yet. When we know it, it will somehow explain everything. Ever dream you have discovered the
ultimate answer to everything and wake up with it just on the
edge of your mind?"

"What goes on here, at this place?"

"You get your hut and they organize your day like it was a
YMCA summer camp. Do this, do that. A few physical skills.
And mostly mental skills. They stretch hell out of your brain.
Memory, analysis, and so on. Things come back in a funny way. I
can replay from memory every chess game I ever played and

every bridge hand I ever held. A year ago that would have been a crazy thought. Right now we're struggling with something called a Pack B."

"What's that?"

"Something you'll have to experience for yourself, baby. Another thing. Have you ever had such an almost overpowering feeling of physical well-being?"

"I hadn't thought of it. I . . . guess not."

"Has air ever smelled as good, or food tasted as good? Every day seems like Saturday."

"You sound happy here. What have you done, Tommy? Found a home?"

Tommy gave him a bland look. "Maybe. I'm waiting for the great revelation. We all are." He stood up, looked soberly down at Dake for a moment. "Here is one clue to think over. We see quite a few people around who never came off earth. They're all manlike. Just funny variations here and there. All in the same general form, however. And, Dake, listen. Every single one of them treats us as though we were all little tin Jesuses. Come on. Join the group. Marina's ready to howl."

They rejoined the group. Marina formed them into a hollow circle. Practice in cooperative illusion, she said. Marina created the illusion—an exceptionally lovely girl who strolled around and around inside the formal circle. At any moment, just as the girl walked in front of you, Marina might cancel the illusion. It was up to the nearest student to recreate her so quickly and perfectly that there was barely any hiatus of nothingness. Dake was clumsy the first time. He saw that it had to be done in such a way that the stride was unbroken. The second time it happened directly in front of him he did better. A second girl joined the first and they walked hand in hand. And then a third. Marina made their costumes more intricate. She made them walk faster. It became an exhausting exercise in hair-trigger reflexes, in memorization and visualization of all details. After over an hour of it, Dake felt as though his head would burst.

There was food, and rest, and another session. Mass illusion this time. Create as many people as you can, to the outermost limitations of your resources, bearing in mind constantly that each individual thus created had to be remembered and concentrated on *in toto* or the illusion would become evanescent. At first Dake could handle no more than six. By the end of the session he had more than doubled it, and was rewarded with Marina's sour smile.

There were variations on those games day after day. At night the alien stars would pinpoint the sky with brightness. He spent the rare leisure hours with his friend, Watkins. They guessed and pondered and found no rational answer.

Apprehensive beings were brought to the game fields. They were not quite human when examined closely. They did not seem so much frightened as awed. And, using them as subjects, Marina taught the class the fundamentals of control. It required a more massive concentration of energy than para-voice, or illusioning, and it was most difficult to give proper neural directions. Even Marina could cause only an approximation of a normal walk, and balance was difficult to maintain. The controlled beings often fell onto the soft turf. Range was slowly increased, and when the class was adept, they were permitted to practice control on each other, being careful always to take both screens out of the way before accepting control. Dake found that he did not like the feeling of psychic nakedness that came when neither of his two mental screens protected him. After he had run Tommy awkwardly into the side of a hut when trying to control him through the door, Tommy had rubbed his bruised nose and said, "As a superman, kid, you're a waste of time."

It gave them a new description of their abilities. The supermen. The endowed ones. The little gods who would, they hoped, walk the earth. The best daydreams were about what could be done with the new abilities.

Tommy said, "Nobody has ever been able to get my brother-in-law off the bottle. I'm going to give that boy such a roomful of snakes and little pink elephants that he'll gag whenever he sees a liquor advertisement."

Dake said, "I'm going to control every Pak-Indian I meet. Make them drop to their knees before the Great Lorin."

"Seriously, Dake, what are we going to do with all these . . . talents?"

"We don't have to earn a living. Just control the cashier and have him hand you the money. Or give him an illusion of a few thousand rupees for deposit. He'll mark the book and when you walk out of the bank it will disappear out of the drawer."

"You have larceny in your heart."

"Tommy, I keep remembering a brown-haired girl named Karen Voss. I know now that she was trained here. Most of the things she bewildered me with, I think I could do. But she helped me get out of a bad spot, and somebody stronger than she has ripped her screens."

"Gives me a headache to think about it."

"Think a minute. Was the person who damaged her trained somewhere else? Are there two groups raising hell with each other? Is earth a battlefield? If so, we're just a couple of likely recruits."

"I'm not fighting anyone else's war," Tommy said firmly. "I had a dandy of my own once."

The next day, control was dropped and instruction in the Pack B's began again. Dake quickly learned the sequence of the control wheels and how to use them. Visualization was something else again. A hundred times he tried. A hundred times he tried to cover a distance of ten feet, and each time felt the sickening sensation of negative mass, and each time achieved plus mass in the exact place where he had started. Marina explained that the visualization of the intended destination had to be far stronger than the visualization required for illusioning. He would memorize each blade of grass, each irregularity of the earth, step back and try again. Tommy suddenly learned how. He was ecstatic with this new sense of freedom. He was obnoxiously ecstatic. He flicked about, endlessly, pausing only to wave derisively toward where Dake stood and struggled.

Dake tried again and again and again. And another failure. He was about to try again when he suddenly realized that he had covered the distance. He backed up and tried again. Slowly he discovered that the strength of the visualization was actually more important than the exactness of it. He set off after Tommy, slowly improving his skill.

For days the class played a mad game of tag around the huge game fields. Then they were taken into open country and permitted to use the full range of the Pack B. There were races across empty miles of landscape where the high trees formed the only reference points. They learned that you could visualize the face of a friend as though it were a yard in front of you, and then make the shift. If the friend was within range of your Pack B, you would suddenly appear in front of him. The sequence of days was confused. New skills, new abilities, and something else, too. A group pride.

In one of her rare informative moods Marina said, "Selection has to be a trial by fire. If you can be broken, you will break. None of you did. And thus we can be assured that you will not break in quite another way—that you will not begin to think that these new powers set you apart from mankind, that you will not misuse them for personal gain. We are called Earthling. It is a good title."

There was a day of pageant, of intense competition. The illusions were watched by vast crowds, who made sighing sounds of approval.

After the crowds had gone, Marina said, "There is nothing more I can teach you. There is only one last thing for you to learn. Those who are already on tour must instruct you in that. We will see you here twice again before you are . . . ready."

They went back to the long low black buildings of first instruction. They did not plod across the fields in the gray dusk. They flicked across the flat plains, appearing, disappearing, appearing further on. They projected to each other, writing the questioning words bright in each other's minds.

They were given rooms. In the middle of the night Dake was awakened. The clothes he had arrived in were waiting. He dressed on command, and was taken to the place of the cubes. Hard pain struck him. He clambered through the orifice into the rock cavern. He walked up the slanting glow of the tunnel and into Miguel Larner's dioramic garden. It was late afternoon. Karen sat alone, and she smiled at him.

He went to her quickly. He tried to project to her, to ask her if she was well. He felt the projected thought strike screens rigidly drawn, rebound as though from metal. The rebuff angered him.

"I suppose I report to Miguel," he said.

"He's gone, Dake. It was a very impressive funeral."

"Dead!"

"An illusion was buried. Miguel has . . . gone. He finished what he had to do. Martin Merman is in charge."

"Do I report to him?"

"He's not here. What gives you the idea you have to report to anybody?"

"I thought . . ."

"Go to the same room you were in before. Stay there until called."

12

DAKE WENT TO THE ROOM. HE FOUND CLOTHES THAT WOULD FIT him. He set the diorama on automatic control to give him an approximation of day and night. Food was brought at regular intervals. There was a projector, micro-books, music. He exercised to keep himself fit.

Stay there until called.

He had detected a warmth, a friendliness in her before. It had disappeared. He felt put-upon, neglected. And he was indignant.

At times he would drop both screens and listen, almost trembling with the effort to be receptive. He would get merely the vague awareness of others somewhere near him. No thoughts ever came through.

One evening she tapped lightly at the door, came in, unasked, and sat down.

"Are you getting impatient?"

"I'm bored."

"The other night you made a detailed illusion of me, and had me sit and talk nicely to you for a time. I'm flattered, Dake."

"I didn't know I'd be spied on here."

"We're all very interested in you. We're interested in all fresh new dewy-eyed Stage Ones."

"You've changed, Karen."

"Karen Voss? That was a hypno-fix. A nice cover story. You can call me Karen if it will make you feel more at ease."

"Thank you," he said with grave dignity.

She laughed at him and he flushed. He said, "I learned enough to know that you made a considerable sacrifice for me."

Her eyes changed for a moment. She made a vague gesture. "It is everyone's duty to recruit. Material is scarce, you know. It always has been. You were my little gesture, so Merman has made me your house mother. Rather unfair, I think. Stage Ones are dull."

"I had an old friend. I met him at Training T. He kept talking about an ultimate answer. Does giving any ultimate answer come under the heading of responsibilities of the house mother?"

"It helped you, Dake. You're not quite as stuffy."

"I'm getting damn sick of mystery."

"We'll take a walk. Come on. See the great world outside. Now see if you can remember the lobby well enough to shift to it. Wait a moment. I'll check with Johnny to see if we have any strangers around." She paused a moment. "It's all right."

He made the lobby as quickly as he could. Yet she was there ahead of him, smiling at him.

"See what we have, Johnny?" she said, taking Dake's arm.

"In spite of all wagers to the contrary," Johnny said. *Welcome home.*

Thanks.

"I sometimes think you Ones are the worst snobs of all," Karen said. "I'll have to orient you, Dake. A June evening. 1978. That article you published last year made quite a stir. Don't walk so fast! But you repudiated it. So all the excitement died down, and people forgot about it in the excitement of George Fahdi's assassination. You were convicted of a Disservice and sentenced to ten years of hard labor. The lovely Patrice was in a nursing home and couldn't bribe you out of it. A poor little Stage One had a hideous time keeping the illusion of you going through the quick trial, sentence and shipment. As soon as you were in the labor camp, he quit, of course, so now you're a fugitive from justice. But they aren't going to hunt too hard. Martin bribed the right people."

"You're going too quickly, Karen. I don't . . ."

"Don't try. We'll just have a little stroll."

He held his screens firm, so that there was no possibility of her catching any fragment of his plan. He casually slipped his hand into his pocket, built up a powerful visualization of the hotel room where he had last stayed in New York. He worked the small wheels with his thumbnail. The shift to the hotel room was instantaneous. A puffy white-haired man in a dressing gown gaped at him. "How did you get in here, sir?" A pretty vacant-eyed girl wearing very little of anything came to the bathroom door and stared at him.

"Wrong room," Dake said. "Sorry."

"Couldn't you knock, dammit?"

"Sorry," Dake said. He moved to the door, unlocked it, hurried out into the corridor.

He went down the hallway, conscious of his conspicuous height. He went down the stairs and out into the warm June evening. He was painfully aware of how the months of Training T had heightened all his perceptions. Sounds seemed too loud, impressions too vivid. The world was a swarming mass of lurid, confusing detail. He had to get away from it, get away to some quiet place where he could think and plan.

He went to another hotel, gave illusion money to the clerk, pocketed his real change, tipped the bellhop with some of it. The room was small, depressingly dingy. He turned off the lights, put a chair over by the window and sat in it, looking out at the skyline.

Funny how this was supposed to be home, yet he felt a strangeness here. As though he were no longer a part of it. He remembered his original resolve, that resolve that had never weakened —learn everything you can and come home and use it to expose them. Let the guy in the street know that he was being pushed around.

And the men in the street would ask WHY?

Dake did not know why. The thing seemed planless. Another extension of the game fields.

Now be coherent with yourself. Collate the data. Set up an operating plan. Through the use of illusion you could land a space ship in New Times Square, march a goggle-headed crew of Martians down Broadway. That, perhaps, would start men thinking about interference—on an extra-terrestrial basis.

"You're a hard man to find," Karen said, behind him.

He turned quickly, almost relieved at momentarily escaping the necessity of making a plan.

She said, "That illusion with the money did it. I caught the direction of that. You can't use anything you've learned, Dake, without it being detectable."

The meager light of the night city touched her face, her cool alien eyes. She looked at him with that remote speculation of an entomologist awaiting an emergence from the cocoon.

He tried to project, to probe her mind. The screen was like metallic rock.

"All your tricks," he said, almost incoherently. "All your dirty little inhuman devices. They———"

"All *our* tricks, Dake."

"Not mine. I didn't ask for it. I went along with it. No choice at all." He stood up, towering over her, his back to the light. "Now the tricks make me ashamed. They make me a . . . mutation. They destroy the meaning of being a man."

"How noble!"

"You can't trace me if I don't use them, can you?"

"Can a man will himself to stop using his arms?"

He half turned from her to conceal the hand he slipped into his pocket. He thought of a ruse. Phone booths have a cookie-cutter similarity. He visualized quickly, flipping the wheels, feeling the surge of sickening nothingness, the sudden recapitulation of himself staring at the black phone a foot from his eyes. He stepped out of the booth, saw that he was in the hotel lobby downstairs, that the Pack B had selected the most immediate target visualization.

He walked out onto the street. Just as he tried to lose himself in the crowd, the thought arrowed faintly into his mind. *Dake! Run and we will kill you. We will have to. If you can hear me, come back.*

His stride faltered for a moment, and then he moved on to lose himself in the crowd. He instinctively hunched his shoulders, walked with knees slightly bent to reduce his towering height.

Learn what they can give you and use it against them. He had spent his life fighting. The equation was clear. The logic was impeccable. If *they* had the abilities he had learned, then they could put an end to the conflict on earth. They did not. Thus they were unfriendly to mankind. And man would have to know and learn. Man would have to recognize the enemy within the gates.

He remembered the one who had injured Karen, injured that previous, more understandable Karen. They seemed to fight among themselves, but with grotesquely gallant little rules. So Earth was an extension of the game fields. A place where you could be aware of your own superiority. Make the silly little creatures jump. They had made him jump, had killed Branson, had driven Patrice mad. They were like cruel children let loose in a zoo with loaded rifles.

A slow-moving prowl car slid a spotlight beam across him, went on. He could hear the metallic chatter of its radio. There would be danger from two sources. According to Karen, Martin Merman had arranged it so that the authorities would not be too eager to recapture him after his supposed escape. Merman could easily reverse that. His great height made him feel naked on the streets. He knew that through his newly acquired talent of control, of illusioning, or para-voice, he could make any attempt to take him a heartbreaking matter to any federal officer. But his escape attempts would, as Karen had told him, enable them to find him easily. As long as he used none of his new abilities, they could only recognize him visually, and confirm it by projecting against the first screen in his mind.

The faces of the people on the night streets depressed him. The months on Training T seemed to have given him a heightened susceptibility to mood. He could feel the waves of tension, and despair, and aimless discontent. Cold taffy faces and metronome eyes and life-broken mouths. An animal walking the city, with the tired inviting flex and clench of buttocks, with soupy opacity of eye. He walked through futility, drowning in it. And then, slowly, began to see other things. Small things. A young boy with a rapt, dedicated face, eyes of a stricken angel, looking upward at one of the pre-war buildings, at the simple perfect beauty of structural integrity. A couple, hand in hand, who would have been alone on the busiest street in the world. An old man shuffling along—the light slanting against a face that had been twisted and torn and broken by life, leaving nothing but a look of calm and peace, a look in which there was that beauty which is sometimes the by-product of torture. Pride made his eyes smart. Try to smash them utterly, and there was always something left in the ruins. Something priceless, eternal.

As he walked, wondering where he should hide, he remembered a column in a lighter vein that he had done long ago, in, it seemed, someone else's lifetime. Dr. Oliver Krindle, psychiatrist, whose hobby was psychic research. He remembered Krindle as one of those rare, warm men not damaged by too much knowledge of the human soul. The column had been about Krindle's endless and skeptical effort to track down psychic phenomena, about the two incidents out of all those years which Krindle felt did not lend themselves to any satisfactory explanation—except the obvious one that the persons reporting them lied.

He looked up Krindle's address in a phone book, walked fifteen blocks to the narrow lightless street. He had remembered that Krindle lived alone over his office. He remembered the good and ancient brandy Krindle had served, making a ceremony of the little ritual. Brandy in a room lined with books—as though Krindle had found some special way to preserve the good things in a world in which good things were no longer understood.

There was a dim light in the hallway. He pressed the button, heard a distant ringing. Across the street, shirt-sleeved men and weary women sat on front steps, their voices slow in the warm night, their laughter oddly dreary.

Dr. Oliver Krindle came down the stairs. Dake saw the thick naked ankles, the worn slippers, the battered robe, the deceptive face of a shaven Santa. Krindle turned on the light over the door and peered through, then made a great rattling of chains and bolts.

"Come in, Lorin. Come in! Damn careful these days. Hoodlums, cretins. Violence for its own sake. That's the kind that frightens you. For profit, that is understandable. Too many people like to look at blood. Maybe it's always been that way. Come on up. I've been listening to music. Choral stuff tonight. Lots of voices in my room, eh?"

Dake followed the man up the stairs, to the quiet room he remembered. Dr. Krindle waved him to a chair, said, "I'll start this one again from the beginning. No one is in too much of a hurry for this, Lorin." He turned on the player again.

Dake leaned back in the chair, let the music sweep over him like a vast warm tide. Krindle moved slowly, making two drinks, setting one down at Dake's elbow. The music was a rich sanity, a reaffirmation of faith in man, a denial of the things he had learned.

The music stopped and Krindle turned it off. They sat in the silence for a time. Ice tinkled in Dake's glass as he raised it to his lips.

"I have read about you, Lorin. You've been busy. Disservice, sentence, escape. I knew you would be a fugitive someday. I did not know when or how."

"But you knew why?"

"Of course. You meet environment in too direct a manner. So your environment is embarrassed. It doesn't like defects pointed out. So it destroys you."

"Martyr?"

"Yes. Without purpose. Your defeat does not add impetus to any creed or group or movement. The solitary man. The flaw, possibly, is in believing too much in yourself. If that is a flaw. I don't know. Once upon a time I told myself I would never compromise. Oh, I was young and brave. Now I look back on life. A life of listening to the anxious daydreams of neurotic women. Little minds so shallow that they present but one surface, Lorin."

"What is normalcy, Oliver? Stability?"

"It doesn't exist. Just a convenient line you draw. Everybody overlaps that line at some point, and deviates widely at another. Add up all the aspects of an individual, and you can only classify him as an individual. No two men have ever been mentally sick or mentally well in the same way—with the exception of physiological mental illness. We are all, unfortunately, unique. How simple my profession would be if I could type people, safely and accurately!"

"Suppose it were your function to drive a man mad. How would you go about it?"

"First I would change your terminology. How would I go about creating a mental illness? The classic way is to present him with an insoluble problem, and make it necessary for survival for him to solve that problem. The rat in a maze with no exit."

"Suppose you could make his senses give him . . . nonsense messages."

"Wouldn't that be another aspect of the same classic problem, Dake Lorin? To survive, it is necessary to be able to trust what your eyes and ears and touch and smell tell you. If the data they present to the brain are patently impossible, then the subject has a classic problem. I must trust my senses in order to survive. My senses cannot be trusted. What do I do? But aren't you thinking of a result rather than a cause? A patient will hallucinate when he can no longer stand the sane messages his senses give him. A wife is unfaithful. So he hears a voice coming out of the fireplace. It says to kill her."

"What happens if the cart is before the horse?"

"Will he kill her, you mean? That depends on how dependent he is on his ears and eyes and sense of touch. Roughly, I would say the more meager the intelligence, the more likely the patient is to obey a false message. What have your false messages been?"

Dake studied his thick hard knuckles. "I looked into a mirror. The left side of my face was a naked skull. I touched it. It was hard and cold. Two persons with me saw it, too. One went mad and one fainted."

"I would say that you had subconsciously recognized the duality of your life, recognized a death wish."

"If two others saw it?"

"Once I had a patient who resented the way people on the street would stop and pet his three-headed purple dog. It followed him everywhere."

"Suppose I told you, Oliver, that I can make you stand up against your will, pick up that record off the turntable and break it on the hearth."

"Perhaps you could, if I were willing to submit to hypnosis."

"Suppose I tell you that I can create a . . . three-headed pur-

ple dog right here and that you will be able to see it. Or tell you
that I can project words into your mind, so that you can know
what I am saying without my speaking."

Oliver Krindle took a slow sip of his drink. "I would say that
you have had much strain lately. You were trying to help the
world. The world destroyed your effectiveness. You cannot admit
that you are ineffective. The struggle is too important to you. You
compensate by endowing yourself with strange psychic gifts which
seem to restore your effectiveness."

"Why have you always been interested in psychic research?"

"For the same reason that a man who is trying to grow an orchard will be interested in a thick dark woods next door."

"Then you believe, Oliver, that there is much that you do not
know."

"Do I look that arrogant? Of course there is much I do not
know."

"Have you ever wondered if all the mystery in our world might
come from one special source?"

"God, Martians, Irish visions?"

"What if the world we know is a test tube? A culture dish? A
continuous bacterial conflict?"

Oliver half closed his eyes. "Interesting from a speculative
point of view. But it has been done too many times before. Show
me the agency."

"I'm one of them."

Oliver opened his eyes wide. "It would please me, Dake Lorin,
if you would stay here tonight."

"I'm one of them, but I don't want to be one of them. They're
after me. They'll kill me, and mankind will never know what . . .
opposes it. I can't demonstrate talents, because they are sensitive
to that. They can find me."

"Lorin, I . . ."

Dake leaned forward. "Shut up a minute. I'm going to take a
chance. But I am going to make it very quick. You'll have to get
whatever you can get from it in a very few seconds."

"Have you thought what you would do if your . . . mysterious
powers fail?"

"That's why I came here. If they fail, I've been mad for months on end. But they won't fail. Do you see that corner of the table, directly under the lamp? There is nothing there, Oliver, is there?"

"Of course not, but . . ."

"And you are resisting any attempt at hypnosis, are you not?"

"Yes, but . . ."

"Watch the corner of the table," Dake said softly. He did the simplest illusion he could think of. A featureless white cube, about three inches on a side. He let it remain there on the corner of the table for no longer than two seconds, and then erased it utterly.

He had watched the cube. He turned his eyes to Oliver Krindle's face. Under the cheerful red cheeks the flesh tone had gone chalky gray. The glass trembled violently as he lifted it to his lips. Some of the drink sloshed out onto the ancient dressing gown. The glass chattered as he set it back down on the broad arm of his chair.

"I may not have much time, Oliver. They may come for me. I want you to know . . ."

"One of the most startling demonstrations of hypnosis," Krindle said, too loudly, "that I have ever seen."

"I came to you because of all the men I know, you are the most likely to react to this in a sane and competent manner."

Krindle chuckled, too loudly, artificially. "Sometimes the sick mind can perform startling things, Lorin. Think of the cataleptic trance, for example. Think of the classic sign of the stigmata, induced through auto-hypnosis. You startled me for a moment, but I can readily understand that it is nothing but the manifestation of . . ."

Dake felt a faint warning touch against his mind. He stood up quickly. "There's no time left now, Oliver. Watch my lips." *I do not speak but you can hear my words.*

His fingertips worked the tiny wheels quickly. As the moment of nothingness weakened him, he saw Oliver still sitting there, eyes bulging glassily. The phone booth was dark. He stepped quickly out into the dark tiled corridor of a locked office building. A car rumbled by outside. He stood, holding his breath, waiting for some faint touch of awareness against his mind. There was nothing. He went up the dark metal treads of the stairs. He found

a doctor's office. The door was locked. He chinned himself on the
top of the frame, looked through the transom. The room was
faintly lighted by the reflection of the city against the night sky.
He visualized the interior and then, barely in time, realized how
this would be a mistake. He broke the door lock, stretched out on
a couch in the inner office. He was exhausted, and sleep came before he could plan the next day.

13

IN THE MORNING DAKE LEFT THE OFFICE WHEN THE BUILDING
was just coming to life. The sky was gray, the air filled with the
threat of thunder. He had no money. To acquire some by extra-
human means would be a grave risk. On impulse he risked turning back into the office. He found a locked tin box in the recep-
tionist's desk. He broke it under his heel, pried the lid off,
pocketed the few bills and plastic coins it contained.

There was more than enough for breakfast. He found a small
grubby place, picked a morning paper off the pile by the cashier's
cage.

The notice of the death of Dr. Oliver Krindle was on page
three, a single paragraph. "Dr. Oliver Krindle, noted psychiatrist,
phoned his intention of hanging himself to the police last night,
and by the time he was cut down it was too late to revive him.
The suicide note stated that his long work with the insane had at
last broken his mind, and that his own prognosis was unfavorable. Police report evidence that Dr. Krindle had a visitor shortly
before his death, but the identity is not known at this time."

Dake ate mechanically, not noticing the taste or texture of the
food. If the sanest, soundest man he knew found it impossible to
accept the disconcerting proof of inhuman deviation, to accept
the knowledge of skills previously limited to legend and oddly accurate fairy stories, then who would accept it? What would a

group do? Check it off to the great realm of table levitation and ectoplasmic messages from Aunt Dorrie?

He remembered one of the very ancient moving pictures to which Darwin Branson had taken him. Old pictures fascinated Darwin. He remembered the one where a tramp was given a legitimate check for one million dollars. An uncertified check. He had a fortune in his hand, and no one could accept the reality of it. Just a bum with a delusion of grandeur. In the end, he had had to tear it up, or go crazy.

And he remembered a particularly infuriating incident of his youth. One summer he had gone surf casting near Marblehead, alone on the gray dawn beach, using borrowed equipment, heaving the cut bait out as far as he could, retrieving it slowly, the surf smashing against his thighs. He was using hundred-pound test line. Suddenly a massive tug had yanked him off balance, nearly yanking the rod out of his hands. He clung desperately, thinking of the cost of replacing rod, reel and line. He had floundered in the surf and the reel had locked somehow. He wanted to brace himself and break the line, but he was yanked forward again, yanked off his feet, towed straight out with ominous speed and power. He saw at once that he would have to let the rod and reel go and swim back, or risk being drowned. Then he discovered what had locked the reel. The end of his water-soaked sweater had caught fast in the reel. He tried to rip it loose and it would not give. He had yelled in panic at the empty seascape. He was moving faster than any human could swim. The monster at the other end of the line swam steadily out, and then miraculously made a long slow turn and headed in again. It was evidently its intention to scrape the hook off on the rocks near shore. Dake at last slammed into the rocks painfully, and the line parted in that instant. He floundered to shore and sat, bleeding, panting.

It had been an exciting experience . . . until he tried to tell someone about it, experienced the blank incredulous stare, the roar of laughter. There was no proof. Nothing but wet clothes and gouged hands. You just took a tumble in the surf and thought a fish yanked on the line, boy. There's nothing in here to tow you around like that.

No one had believed him. Ever.

No one had believed in the bum with a million dollars.

No one would believe in the powers he had acquired.

And he could not use them and remain alive. Unless . . .

In late afternoon he found what he wanted. A twenty-five-year-old rust bucket of a War II Liberty ship, under Panama registry, which meant, of course, Brazilian control. They signed him on as a deck hand, looking only at his powerful frame, not at the lack of identification. At dusk they wallowed slowly by the shattered stub of the Statue of Liberty, heading for Jacksonville, Havana, Port au Prince, Rio. He knew that ten thousand yards was the ultimate limit of the Pack B. He knew that there had to be some limit to the space over which they could detect the psychic radiations of any extra-human application of mental force. At no time did he doubt that they would kill him if they could. It is more difficult to lie in the mind than with the lips. He wanted a chance to think. He wanted labor that would exhaust his body. He had the vague, unformed idea of taking an isolated group of people, such as the crew of the ship, and somehow forcing them to believe in what he would tell them.

The captain was a remote little man with a twitching face and two fingers missing on each hand. His name was Ryeson. The first officer ran the ship. He was a round muscular Dutchman with tangerine hair, radiation scars on his face and throat, and his name was Hagger. It was a sullen ship, a floating monument to slovenliness, dirt, unidentifiable stenches. They worked long into the night battening hatches under the incomprehensible cursings of the first officer, under the roll of the ship lights, driving wedges, lashing the canvas tight.

The next morning, cramped from the short narrow bunk, Dake was put to work by Hagger chipping paint. He and the other green hand were so elected. The other man was a professorial-looking citizen in his late thirties, with the long slow tremblings of alcoholism complicated by prono addiction. His name was Green and he had nothing to say. His reflexes were so uncoordinated that he kept hurting himself, though there was not enough strength in his blows to damage himself severely.

Dake stripped to the waist and let the June sun darken his back as he worked. As he worked monotonously he tried to organize some plan. There was one alternative. To hide for the rest of his life. Never use the new skills. Work in far places, keep quiet, let the knowledge eventually die with him. That was a remarkably unsatisfying solution. He wondered how Watkins had accepted his return to Earth. Watkins would, he guessed, conform to whatever had been asked of him, expected of him. Somewhere along the line Watkins had lost the intense need to revolt.

So lost was he in thought that he stopped working for a time, squatting on his heels, looking squinch-eyed out across the blue sea. A heavy kick in the shoulder rolled him across the greasy deck. He jumped up and faced an irate first officer.

"You take a break when I give you a break. When I don't give you a break, I want to hear that hammering."

"I'll work. But don't ever try that again, my friend."

The first officer was standing close to Dake. He glanced at the chipping hammer, shrugged and turned slowly away. He spun back, putting his weight into the spin, his meaty fist landing high on the side of Dake's face, knocking him down. As Dake tried to scramble up, the heavy kick took him in the pit of the stomach. He could see, as in a haze, the wide scarred face of the first officer grinning down at him. The foot swung back again and this time Dake, half helpless, expected that it would catch him flush in the mouth.

Dake exerted the full thrust of control, taking over the chunky body, marching it back. He pulled himself to his feet, one arm clamped across his belly, gagging for breath. The first officer's eyes had a glazed look.

"What's going on down there, mister?" the captain asked, peering down from the bridge onto the boat deck. His voice was dry, puzzled.

Dake looked up, quickly released Hagger. Hagger swayed, braced himself, made a deep grunting sound in his throat and charged directly at Dake, who had to admire his single-mindedness.

Dake caught him again, and, still angered by pain, not thinking of consequences, he set Hagger off on a blundering run toward the rail. Hard thighs hit the rail and Hagger plunged forward. As he toppled into space, Dake released control. A head, orange in the sunlight, bounced in the stern wake. A yellow life-preserver arced out from the fantail, hurled by some alert seaman who had heard the captain's surprisingly loud bellow of "Man overboard!"

They swung a boat out, manning it in a sloppy way, and recovered the first officer. He seemed remarkably chastened. Dake went back to work. He was aware that the first officer and the captain were on the bridge, talking in low tones. He could sense their eyes on him.

"Stand up, you," the captain said, startlingly close behind him. Dake stood up and turned. Captain Ryeson stood six feet away. He held a massive ancient automatic in a white steady hand, the muzzle pointing at Dake's belly. Dake was aware that the rest of the ship was disturbed. There was a clot of a dozen hands forty feet down the deck. The first officer stood just behind Ryeson and a bit to one side.

"Mister Hagger is going to knock you about a bit. I want to see what happens. He says you made him jump over the rail. Try that again and I'll blow a hole in you."

"You better forget the whole thing, Captain," Dake said quietly.

"A thing like that can bother a man. Go ahead, Mister Hagger. The whole crew is present." Hagger balled his fists, licked his lips and came tentatively in toward Dake, walking uneasily.

"Forget it, please, Captain. I won't be beaten. And I won't be . . . accountable for what I'll do to stop a beating."

"I want to know what I have aboard my ship," the captain said.

Dake was in that moment aware of the full impact of the fear and horror that normal man has for any entity that is alien. He knew that if they couldn't understand him, they would destroy him. He saw that what he should do was to cow them utterly, and quickly.

Hagger took another cautious step, his shoulders tightening. Dake's refusal to defend himself was troubling the first officer.

The captain turned quickly and jumped back away from the maraca rattle of the tail of the colored diamondback. It struck at him and he fired. The slug screamed off the iron deck, high into the blue air. The snake was gone and the muzzle swung quickly toward Dake. He took over the captain's mind, finding it tougher than the mate's, finding it a bit harder to exert control. The mate's eyes bugged and the captain slowly put the muzzle of the gun into his mouth, closed his lips around it. The vast warted weedy head of a sea serpent shot up off the starboard bow, throwing sparkling drops into the air. It made a bass grunting noise. Dake felt quite impressed with it. The mate stood fixed in horror. Dake released the captain, who snatched the muzzle out of his mouth, once again tried to aim at Dake. Dake made him throw the automatic over the side. Dake backed until he was braced against the bulkhead. He peopled the bridge with illustrations from the books of boyhood. Blackbeard, with twists of powder that crackled and flared and stank in his beard. Long John Silver, banging the peg leg against the bridge railing. Captain Bligh, with eyes like broken ice. A dead sailor, clad in conches and seaweed. For artistic balance, he added a creature of his own devising—a duplicate of Captain Ryeson who carried under each arm, like a pair of pumpkins, two grinning heads of First Officer Hagger, the tangerine hair aflame.

And he had them all lounge against the bridge rail and look down and yell with thin, hollow, obscene laughter.

Dake turned back. The mate had gone over the rail again, on the opposite side of the sea serpent. The captain stood with his eyes closed tightly. Dake heard the ripe fruit plop of seamen going over the side, dropping into the blue sea. Several tried to lower a boat, and the lines fouled, and they went over the side.

He dispersed the illusions, seeing at once that he had gone too far. They were swimming west, away from horror, toward the faint smoky line of coast. He could control the nearest ones, but his control was not expert enough for the complicated task of swimming. Each time he would release them to avoid drowning them, they would turn like automatons and swim away from the ship. They were dwindling astern, out of his range. The captain had fallen. His face was bluish. He died as Dake was trying to revive him. Dake ran to the wheel, tried to bring the ship around. Midway in the long arc the muted thud of driving power faltered, stopped. The ship coasted, powerless. The heads had dwindled astern. He found the captain's glass and steadied it. Even as he watched, powerless to help, he saw them going under, one by one. Their initial frenzy had exhausted them. The bright head of the mate, bright against the blue sea, was the last to go. And the sea was empty. He went over the ship from end to end, carefully. A cat sat on the galley table, mincingly cleaning its paws. The engine room was empty. He and the cat shared the ship. It rolled in the ground swell, and dishes clinked. Food cooled at the long table. A wisp of smoke rose from the last fragment of a cigarette. He had overestimated their capacity to absorb horror. He dragged the captain to his cabin, tumbled him into his bunk, straightened out the dead limbs. He found the ship's safe ajar. He crammed his pockets with cash, pried fouled lines loose and managed to awkwardly lower a boat. He slid down a line and boarded it. The cranky motor started at last. He moved in numbness, in consciousness of the unpremeditated murder of twenty-one men. He thought of the one who, as he was sinking, turned and made a sign of the cross toward the devil's ship.

Blue water sparkled and danced. The boat chugged obediently toward the smear of land against the west horizon. Closer in he came on private fishing boats and gave them a wide berth. He turned south, away from an area of summer camps, away from the bright specks of colorful beach costumes, and at last found a place where he could land unobserved. The ship was out of sight, miles off the beach. This would give the world another mystery of the sea, another Marie Celeste, as inexplicable as the original. And all he had learned, through twenty-one deaths, was that it was far too easy to overestimate the capacity of man to accept horror, particularly horror that dances in the bright sunlight.

He drove the bow against coarse sand, leaped ashore and abandoned the boat, striking up across rough dunes, finding a narrow road. He turned north, walking along the shoulder, clad in the ill-fitting work clothes he had borrowed aboard the ship. Cars passed him. He found that he was near Poverty Beach, just north of Cape May. He walked to Wildwood. By mid-afternoon he was in Atlantic City. He bought clothing in a shoddy ersatz wool, waited for alterations. At nightfall he was on a crowded bus just entering the city limits of Philadelphia. Regret was a dull ache within him. If only he had been more restrained . . . perhaps it would have all been possible. A slow indoctrination of the men aboard the ship. Teach them the nature of the enemy.

But if Krindle had been unable to accept it, could he ever have gotten the men aboard the ship to accept it? Who would accept it? He recognized the blindness of the instinct that had taken him toward Philadelphia, toward Patrice. The inexplicable had broken her. Perhaps an explanation would heal her. She would be anxious to be healed. She had accepted the world as a jungle, believing only in her own strength. When her strength had failed her, she had no other resource. Nothing else in which she believed.

The danger, he knew, was that "they" would anticipate his need to see Patrice, would be waiting for him. Though he recognized the danger, he knew at the same time that there was nothing personal in their attitude. Perhaps they had found that some people identified themselves so closely with the known world that even after training they were incapable of accepting an assignment that was—in essence—merely a wry and confusing game with no discernible purpose or rules. A children's game where all were blindfolded except the agents themselves.

As night came the streets of Philadelphia began to fill with the pleasure seekers. Electronics had played the rudest of all jokes on the people of the United States. By 1955 television had developed from an interesting drug into a vast obsession. Most children had had almost five years of it. It was not necessary to develop any resource of self-amusement, any intellectual curiosity. It was only necessary to sit and watch and be amused. The electronics industry met the vast challenge of millions of home sets, hundreds of stations. The war diverted the capacity of the electronics industry into military channels, and decimated technician personnel. One by one the stations began to fail, unable to replace essential parts. By hundreds, and then by thousands, the home sets became silent. After the war, amid economic exhaustion, there was a short period of resurgence, with stations reactivated, with home service available in meager amount. But it slowly tapered off again into the increasing silence. The triditoriums cornered the small capacity of the electronics industry. A few channels were still active in major cities, but there were no more networks. Just individual stations showing old films, over and over and over again.

In millions of front rooms there was a cubical object of polished wood and white lightless tube. But the resources of the individual to amuse himself without commercial assistance had been sadly weakened, weakened by the years of the glowing tube. So they went out onto the streets at night to escape the silent homes, to escape the doom of sitting in silence, with nothing to say to each other. There had to be some answer to boredom, and the answer became fleng and prono and tridi and violence. Ten-minute divorces and gangs of child thugs. Yet it couldn't be criti-cized too bravely or too loudly. Criticism was a Disservice to the State.

Telecast of India had made a survey to determine whether it was economically feasible to reactivate the industry in the United States. But with the breakdown of transportation, the decline of the technician class, the trend toward regional self-sufficiency, there were no longer commercial sponsors able to afford the high cost of network television. And Telecast of India was not con-cerned with any project which would fail to show a profit.

Dake walked tall and alone through the brawling night streets. Large areas of the city were in darkness again. He tried to tele-phone Patrice. It was a half hour before the call went through to the right number. He heard the distant ringing of her phone. He hung up after ten rings. At last he remembered the name of one of her lawyers, and found his home phone listing.

The lawyer was hesitant about giving her address. Dake identified himself as a Mr. Ronson from Acapulco, phoning about a hotel investment Miss Togelson had been considering.

"I suppose you could talk to her, Mr. Ronson. But she is taking no interest in business matters these days. We're handling her in-vestments for her."

"She was very interested in this property."

"If she is still interested, we'd be very pleased. It's most difficult to please a client who . . . gives us no clue as to her wishes. She is at Glendon Farms, Mr. Ronson. It's a private con-valescent home outside of Wilmington. But you won't be able to contact her tonight. Visiting hours are, I believe, in the after-noon."

Dake thanked him, hung up. He ate from a sense of duty, not hunger, and found a cheap hotel room. He lay on the bed in the darkened room and thought of his motives in trying to see Pa-trice. To find just one person who would accept, who would be-lieve, who could be made to look at the shape of the enemy. . . .

To have suffered those incredible alterations was to become

desolately lonely. He had never been particularly dependent on emotional attachments. But to have the certain knowledge that to human man he was an object of fear and dread, and to extra-human man a rebel to be immediately eliminated—it gave him a sense of apartness that shocked him, it was so unexpected. He knew that he could go down into the streets and find a woman and bring her back to this room. Yet any such intimacy would be a farce. A gesture as strangely indecent as those photographs showing a cat and a canary in precarious comradeship. He could go to a bar, and force himself into some group, and talk all night, without ever saying anything.

He knew, then, that the only true intimacy of the spirit was that intimacy possible only with those who had been trained as he had been trained. Only with those who had learned to focus and direct that incredible energy of the brain cells. With all untrained humans he would be a civilized man who had gone to live among savages. He could go native, but it would be a denial of his abilities. He would take to that savage tribe a knowledge of customs and abilities beyond their power to conceive, let alone understand. And never would he be able to forget the thought of waste, of dispersal of power, of abnegation of destiny.

The closest friendship he had ever experienced had been with Watkins during the brief training period. In trust and friendship they had lowered screens, permitting an exchange of thought subject to no semantic distortion. It had been easier, more relaxing, to use speech rather than para-voice, but in any particularly difficult concept, where there was a misunderstanding, para-voice had been available. The thought changed itself into the words the listener would have used to express the exact shade of meaning.

Maybe, he thought, the agents are right. If a man could not accept the implications of training, he might be better off dead. Death could be no greater loneliness than this knowledge that you were forever cut off from other minds attuned to yours in a way that, once experienced, became forever necessary.

But he could not reconcile himself to defeat. The answer was clear. Make Patrice understand, and she would divert all her resources to the task of making the world see what was happening, what apparently had been happening for years without end. Perhaps untrained man could find a way to fight them, to keep them from toying like careless children with the destiny of man. But the first job was to expose.

He thought of the heads of swimming men, tiny against the wide flat sea. He thought of those who would be waiting, in delicate awareness, for some indicative display of his new abilities, then using that detectable emanation to track him down, with an objective, functional mercilessness.

And he was honest enough with himself to wonder if he would have revolted against them if Karen had met him with the warmth he had expected of her.

14

A NURSE WITH A HEAVY, PLACID FACE MET HIM AT THE DOOR of Patrice's cottage on the fenced grounds of Glendon Farms and took his visitor's card and asked him politely to follow her. Her starched uniform rustled, blinding white in the sunshine.

There was a long slope behind the cottage, down to a small formal garden. Patrice lay on a dark blue blanket spread on the tailored grass. She wore a brief black sunsuit.

The nurse paused with him, out of earshot, and said, "Please don't say anything to disturb or excite her. If you see her beginning to get nervous, call me. I'll wait here."

Dake walked down to her. Patrice was face down, her back deep gold in the sunlight. He sat on his heels beside the blanket and said, "Patrice?"

She turned quickly, raising herself on her elbows, a sheaf of the bright hair masking her eye for a moment before she threw it back with a toss of her head.

"Dake, darling," she said warmly. "How good to see you!"

"You look well, Patrice."

"I'm very well, dear."

He studied her curiously. There was something subtly wrong

about her face, about her expression. A bland childishness. Her mouth and eyes were soft, but something had gone, utterly. He saw what it was. There was no firmness, no resolution, no strength of will or character left.

"Patrice," he said uneasily, "do you remember the . . . last time we saw each other?"

"That night when I got sick? They told me you were there, dear. Was I too awful?"

"No. I mean, you weren't really sick, Patrice. You just saw something you couldn't explain to yourself. But I could explain it to you."

She glanced up to where the nurse stood fifty feet away, guardian white against the green of the clipped grass.

She said in a low tone, "Don't let her know that I wasn't really sick. They're doing this for the money."

"What do you mean?"

She gave him a childish smile. "Don't be dull. If they find out I know what their little game is, they'll kill me. You certainly know that." Her voice was perfectly calm, matter-of-fact.

"What . . . do you plan to do?"

"Oh, there are too many of them! I can't do anything. You know that! But I have to let them all think I believe them. They give me warnings, you know. They put electricity in my head, and keep telling me it's going to help me, but it's just a warning about how they'll kill me if I don't do exactly what they say. Now you're in here and they won't let you out either. Because now you know, and you could tell about what they're doing. You were silly to come here, Dake, dear. Terribly silly. There are too many of them."

"Patrice, I . . ."

She sat up all the way and her voice became shrill, and her eyes were filled with sharp excitement. "Run, Dake! Run before the men come!"

The nurse came quickly down the lawn. Dake stood up and backed away from Patrice. The nurse said, "Now lie down and get some more sun, Patrice. That's a good girl."

Patrice smiled at her and stretched out obediently. She yawned and closed her eyes, said in a sleepy mumble, " 'Bye, Dake, darling."

He walked back to the cottage with the nurse. "How is she?"

The nurse shrugged. "She'll improve for a time, and then retrogress overnight. There seems to be something, some memory she won't face up to. She's had two full series of shock treatments. They seem to help for a time, but the effects aren't lasting. She's sweet, really. Mild and cooperative. We never have to use restraint, except when she realizes she's due for another shock treatment. She thinks she's some sort of a prisoner here. That isn't uncommon, you know."

"She always had such . . . enormous energy."

"She seems quite content to vegetate, sir. That is common, too. A complete avoiding of decisions, or the reasons for making any."

He went back to Philadelphia, back to the cheap room. Branson might have understood. He was gone. Patrice was gone. Oliver Krindle was gone. In a sense, Karen was gone.

He sat on the corner of the desk, lean ankles crossed, and tried to plot his future actions. "They" would be spread quite thin. There would be many places in the world, many places in this country, where he'd be out of range, free to work out some plan of what to do with the rest of his life.

Someone had to believe! Odd, how important that had become. He could not risk it with anyone he had known. It would have to be a stranger. Someone carefully selected. And the demonstration of his abilities would have to be carried on where the chance of detection was remote.

He walked in the city, looking at faces, looking into the eyes of strangers with an intentness that made them uneasy. His training had made faces more readable. He saw shallow concerns, and fear, and aimlessness. He walked long miles through the city. He found no one in whose stability he could believe. At dusk he walked out on the rusting mass of the Delaware River Bridge, wondering if all the cities would be like this, if there would not be a face in all the world to trust, instinctively.

The bridge lights were out and the girl was a vague gray shadow a dozen yards away. There was a pale hint of her face, and then she began to climb the parapet. He ran as quickly and silently as he could. She heard him and tried to move more quickly. He caught a thin wrist, pulled her firmly back and down to stand by him, his arm around her slim body. She stood very quietly, her head bowed, trembling slightly.

"Are you certain you want to do that?"

"Yes." It was a whisper, barely audible.

He took out a match, struck it, shielding it from the fitful wind, tilting her chin up calmly to study her face. It was a young face, haggard, frail, vulnerable. She turned away from him.

"I'll do it anyway," she said. "Sooner or later."

"The reason is good?"

"Of course."

"I won't try to question you about it. I'll accept that. Your reason is good. Do you have a name?"

"Mary."

"Suppose you were given a chance to do something . . . that might be constructive, and then be permitted, later, to destroy yourself. Would that interest you?"

"Constructive. That seems an odd word for you to use." Her voice was low, the inflection good, articulation crisp, clean.

"You would have to take it on faith. I can't explain, yet."

"Hold a light by your face. I want to look at you."

He lit another match. She looked up at him. "The heavy sorrow of all the world," she said softly.

"What do you mean?"

"In your face. In your eyes. I work . . . used to work, in wood and stone and clay, and anything else that will take a form." In the last dusk light he saw her hold her hands out, clench her fists. "Your face would fit a heroic figure. There aren't many faces left like that. It's a good face. Do you have a name?"

"Dake."

"I'll do what you want. But no questions. Will it take long?"

"A week, perhaps less. I don't know."

"I didn't know it would take that long."

"I have to tell you one thing, Mary. You have to be a person who . . . has very little to lose."

"I have one question. Is it something criminal?"

"No."

"All right. But first you better buy me something to eat. I'm pretty shaky."

In the small, lamp-lit restaurant he had his first chance to look at her. Her hair was straight, dark, worn long. She wore a gray suit, a white blouse, both of casual good quality, but rumpled. She wore no makeup. He sensed her lack of pretense and vanity. She had a style of her own, a directness. It was her hands that interested him most. Good square firm hands, with short, competent-looking fingers. They were as immaculate as a surgeon's.

She ate with controlled hunger, and with the precision of a starved house cat. He sat, smoking, and watched her.

At last he said, "I'm not asking questions about you. But in order to explain my position, I have to refer it to your customary frames of reference. Otherwise I might make myself meaningless to you. How do you . . . think about life, about the place of man in his environment?"

She made a face over her sip of substitute coffee. "Man," she said, "as a free spirit, has never had the freedom he deserves in his environment. He just drifts from one form of collectivism to the next. Taboos change—lack of freedom of expression is a constant."

"What causes his lack of freedom?"

She shrugged. "Ignorance, I suppose. Superstitions. The yen for the master-slave relationship. Or maybe plain bullheaded perversity. Let any person stand out as an individual, and the herd pulls him down and tramples him."

"Progress?"

"We wiggle back and forth in a groove, like a phonograph needle. On a flat surface."

"What if that's the plan?"

"Are you being a mystic?"

"No. Suppose it is an arbitrary plan, a definite suppression, for an unknown reason?

"Presumably, then, by some definite entity, some thinking aura of fire-ball or nine-legged Venusian?"

"By men who have been trained in . . . abilities you would think impossible."

She clapped her hands once. "What a lovely excuse for all defeatism! We can't possibly get anywhere because we're . . . breeding stock, or something. A rather poorly run stock farm, I might add."

"I have been trained on another planet."

She stared hard at him in a long silence. She picked up her spoon, put it down again. "This is where I should say I'm Mary, Queen of Scots, I suppose."

"If you'd like."

"They say madmen come in the most credible shapes and forms. I'm supposed to be mad, too. Suicidal. By the way, did you know the list of living creatures who do away with themselves? Lemmings, of course. That's common. And man, bless him. A scorpion, when infuriated beyond reason, will sting himself to death. And there is a species of white butterfly that flies straight out to sea. Those are the non-functional deaths, as opposed to the dying of, say, the male spider, or the winged ant. Yet . . . somehow I cannot believe that either of us is mad, Dake." She smiled and took a small glossy photograph from her pocket, slid it across the table to him.

He picked it up and looked at it. It was a photograph of a carving, in some dark wood, of a starving child. Spindle limbs, bloated belly, an expression of dull acceptance, without either pain or fear.

She said quietly, "I wasn't going to tell you. I planned not to. I've been working too hard. I've been doing too many things which . . . disturb my public. Apparently I've been critical. And criticism is a Disservice. Yesterday they came with a writ. They smashed my work. Every last bit of it. Hauled it away. Gave me an appointment with the Local Board for this afternoon. I didn't keep it. Suicide isn't a gesture of protest. Not in my case, Dake. It is very simply a statement. I refuse to permit myself to live in my environment. Am I mad?"

"I . . . don't think so."

"I'm not afraid of labor. I'm not afraid of being sentenced. You must believe that."

"I do."

She lifted her chin with a touching pride. "I've never been afraid of anything that walks, creeps or crawls."

"For myself, I would qualify that."

"How?"

"I've been frightened, but never afraid."

She tilted her head on one side. "I rather like that, Dake. Now what do you do with this training? Spread your filmy green wings and take off? Forgive me for sounding so flip. The food, I guess. Intoxicating after so long. I ate yesterday, before they came. That was the last time."

He leaned forward a bit. "You see, I have to make someone believe me."

"Or cease believing in it yourself? Maybe it's necessary for you to keep believing in it."

"That sounds like you're thinking of insanity again."

"Blame me?"

"No. But I want you to be . . . objective about proof."

"Start proving."

"I can't. Not here. I can't even tell you why I can't do it here. It will sound like a persecution complex running wild. If you're through, we'll leave. We're going to fly west."

"By flapping our arms? Oh, forgive me! I feel right on the edge of tears or hysteria or something. Let's get out of here."

They sat in the deep comfortable seats of a CIJ flagship awaiting takeoff. Dake noticed that, under the terminal floods, the stairs had been wheeled back into position. Two men boarded the plane and came down the aisle toward them. Mary made a small sound, like a whimper. He saw the pale, flat, expressionless faces of Disservice agents, saw that they were staring at Mary, saw the eyes of the lead one widen as he glanced at Dake. A pink tongue flecked quickly at pale lips, and the hand slid inside the neat dark jacket.

He thought quickly. Takeoff was already seconds behind schedule. The Indian co-pilot glared at his watch.

Dake closed his hand over her thin wrist. "I have to demonstrate sooner than I wanted to," he said, barely moving his lips.

It would be too puzzling to the other passengers if the two men, whose profession was so obvious, should turn and leave the aircraft without a word. He selected a man across the aisle, an overdressed toothy man with a shyster look. He saw dullness replace alertness as he enfolded their minds in his will, thrusting volition aside ruthlessly. They turned, their movements awkward and poorly coordinated, and grasped the toothy man and hoisted him roughly out of the seat.

"Hey!" the man yelped. "Hey, what are you doing?"

Dake made them shove and thrust him up the aisle. He had to stand to see the wheeled steps. The struggling victim made the task difficult. The balance could not be maintained, and the three of them tumbled down the steps. The victim got up, was grasped again, and marched off toward the main terminal buildings, across the concrete apron.

The steps were wheeled away, the doors slammed and latched. The jets flared and roared, and quickly faded into silence as the flagship, turning above the city, arrowing upward, passed the sonic barrier. He realized he still had hold of Mary's wrist. He released it. She was looking up at him, her eyes unfrightened.

"They were coming after us, weren't they?"

"Yes."

"They wanted you too. I saw it in their eyes."

"Yes."

"You hypnotized them. I could see it in their walk. Such an odd walk. Will they . . . stay that way long?"

"As soon as they were out of range, they got over it."

"Won't they have the tower call the plane back?"

"I don't think so. They don't like to inconvenience CIJ in any way. And I know how their minds work. That man. I had to pick him quickly. They won't be able to explain what they did, or why. So they'll take particular pains to find some recent act of that man which can be classed as a Disservice. I'd be willing to bet that they'll report that you weren't on the plane. And they'll conveniently ignore having seen me. Any failure of a Disservice agent is in itself classed as a Disservice to the State, you know."

"Then we're safe?"

"From the Disservice agents. But not from . . . another group."

"Who are they?"

Do you believe me when I say I was trained on another planet?

"Yes, Dake, I——How in the world did you do that?"

In this world but not of it, Mary.

"Hold my wrist again. Hold it tightly. Hurt me with your hand."

"Why?"

"I have to believe that I didn't go off that bridge. I have to believe that all this isn't happening in some . . . gray place between the last life and the next."

He held her wrist tightly, made her gasp with pain. She smiled. "That's better, a little."

"The other group . . . they are the people who have been trained in the same things. I think they control the world. I can't make myself believe in . . . their motives. I think they are evil. And apparently, the penalty for misplaced loyalty is death."

"Wasn't there a myth about a god who left Olympus, who preferred to live with man?"

"Men hate gods and fear them. I learned that quickly."

"I don't fear you. I don't hate you. There's just . . . a very definite awe. Can the others . . . find you?"

"They may be there when this plane lands. The first stop is Denver. So there isn't much time for us."

"What else can you do?"

"What did we do while we were waiting for the plane?"

She frowned. "Walked, talked."

"Did we?"

He took over her mind quickly. The life left her eyes. Her hands rested flaccid in her lap. He gave her a better memory. He brought the memory up out of the good years. A great glittering ballroom, open to the sky, an orchestra, playing for the two of them. He dressed her in silver blue, a dress sheathed perfectly to the uncompromising perfection of her body. Music of Vienna, and a sky with too many stars, and the long dance as he looked down into her eyes.

After a time he released her. Her eyes focused on his with a slow fondness, and then she gave a little shudder and flushed.

"Lovely, Dake. But like dancing in a dream. Light, effortless. I always trample on my partner's feet."

"But it was real, Mary. You believe it happened. So it happened."

She nodded, solemn as a child. "It happened."

"Would you like more magic?"

"Much more. All there is."

"Look at your hands."

He had covered her fingers with great barbaric rings, with the emeralds and fire diamonds of illusion. She touched the stones.

"They . . . exist."

"Of course. But all magic isn't gay." He dissolved all the rings but one, an emerald. He turned it into a small green snake curled tightly around her finger, its head lifted, eyes unwinking, forked crimson tongue flickering.

She flinched violently and then held her hand steady, stared at it calmly. "Magic doesn't have to be gay. It has only to be . . . magic."

"Do you believe?"

"In legend, Dake, it was necessary for you to sell your soul to the devil to be able to do this."

"I refused to sell. That's why there is a forfeit I have to pay."

"The same forfeit I'm paying voluntarily. When you're through with me." She bit her lip and said, "I'm like a child with a new toy. I don't want it taken away from me. Those two men back there—will they remember what happened?"

"Not what happened while I was controlling them. Just before and after."

"Would the crew of one of these liners admit they had made an unauthorized landing?"

"They . . . might not, but . . ."

"Can you control all the passengers?"

"Not at the same time. I can put them to sleep, one by one, and give them a strong suggestion to remain asleep. But I can't fly one of these things. I can't therefore control the man flying it."

"Could you make him believe he'd heard orders to land somewhere else, the way you made me believe in that . . . dance?"

He thought it over. "That might be done. It's a case of erasing the memory later, though."

There had once been a vast bomber base near Cheyenne Wells. One strip was kept lighted as an emergency strip. The flagship rolled to a stop. Sweat stood on Dake's forehead with the intensity of his effort, with the diversification of it. He got the doors open. It was a thirty-foot drop to the hard surface. All around them the passengers slept. Up forward the crew slept, heavily. They walked on their toes inside the plane, talked in whispers. Dake let the emergency ladder down, climbed down and held the bottom steady as Mary clambered down.

A light came bobbing and winking toward them. A heavy man

in khaki came out of the shadows. "What goes on here?" he asked.

Dake wasted no time on him. He took him over with punishing abruptness, made him stand aside, his eyes glassy. He took Mary by the hand and they ran across the runway. He turned and looked back at the aircraft, at the lighted control room. The crew stirred, came awake, looked around.

Dake and Mary ran and hid in the grass, watchful. After a time the flagship wheeled ponderously around, raced down the runway, lifted toward the stars.

15

IN THE DESERT THE NIGHTS WERE COOL AND DRY, THE DAYS CRISP, blinding. It was a miner's shack, abandoned when the claim was worked out. Mary drove into town eight miles away once a week for supplies. Fuel was a problem, water was a problem, money would soon be a problem. But each day was an idyll, each night pale silver with too many stars. They would sit on an outcropping of rock, still warm from the sun of the day. He would wonder where he had been—which exact portion of the big sky.

She wore jeans and white shirts and went barefoot gingerly until her slim feet were brown and toughened. The sun bleached the ends of her hair, whitened her brows and lashes, and turned her face a deep ruddy brown. He liked to watch her. She had a cat's grace, a cat's ability to relax utterly. They walked miles across the harsh burned land. They talked of all things under the sun.

Mary never tired of making him perform. The tiny Pack B fascinated her. He taught her the sequence of wheels, tried to teach her how to use it. She tried until she was on the edge of tears, saying, "I can't get rid of that last tiny little feeling that it's impossible. If I could only accept it completely. . . . Do it again, Dake. Let me watch again."

And finally she refused to try any more. Her smile seemed a bit strained.

There was another game. She would say, "I met this one when I was studying in Sarasota right after Korea. About five foot six, a hundred and seventy pounds, I'd say. Balding, with very silky blond hair. Big bland blue eyes, and a snub nose and a puckery little mouth, and two chins. He stood very straight, with his stomach sticking out, and when he was thinking of how he would explain something, he'd suck his teeth. He used to wear white slacks and a beaded belt and dark shirts with short sleeves, navy or black."

"Like this?"

And she would clap her hands with sudden delight, or she would frown and say, "He's wrong, somehow. Let me think. It's the forehead."

And he would alter the illusion until she was satisfied, and he would fix the man in his memory, ready to reproduce him at any time she desired. Once they had a party. He produced the illusions of a round dozen of the people she had described. He created them to the extent of his abilities, sitting taut with the strain of managing so many of them. And Mary walked among them, burlesquing the considerate hostess, saying outrageous things to them.

And suddenly she began to laugh, and she sat down on the sand, and laughter turned to tears, her face huddled against her knees. He dissolved the illusions and went to her, kneeling beside her, touching her shoulder.

"What is it?"

She lifted her wet face and tried to smile. "I . . . don't know. It's a crazy thing. I started feeling as though I'm . . . here with you like a favorite puppy, or an amusing kitten or something. And what you were doing was like throwing a ball for me to fetch it back to you, panting and wagging my tail."

"Not like that."

"Dake, what are we doing here?"

"I had to have someone accept what I could do. Take it without fear and without horror. It seemed necessary to find someone, to find you."

"But I'm shut out, aren't I? I'm . . . like that puppy."

"How honest do you want me to be?"

She was solemn. "All the way, Dake."

"I have a feeling of guilt, about the things I can do and you can't. Guilt makes me resent the fact that you can't. I'm dissatisfied with your lack of ability."

"I'll be honest too. I envy you. And it's a very small step from envy to resentment, from resentment to hate. I keep saying to myself, 'Why did they take him? Why did they train him? Why wasn't it me?' Do you see?"

"Yes, I see, Mary. I've told you . . . every part of the story. Every part of my life, I guess. You know how it happened."

"I know how it happened. And I've watched you, Dake. I've watched you sitting, staring at nothing, that puzzled look on your face. You haven't told me the whole thing, have you?"

He sat back on his heels, picked up a handful of sun-hot sand, let it slide through his fingers. He said, "These weeks here . . . it's the first breathing space I've had. The first time to think. My mind goes around and around in a crazy circle and then always ends up flat against a paradox that I can't solve, can't see around. A featureless thing like a wall."

"I think I know what it is, Dake. You tell me."

He picked up more sand, tossed it aside irritably. "Just this. The mind and the spirit are perhaps . . . indivisible. On Training T, I was trained by humans, in an alien series of mental techniques. Their method of conquering space, this Pack B, the buildings and methods I saw—all those came from some alien technology far superior to anything on earth. But their greatest advances are in the realm of the brain, and its great unused power. If the mind and the spirit are—instead, I guess I should say the mind and the soul—if they are indivisible, I should think that any increment in the power to use the mind would presuppose a greater understanding of the human soul. And if that is true, why is the influence of the trained ones inimical to mankind? Greater knowledge should mean greater understanding. So why haven't they made of Earth a decent, safe, sane place to live? I know that with the powers I have, if I could be the only man on Earth with these powers, I could lead this planet into the greatest period of prosperity and peace it has ever seen. If I could do it, by crumbling away the rotten spots, reinforcing the good spots, why don't *they* do it? I certainly have no corner on good will. I saw the people trained at the same time I was. I saw them change. I saw an ignorant Spanish Gypsy girl change utterly from a person who functioned on the instinctual animal level to a person who began to have sound, sincere, abstract thoughts and concepts. I've labeled the entire operation as something evil. And I doubt whether my label is . . . accurate. I have the feeling of some chance slipping away from me."

"I've had that feeling for some time, Dake."

"Then what is the answer?"

"There has to be some answer that you haven't seen yet."

"Then why didn't they tell me the answer?"

"Maybe you had to decide it for yourself. Maybe they gave you enough clues."

He smiled crookedly. "Then I should keep thinking?"

"Of course. And if you find the answer, you should go back." She stood up, brushing the sand from herself. "Walk?"

"Sure."

"Make me a mirage, Dake."

"What kind?"

"On that hill. Something cool. Something inviting."

He made heavy old trees and black shade and a limpid fountain. She took his hand and they walked across the desert floor.

"Not a puppy," he said suddenly. "Something special. Something I need. Patrice had a portion of it, once. Karen had some of it. Even the Gypsy had some of it. I don't know how to tell you what it is. Strength and warmth. The strong people never seem to be warm enough. The warm people too often have wills like suet. My wife was . . . right. So are you. I love you."

"Scratch me behind the ear and throw a ball and I'll fetch."

"Stop that!"

"Don't you see? Remember what they told you when you were learning arithmetic? You can't add apples and oranges. You have to change the bottom halves of fractions before you can add them together. I can't become like you. You can't retrogress to me. I'll be around as long as you want me, but my attitude will be . . . sacrificial."

"That's a hell of a thing to say."

"I want you to realize your 'apartness.' You can't love a human except condescendingly. You want desperately for me to be able to insert my thoughts into your mind, as you can into mine. But I can't. So we'll never have the sort of communication that you depend on, that you have learned to depend upon. Without that, I'm just a warm, articulated doll. Press the right switch and I'll say, 'I love you, Dake.' Flat and metallic and mechanical. But I cannot ever say it . . . in your way."

"But you do?"

"Of course. Puppies have a traditional attachment to their masters. A revolting adoration."

In anger he walked rigidly ahead. He glanced back and she was standing quite still, watching him. He turned and climbed across brown rock.

Look out! Snake!

He caught the glint of sun on diamond coils and jumped wildly away, feeling the faint brush of blunt head and fangs against the leg of his trousers. It was a gigantic rattler, as big around as his upper arm. He moved warily away from it. It coiled, then turned slowly and slid, like oiled death, off into the raw brown rock.

It was only then, his heart still thudding, that he realized the implication of what had happened. He turned and looked at the girl, a hundred feet away. She stood with her chin up, her arms pressed tightly against her sides.

He walked slowly down toward her, faced her. Her expression told him nothing.

"That night on the bridge?"

"I was never far from you, Dake, from the moment you left Glendon Farms."

There was a sick taste in his throat. "So I'm an assignment. Is that it?"

"Yes. I should have risked shouting. I didn't think of it. Para-voice was quicker and . . . it saved you. I could only think of saving you."

"Will you explain . . . everything to me?"

"Let's go back."

They walked in silence to the shack. They sat on the ground in the intense desert shade, in the dry coolness.

He laughed flatly. "I must have been pretty amusing, showing you all my little tricks."

"Quite sweet, actually. A strain, though, not using my screens for so very long."

"That's a nice word. Sweet. And you were a sweet puppy, Mary."

"Get all the bitterness out of your system, Dake."

"And very amusing that the subject of your assignment fell in love with you."

"Are you through?"

"What is it all about?"

"You were studied very carefully. There's a paradox you don't know about. Those who barely manage to get through without cracking are the ones who are eventually the most valuable. Take the Gypsy. She withstood it easily. And she very probably will never go beyond Stage One. It is the borderline ones who eventually become the Stage Threes. You will be a Stage Three someday, Dake. I know I'll never go beyond Stage Two. So you see, you are rare and valuable."

"Thank you," he said, with irony.

"It was Karen's duty to start you running. She did it very neatly indeed. You weren't as much afraid of death as you were afraid of dying without ever knowing what Watkins called the ultimate answer."

"Why was I supposed to run?"

"Because there is an attitude which you will have to maintain for many years. It can't be superimposed on you, without limiting your effectiveness. It is a balance and a philosophy that you have to acquire by yourself. Only then are you ready for assignment. You have acquired a large measure of that philosophy here on the desert, with me."

"This philosophy has dimensions? Standard parts?"

"They vary for the individual, Dake. One of the primary attitudes, however, is an awareness and appreciation of 'apartness.' I think you have that. Man hates and fears deviation, and will destroy it if he can. Thus your relationship to man, in your role of induced mutation, must be in somewhat of the nature of parent to child."

"I've felt that. A . . . pity. A remoteness."

"You can achieve identification with only those of your children who can be induced to aspire to . . . adulthood. You are a true adult."

"With a pretty callous attitude toward the children?"

"There has to be a lot of attrition, a continual thinning of the ranks in order that others may grow."

"Why?"

"What would the answer to that question be?"

He thought for a moment. "Would it be Watkins' ultimate answer?"

"Yes."

"Where is he?"

"Running, as you have been. Maybe he is back by now. Running, not from the fear of death, but from the fear of never knowing."

"Can you tell me the answer?"

She looked at him for a long time. "I have to know if you're ready, Dake. I have to know if you can accept it. Take my hands."

They turned, facing each other. Her lips moved quietly, "Screens down, Dake."

He was utterly lost in her eyes. Gone. Taken into some warm place. Taken into secret depths of oneness, of togetherness, of warmth, that he had never imagined could exist. This was a closeness far beyond that which could ever be achieved by the body. This was a spiritual mating, a clinging and mingling of souls, a high, wild, hard emotional experience that was beyond space and time. . . .

Then he was aware that they were releasing each other, that they were separating slowly into separate entities.

"I've wanted that for so long," she said gently. Her voice trembled. Her eyes were brimming. "I knew it would be . . . right."

"Am . . . I ready?"

Her lips twisted. "Your ultimate answer will be anticlimax, Dake. Now."

"I think I sense that. Maybe the obvious is always an anticlimax."

She stood up lightly. "No, stay there. This is history, Dake. Human history. History of galactic man, and his adjustment to his environment, and his answer to decadence. There is more than a hundred thousand years of recorded history. Someday you will learn more of it. It is part of Stage Two training. The heart worlds grew and learned and warred on each other, and combined, and found peace, and added to themselves those other planets and star systems as they achieved cultural maturity. Each manlike cultural system made its own contributions to the whole. For the sake of simplicity, we shall call the entire unity Empire. Examine that word *manlike*. If I had a complete adjustment, I would not use that word. Physiological deviations are small throughout the galaxy. We are all men. You saw several varieties on Training T."

"Acting a bit . . . servile."

"Of course. One cultural group, part of the unity of Empire, is called the Senarian. It was that group which carried mathematical calculation to the inevitable pitch where it can make a sound prediction of the future. Perfection of extrapolation, the inevitable end result of all mathematical science. The parsing of time. Many thousand years ago the calculations of the Senarians were directed at a problem which was growing more serious. It had started in a very subtle way. It was noticed that, as new cultures were added to the unity of Empire, there followed a period when the top administrative jobs of Empire, the crucial decision-making positions, were all manned by citizens of the most recent culture to join Empire. After a few generations of the peace and sanity of membership in Empire, the descendants of the newest culture would lose their competitive drive, and no longer be of valid worth for leadership purposes. This was not a pressing problem so long as there were a sufficient number of barbaric cultures forging ahead toward Empire membership, as they would provide the future leadership, the future vitality which would avoid stagnation. But, the Senarians asked their vast computers, what will happen when there is no longer such a supply?

"The answer was disheartening to Empire. Leadership cannot come from any environment where there is peace and plenty. Leadership can only be developed in an environment where there is conflict, savagery, violence, hate. Leadership is the answer to a competitive environment. Empire is not a competitive environment. Empire will eventually be without leadership. Progress will cease.

"The computers were asked a second-level question. What will be the result of the cessation of progress? The answer was destruction. Destruction by life forms of neighboring galaxies. Life forms so alien that there could be no communication. Only through progress could there be a continual increment of strength sufficient to keep the species alive.

"A third question was asked. What can be done? The answer took much longer. And the logic of it was inevitable. Keep one planet in a barbaric state. Keep it in continual conflict. Permit it no knowledge of the existence of Empire, and no knowledge of its function. Do not permit it to destroy itself. Deny it any more than token space travel. Keep it in insane and continual conflict and that planet will provide you with your leadership. Take those men and women who rise to the top of the boiling pot, and skim them off, and train them, and use them."

He stared at her in the silence. "Then all this . . . all this that has tortured men for thousands of years . . . it is just a . . . trick? A breeding ground? A training ground?"

She looked at him proudly. "More than that, Dake. Much more than that. Earth is the heart of Empire. The ruler. The destiny of the galaxy. Men of Earth rule all the countless stars. They rule justly, firmly, ruthlessly. Under the leadership of Earth, Empire moves on up the infinite ladder of progress, up to a strength that will keep us free forever."

"Why was Earth selected?"

"Because here man was stronger than elsewhere. His natural environment had been harsher, gravity stronger than the norm, climate more extreme, nature more violent."

"But I——"

"No more, Dake. Not now. You have to think over what I've told you. You have to understand how you must transfer your loyalty from Earth man to Galactic man. But transfer it with an increment in pride in Earth, and in yourself. I will talk to you later, after you have had a chance to think it over."

16

HE WALKED ALONE, AND DID NOT KNOW WHERE HE WALKED, OR how far. He stood on a hilltop and watched the sun slide red behind the far blue of the mountains. It made such a complete reversal of all his concepts, of all his adjustments to the political and emotional climate of his environment, that he felt as though someone had taken his brain between two hard hands, and twisted it like a sponge.

There was no segment of his beliefs that did not need reorganization, reevaluation.

Earth had a history. There were names in that history. Alexander, Hannibal, Napoleon, Hitler, Stalin, Mussolini. And, he thought, Christ. And Buddha and Muhammad and Vishnu. Good and evil, fighting an endless battle, to a predestined draw. Keep the pot boiling. Keep the four horsemen riding across the ravaged lands. A million men broken and burned and dying for each one selected. Massive, callous, mathematical cruelty, for the sake of . . . the greatest good for the greatest number.

He sat on the hilltop rocks and watched the stars come out, watched the quick desert night fall like a curtain. Men of Earth, being led in a crazy dance of death, for the sake of the high, wide ballroom of the skies.

He heard Mary's foot touch a loose stone. She came up behind him. He did not turn. He felt the soft warm pressure of her hand on his shoulder.

I know how difficult it is.

What is the final adjustment? What do I feel, afterward?

"Joy, Dake. Gladness. Pride. Humility. All the best attributes of the human spirit."

"Will you answer questions? I've been thinking in circles again."

"Of course."

"What did I have to be sent back here?" *why*

"Assignment here is part of your training for your future responsibilities. Part of your training in logic, in analysis, in action, and in humility. When your work is valid, you will be credited for it. After you have acquired enough credits, you will be given Stage Two training and returned here. Later, perhaps, you will be accepted for Stage Three training. After three tours here you will be assigned to the post in Empire that you are best qualified for."

"How long will I have to be here?"

"That depends on your progress. Twenty-five to thirty of their years."

"Their years?"

"Earth years. Two and a half to three of ours, basing it on effect of time."

"I want to gloat about that. And feel guilty. That's a very precious gift."

"But not mystic. Just one logical result of an advanced medical science. A continuation of the trend you've seen here on earth."

"Another question. There are two groups, apparently, or more. In conflict with each other. I don't see why that should be necessary, or even advisable."

"Is any untrained man a fair match for you?"

"N-No, but . . ."

"Did any man ever play a great game of chess, alone?"

"No."

"Conflict breeds ingenuity. Competition, also, gives a more random result, one that is less predictable, less likely to be detected by the ordinary thinking man as the result of extraterrestrial interference. You get credit for accomplishment, and you pay, as Karen did, a penalty for failure. And always you must watch. You watch the top people in every possible line of endeavor. The most successful crooks, as Miguel Larner was. The best statesmen, the best politicians, the best artists, designers, salesmen, engineers. People at the top of every heap got there through conflict, through a compensation for some type of psychic trauma. If the incomprehensible doesn't drive them mad, they become our best recruits."

"Why wasn't Darwin Branson recruited? He was killed, wasn't he?"

"He had an organic disorder that was too far advanced for treatment. It would have killed him within six months. Besides, it was only during the last three years of his life that he achieved more than a pedestrian impact on his environment. So he wasn't noticed until too late."

Dake absorbed that in silence. He stirred restlessly. She sat on the rocks beside him.

"There are so many loyalties to give up," he said. "Loyalty to my country. That was pretty strong, you know. And now I can see that its weakness is due to what . . . we have done to it."

"That word was good to hear. We. It's an acceptance. Here is something you should consider. The number of recruits we obtain from any one country is in direct ratio to the extent of hardship that country is undergoing. During India's years of poverty and exploitation and death we obtained many recruits there. During the fattest years of the United States it was difficult to find people sufficiently toughened, hardened. Sword steel is treated in flame. Civilizations rise and fall. Those on top are poor breeding grounds for leadership. See, you have to reverse all your concepts, Dake. Good becomes weakness. Evil becomes strength."

"And isn't it all a vast rationalization?"

"So is the life form itself. A rationalization of the means of survival."

They walked back to the shack, walking in the starlight that silvered the sand underfoot. A coyote cried far away, cried of unmentionable woes and wrongs. He felt the girl shiver.

"We'll start back in the morning," he said quietly.

"In the morning, Dake."

They stood for a time and watched the stars, near the dark hulk of the shack. He held her hand, felt her mind touch gently at his. They stood again in the climactic oneness, and later he began to feel the first faint stirrings of dedication, the first wary reachings toward a philosophy that would have to support him, amid cruelty, for long years of service to a barely comprehensible dream.

17

THE CABDRIVER WAS SWEATY, IRRITABLE, AND TALKATIVE.

"Guess you folks have been out west. I can tell by that tan. You don't get that kind of tan here in summer, or in Florida, or anywhere except out there. Jesus, it's been a hot August here. Wet. I wish to hell I was back out where it's dry heat."

"It's more comfortable," Mary said.

"You bet your elbow it is, lady. This town goes nuts in the summer. All the rummies start sleeping in the parks. Bunch of pronies running around cutting up people. Another fleng joint war, with them throwing bombs in each other's joints. Gawd, what a month. You hear the knock in this thing? I'm running it on kerosene, and damn poor kerosene at that."

The driver cursed and swerved wildly to avoid a big Taj full of Pak-Indian tourists. "Think they own the damn world," he said viciously. He shrugged, arguing with himself. "Maybe they do, come to think of it."

"Have there been many tourists around this summer?" Dake asked.

"Too many, if you ask me. I don't know why they come over here. I got a pal with connections. He's all lined up to emigrate. Going to run a hack in Bombay, with a Sikh partner. He's never had it so good. They got those quotas so tight, it's almost impossible to get in over there."

"You'd like to do the same thing?"

The man turned in the seat and gave him an angry glare. "Why the hell not? What is there here? Three days a week I get fuel. I get four deadheads for every tipper. I don't even own this hack. Where's the opportunities here? I ask you that. When I was a kid it was different. My old man owned six cabs. He had it nice. All the gas he could use." He stopped for a light and turned around and gave Dake a puzzled stare. "What happened to us? You ever try to figure that out? Where did it all go?"

"The war."

"That's what everybody says. I wonder. Seems like soon as we start to climb up there again, we get knocked down. Something always tripping us up. Somebody always tripping the whole world up."

"And then picking it up again?" Mary asked, smiling.

"Lady, in this world, you pick yourself up." He started up slowly, cursing the cars that passed him. "You know what I figure?"

"What?" Mary asked obediently.

"I figure we got to depend on those atom rocket boys. They're working day and night, I understand. What we haven't got is resources. Now you take Mars, or Venus. I bet those places are loaded with coal and oil and iron and copper and every damn thing we need. We just got to get there first and stake a claim. Then we'll be okay."

"And if we never get off the Earth?"

The driver's shoulders slumped. He said, in a dejected voice, "You know, mister, I just don't like to think about that. It means we're stuck here. And things aren't the way they used to be. My old man used to take me out to Yankee Stadium. Yell his fool self hoarse. Can I do that? Who wants to yell at a bunch of silly broads playing softball, I ask you? Those good old days, mister, they're gone. Believe me. TV we had, and baseball, and all the gas you wanted. Every time I see those Indians around, I feel like maybe we're one of those kind of tribes, with bones sticking through our nose, and big spears. We're for kicks, mister."

They rode in silence for a time, nearing the apartment. The driver said, "When we used to have all them saucers around, my old man used to say it was time the Martians landed and took over. The old man had something, you know. Know what I think?"

"What?" said Dake.

"I figure those Martians took a good long look around and said to each other, boys, we better go away and come back in ten thousand years and see if these folks have grown up any. Man, it's dangerous down there. Is this place you want in the middle of the block?"

"Right over there on the right, driver," Mary said.

"Class, eh? Isn't that where that racketeer used to live? Larner? Mig Larner?"

"That's the place, driver."

They got out. The driver took the fare, grinned. "I didn't figure you to deadhead me. I can almost always tell. Be good now. Watch out for them Martians."

They walked into the coolness of the air-conditioned lobby. Johnny came around from behind the desk, hand outstretched. "Here for good this time, Dake?"

"I think so."

"Little stubborn, was he, Mary?"

"Did I take long?"

"Last ones in, dear. Martin Merman suddenly became interested in your space requirements the other day."

Mary smiled. "He's a hideous person. What he doesn't know, he can guess."

Johnny went back around to his side of the desk. "Both of you in suite 8 C then?"

Stop blushing furiously, darling.

"Yes, Johnny," she said.

"And so he'll twin you on assignments. You'll make an ominous pair, kids. Shard will have a happy time assigning the equivalent. Now Martin is expecting you for a couple of brief impressive ceremonies."

They went down to the dioramic garden where Dake had first met Miguel Larner. Merman got up, his young-old face smiling, his handshake warm and firm.

He said, "It isn't something we can give you, Dake. It's something you have to find for yourself. You found it with Mary's help. Are you ready to accept?"

"Completely."

"That's the only way we can . . . accept your acceptance. Without reservation. Raise your right hand, please. It isn't necessary to repeat the phrases after me. Just say 'I do' when I have finished. Do you, Dake Lorin, agree in heart, mind, and spirit with the eternal obligation of Earth, the planet of your origin, to provide leadership for Empire? Do you agree to accept dutifully all agent assignments given you with the full knowledge of the end purpose of those assignments, to provide leadership through keeping Earth, the planet of your origin, in a savage and backward state, where neither progress nor regression is possible? Do you promise to bring to this duty every resource of your mind and spirit, not only those resources recently acquired, but those developed in you by your environment prior to your association with us?"

Martin Merman's eyes were level, sober, serious.

"I do," Dake said.

"For the sake of all mankind," Martin Merman said.

"For the sake of all mankind," Mary repeated softly.

"Now you are one of us, Dake. I'll break your heart a hundred times a year, from now on. At times you'll be sickened, angry, resentful. You will be called on to do things which, in your previous existence, you would have considered loathsome. But you'll do them. Because the purpose is clear. Cold. Inevitable." He grinned suddenly. It was an astonishingly boyish grin. "Anything else, Mary?" he asked.

"Another . . . little ceremony, Martin."

Now who looks like a beet?

"This is a tribal ceremony, Dake," Martin said. "A uniting. It has no legal status among us. Only a moral and emotional status. Either of you can dissolve it at any time by merely stating the desire that it be dissolved. However, in our history, no such a uniting has ever been dissolved. It is, to pun badly, a mating of the minds. And in that field there can be no deceit, no unfortunate misunderstandings, no secrets, each from the other. You will live and work together as the closest possible team. You will complement each other's efficiencies, and heal each other's distress. Any children you may have will be taken from you and raised on one of the heart worlds, and you will renew your relationship with them once your duties here are over. They will still be children, still need you. And your eventual Empire assignment will be as close as your assignment here. Do you accept that?"

"If Mary does."

Mary nodded. Martin said, "Then we must have witnesses." He K25 smiled.

There was the faintest shimmer and Karen suddenly appeared near them. And then Johnny. And Watkins. And one by one, others from his training class. And the persons he had seen in the lobby that night long ago. And strangers. Many of them. All appearing, grouping themselves in the bright garden, their faces reflected in the garden pool.

Dake had always been a lonely man. He had never been a part of a group, never relished it, except during the months on Training T. There, for the first time, he had experienced the vague beginnings of group warmth and group unity.

And the warmth of all these people suddenly surrounded him, enfolded him. They had proud faces, and level eyes, and something unmistakably godlike about them. Super-beings who walked among men with sadness, with pride, with humility.

That group identity caught him up. He was a part of it. He knew that never again would he have the feeling of walking alone.

He stood for long moments, tasting this final acceptance, sensing the challenge of the years ahead, knowing that at this moment he began his apprenticeship.

He reached and took Mary's firm brown hand, and turned just enough so that the two of them stood, side by side, facing Martin Merman. Her fingers tightened on his.

Dake Lorin squared his shoulders and stood quietly, awaiting Martin Merman's words.